This book is for my wife Barbara Jean, my first and last true love.

Acknowledgements

Many writers begin their acknowledgements by stating that "no book is written alone." I have never understood the reason for that phrase, and I consider it to be completely false. Books are written alone, in the silence and solitude of the imagination. I wrote ELAINE THE FAIR in just this way, over the course of six years. The book is mine own, as is all credit or blame.

Yet the writer often does need help from others during the course of his labors—help in the most basic sense, being that which keeps his body and soul together. I want to thank my friends, Arthur Smith, Paul Fielding, Bobby Dudley, Alan and Elaine Hosfeld, Ed and Betty MacNamee, and Bill Goichberg, all of whom were both generous and forgiving during my years of unremunerative toil.

A writer often feels that his troubles are over when he can finally, with a clear conscience, place 'The End' on the last page of his manuscript. This feeling is, most often, a fallacy. It is at this point—as he attempts to get his work published—that a writer needs help more than ever. I was fortunate to get more than my share of these good services. I can say truthfully that ELAINE THE FAIR would never have been published had I not been given the help of Elizabeth Hawkins and Ellis and Jean Wall.

Finally, I must say that I might never have begun this book at all had I not met Aileen Louise.

Author's Note:

The story you are about to read is a legendary tale, not a collection of cold facts. While the general course of history has been accurately conveyed, there are various deviations from the official record. These deviations always occur in any story that has been told and retold down through the centuries. It is my opinion that the truth of legend is often more meaningful than the "correct" truths of the textbooks.

Elaine the Fair

Part I

History

Chapter 1

THE LADY

Once upon a time, in the year of our Lord eleven hundred and ninety-four, there lived a lady of the English court who was known as Elaine the Fair. On this the twelfth of May, a Tuesday night, a night no different from so many others, she woke up screaming. She thrust her hands out violently—and the surprise that her arms worked broke the spell of the dream. It hadn't touched her—no, it hadn't touched her—just that one small prick and ribbon of blood—she reached up with an unerring finger to feel the tiny white scar an inch below her left eye. In five years time it had never gone away—she knew she would bear it forever, like a brand. Elaine didn't know that the slight jar of this imperfection was the only thing that made her beauty bearable to mortal man.

The room was dark—a single candle was flickering its last— and a little cold. Elaine always seemed to feel the cold worse than other people.

She sat up in bed, shivering in her thin nightgown, and slipped her feet into her rabbits fur slippers. She pulled a heavy woolen robe about her shoulders, and got up to light a fresh candle from the dying light.

She walked without hope to the door of her husband Arthur's room. She opened it, and was greeted by the smell of his unwashed body. This was worse. She had expected him to be out, drinking and gambling with his cronies and those seeking his favor. Instead he lay here, oblivious of her screams, of her need. Why had he not come to her? Yet she knew he gained little pleasure from the act of love.

Elaine looked at her husband, sleeping in his wine stained

clothes, the pack of cards he always carried spread out on the bed near his open palm, the pages of the old Book of Doom scattered about the floor. She did not think of him as the Chancellor of the Exchequer, Arthur the Assessor, the most feared man in the land—she thought of how she literally owed him her life. She touched the silent white scar again, and she thought how she could love Arthur, if only he would hold her. Never mind about the desires that were so much stronger now—if he would just hold her . . .

I could slide into bed next to him, Elaine thought, and put my arms around him. But the smell stopped her. She tried to tell herself it meant nothing (even here in the palace of Bermondsey cleanliness was as rare as Godliness) but her arguments lost conviction as she stared at Arthur's sleeping form. She wanted to be enfolded in a man's strong arms—not the loose fat and pudgy fingers of the man her husband had become. If she felt a man's sweat against her skin, she wanted it to be the honest sweat of effort—not the unhealthy moisture of a body that has eaten and drunk far more than it needs or even desires.

Elaine thought of her own body, bathed and caressed by her lady in waiting this afternoon—she was ready for Arthur to save her life again, and she would give him the reward he had never really accepted.

She touched her breasts through two layers of cloth, and then moved her right hand up to her throat. She could still feel the rawness inside from her screams.

Once Arthur had comforted her whenever the dream came, but now he no longer heard her. What desire there had been was also a thing of the past.

Elaine thought, if you can not be my man, then although I will do my duty, in my heart I will no longer be your woman.

And so, after five long years, after a gradual starvation of affection, she finally said the long suppressed words aloud—but she said them very, very softly.

"I won't try to love you any more, Arthur."

Once she said that, it was easy to walk into the room. She moved gracefully to the head of his bed, and against her will felt her heart pounding. She bent down to kiss his cheek, expecting—no, hoping that at any second he would reach out and wrap an arm around her legs and pull her close—but his heavy breathing did not change.

She stood up slowly and waited for her heart to calm down.

Now it was as hard to leave the room as it had been to enter. Nothing awaited her save her own empty bed.

Elaine felt the same as when she was a child, twenty years ago. She had been just four years old, and they had taken her mother away. She had been alone then, and she had longed so much for a guiding hand—as their hard eyes accused her—but there had been no guardian, no savior.

She remembered it now with a touch of pride—for even as a child she had made the right decision. Elaine entered her own room, leaving the wreckage of her love behind her.

The thickness of her loneliness was no protection against the cold. She shivered as she got into bed without taking off the robe. Her spirit felt like an ancient empty tunnel—wind whipped through it and the walls were scarred by claws of guilt. She thought that she must have failed Arthur somehow—but she knew she could not go on like this without failing herself.

She pulled her blanket up around her shoulders and waited for the dawn.

Chapter 2

THE DUKE

Halfway across Europe, Roland, Duke of Larraz, was also having a sleepless night. There was no outward reason for this. He was thirty-three years old, in the prime of health, and he had led an extremely successful life.

The Duke's ancestors had mainly been warriors. His great uncle, Godfrey of Bouillon, had been one of the leaders of the First Crusade—indeed, he became the first Christian King of Jerusalem (a vacant title now, alas, for the Holy City was back in Moslem hands). Still, Roland chose not to follow the martial example of his forebears. His talents led him in a different direction.

Roland liked to think of himself (despite his exalted station) as a simple merchant. The Duke preferred to supply the Crusaders rather than fight with them—and he was the perfect middleman when they wanted to dispose of their booty.

His duchy, situated midway along the eastern border of France, had become a center of trade for all European commerce. So while other peoples were taxed beyond their ability to pay, and knights themselves often hopelessly in debt to their usurers, the fortunate citizens of Larraz were prosperous—and Roland himself was immensely wealthy.

The Duke combined his financial ability with a genuine (and some said, almost unChristian) love of peace. The hotheads in his duchy were always free to volunteer for the Crusades—yet in the twelve years of Roland's reign, Larraz itself had never been involved in war.

Heads of state remembered Roland's conciliatory mien—he was the enemy of no man. They respected his political acumen—when the dust had settled on each conflict of Europe's bloodstained whirl, it always seemed that Roland had been supplying the winning side.

None of his equals could emulate Roland's success—nor did they truly want to be like him. How terrible it would be to stand on the sidelines, never to lead an army into battle! Roland's secrets were open ones—but no one coveted them.

It was a time when men acted on faith, not reason: when a leader's highest act was thought to be leading an army of believers into a faraway desert in an attempt to recover the Holy Sepulcher—and never mind about sweltering knights in heavy armor suited only for northern climes, or two thousand mile supply lines, or an entrenched enemy with mobile cavalry . . .

Men kept the faith, and died.

Roland looked at the facts, and thought, and prospered. Then with his great wealth, he bribed the local representatives of the Christian church (thought to be sure, his gifts were not labeled so baldly) and the wise priests blessed their Duke, and left him alone.

It was not reason alone, of course, that kept Larraz in its favored position of peace and trade. It was reason based on knowledge. Roland traded not only in goods, but also in information.

It had gradually become known that the Duke of Larraz would pay well for information from foreign lands. Pilgrims on their way to the Holy Land, wandering knights, traveling minstrels, even men fleeing their crimes—all made certain to stop at the palace of Larraz, where stories could be exchanged for gold.

None were turned away.

Roland made himself personally available to these men: he listened to their tales every afternoon, and rare indeed was the day when he did not have a visitor. The Duke listened, he rewarded, and he remembered.

Over the years, Roland figured out how things worked. While other leaders waited for signs from heaven, Roland learned the price of bread—and predicted the future far more accurately than a dozen mystic priests.

He was a man of reason—but this afternoon an English knight had brought him information that tore open his heart where he had been wounded long ago. He lay awake in bed and watched as reason fought with love—he kept his eyes wide open as the former was overwhelmed.

The news that Roland had received was this: the English had finally raised the last of the money required to free King Richard Lionheart.

The renowned English King, returning from his failed Crusade in December, 1192, had suffered shipwreck in the Adriatic Sea. He had been taken prisoner by forces of Leopold of Austria, who in turn handed over his royal captive to Henry VI, the Holy Roman Emperor—a man whose greed so far outstripped his holiness that he had demanded a ransom of 150,000 marks: twice the annual revenue of the English crown. Richard had been held in a castle in Germany for over a year while his people struggled to raise the funds—now somehow that astonishing sum had been collected.

The money was on its way—the Lionheart would soon be free.

Richard would have to go back to England first—he would need to gather his forces—but then he was bound to come storming back on to the Continent.

Roland did not fear for Larraz—he had met Richard before, flattered him well, and contributed generously to his Crusade. No, it was France that would get the attack, France, where King Philip II had been busy gobbling up English possessions while Richard was imprisoned, France, which stood in the way before any direct vengeance against Henry VI's German empire.

Roland knew he could not be wrong about this.

It was not a serious political problem. He could watch the way the wind blew, and throw his support to the winner (Roland's relations with Philip II were also quite good).

It was not politics that kept the Duke wide eyed and awake in the middle of this night in May.

It was a vision that shattered sleep, a dream that ached in his heart. Roland was in love with an English lady, a married lady separated from him by a nation and a sea. Yet even so he could imagine himself setting out on an expedition (in his dreams he had often done so). Well guarded by armed knights, soundly provisioned, he could ride across France and hire a boat to take him to England. He had made this journey nearly five years before, when he had attended Richard's coronation.

But now England and France would soon be at war. Before long, passage would become impossible—and who knew how long the war would last?

He would be cut off from his dream—the memory of a lady

who left no room for others in his heart. He might never again see Elaine the Fair.

Roland thought again of his first sight of that lady, a vision of beauty and mystery yet haunted in the background by memory of death.

It was September 7, 1189 (Roland would never forget that date), a week after Richard Lionheart's coronation. Roland had journeyed to London to personally pay his respects to the new King. In dealing with powerful men, it was Roland's style never to set himself up as a rival. He was very convincing as the loyal friend, a little in awe of the hero's accomplishments, and eager to help him in any way possible. In just this way he flattered Richard, pledged his support to the coming Crusade, and gained a few valuable trade concessions in passing.

After his audience with the King, it was necessary to obey the royal suggestion and take in the jousts that afternoon. Roland hated that "entertainment"—he attended the theater of combat as little as possible—another thing that distinguished him from the nobility of his time.

The Duke's eccentricity was founded in experience. He deplored sacrifice and wasted life—and as Roland would never forget his first sight of Elaine, so he had never got over the tragedy of his younger brother Charles.

It was strange when he thought about it, but both of the most profound happenings of his life had occurred at those hateful, barbaric jousts.

Roland and Charles had loved each other.

Physically, they had been opposites: Roland, big and burly, a bear to Charles's slender, beautiful stag. Charles had been a high-strung child—he fussed constantly as a baby and cried frequently as a young boy. He often angered their father, the old Duke Bernard, who had no patience for his second son's tantrums. Almost by default, Roland became a father to Charles. Though only four years older than his brother, Roland always had a calm and mature character. When the younger boy went wild, thrashing and screaming, Roland would quickly challenge Charles to wrestle. It was the only way to calm him down—the stag would charge wildly at the bear only to be enveloped by his big brother's strong arms and gradually borne to earth. The tears were hidden in Roland's embrace, and Charles would emerge, ready again to face the world.

As Charles grew older, he began having frenzied martial

dreams. He would slay the infidels single-handedly, he would restore the cross to Jerusalem, and just like their famous ancestor Godfrey, he would finally sit on the throne at the Holy City.

Charles prepared for knighthood with bright enthusiasm and black depression. In his speech he claimed a prowess that no boy of sixteen could truly possess—yet in his heart he knew the falseness of his boasts and feared that he would prove a total failure. He was unable to adjust his aim to a realistic level—he could confide in no one—not even Roland.

All Charles could say, on a summer's day in 1181, on the eve of his first public joust, was this: "You will come and watch, won't you?"

Roland had agreed, of course, struck by the beseeching look in his brother's eyes.

The future Duke of Larraz stood in the front of the crowd that day, brightly clad in gleaming scarlet, so that Charles would see him and gain courage as he rode.

Roland could remember his thoughts on that day even now. He had tried to cheer himself by reflecting that jousts were a game of war, not war itself. The object was to unhorse one's opponent, not to kill. The wooden lances were unsharpened—the men were protected by armor—and in any case, direct hits with the point of the lance were rare—the speed of the closing horses and the length of the unwieldy weapons made accuracy exceedingly difficult—probably Charles and the opposing knight would make a few fruitless passes, and then one or the other would simply swing his lance sideways and sweep the other off his mount in that less dramatic fashion—Roland remembered those thoughts, and the feeling of impending horror that had hung over them—he remembered Charles's last ride.

Charles rode past the gallery at full gallop—he raised one gloved hand to Roland as he flew by—he aimed his lance at the other knight, who was riding toward him at equally great speed—Charles missed, yet some cruel quirk of fate guided his foe's lance so that the dull point struck Charles full in the throat—the light mail covering the boy there barely cushioned the blow—Charles's neck was snapped on impact, and he was dead before he hit the ground.

He was innocent of women, of life. He was dead at sixteen.

After that Roland never went to a joust again of his own volition—but he was too good a politician to refuse King Richard's invitation.

September 7, 1189—eight years after Charles's death: it was a hot day, hotter still for the knights performing in their heavy armor. Roland endured the spectacle—fortunately there were no deaths. Afterward—duty fulfilled—he was hurrying to where his horse was tied when he was struck by the sight of a lady of the court. Alone in the bustling crowd, not more than ten feet away, she stood stock still, staring at something—or someone.

Roland looked quickly in the direction of her stare, but he saw nothing save the swirling, indifferent throng, and over by the fence, a dark greasy man with his arm around a serving girl.

Roland looked back at the lady—she hadn't moved, her face in profile, and he felt the deep rare pleasure of studying a beautiful woman while she was unaware of him.

She was bareheaded in the heat of the sun, blond hair gleaming, a pale blue silk dress blown tight against her slim body. She was caught in the midst of a smile—as though her lips could not finish their expression until her eyes had looked their fill. He watched her until he knew her mouth—a thin upper lip and the promise of sensuality in the lower. He discovered the deep line along her cheek that testified she smiled often. His gaze flickered to a nose that asserted itself, with a slight upward tilt—and then he noticed the unbearable poignance of the tiny scar under her left eye.

He had to see her from the front now, and he stepped slowly, heavily, to his left, feeling the weight of his body as he moved, and he learned the colors of her face, a pale complexion but eyebrows almost brown, a good shade darker than her hair—and he never knew whether she noticed his movement or his stare, but she turned to face him squarely—and he saw her clear blue eyes turn suddenly cold and it was as though a dagger had plunged into his heart.

In Larraz now, in his ornate bed with a servant sleeping outside his door, with his chests of gold and wearing his silken robes, with women who would serve him and ladies who pined for him, he still felt the dagger of love in his chest.

His heart ached.

Roland remembered: she came toward him with those eyes like priceless blue gems and then she was looking through him, past him, there was no connection, no intimacy—she went past him with a long graceful stride that was so smooth one didn't notice at first how fast she was moving—she was past before he could think of anything to say except "I love you," and that in

the Larrazian dialect of his childhood that she wouldn't understand—she was past and he wanted to spin and race after her
but some vestige of dignity made him turn heavily, slowly, and
he was just in time to see her bright beautiful hair disappear
into the throng.

He knew his expression was one of abject longing, but before
he could change his countenance he felt the touch of a hand on
his arm. Roland jerked violently, only to see the grinning face of
an insolent young knight.

"She is known as Elaine the Fair," said the young ruffian.

The dignity Roland had tried to assume broke in the face of
those words—no Duke any longer, he was just a desperate man
hungering for information, for connection. He didn't try to hide
the longing in his face as he asked, "Is she . . .?"

The knight's grin deepened into a smirk. "She is married to
the Chancellor of the Exchequer, a gentleman known to one and
all as Arthur the Assessor." The young man swung and pointed
with a knavish forefinger. "Yon gentleman up on the hill, in the
fine golden cloak—you see, he has taken her hand."

Roland looked, and the dagger in his heart twisted, and he
wanted to howl like a wild beast—but he would not give the
younger man that satisfaction.

"I trust she is happy," said Roland.

The smirk deepened, if possible. "She is said to be very loyal,"
said the knight.

Roland was used to living with pain. It had been his constant
companion since the day his brother had died.

He straightened up to take his leave.

"Thank you, Sir . . .?"

"Sir Guy of Sussex," said the knight, with a self-satisfied air.

"Yes, Sir Guy. Thank you very much, but now I must leave,
for I have urgent business with the King."

With this white lie (for his business with King Richard was
well concluded) Roland made his exit. He took off with a wide
shambling walk, a wounded bear zigzagging over the countryside, his horse forgotten, remembering only her lovely hair, her
hard eyes, her soft body under her dress and then her mouth,
both arrogant and sensual, and he wished just to touch her lips
with his own, but then the dagger twisted again and he wandered through fields and soaked his feet in streams, a heavy,
heedless, monstrous, gentle bear, and finally he came up with a
plan that would put him next to the lady, if only for an hour.

There are men of great ability but common stock who spend their lives in political maneuver, manipulating, twisting along any circuitous route that will bring them to the heights to which they aspire. For Roland, on the other hand, politics had always been external. Born the eldest son of a Duke, he understood from his first awareness that he *was* Larraz. His deft manipulation of heads of state was always done with his country's interests in mind.

Wandering on that day in September, his life changed by chance and beauty, Roland began, for the first time, to think only for himself. King Richard had announced a great feast to herald the beginning of the Third Crusade. Roland (along with every knight and noble in the land) was invited. Elaine would surely attend. There would be servants by the hundred—and where there are servants, one can always bribe.

Roland spent the week before the feast moving among waiters, cooks, and royal place setters—and when dinner was served, he took his place at the right side of Elaine the Fair.

He bowed to this lady of dreams, and kissed her hand, and for the first time saw her smile completed. He thought there was recognition in her blue eyes, recognition and amusement. He wondered what she was thinking—perhaps, 'Another one—just another one who loves me,' but he did not care. He wanted only to reach out and run his fingers through her shining hair.

The first course was beef, taken from the royal herd, freshly butchered that morning. A smiling waiter laid a large chunk on Roland's plate (the server's palm had been liberally greased so that the choicest cut would come directly to Roland). It was the custom of the time that the gentleman on a lady's right should cut her meat for her—first, because handling a large edged weapon is not a particularly ladylike activity, and second, it must be admitted that even the choicest cuts of meat tended to be rather tough—it frequently took a soldier's strength to slice it.

Roland was helpful without being servile—he passed Elaine a bite or two at a time on his fork, and the fare agreed with her.

He liked the neat way she chewed her food, and the smile she would give him after swallowing. He was very aware of the closeness of her body, the proximity of their thighs on the hard wooden bench. There were many long banquet tables—the Lionheart himself sat at the head of this one, and his Chancellor of the Exchequer sat across from his wife a few places down—but Roland was hardly conscious of Arthur or even of the King—only *her* smile mattered—her smile, and the scent of flowers that lingered about her hair and shoulders—as he breathed in her spirit he provided her with physical sustenance—and it was only long afterwards, after he returned to Larraz, that Roland realized he had not truly come close to Elaine at all that night.

In the years following, he returned again and again to his memories of that feast—and he finally came to certain conclusions that were not as agreeable as he would have wished. He had originally taken the smile lines on Elaine's face as signs of happiness—but that was not quite true. Her smile never really varied. It served equally as an answer to a witty remark, or to show her satisfaction with a choice morsel. It was a political smile, a court convention—and being conventional it robbed her beauty of its savage force. One could eat, converse, and go about one's business with that smiling Elaine—one was kept at a formal distance. Yet Roland had been fortunate at their first meeting to see her caught by emotion, smile unformed, unfinished, her face open and her only defense those marvelous eyes—windows to her soul.

There was comfort in her smile but no soul—her soul was wild and passionate and chained—her beauty was ferocious but reined in—a beauty that could root men and uproot nations—she knew about it—she might not understand it, but she knew about it—so she smiled, and kept everyone, including herself, safe.

At the end of the feast Roland had wanted to kiss her hair, her mouth—but he kissed her hand instead, politely, for even then he realized that while he was lost in her smile, she was not lost in his.

Still, he had felt very close to her, and the last words he said to her that night were, "We must meet again."

She replied, "I'm sure we will," and then her husband took her arm and she was gone—save for a faint perfume of flowers that lingered like a trace of a goddess.

He remembered how he had stood there, lost, foolishly lost— and then a great sadness had overcome him: a married lady of another country, in a time when marriage was nearly indivisible—there was no hope.

And yet, when he returned to Larraz, he found he still carried memories of Elaine's fingers in his and of the back of her hand against his lips. It had been a thin strong hand—when he thought about it Roland was certain that those hands had not always been the hands of a lady. She had done hard work at one time.

She was beautiful and mysterious—nothing he did could make him forget her. Roland tried other women—he tried travel—he tried to immerse himself in the business of government— he even donned armor and took part in a joust, half hoping for death—but he lived, and wished only that she had been there to watch him.

The dagger stayed in his heart: a jewel, a curse, a constant ache.

Roland thought of Elaine every day. He would go over all the details of their two meetings, and then, in his logical style, he would imagine how he could set up a third. First, he would have to organize an expedition—there were questions regarding supplies, armament, the number of knights he should bring . . . He came up with different answers over the years, according to season and circumstance—it was his favorite waking dream.

There was, however, one part of his planning that was not a dream. Roland had made arrangements with various noble trading partners from Larraz to the Norman coast—if he *did* ever lead such an expedition, he had guarantees of safe conduct and sleeping quarters for his men all the way to the English Channel.

He had been planning this trip for more than four and a half years now—he had never set out.

What good would it have been to go? Roland's informants reported on the solid power of the English Chancellor of the Exchequer, and occasionally mentioned his beautiful wife. There was no hint of a breach.

Then too, there was no good political reason to visit England—but there was a very good reason *not* to go. Some six months after that feast that heralded the Third Crusade, Richard Lionheart had indeed set off for the Holy Land, and he had not set foot in England since. Only now, after capture and ransom, would he return. It would have been a terrible blunder for Roland to have visited England when the King was absent. Such a visit could only be interpreted as treachery, as though the Duke intended to ally himself with Richard's amoral brother John, who coveted the throne for his own. (With Richard imprisoned, John had tried to convince the populace that the King was dead—when no one believed him, he had tried to bribe Henry VI to *keep* Richard captive—but evidently that plot had failed as well.) The Duke knew well that even the appearance of alliance with John could eventually lead to the destruction of Larraz by England's violent King.

So Roland had kept to his waking dreams—but history waits not for love. With England and France soon at war, with France as the battleground, the guarantees of safe conduct would be worthless. Roland's small force could hardly fight its way through the entangled armies of the great powers—there could be no expedition.

The decision had to be made now.

There was a month, or perhaps two, before Richard would return to England.

Roland thought of knights and horses and provisions. He thought of his learned and capable sister Isobel, who could handle administration in his absence.

He did not think of Elaine as the unobtainable married lady of another land—he did not think of the hopelessness of his quest.

He just knew that now he had to go, or else take a real, jeweled, steel dagger and plunge it into his warm beating heart.

He saw with bright memory the image of Elaine by the jousting field, and he wrapped his arms about his pillow and bit into its softness with his powerful jaws—he cried softly against encased goosedown: "Elaine, Elaine, Elaine the Fair . . ."

Then he got up, face unmarked by tears, and walked to his door and opened it. He woke his sleeping servant and began to give orders.

Roland pushed aside the thought of Richard Lionheart's anger—leaving now the Duke would arrive well before the English King, and would of necessity be greeted by the usurper, John—Roland didn't think of what could happen if he succeeded, and stole away the flower of England just before the return of a warlike King—he didn't think of an English army that could sack and burn Larraz.

He gave orders for himself. His country was as nothing to his love.

Chapter 3

THE KNIGHT

At the English Palace of Bermondsey, the first weak rays of sunlight played over Elaine's face—she had finally gone back to sleep—her countenance was serene. In Larraz, the Duke had roused his knights—he was asking them if they wished to go on a quest. In a stable in England, not far from the palace and the royal jousting field, a knight known as Sir Thomas the Silent wished his groom "Good morning"—and nearly caused that gnarled old yeoman to fall to the straw in a faint. It was not that Sir Thomas never spoke—it had been a year and a half since his vow of silence had ended—it was just that, until this minute, he never spoke unless he had to.

Greetings, small talk, politenesses, and congratulations were all foreign to him.

No one at the court had any more than a vague recollection of what Sir Thomas had been like before he had sailed off with the English wave of the Third Crusade. There was generally just a slight memory of a country fellow, a quiet, pious young man—those who racked their brains further might recall that he was the last descendant of a noble but impoverished family. No one had noticed anything remarkable about him.

Thomas had sailed away as one of King Richard's Christian army on March 3, 1190, destined to do battle in the Holy Land.

The English army was still fighting Saladin's Moslems when Thomas returned to London on January 12, 1192.

This time he was noticed.

He came back alone. There was no squire, groom, or servant with him.

He rode a most unusual horse: a tall, black, narrow-bodied,

long legged Arabian stallion. He was armed with the traditional knightly weapons of sword and lance, but he also carried a peasant's longbow slung over one shoulder and a pair of green tapestries tossed over the other. Completing the curious picture, it was noted that he wore no armor.

There was considerable excitement as this strange knight presented himself to Prince John at the palace court. The ladies observed a tall thin young man whose gray eyes were marked by pain—men picked up on their visitor's air of controlled violence.

The knight said not a word—he simply walked up to the Prince and handed him the first of the two tapestries. A message was embroidered in white thread on the green background. John scanned the words and then gestured to his royal crier to read the declaration aloud.

The crier read loudly, with the booming voice of his trade: "I, Sir Thomas, knight in the service of His Majesty Richard Lionheart, do take a vow of silence for one year, beginning this day, August 20, 1191, and witnessed before God by Father Christian of the one true church,"—the crier dropped his voice for the last word—"Acre."

The word reverberated in the crowded room. Acre: the site of their King's great victory in the Holy Land. The assembled nobility stared at Thomas with new respect, and sympathy, and curiosity. What loss had he suffered in battle that he had to leave his comrades, without even words to speak of his misfortune?

Thomas seemed oblivious of the many staring eyes on him. He handed the second tapestry to the Prince.

John scanned it as before, and passed it on to the crier.

The strong voiced man read: "By order of His Majesty Richard Lionheart, I, Sir Thomas, take on as my sacred duty the protection of the ladies of the English court, that no harm may come to them from nature, men, or dragons."

The crowd looked at this stalwart knight. None could doubt his commitment—for who would bear false witness before both God and King?

The ladies stared even more avidly than the men—more than a few began to feel a strong need for protection.

John spoke. "Do you have a place to stay?"

Thomas shook his head no.

John reflected: While it was unfortunately still necessary to

Elaine the Fair
A novel by Timothy Taylor

Horseshoe Press
Jacksonville, North Carolina
1991

Library of Congress Catalog Card Number: 91-71232

ISBN 0-9628943-0-3

Published by Horseshoe Press, 5326 Richlands Highway, Jacksonville, North Carolina, 28540, Tel 919-324-1110
Printed and bound in the United States of America

honor his brother's little whims—and so this strange knight would have to have access to the court—still there was no reason to put up this interloper in the palace.

"Do you know the stable for landless knights?"

Thomas nodded yes.

"You can live there, and carry out my brother's orders as you see fit. I will assign a groom to take care of your horse."

Thomas bowed formally, turned, and left.

And so the silent knight had moved into that empty stable. It was full of old damaged equipment: bridles with straps missing, saddles with broken girths, weak rotted ropes and other debris that had been left behind by a successions of poor knights—though it did not appear, judging from the spiderwebs, that anyone had lived there for a long time. Thomas cleared a space on the floor, and laid down a blanket to serve as his bed.

The Prince sent over a crotchety old groom named Jim—the black stallion moved into a stall, and for the first time in many long months the horse enjoyed regular meals.

By way of proving himself worthy of carrying out his royal orders, Thomas entered every joust and tournament that came long. The tournaments were spectacular affairs—they incorporated duels with the sword as well as the lance, and they were designed so that a series of combats would gradually eliminate losing contenders, finally leaving one supreme winner. Knights came from all over the country to participate in these events.

Thomas was a shocking figure at these celebrations of combat: he wore no armor. There was only one other noble in all the Kingdom who wore no armor in battle—and that man was King Richard Lionheart. This was not so risky for the King, who was protected by the reverence for his high station (who would dare strike at him?)—but it seemed nearly crazy, or else incredibly arrogant, for Thomas. Nothing protected *him* save his skill. Nearly every week the best knights in England rose to his provocation and tried to kill him—but neither sword nor lance ever touched his unprotected flesh.

In every joust Thomas unhorsed his foe. In every tournament Thomas emerged as sole victor.

Those who could remember Sir Thomas from before the Crusade could not account for this power at all—indeed, no one could recall Sir Thomas battling even once—*before*.

He had been changed somehow by his experience in the Crusade—in some terrible way he had been transformed into a fighting machine. There was no warmth in the man—just a cold and remorseless beauty of movement.

And yet Thomas never killed in those tournaments. He unhorsed his opponents—but his lance always seemed to strike where the armor was thickest. He chopped swords off at the hilt—and brought his own to his foe's throat—but there was no uncontrolled follow-through.

He won without passion, with a kind of icy purity—he stood silent, removed from human contact—always alone, no matter what the size of the crowd around him.

As for the ladies, Thomas took his job as guardian seriously— so seriously, in fact, that the ladies found they could not tempt him—but it was only natural that they tried. These privileged women were used to sonnets and ballads, flowers and protests of everlasting devotion. It was the time of courtly love, when a married woman could indulge in every sort of blithe romance— so long as she eschewed the final union. The English court was a hotbed of passion and deliberately thwarted, and thus inflamed, desire.

Sir Thomas's very coolness was an attraction for these hot-blooded ladies—his silence was a challenge—his strength an excitement. But then excitement often turned to anger when their charms were—not rebuffed, but worse—ignored.

There were some who allowed poisonous seeds of rejection to grow into fullblown, hardened hatred—but there were more who came to regard Sir Thomas with a sort of confused wonder. They could admire his feats of arms—but about his character, no two could agree.

Thomas's vow of silence came to an end eight months after his arrival in London. If people thought he might reveal himself then, they were disappointed. Yes, Thomas spoke—but he did not converse—he did not explain.

There was a story about Sir Thomas that was whispered still throughout the court. It concerned an adventure that had occurred just two years ago, during those first silent months. All agreed as to the truth of the story—for the Baroness Louisa had told it herself—but none could define its meaning.

Louisa was a plump and cheerful lady, a buxom lass who enjoyed a frolic. She had gone out to picnic with several similar-ly inclined acquaintances, and their admirers, during the May Day festivities. All the ladies were married—though there was not a husband to be found among the bold young knights who accompanied them—after all, it was May! This day would certainly know heartfelt sighs, burning looks, perhaps a kiss or two in the quiet woods—but all this was sanctioned by God and man, provided temptation did not sweep the lovers away.

Louisa enjoyed these games (she was the wife of the wealthy but inattentive Baron of Nottingham, an older gentleman who preferred his quiet country estate to the intrigues of London) and on this day she was set to meet Sir Guy of Sussex (the very knight who had so enjoyed tormenting Roland) for a bit of dalliance. She wanted to tempt Sir Guy—admiration brought a glow to all her features—but she didn't want any more—or perhaps she did want something, and couldn't admit it to herself—in any case, she was sure the code of chivalry would hold firm.

The party stopped by a wandering stream in the woods, and the servants set out food and drink.

Louisa whispered to Sir Guy—and leaned against him for a moment—and then she walked off, following the stream deeper into the woods. She took off her loose dress and kicked off her shoes—she stepped naked into a clear wading pool. She threw her head back, and let the bright noontime sun beat on her face and her voluptuous breasts. The water had been cold at first, but now it felt warm against her thighs and she opened her legs and stood like a glorious pagan goddess—and then she knew she was not alone.

Louisa shaded her eyes against the sun, and looked for Sir Guy—she later learned that another lady had seen their whispered colloquy and had jealously drawn him aside—Louisa froze, for there were four rough and ragged men staring at her, with dirks in their belts.

At first she felt only shock—not fear. Louisa had been taught from birth that her femininity and her rank protected her from the violence of men—and she was proud of the fullness of her body. She did not shrink from the ruffians—but her breath became short and her heavy breasts tingled from the heat of their gaze. She tried to place these ragged, nearly starving men; she saw their clothes, torn as they were, had been designed for colder climes. She observed their leader, ragged as the rest, but strong and black bearded like the Devil himself—and then he stepped closer to her and drew his dirk.

The blade's gleaming reflection flashed on her body and she saw the leader looking down at her soft belly and her softer breasts, never looking at her face, her eyes, no attempt to communicate on a human level even if only to intimidate—and then suddenly she *knew* and she remembered the horror stories told to her as a child about the heathen Picts from the north, stories for nightmares but suddenly true and she knew it was not pleasure they wanted, not the pleasure of her body but literally her flesh, and she could feel the knife cutting into her and she could see their teeth tearing into her breasts and she screamed to set every bird in the forest aflight and the horse crashed into the clearing and the heads flew.

She thought afterwards that there had only been three strokes: he got the two on her left with one blow, the one on her right with a follow through, and a backhand chop beheaded the leader. He wheeled the horse, sword dripping, and Louisa recognized Sir Thomas the Silent, bareheaded, without armor as usual.

Her hands went to her breasts, and she held them, and then she moved one hand down over her belly to where her soft curls met the water at the juncture of her thighs. She was whole, untouched—she looked at the bodies of the Picts, at the bulging eyes of their separated heads—and then she looked up at Sir Thomas, and opened her arms to him.

He guided his horse over, cleaning his sword as he rode, and then he put it away and took her hand. He helped her step up on the bank and then he walked her a dozen steps away from the carnage. He did not dismount, but he let her lean against his thigh, and he stroked her hair until her breathing calmed. Finally he gestured to her dress, and she put it on.

He had made no pretense of averting his eyes from her nakedness, and Louisa was sure that he knew that in the moments after the rescue he could have done whatever he liked with her—but he did not so much as try to kiss her. When he was stroking her hair, she had looked up at his face once. He was looking far away, and in his eyes was a deep and unknowable sadness.

Elaine, of course, heard this story—and she, alone of all the ladies at the court, began to understand their silent protector.

Other people looked at Thomas's feats of arms and said, 'What a strange and magnificent creature.'

Elaine, on the other hand, looked at what he did *not* do. He didn't speak, so he never had to explain himself; he didn't love, so he never had to give; he didn't drink, or enjoy the pleasures of the flesh, so he never had to expose himself. She was sure that he had a great deal to hide.

She was also sure that the victories he had so far won were just a prelude. While others thought he was extending himself to perform his amazing feats, she realized (as one exceptional person always understands another) that he was holding himself back. She thought that one day his name would be known as well as King Richard's—or better.

He waits in his cocoon of silence, she thought, as I wait in my beautiful chrysalis. Neither of us has yet begun to fly.

Elaine had taken an interest in Sir Thomas, often he had guarded her, and yesterday she had finally spoken to him.

And though Elaine had come to some understanding of Sir Thomas, she had no idea of how much her few words would change his life—and hers—for sometimes, not being able to see or feel it herself, she forgot the effect of her own beauty.

In the stable now, on this the thirteenth of May, the first effect of Elaine's words could be seen: though the sky was overcast, Thomas had wished his groom "Good morning," and now the happy knight looked at the old man's shocked face and went on, "Jim, why don't you get Saladin ready this morning."

The groom looked at Sir Thomas to make sure this was really happening—he had never been allowed to touch the horse before (his duties only concerned food and excrement) and until this moment he had not even known (nor did he think anyone else knew) the animal's name.

"Yes Sir," Jim said, and he turned to the big black stallion with the intelligent sly face and the white snip on his nose. "Saladin," he said softly to the horse, and he wondered at that strange, almost sacrilegious name. Was it not heresy to name a trusted horse after the leader of the Moslem infidels?

Jim had great difficulty putting the bridle on, for Saladin— the black devil—would stay perfectly still as he approached— but the horse would watch him intently with one great wary eye—and then as soon as the leather was raised over his head, the big Arabian would shy violently, head tossing far out of Jim's reach.

The groom would have given another horse what for, but he could do nothing with Sir Thomas there—Jim was confused by the knight's sudden friendliness and humiliated by his own failure with the horse.

"Maybe that was a bad idea," Sir Thomas said, moving up to take the bridle from Jim.

"I can handle him, Sir," the groom said, but Thomas gently pushed him aside and took the bridle.

Jim backed away and then turned on his heel so he wouldn't have to see the way the fickle stallion peacefully accepted his bridle—the groom silently cursed the knight with all a proud man's accumulated hatred for the gentry. He thought: Not a word for me in over two years, not even after the bloody stuck-up bloke started speaking again, not one word for old Jim, and now he thinks it's 'Good morning' and everything's fine and set me up with this crazy horse—Saladin—I have a mind to drop that little tidbit where it will do the most harm—there he goes, smiling—the bastard!—he can't treat me like this!

Thomas did smile and wave as he rode out, and Jim waved back with a servile grin—Thomas was completely unaware that he had left behind another person who would hate him forever.

There were many people who hated Sir Thomas: ladies whose finest glance had been spurned, knights whom he had bested without half trying, courtiers whose favor he had ignored—Thomas was oblivious of them all, for there were only three that he truly cared about now—the memory of his parents was faded and the pain mostly gone—three that he cared about since he had become a man, and of those three two were dead in the Arabian sands, they died August 20, 1191, and now there was only one living person to love, a lady more beautiful than imagination—and she had spoken to him.

As Thomas rode, unconsciously guiding the big horse that he had won in single combat with an Arab warrior, he went over again and again yesterday's scene with Elaine. He could remember every word she said to him—and how she said it: the tilt of her head, her smile, the laughter dancing in her blue eyes when she saw the nakedness of desire in his—and always in the background, the faint scent of flowers, like a meadow field baked by the summer sun.

Some ladies and gentlemen of the court had gone out to the open fields south of the palace to watch an exhibit of falconry. A new crop of the finest and fastest hunting birds were to be tried. Thomas had ridden Saladin restlessly about the group, always looking for danger, taking no part in the cheerful conversations he encircled. Elaine had moved her horse out of the pack—like all proper ladies she rode sidesaddle, both legs on the left side of the horse—she deliberately rode up behind Thomas and to his right, so that when he turned, her horse would not block any of his view of her.

Thomas had been aware of her approach with every sense of his body—but he did not dare to look around until he heard her voice.

"Sir Thomas."

He turned his head and looked, not at her body but just at her face, her face was enough—he saw her eyes and her smile and her held in laughter and he felt her beauty break over him like a wave, pulling and tugging at the moorings of his heart, and then he felt his love break free and go to her and he felt light and loose and crazy happy and his first smile in years nearly cracked his haunted face.

"Milady?"

"You defeated all comers in the joust yesterday."

"Yes." He hardly heard what she said—at that moment he would have agreed to anything.

"And the day before you were victorious in hand to hand combat."

"Yes." The wind had blown Elaine's hair loose as she rode, and Thomas imagined reaching out and catching an errant golden lock—he'd smooth it back where it belonged, his trailing fingers grazing her warm cheek . . .

"It is said that you are the strongest knight in the Kingdom." Elaine was serious, and Thomas was startled, for he rarely thought of himself as others saw him. He looked into her eyes, the laughter gone, and for a moment he saw into her soul, saw something deeper than the shocking aura of her beauty—he had just a glimmering that her life as well as his had not been easy.

He answered carefully. "Not the strongest, Milady. Possibly the most adept."

She looked at him a moment longer in that serious way, and then she smiled as though it were all a lark, and she asked, "Will you teach me?"

"What?" Thomas was quite taken aback.

"Will you teach me to use weapons. I would like to have the ability to defend myself."

The request was unheard of. A lady whose meat is cut for her wants to handle a sword? Thomas could think of no other woman who would broach such a request—nor could he imagine acceding to it with any other. He looked down at Elaine's tense hands on the reins—not at her "carefree" face.

"It would be an honor, Milady."

This afternoon they were to meet for her first lesson.

He went over the scene again and again: her questions—his answers. He worried that he had not said the right things—but then he told himself that none of that mattered now. He would see her this afternoon. That was the miracle.

He seemed to see her face before his eyes—he reached out and caressed the air.

And then he smiled with the bright prideful thought that burst free: She chose me—of all the knights at the court, she chose me!

He rode with that smile on his face, and let the giddy happiness lift him like a swirling zephyr.

He had watched Elaine for years. He knew her walk, her manner—he could identify her from a lock of hair disappearing round a corner—but he had never before even dared to dream of her. He had loved another—but she was gone to the mercies of her God.

He had longed for Elaine—but longing is not the same as love, or even the possibility of love. Now everything was changed. He had begun to know Elaine. He saw in her, as she had seen in him, the banked, smoldering fire.

He would teach her to use the sword. He wanted to see the flames.

Chapter 4

BEDTIME STORY

Twenty years ago . . .

Elaine was frightened as she looked down at her mother. Her mother had always been a large, warm, loving person to her; even through the sadness a child can sense, even when she drank cup after cup of wine and laughed strangely, still—when little Elaine cried, her mother's eyes would focus sharply and she would take her daughter to her bosom, and hold her and kiss her finespun hair, and rock the beautiful little girl in her arms. Then, safe and comforted, Elaine would talk in her private language, and her Mama always understood her.

This morning her mother had been taken away, and Elaine, just four years old, had been lost in terror for endless hours.

Her father had died before she was born—she was alone, and no one in the small village of Firfleet came to comfort her.

Finally, late in the afternoon, she was taken to her mother. Rough men grabbed the child, and yanked her hands—these were local folk, but she didn't recognize them in her fear and in their vicious handling of her. They dragged her through the village and pushed her into a hut, where she saw her mother, who was chained. Elaine was told to speak, and she made her decision—she said the right words in her small voice, and they let her Mama go.

Now Marian (for that was the suffering mother's name) lay on her low wooden bed, and Elaine stood above her, looking down at the tear tracks over the red blotches on her mother's face. It seemed all wrong to the child, for she felt bigger than her mother, and she wanted to go back to yesterday.

Elaine sank down to her knees, and said, "OOah," which was

her word for 'Mama', and her mother pulled her close and held
her, but her grip was not strong, and they ended up lying next
to each other on the narrow bed.

Marian didn't want Elaine to sleep, for there was a story that
she had to tell her daughter. She had planned to wait until
Elaine was older—but now she knew she would have no other
chance.

It was only much later that Elaine realized how much pain
her mother had been in just then—as a child she only knew that
something was terribly wrong—she knew somehow that her
mother was going away.

"I will tell you a story, my darling, my dearest one. Can you
understand me?"

This was a little better. Her mother told her a story every
night.

"Aya."

"Can you say it the other way"—a heartbreaking pause—"like
before?"

Elaine tried to make her Mama smile.

"Yes!" she piped.

"You're a dear good girl, and now you must listen, and never
forget, for I will tell you how you came to be here, and of the
lady who sailed across the sea on the power of love, and how she
bore a daughter, and how through the generations her love was
passed on, until you see your own poor Mama, who loves you.

"There are many things in this story that you will not understand now, but you will remember them when you are older,
and then you will understand everything.

"And there are sad parts to my story, but you will learn that
love goes on and is never lost, and you know your Mama loves
and will always love you."

The beautiful little girl snuggled closer and felt the warmth of
her mother and the stronger grip of her arms. She didn't know
that Marian was using the very last reserves of her strength.
Elaine thought her mother could never go away now.

Marian kissed her child's hair, and let her lips linger for a
long moment against those fine golden strands.

"Now here is the story.

"Once upon a time in the year of our Lord one thousand and
sixty-six, there lived a beautiful young girl in a land called
Normandy, which is across the sea from where we live. This girl
was named Elaine, just like you, and she looked like you too.

She had blond hair and blue eyes and at the time of this story she was twenty years old.

"Now without her there would be no me and no you, for she was my great great grandmother and your great great great grandmother.

"This Elaine was also much like you in other ways besides looks"—Marian smiled slightly at her daughter—"she always wanted her own way. This caused many problems when it came time for her to marry. She was the daughter of the Count of St. Valery, and so, given her noble lineage and remarkable beauty, there were of course a great number of suitors. Knights and nobles, not just from Normandy, but from all of France, came to woo her.

"Yet the young Countess would have none of them. 'This one is too fat,' she would say, 'And that one is too thin, and this other one is worst of all, for how could he protect me, when I am braver than he is?'

"All these refusals made her father, the Count, very angry. He was nearing the end of his days, and he wished to see a grandson before he left this earth.

"One day he summoned his daughter, and laid down the law to her. 'My dear only child,' he said, 'I have been very patient with you. I have not forced any suitor upon you, and I have let you follow your heart's desires. But I do not have that much time left.

" 'You know our Duke William is building a great fleet so that he can cross the sea and conquer the deceitful English. The finest nobles from all of Europe will assist in this grand enterprise. Before the fleet sails, you must choose your husband—I ask only that he be a gentleman, so that our family name will not be besmirched.

" 'If you can not make a decision in that time then I will know that you are above all men, and must therefore serve God. The good abbess here in St. Valery, Mother Catherine, will be pleased to take you in and instruct you in the ways of a bride of Christ.

" 'I do not wish to go against God's will, but it would please me better, my daughter, if you would marry and bring forth a child into the world.' "

Marian had seemed far away, speaking in the voice of the old Count, but now her gaze focused again on little Elaine, and her eyes were bright with love—because with an effort only a mother could manage, she kept all pain from showing.

"You see, my child, Elaine's father was a good and just man, but headstrong and spoiled as his daughter was, she did not appreciate him. She was angry that he had set a limit—no matter how generous—on her, and she certainly had no desire to become a nun, for though she believed in God, formal piety had no attraction for her.

"Still, she was pleased by the thought of all these brave men coming to St. Valery, and perhaps in her mind she thought they were coming for her, rather than the English prize.

"The army gradually assembled—a sight such as had never been seen before in that small town. The Duke had decreed that any brave man could join the enterprise—provided he was willing to gamble his life for a share of the prize. The bravest—and strangest—men of Europe descended on St. Valery. There were heavy bodied, powerful knights from Flanders, wild Magyar cavalry, even a group of Italian archers. There were second and third sons, deprived by primogeniture of any hope of inheritance, who suddenly had a chance to seize land with their own courage. There were peasants never content with their lot, ready to lay down their lives rather than stagnate in the feudal society's grip. They were all eager to conquer, and fittingly led by Duke William, a bastard himself, the son of Duke Robert and his mistress Arletta, the daughter of a tanner.

"While the Duke attended to the organization of this vast expedition, while horses were secured and ships built and even wooden castles constructed piecemeal (to be erected on English soil), the soldiers found themselves with time on their hands. It did not take long for the word to spread that there was a lady of quality in the town, a lady of extraordinary beauty, who was seeking a husband.

"And so it came to pass that whenever the young Countess left her father's castle, she was showered with flowers by eager swains. Her windows were serenaded at night, and talented minstrels earned great sums, as hopeful gentlemen paid them to devise songs in her honor.

"There were jousts and tournaments as the knights prepared for war, and there was one man who gained the ascendancy on the field and in Elaine's heart. His name was Oliver, and he was a sophisticated Parisian knight, and Elaine's father was well pleased, as other suitors fell by the wayside, and she spent more and more time with this dashing hero.

"At last the deadline approached. It was a Sunday afternoon. Duke William gave the order that the fleet would sail on the morrow. Elaine spent a last evening with Sir Oliver. They walked together through the public square, and spoke of their future. Oliver predicted great feats of battle—the knight was certain that besides the land that was his ordained share, Duke William would also heap gold upon him in recognizance of his valor. Oliver continued on in this vein for some time, unaware that Elaine was gradually moving away from him—not physically, for she was close by his side—but rather, she was listening to him as though he were a stranger. He mentioned in passing that they would get married after his victories, but Elaine could feel no happiness at the prospect.

"At such a moment as this, one sentence can change a life, and with his next few words Oliver lost his greatest prize.

"He said, 'I will build my castle on land that I have won,' and Elaine looked sharply at his oblivious face, and she saw that he could never love her, for his one true love was himself.

"She jerked her head away, for suddenly the sight of this man was loathsome, and she found herself caught in the insolent stare of an Italian archer. It was evident that his eyes had already cut away her clothes, but he did not turn his head—as did so many other men, ashamed of their own desires—he just lifted his eyes to her face, and smiled with bright white teeth under a black mustache.

"Without thinking at all, Elaine pursed her lips, and blew him a kiss, and then continued walking with Oliver.

"Elaine was radiant when she came home that night, and the Count was certain that she had made her choice, and equally certain that the worthy addition to their family would be Sir Oliver.

"However, when he tried to confirm this, his daughter put him off with a gay smile, and said that she had made her choice, but she would tell him on the morrow, an hour before the ships sailed.

"My dear child, this next I will tell you may seem strange, but when you are older you will understand that the river of passion often takes a surprising course. For now, I will just say that Elaine had fallen in love, and very early the next morning the archer met his Countess and took her off into the secluded forest. The archer, whose name was Anthony, made a bed for his love with beautiful wildflowers, and they came together joyfully, and the love they shared that day was the seed of a new life, a new person who would come into the world.

"When Elaine came home later that morning, she was wearing a garland of flowers around her neck, and a smile on her face. She might have even told her father all, right then, had she not heard him speaking in low tones to her mother.

" 'The wind has shifted to the north,' he said. 'A bad omen— the ships will not be able to sail today. I have begun to have my doubts about this expedition, which I once thought so grand. Now I fear that even God himself is opposed. Perhaps it is true that blood will tell: William the Bastard—only a tanner could feel comfortable with that mob of ruffians he calls an army. Have you seen those Magyars, dear wife, shrieking down the street? Or even worse, those Italian peasants, who in their insolence know nothing of the respect due a lady.

" 'I am only glad that young Elaine is protected from such riffraff by a fine French knight.'

"You can imagine, my child, how your ancestor felt on hearing this. Her face turned bright red, and for one horrible moment she thought of killing her father—and then she ran to her room and flung herself on the bed in tears.

"She swore to herself that she would *never* tell her father the name of her lover.

"When she was finally composed enough to appear before her family, Elaine again put off her father's questions, saying that she would speak an hour before the ships sailed, and since they were not leaving today, he would have to wait for the morrow.

"Each day of rising tension followed the next, and every day took the same course. In the morning Elaine would slip off to see Anthony, and they would make the love of young people who feel they are alone in the world.

"She would come home, while Anthony would go to the shore—and each day Elaine would ask her father about the wind.

" 'Steady from the north,' he would reply, with growing exasperation.

"Then in the afternoons, as the expedition was once again postponed, Elaine would see Sir Oliver, for form's sake. It was easy to accompany that knight. He had his own dreams, and she had hers. They were the perfect couple.

"So the days went on—Elaine and Anthony's love grew deeper, and each day on parting they would kiss good-bye—and silently pray that the wind would not change.

"Two weeks went by and the wind stayed from the north. The soldiers began to mutter in discontent.

"Four weeks went by, and there was open talk of mutiny. Who wanted to stay in a cause openly cursed by God? Only William's character kept them together to wait a little longer.

"Finally, it had been six weeks, six weeks of an unchanging north wind. Two were happy—thousands were filled with discontent, confusion, anger. William knew he might not be able to keep these men together even one more day.

"He took his greatest gamble.

"The Duke ordered the bones of the revered St. Edmund to be dug up, and carried with proper ceremony on a procession along the beach, as every soldier and all the townsfolk watched. Even Elaine and Anthony abandoned their lovemaking to watch the ceremony.

"They listened to William implore God for a change of wind, and it was as though they could feel the answer of heaven on their own quivering flesh.

"Elaine spoke to Anthony. 'I believe I am with child. The blood that comes with the moon has not appeared this month, and my breasts are swollen and taut as never before.'

"She looked at her love, and saw happiness on his face, although the sudden weight of responsibility sagged his shoulders for a second, but then he straightened up like the honorable soldier he was.

"He hugged her. She went on, 'I have come to love you so that you are part of me, and I am part of you. It is only right that the best of us shall make a child. But now I cannot be parted from you, and I cannot stay here with my father. May I come on the ship with you?'

"He answered, 'Yes,' immediately, for his love was the equal of hers.

"As they knew it would, the wind changed within the hour to the south. Elaine had prepared for this day. She carried both a costume and a wedding gown. And so, without returning home, or saying good-bye to her father, Elaine stowed away on Anthony's ship, disguised as a stable boy. She hid down in the hold with the giant war horses, and stroked their hot bodies for comfort.

"The journey across the sea was not easy for Elaine. She was already having sickness in the morning, a sickness that the pitching ship and dank hold did nothing to alleviate. She did not dare go up on deck, for fear of discovery, so she was forced to retch painfully into a bucket that Anthony had procured for her.

"Anthony brought her food, and told her she must eat, for she had to nourish two—but she could keep nothing down. She was pale and thin, haunted and beautiful.

"In the small confines of the ship, it would have been impossible to keep Elaine's presence entirely secret. Someone had to cover for Anthony on his trips to the hold, and he could not always go himself. Anthony had confided in his closest friend, a fellow archer named Luigi—sometimes it was this kind man who brought food for the lady, or, ignoring her embarrassment, removed or replaced the bucket.

"At last they came to the English shore, and landed without opposition. There a famous incident occurred, much recounted in song and story—Elaine did not see it, hidden as she was, but Anthony gave her a full account that night. Duke William had leaped ashore, eager to be the first on this land he would conquer—and he immediately tripped and pitched forward on to his face. He broke his fall at the last moment with his hands, as the soldiers looked on aghast. Could nothing go right? Then they saw their leader spring lightly to his feet, and with muddy clumps of earth in each of his hands he cried, 'See my lords, by the splendor of God, I have taken possession of England with both my hands. It is now mine, and what is mine is yours.'

"All the men were greatly cheered—it seemed as though the winds had changed in more ways than one, and that their ultimate victory was assured.

"The date of this landing was September 28—the great battle of Hastings was not joined until October 14. Harold, the King of the English, had just been attacked from the north—with great skill he destroyed the Norsemen at Stamford Bridge. Now he hurried with his army to meet William and his buccaneers.

"Every day on shore brought victory and land—or death—closer. Elaine hid in confiscated stables. Days went by when Anthony could not see her for even a moment, for all the men were constantly on call.

"At last they heard the jingling of Harold's armor on the night of the thirteenth.

"The fate of a nation and a love, the destiny of a child—all would be decided on the field of battle.

"Anthony came to Elaine in the middle of that night, and he

took her in his arms and kissed her. He told her to stay inside, where she would be safe, and he would come for her in the evening.

"He told her to fear not, but think of the land he would win for her, the cottage they would build with their hands, the free and happy child they would raise.

"He told her he loved her, and she answered him in kind, and they spoke the truth.

"He kissed her one last time, and then he took his leave.

"The young Countess, protected and cherished all her life, had never seen death.

"From her hiding place she could not see the battle. But all day long she heard the dreadful screams of the hurt and dying; she heard the clash of armor and the worse sound of swords cleaving flesh.

"She would have run out on to the field, and taken a sword herself to fight by her man, but the call of the life she carried inside stayed her, and so she waited with the terror of uncertainty, one hand always against her beating heart.

"She waited, and nightfall rang with the sounds of Norman triumph—but Anthony did not come to her.

"Elaine had not slept in two days. In the middle of that terrible night, she took off all the rude clothes of the stable boy costume, and she walked into the cold sea, and bathed and purified herself. Then she dressed in her white bridal gown, and prayed to God until morning.

"Luigi came to her an hour after dawn. The experience of battle had put years on his face, and his bulky body seemed terribly diminished, until Elaine realized that he was simply missing an arm.

"The wound had been cauterized with a hot iron to stop the flow of blood, and bandaged with a torn shirt.

"Elaine stood up to offer him comfort, but she saw that the pain in his eyes was not for himself.

"'I can not find Anthony,' he said. 'He has not come to me, nor, I can see, to you—yet I can not find him on the field. There is terrible butchery. Many can not be recognized. English monks are searching for their fallen King—they can not find him. I can not find my friend.

"'I can not find him,' he repeated, and he began to weep and embraced Elaine with his single arm. She held him for just a second, and then bade him sit where she had waited.

"'I will find him,' she said, and she set out toward the plain of death with no other thought in her mind, wearing the white dress of a bride.

"The two monks that Luigi had mentioned were from Waltham Abbey, which had been established by King Harold when he had ascended to the throne. The monks had searched diligently, with Williams's permission, for the body of their benefactor, but they could not recognize his form, for the bodies of the dead had been stripped for gain and mutilated out of blood lust—they could not recognize their fine King in the piles of torn nakedness.

"They returned to William the Conqueror (who would never again be known as William the Bastard) and begged one more favor. They asked that the late King's mistress, Edith the Swan-necked, be brought out to the field, in the hope that her eyes of love would prove keener than their own.

"William was intrigued by this proposal, for he had heard of this proud beauty, and he gave his assent.

"Just as Elaine, coming from the rear of the Norman camp, crested a small hill and looked down on the aftermath of battle, so Edith was brought out from the wreckage of the English camp on the other side, guarded by two burly Norman men at arms.

"Elaine looked across the red torn bodies and saw on the other side the most beautiful lady she had ever seen in her life. Edith wore a black mourning dress, and her hair was midnight black as well, and she carried her head high on a long columnar neck, and her piercing black eyes looked out over the field and up to Elaine.

"She saw a bride seem to come out of the clouds, a vision in white with sun on her blond hair, and huge haunted blue eyes.

"The women walked toward each other, shrinking not from death, stepping carefully around the corpses, always coming closer. Not a man moved or spoke on the whole battlefield. William was as stunned as anyone, and as he stared, he whispered the thoughts of all.

"'God has sent his angels.'

"And he watched—all the living watched—as the visions of beauty, one in black, one in white, slowly approached each other in the midst of the carnage. The Norman guards felt the sacred moment around them, and they fell back, so the ladies were alone when they met in the exact center of the field, and then black and white merged and the ladies embraced, each God given face buried in the other's long soft hair.

"Tears flowed on to one another's cheeks, and they spoke in the Latin they had both learned as children, and then Edith took Elaine's left hand with her right, and their fingers entwined, and they walked closely so that their bodies might touch to give each other courage, and they began the search.

"It was necessary to look, and look closely. Where modesty would have precluded such examination of living, naked men, the dead offered all in their final, pitiful agony. And where faces were shattered and necks severed, then it was the bodies themselves that had to tell the tale.

"Suddenly Edith squeezed Elaine's hand with a terrible unconscious grip. Elaine squeezed back, both to aid her new friend and to keep her own hand from being crushed, though she could see no man who looked like a King.

"Edith abruptly released her grip, ran two awkward steps, and threw herself down, resting her cheek on the powerful chest of a naked man with a horrible face. His left eye was almost popped out of its socket, while the right was totally gone, for an arrow had been driven through the orb and into his brain.

"Edith kissed the skin above his silent heart, and Elaine turned away in terror and shame, for she thought that Anthony might have shot that arrow, and then she did the hardest thing she had yet done in her young life. She turned back to Edith, and knelt down beside her, and put a warm arm across her heaving back, and kissed her friend's soft hair and whispered between the sobs that she would go on alone.

"Edith jerked her head around at that, all pride gone from her tear stained face, but Elaine stood up and gestured for her to stay, and left the dark lady with her love.

"Then Elaine searched alone, and it was not long until she saw the black mustache, gleaming bright as ever, and under it the red and shattered mouth that would never more kiss her, and above it staring eyes that would never see their babe, save only if God should give him eyes to see from Heaven.

"So, my child, that is how you came to be in this land.

"Edith was taken by right of conquest by Duke William—she served him well for many years, though she never loved him. She was able to ask one favor of him, that greatly helped your namesake.

"Elaine was in an even more perilous situation than her

friend. She had broken the commonly accepted laws of God (though in my heart I believe that true love *is* cherished by God) and the far harsher laws of men. She had had unconsecrated intercourse with a peasant, she had illegally stowed away on a warship, and after leaving her father without a word the Count (as she would later discover) had died of a broken heart. She knew she was a disgrace to her family and she could expect no help from them.

"Now that Anthony was gone, she had no man to protect her.

"Oliver *had* distinguished himself in battle, but she neither wanted nor expected his help—in any case he did not offer it.

"Luigi had no influence, as a foreign archer of Anthony's class, and besides he was returning to Italy with gold in his pocket for a childhood sweetheart.

"Elaine faced whipping at least, and death at most, yet Edith interceded, as I have said, and I believe William himself was so impressed by the miracle he had witnessed on the battlefield that he was inclined to show mercy. So Elaine was quietly brought to Edith's old village, and taken into the cottage of the Swan-necked one's mother, and there she lived and bore a beautiful girl child whom she named for the friend she first recognized across a battlefield—the child had dark hair, like her father and Godmother (for the proud mistress was pleased to take that position) and she was called Edith.

"And since then our generations have lived in this village, outsiders by choice, love, or fate, but of a noble lineage.

"And all our children have been dark, until you, my dearest one, and it is you who will rise again among the nobility of the land, and that is why I gave you the name Elaine.

"Now in the morning you will find a sack of gold buried under the sunflower. You will dig it up, and take it to the good Father Ashendon, and he will know what to do.

"I have spoken long, sweet Elaine, and you are young, but you will always remember your great great great grandmother, the beautiful Countess whose name you carry. You will remember that she loved a man and made a child; that she comforted a friend when she was needed; you will remember that she showed courage and did not shrink from the face of death.

"You will remember all these things, for one day you will tell this story to your own child, just as my mother told it to me.

"Now kiss me, little one, and give me a hug, for your Mama loves you more than anyone else in the world. And remember too, your father watches you from Heaven, and loves you, and sends his kisses with every moonbeam. Now sleep, little one, and dream of a future as gold as your hair . . ."

Marian rocked Elaine until she slept, hugged her close and kissed that so fine hair. Then she deliberately unfolded her arms and separated herself. She had heard that the grip of death was strong, and she did not want her child to wake up to the horror of being locked in the arms of a dead mother.

Marian knew she didn't have long, but it had been necessary to tell the story that had been passed down. Now she could rest.

Marian lay her head down and closed her eyes. She felt the soaked rag that she had stuffed between her legs to hide the wound. There was a last flash of anger at the brutal, cowardly men—afraid she was a witch, they had not raped her in the ordinary way (if such an act can ever be called ordinary)—they had stuck their steel pikes inside her, and her life's blood had dripped away all day.

Praise the Lord her child had spoken English and brought her home, so giving her time to tell the tale.

Praise the Lord the beautiful child lives on.

Chapter 5

THE LADY WAKES

May 13, 1194, midmorning . . .

Elaine the Fair slept through the morning mass, something she did ever more frequently these days. She wondered sometimes if she had any religious feeling left at all.

It was true that she owed a debt to Father Ashendon. He had taken her in, educated her, and protected her for as long as he lived—yet in some way she had always realized that guilt lay at the root of his kindness. His care of her was one long expiation for not speaking up on behalf of her mother—yet in the most important way his atonement was unsuccessful. He did not vanquish evil—he simply ignored it, let it lie quietly, waiting—it rose again after his death.

Elaine thought then, and still now, that if the priest had spoken out against the crazed violent superstition—if he had fought that simplistic human desire to blame external calamities on one poor scapegoat (perhaps some "foreigner" who could be branded with the curse of witchcraft)—if he had defended Marian, then she might have lived.

And furthermore—if even afterward he had called down God's judgment on both her murderers *and* the men and women who had kept silent (for all knew—there are no secrets in a small village), if he had made the people ashamed of their sins, if he had guided them, taught them—then perhaps they would not have moved later against Elaine herself.

Perhaps they would have resisted the false priest . . .

Father Ashendon never did speak out. He lived a "good" life— he walked a narrow path, and never confronted the evil around him.

Elaine's nineteenth birthday present was a mob bent on murder . . .

She had dreamed of that horror again last night, and she woke up wanting Arthur who had saved her—but even half asleep she knew enough not to reach for him—it had been years since they had slept in the same bed—"Damn you," she said aloud, and the sound brought her fully awake and she rolled over on her front and pressed her face into her pillow (as if to deny that she had said the words) and she reached out blindly with one hand to ring the bell for Sandra, her lady in waiting.

Adjusting to life with a personal servant (one who assisted at her bath, brushed her hair, helped her dress, and so on) had not been difficult for Elaine. Yes, she had grown up as a housekeeper for an elderly priest. As Father Ashendon had grown older and weaker, she had taken on more and more of the chores. She had milked the cows he kept, carried water for bathing and cooking, carried logs for the fire—it was no wonder that Roland had noticed the strength of her hands. Yet in her heart she always kept the image of her great great great grandmother coming over the hill above the battlefield, a vision of beauty overcoming death, and she remembered the nobility of her mother's last hours.

She felt herself truly to be the daughter of a Countess, and it was as nothing to take on that role in life—it was almost as if she had lived it before.

So she let Sandra dress her, and absently reached down to stroke the seventeen year old girl's brown curly hair, and she looked down to see the adoring look in Sandra's soft brown eyes.

Elaine knew that it was not uncommon for the noble ladies of the court to use their ladies in waiting (who were, in fact, mainly young girls of good family but little money) for their pleasure. It was almost inevitable, given the heated atmosphere of the court and the intimate nature of the girls' duties. Sometimes, on days like this when she was filled with desire, Elaine thought of pressing Sandra's pretty face to her body and making the girl kiss her all over. She knew that Sandra's lips would be as adoring as her eyes—and yet she never exercised that power.

When lost and alone, Elaine would sometimes fantasize about being with another woman. She took the images from her mother's story: she thought of herself as the Countess Elaine from Normandy, and she thought of the proud and darkly beautiful Edith the Swan-necked, but instead of a battlefield she imag-

ined them coming together on a secret, silken bed—she thought
of kissing a tender beautiful woman—she thought of a sweet
and gentle love.

She could use Sandra—but she wanted more than that—she
wanted love, passion, desire—she wanted—Damnit! Damnit!
Damnit!—her husband. As always, her fantasies of being with a
woman swung back around to the burning desire to be taken by
a man—she would always need a man to love—she had a man
to love—and he did not want her.

Elaine remembered the sweaty wrestler at the joust five years
ago—she remembered what the serving girl had said to him—
she remembered how the girl had said it with her legs apart . . .

Elaine thought of making that offer to her husband.

She shook her head slowly, and felt the desire inside her
recede.

She helped Sandra arrange her dress, and bent down to kiss
the girl's cheek, and sent her on her way.

Elaine walked alone to her breakfast, for she had looked to
see that Arthur was still sleeping. In the night, her marriage
had been over—but now, walking in the light of day, there
seemed to be fresh possibility. She knew that Arthur would
come down to join her soon, and she knew they would get along
well. They had so much in common! They were two outsiders
from a remote village, with claims to nobility distant on her side
and nonexistent on his—and yet here they were, led by bluff
and beauty to the top of the heap.

They would laugh together at the court follies, and Arthur
would take her hand, and those passing would smile and say, 'A
marriage made in heaven.'

Elaine didn't think of yesterday, but if she had tried, it would
have seemed eons ago.

Children were playing in the courtyard of the castle, and as
she walked through a boy ran fast toward her, looking over his
shoulder in pretend fright of a make-believe dragon. Elaine
caught him before there was a collision, ruffed up his hair, and
sent him off with a smile.

She didn't think at all of the desperation that had seeped
even into the daylight yesterday, a desperation so terrible that
she had been driven to seek a knowledge of killing—a knowledge that she had felt might sometime keep her alive.

No, it was as though all that terror had been screamed out
into the night—and likewise, this morning's burning desire was

calmly banked. She was held in, restrained—but she had put the leash on herself.

She didn't remember her lesson with weapons, planned for this afternoon—she did not think of Sir Thomas at all—though it can hardly be imagined that he did not think of her.

Chapter 6

THE FAT BOY

Sir Thomas did, indeed, think of nothing but Elaine this day. He rode with rising anticipation, he mused, he dreamed, but he never gave one thought to the lady's husband, Arthur the Assessor.

That gentleman slept on, unaware of Thomas's dreams, equally unaware of his wife dawdling over her breakfast, waiting for him.

Finally (it was but one hour before noon) Arthur came to his slow and sore awakening—yet happy withal. So what if his head buzzed and his stomach rumbled uncomfortably—the one could be cured by fresh wine and the other by a breakfast fit for a King. He could eat as much as he liked now—and more! No one would ever again call him The Fat Boy.

That's what they called him in the little village of Firfleet where he grew up with Elaine: The Fat Boy, or sometimes just plain Fatty. He was the son of a small farmer who had named his firstborn Arthur in the hope of having a soldier for a son— but the father was soon disgusted with the weak soft boy who would rather play in the kitchen than fight mock battles in the fields.

Arthur proved to be inept at every skill a farm boy needs: he could not ride, or milk, or plow. Another lad might have been beaten for his failings, but Arthur was the dumpling of his mother's eye, and he quite literally hid behind her skirts.

His father gave up on him—younger brothers and sisters came along—but his mother continued to dote on her eldest. She kept him with her in the kitchen, fed him snacks all day, and gave him first choice of foods before the meals were served. She always told Arthur he was special, and he knew that it was true.

He tried never to play with the other boys of the village, for they tormented him. Every now and then it was necessary for his mother to send him out on an errand, and his heart would pound with fear lest he be caught—and sometimes his fears were realized. A gang of boys would surround him and hurl insults—when that palled, they would dart in on him like birds of prey and cruelly pinch his extra flesh. They marveled at his fatness in those lean times—their bony strong fingers would dig in and twist, and then they'd bounce back, hooting while another attacked, while Arthur cried and screeched from inside his helpless body.

When he finally made it home, his mother would give him extra sweets, and he would eat them with self-loathing, and then he would think and think of how he would get his revenge, for he was special, and smarter than them all.

His mother took him to Father Ashendon for his education. Arthur learned to read and write, and he showed a particular facility for mathematics. He met Elaine, for she shared his lessons, and the two outcasts—the orphan beauty and the fat boy—became fast friends.

Given Arthur's intelligence and ambition, the two year difference in their ages (Elaine was the elder) meant nothing to them. They shared their dreams—but it was the iron laws of mathematics that first gave Arthur a glimmering of a way out.

There was not much entertainment in Firfleet. There were no tournaments or jousts to attend, for the village was far from any baronial seat. Life was monotonous and dour—people spent their lives battling the soil.

Yet man cannot exist without some kind of game, some way of challenging fate outside of the deadly serious battle for survival. It was the pleasure of most of the men to play cards in the evening. After a good draught of wine, they'd sit out in the late summer sun, or inside by the light of flickering candles in winter, and wager small sums back and forth. Those without coins might bet a shirt, or a shoe—one unlucky gambler named Simon could never win back his proper pair, and he could not afford another, so he limped with mismated shoes, much to the coarse amusement of his fellows.

Cardplaying was considered a sport for men, not boys—there did not seem to be enough violence in it for the village children—so Arthur was often able to watch the games unmolested.

He was fascinated by the worn wrinkled paper fluttering, the crudely drawn faces of kings buried in shuffled heaps, the red promise of bursting hearts.

He learned the rules—and the odds—for each and every game. One winter's day it came to be Arthur's father's turn to host the card game. Arthur, twelve years old, watched from the shadows for hours—watched his father lose, and lose again.

Finally the boy gathered his courage and made a request that would change his life.

He asked, "May I play?"

The men snorted in derision, and his father, in no good mood after his losses, snarled, "Get back in the kitchen with the women!"

Arthur trembled before his father's harsh look, and his high voice came out in a plaintive squeak as he begged, "Please Father, let me borrow a coin and play."

"I said, Get Out!"

Arthur looked at his father and hated him—any other time he might have run away, but now his hatred gave him fresh courage—and a son must always challenge his father if he is to become a man.

Arthur's voice was still high, but it didn't quaver this time. "You made a mistake in the bidding on the last hand—if I had played, I would have won."

His father rose from the table, and in his eyes was a hatred to match his son's. He would have struck the boy had not one of the men called out, "Hey Dick, let The Fat Boy play. You needn't waste any money on the whelp—we'll win the shirt off his back!"

Dick's hard face twisted into a malevolent sneer. He never took his eyes off Arthur. "Mind what my friend says, boy. Take my place, and wager your shirt. And listen—I don't care if you lose every cloth on your body—you lose, and you can go naked for the rest of the winter, because I won't get you any more!"

Arthur was shaking with fear as he walked up to the table. He wasn't afraid of the game—he was afraid his father would hit him as he approached. But Dick just stared with the cruel desire to see his son humiliated—Arthur got past him safely, and then everything was easy.

For all the others, cardplaying was just a game, a diversion—for Arthur it was a mathematical exercise, a test of memory that he passed like the simplest of quizzes. He knew where every card was in the deck. He won so easily that at first the others thought he was cheating, and then they shook their heads wisely and ascribed it all to beginner's luck.

Arthur won all the coins they had, but they laughed and told the boy it would all be different next time. Dick saw his friends out, but he looked back once with a puzzled expression—he saw his son, somehow different now, with a small heap of coins in front of him. Dick suspected that the next time might *not* be any different—and he was quickly proved right, for the next time was only more of the same, and nothing changed no matter when or where they played.

The Fat Boy always won.

A grudging accommodation was reached between father and son. Dick forced Arthur to give up all the coins he won—in return, the boy was given a little respect.

Of course, success as Arthur enjoyed could not last long in such a small village. Before long, no one would play with him— but his status had changed. He was still resented for his intelligence and despised for his fatness, yet in the final analysis he had something that Elaine could never achieve: he was *of* Firfleet. Elaine would always be the daughter of a witch and a descendant of foreigners—Arthur's ancestors had tended the land there since time immemorial. *He* could be accepted.

So while people were contemptuous of the lad in their daily rounds, their manner changed in a flash when a visitor—a real outsider—came to town.

It was always a big event when a stranger stopped by—but it became especially festive when the village folk succeeded in luring their visitor into a game of cards. Then Arthur was the toast of the town as he mercilessly picked their guest clean.

As always, Arthur gave all the money he won to his father— that is, all except for one or two coins he managed to hide—but less tradeable winnings he was allowed to keep. These became his private treasure.

Arthur liked to remember his victories—and his victims. There was the fierce knight with a helmet that covered all but his eyes—Arthur won that helmet and the shamefaced knight left bareheaded, his ferocity all gone. There was the gallant lover bringing a silk dress for his lady—but she never saw it for now Arthur owned that lovely gown. There was the King's messenger who was finally left in rags—he simply could not believe that this fat child with the squeaky voice could best him.

Arthur never wore the clothes and armor he won—he just hid his treasures away, and showed them to no one save his one true friend, his orphan classmate. He and Elaine would hide sometimes, and run their fingers over the heavy mail, and smooth silk, and play at being lord and lady of the court.

But then Elaine turned sixteen, and Father Ashendon died. She mourned the priest who had taken care of her—he had always been kind to her—whatever his faults he was the only father she had ever had. The sorrow that she felt settled on her features—it was the last perfect touch that completed the picture—and her beauty suddenly burst on the village like an explosion of light.

Every man who saw her wanted her—every man who heard of her wanted her—and suddenly she had no more time for the fat, younger boy whose high voice stubbornly refused to change.

By accidents of death Elaine had freedom of choice. There was no one to give her away, and a myriad of suitors.

Arthur, ever watchful, saw her desire. She wanted, wanted— she was touched, and kissed, yet she maintained her purity, for there was something she wanted more than love. She had told her mother's story to Arthur, and he knew that she had to fulfill that prophecy. She *would* rise among the nobility.

And so she refused them all—Arthur watched as the men's desire turned to anger, and resentment, and hatred. He knew those emotions well, turned against himself—he bided his time—he was watching when the spark of evil ignited.

When they came to kill her, he was ready—he saved her, and not only that—he brought her to the court, and there her mother's words came true.

Chapter 7

ARTHUR AND ELAINE

March 1, 1189, Elaine's nineteenth birthday . . .

After the rescue, Arthur and Elaine rode hard for London on his father's two best horses. The young man had left a note (it amused Arthur that his father would have to take it to the village scribe and have it read to him) which said: "The horses are mine, long ago paid for by the coins you stole from me. I leave you in peace, but if you come after me, I can only hope that God will have more mercy on your soul than the King's justice will have upon your body."

It was signed "Arthur of London", because Arthur knew that only the capital city could answer his ambitions.

He did not leave a word for his mother.

After a good twenty miles, the fleeing pair settled into an inn to rest for the night. A gold coin that Arthur had hidden from his father procured the best room—the garb of a King's messenger and his lady (Elaine had changed her torn dress for Arthur's silk treasure) put them beyond reproach.

The innkeeper lit a few candles in their room and left them alone. Arthur did not move toward Elaine. He began to talk.

He explained to Elaine everything he would say to their good King Henry II—and she believed he *would* persuade the King. She was certain that Arthur would earn a position among the nobility, and she would rise with him and be his lady.

She listened to his deep voice—it had finally changed, which was why no one had recognized him when he had come to save her—it was a big heavy man who had saved her, not a fat boy.

She felt the terror just behind her and she saw the leering screaming face of the priest—no, no real priest—she would not

believe he was a servant of God—the madman in priest's robes
with foam on his lips howling—

She shuddered and listened to Arthur explain how he would
revise the tax system—

The cries of 'Witch! Witch!' were still ringing in her ears, trying to drown her friend's voice—

Her friend, her man, her love—

They were tearing her dress—

She needed the safety of Arthur's embrace—

They were tying her hands—

She had to get close to her man, had to feel his body against
hers, for only then would she know she was safe, know she was
free of the mob—

She walked across the room to Arthur—

She kept the mob behind her by an effort of will—

At the last second she almost saw the nails again before her
face, but then she hugged Arthur's big body and buried her face
against his shoulder—his shirt burned against the just closed
cut under her eye, but it pleased her, she pressed even closer to
his warmth, the burn telling her she was alive, and she said—

"I love you. I love you."

Elaine gave herself without reserve.

Every tremoring inch of her body cried out to be taken.

Arthur never liked to remember that night.

He had been fine when he faced down the mob. He was fine
when he talked to Elaine and told her his plans—he knew he
would have no trouble dealing with the King.

But he undressed Elaine almost reluctantly, though he knew
that she wanted him with all her heart and soul. He was frightened as her body came into view—he saw the gentle slopes of
her breasts crowned by her hard pink nipples—and then she
pressed them against him, and he saw the smooth lean lines of
her back, curving in at the waist and then blossoming into perfect round soft buttocks that were made for a man to caress—
and he almost shook in his fear, though it was not truly her
beauty that frightened him—it was that he must reciprocate,
must bare his own body, the body that shamed him, and he
cursed the addiction that made him eat in response to all troubles, and he cursed his mother for starting him on that path,
and he cursed his own extra flesh that hung over what should
have been his male pride—and behind the anger was the terrible fear that he would not please this most beautiful of all

women, that he was not really a man . . .

Elaine helped him. She cared nothing for the fact that he did not have the body of an athlete, but she sensed his troubles, and she pressed her body against his bare skin and kissed him. She told him again and again, "You're my man, you're my man, my big man . . ."

And once she had a flash that she was a mother dealing with a child, but then that passed as he finally rose to the occasion, using all the confidence he had left and all the love she gave him—the deed was done, in sweat and gasping, and her virgin's blood colored the bedsheet, and Elaine was so proud.

She felt that she had left the past behind, which until a few hours ago had often been so terrible—she was in love, and she wanted to be held.

Arthur felt shamed by his body's near betrayal—he knew that he would not have been capable without Elaine's help, and he could not bear to think of himself struggling and naked.

His manhood was small now and best hidden—his stomach rumbled painfully. He put on his clothes and said, "You must be hungry, darling. I'll see if the innkeeper can fix us something special."

Arthur kissed Elaine on the cheek and left the room.

Chapter 8

HENRY II

The meeting with the King would turn out even better than Arthur and Elaine had anticipated. With another monarch, they might have had to wait weeks for a royal audience—but Henry II prided himself on his accessibility.

There were both light and dark sides to the King's free and easy acquaintance with his people. It was good that Henry knew what the citizenry were thinking; it was good that he was always open to new ideas. Conversely, his black moods were presented undiluted to his subjects—there were those who obeyed their King too well, and with their obedience came tragedy.

The tragedy that would never be forgotten occurred nineteen years ago during the year of Elaine's birth: it was the murder of the Archbishop of Canterbury, Thomas Becket.

Becket and Henry had grown up in Normandy together, lifelong friends, living proof of the attraction of opposites. Becket was chaste, unworldly, a true Believer—Henry was vibrant, virile, a lover of the sensations of life. They rose to power side by side—Henry in the temporal sphere, Becket in the spiritual. In time Henry became King of England, and eight years later, in 1162, Becket assumed the equivalent religious office: Archbishop of Canterbury.

Henry thought that with Becket by his side England would be insulated from papal power—but the King was wrong—perhaps he never really understood his friend.

Becket wanted to be a saint—that was *all* he truly wanted. Nothing else—certainly not his life—mattered.

There were conflicts between church and state: land that

rightfully (according to earthly laws) belonged to the crown was claimed by the church, ecclesiastical courts claimed sovereignty over temporal ones, the responsibility for investiture was disputed and so on.

It was in 1164 that the truth became clear.

Henry found that Becket sided with Rome on all these issues—the Archbishop would accept no compromise.

Becket looked to Heaven, and placed himself above the law, above his friend.

For six years the issues remained unresolved. Tension gradually built up in the King, whose mind was also beset by domestic troubles.

Becket sensed the change in his former friend's mood. He knew the end was coming—and he embraced it. He gave his last sermon. "I am come to die among you," he said. "In this church there are martyrs, and God will soon increase their number."

Henry was given news of Becket's defiance—it was evident that the Archbishop would hold his position to the grave.

Another King might have reacted calmly, judiciously—but that was not Henry's way. He enjoyed his personal relationship with his subjects—he felt free to speak his mind—he did not hide his rage.

He roared, "What a pack of fools and cowards I have nourished in my house, that not one of them will avenge me of this upstart clerk!"

The words were spoken in anger, without reflection—but they were carried out in blood. Four knights rode out to the cathedral, and on December 29, 1170, they cut Thomas Becket's mortal body to pieces. They made him a martyr, as he had foretold.

Three years later he was canonized as Saint Thomas Becket.

The murder—and his own complicity in it—would haunt King Henry for the rest of his days. For years afterward he traveled the country to do public penance. He bared his back in any number of town squares. He let the people watch while he was flogged by their local monks.

It is true that there may have been other sins on his mind when he felt the sting of the birch branches—for the King was a man who loved women.

When Henry was just nineteen, Duke of Normandy, he had come to Paris to pay his respects to his patron, Louis VII, King of France. He bowed to the King—he looked at the Queen, Eleanor of Aquitaine—and as his eyes met hers, he lost all respect for his sovereign. He saw a beautiful, powerful, ambitious woman—he saw in her eyes a yearning barely hidden by her royal demeanor—he saw that she was neglected in the most fundamental way—and he looked back at King Louis almost with pity, as a fully armed soldier might gaze at a half prepared enemy.

Henry met Eleanor in secret—the thirty year old Queen put her arms around the nineteen year old Duke with the fiery red hair—she pressed her body against him and said, "I am married to a monk, not a King."

Henry said, "It is not a King that you need—but a man."

Then he took her with such violence the first time that she cried—he took her the second time more gently, so that her pleasure might bind her to him—but then when she bowed her head to raise his passion again he thrust her away roughly—she fell back on the bed, naked, still wanting, yearning—he dressed calmly, and said as he left her, "Free yourself of the King, and I will see you again."

Eleanor journeyed to Rome—and who knows what manner of persuasion she applied to the Pope, but very shortly her marriage was annulled on the grounds of consanguinity.

Two months later Eleanor married Henry. She gave herself—and her lands of Aquitane, Gascony, Poitou, and Anjou—into his hands.

In a stroke Henry's power doubled—and with passion roaring through his veins he vowed to recover the legacy of his great grandfather, William the Conqueror.

England had slipped from Norman grasp (for lack of a male heir to William's son Henry I)—but no one had control. The country was nominally run by a usurper named Stephen—but the reality was anarchy, civil war, famine . . . There was no law in the land—the rich and powerful robbed the poor—and the poor died.

A monk of Peterborough wrote, "Every powerful man made his castles and held them against the King—and when the castles were made they filled them with devils and evil men. Then they seized those men who they supposed had any possessions, both by night and day, men and women, and put them to prison for their gold and silver, and tortured them with unspeakable tortures. Many thousands they killed with hunger. I neither can nor may tell all the horrors and all the tortures that they did to the wretched men of this land. And it lasted the nineteen winters while Stephen was King; and ever was it worse. They laid taxes on the villages from time to time and called it 'Tenserie'; when the wretched men had no more to give they robbed and burnt all the villages, so that you might go a whole day's journey and you would never find a man in a village or land being tilled. There was corn dear, and meat and cheese and butter, because there was none in the land. Wretched men starved of hunger; some went seeking alms who at one time were rich men; others fled out of the land. Wheresoever man tilled the earth bare no corn, for the land was all ruined by such deeds; and they said that Christ and his saints were asleep . . ."

Henry landed on the English coast on January 24, 1153.

He was still but nineteen years old, married to Eleanor for less than a year.

His first act in England was to seek a church, and there he knelt to pray. The priest came out to see this foreign noble—and suddenly stopped still, for in a way he couldn't explain, he recognized this man that he had never seen before. Tears started in his eyes, and it seemed a voice invaded his ears. He raised his arms aloft above the kneeling young man, and spoke the words that would soon echo throughout the country: "Behold there cometh the Lord, the Ruler, and the Kingdom is in his hand."

Men flocked to Henry's banner (Sir Thomas's father was one of those men) and victories were won as though preordained.

On January 24, 1154, a year to the day following Henry's landing on English soil, he was crowned as King Henry II. By his side stood the lovely Eleanor, and in her arms she carried their first child, Guillaume (named for Henry's personal man at arms), who was only six months old.

Greatness was expected of the new King—and he delivered. He restored order to the land. He began a system of civil law that endures to this day. Well aware of his own capacity for impetuous action, Henry vowed that his subjects would not have their fortunes decided by the capricious whims of their lords— he established trial by jury: "twelve good men and true"—and thus gave his greatest gift to the English people. By slow and steady increments, prosperity returned to the country. The King would listen to any man, noble or commoner—he loved, and was loved in return.

Henry and Eleanor had more children together. The King gave his own name to his second son: young Henry was born in February 1155—Guillaume sadly died in the spring of 1156, but

then Matilda came along in June of that year—Richard was
born in September 1157—Geoffrey arrived in December 1158—
Eleanor followed her husband's example and gave her own
name to her second daughter, born in September 1161—more
than four years later Joanna was born in October 1165—and
the last young Prince, John, was born in December 1166.
Four years later Thomas Becket was murdered.

Henry remembered the beautiful blessed days before that
dark tragedy—but those days were gone now. Old and embattled in this year 1189, the King prepared himself for death by
remembering his life. He thought of his children with sorrow,
and he thought of their mother: a woman that he had once loved
with such passion that they had thought the earth itself turned
to their pleasure—but now Eleanor was in exile—she was an
enemy, filled with hatred.

Eight children all borne after the age of thirty had taken their
toll on her beauty. Thus it had come to pass that there was a
young King in his thirties, a robust and powerful man addicted
to the chase—of both foxes and women—and there was a Queen
in her forties, whose closest ties were to her children.

Henry was thirty-seven at the time of the murder in the
cathedral.

Eleanor was forty-eight.

The King sought forgiveness, forgetfulness, escape.

Henry traveled the country to do penance—and to sin even
more with the fair maidens of the countryside. He raised an
army to conquer Ireland—and if Henry's name will always be
blessed by the English people to whom he brought justice, then
also he will always be cursed by the Irish, who received no justice, but only oppression. Henry declared himself Lord of
Ireland—but in truth he never entirely subdued that proud
island. There were pockets of resistance that escaped the
English King, and a rebellion was begun that has flamed now
for eight hundred years.

Henry left behind an occupying force in Ireland—he returned
to England sick at heart. He had taken pain like a sacrament,
he had taken women, he had taken a whole country—but still
the only heart's ease he could recall was love.

When he had been away he had dreamed of Eleanor, and in
his mind she had always been the young passionate Queen he
had stolen away from the French court—but he returned to a
middle-aged woman embittered by her husband's infidelities—a

woman who pointedly ignored him in favor of their children.
Henry turned away from his Queen, not knowing the hidden
depths of her rage.

He searched for that woman to whom he could give his love,
and he found someone truly worthy in the person of Fair
Rosamond—a lady of pure character, noble birth, and surpassing beauty. He made her his mistress above all others—he kept
her safe, as he thought, in a maze at Woodstock, navigable only
with the clue of a silken thread. Yet even so Eleanor found this
woman he loved, and announced the end of her life by offering a
hard choice: a dagger, or a cup of poisoned wine.

Rosamond chose the cup. Eleanor watched her drink—and
watched her die.

The year was 1173. In Rome, Thomas Becket was declared a
saint.

The spirit of his old friend did not comfort Henry. The King of
the English would never again know heart's ease until the last
few minutes of his life.

Henry could not kill his Queen, the mother of his children, the
woman he had once loved. He sent her back to her native
province of Aquitaine. She took their children with her. She
would not return to England until long after her husband's
death.

Henry mourned Rosamond alone.

In Aquitaine, the Queen told her children that it was their
father's will that they had been sent away. (Actually it was
hers, and Henry had been too consumed by grief to oppose her.)
She said he did not love them.

In time Eleanor turned her children, especially the ambitious
boys, against their father.

In time they came to see him through their mother's bitter
eyes: he was an adulterer, and worse still, the evil murderer of
St. Thomas Becket.

In time they decided there was no need to wait for their
father's natural death.

And so on this day in March, in the year of our Lord eleven
hundred and eighty-nine, on this day when King Henry II would
meet a woman the equal of Eleanor in her youth, a woman as
beautiful as Fair Rosamond in the hour before her death—on
this day the King thought of all his life, and of the rebellion just
begun, a rebellion led by his sons, who had come to kill him.

Chapter 9

A COUNT AND A COUNTESS

The court convened as usual in the Palace of Bermondsey, despite the nervous reports of the Princes' rebellion across the Channel in the Continental provinces. Still, few people thought it wise to try to deal with the King during this tense and sorrowful time—Arthur and Elaine did not have to wait long before the royal crier announced their names.

They stepped forward smartly—Arthur bowed, Elaine curtsied—but the King only looked down at his lap through half closed eyes—he did not seem to notice them at all.

They straightened up, and stood waiting—the moment stretched ever longer. Elaine wore the silk dress that Arthur had won years ago—she realized now it was both out of fashion and badly soiled by three days hard riding. She looked over at Arthur—his messenger outfit was going to pieces, for his extra weight had strained it severely. Elaine fancied she heard titters from the courtiers behind her—but then she looked up at Arthur's face and saw his calm confidence. The sight of her big man filled her heart with love. She could ignore the foolish courtiers now—she looked boldly at the King.

Somehow she had never expected him to be old. She knew Henry had ruled for thirty-five years (nearly twice her lifetime), knew that he must be in his fifties now—but in her mind she had always pictured the bold red-haired King of legend, his cheeks bright with brazen freckles. Instead she saw a sad old man with little hair left (and that little was white); the freckles were long gone, replaced by the dark spots of age.

She felt sad, looking at his bowed balding head—and then he slowly raised that big head and looked her full in the face and smiled.

It was the bright smile of the man he had been, always on the chase—Elaine blushed—Henry said lightly, "Good morning, my beauty." Then he turned to Arthur and said, "Good morning, Sir. Now state your business, and be quick about it."

Arthur was not quick at all. He had prepared this speech for years, and he was not to be denied his full measure. He was also well aware of the difference between begging and selling. He was not asking the King for some favor—he was laying out a proposal, and he was presenting it with confidence and precise detail.

On the other hand, Arthur had not counted on the King not looking at him at all. He had hoped to read some answers, even as he spoke, in the royal gaze. However, after Henry had spoken his hurried command to Arthur, his eyes had shifted back to Elaine and they had not wavered since. Elaine stood calmly, hands clasped in front of her, eyes downcast, the slight blush of innocence on her face burned through by the fresh red scar on her cheek: she was sweet and pure and dangerous. The King could not look away.

Arthur almost lost his voice when he truly realized the intensity of the King's concentration—but then he caught himself, for he was certain that a man as often embattled as Henry must surely be able to utilize more than one sense at a time. Though his eyes were dazzled by Elaine, Arthur had his ears—Arthur fingered the deck of cards concealed in his big soft hand and went on with a sure voice. He explained the weaknesses in the crown's manner of taxation—he offered his own plan in its stead.

As Arthur spoke, the crowd of courtiers and knights and ladies gradually noticed their King's intentness. They pressed closer, the better to see what he saw.

Arthur's speech rolled on, full of the mathematical flourishes that go over any audience's head, royal or commoner. Henry paid no attention to the numbers, but eyes fixed as they were, he still caught the main details of this revolutionary plan.

Essentially Arthur said that the present tax system failed for two reasons. The first problem was that it was still based on the Doomsday book of 1086. One hundred and three years of war, both internal and external, had made those census and assessment figures valueless. Secondly, the collection of taxes by local lords and Barons, who were then supposed to forward the money on to the King, was, in Arthur's view, a hopelessly naive process. The system could be easily undercut by Baronial greed, or even worse, outright disloyalty to the crown.

Arthur proposed an active Exchequer that would make a census and an assessment of property each year. Each citizen would be personally responsible for his tithe to the King. Payment would be made directly to the King's representatives in the Exchequer. The Barons would have no part in the process—and thus their power would be weakened, while the monarchy would be strengthened. The people would be content—they would certainly prefer to pay their fair share directly to the King who gave them justice, rather than to the Barons who often exploited them.

Arthur finished on this note. There was a long moment of silence as Henry considered the proposal.

The King knew the present system was inefficient—but he had never been unduly concerned about it. The Barons feared him (he had dealt out some rough punishments to those who had been markedly evil during Stephen's reign), and so they never stole very much.

But what about when Richard takes over, he thought to himself. Should I let him deal with the Barons on his own? Or should I smooth the way for that boy who plans to kill me?

Yes, he thought, I will help him, for he is my son, flesh of my flesh. When he goes off on his Crusade he will not need disloyal Barons behind his back pulling the purse strings. This new plan will put the power safe in his hands, after I'm gone . . .

The decision was made, but Henry decided to let the young man wait a little while. He looked only at the beautiful girl before him. The crier had said her name, but he had not been listening then. The King spoke softly, only to her.

"Come closer, fair lady. What is your name?"

"Elaine, Your Majesty."

"Elaine, Elaine, Elaine the Fair," murmured the King, and though his voice was low, the close pressed crowd heard every word—and from that day on she was called nothing else at the English court.

Henry looked over at Arthur for one quick moment.

"Your wife?"

Arthur did not hesitate for even an instant. The card had been dealt—he played it back smoothly. "Yes, Your Majesty," he said with a firm solid voice.

Elaine smiled, for Arthur truly had made her his wife that first night at the inn. They had had two more nights together, on the way to London, but Arthur had been considerate (in view of the exhausting journey) and had not demanded anything more of her.

They would have time later to get to know each other as man and wife.

Elaine thought of her big man—her husband!—and she was sure that life could only get better.

At least for this day, she was absolutely right.

Henry looked at Elaine again, as though he had lost all interest in Arthur and forgotten whatever he had said.

"Dear lady, do you know of the great painting I had commissioned for my retreat at Westminster?"

Elaine shook her head slowly, amazed at the pain in his voice. A lock of blond hair fell across her face and caught against her lips—her fingers traced her lips as she brushed it back, and Henry spoke, only to himself though again all heard: "Ten years ago I would have tossed my crown aside and dueled for you— but now, no, I'm old"—his voice grew firmer—"and I'm dying. Anyway, my dear, you truly know nothing of this painting?"

"No, Your Majesty."

"I would have thought the story of my death would have more appeal. But in any case, let me describe it to you.

"There is an old eagle in the picture, a bird of prey not unlike myself. Once he flew high above the clouds, but now he is missing some feathers and his wings have lost their strength. In the picture he is beset by foes—four young eaglets, his sons, are attacking their sire with claws and beaks. Three are tearing apart his body, while the fourth, the youngest, is perched on the old bird's neck, beak poised to peck out his father's eyes.

"That is my son John, the one I love the most."

Henry smiled at Elaine, but his pale blue eyes were so faded by pain they seemed almost white, as though the sight of the world had driven him blind.

"But my dear"—he took Elaine's hand—"the painting is no longer correct. Where once there were four, now there are only three.

"Henry, my namesake and eldest child, was stabbed in the back two weeks ago. He's dead. Richard is now my heir—and it is Richard who leads the army of rebellion.

"Do you think Richard killed his brother?"

"No, Your Majesty."

"You are a sweet girl, and you answer only as you can. I will not ask you any more such questions, for I would prefer that you speak the truth of your heart rather than what you think would please me.

"However, in this case you are correct. Richard didn't do it. Richard Lionheart sees the world in black and white. I am an adulterer and a murderer—therefore I must die. He wishes to lead a Crusade because that also is a simple moral issue to him: he is the heroic bearer of the cross, while the Saracens are heathens who must be converted or killed.

"He could not keep his purity if he killed his brother—but at the same time he believes his destiny is to be King. Henry's death must have been a gift of God to him—another sign that he is Chosen. I am sure that he has made no investigation of the assassination—he would not want to discover any unpleasant truths. Young Henry was just an impediment who can now be forgotten.

"But I can't forget him. Henry was my son. I favored John and yet I knew that Henry was the best of them. Henry"—the King stopped and then tried to go on with an agonized voice—"young Henry"—he stopped again, and it was as though he might never go on. He gripped Elaine's hand with all the strength of his old fingers, and she wanted to put her other arm around his thick neck and gently pull his suffering face to her bosom—but she dared not treat the King as a man, and in that moment she learned of the terrible loneliness of power. She looked down into his pale, barely seeing eyes, and she tried to put all of her compassion into her gaze, and she answered his grip of her hand with her own pressure.

She felt the crowd around them, pressing close, barely breathing, watching for signs of weakness in the aged ruler. They too were ready to fall upon him.

She held his hand tight and tried to pass her youth into his body—the crowd sighed and she smiled as the King's eyes focused—he ignored the crowd and spoke to Elaine in a clear controlled voice.

The court stepped back, cheated of tragedy.

"My son Henry never wronged Richard.

"He was a good Christian, a gentle lad . . ."

Elaine felt the King was slipping in and out of this world, and that his only anchor was his grip on her hand. She had heard those faraway tones before, in the voice of her mother, and she knew that Henry also was reconciled to his death, and that it would come soon. He came back again, squeezing her hand, but his eyes were still lost.

"You see, it will be much more fun to serve Richard. He has that simplicity that men call greatness—he will be a hero, win famous battles, conquer many lands—his followers will find plunder and women in abundance—but nothing of the sort would have happened if Henry had lived a long and quiet life. Yes, the boy might have killed me, to avenge his mother—but then there would have come a long period of quietude, of remorse—a quality that is absent in Richard.

"So you see, Henry had to go," the King made a smile with his mouth, and looked up at Elaine with those pain seared eyes, "for the glory of England. Such, I'm sure, was the thinking of those ambitious men who surround my present heir. I should imagine the deed was actually done by one Brian, a man who has earned a certain reputation in such matters.

"In any case, the way is now clear for the hero Richard Lionheart, and I am left with a political problem."

The voice was steady and the eyes clear. This time as he looked up there was genuine warmth in the King's smile.

"My son Henry was the Count of Anjou. Now that title is vacant, for he left no heir. In these last two weeks there have been few who comforted me in my sorrow—but many have put on masks of bereavement in the hope I would lay my dead son's title on their undeserving shoulders."

The *King* was speaking now. The court snapped to attention.

"Elaine the Fair." Henry looked at her face. He chose to ignore her scar—neither then nor later would he ever mention it—he concentrated on her beauty. He observed her high cheekbones and assertive nose—he spoke kindly, thinking she was perhaps some Baron's bastard. "I see you are of noble blood."

"Yes, Your Majesty. My great great great grandmother was the Countess Elaine of St. Valery, in Normandy. She crossed the sea to this land with your own honored great grandfather, His Majesty William the Conqueror."

Henry's mouth dropped open in shock.

Few things could surprise the King at this hour of his life, but this revelation, at least for a moment, drove away all royal cares. His eyes lit up from within—a child's memory, almost forgotten, became real—beauty once told was suddenly before his eyes, and her warm hand was in his.

" 'God has sent his angels,' " he whispered, and Elaine smiled but Henry saw the tears start in her eyes and he felt her hand tremble in his.

He held her tight—now he was the one giving comfort—he went on quietly, "My great grandfather passed that story on to his son, the first King Henry. He had no living son—he told the tale to my mother, Princess Maud, as an example of woman's courage, and she always cherished the story.

"She told it to me often when I was a young boy—'the bride who came out of the sky'—I never knew whether the story was true, but I liked to think it was, and I used to dream of that fair Countess Elaine.

"Now I hold your hand—the story *was* true—you are real, and as beautiful as your ancestor, God rest her soul.

"Dear Elaine the Fair," he smiled, and then looked down as she turned her head to wipe her eyes.

The King reflected that at least some good could come of his son's death.

He bent his head and kissed Elaine's hand, and then released it. He turned to face Arthur, who had waited quite patiently.

"Sir! Come closer and state your name."

"Arthur, Your Majesty."

"Your lady's rank is clear, but I would not raise a woman above her man.

"Do you promise to revitalize the Exchequer as you have proposed? Will you serve me to the end of my days—and when the time comes, will you obey my son Richard?"

"I will do those things, Your Majesty."

"That is good, for Richard will have need of men like you. Much gold will be required to accomplish his heroics."

The King got up slowly, a dignified rising that did not show his age.

"Give me a sword," he said quietly, to no one in particular. A young knight who was standing nearby pressed the hilt of his weapon into the King's open palm.

Henry looked at Arthur and Elaine. They stood so still they hardly dared breathe.

The court was absolutely silent.

The King's voice finally came like the slow measured boom of a heavy drum.

"Kneel."

Arthur and Elaine knelt side by side on the luxuriously carpeted floor.

Henry gently placed the edge of the sword against Arthur's broad right shoulder.

"By the right of the Crown, I confer upon you, Arthur, the title of Count of Anjou—and furthermore, I name you to be my Chancellor of the Exchequer."

"Thank you, Your Majesty."

Henry raised the sword and stepped a careful pace to his right. He admired the gleaming waves of Elaine's golden hair and her white shoulders left bare by her dress. He lowered the blade carefully until the edge just touched her skin.

"By the right of the Crown, and recognizing your own noble birth, I confer upon you, Elaine the Fair, the title of Countess of Anjou."

"Thank you, Your Majesty."

The King handed the sword back to the young knight, and sat down carefully.

"Rise, my friends."

Arthur and Elaine stood up, caught in a dream they had long imagined, but barely able to believe it had come true.

The King's roaring voice woke up the stunned court.

"Fools, do not stand there gawking! Are there no ladies in waiting? Take care of the Countess and find fresh rainment for her.

"There will be no more audiences today.

"Arthur!"

"Yes, Your Majesty."

"I will see you privately now. Your plan must be implemented at once. I want it running smoothly, in time for the succession."

"It will be, Your Majesty."

Henry thought he was providing for his sons, especially Richard. He did not realize that he was placing the English people in jeopardy—he did not see the potential consequences of his last impetuous act. Centralizing the awesome power of taxation in this way could lead to a corruption far worse than that of a few petty thieving Barons. The whole machine could now be directed by just two men: the King and his Chancellor of the Exchequer.

If just those two men turned evil, they could strip the whole countryside bare.

Chapter 10

THE CHANCELLOR OF THE EXCHEQUER

Arthur enjoyed his new position.

Henry drove him hard, for the King was racing against his own death. Henry ignored the reports of the huge army that Richard was amassing on the Continent. He ignored the rumors that his remaining sons, Geoffrey and even his favorite John, had joined that murderous force. Even though the King had hinted to Elaine that John would strike the final blow, still one could see that in his heart he did not wish to believe it.

The King dispatched Arthur on one mission after another. The new Chancellor, well guarded by armed knights, traveled to every corner of the Kingdom. He recorded all the changes in property ownership that had occurred since 1086. He determined the current value of the land with a keen and searching eye.

In just a few short months he picked up the sobriquet Arthur the Assessor, a title that would never leave him.

In practice this title meant that Arthur could enter any house, count any livestock, inspect any crop.

The result of his inspection could determine a family's future. Arthur was feared.

He buried the memories of The Fat Boy—and enjoyed.

He was seventeen years old—he had a round pudgy face and prematurely thin brown hair—he was the second most powerful man in England.

Arthur's travels kept him away from London for days at a time—and when he did return, he was often in close conference with the King. He had little time for Elaine.

She needed more than he gave.

Elaine had her own success at the court, but that meant little to her—and perhaps that was one of the reasons for her success. She was aloof—she did not attempt to ingratiate herself. She just glided through the Palace of Bermondsey as though she owned it. She stunned men and women alike with her beauty. No one dared to ask about the mysterious scar that gradually faded from red to white.

Some tried to snub her—harsh whispers of "bastard" were heard—but such low tactics had no effect. Elaine ignored minor distractions—she effortlessly projected the haughty style of a Countess by birth.

Some ladies tried to befriend her—Elaine enjoyed their racy conversation—she picked up some interesting tips for the boudoir—but she gave nothing back, and so the ladies retreated, and Elaine did not find a friend.

Elaine needed a lady in waiting. She was fortunate to find just the right person less than two weeks after her arrival at the court. A young girl named Sandra came then to the palace. She was a pretty lass, just twelve years old, with bouncing brown curls and sad brown eyes. She had a note for the King. The note had been written by Sandra's father on his deathbed. He was an old knight who had served King Henry well when both of them had been young. The knight had retired to the countryside near Salisbury some years ago. His first wife having died, he made a second marriage to a pretty country girl, and soon after was blessed with a daughter, Sandra. Tragically, the young wife died of fever when her daughter was only five years old. Seven years after that, the fever swept across the low lying plain again. Death stole upon the old knight so fast that he only had time to bless his daughter and write a short note to the King he had served, begging him to provide for the young girl.

Sandra made the long day's journey to London alone, on her own little horse.

As soon as Elaine heard about the brave young girl she went to the King and asked if Sandra might serve as her lady in waiting, and sleep in the room next to hers. Henry was pleased to agree—and Sandra adored her mistress from the start.

Elaine was very kind to the girl—she understood much of what Sandra was going through—yet in some way Elaine still remained aloof, just as she was with the ladies of the court.

Elaine was not ready to love anyone except her husband—but Arthur was not her lover—he was her friend.

When Arthur came back to the palace, he would tell Elaine of his adventures, and she would tell him of hers. They were kind and supportive of one another. They got along famously (as everyone noticed) in the daytime.

The nights were different. Rarely did they sleep together, and when they did, Arthur used the excuse of exhaustion to forestall the chance of lovemaking.

Elaine was frustrated.

Arthur was afraid.

The power he accumulated was never enough to stave off his doubts about his manhood. He kept busy—he stayed away from Elaine—he filled the emptiness in his spirit with food and drink.

Elaine applied the secrets of seduction that she had learned. There were nights when she presented herself to her husband in such ravishing disarray that even he could not resist her. But such nights became less and less frequent as Elaine realized that she must *always* initiate—and each time, she had to go farther to reach him.

It was when she realized this that the first nightmare came. She relived the day on which Arthur had saved her, and her screams brought him to her side. Yet Elaine felt shamed—it seemed as though she could only trap her husband with cunning silk or desperate screams. She wanted him to come to her of his own desire—she wanted to be taken—she wanted to be held close through the night.

She thought that all might be better when the old King's race was done—when he would find peace and stop the ceaseless driving of her husband.

Then Arthur, with his administration in place, could find time to relax with her. He could discover the joy of love, and give to her as she would give to him.

Chapter 11

THE DEATH OF A KING

July 1189, four months after Arthur and Elaine came to London . . .

Henry finally pronounced himself satisfied that his country's finances were in good order. In any case he could no longer ignore the massive threat of that army led by his eldest surviving son.

The King had a choice: he could wait for Richard to invade England, wait for destruction and civil war—or he could raise an army and go himself to meet his son, and his destiny.

Henry chose to go forth.

He left with a sorrow that was past despair—and yet it could be borne. To be killed by the simple, forthright Richard—avenging the betrayal of his mother—yes, that was terrible, but it could be borne.

Yet that other thought—those insistent rumors—those terrible thoughts that he had whenever he looked at that monstrous painting in Westminster—those terrible thoughts that he had let out without volition in the grip of his last young beauty—ah, he remembered John, his dear clever youngest baby, the last and all the more missed for having been so soon snatched away—snatched away and raised by a vengeful mother—could John be in the enemy camp?

That thought could not be borne.

Henry crossed the Channel nevertheless.

He arrayed his forces.

The battle was joined at Chinon.

Richard Lionheart rode defiantly at the head of his troops, mounted on a magnificent black stallion. As was his wont, he scorned the wearing of armor—he presented a perfect target to his father's men.

Any of Henry's experienced archers could have killed the young Prince with a single arrow—yet none dared aim at the heir to the throne. A few desultory arrow showers were sent over the Lionheart's head—they fell harmlessly against his mail clad followers.

Some knights engaged in single combat—but those who struck with real violence were most likely settling some private grudge.

These knights, these soldiers knew each other. They served the same Kingdom. Few were truly willing to fight the battle between father and son.

Henry himself rode up to the front line—but far away from where Richard postured. The King dismounted, and singled out a young knight who was wearing a bright red scarf—doubtless the gift of a lady.

Henry drew his sword and called out, "Red Scarf! Come fight me, noble knight."

The young knight dismounted and drew his own weapon. "En garde, Your Majesty," he cried.

The two crossed swords like a pair of traveling actors.

Henry blocked the young man's thrusts and chops with the ease of a lifetime of practice—his hand automatically came up with the parry as his old eyes searched the ranks of his son's army.

It took a minute or two, but then he made out the figure of Geoffrey. The boy, looking like a younger image of poor dead Henry, rode nervously in the rear of Richard's troops. The King's heart went out to Geoffrey—he felt the pain any father feels when he sees a catastrophe looming for a child and is powerless to prevent it. Henry remembered teaching the boy to ride—it had been terrible watching Geoffrey slip to the side, balance lost—to know that whatever one yelled was too late, that each stride of the horse sent the boy further over, until finally there came the inevitable crash to earth.

Yet it was possible then to walk out onto the field, and raise the boy with a gentle hand, and kiss him and brush away his tears with a careless gesture as though they hadn't really been seen. One could tell the boy what he should know of the ways of horses, and boost him again into the saddle, and watch with pride as this time—perhaps this time, he rode.

Henry blocked the slash, knocked away the stab, feinted lightly toward the young knight's heart.

He thought, It's all gone now, I can not pick him up again. He
is caught between the Scylla and Charybdis of his ambitious
brothers—he has neither the ego of the one nor the cunning of
the other. Poor son, do not ride in front of John.

He blocked, he parried, he chopped hard at his foe.

He peered through the ranks of Richard's men, pain insupportable now, for he had suddenly discovered the truth of his
feelings for John—the young man he feared now might murder,
the boy who had only taken, never given from the moment of his
birth—the cunning lad who let no one close, let no one see his
true face—and now Henry realized that he wanted to be loved
by that boy, wanted desperately to know before the end that
John loved him, and as this thought broke free the ranks behind
Red Scarf parted for a moment, and there just for a second was
Richard's camp, and there was the black helmeted head of
John—a serpent's head testing the air with its forked tongue—
there was death peering around a tent flap and Henry missed
with the parry and his foe's low swung sword sliced into the
light jointed metal at the King's thigh, and cut through it, and a
bright crimson gash spouted before the horrified eyes of the
young knight who had inflicted it.

Henry staggered back, still staring far away, and two of his
attendants speedily helped him mount. The King's faithful man
at arms, Guillaume the Marshal (the old comrade for whom the
King had named his first son), rode forward in a rage and slew
Red Scarf where he stood.

Henry did not see that revenge. Once mounted, he immediately turned his horse and lashed him with his whip. He rode hard
for the rear as though the Devil were pursuing him.

His men saw their leader's flight, and they hesitated a
moment in uncertainty—and then they too turned to follow,
wishing only to get away from this ill chanced field.

Richard, high on his great stallion, saw his father's desperate
flight. The Prince did not stop to think of the reason why—no
expression of sorrow crossed his face. He waited just long
enough to see the enemy troops break rank and then with a
lion's roar he personally led his own charge. As always, he rode
well ahead of his troops, unprotected by armor, yet terrifying in
his strength and singleness of purpose. The crown's soldiers
raced away in a panicked retreat, none daring to give the Prince

battle—but Richard had forgotten one thing. There was one man in his father's army who was not part of that retreat. The faithful Marshal had paused (after running Red Scarf through with his lance) to chop off that youth's head as penalty for his impudence. After doing his duty by the King, the honorable retainer looked up to see his fellow soldiers in desperate retreat—with Richard hot on their heels—he felt Richard's men beginning to swarm forward—his own life would be forfeit in a second! Guillaume swung his mount around and put spurs to the beast—he raced back toward his comrades—and thus by a strange quirk, he came up *behind* Richard. The bloodstained lance was in his hand as Guillaume's panicked horse, chased by the army behind, gained on the black stallion. With the strength of desperation, Guillaume swung the bloody oak—and knocked the Lionheart to the ground. The black stallion skidded to a stop, as he had been trained, but Guillaume wheeled too quickly for Richard to remount. The future King of England was at the mercy of his father's most trusted servant.

The bloodstained lance aimed straight at the Prince's unprotected heart. Richard's men stopped their charge. They knew that any attack on Guillaume would mean the death of their leader.

Richard looked at the sharpened point of that heavy lance, already marked with the blood of one of his own knights—he saw that the weapon did not quiver at all and he looked up into the cold eyes of the man that he had known all his life to ride behind his father, the man who taught all the boys to use weapons, the one man who, despite his low rank, his father might call friend—he looked up and saw no pity in those green incurious cat's eyes and Prince Richard Lionheart begged for his life.

"Spare me!" he cried. "Spare me in the name of God!"

The cold green eyes showed no emotion. One could almost see the cat's tail twitching.

The troops behind Richard held their breath.

The Marshal's horse snorted and pawed the earth, ready to charge—the lance aimed true at the Prince's heart—Guillaume tightened his knees and his horse burst forward upon Richard—the Prince opened his mouth to scream but then at the last second Guillaume yanked his horse over, jerked the lance around toward a different target, drove it with all his strength and all the speed of his horse, drove it deep into the chest of Richard's black stallion.

Richard watched in horror—and let his lungs slowly empty in relief—as the brave horse he had trained from a colt sank to his knees, sank to his knees with his heart pierced, and then the stallion's eyes rolled up, his mouth opened to whinny but no sound came out and he jerked one last time, wrenching the lance out of Guillaume's hand, and then he fell heavily to his side in death.

Richard looked up slowly, fearfully, and saw again those cold cat-green eyes.

"I will not slay you," the Marshal said with contempt. "The Devil may slay you."

Then Guillaume turned his horse and rode away at a steady pace. No one gave chase. He rode a few miles to where his King was resting in a commandeered cottage, and he was brought in to see His Majesty right away, for Henry had been calling for him.

The King sat up in bed, clad only in his shirt, a blanket thrown over his legs.

"Are my sons safe?" Henry asked.

"Yes, Your Majesty," Guillaume answered in good conscience, for he had no way of knowing that Geoffrey had fallen during those few violent moments when Richard's army had pressed forward. It was a little strange, for the Prince had been struck by an arrow in the back of his neck. Various explanations of the death were offered later: perhaps one of Henry's men had shot a last bolt into the air as he retreated, perhaps Geoffrey had had to turn his horse to get around some obstacle, perhaps he had turned to look behind him for some reason—but no one knew the truth, for all eyes had been on the drama of Richard and Guillaume. No one had seen John raise his bow . . .

The youngest Prince had almost been completely successful— if Guillaume had killed Richard then John would have been heir to the throne.

But Guillaume knew none of this, and so the King did not learn of this evil in his lifetime.

"Thank God," said Henry.

He paused, and then went on quietly, as though speaking to himself, "But perhaps I ought not to thank Him, or think of Him—perhaps I am beyond his forgiveness."

He looked at Guillaume. "Did you see the doctor and the priest at the door?"

"Yes, Your Majesty."

"You have served me well, my friend. Now let me give you my last order. Do *not* let them in, under any circumstances. If I cry and scream and rave at the end, still do not let them in. I will die a soldier's death, with only a soldier's companionship.

"You see, I haven't let them touch it." Henry threw off the blanket and Guillaume started at the sight of his master's bloody leg, drying down toward the knee but a fresh seepage bubbling up over the thigh with each pumping of the King's heart.

"But—"

"No. I understand that you could bandage it, that I might live another hour—another day—another year, no I could not bear it. It's easier this way—now there are just a few more minutes.

"You saw John, back behind the battlefield?"

"I saw him," Guillaume said coldly, not referring to the Prince by title.

"Then you understand," said Henry. He was no longer speaking to Guillaume directly, he was addressing someone else, perhaps God.

"Should I have stolen Eleanor away from a loveless marriage? I gave her love and children, and she wanted both. Then there were women—I discovered all the delights of earth in their kisses. And then Rosamond—ah Rosamond was so so beautiful! I only wanted to protect her—I didn't want her at the court, I didn't want her at the castle—just a small warm cabin for the two of us and our love, a place where no one could harm her beauty"—tears were streaming down the old man's face—"her beautiful face, her soft skin"—he stopped suddenly and brusquely brushed away the tears with one hand. He looked hard at Guillaume, but the Marshal didn't think the King saw him. The pale old eyes were looking through his friend, looking beyond to whomever he was addressing.

"I failed. I could not protect her, and Rosamond was never twenty. And thus I lost my wife, and my children, and finally my life.

"But I have learned, you see. I have been fortunate to live long enough to know the truth, and I know now that having this life to live over I would do the same.

"I discovered this truth just a few months ago, when I could already see death approaching. A young lady came to the court and I made her a Countess for no other reason than love. I have loved three women in my life, and this lady—whom I have never known in the bedchamber, whom I have never kissed—is the last, yet just as true a love as the others.

"I held her hand, and looked into her eyes, and she gave me all that she could, and I learned then what is important. The pride and sorrow of children is great; a friend like Becket is a stirring challenge and yes I still feel guilt for what was done to him; but the love between man and woman is the only joy on earth."

Now he did not see Guillaume at all.

"I love you," he said very quietly, and then he screamed, "ELAINE!"

The doctor and the priest tried to charge through the door, but Guillaume knocked them back with a hard forearm and then braced himself in the doorway.

He watched the King lay back calmly on the bed, a faint smile on his face, and Guillaume saw the blood pumping very slowly through the open wound and he heard the King say, "Elaine," and in his soft voice there was acceptance and then still more quietly, "Elaine," and then softer than a whisper, "Elaine, Elaine, Elaine the Fair," and then there was no more to say and his heart stopped and the half smile froze on his lips and his eyes stared toward his last vision of beauty.

Guillaume walked slowly to the head of the bed, and gently closed his master's eyes—and he felt the soul of the King take flight from under his fingers.

King Henry the Second was dead.

Chapter 12

RICHARD LIONHEART

Richard was very busy in the weeks following his father's death. First there was the funeral to get through—Richard knelt by Henry's bier no longer than necessary, and wished that others could have had the same dispatch—and then it was on to England to prepare for the coronation.

This would be a grand event—the first uncontested succession to the crown in living memory (even Richard's father had had to wrest the crown from the usurper Stephen). Every bit of pomp and circumstance available to church and state would be brought to bear, for not only was a new King to be anointed—he was also a Champion of God, poised to lead his Christian soldiers into the Holy Land. There, by the grace of God, he would recapture Jerusalem from the Moslem infidels—he would return Christ's sepulcher to Christian hands.

Richard had aimed for that heroic destiny all his life.

It was, indeed, a common enough dream, one that struck most boys of Christian Europe at some time in their adolescence (Charles, Roland's unfortunate younger brother, was a good example of this). But boys grow up to be men, they marry and have children—the thought of sacrifice in distant deserts grows less and less appealing.

Not so for Richard. He would soon be thirty-two years old and he had never married—he scorned the softening company of women—he held tight to his dream of glory.

It was this vision of greatness, blessed by God, that drove Richard to always lead his troops—he simply could not see himself as the careful general, safe at the rear. For the same reason, he refused to wear armor—he was protected by God and his own invincible faith in himself. If that faith had wavered, just for a moment, when he had looked up at the Marshal's cold cat-green eyes; when he had seen that unwavering bloody lance; well, then he had his answer when Guillaume turned his weapon. Richard was certain that he was being saved for something special—only the greatest victories awaited him now.

And so the coronation took place on September 1, 1189. No one would ever forget the magnificent ceremony. It seemed as though every man in England turned out to wave and shout, "Long live the King!"

Richard accepted the adulation—but it was only the final ceremony that truly moved him. Hubert Walter presided. This was the man who had succeeded the sainted Becket as Archbishop of Canterbury—this was the man who was now God's formal representative on English soil. When the Archbishop's fingers anointed the King's head with oil, and placed the crown thereon, then Richard knew that his father's sins had finally been forgiven. The Lionheart accepted the Archbishop's blessing with a great happiness. He was now free of the shadow of his father—free to do his duty before God. He was ready, body and soul, to lead this Christian Holy War: the Third Crusade.

Richard would have liked to leave for Jerusalem the next day, but even as his great great grandfather, William the Conqueror, had had to wait for a favorable wind, so Richard also had to bow before the weather. It was September already—there was no time to organize and begin the great expedition before winter would come.

The delay could be counted fortunate. Each passing day brought new emissaries from every capital of Christian Europe, all happy to be of service to God's chosen warrior. Soldiers were promised from Germany, France, and Spain. Small duchies like Larraz came through with gifts of gold and promises of volunteers.

Richard decided to leave in March. He would have six months to raise and train the finest army imaginable.

All was going well—and yet the King still needed something more. The extra ingredient was money: specifically, gold in great quantities. The contributions he had received so far were welcome but hardly adequate for such a huge venture. Food could not be kept on such a long slow trip—especially one that ended in a hot climate—so provisions would have to be bought every step of the way. Also, even "friendly" potentates might need their palms greased to allow the Crusaders safe passage. Finally, the men had to be paid. Richard knew that he could hardly keep a fighting force in the field for over a year unless the soldiers had coin for a bit of diversion now and then.

The sum required was extraordinary—and Richard needed it in six months. He turned to the only man who could get it for him, his father's choice for Chancellor of the Exchequer, the man who knew where every penny dropped in the Kingdom: Arthur the Assessor.

Chapter 13

RICHARD AND ARTHUR

"I have come to speak with you about the Holy Expedition, but first I need your help with one other matter."

"Yes, Your Majesty."

"I am looking for an unmarried, wealthy woman, who ideally lives far from the capital. Do you know of any such person?"

Arthur's gambler's eyes showed nothing, but his mind raced. Could the King want a bride for himself, when all knew he was engaged (if only for political convenience) to Alice, sister of Philip II, King of France? It might be possible, for that marriage had long been postponed. Alice was said to be beautiful, but steamy rumors drifting across the Channel left little doubt that she was no longer chaste. Perhaps such a hot-blooded Princess was not right for a soldier in God's cause—though again it was hard to say what sort of woman would be right for Richard, since he had never shown any interest in the fair sex, whether chaste or not.

Richard liked his orders obeyed at once—he much preferred the battlefield to the court, for on the former a single barked command could move thousands on the double, while here these fat fops barely condescended to speak to him.

"She's not for me, my dear Count," the King snarled, "so cease your idle thoughts and give me your answer—and be quick about it!"

Arthur smiled, hearing the echo of the father in the young King's voice—and just as with Henry, he took his time. No one, not even a King, would ever push him around again. His hands were on the purse strings—he would open them at his leisure.

"On one of my last surveys, I did encounter such a lady as you speak of, Your Majesty. She is the Baroness of Pembroke, recently widowed as a result of a hunting accident that took the life of the late Baron. She has inherited his lands, and indeed, her family is quite wealthy in its own right."

"Fine," said the King without expression. "And now on to God's business."

Richard said that with complete seriousness, and Arthur had to work hard to keep the amazement off his face. He thought, you, who eat and urinate and defecate the same as I, think that you are chosen of God. You believe in this fallacy for no other reason than the luck of the draw, the luck that caused you to be born a King's son. You think, because of this luck, all should serve you—but I serve you because it suits my interests, because I like my position. I have no loyalty to you—I will be ready to move on when you die. Indeed, your fallacies will *speed* your death—and then perhaps you will tremble to really meet your God.

Then Arthur had to turn away, for he could not disguise his loathing. Richard reminded him of nothing more than the biggest and cruelest of the village bullies.

Arthur did wonder about the request for the woman—it took him some time, but with Elaine's help he finally put the whole story together—and the two of them had a good private laugh about it.

Soon after this meeting, the Baroness Pembroke was summoned to London, and there by express order of the King, she was married to that faithful old soldier, Guillaume the Marshal—Guillaume also received the title of Baron from the King. This act was everywhere applauded: what a gracious, forgiving, chivalrous King!

As Arthur learned the exact details of the incident at Chinon, he wondered why Richard had not simply had Guillaume killed. He doubted the gifts were a way of showing mercy and magnanimity, as the populace believed. Arthur couldn't see a bully acting that way. The Assessor realized that Guillaume, at least for a moment, had really put the fear of God in Richard. It was terror that moved the King. He was afraid to go after the man who had had him down, and yet he needed to get the Marshal out of his mind, out of his way. So he paid Guillaume off with a title and a rich and pretty widow. He put the old soldier, quite literally, out to pasture.

But Arthur would only know of this later. For now, he had to please his King, and pleasing him meant accumulating gold.

The Assessor had his plans ready.

Arthur suggested that they levy a special "Saladin tithe" on every man over the age of eighteen. This tithe would be extremely high, perhaps three times a gentleman's normal assessment, but it would be invested with such holy urgency that it would be a mortal sin not to pay (and the hangman would stay close, lest there be some who lacked true religious motivation). There would be only one way to avoid the tithe— and that would be to volunteer for the Crusade oneself.

It was a simple stroke of genius. The young, strong, and poor would give their bodies—the old and infirm would give their gold. Arthur waited to be congratulated, but Richard said only, "Fine. Now what else do you have?"

So Arthur pressed on with a further plan to tax *all* land by the hundred acre—forest and fallow land alike, rather than just cropland, as had previously been done.

The King approved both proposals, and told Arthur to get to work at once. Then His Majesty rushed off, undoubtedly called by God.

Chapter 14

THE GOLD SOVEREIGN

Arthur cared not a whit about the Crusade, but he loved making the squeeze. Money poured in from Barons and peasants alike. Arthur orchestrated it all with his well tended hands—soft hands, but full of power.

Richard set out for the Holy Land, with his army of Crusaders, on March 3, 1190. He left his brother John to watch over the country while he was gone.

John wasted no time in cloaking himself with royal robes and royal vices. He became known for debauched parties that featured pliant girls, and boys as well. John felt confident in his amusements. With any luck, his brother would soon be a Holy Martyr—and he would become King (since Richard did not like women, there could be no son to dispute John's succession to the throne).

Arthur was also well aware of this possibility. John's vices cost money—but it was not difficult for Arthur to divert a small portion of the Exchequer's funds into the hands of that corrupt Prince. In this way, the Assessor's bets were finely hedged—he would always be indispensable, no matter who ruled.

As years passed with the King gone, Arthur grew ever more amazed at the fortitude, and the pious naivete, of the English people.

Every year Arthur had to raise the taxes (this on top of the Saladin tithe that in itself was almost unbearable) to meet Richard's ever more desperate demands—and every year the news from abroad was bad.

First of all, it took Richard more than a year just to *get* to the Holy Land—he kept getting involved in minor conflicts on the way—he didn't arrive on the beach near Acre until June 8, 1191. Was the Lionheart afraid to go up against Saladin? Then there was that one quick victory at Acre—but not a single additional success.

The Northern European army found itself on alien ground. Mail clad knights roasted inside their armor. Foot soldiers were burned by the sand that lashed their unprotected faces. Water was dearer than blood.

As if the physical conditions were not bad enough, Saladin utterly outgeneraled Richard. The Moslem leader avoided pitched battles that could be decided by the Crusaders' iron might. He refused to 'stand and fight'—he preferred to harry the Christians with his mobile cavalry, to bleed them bit by bit. Saladin knew time and geography were on his side—so he used diplomatic weapons as well. He confused the Lionheart by offering negotiations like tantalizing fruit—he held up the keys to Jerusalem and then snatched them away, leaving Richard grasping at a mirage.

Jerusalem might just as well have been a mirage. The Crusaders, bitten on the flanks whenever they tried to advance, were never able to get close.

Yet each month Richard sent his messages. 'More gold—and more! Just a little more gold and we will take the Holy City!'

And the people gave, and gave, and gave again.

Arthur watched with cynical amusement as the beloved monarch ripped the English economy to shreds. In three short years Richard destroyed all the prosperity that had taken his father thirty-five years to build. There was no money to invest, none to build, no way to get ahead when every year more was taken to feed the bloodsucking leech of Glory. Already there were intimations of famine, as farmers had their land seized for failure to pay their taxes—and then there was no one to work that land—less food in the markets, more and more beggars on the roads.

Yet if there was any resentment at all, it was never directed at the great Lionheart, but only at the perverse John. Arthur had to laugh at the people's stupidity—for it was Richard who sucked their lifeblood—the foreign war cost a thousand times more than John's petty vices—but then the people preferred to suffer for their piety.

The situation reached a new height of absurdity when Richard, in his fashion, came to his senses. It was the fall of

1192, and Richard, weakened by fever, had barely survived the deadly summer heat. He realized that more of this inhospitable climate could easily prove fatal. He also realized that he was simply facing a stronger foe—a most uncomfortable situation for any bully. It hardly gave him pleasure any more to recall how he had massacred those prisoners before their comrade's eyes— that was well in the past now, and there had been few enough prisoners since. It was time to get out, to fight in France, where war was fought by the rules and castles didn't move.

Yet before he could go, he would have to appease Saladin— Richard knew well he would be most vulnerable in retreat.

The Lionheart looked for a way out. Unburdened by principles save his own divine right, Richard came up with the deal most likely to save his own skin. He offered his sister Joanna (she was in his camp, ostensibly under his protection) in marriage to Saladin's brother. That fellow was quite delighted—a European Princess would make a piquant contrast to his other three wives. Joanna, who of course had not been consulted, was not at all pleased by the prospect of being bound over to an infidel. She confronted her brother—but he denied even her most elementary rights. To him she was not a sister—just a subject, like the Baroness Pembroke, to be married at his convenience.

Joanna, the daughter of Henry and Eleanor, refused to submit without a fight. She rallied the priests to her cause, and they raised such a cry of outrage that Richard was forced to renege on the deal.

Joanna remained free—but now Saladin was both angered and insulted.

Richard needed a grand gesture—and he found one: peace. Saladin, holding all the cards, decided to be obliging. Indeed, a formal recognition of Christian defeat was quite toothsome.

A truce was agreed, with each side keeping the territory it already held. In other words, the Christians kept Acre and a few rocky beachheads here and there. The Moslems kept nearly all the Holy Land, including Jerusalem, including all the Christian holy places—they continued to keep watch over Christ's Sepulcher.

Richard had failed—but then he still lived, he was still Chosen.

Saladin gave Richard a golden sword as a going away present.

The King sailed away with a remnant of his army. He left behind 200,000 Christian dead, young men who had done their duty (as they had been told) before Church and King—young men who had died for the Glory of God, or perhaps the Glory of Richard, or perhaps they had died for nothing at all.

Arthur gave a sneering laugh when he heard the news of Richard's retreat. The great hero! He fails in battle, tries to sell his sister, and finally slinks off with his tail between his legs, having failed to obtain any of his objectives (O yes, he did get the concession that small groups of unarmed pilgrims could come to Jerusalem and pray at the Holy Sepulcher—the same right they had *before* one hundred years of war!).

Arthur braced for the insurrection—he was ready to throw his support to John at a moment's notice—but there was not even a murmur of discontent against King Richard Lionheart. It seemed that his *image* as God's chosen warrior was so fixed in people's hearts that his *actions* could do nothing to change it.

The English people were on the rack, and they had stretched mightily to aid their torturer. Now came a twist of fate, a chance to break their bonds—but they asked only for another turn of the wheel.

As has already been recounted, Richard met misfortune on his way back to England. His boat capsized while crossing the Adriatic Sea. The King was captured by Leopold of Austria (this was in December, 1192) and soon turned over to Henry VI, the Holy Roman Emperor. The Emperor demanded a giant ransom for the King. The tortured English populace might well have replied, "Let him rot!"—but instead they chose to suffer still more. They gave, when there was no more to give. Arthur did not have to squeeze—money poured in from the barren counties like the last blaze of a dying fire. God knows where it came from—socks, mattresses, hidden in wells—it was the last reserves of a hungry populace. Arthur wondered if the people would remember these gifts when their children were begging for food in the next winter.

Arthur was often a cruel and vindictive man. The hate in his heart for the loutish villagers who had abused him as a child was still strong. Indeed, by extension, Arthur had come to despise all of rural England. Yet lowly as these people were in his eyes, he wondered if this last royal extortion was not too much. He saw clearly what others did not—he saw famine and slow starvation coming, as the people stretched out their hands to aid their murderous King.

There are only two responses to cruelty on a vast scale: one weeps, or one laughs.

Arthur chose to laugh.

He invented a macabre game that pleased him perhaps too much. No one but Arthur knew it was a game. No one else knew the rules.

Arthur had a lucky gold sovereign: it was the first that he had ever kept from his father. He had hidden it inside a fat cheek all day, and not even a box on his ears that night had loosed it.

He had saved it all these years, but as the insanity mounted around him, he chose to gamble it—but on his terms.

Arthur would travel with all the pomp and circumstance of his office to some hard pressed village. There he would make an entirely unnecessary assessment—he already knew just how broke all the villages were. Then, just before leaving, he would, as if casually, choose a victim. This would be a man who owned a few chickens, or ducks, or geese. Arthur would compliment the birds, and ask if one was for sale. The man, who needed the fowls for his family, would usually say no, whereupon Arthur would flash the gold sovereign. He would ask if he could buy the bird with that coin. At this, the villager's eyes would light up, for on the open market one could probably buy twenty birds for that price. Turning obsequious, the man would load the bird into Arthur's coach and Arthur would give him the coin. The man would thank Arthur profusely, and then the game would begin in earnest. The dialogue hardly ever varied.

ARTHUR: (Roaring) You know that bird isn't worth more than a shilling, now where are my nineteen shillings change?

VILLAGER: (Shocked, frightened) Sir, I didn't know, I thought—

ARTHUR: You thought you would cheat me!

VILLAGER: (Begging) No Sir, not me Sir, but I have no money for change Sir.

ARTHUR: You were going to steal from the lawful representative of His Majesty Richard Lionheart!

That name broke them every time. The man would cry and plead for mercy, and Arthur would take his time, but finally allow that the fellow's life might be spared, provided of course that he gave back the sovereign—while Arthur would naturally keep the bird, as a penalty for the man's dishonesty.

In fear and trembling and sorrow (for the loss of the bird *hurt*) the coin would be returned, and Arthur would ride off with his knights. Once safely out of sight, he would toss the bird out of

the coach—perhaps to wander back to its master, perhaps not—
Arthur never went back to the same place to check.

Though the dialogue was the same, the villages almost inter-
changeable, still Arthur could remember each individual face of
the men he had broken. He could picture them, one after another, begging for mercy. Some went to their knees when he
invoked the name of their King.

Yet Arthur was prepared to play fair, by his rules. If any man
would have the courage to say (after the Lionheart's name had
been invoked), "Considering all the extortionate taxes I've paid
to let our good King fail in the Holy Land, I say the crown *owes*
me a gold sovereign," then Arthur was ready to return the bird
and let the man keep the coin.

He had yet to find such courage. He still had the lucky gold
sovereign.

So Arthur traveled far and wide to play his game. It was an
unhealthy pleasure, the breaking of men—but it amused him.
He deliberately stepped over the line that passes between good
and evil—and he laughed.

Arthur could not tell Elaine about any of this.

She lived in her magical beauty, in the unreal atmosphere of
the court—she knew nothing of the pitiful state of the countryside.

Arthur knew too much. He had gotten drunk last night to
hide from that knowledge, to hide from his wife—to hide from
himself.

But now it was noon on a bright glorious day: the thirteenth
of May, in the year of our Lord eleven hundred and ninety-four.
It was time to get up and seek out Elaine. He liked to see her in
the daytime, in company. He liked to see the desire in other
men's eyes—and their failure.

He called his manservant.

Soon he would be with Elaine, and all would envy him.

Chapter 15

IVAR THE HEARTLESS

Arthur's manservant dressed him in the finest clothes available. He walked slowly to the royal dining hall. He was sure Elaine would be there—perhaps some foolish knight was wasting his time trying to court her.

Arthur the Assessor felt secure in his possessions: his gold, his wife, his power. He could, if he chose, squeeze the last shilling from every last citizen in the land. He believed that he controlled all the world he knew.

Yet there was another, in a part of the world that Arthur didn't know, who would soon have a profound effect on the Assessor's life. In a rough hut on the Norwegian shore, a Viking chieftain named Ivar the Heartless tore at a chicken leg while his women lay bleeding behind him.

He had been born Ivar Ragnarsson, but no one had called him anything but 'the Heartless' for many years. Ivar had invented the sobriquet himself. He had been addressing his men, at the outset of a raiding party—the end of the speech went like this: "... what beats in my chest is but the sound of oars turning in steel locks. I have no feelings. Beware, my Champions, for I am not inclined to mistakes of compassion. But if you do your part, then there will be plunder and slaves aplenty—and nought but smoking ruins will be left where Ivar the Heartless has landed."

The men had cheered, the name had stuck, and their Chief, then and now, was as good as his word.

Ivar was one of the most successful of the Scandinavian raiders who called themselves Vikings (though the English called them Northmen). He had pillaged from Muscovy to the Italian peninsula—but his success meant nothing to him.

Onshore, he lived in a shack like the poorest seaman.

No emotion touched him—he could feel nothing—yet like a man with a missing limb, he constantly searched for the lost extension.

Ivar first realized how different he was from other people when he was a boy of fifteen, just one year too young to join the raiders. He was playing chess with his friend Sigurd, who was just a few days shy of his sixteenth birthday. Ivar's father, the famous Chief of Champions Ragnar Lodbrok, had sailed three weeks before to raid the English town of Marvelsville. He hadn't come back yet—he was overdue.

Sigurd made a weak move. His mind was not on the game. Ivar concentrated. There was a forced win in the position, he was sure of it.

As he deliberated, both boys heard a fierce roar come up from the harbor—a roar that quickly changed to cries of lamentation.

Ivar didn't move, but Sigurd jumped up and ran down to the sea to investigate. He saw Ragnar's longboat, barely making headway as it limped toward the dock. It was propelled by a mere twenty men when the usual crew was fifty.

When Ragnar's boat had returned on other days, it had always been heaped with plunder and stuffed with slaves— there were often twenty-five or thirty captives, most of them comely young women. Now there was no one on board save the exhausted, decimated crew.

Sigurd saw that there was a twenty-first man on board who was not manning an oar—this man had clearly been badly wounded.

Ragnar was not in sight.

Ivar barely heard the ever louder cries of sorrow. He concentrated—and then finally he found it—a killing maneuver with the bishop. He made the move on the board, and then got up and walked slowly down to the dock. He was met by a sea of tearstained warlike faces. He was told that his father was dead—killed by the English.

There was only one form of revenge in the Viking creed that could wipe out the insult of a father's murder. Ivar said the proper words in the voice of the man he had become: "I shall cut the Blood Red Eagle into the flesh of the villain who killed my father."

The vengeance seeking faces around him showed a savage approval.

Ivar saw himself with crystalline clarity, alone in the midst of the raging throng. He analyzed his feelings—he realized that while he felt some satisfaction about finding the correct move at the chessboard, his father's death caused neither pain nor sorrow. It just meant that he would get his command a little earlier than he had expected.

As for these men, beating their breasts and swearing oaths on the old gods—he did not care to be one of them. They would be easy to rule.

Ivar walked coldly among them, and listened to the story of his father's last hours.

Ragnar had picked out Marvelsville as his target mainly because it was said to have an elegant cathedral. The Viking chief was sure there would be golden religious plate and tender virgins alike, ripe for the plucking.

Ragnar sailed his longboat quite openly into the town's harbor on a Sunday afternoon.

He disembarked with thirty men (a skeleton crew of twenty was left on board, oars at ready, set to flee in an instant). The thirty who landed showed grief stricken faces—they were dressed for a funeral, with no weapons in sight. They carried Ragnar on a litter—it seemed their chief was so weak that he could not even sit up.

This was an old Viking trick, many times successful, that played upon the gullibility and piety of the English people. The Vikings would claim that their leader was deathly ill, and that he wished only the blessing of the last rites of the Church before he died.

Delighted with the Christian repentance of these savage Northmen, the people would open up their town, and lead the grieving men to the church—yet once inside, the Viking leader would spring lightly to his feet (miraculously restored to health by the atmosphere of Christian charity), and his comrades would pull swords and axes from beneath their robes and immediately set to murder and pillage.

The plan appeared to work well at the start. An English delegation listened gravely to the Northmen's sorrow, and expressed sympathy, and offered the hospitality of their church. The pious English led the Vikings in a slow, sad procession to the town's gate. There, after some discussion, the gate was opened. The grieving Northmen were ushered in with a slow and formal courtesy—and all the while the town's best archers had been scrambling for the rooftops, for this particular ruse had now been tried once too often.

The Vikings were led in a solemn procession to the main square in front of the church—and then the English delegation suddenly dashed off. The Vikings were exposed in the barren square, and before they could react the Mayor of Marvelsville gave the signal. A deadly arrow shower flashed down from above. Twenty-five Northmen were killed at once. Five were wounded, and of these, four were hacked to death by the enraged townsfolk (who saw the hidden weapons come rolling out as the villains fell). One grievously wounded Viking, Fridriksson by name, was allowed to live to fill out the role of witness—and Ragnar Lodbrok was taken prisoner, so that a fitting death might be prepared for him.

Marvelsville closed in on itself for the next three days. The sturdy archers manned the walls so that the remaining Northmen could not rescue their leader.

By late afternoon of the third day all was in readiness. A pit had been dug in that main square, and Ragnar's legs were broken, and he was tossed in. All the townsfolk watched—the wounded Fridriksson was forced to watch—the snakes that had been collected over the three days (every boy who caught one was given a shilling) were brought forth—the Mayor joked, "We have all the serpents here that fled St. Patrick!"—and then those venomous creatures were thrown in the pit with the Viking chief.

Ragnar tried to beat off the snakes with his hands at first, but they bit his fingers, his palms, and their poison started to work in his body. His motions slowed, he realized he could no longer fight them off, other vipers bit his useless legs that could not even twitch away—he tried to crawl up the loose dirt side of the pit, dragging his broken legs behind him—the dirt crumbled beneath his hands and he fell down again and again, snakes clinging to him, their fangs embedded in his skin—finally he fell down to the bottom of the pit for the last time and his body was covered by the squirming black mass of the serpents . . .

Fridriksson was set free, so that he could tell his comrades of their leader's death—so that he could tell of the greatness of the English wrath.

This was the tale that Ivar heard, one that stirred the blood of Vikings for a hundred miles in either direction along the Norwegian coast. The story had the opposite effect to the one intended by the English—the Vikings were not frightened—instead they were nearly frantic with the desire to strike back.

Ivar took command of the mission of revenge, as was his right and duty (though he was still technically underage, by common consent it was assumed that the tragedy had aged him at least a year). He planned the attack with the cold precision for which he would later be noted.

Ivar landed his army (ninety men, from three ships) in the dead of night on the beach below Marvelsville. All were clad in black at Ivar's command.

Ivar led a small picked unit of six men that moved ahead of the main body of the army. In these six were included the now sixteen year old Sigurd, and Fridriksson, the latter nearly healed of his wounds, his blood on fire for revenge.

The six men carried a heavy battering ram.

They stopped about ten yards before the town's gate. No one gave an alarm. The black clad Vikings were nearly invisible on this overcast night.

Ivar let Fridriksson take the lead and aim the steel capped oak. The ex-captive knew just where the lock was located on the gate.

He lined it up, and nodded once to Ivar. The young commander turned and looked back at his men. He could sense their eagerness more than he could see them.

Ivar picked up his share of the battering ram and turned forward again. He let the tension build for a moment, and then he screamed, "NOW!"

They charged forward and smashed through the gate—and then with hellish, guttural cries, the rest of the army swarmed through the opening. The Vikings went mad as they tore into the town. They killed the watchmen and grabbed their torches—they set fire to every building in their path, and in that deadly light they cut the English down like beasts.

Only the Mayor's house was spared the flames—Ivar took that himself with his picked band—soon his men had seized the little family within: father, mother, daughter.

Ivar ordered the women tied—he told Fridriksson that he could do whatever he liked to the older woman later—he ordered his men to hold the Mayor down.

Ivar tore off the Mayor's nightshirt—and then he drew his knife, and cut the pattern of an eagle into the flesh of the screaming victim's chest. Ivar made the cuts deep and wide—he

exposed the bone beneath—and then he took out the saw that
he had brought for this occasion. He cut through the ribs, following the eagle's outline that he had drawn, and then he
yanked the broken bones apart. He reached into the bloody cavi-
ty and tore out the Mayor's lungs—and thus the revenge of the
Blood Red Eagle was accomplished.

Ivar had his first woman then too. He took the daughter
upstairs to her own bedroom, and a pretty lass she was, perhaps
a year older than the bloodstained boy who held her. He raped
her on her own bed, and when he broke through her virginity he
thought he saw something in her eyes that moved him, but then
there was nothing save his own physical release, and he slew
her when he was through.

Now it was fifteen years later, and Ivar still wondered why he
had felt nothing when his father died, why even his revenge had
been devoid of satisfaction. He had only been touched by the
girl's eyes when he had broken her, and over the years he had
learned to prolong that single pleasure.

Ivar took slave girls now, like the other men, but there the
similarity ended. These captive beauties were quite a treat for
the rough Vikings (they kept only the best for themselves—the
rest they sold in the slave markets of the East). Though the
relationship began in pain and terror, it did not often end that
way. It was a delight to find beautiful women waiting for the
sailor home from the sea—there is a natural reverence for the
lovely form of woman. Then as time went by, children were
born, handsome sons, beautiful daughters—there was a gradual
change from slave to wife. Ivar's mother was a good example: a
lovely French girl, seized on one of Ragnar's Parisian raids, she
had fought at first—but she had been loved by her master, and
she had finally come to love him in return—she gave herself
with a wild abandoned sensuality when she realized that this
was the only life she would ever know.

She had wept when that half empty ship came in—but her
only son shunned her, then and now.

Ivar did not keep women for love, or to make children. And if
it was pleasure he kept them for, then it was a pleasure so terrible that it would not have been countenanced even by his savage brethren, had he not been their trusted leader on so many
successful raids.

Ivar enjoyed the breaking of women. It was the only thing
that made him feel. It moved him in some dark way, this feeling

that he had first had atop a terrified virgin—he repeated the process again and again, searching for that part of himself that was lost.

He would bring his captives home to his rough and gloomy hut—there was no love to brighten this abode, and the riches he had accumulated moldered in a corner—and then he would chain the women to the rusty iron supports that held up the leaky roof.

He always tortured the women slowly and carefully to put off the moment when they broke—he used knife and rope and simple twisting merciless fingers—he prolonged the act as long as possible (as he discovered, torture could be made to last far longer than rape)—days might go by—but finally the victim's head would sag in utter submission, and then Ivar gained his fleeting pleasure, as he broke another's will.

If Ivar had known Arthur the Assessor, the cruel Viking might have sensed a kinship with the tax collector—but while their games may have been alike in kind, they were vastly different in degree.

Once the women were broken, Ivar killed them.

Ivar had almost finished the chicken. He took a last bite, and then threw the scattered bones to the four women who cowered in their chains. They were a new bunch—Italian girls—there would be plenty of time to work on them.

For now he waited for Sigurd Sigurdsson, his childhood friend, the one man in the world he could trust. He tried to imagine Sigurd dead. Would that affect me? he wondered. He pictured Sigurd with his throat slashed, but the image meant nothing.

I *am* heartless, Ivar thought. I am—unless . . .

There came a knock at the door.

Ivar said nothing.

A moment later the door opened and Sigurd stepped in. He was thirty-one years old now—he had grown to be a handsome fair-haired man. He had three wives whom he loved. He did not greet Ivar. He stood quietly, just inside the door. He stared at the floor, for he did not want to see the piteous creatures in the back of the hut. He knew of their fate.

Ivar savored his friend's discomfort for a long moment, and then he began to speak.

"Friend Sigurd, you have known me all my life. You were there when my father's ship came home without him—you were there when I cut the Blood Red Eagle. You've seen me rise to the position of Chief of Champions—you know the best men vie to sail with me, for never have I failed to come home with riches and slaves.

"Yet now I have decided to end my life."

Sigurd looked up in shock. Ivar smiled triumphantly as though he had won a bet with himself.

"I see that bothers you. Even though you have come to despise me, still you care about my life.

"Yet I care for myself as little as I care for these chattels." Ivar gestured backward toward the frightened girls huddling in near darkness.

"If you were killed, would your women weep?"

"Yes, I believe they would," Sigurd answered.

"And you, what of your Spanish girl—the one who fought you for months—yes, I saw the scratches—I have also noticed that she is now big with child—what if she died giving birth?

"No, you don't need to answer. I see it in your eyes. It would"—Ivar enunciated his next words with an exaggerated care—"break your heart.

"But it seems that *I* have no heart, and thus, none to break.

"I have never given life, and my only pleasure is the taking of it—but even killing bores me now. I thought, as I said, that I would take my life and be done with it—but then I changed my mind. You see, Sigurd, you may rest easy. I spoke of suicide only to shock you. I will live at least a little longer, though how much longer is to some extent dependent on you.

"Will you go on a quest for me?"

The question was asked in the flat emotionless tone that Ivar always used, but Sigurd heard the very real despair under it. He saw Ivar searching for that something beyond his grasp— Sigurd remembered his boyhood friend, and forgot the present day monster.

"Yes," Sigurd replied.

"Good. I think of the women I've had, those I've killed"—the chains rattled behind him, but Ivar paid no attention—"and I realize that I can not remember even one of their faces.

"I want to remember one.

"I want to discover this delight in one special woman—this special feeling that you know, that even my humblest sailors know—but which I have never felt.

"I decided to put off my death, so that I would have one last chance to discover love.

"I do not know the name of the woman who can lead me to this secret. I only know that she must be above all others—she must be the most beautiful woman in the world.

"You will find her, Sigurd.

"You need not search all continents, my friend. I have already had a presentiment. I *know* that she must be an English woman. Only the land that killed my father could also nourish the pinnacle of beauty.

"You will sail with Bjorn tomorrow on his Irish raid—"

Sigurd interrupted, "You arranged it already—you never thought I wouldn't go, did you?"

Ivar smiled fondly at his friend. "No, I never did," he said. Then he went on, "Bjorn will let you off on the English coast. You can arrange with him the time and place for you to be picked up on the return voyage.

"I know that your English girl has taught you her language. I also have made a point of learning that tongue. Anyway, your job is simple. You will ask of everyone you meet, 'Who is the greatest beauty in the land?' If there is such a woman as I imagine, you will doubtless hear the same name many times. You will seek this woman out. You must see her with your own eyes. You will know if she is the one I seek.

"Then you will go to your meeting place, and Bjorn will pick you up on his return voyage, and you will come home and tell me her name—you will tell me all you know of her.

"I will mount an expedition, and I will capture her, and bring her here.

"Perhaps then I will find love, with this one finer than all others.

"Or perhaps not—I may discover that I can *not* love—I may discover that I am fated always to be a cripple. If such is the truth, then I *will* kill myself—but I will kill her, first."

Chapter 16

THE CIRCLE OF STONES

Ivar the Heartless knew the coast of England quite well from the many raiding parties he had led. He could probably have drawn a reasonably accurate map showing the outline of that island. On the other hand, he knew almost nothing of its interior. He had never even heard of the most notable monument in the land—but he would come to know it, in a month's time.

Not far from Salisbury, in south central England, there stands a gray circle of monstrous stones. Inside that circle is a horseshoe arrangement of smaller blue stones, and inside that is an even smaller blue horseshoe. The whole is surrounded by a ditch. There is but one break in the ditch, and thus only one entrance to the charmed circle. The entrance path is a narrow avenue guarded by two stones that stand one on each side like sentinels. The avenue is lined up exactly with the rays of the rising sun at the summer solstice. In other words, one must come from due east to enter.

This construction was completed three thousand years before the reign of King Richard Lionheart.

The stones in the outer circle are twice the height of a man and each one weighs fifty thousand tons. No one knows how those ancient builders dragged the stones twenty miles to the site they selected. No one knows why they chose that site so far from where the stones could be found.

All anyone knows is that the stones are there—a temple, rising from the edge of the vast flat Salisbury plain.

It must have been beautiful once. Originally, the colossal stones of the outer ring had all been joined, one to the other, by massive rock lintels, each one expertly fitted. If a man and a woman could have climbed to the top, the lintels were wide enough that they could have linked arms and walked, side by side, all the way around the magic circle. Perhaps such a couple circled the blue stone horseshoes three times for luck. Perhaps they made love in the night, raised up above the earth, close to the turned over bowl of sky and stars—the woman might have looked into the eye of the moon as her man filled her . . .

The beauty was gone now. The weight of three thousand years had toppled many of the stones. They leaned against each other at odd angles, or else lay helpless like beached whales on the ground.

Most of the lintels had fallen.

The circle was broken. No more could lovers, real or imagined, walk all the way around without touching earth.

There was just enough left—a number of standing stones, some fitted lintels still suspended in air—that one could imagine the greatness that man had once created.

Many feared that greatness. Most people thought that since the stones were preChristian, then the site itself was by definition heathen and evil.

Yet that was a false appreciation of both history and religion. A circle of stones is not evil—but man can bring his own evil to the stones.

In a month's time, the gray stones would run red with blood.

Elaine the Fair would watch six men die inside that sacred circle called Stonehenge.

PART II

Romance

Chapter 17

A LESSON REMEMBERED

Wednesday, May 13, 1194, a few minutes after noon . . .

Elaine had long since finished her breakfast and her dishes had been cleared away. She knew she had been waiting too long but she couldn't make herself leave. She kept her mind fixed on one point—she allowed no distracting thoughts—she convinced herself that her husband would come soon.

Two knights on the other side of the dining hall were watching her while they pretended to converse. Elaine didn't want to look up because she didn't want to smile at them.

She stared down at the table before her and waited.

The knights stared at her and dreamed.

Arthur, like many fat men, was quite light on his feet—but still Elaine heard his footsteps as he came up behind her. A smile lit up her face—a clear, unforced, uncalculated smile. Her big man had come.

The knights saw that smile, and they froze like comic wooden soldiers, because for just one second they thought her smile was for them—and then they saw the hulking figure of the Chancellor of the Exchequer coming up behind his wife. They saw Arthur bend down to kiss Elaine's cheek, and the image of his grossness blotting out her beauty was too terrible to contemplate, and so the knights turned away as one man before the kiss was fairly completed.

The knights walked away, cursing themselves for dreaming—they knew there was no hope.

They should not have given up so quickly.

If they had kept looking at Elaine, and if their eyes had been discerning, then they would have seen that lovely face grow taut as her husband kissed her cheek. They would have seen her smile freeze and then disappear, only to be quickly replaced by that other pretty smile, the political smile that helped Elaine through her days, the one that charmed Dukes and Kings and lustful knights like themselves—the smile that was not a sign of happiness, the smile that revealed nothing of her soul.

If they had seen all that, they might have wondered what wall had come between England's perfect couple—it might have pleased them to see Arthur, like themselves, on the wrong side of that wall—it might have given them hope that someone else might replace her husband in Elaine's affections.

But they learned none of this, for they walked away without turning back.

It was the smell again that wounded Elaine. She had felt her man come up behind her, she had loved the weight of him, the feel of his big soft hand on her shoulder, the expensive heaviness of his cloak against her back—and then he leaned down, and her nose was assailed by the odor of last night's wine.

He had not bothered to clean his face or his mouth for her—she steeled herself to accept his kiss—she was only glad that so rarely now did he ask for her lips.

He sat down across from her and said something, and she smiled and answered—an automatic reaction from years at the court—she answered as though making small talk with any courtier.

Elaine studied Arthur. She saw that he didn't notice anything. He talked on as though nothing had changed between them. She wanted him to *see*, to ask her what was wrong—she wanted him to reach out and touch her but she didn't want his offensive breath!

She was heartbroken and infuriated all at once.

Arthur seemed so far away—and then she realized that her vision was blurring. Elaine turned her head sharply and just managed to fight back the tears.

She wondered how Arthur saw her now. She knew her face was taut and strained—and she had never been that pleased about her profile anyway. She thought her nose was too prominent and the lines of her face too sharply drawn. She didn't know that any man worth his salt would read the character in those clear bold lines of her face. It was evident that she had none of the amorphous quality of other women, waiting to be molded by a man. Instead, there was a nobility of spirit, an inherited grace refined in pain, a fierce desire for love. That whole perfect face was stretched taut by the pain in her soul.

She had turned her head to the right, so Arthur was looking at her scar.

He kept talking. Perhaps it was a funny story.

Elaine began to realize that her love had not yet been won. The thought was unbearably sad. She knew that if she faced Arthur again she would be unable to restrain her tears.

He kept talking—a rush of anger gave her strength, cleared her brain to think—she saw a way out.

Her womanhood was always a mystery to Arthur—he had not had a girl before her, and in general he knew little about women. He had never bothered to learn her cycle, for he did not wish to know of the mood changes that overtook her each month as the blood flowed from her empty womb.

Her menses was not due for a while but she was sure her husband wouldn't know that.

Elaine turned to face Arthur, and held both hands to the pit of her belly, and as she looked at him she felt the tears start just as she had predicted. He stopped in midsentence and she whispered, "I hurt."

Her eyes were pleading through their fog of tears, but he saw where her hands were, and he did not want to get involved in that somehow unclean mess of pain and blood.

He asked tentatively, "Would you like me . . .?" and then he paused, for he wasn't sure what he could do—he wasn't sure what he wanted to do—he knew he did not want to be with her when she was like this.

Elaine helped him, as always. She got up.

"I'll just go to my room for a while, and then I'll feel better."

Arthur got up too, but he was relieved when she waved him off. She turned quickly and began to walk away, still half blinded by tears.

She could hardly see where she was going, and this time it was she who nearly caused an accident. Halfway across the courtyard she almost crashed into that same little boy that she had met on her way to the dining hall.

He was very quiet at first, seeing this sad grownup. Elaine knelt down and kissed him—but the valiant boy could stand this for only a second, and then he squirmed out of the lady's embrace and raced off with a gleeful shriek.

Elaine stood up slowly and wiped her eyes—the pain in her heart was insupportable. She wanted to put her hands over her breasts—they were too small—she wanted them to be big and full and heavy with milk—she wanted a baby to suck them.

She looked at the boy as he played happily—she thought of having a son with Arthur—a baby who might grow to be just such a sturdy manchild—she even thought that she could see a likeness of both Arthur and herself in this boy—and then the pain drove her away and she made it to her room and lay down and waited for the torrent of tears that didn't come.

She was all alone and desperately sad and she couldn't cry.

She thought that if a man held her, if she could bury her face against his shoulder, then she could cry. She thought if she held a child, then she could look down at that baby at her breast and tears of joy would flow down her cheeks. She thought that if a woman kissed her tenderly, then she could weep softly and mingle her tears with those of a loving friend.

She could not cry alone.

Would she ever have a baby with Arthur? When they had been married that night in the inn in the eyes of God (if without benefit of his earthly servants), Elaine had assumed, quite happily, that she would conceive soon. King Henry's sanction of their union only leant weight to this opinion.

But then she had not become pregnant during those last months of the old King's reign—she had ascribed this to Arthur's busy schedule, which left them so little time to come together.

Then came the calm transference of power to Richard, and Arthur's seat in government was firmly assured. Elaine had hoped for a change.

Yet Arthur always seemed to find reasons for travel—new expeditions were constantly required in order to unearth gold for the King's Crusade.

And then there was worse: her husband's desire, which she had always to coax, finally dropped to the vanishing point. He never wanted to hold her now save in public—when she could not make uncomfortable demands on him.

They had been together for more than five years now.

She thought of the little boy she had met today, and how he looked like a son they might have. She thought if only she could bring Arthur to her bed, then maybe they could make a child like that—she put a hand over her left breast, she felt her heart

race and her nipple harden—but then she wondered if Arthur
would be indifferent to the child too, and then she wished to
God she could cry.

She remembered how Arthur had come up behind her today,
and she realized that it was not merely an odor that had wounded her heart.

It was memory.

The scent of stale wine was still in her nostrils, and the scent
brought back the night and the dream and what was worse than
the dream—she remembered her pilgrimage to Arthur's bed,
her lonely vigil and retreat.

'I won't try to love you anymore, Arthur.'

She had hidden the night, tried to leave it behind like a
dream—but she had started to remember in the dining hall, and
it was all clear to her now, she remembered everything and she
could no longer hide from the truth.

There would never be a child with Arthur.

Elaine remembered, not just the night but the day before. She
remembered the terror that had gripped her even in broad daylight. In the midst of convivial acquaintances she had felt utterly alone, sure in the awful presentiment that she would soon
have to fight for her life, with no husband to protect her.

She had ridden up to Sir Thomas.

She remembered the planned lesson.

There was still time to go.

Her hands were strong. She would learn to use the sword.

Chapter 18

THE ARTICLE OF FAITH

Sir Thomas was early. He rode Saladin nervously through the sculptured wood that surrounded the King's stables. He rode around and around on manicured paths, and down long alleys flanked by carefully trimmed trees. He was blind for once to danger—blind to the magnificent scenery—he saw nothing save for the path that led from the Palace of Bermondsey—the path down which Elaine the Fair must walk.

His seemingly aimless wanderings were always designed to keep that path in view.

A light rain was falling. There was no one else about.

In former times the royal stables had been the staging area for hundreds of lavish hunting parties. Henry II had loved to hunt and Richard had carried on the tradition during his short stay in England.

All that changed when Prince John assumed command. Unlike his father and elder brother, John had no love for the so-called manly arts. He disliked riding, hunting, jousting, war— he liked private pleasures (it amused him that these were paid for by the holy tithes supposedly earmarked for his brother's Crusade); he liked to kill from the shadows.

The Prince sponsored no hunts and refused to let the nobility use "his" stables. (Why let others have a pleasure that he could not share?)

The Prince's perversity worked in Thomas's favor—there were no other knights around to challenge him.

Thomas kept moving, riding through the rain, eyes on the path.

Saladin felt his master's tension and reacted in kind with

bunched up muscles and a stiff gait. The horse didn't like the footing either—it had been a drizzly cold May—the carefully laid out paths were turning to mud. Saladin slipped and bounced along, and laid his ears flat to his head to show his displeasure.

Thomas began to speak to Saladin in a low comforting tone, he kept one hand on those tense neck muscles, he soothed and guided the big horse—but he never took his eyes off the path.

Thomas knew that Elaine was late by now—they had agreed on one by the clock, and even the half seen sun showed that that time was passed—but he didn't wonder when she would come. He didn't consider the possibility that she wouldn't come. He didn't wonder what he would do after she came.

He just watched, as if that act alone could consume nearly all his energy—he watched, and cared for his horse, and if branches did occasionally burn his cheek, he took no notice—he did not turn his head for trifles.

He watched—and she wasn't there.

He watched—and Elaine the Fair was there before his eyes.

He hadn't seen her approach. He realized later that she must have taken a shortcut through the royal gardens—but he couldn't figure that out now. He could only stare.

Thomas watched her walk—she hadn't seen him yet—and a belief formed in him that would forever alter his life.

She had made her request to him, and to him alone. Now she had come to him. This was all he needed to know.

He did not consider her thoughts and feelings. He did not consider her marriage.

He just watched her walk—she was wearing a deep blue coat and a pretty black hat—a hat too fashionable to be really effective—he saw her long blond hair escaping its protection, the hair turned dark by the rain—he saw the light blue dress she wore peeking out from under the darker hue of the coat—he knew that dress was the color of her eyes.

He watched her—and the belief formed solidly in the soul of this man who was without religion—the belief formed like an article of faith, and if he had put it into words, he would have said this: "There will come a day when Elaine will love me as I love her—she will be my woman, and I will be her man."

He did not say those words—he did not need to. The belief had formed. It was part of him now. He understood it without expression.

He said only, "I love you," and though the words were spoken softly, he said them not with hopeless longing but rather with patient confidence.

Sir Thomas truly believed that someday he would have Elaine the Fair.

Chapter 19

CUPID

Sir Thomas got off Saladin so that he could walk up to greet
Elaine. He did not wish to talk down to her from his mount—he
wanted to be close enough to touch her.

Elaine heard the man and the horse coming down one of the
alleyways. She recognized Sir Thomas and his black Arabian—
the horse snorted and pulled as he was led along—he seemed to
be protesting his master's strange behavior.

Elaine smiled.

It was nothing special, just this lady's normal smile of greeting, and even this only half seen through the light drizzle—yet
it entranced Sir Thomas, just as Elaine shocked the hearts of all
men, save only her husband.

Thomas could not even manage 'Good afternoon'. All he got
out was "Countess," and that in the low caressing voice of a man
hopelessly in love.

It was doubtful whether Elaine even heard him in the rain—
but she understood his greeting all too well. He loves me, she
thought, he loves me without knowing me. Then she felt a touch
of fear, for she had told no one about the lesson—she was alone
with this powerful man.

She kept smiling, but she looked searchingly at this knight.
She tried to look into his soul to see whether his intentions were
honorable. Thomas met her gaze.

Elaine did not see the fear she often saw in men, fear of her
beauty and her position—instead she saw a look that brought
back the never forgotten memory of the sweaty wrestler at the
joust—Thomas looked at her like that man had looked at the
serving girl. Yet there was more than desire in Thomas's eyes—

Elaine saw love, and tenderness, and courtesy. She would be safe enough with this man—and yet never completely safe.

She thought of leaving now and returning to her husband—but that thought was too awful. Pain flashed through her eyes and she saw Thomas notice it and stretch out his hand to her as he quickened his approach—she felt his kindness, his concern, but she had not come here to be helpless, she had come to learn how to defend herself.

She thought, Perhaps it is best for me to be brave. She took Thomas's offered hand and looked boldly up into his face.

"I am ready for my lesson," the Countess said.

This surprised Thomas. For a moment he had been ready to take her in his arms—for a moment he had thought that that was her only wish.

Now he held the firm hand of a lady of quality—a lady who smiled at his consternation—a lady who was ready for serious instruction.

Thomas switched gears smoothly—he was, after all, a master of arms. He would teach her—there was no hurry. The solid belief hung well anchored in his soul: in time she would come to love him.

He let go of her hand and spoke with quiet authority. "There are three main weapons that you need to understand, Milady: the sword, the lance, and the bow. Of these, the one best suited for you is the sword.

"I know of a small clearing past the dog runs where we will be somewhat sheltered from the rain. It's an ideal place to practice but it's a little far for you to walk. Did you tell them to have a horse ready?"

"No, I wasn't sure where we would be going—and I don't have a sword."

"I took the liberty of bringing one for you, Milady." Sir Thomas turned slightly, and unclipped an extra sword, sheathed, from his belt. He handed it to Elaine.

"Take this, Milady, and let us go in out of the rain. I'll tell the man to get a horse ready for you."

Thomas turned back to Saladin. "Wait here till I return, my friend," he said in a calm, loving voice. He stroked the horse's neck and pressed his face for a moment against the soft short hair of Saladin's black cheek. The horse stood quietly now—once again all was well with his master.

Thomas and Elaine walked over to the royal stables—actually

a large barn that showed the ravages of four years of neglect. They stepped into the wet, moldy interior—and had to dodge a drip coming down from the leaky ceiling. There was a long dim hallway with stalls on either side—Thomas noticed that there were only four horses present, where once there had been thirty or more.

The knight and the Countess could just see the backside of a young groom as he worked—not too hard—at mucking out the last stall on the right. He had probably heard them come in but he didn't seem at all curious about his visitors.

Thomas touched Elaine's arm, indicating that she should wait, and then he walked on down the hallway. She stood there in the damp, holding the unfamiliar sword—so deadly and yet lighter than she had expected.

She watched Thomas walk down toward the groom, and she thought how her husband would have yelled, 'Groom, get a horse ready now!' Arthur would never have walked to the servant as Thomas was doing.

She saw the knight reach the far stall and say a few words to the groom. The lad stopped his pitchfork in midstroke and quickly propped it up against the manger. He stepped out into the hallway and took a long look at Elaine—then he almost ran down the hallway to the tackroom, which was but a few stalls up from where Elaine stood—he took another long look before he ducked into that room, and still another when he reemerged with sidesaddle and bridle.

Unfortunately for the lad, he then had to walk away from the beautiful Countess—as Thomas had walked by the horses he had picked out a gentle bay for Elaine—this horse was in a stall about fifty feet down the hallway.

Thomas, walking slowly from the other end, met up with the boy again as he set the tack on the mare's stall door.

"Why don't you take her out here and outfit her in the hallway," Thomas suggested. He wanted to make sure the boy put the equipment on properly—given the general atmosphere of disuse, there was no telling when the lad last had practice.

The groom caught the implication but he didn't mind too much—"Yes, Sir," the groom said—this way he could look even more at Elaine the Fair!

Thomas, smiling, walked back to Elaine.

"What's so funny?" Elaine asked, grinning herself.

"The lad is an admirer of yours. While that is hardly unique, still, I am always pleased to meet another who shares my good taste."

Elaine had to laugh at the oblique way he presented the compliment, and then in the midst of her laughter she realized that he had entire left off any formal form of address—not the 'Milady' he had used before (which was commonly applied to all ladies of quality), and certainly not 'Countess'. He no longer considered her rank—he was treating her like a village girl out for a frolic. Elaine suddenly remembered the sweetness of being seventeen—she remembered the boys who had chased her during that brief golden flowering before all the horror returned. She looked at Sir Thomas and thought of being kissed.

Sweet memories were in her voice when she spoke to him, but the subject was once again the lesson.

"Why am I only suited for the sword?"

The groom had the mare out in the hallway now and he was putting on her bridle. Thomas kept his eyes on the lad as he replied. "The lance is too long for you," he said cooly. He paused. The groom had the bridle on and now he set the saddle on the mare's back. "As for the bow . . ." Thomas shrugged his shoulder and let his longbow slide down his arm. He caught it with one hand and gave it to Elaine.

She took it with her free hand—Thomas reached out and took his extra sword back. He handed Elaine an arrow from his quiver.

"Shoot the groom," he said.

"What?"

"Shoot him. He won't feel any pain, my dear E—um, Countess. Doubtless he will think of it as a bolt from Cupid's bow."

Elaine smiled at the way he had almost lost himself with her name—but then as she fitted the arrow she wondered what he truly meant by his roguish command.

"There, go ahead—you've got the arrow nocked—draw back and let fly!"

Thomas didn't let any sound out but it was obvious that he was laughing at her. Elaine decided to make the pull and aim the arrow at *him*. That would take the smile off his face!

She pulled back on the arrow with her right hand. Nothing happened. She braced her left hand against the bow and pulled harder. Nothing. She pulled with all her might—strong hands, yes, but she did not have the trained muscular arms of a warrior—she pulled and she pulled, but she could not bend Thomas's mighty bow—she yanked in frustration and her fingers slipped and the arrow came loose and fell to the stone floor with a clatter.

"That's why the sword is best," said Thomas.

He clipped on the extra sword, picked up the arrow and casually took the bow from Elaine. He pulled the arrow back, bending the bow seemingly without effort, and let fly. The arrow struck a wooden post about a foot above the groom's head. It stuck in, quivering.

The groom jerked around in alarm.

"Cupid missed," said Sir Thomas.

The groom said something under his breath and turned back to the mare. He impatiently yanked the saddle girth up around her without checking whether she was relaxed. Even from where he stood Thomas could see that the mare was puffed up with fright from the arrow—when she relaxed, probably with Elaine on, the girth would hang loose and the saddle would slip. The Countess could easily suffer a nasty fall.

Thomas was angered by the groom's carelessness—especially since Elaine could be hurt—he did not think of the role that he had played with his boastful shooting.

He started for the groom.

Elaine looked back and forth between the two men. She saw how Thomas's politeness (walking down earlier to speak to the groom) was overshadowed by his careless disregard of other's feelings. He could be, almost unconsciously, very cruel. She understood now why he had no friends—yet at the same time she was in awe of his physical prowess. He's just a boy, she thought, well meaning yet unaware of anything save his own desires.

She wondered what it was that had frozen Thomas in this sort of magnificent adolescence. He had all the strength and generosity of youth—yet without mature wisdom or understanding. He clearly loved women, as attested by his daring feats in protecting the ladies of the court—yet he had not the maturity to take a woman of his own and keep her. Like a lovesick boy, he preferred to desire one he couldn't have—Elaine knew well that she was the object of his desire.

She was impatient with this knight—she guessed that he was about the same age as herself but she thought of him as the younger. She knew she had an old soul—she had been a grownup since she was four years old. This young knight could never match her.

Elaine decided that Sir Thomas was not the man for her.

The thought came as a shock. She had not been aware of the direction of her own musings. I should not think this way, she thought, so of course she pushed on. She wondered if Thomas *could* be the man for her—she still expected greatness from him—she wondered what force could break the youth and bring on the man—she thought he must know sorrow, and learn compassion—if then he could keep his strength, then just maybe . . .

Elaine smiled at Thomas's back as he dismissed the groom and adjusted the girth himself.

She was glad she had requested the lesson.

Every inch of her body felt alive, quivering like the arrow in the wood.

Chapter 20

THE FIRST LESSON

Sir Thomas and Elaine the Fair rode up away from the King's stables, past the dog runs full of desperate beagles. The dogs barked hopefully, excitedly. They all ran over to the fence to watch the riders. They climbed over one another's backs—some lifted legs and sprayed their friends in their excitement—they entreated with voices and soulful eyes. They hoped that this time they would be let out to hunt.

"I hate to see dogs like that," said Thomas.

"Why are they so upset?"

"They were used to hunting once a week, and plenty of good training runs between times. That was the way under King Henry, and in Richard's early days. Even when I returned two years ago it was still common for gentlemen to ride out with these dogs for a day's hunt. But as the Prince has gained power, he has gradually eliminated access—now he doesn't let *anyone* hunt with "his" royal dogs. Prince John doesn't hunt himself, so he stopped the training runs too. The dogs are locked in—they have to live on hope, you see."

Elaine studied Thomas from her ladylike, sidesaddle perch. He was indignant about the dogs, but was he even aware that he had committed a grave political heresy? There was no sign of it in his face. He had referred to the King just casually—Richard—just the name, without majesty or title.

What if the King heard of this?

Thomas was risking his life!

She remembered his famous tapestries: "in the service of His Majesty Richard Lionheart . . ." Why did Thomas show no respect now? At least he had referred to the Prince properly, despite his obvious contempt—why did he denigrate the King? And furthermore—why did this knight, known everywhere for his silence, talk so much? Even the dogs moved him to speech—it seemed he cared more about them than people. Elaine thought her escort was acting almost crazy—she had never expected this provocative, foolhardy, contemptuous man when she had ridden up next to the famous silent knight.

The explanation of Thomas's behavior was really quite simple. He was just incredibly happy. Being next to Elaine put him almost out of control. Speaking to her was an intoxicant—and she even answered him! Elaine was right on two counts, but she hadn't put them together. He was in love with her, and he was crazy. He was crazy in love with her, and the feeling swept over him every time he looked at her. It never occurred to him to restrain his speech in any way. He spoke his mind (save only his declaration of love, which even Thomas realized was a trifle premature) and never thought once of betrayal—after all, she would come to love him!

As for Richard, Thomas hated him—and with good reason. The knight saw no reason for false humility in the company of his love.

Elaine contributed to all this, though not on purpose. It wasn't just her beauty that was driving Thomas mad—her voice was having quite an effect too. It reflected all the changes that she had gone through today. There were her screams in the night that had left her throat raw—there were her unshed tears after meeting Arthur—there was the exhilaration of being with Thomas—and the fear that hadn't quite left her. She hardly had any voice left, but what was there might even have challenged a saint. She spoke with three parts breath to one part voice—it was a husky whisper that Thomas had to lean in to hear—a voice that belonged in the bedroom—Thomas's heart nearly stopped when he pictured her there, breasts peeking atop a silk nightgown, legs bare to the thigh, that voice like kisses down his spine . . .

The two adventurers, lost in their private worlds, reached the spot that Thomas had chosen just as the rain drizzled to a stop. It was a wide clearing in the midst of tall pines—their rain softened needles made a fine carpet over the mud.

They dismounted—Thomas handed his extra sword to Elaine—they drew their weapons.

Thomas was a good teacher—a close and attentive teacher—

he showed Elaine how to set her feet and balance so that the sword became part of her. He told her that the sword was an extension of her arm, an extension of her will. He guided her, he touched her shoulders, her arm, her wrist, his big hand curled over hers as he demonstrated each stroke.

Every time he touched her a thrill shot through his whole body.

He spoke to her in that hopelessly loving voice that he did not try to disguise. He called her 'Dear lady' and once 'My love', though she affected not to hear.

He dreamed.

The shadows lengthened. Elaine told Thomas that she had to go.

Thomas told her the truth that she was a fast learner—he asked if he might teach her more on the morrow.

Elaine looked into his eyes—this crazy boy-man—she wasn't ready to see him again so soon, but she did not want to lose this dangerous feeling. She asked if she might meet him again in a week's time, at the same place.

Thomas gladly gave his assent—he gave the Countess a smile that outshone the dying sun.

She wanted to see him again—he believed that all his dreams would come true.

Chapter 21

ELAINE AT NIGHT, AND THE MORNING AFTER

Everyone at the court knew about the lesson—though some called it an assignation—by the next morning.

Elaine thought that Arthur even knew about it before she got home—that groom must have wasted no time—but her husband didn't say anything more to her than he usually did. Still there was something different in his eyes. She liked having an effect on him, and yet there was nothing that she needed to conceal. Elaine smiled brightly as she went into her room to change her rather muddy clothes. She felt light-hearted and gay for the first time in months.

Elaine wondered if Arthur would come to her that night. She made herself especially beautiful, and they had dinner together—but after dinner Arthur went off drinking with his coterie of sycophants—Elaine was left to go to bed alone.

Elaine lay awake long into the night. She heard Arthur come in—he did not look in her room—he went directly to his bed—soon she heard his snores.

Elaine resolved not to become unhappy. With an effort of will she changed the direction of her thoughts. She remembered her lesson with the sword.

She had discarded her coat and hat when the rain stopped, and she pictured herself now, all blue and gold against the dark wet green of the trees and the soft brown of nature's carpet—she saw herself move, sword in hand—she remembered Thomas's eyes on her body—she heard his caressing voice—she felt his strong hand again, as it guided hers—and right then she did not care that he was not the one—he made her feel beautiful, he made her understand what others had always told her—

she was beautiful, so, so beautiful . . .

Elaine was lying on her back. She brought her hands up to her face, and studied her fingers in the light of her last flickering candle. She kissed just the tip of each finger, lingering for a second over each one, and then she put her hands down below her breasts. Who was she teasing? She slid her hands slowly upward over the silk nightgown that clung to her body. Her nipples were like little hills in the silk—she caught them between her fingers and squeezed until she moaned deep in her throat. Then she moved her hands up a little further until she cupped each lovely breast—until her hard nipples were comforted by each protecting palm. She loved her breasts now—at this moment she did not care a whit about their small size, they were perfect, all of her was perfect—she saw herself in the clearing again, the bright sword flashing—and then she moved that sword hand, her right hand, moved that hand down over her soft belly, down over her mound of Venus—she explored her own feelings, she let her mind roam—and then she rolled over slowly and her hand was trapped, a prisoner of love between her thighs, and she held it there for a long time and then finally she fell asleep, and her dreams were happy.

As usual, Elaine woke up well before Arthur the next morning. She stretched and smiled at the sun pouring in through her window. She thought of the day to come with bright expectation. She called Sandra, her lady in waiting, and the girl (who had been listening for her mistress) came at once.

Sandra brought water for her—Elaine washed her face and rinsed her mouth clean of the taste of the night. Sandra brushed her mistress's hair, and then Elaine made the girl dress and perfume her as though for a King's feast, rather than Thursday's breakfast. Elaine enjoyed the whole procedure—her body felt exquisitely sensitive to every touch of her lady in waiting.

When Sandra was finished, the Countess stood up to admire herself in her floorlength mirror. What she saw pleased her— she smiled at her reflection, and Sandra smiled too.

Elaine saw that smile. She turned, blue eyes sparkling, and cupped Sandra's chin with one hand. The Countess deliberately tilted the shorter girl's head back—there was a sudden fear in Sandra's eyes, but Elaine just laughed and bent down and kissed the girl on the mouth.

Elaine stepped back and was out the door before Sandra could even react.

Sandra could barely move for a good minute.

Elaine fairly skipped on her way to the royal dining hall.

Once there, Elaine tried to act as though this were a normal morning. She ordered her usual breakfast of a single egg and a roll (she didn't know that there were already shortages of chickens and bread in the countryside, and the conditions were getting worse—Arthur didn't tell her, and others at the court didn't know or didn't care to know—why worry when there was plenty at the court?). The food came, but she never ate it. A waiter finally took the plate away when it became apparent that this morning Elaine the Fair preferred admiration to nourishment.

In former days it had not been uncommon for lovesick young knights to wander by Elaine's table and wish her 'Good morning'. She had always smiled at them—her good calm political smile—and replied in kind, but she never encouraged them to stay. There was never any real conversation.

Today the form changed.

Knights had talked of little else besides their favorite Countess last night, and Elaine was hardly the only one who dressed in her best this morning.

Elaine had been present at the court for five years—but now for the first time her gallant admirers had real hope. She had left her husband (if only for an afternoon) to go off alone with another man. If she had done it once, might she not do it again? Each knight hoped to supplant Sir Thomas in her affections.

So they came by the royal dining hall this morning, wondering inside if they were being foolish, if they were the victims of a false rumor—and then they saw Elaine the Fair. They spoke to her—and she answered them in a voice they had never heard before. When they heard that voice they knew their world had changed.

Perhaps Elaine had noticed the effect of her voice on Thomas—perhaps it was simply the voice of her new happiness—in any case, she continued to speak in that breathy whisper that made strong knights bend over her table to hear while their knees shook below. Her voice just seemed to pull them in—and when they were close, helpless in her power, she raised her eyes and looked into their souls.

Elaine received twenty-five men over the course of two hours. She saw callow youths and battle hardened veterans. She saw men who knew every strumpet in London and men who had only loved with words. She listened to all of them, for each had a proposal for her.

"Milady—

"The Prince has appointed me to judge the annual cattle show in Islington next week. It's really a country fair—there will be many amusements—might I escort you there?"

"I understand that you have an interest in weapons. I captured this curved scimitar from an infidel that I sent to hell. Perhaps you would like to give it a try with your good Christian hand."

"I have a lovely young filly that I'm training to be a lady's mount. You would be the perfect person to try her out."

Twenty-one of the proposals were different variations on those themes. Elaine did not say yes to any of these men—but she didn't say no either.

She said, "Perhaps", or "Maybe"—she whispered those words and smiled—a true smile from the heart for each man as she came to know him.

No matter what words she used, all convinced themselves that she meant yes.

Elaine gave a more definite reply to the other four men, all of whom had made the same request.

They spoke like this: "Countess Elaine, I will challenge Sir Thomas to a duel with sword and lance. I would be honored if you would come and watch the battle."

Elaine gave the same reply to each warrior: "You must understand, brave knight, that I have made no breach with my husband. If he forbids me to go, then I must obey. But if I can, then yes, I will come and watch the battle."

The men appreciated Elaine's candor. They understood that her answer was the best they could expect. They bowed, and took their leave—they prepared to put their lives on the line.

Never before had there been a duel fought over Elaine. She had always put her husband above all—other men she treated exactly alike. They might love her, if they chose, but that had never affected her—she had no favorites.

Now she had singled out Sir Thomas—the balance was gone—violence had to follow.

With the violence, there came the possibility of passion.

The goddess had revealed herself to be woman.

Every man who leaned over to hear Elaine's voice, every man who saw her eyes watching him—every man there learned the truth that morning, a truth that Elaine was only gradually admitting to herself.

The Countess of Anjou, that lady of surpassing beauty christened by a King as Elaine the Fair, the lady of unfathomable blue eyes and unexplained scar, the lady of dreams come to earth—this woman would soon take a lover.

The men offered their possessions, their privileges, their honor, and even their lives—and each felt the gamble was well worth the possible reward.

They didn't know of the man who had set out to win Elaine with even less encouragement than themselves. This man was wagering not only his own life but also the future of his nation.

No man at the English court would have considered him to be crazed. He was like them, no different in spirit despite his wealth and the magnitude of his risk.

Roland, Duke of Larraz, had begun his quest.

Chapter 22

ROLAND SETS OUT

Thursday morning, May 14, 1194 . . .

In England Elaine received her admirers, considered their proposals, and spun the English court on its axis.

In Larraz Duke Roland kissed his sister Isobel on both cheeks and bade her farewell.

He rode off at the head of a column of twenty handpicked knights. The men were armed with swords, knives, and the occasional mace. They had no lances, for that weapon was too awkward to carry over a long journey. None wore full armor because they were traveling, at Roland's decree, without squires (full armor can only be put on by an assistant). Instead they wore light vests of mail which offered some protection without weighing them down too much.

The little troop was the final result of five years of Roland's planning—the best compromise he could manage between speed and military might.

The knights knew that on this trip they would have to do menial tasks like grooming their own horses and greasing their own weapons—but none of them minded. Indeed, these twenty were the happiest men in Larraz. It had been their misfortune to have been born in this peaceable Duchy—now after years of training and jousting they were finally going into real action.

Roland had spoken to each man individually on yesterday's morn—the morning that followed his sleepless night. Some he had awakened with a touch of his hand—it pleased him to see their reactions, though the knights were shocked, as can easily be imagined: a fighting man is touched by an intruder at dawn—he rolls over, sword in hand, and brings the blade to the intruder's throat—and there above his weapon he sees (with disbelieving, sleep-cobwebbed eyes) the grinning face of his liege lord—he lowers his sword with embarrassment, and hears his Duke say, "Well done, Sir. Now I would like to ask you a question."

Roland had asked the men if they wanted to go on a quest, of duration undetermined, of danger extreme. To a man, they had answered yes.

Roland had told them that they would have one last day with their wives or sweethearts. They would leave Thursday morning.

Now the quest had begun, and they rode off as fast as possible, given due consideration to the strength of their horses. The *men* received no such consideration. After a time Roland called a halt so that the horses could rest—while the animals grazed, the Duke ordered his men to engage in mock combat. The Larrazian warriors set to with a will, for they felt the certainty of impending battle—what they didn't know was who their adversaries would be.

Roland knew that his men trusted him, knew that he could go on for some time without revelation—yet he was too wise a leader to take that course.

He knew that men follow a commander best in the light of knowledge, not in the darkness of unanswered questions. When he thought they had battled enough, Roland called a halt and bade his men arrange themselves before him.

He spoke in this wise: "Gentlemen, we are but a few hours ride away from Larraz. After you hear what I have to say, there may be some of you who wish to return there. I say now that you can depart with no ill will, without dishonor."

Roland looked over the group of steadfast knights. There were murmurs of "No, Your Grace," and "Never, Milord." The Duke waited until there was quiet again, and then he continued.

"I am thirty-three years old, and I have not yet taken a wife. You may have wondered why I never married, why I still have no heir.

"The answer is simple. For many years I was searching for a great love, a woman above all others. Then five years ago, in England, I found her—but she was married to another man."

A shiver went through his audience. Some of these same knights had been with Roland when he had attended Richard Lionheart's coronation. They held their breath as they waited for their Duke to go on.

"The lady's title is the Countess of Anjou; her husband is Arthur the Assessor, England's Chancellor of the Exchequer; her name is Elaine the Fair."

A sigh came from the men, as the breath they had held was slowly expelled. Those who had seen this lady had told their fellows of her—but over the years her existence had become more mythical than real.

Roland's words brought her back to life.

The Duke went on: "Years have gone by since I have seen her, yet the time has served me well. I know now that I love this lady more than any other man on earth. I know that she has no children to root her to England. We will go to her country, and I will win her away from her husband. We will bring her home, and she will sit beside me as the Duchess of Larraz!"

There was silence for a moment, and then the men erupted with yells and cheers of affirmation.

Roland cut the demonstration short with a wave of his hand.

"There are dangers. The Countess's husband is very powerful—he could easily raise a large army of knights against us. Prince John is an unpredictable political animal—if he feels that we threaten his authority, he may strike, and given his penchant for duplicity, we shall have to watch our backs. These two hazards you could have figured out for yourselves. Now I must tell you something you don't know."

The Duke paused. His face was grave. The men waited.

"I learned just two days ago that the ransom money is on its way to free the English King, Richard Lionheart. He is certain, following his long captivity, to return to his homeland in a violent mood. I estimate that it will take King Richard at least a month, probably more, to reach the English coast. We should get there in half that time.

"Then, of course, I have to win my chosen lady.

"The timing is very close. The English King may return in the midst of my activities. He may not approve of my quest.

"We may have to fight our way past the Lionheart to bring my love home."

Some fear had come into the men's eyes when Roland had first mentioned the name of the English King. They had fought that fear as the Duke had continued to speak. By the time he finished they had it under control.

Roland looked at each man in turn, and each man met his

eyes with courage and steadfastness. None faltered or looked away. This was what they had trained for all their lives.

Roland spoke softly. "If any man wishes to go, he may leave now."

The knights stiffened their spines. No one took a step. From the outside there was no way to tell that each man's spirit was vibrating with fear. Each man heard that inner voice that speaks only truth. The voice whispered, "You are mortal—you may not come back from this alive."

Every brave knight knew that some of their number would die before they returned to Larraz. No man showed a hint of that knowledge—and in that act displayed the essence of courage.

The Duke of Larraz smiled once. "Mount up and follow me," he said.

The knights obeyed.

The Duke led his troop at a brisk pace—when they stopped again (at a bustling market town) there was food and wine waiting.

The route was all set—Roland had been paying people off for nearly five years in preparation for this expedition. Yesterday he had sent out a fleet messenger to ride ahead and inform each trading partner and friendly noble that Roland and his men were finally coming.

The Duke was confident that, as planned, there would be food and shelter waiting for him at every stop on the way to Calais on the Norman coast. His confidence would prove to be justified.

When Roland retired that night in a friendly castle, he felt that he had everything about the expedition under control, saving of course Elaine herself. The journey was going smoothly, he was pleased with the bravery and fighting qualities of his men, he knew his enemies and he was prepared to face them.

It had been a relief to finally begin the long imagined quest. Now at last he was on his way. Roland fell asleep easily—his mind was at rest. He might have expected an unvexed slumber—but such was not to be.

A nightmare woke him just as dawn broke in the east. His hands shook with terror. His body was covered with sweat. Fear rasped like a physical presence inside his dry throat.

The Duke forced his eyes open. For a moment the terror continued—he didn't recognize the room. Then he remembered his quest—he remembered that he was in a guest room at the

Count of Belfort's castle.

The strength came back to his body. He sat up. He tried to remember the dream, but now all that he could recall was a single terrifying image: a black cross floating in the air.

Chapter 23

CHALLENGES

London, Thursday morning, while Elaine still received her admirers . . .

Sir Thomas was returning from his normal morning ride. He was but thirty yards from the stable when he saw a knight step out in front of him. Thomas recognized the man as Sir Gareth, a lanky young fellow from the north country—but what business did that rich young man have here, hard by the poor abode of landless knights? Thomas looked past the knight at his own surly groom, who stood outside the stable. Jim was watching with interest—was there a smile on the old man's face? What was going on? Thomas looked hard at Gareth, but the young man didn't flinch. He just held his ground a pace in front of Saladin, deliberately blocking the path.

Gareth had been one of the first men to approach Elaine this morning. He carried the curling whisper of her voice in his heart. He knew no fear.

Gareth was wearing heavy leather jousting gloves. Now he took one off with a deliberate motion—and then he threw it down hard on the dirt just before Saladin's feet.

The high-strung horse reared slightly and then backed up when Thomas pulled him down. Thomas looked down at the glove on the ground—raised his eyes to see Jim, who was obviously grinning now—and then Thomas looked back at Gareth's stony face.

He was being challenged.

Thomas had not had a personal challenge in over a year. His dominance, continually reasserted in the regular tournaments, was unquestioned. Then again, once his high position was acknowledged, there was no particular reason to challenge him. Thomas was not a rival for any man's lady—and he had no claim on a lady of his own . . .

Thomas looked more closely at Gareth's brave young face and he saw the exaltation of love in his features.

Thomas understood.

He dismounted, walked slowly around Saladin, and picked up the glove.

"What weapons?"

"Sword and lance," Gareth replied.

Thomas nodded. "You have spoken to the Countess?"

"Yes. She says she will come, save only if her husband forbids her."

Thomas considered that for a moment. He realized, like the other knights, that Elaine was moving away from her husband. Despite her disclaimer, he doubted that Arthur still had any real power over her.

That meant she would be there to see the battle.

Thomas could barely keep his voice steady. "Tell the Countess that as the one challenged, I have choice of both time and place—and I say tomorrow, at one by the clock, on the great lawn before the palace. Tell her that I will expect to see her there."

Thomas handed the glove to Gareth.

The young man took it, bowed formally, and turned to walk toward his horse. Thomas noticed the animal now for the first time—it was a big strong war horse—it waited contentedly beneath a tree. Thomas looked from horse to knight and back again—they both looked to have the same straightforward, earnest character.

Thomas could feel no anger toward his young challenger.

He has the courage and foolishness of any youth in love, Thomas thought, and the strength of an oak. I may have to kill him.

Thomas watched as Gareth mounted his horse with a light springy leap.

A deep sadness came over the silent knight, a sadness such as Louisa had noticed after he had rescued her—a sadness that had its roots in the Holy Land. He remembered a shallow grave, and a body in the street, and a blood soaked enclosure . . .

Gareth rode off.

Thomas whispered, "I may have to kill you."

He watched Gareth ride away, and he let that last memory come back—just for a second he saw the hanged men and the whirling knights with bloody swords . . .

Thomas shut his eyes, for he did not want to recall what came afterward. Part of him had been killed that day.

The challengers came one by one. The last, who needed several hours to screw up his courage, arrived just before nightfall. There were four in all.

Thomas said almost the same words to each knight: "Tell her that I will expect to see her there."

Given the choice of timing, he scheduled one battle a day. Thus he would duel tomorrow and Saturday—then the Sabbath would be a day of rest—and then the last two would take place on Monday and Tuesday. It pleased Thomas that he could fit in all these battles before Elaine's next lesson. They would be good visual instruction for her!

It never occurred to Thomas that he might not live until that Wednesday.

He was only concerned about the lives of the brave knights who had challenged him.

Chapter 24

"RUN ALONG . . ."

Friday morning, May 15, Sandra attending Elaine the Fair . . .

Once again Sandra took special pains to accentuate the beauty of her mistress. These were hardly normal days. Sandra had heard about the duels. She wondered if someday men would fight over her—and then she brushed aside that silly thought.

She concentrated on Elaine—she lost herself in her sensual tasks—and then she stepped aside and waited nervously while Elaine inspected herself in the mirror.

Sandra held her breath until Elaine smiled, and then she relaxed, and smiled herself—she remembered yesterday—she looked up to be kissed.

The kiss didn't come. Elaine was thinking of the men she would see at breakfast—she was thinking of the morning ride she would take, on a knight's well trained filly (while he rode his stallion alongside, of course)—she was thinking mainly of the duel she would witness this afternoon.

Elaine noticed Sandra waiting there, and she said absently, "Run along, dear, and I'll see you again before dinner."

Elaine didn't notice the tears that started in Sandra's eyes as the girl curtsied clumsily and turned to leave—Elaine didn't know how much she was loved.

Chapter 25

THE POINT

Friday, in the stable for landless knights, high noon . . .

Thomas had given Jim the day off so that he could be alone. He paced around the empty stable—he stepped outside and checked Saladin, who was grazing peacefully—he looked up at the sun, and ducked back inside.

He picked up his lance and laid it across his long worktable. The table rocked—he bent down to stuff a rag under one leg. He stood up again and looked at the lance. The point was dull, as was customary for any friendly joust. Thomas took out his knife. An expression of sadness settled over his countenance. He began to sharpen the point.

Chapter 26

THE SCARLET SASH

One o'clock.

Brightly colored chairs dotted the great lawn before the palace. Brightly dressed ladies sat in those chairs, attended by pages, courtiers, and handsome knights. Everyone chattered away quite merrily, but no one paid any attention to what they were saying. They were waiting.

The palace doors opened. Everyone looked back to see who was coming so late. They saw a strapping page appear, carrying a chair—they looked even more keenly—they forgot to continue their insubstantial conversations, for behind the husky lad they saw a flash of gold—the Countess of Anjou had come to take her place.

Elaine walked up next to her page. She was elegant in a simple but beautiful white dress, accented by a scarlet sash pulled tight around her waist. She brought her lips to the lad's ear and whispered something. He nodded purposefully and set off across the lawn at a brisk pace, Elaine following behind. He carried the chair right through the assembled crowd and set it down before everyone—he centered the chair precisely, as though on an imaginary line bisecting the center of the lawn.

Elaine walked up to the page, thanked him, and pressed a coin into his palm. He walked back to the palace. She sat down.

The horses would most likely cross directly in front of her. No one could block her view.

The three knights who were to challenge Thomas in the next few days came up in a group. She allowed each one to kiss her hand—but she did not encourage them to stay.

They melted back into the crowd.

Everyone had been watching Elaine. The small talk had not had a chance to get started again. Ladies squeezed their lovers' hands and shifted nervously in their chairs. Knights stood on tiptoe and peered into the distance, looking for the approaching horses.

The lawn sloped gently downward from the palace, until it ended on the shores of Green Pond—actually, a large, well kept lake. Widely spaced trees bordered the lawn on either side—the lawn spread out as it sloped, but at the point where Elaine sat, it was about one hundred yards wide.

The sun beat down on the open lawn. The trees had black shadows beneath them that defied vision—no one saw the knights until their horses stepped out into the sun.

Sir Gareth emerged from the wood on the right, a squire walking alongside his horse. Sir Thomas appeared from the left—Saladin took one look at the assembled throng and tried to bolt back into the trees. Thomas only restrained him after a number of sideways jumps that brought laughter to the tense spectators.

Elaine was amazed at the contrast between the two horses. Thomas's black Arabian was approaching now—in his fashion— the gait was some kind of quirky trot interspersed with unpredictable zigs and zags—one got the impression that the horse was taking as many sideways steps as forward ones—Thomas seemed to be just barely in control. On the other hand, Gareth was astride a solid and menacing war horse which marched forward imperturbably, its vision limited by blinders that allowed it to see only straight ahead.

The knights rode up before the Countess to pay their respects. Saladin tried to bite Gareth's bay—Thomas reined him in with great difficulty.

Elaine still looked only at the horses. She saw that Thomas's stallion gave an impression of size more through height than breadth. The black was a bit taller than the English bay—but the latter's powerful chest was far wider; Gareth's horse was clearly the stronger.

Given the blinders, Gareth's horse would surely charge straight—then she looked at the Arabian's rolling, unobscured eyes. How could Thomas control that wild beast and fight at the same time?

She looked up at the man. Though she had not really expected Thomas to change, still his attire was a shock: even for this most dangerous battle, he still scorned the wearing of armor. She looked at his body, shielded only by light summer clothes— she did not raise her eyes to his face.

She turned her head carefully to look at Gareth. He was encased in armor from head to toe. Only the visor of his helmet was open—she could see a square of his face from eyebrows to just below his lips. She looked at this small patch of vulnerable skin, at his fair nose and brave loving eyes, and she felt terribly sad and yet excited all at once.

Elaine stood up and undid her scarlet sash. She looked into Gareth's eyes—her heart fluttered madly and her lips parted as though for a kiss—she let all the heat of her desire show in her face—she held out her sash to Gareth, and he took it with his gloved left hand.

Gareth never took his eyes off Elaine, but he gestured to his squire, and murmured, "The lance."

The squire nodded and took the sash from his master. Gareth had planted the heel of his lance in the grass on his right side. The squire stepped around the horse and tied the scarlet charm about two thirds of the way up the weapon.

Elaine turned away from Gareth's intense stare. Now it was his desire that followed her. She felt frightened—she looked at that long upright lance—she followed its course up past its fragile decoration, up to the point—she felt her heart stop for a second as she realized that Gareth's lance had been sharpened to a point as fine as a needle. She thought of that point tearing through Thomas's unprotected flesh.

She turned her head, and looked right up at Thomas's face. He had seen her notice the point of Gareth's lance—he met her eyes, and smiled, and gestured to his own needle sharp weapon.

Elaine shook her head, she tried to smile but she couldn't, she closed her eyes for a moment and then looked up at Thomas again. Now he wasn't smiling.

She realized that she had never really examined his face before. The horrible thought struck her that this might be her last chance. She made herself become calm. She looked him over.

His hair was auburn, poorly combed—it traveled in three directions when he probably desired only two. His mustache had been long untended—it grew over his upper lip and straggled down around either side of his mouth. His nose was long and crooked. His face was narrow and could easily be cruel. His eyes were extraordinary. They were a slate gray like that of a clear winter's sky on a day when the wind comes howling from the north. They were calm eyes—and yet one imagined there were explosions going off behind them.

Elaine could not tell whether he hated her or loved her. All she knew was that she could not meet his gaze even one moment longer.

Elaine turned and looked at Gareth.

He worshipped her with his eyes.

"God be with you, Sir Gareth," Elaine said.

Sir Gareth bowed formally and closed his visor.

Elaine turned back to Thomas. His eyes pierced her as though they would read the secrets of her soul.

"God be with you, Sir Thomas."

He bowed and turned his horse away.

Gareth had already started riding in the opposite direction.

Elaine hugged her own body. It was out of her hands now.

Elaine watched—first one rider, then the other, as they spread out to make their run. Something was different. She realized that Thomas's horse was perfectly under control now. He was making good speed—better than Gareth's heavy steed— Thomas turned his horse quickly at the edge of the woods and brought his lance forward. Gareth turned at the opposite end. It took a moment for that knight to capture Thomas in the narrow field of vision provided by the slit in his helmet—like his horse, Gareth had only tunnel vision.

Gareth put spurs to his mount, and the heavy war horse rumbled forward, charging straight as a die.

Thomas gave an unearthly shriek. Saladin jerked forward as though he had been shot out of a catapult.

The horses closed at incredible speed.

Elaine saw the heavy power of Gareth's horse, saw the sharpened point of that knight's lance aimed straight and true at Thomas's heart, saw her lovely sash blown back along the deadly line of that weapon, she saw nothing to save Thomas, she wanted to scream, but when it happened, it was too quick for her to scream.

Thomas saw the lance coming, didn't try to avoid it, charged as though racing to his doom and then at the last second he turned his narrow bodied steed *inside* the lance, he was between Gareth's lance and his horse, and his own sharpened lance was held low, razor point scoring Gareth's saddle and then driving upward at the one place where man cannot abide armor, and yet that is the one place where he needs it most.

The point of Thomas's lance tore right through Gareth's groin and drove him straight back over the rump of his still charging horse.

Saladin flew past the wrecked man and Thomas threw down the bloody lance and then he heard the screams. Thomas stopped Saladin and wheeled him around.

Gareth had landed on his feet. He was still upright. He was screaming—but he had drawn his sword.

Blood poured down his legs. Just one single thought kept him upright. He was afraid that if he fell down Thomas might let him live.

Thomas dismounted and drew his sword.

Gareth felt the shrieking pain of his ruined manhood and he tore off his helmet and howled with all the rage in his soul, "Kill me! Kill me, Goddamnit, or I swear to God I'll kill you," and then his words became unintelligible screams again, he tried to take one lurching step toward Thomas and blood spattered his metal shod feet and he screamed and raised his sword high.

Thomas came toward him, moving slowly, deliberately, sword at ready—it seemed an eternity to those watching, Elaine couldn't bear it and couldn't stop looking and the screaming filled her head and still Thomas took his time and then he stepped into Gareth's range and the horribly wounded Knight swung that high held sword with all his might, but Thomas dodged as easily as he had maneuvered Saladin inside the lance, he let the sword go by on his left, he waited one more terrible second until his foe's wrist passed the center of the curve, Gareth could no longer switch direction, Thomas stepped right into the empty arc the sword had swung through, he led with his left foot and pivoted, he brought his sword around with all the strength of his body behind the stroke, a stroke so powerful that it completely severed Sir Gareth's neck.

The head of the late knight toppled loose of the body it had graced. Elaine only realized the screaming had stopped when the head hit the ground. She watched the headless body fall too and then suddenly it was far too much—far too late, the Countess of Anjou covered her eyes.

When she opened them a minute later, she saw Thomas with his back to her, working at something on the ground. Then he turned around, and he was holding her scarlet sash.

He walked over to Elaine, and bowed, and held out the sash to her.

Elaine made no move to take it, but she stood up and looked into his eyes. She saw sadness there, and the sadness spoke to her and she knew then it was love and not hate that drove him—but she could not forget what he had done and she looked down and saw the spattered blood on his shirt—she remembered her mother's wound and she remembered her mother's prophesy: "and it is you who will rise again among the nobility of the land"—she could not imagine herself with this silent killer—she wanted to shake her head back and forth and say 'No, no, no you are not the one'—but he loved her, he had shown great courage—she would treat him honorably.

She looked up at his sad eyes again and then she reached out and took the sash from his hand.

"Thank you," she said.

Thomas gave another slight bow. "Until tomorrow then, Milady," he said.

Elaine felt her heart racing again, she had completely forgotten there would be *more*, she wanted to stop this madness—and then she thought of how much she had lived in these last few days, how much she had lived in these last few minutes, and she knew she wasn't going to stop it.

She felt a terrible excitement race through her body but she made her voice cold. "Until tomorrow," she said.

She tied the scarlet sash tight around her narrow waist, and turned to walk back to the castle.

Only after she had taken many steps did she realize that Thomas had wanted her to present *him* with the sash in honor of his victory—but by then it was too late, and in any case, he was not the man for her.

Chapter 27

THREE MORE FALL DOWN

Saturday's knight, Sir Hugo by name, had learned from his unfortunate predecessor: he cut the blinders from his horse's bridle and he did not charge nearly so close. Even so, Sir Thomas unhorsed Hugo with a sweeping movement of his lance. The swordfight that followed was brief. A mighty chop of Thomas's sword amputated the last two fingers of Hugo's right hand. Hugo could no longer hold his sword with that hand—he dropped his weapon and begged for mercy.

Thomas spared Hugo's life. It was understood that the latter would no longer pursue Elaine the Fair.

The last two duels were similar, though no physical damage was done. Once placed at a disadvantage, each knight chose to give up rather than risk life and limb further.

One odd aspect of these battles was Elaine's seeming coldness to the victor. She hardly spoke to him—she gave him no token of her esteem, no talisman to wear into battle. Likewise she did not stop seeing the courtiers who vied for her attention daily— she spent far more time with those men than she did with Sir Thomas.

It was evident that, regardless of the result of the duels, Elaine still had not made her choice.

Thomas was not unhappy. It was true that he had wanted Elaine to present him with her scarlet sash—he would have loved some such special gift. On the other hand, after Sir Gareth, she did not so single out any other foe.

Thomas retained the sure belief that Elaine would eventually come to love him, and his faith was reinforced even more after the last duel. Elaine promised once again that she would see him on the morrow for her second lesson.

For Thomas it was all very simple: she would come to see him—in time she would come to love him.

Chapter 28

A LESSON LOST

Wednesday afternoon, May 20, by the royal stables . . .

Thomas had been waiting long for Elaine the Fair, but the fact that she was late did not concern him. This time there was no restless riding. He had long ago slipped off Saladin's bridle and saddle—the black stallion was calmly grazing. It was a beautiful day—Thomas let the warm sunlight soak into him—he waited, as he thought, suspended in time.

Elaine had promised.

She would come.

The sky would stay blue forever, and the sun would never set . . .

Young Harry, the groom who had vexed Thomas last week, was again on duty. He peeked out at Thomas now and then and smirked.

Thomas paid no attention to him, but perhaps he should have—perhaps the lad was better informed than he was.

The sun traveled across the sky without the guidance of Elaine the Fair.

Harry left at sundown.

Thomas waited two more hours.

Finally he put Saladin's bridle and saddle back on.

England's climate is never long free of cold and rain. Thomas hadn't noticed the clouds gathering in the dark. A sudden thunderstorm caught him before he made it home.

Thomas was still wet and cold when he wrapped himself in his blanket that night and tried to go to sleep.

He neither cursed nor shivered.

He was numb—on the surface. Deep in his heart, the hard knot of his belief burned like a red hot coal.

Chapter 29

NO PLACE TO HIDE

Arthur, uncharacteristically, had stayed home with Elaine during the week of the four duels. Elaine was certain that he knew everything that was going on—but he didn't say a word about her new interests until Tuesday night, the last night before her scheduled second lesson with Sir Thomas.

Arthur came into her room late that night. Elaine lay on her back in her bed, naked under a single sheet. Her hands were down under the sheet, touching her own softness—she was dreaming with her eyes wide open, dreaming of a man, dreaming of some man that she didn't know . . .

Arthur's arrival shocked her out of her fantasies. She felt frightened and vulnerable, for her nakedness was obvious: her nightgown hung by the head of her bed, and the thin sheet hardly disguised her body. She felt ashamed that she had been caught caressing herself—she closed her eyes—she wished O she wished that he had come to love her—was Arthur her husband?—was he really her husband?—her thoughts raced on while her eyes stayed closed—she dared even to think the one thought that she usually kept carefully buried: she was *not* legally married to Arthur—she was, perhaps, free.

She did not want to be free.

Elaine opened her eyes and gave Arthur a look that would have melted a saint.

He might have kissed her or slapped her—Elaine would have understood either—she was still ready to give him her love.

Arthur looked away. He looked away for too long and when he turned back to Elaine her eyes were like ice and her nakedness was armor.

Arthur asked, in a strange hollow voice, "Are you going to see Sir Thomas tomorrow?"

Elaine answered cooly yet with a trace of amusement. "I will ride with Sir Guy in the morning, and I will have lunch with Sir Robert."

Arthur asked again, with that same unsure voice, "Are you going to see Sir Thomas?"

It is the warrior he fears, Elaine thought. The courtiers with their presents mean nothing to him, for he can always outreach them—but Thomas does what he cannot do. That scares him. Yet Arthur doesn't know that when I am drawn to Thomas, it is not his skillful violence that attracts me—instead it is the sadness, the mystery, the childlike kindnesses—all those qualities one would not expect from a man of war—those are the qualities that move me.

Elaine answered, "Sir Thomas has been kind enough to teach me how to use the sword. I will go to him for my second lesson tomorrow afternoon."

Arthur had been wearing a timorous expression to go with his unsure voice. Now Elaine realized that had been a sham. He peeled off the expression as though it were a mask—he let Elaine see the coarse triumph underneath.

Arthur laughed, and then he said in a clear booming voice: "You won't see any of those men tomorrow, dear wife." Arthur smiled and continued, "No ride with Sir Guy, no lunch with Sir Robert, especially no lesson with Sir Thomas.

"My duties take me far this week, sweet Elaine. I must inspect the estate of the Baron and Baroness of Pembroke. I must see if the gallant Guillaume is paying proper taxes to the King he nearly killed. And since I will be visiting such an honored host, and such a lovely hostess, it must certainly be my duty to bring with me my faithful wife.

"We'll travel at dawn."

Arthur looked down at Elaine with a smirk of satisfaction.

Elaine looked back at him with hatred. She flung her beauty at him like a weapon.

Elaine slowly sat up in bed—the motion compelled him to watch—as she moved, the sheet slipped lower and lower—finally it rested just on the tips of her breasts—and then with a defiant gesture she tossed back her hair and her breasts came free—they were white and soft and perfectly formed and perfectly crowned by her hard pink nipples—each breast was a challenge that demanded to be touched.

Elaine ran her hands through her hair—she did not make the slightest move to cover herself.

"Am I your wife?" she asked.

The Chancellor of the Exchequer turned and walked over to the door. He stopped with his hand on the knob, and looked back over his shoulder. "You'll do as you're told," he said coldly. Then he opened the door and left the room.

It was a difficult night for Elaine. Her breasts were so taut that they hurt—and yet when she covered them with her own hands, she found that she could not comfort herself.

She moved a step closer to the knowledge that the court already possessed: soon she would take a lover.

She could not assuage her desire, nor could she ease the piercing guilt that she felt concerning Sir Thomas.

This second lesson had been long planned and today confirmed. Ever more separate from her husband, removed from his protection, Elaine did want to learn more about the sword—and she knew that it gave Thomas great pleasure to teach her. He had certainly earned that pleasure with his own valor.

Elaine thought of ways to get a message to Thomas—it was possible, but then the necessary use of an intermediary would likely bring the matter to light (Elaine remembered how quickly the news of her first lesson had traveled). Everyone would know that once again she had singled Sir Thomas out—it would be assumed that he was her lover.

She refused to let herself be locked into that role.

She would choose for herself.

Yet still it bothered her. It was an unintentional lie—but a lie nonetheless. Thomas would come out for the lesson—he would wait—O he would wait a long time, for he was a steadfast knight . . .

Elaine resolved to apologize properly when she saw him again.

She tried to sleep—but when she finally succeeded, it seemed hardly worth it. No sooner had she closed her eyes (or so it seemed) than she felt herself being gently awakened by Sandra, who was acting on Arthur's orders. Elaine's reaction was far from gentle—it was an exceedingly cranky mistress who was dressed this very early morning by her lady in waiting.

Arthur was true to his word. They did leave at dawn.

And so it came to pass, that after Thomas *had* waited a long time, after he had finally taken his horse to stable, as he lay cold and numb on his blanket—so Elaine the Fair took off her clothes in a warm and comfortable inn many miles from London.

She got into the inn's comfortable bed from one side, and Arthur climbed in from the other. He looked at Elaine's face in the candlelight, and then he looked around the room—he realized his mistake.

There was no place to hide.

A large and luxurious room was his, yes—with just this *one* luxurious bed.

It was dark outside.

There was nowhere to go.

No place to hide.

They were both wide awake, keyed up by the tension between them.

There was nothing else to do except make love.

To Arthur's credit, he tried. Yet yesterday had really been his last chance. He had failed then to meet Elaine's challenge. Now he lacked the strength of desire to force his wife—and she would not help him.

She was tense and withdrawn and his touches could not move her—they did not move himself.

It was an agonizing week.

They returned on Tuesday, feeling like veterans of a war. There was a new understanding between them. Elaine would see Thomas once a week—no more. Arthur would not interfere with that rendezvous or with her more casual meetings with other men.

Elaine promised that she would not dishonor her husband. She knew that she lied even as she spoke. It was the first *intentional* lie that Elaine had ever told.

She did not try to take it back.

She did not try to convince herself that she spoke the truth.

Chapter 30

MISSION ACCOMPLISHED

Wednesday, May 27, Thomas riding, once again, by the royal stables . . .

It was raining hard. The weather suited Thomas's mood. Saladin, who had grown up under hot clear skies, was just as cheerful as his master. The horse bucked through the mud and snorted. The knight thought of the agony of last week's lost lesson.

When he had finally gone to sleep that awful night, he had known only that Elaine had not come to him—he had no way of knowing that she had left the palace. For all he knew, she might have gone to see another suitor.

He awoke that next morning determined to learn the truth of her movements—but he could think of no one to ask. He was not really on speaking terms with anyone at the court. He had always been contemptuous of the gossiping courtiers that he needed most now.

Thomas spent Thursday searching every place the Countess was known to frequent, but not only did he not see her—he did not feel her presence. He felt that she had gone—but he didn't know when or why. He was alone in his terrible uncertainty—he didn't learn the true story until he overheard two knights talking late Friday afternoon.

Then when he knew her husband had taken her away, he felt terrible that he had doubted his lady for even a minute. Elaine would have come, if she could have. Her word was as good as her strong hands, as clear as her beauty.

He could wait in peace—or so he thought. The reality was different. The knights had not said when she would be coming

back—each day became a racking trial for Thomas. He spent
nearly every waking moment in the saddle, watching for Elaine.
Finally, last night, she had returned. Mounted on Saladin,
wearing dark clothes, Thomas was nearly invisible as he trailed
the Assessor's coach as it made its way to the Palace of
Bermondsey. Thomas veered off when the guards opened the
palace gate for the coach, for he did not want to be caught in the
light of their torches. He rode up a small hill, and looked down.
He saw how the coach horses were led by hand into the palace
courtyard. He saw the servants come out with their own torches, ready to assist the noble couple—he saw the gleam of
Elaine's golden hair in the torchlight—he saw her walk into the
palace ahead of her husband—Thomas noticed the distance
between them, and he smiled, and he leaned down and whispered all his dreams into Saladin's alert and twitching ear.

Now in the day with the rain pouring down—two weeks past
the first and so far only lesson—one week past last Wednesday's
terrible disappointment—on this day Thomas rode about desperately, with no hope and no expectations—with only faith in
his heart.

He reflected that he and Elaine had no contingency plan for a
missed lesson—it seemed logical to him that they should continue on a weekly basis—but there was no way of knowing whether
Elaine thought the same way—and even if she did, would she
venture out into this drenching rain on the *chance* that he
would be waiting for her?

Thomas cursed his luck—he loosened his grip on the reins—
Saladin tried to run for home—Thomas yanked him to a stop
and cursed his horse—he turned Saladin away from the path
down which Elaine might come—he kept his back to hope, and
he ran through the litany of soldier's imprecations—and when
he finished, he still felt the hard knot of his belief burning in his
heart.

He turned Saladin around, and he was not really surprised to
see Elaine the Fair walking down the path toward him.

He just smiled, and relaxed all over. The second he recognized
her he became the happiest man in the Kingdom.

Thomas patted Saladin cheerfully on the neck, and urged him
forward. The horse, ever sensitive to his master's moods, raised
his head and pranced toward Elaine, showing off in his own
way. This strut had an unfortunate side effect—just a pace
before Elaine, one high-stepping hoof kicked up a gob of mud

and sent it flying forward like a bad review in the theater. The gob struck the front of Elaine's brown (fortunately!) woolen cloak, and splattered.

Saladin seemed pleased.

Thomas was aghast.

He leaped down. Two giant strides brought him next to Elaine. He put out a bare hand to try to wipe off the mud—which would have only spread the damage—but Elaine reached out and caught his hand.

"It doesn't matter," Elaine said.

Thomas looked at the Countess. All of her was covered by the brown cloak—there was even a cowl to shield her head—only her face was visible. He felt his hand burning where she held him.

"I'm so sorry—" he began.

"No." Elaine cut him off firmly. "It was an accident of no importance." She let go of his hand and looked up into his eyes "It is I who must apologize. I hope that you can forgive me—"

Thomas had felt increasingly uncomfortable as soon as she had started to apologize—he could not bear to see her go on when there was no need. He simply reached up and placed a finger across her lips to shush her.

The unplanned intimacy of the gesture shocked both of them. Thomas felt her soft parted lips under his finger. Elaine barely breathed as she looked up at the powerful man who had so delicately silenced her.

Thomas brought the tip of his finger down across Elaine's lips. He lingered—pressed—just for a second on her lush lower lip, and then he took his hand away.

"Don't be a silly girl," he said. "I know why you couldn't come last week. You have no reason to apologize."

He needed to say that to clear the air. Now he was ready to kiss her.

Elaine said sharply and rather coquettishly, "I'm not a silly girl. I've come here for a serious lesson in swordsmanship."

With that, she made an abrupt half turn and set off at a good pace toward the royal stables, fifty yards away through the rain.

Thomas was left grasping air.

Then he had to run to catch up with her.

Then he found he had to lengthen his stride to keep up with her amazingly fast walk.

Elaine had maneuvered very neatly to make an embrace

impossible.

Still, the Countess had not rebuked Thomas for his utter familiarity. Another milestone had passed.

They were almost to the royal stables when the door opened and a groom came out, leading a horse that was saddled and ready for Elaine. This was a different groom, an older man—Harry would never have acted with such efficiency. This new fellow must have seen Thomas riding about, Elaine thought, and he's probably heard about me visiting Thomas here—everyone else has!

She smiled at the man, but he did not smile back. He just studied her face with an intentness that one would not expect in a servant—and his look had nothing in common with young Harry's yearning glances. This was more like an inspection than a look of desire.

Elaine returned the look with cold hauteur. The man was unfazed. He met her eyes briefly—an expression of pity seemed to flash across his countenance. Then he turned without a word and went back into the darkness of the stable.

Thomas was pleased that the horse was all ready and equally pleased that he didn't have to deal with Harry again. He checked the girth, which was tight, and then he helped Elaine mount. He got on Saladin, who had been following them. They rode out toward the somewhat sheltered practice area that they had visited two weeks before.

The dogs came out to bark hopefully as they passed.

Thomas hardly heard them. He was thinking of touching Elaine's lips. He wished that he had grabbed her right then and stopped her voice with his mouth.

Elaine was thinking of the strange groom. Why had he looked at her like that? Then she heard the dogs, and she looked over at Thomas—one glance and she *knew* what he was thinking. She smiled to herself and her thoughts began to move in another direction.

Thomas did not think of the groom at all. He had been pleased by the fellow's competence—but beyond that, he had not even really looked at the man.

Thomas should have been warned by that competence—Prince John's servants were rarely so capable.

Thomas should have taken a long look at that man just as he stepped out of the stable, before the rain turned his fair hair dark.

If he had looked then, he would have seen that the man's hair was even lighter than Elaine's—a color that is extremely rare, except in the countries of the far north. If he had watched closely, he might have noticed the slight rolling quality of the man's walk—and if he had followed that clue further, he would have noticed that the man had the windblown face and clear farseeing eyes of a sailor. This fellow had clearly not spent his life mucking out dark stables.

Perhaps if it had not been raining—perhaps if Thomas had not been so drunk with love—perhaps, perhaps, perhaps . . .

The fact is that Thomas noticed nothing. He failed to pick up a sense of danger from this "groom"—and so he missed his chance to block Ivar the Heartless's quest before it even got started.

As Thomas and Elaine rode off, so Sigurd Sigurdsson (for that was the true identity of the groom) saddled up the best one of the three remaining English horses. He set off toward his rendezvous point on the coast. Bjorn would probably not get there for another day or two—but there was no reason for Sigurd to stay around any longer and risk discovery.

That one long look had been enough.

Sigurd had found the most beautiful woman in the world.

Chapter 31

THE SECOND LESSON

The wind came up as Thomas and Elaine rode to their practice area. They made it to that sheltered spot—made it inside that protective circle of evergreens—only to find that a gap in the trees coincided with the angle of the wind. The rainstorm had become a howling beast of a gale—it tore through the gap and clawed their faces with its icy spray.

The Countess turned her face away from the onslaught—but now she could not see where she was riding. Her poorly trained "royal" horse was ready to bolt. Thomas jumped off Saladin and ran to Elaine. He took her horse's reins with one hand—he took Elaine about the waist with his other hand—without so much as a "By your leave' he lifted Elaine off her sidesaddle perch and set her down on the ground. She stood on the soaked pine needles, protected by her held horse and Thomas's body—the knight held her close, his one arm tight about that slim waist—he looked over her horse's back at the surrounding trees, searching for some shelter.

The royal horse jerked her head trying to escape—the mare just wanted to race back to the stable—but she could get nowhere against Thomas's firm grip on the reins.

The "temperamental" Saladin turned his back to the rain and waited patiently for his master's orders.

Elaine looked up from her soaked cowl.

Thomas spoke. "There's a good strong fir to the right that's out of the wind. There's still a dry spot underneath it. Let's go over there and wait out this rain."

He started to turn her toward that tree.

Elaine took his arm and quite firmly removed it from her

waist.

Thomas let her do it—his arm seemed to lose all strength when it lost contact with her body. He looked down—he felt confused—the rain lashed his face.

Elaine bent her head so all Thomas could see was the brown cowl. She looked down at the two swords he carried in his belt. She took the hilt of the one he had brought for her, and drew it from its sheath. She spun the weapon in an arc, so that the blade was toward Thomas and the point was just an inch before his chin.

Now she looked up and met his eyes. "This is no time for lollygagging under trees," she said. "You must teach me of the sword, Sir Knight."

Thomas's face was that of a child who has just had all his sweets taken away. He could not hold her gaze. He said, "I'll take care of the horses," and turned away from her.

Elaine watched as he called Saladin and then led both horses over to the line of trees. He used the saddle ropes to secure them to the pine next to the fir he had suggested for their own shelter. Perhaps he still hoped!

Elaine stood watching in the pelting rain, holding her upraised sword. She let her thoughts run.

What if I had allowed Thomas to lead me under the fir? I can see that it is dry on one side near the trunk, under the tight laced branches—but that is a very small space. I know that is what Thomas wanted: the elements outside, the two of us snuggling tight together . . . Would I have left his warm embrace then and run out into the rain? No, I would not—I knew I would not—I had to decide before he took me there. Is there harm in thinking what if? I like the way he holds me. I would have let him kiss me—I could not have prevented him from kissing me. Would he have taken me right there under the tree like the savage he is?

Elaine saw again the death of Sir Gareth. She shook off the vision—only to see the reality of her own naked sword before her eyes.

She shuddered, she felt weak—and then she noticed that Thomas was coming back.

She was a Countess, destined to rise still higher in the world—she took the stance Thomas had showed her, and held her sword high. "En garde!" she cried.

Thomas drew his own sword.

It was almost impossible for him to instruct in the midst of the gale that buffeted them—but then Elaine did not really want to be taught.

She just wanted to fight.

She came after Thomas, laughing and slashing—she would have killed him if she could have, and several times he had to knock her sword away before it struck his body. Finally she made a furious lunge at his heart—Thomas chopped sharply, reflexively, much harder than any of his previous parries—he knocked the sword from Elaine's grasp—she watched it fly, spin twice, and then stick blade first in the needle covered muddy earth.

Thomas dried his own sword and sheathed it.

Elaine was no longer laughing. She swayed—Thomas took a step toward her—she fell into his arms.

Thomas held her and stroked her wet hair. Elaine buried her face against his shoulder. She had known two weeks ago that she could cry if only a strong man would hold her. She cried now: tears for a loveless, childless marriage, all broken and gone now; tears for herself, adrift in the world of men, with only her mother's dying words to guide her; tears for Sir Thomas, who loved her and held her so well and yet still could never be the man for her—she cried until there were no more tears, and then she just hugged Thomas for a long time until she felt the rain slacken around them, and then finally she raised her face to his, her eyes as vulnerable and trusting as a child's, and Thomas kissed her on the cheek instead of on the lips, and Elaine was grateful.

A few minutes later they began their ride back to the royal stables.

When they got there, Thomas called for the new groom, but there was no reply. Thomas dismounted and helped Elaine down. Then he walked into the barn and looked around, but he didn't see anyone. He stepped back out and called to Elaine, "The groom's gone. Doubtless John got rid of him already. That new man was far too efficient for a Prince who values only subservience."

Elaine laughed. She felt so much better now! She thought of her crazed suitor with his contempt for Kings and Princes. She wanted to yell back at him, 'If you wish to look down upon our rulers, then you must yourself become greater than they. What claim of greatness do you have, O landless knight?'

She wanted to fling the question at him—but she bit her tongue, because she thought that maybe, just maybe, Thomas *would* rise to such a peak of greatness.

What is his destiny? Elaine wondered—and while she wondered, Thomas took the tack off her mare, led the horse back to the proper stall, and gave the animal food and water.

For the moment at least, his destiny was to be a substitute groom.

Thomas himself was concerned neither with his present menial chores nor with some grand unimagined future. He saw nothing demeaning in taking care of a horse. And as for his future, right now he never looked more than one week ahead.

When he came out of the stable Elaine hugged him and this time it was she who kissed his cheek.

She promised that she would meet him again in one week, at one o'clock as usual, at this same place.

Chapter 32

ROLAND CROSSES THE CHANNEL

Thursday, May 28, the day after Elaine's second lesson . . .
The Larrazian force reached Calais that day, the French port
that lies closest to the English isle. Roland hired two fishing
boats to take his men and horses across. As they sailed Roland
saw the white cliffs of Dover welcoming them from across the
sea—what lay beyond that white veil?

The Duke reflected that this short sea voyage marked the end
of his plans, the end of his control. All that followed would be
improvisation in a land of unknowns. Once they landed on the
English shore there would be no more guaranteed shelter, no
more safe conduct—and the menace of the approaching
Lionheart would be ever more real.

Besides all that there was the problem of language. Every
time his men opened their mouths they would reveal themselves
as foreigners. Though Roland had picked his men partly for
their knowledge of English, still, all spoke with an accent—and
only two (besides himself) could be considered truly fluent.

The first of these was the oldest Larrazian knight, Sir Anton
by name: he was a battle scarred veteran of forty who had left
peaceful Larraz in his youth to seek adventure as a mercenary.
Roland trusted his experienced military judgment.

By strange contrast, the other fine linguist was the youngest
knight in the troop, Sir Daniel, who was barely twenty. He was
a romantic lad who had taught himself English after he had
become fascinated by the legends of King Arthur, Guinevere,
and the Knights of the Round Table. Roland smiled slightly as
he thought of this—no doubt the lad imagined himself to be the
reincarnation of Sir Lancelot!

The chalk cliffs were closer but the sunlit whiteness was gone. The afternoon sun had dipped down to the west beyond the cliffs—they were gray shadowed now, forbidding rather than welcoming.

Roland thought of the black cross floating in the air. The nightmare had not come back but the image it had left behind stayed with him.

The Duke could not smile any more about Daniel's youthful dreams. Neither could he feel confident about Anton's great experience. Roland understood that it was finally only his command that mattered. He felt a terrible weight of responsibility for all his men.

What was the meaning of the black cross?

What was this evil omen that hung over them all?

They landed at Dover as the sun disappeared completely behind the chalk cliffs.

Roland found a stable for the horses and beds for his men and himself.

Roland was uneasy as he prepared himself for sleep—but the night passed without incident.

They set off at dawn the next day and reached London in the early afternoon.

The day after that, Saturday, the Duke met with some of the informants that he had dealt with over the years. He got a sense of the political situation—Prince John was said to be in a state of near panic. One moment he would prepare to flee, convinced that his vengeful brother was about to appear—in the next he would calmly assert that the Lionheart was dead, and call for his own coronation.

Roland liked the situation—a desperate man can easily be manipulated.

The Duke was also fortunate in another matter: one of his informants knew of a large house that might be available for rent. Roland inquired, and found the elderly Lady Smythe living alone, in genteel poverty, in her vast mansion. The Duke charmed the lady—or perhaps his gold charmed her—in any case, he was able to obtain a base of operations big enough to house all his men (plus adequate, if rather musty, stables for the horses).

The Lionheart *was* coming—Roland was sure that he lived (having survived the Third Crusade plus German captivity, it seemed most unlikely that the King would die on his way home)—but still the Duke refused to hurry. He observed the Sabbath—only on Monday did he send Daniel to the Palace of Bermondsey, with a handwritten note for Prince John.

While he waited for Daniel to come back, Roland pitched in with his men as they worked to renovate Lady Smythe's stables. The Duke showed no sign of emotion.

It was late in the afternoon before Daniel returned. He handed Roland a folded card that was embossed with England's royal seal.

The knights around Roland diligently pretended to work while they waited for the news.

The Duke broke the seal and opened up the heavy paper. It was an invitation. He read it carefully.

The Duke folded the paper back together and stuffed it in a pocket of his robe. The crackling noise that this made was too much for the waiting knights. Twenty men looked demandingly at their Duke.

Roland looked around at these brave men, and he gave them an assured, confident smile.

"Gentlemen," he said, "in two days time I shall see Elaine the Fair."

Chapter 33

FAVOR

Tuesday morning, June 2, in Elaine's room in the Palace of Bermondsey . . .

Sandra finished preparing the Countess for the day. The girl no longer waited to be kissed. She expected that her mistress would send her off just as soon as Elaine felt satisfied with her appearance.

Today Elaine spent a long time looking into her mirror. She didn't smile. Finally she turned to her lady in waiting and said softly, "Sandra, I would like you to do a favor for me."

Sandra lowered her eyes and said, "Yes, Milady."

"You know that I have met Sir Thomas twice, on Wednesdays, for lessons in the art of swordsmanship. I had planned to see him again tomorrow.

"Now I find I can not go to him. Last night I received an invitation from Prince John. There will be a state dinner to honor the newly arrived Duke of Larraz. I must obey the royal summons.

"I want you to go down to the stable for landless knights and tell Sir Thomas that I will not be able to see him tomorrow."

Sandra noticed that the Countess said nothing about seeing Sir Thomas again in the future. The lady in waiting did not question her mistress. She answered obediently: "I will tell him, Milady."

Sandra waited to be dismissed. Elaine was silent. Sandra raised her eyes to her mistress's face. She saw Elaine staring out the window—her sad blue eyes were lost in some distant vision. Sandra could not look away.

It seemed to be a long time before Elaine noticed that she was being watched. Finally she turned away from the window and looked at Sandra—but even then it seemed to take a good minute before she truly focused and recognized her lady in waiting. It was then that the Countess did a strange thing—at least it was something she had never done before. She stretched out her arms to Sandra—she opened her hands, beckoning the girl into her embrace.

Sandra took a step toward her mistress. Elaine caught the girl's shoulders, and then pulled her close and wrapped her arms around her.

Sandra was still only wearing the thin cotton shift that she slept in. Elaine could feel the heat of the girl's body against her own. Elaine gradually tightened her grip until she was holding Sandra in a fierce embrace, until Sandra was crushed breathless against her—and then she abruptly loosened her hold.

Sandra was left breathing heavily, just an inch from Elaine, frightened and unsure of what she should do.

Elaine ran her left hand through Sandra's brown curls and then tightened her grip on those tresses. She pulled Sandra's head back by the hair, so that the girl's face was tilted up as if for a kiss—but the Countess didn't kiss her. Elaine just looked down at her with hard, cold, unreadable eyes—and then she said, softly, "You should get dressed and go now, my dear."

Elaine let go of Sandra's hair and put her hands on her shoulders. The Countess spun the girl around smartly and sent her on her way with a sharp smack on the bottom.

Chapter 34

ICE

The lady in waiting walked toward the stable for landless knights.

Sandra had watched all four of Thomas's duels from an upstairs window of the palace. Previously, she had often watched him joust at the stadium.

She had never seen him up close.

The young woman, her body already awakened by her mistresses's touch, felt a thrill of excitement at the thought of meeting the dangerous silent knight. She was glad that she was wearing her best dress (actually one of Elaine's that the Countess had given her and she had altered). She imagined herself to be a lady going to meet her lover. She thought of Elaine's sadness—she regrets, Sandra thought, but she has thrown him over. Will he be angry with me for bringing the news? Will he seek comfort with me? I love my lady but I need to *be* loved. What does my body cry out for? What is it like to be loved by a man?

Sandra was almost to the stable. She saw Sir Thomas's black horse grazing peacefully outside. The door of the stable was open, but she could see no sign of life within. Suddenly she felt a man's powerful hand seize her shoulder from behind—Sandra would have jumped two feet had not the hard hand held her down. Only when she had stopped struggling did the man let her go.

Sandra turned around and there before her was Sir Thomas the Silent. She started to smile—but as she did so she looked up at his face—she met his eyes—and her smile never formed. He had gray eyes—slate gray killer's eyes—for one terrible moment she thought that he was going to kill her then and there. She didn't know why she felt that way—he made no threatening move—he just looked at her, and the look alone terrified her.

Thomas smiled then, and the smile was a shock. His eyes changed too, they grew warmer—he said, "Tell me the message, little girl."

Sandra was not at all surprised that he knew her mission. With those eyes he could surely read all her thoughts—and then she remembered what she had been thinking about on the way down here, and she blushed, and then finally she managed to speak.

"Yes Sir, I do have a message from my lady, the Countess of Anjou."

Thomas didn't say anything. He just looked at her, and his eyes began to turn cold again.

Sandra rushed onward. "Sir, there is a state dinner tomorrow. Prince John has given my mistress an invitation"—as soon as she said it, Sandra realized she had made a mistake: 'invitation' was hardly good enough. She stammered on desperately, "The Prince has *demanded* the Countess's presence. She must go, she apologizes but she cannot meet with you tomorrow."

Sandra stopped, breathless.

Thomas just looked at her and then finally he asked, "Does she apologize or do you apologize?"

Sandra didn't answer right away—a fateful moment passed—and then it was too late to answer anyway. He knew. Sandra watched his eyes turn to ice and the fear came back to her and then she suddenly realized she had delivered the message, she was free to go and she turned to walk away but she still felt his eyes on her back and then she started to run and she didn't stop until she was at the door of the Palace of Bermondsey.

For as long as she lived, Sandra would never forget those terrifying gray eyes.

Chapter 35

DOUBTS

Tuesday night, June 2, in Lady Smythe's mansion . . .

Roland lay in bed and considered his successes. The trip across France had gone exactly as planned. He had expected problems once they got to England, but even here everything had gone incredibly well. They had traveled through the country without incident, and they had even secured this wonderful house to stay in. Then the letter to Prince John had been an unqualified success. Roland had suggested a formal dinner to confirm the alliance between their two countries. He knew that the Prince would jump at this—John loved to appear as the "statesman" directing his nation. Then Roland had added a broad request for the company of beautiful ladies at the dinner, pleading a lack of such feminine company during his travels. This bolt also had shot home—John would see the possibility of future leverage there, and indeed, the Prince's reply specified that the most beautiful ladies in England would be at the dinner.

Elaine would be there.

Roland doubled up as if with a seizure. His hands scrabbled feebly at the bedcovers as pain tore through his heart.

She would be there. After five years of dreams he would once again meet the living woman who was known as Elaine the Fair.

Roland slowly straightened his body out on the bed. He threw off his covers. He put a hand over his aching heart.

The truth of his soul was plain to him: he loved Elaine far too much to ever take her by force. He could never abduct her. He could only take her away with him if that was her will.

The Duke remembered Elaine's cold blue eyes from their first meeting and he knew that if he saw her like that tomorrow there would be no hope. He remembered her political smile from their second meeting and he knew that if she kept him at a distance like that there would be no hope.

There was no reason to expect any different reaction from what he had already encountered.

Was there any hope at all?

Wouldn't it be better to call his men together, make his excuses, and leave now before the return of the wrathful Lionheart? Since the situation was hopeless anyway, wouldn't that be the prudent course?

What would he see if he went through with all this? He remembered the peaceful married lady who had sat next to him at King Richard's feast. 'I have come to woo you away from your husband,' he could say. She would reply, 'But Your Grace, I am very happy in my marriage. Do you mean to say you have traveled halfway across Europe on this fool's errand?' Roland could hear her laughter.

He wanted to run—run away—run home. The years of dreaming—how he missed them now! Those marvelous dreams were so much better than reality. Dreams could always be spun off into the future, one could weave tapestries without end, each panel more brilliant than the last—but by taking this trip, Roland had ended his dream.

I shall have to face the truth, he thought. He smiled with a sort of mad good humor. The truth of it is that I shall fail and my life will be shattered. Elaine won't remember me—I'll introduce myself and make some meaningless small talk with the lady—she'll "favor" me with her polite smile—and then what will I do when her husband comes to take her arm? Run him through with my sword and then declare my love for her?

He wanted to laugh at his folly, or weep at the bitter loss of illusion—but then he thought of his men, the twenty brave comrades who had made this journey with him, the men who had offered their lives . . .

He could not dishonor their gift by showing cowardice.

Perhaps it was true that he would fail. Perhaps all along he had been charging straight for the lance. Perhaps truth's spear would transfix him on the morrow.

Yet even so he would show only confidence to his men. He would make his best effort.

After all, Roland thought, history teaches us that Henry II stole away the Queen of France.

Surely I can seduce a Countess!

Chapter 36

"NEXT WEEK . . .?"

Late Wednesday afternoon, June 3, as the state dinner for the Duke of Larraz was about to begin . . .

Elaine was walking through the courtyard toward the royal dining hall. She noticed the guard that Prince John had posted at the door, doubtless to check the guest's invitations. The Countess did not carry her own invitation—she knew quite well that her face alone would open any door in the Kingdom.

The guard squinted into the setting sun to recognize her. He smiled when he realized that Elaine the Fair was alone.

Arthur had been pleased that Elaine had broken her date with Sir Thomas. He quite approved of her going to the state dinner. It was the sort of frivolous entertainment that he felt was suitable for his wife. Equally important was the fact that Thomas could not be there—Thomas was never invited to such affairs—Arthur did not fear the sort of courtiers who would be invited.

Arthur had set out for the countryside this morning. He told Elaine that he needed to make some tax assessments—but the truth was that he needed to play his "game" again. It had become an addiction, like the desire for food and drink that surpassed hunger. The more one had, the more one needed—and even the breaking of men could lose its thrill. Arthur did not really think he would lose his gold sovereign on this or any other expedition. Would he soon have to seek a sharper sensation?

Elaine walked toward the guard, feeling only relief that her husband was not with her—she did not think at all of the countryside she had long since left.

The guard looked appreciatively at the late arriving Countess, and then he stepped back and opened the door wide for her.

There were two steps up to the entrance. Elaine took the first one easily, and then she paused, preparing herself for the gaze of all the men and women inside. She put her right foot on the top step—she felt the hush come over the assembled guests—she heard the horse coming from her left and she could not take the second step that would put her inside. The thudding hoof-beats seemed to shake the stone beneath her feet. She froze, poised in the doorway, one foot in the world of the court, the other planted as though to stroke with the sword—she knew without looking that the horseman was Sir Thomas.

The horse stopped, behind her and to her left, just out of sight of the people inside.

She heard Thomas's voice. He sounded pleased with himself as he asked his question. "Next week, Milady?"

Elaine was caught. She could not argue with him here. Any conversation would give an impression of intimacy that would further link her to Sir Thomas. She was trying to break free of him! She didn't want to remember crying in his arms. She had been so glad to get the invitation from Prince John. It was the perfect excuse and yet—Thomas had kissed her cheek when he might have taken advantage—he sulked like a child when she didn't let him take advantage—he was a gentleman and a lovesick boy—why couldn't she take one more step and leave him? Suddenly Elaine wondered if he would follow her in—she looked at the guard and saw he was frightened—he could never stop Thomas—how can I get free of that knight?

She looked around and yes, there was Thomas on his black steed, smiling. She smiled back. He had touched her heart, he had made her feel her own beauty, he had held her protectively in his arms—he was a savage killer with a past no one knew—he was a landless knight who slept on a stable floor.

It was possible that he would be a great man—but right now he was still a boy. Then again, he was a magnificent boy—"Yes," Elaine said to Sir Thomas, and then she turned away from his smile and stepped into the royal dining hall.

Chapter 37

BURGUNDY

Inside the royal dining hall the Duke of Larraz sat in the place of honor next to Prince John and waited for Elaine to arrive. Roland shivered as the foppish would be monarch laid an arm about his shoulders. The Duke had heard reports of John's perverse proclivities, and now he knew that all he had heard was true.

Roland lived only to see Elaine now—the coming moments would mark the end of his dreams—and perhaps a new beginning—reason spoke solemnly of the death of illusion—yet hope made a desperate stand in his heart—he could not stand the Prince's loathsome touch!

Roland removed John's arm as gently as possible, and said casually, "I find it rather hot, don't you agree, Your Majesty?" The Duke hoped that the gift of a higher title would mollify his host.

"You are wise to acknowledge me," said the Prince. "Truly, I have reports that my dear brother was murdered by footmen as he attempted to make his way through France. Soon the whole world will know me to be King!"

Roland looked quickly at that twisted face, already old with debauchery (though he knew that John was only twenty-eight) and he was sure that the Prince's loose mouth was lying. The Duke turned away so that he wouldn't have to look at the low company he was now forced to keep.

Everyone was seated now, but nothing had started—more than just Roland were waiting . . .

The door opened to admit the red ball of the setting sun. A lady stepped into that light—stepped up to enter, and then stopped in the doorway.

Her appearance drew every eye and stopped every mouth.

Elaine the Fair had arrived.

In a moment Roland would see that she wore a long burgundy dress, but now the light blazing behind her brought out only the red in her fine dress, and beams shimmered through the loose material of her sleeves so that it seemed her body was wreathed in flames, and her hair was a spun gold crown shot through with red, and her eyes caught none of the sunlight, nor did they yet reflect the torchlight inside—her eyes were black coals in the midst of the fire.

Roland stared in horror at this apparition of his love—and then she turned her head and said a word to someone, perhaps 'Good-bye' to some suitor—Roland saw her profile in the flames, and the horror began to recede from his mind—he remembered his first sunlit vision of her—how can the sun bring both beauty and terror?—she stepped inside, and the door closed behind her, and the sun was gone.

Roland saw a beautiful lady with happy blue eyes wearing a warm burgundy dress.

Roland looked down at his hands for a moment. They weren't trembling. He looked up at Elaine again and saw that there was no husband with her—in his heart he felt the victory of hope.

The Countess walked past the tables and curtsied before the Prince. He acknowledged her, and then she looked at Roland and smiled.

This time his hands did tremble and he dropped them in his lap so that she wouldn't see. This was not her political smile—on the contrary it was a small clear gesture of pleasure. She *did* remember him.

Roland bowed.

Then he raised his head and watched her graceful walk to her place, just one table away.

Roland saw a gentleman rise to help the Countess into her seat—he had to smile when he recognized the man: it was none other than that cynical young knight, Sir Guy of Sussex. Sir Guy had quite lost his detachment—as he touched Elaine, his face became a picture of adoration.

Elaine smiled at Sir Guy as she settled into her seat, and if it was a smile of amusement, if she was laughing at him—then still she was laughing at him alone.

Roland watched Elaine respond to a compliment from the

man on her other side—she gave him a look to singe his whiskers.

The Countess had abandoned her safe, conventional smile.

Sir Guy wrapped his big right hand around the hilt of his dinner knife.

No one was safe.

Roland wanted to laugh with relief.

The Duke gaily tossed all his thoughts of an "untouchable" lady out the window. Elaine's unhidden sensuality, her private glances, her fearlessness—all made it clear that she was seeking a lover. Could she even have found one already? No—he watched as she cheerfully acknowledged a compliment from across the way—Sir Guy gripped his knife as though wondering which man to kill first.

She was still looking. No man had yet been able to claim her—they were turned one against the other.

Roland hid a deep sigh of relief behind his hand. The last of his doubts disappeared. It was not that he thought that he could automatically win Elaine now—he knew that his task would still be very difficult, and the danger (from jealous knights as well as Arthur and Richard) was perhaps even more extreme— but the one thing that truly mattered was that now Roland knew that he had a chance.

The Duke of Larraz, a realist, asked no more.

He caught Elaine's eye and lifted his glass to her. She smiled, and answered his silent toast.

I love you, the Duke thought, and I can win you.

What is possible can be done.

Chapter 38

THE STATE DINNER

Prince John finally stilled the tumult caused by Elaine's arrival. He signalled to the court priest, who had been waiting inconspicuously in the shadows, and ostentatiously bowed his head to listen to the prayer. Roland followed suit, as did all the other men and women there. The priest began to speak, in English: he started with a long self satisfied blessing of the ruling class, especially signalling out Prince John for praise.

Roland wondered where John had found this loyal toad. The Duke thought of the changes in the countryside that he had noticed during his ride up from Dover. The prosperity of five years ago was gone. There were abandoned farms, and castles shut up tight for fear of the taxman—the roadways were the beds of beggars.

John had done well indeed.

The priest switched to a long droning Latin prayer.

The Duke thought of his own green and happy country. With hope alive in his heart, he thought: I must take my lady home. She does not know it yet, but I will bring her happiness. She is looking, and I must make sure that I am the one she will find. I will win her, but not just as a lover—I will break her marriage (in any case there must already be a great rift between Elaine and the Assessor: he lets her go alone to this dinner attended by lustful knights, and she encourages them!). I will obtain a Papal annulment for her, no matter what size bribe the Church demands. I will free her of her youthful mistake—and I will take her home with me to be the next Duchess of Larraz.

Roland had his course before him—now it only remained for him to work out his strategy. He looked at the smoldering jealous knights who sneaked glances at Elaine (demure, head down, 'unaware')—he smelled the violence in the air. He did not yet know about Thomas and the duels already fought, but he guessed correctly that there must have been some such, and he reasoned that that could not be his path.

He was the Duke of Larraz, ruler of a rich land, worthy recipient of a state dinner.

He was above the fray.

He had his plan ready before the priest finished his prayer.

The dinner started at last. Sir Guy cut Elaine's meat for her, but Roland paid no attention to them. He was relaxed. He made casual small talk with John (skillful flattery on the Duke's part) and he bantered with some lesser nobles.

There was a knot of tension around Elaine—sometimes heated words—desperate suitors tried to impress her. They felt that Thomas had lost his ascendancy (since she had chosen to go to this dinner instead of to him) but they did not know whom she now preferred.

They begged for her favor—meanwhile, Roland leaned close and whispered in John's ear.

The Prince smiled when Roland had finished, and called for silence. Gradually the room quieted—men stopped looking at the Countess, and turned to their Prince.

"I have just received a proposal from our honored guest, His Grace the Duke of Larraz," John began. "I am happy to grant this request from His Grace." John decided not to mention that it was an easy favor, since Roland was footing the bill.

John continued. "We shall have a grand ball here at the court in one week's time. No expense will be spared!" John grinned at Roland. "The finest minstrels will play for us, the food and wine will be superb—and of course we already have here assembled the handsomest knights and most beautiful ladies in the world!"

The smiling faces below carried John onward—it was as though this were his idea, his grand gesture—hardly knowing what he was saying, glad for a moment to be popular, John continued—"Yes, a grand ball, the finest ever in England, and we shall name it in honor of . . ."

Here John paused, for he had got ahead of himself. He did not want to name the ball for Roland, because it was John's nature never to benefit a benefactor—then again he did not feel secure enough to name it for himself—he looked at the Duke, and that was a mistake.

Roland could not resist the chance to stick in the knife. He leaped to his feet, goblet in hand, and declaimed, "In honor of the King! In honor of His Majesty Richard Lionheart!"

The gentry rose to their feet as one man. "To the King!" they cried lustily.

John looked as though he had been really stabbed—his face was turning green—he grabbed his goblet and drained it, then stood up and waved for silence.

"Yes, by God, we shall call this King Richard's Ball. Our hopes and prayers are with him as he travels the dangerous road home. My brother has served God in the Holy Land. He has survived cruel imprisonment. He deserves more honors than we can bestow.

"Yet we shall not sorrow while he is still gone. All will be ready in one week's time. We shall dance—we shall celebrate his coming arrival!"

As the crowd roared its approval, John fervently hoped that his words were false. But what if they were true? Would Richard have found out that he had tried to bribe Henry VI to keep him imprisoned? Henry had scorned that bribe—he might well have told Richard. If Richard knew, if he still lived—then John knew that his own life might soon be forfeit. The Prince resolved to station some watchers in all the coastal towns, with fleet horses at the ready, so as to quickly report any landing of the Lionheart.

Richard might land with a thirst for his brother's blood.

John shivered, and looked at the Duke of Larraz. Here was the man who had brought on these evil thoughts. Here was the man who had gained his favor and then double-crossed him by bringing up Richard's name.

Perhaps it was for the best. He would be forewarned now, he could take precautions.

John looked at Roland with some respect. He understood now the high regard for the Duke's political machinations. Roland would be a bad enemy. Warriors, who always looked straight ahead, were easy to strike from behind. A player like Roland looked in every direction.

What was Roland's game?

Chapter 39

THE COUNTESS AND THE LANDLESS KNIGHT

Thursday morning, June 4, the day after the state dinner . . .

Elaine was walking toward the stable for landless knights. This time she could not send Sandra. This time she had to go herself, and end it. Perhaps he was magnificent—but he was just a boy, not the man for her. She wanted no more embarrassing last minute questions, no more lessons, no more rainy embraces. She knew the direction of that path, and she would not follow him down into the mud.

She saw the stable before her—a high motion caught her eye. She looked up to see Thomas's old groom forking out hay from the stable loft. The wispy forkfuls floated down, much to the delight of the black stallion below. The groom, in contrast to the horse, looked surly—but he did tip his hat when he noticed Elaine.

The Countess smiled at him, opened the stable door, and stepped inside.

The interior of the stable was brighter than Elaine had expected it to be. The groom had left the trapdoor to the loft open, and sun streamed down through the poorly maintained thatch roof, streamed down through the squarecut hole of the trapdoor, and it illuminated the bits of golden hay on the floor, and in the center of its glow sat Sir Thomas before a crude table, working with some lengths of leather.

His back was to the Countess. Elaine watched his fingers move—he did not seem to be aware of her presence.

Actually Thomas had been attentive to every step of her approach. From the moment he had heard the first footfall he had known it was Elaine. He had been trying to repair a strap from Saladin's bridle—now he kept his fingers moving over the leather, though in fact he could no longer accomplish anything. There was no strength in his hands—just the overwhelming consciousness of her nearness—just the overwhelming pleasure that she had come to him.

"Aren't you afraid that some enemy might attack you from behind?"

Thomas put down the bridle. He felt her voice as much as he heard it. She was with him, in this place he called home.

He stood, turned around, and looked at Elaine the Fair. He could never remember how beautiful she was.

She wore the blue dress from her first lesson, and her long blonde hair tumbled free past her shoulders, and her eyes were pale blue, sad serious eyes, and the uncompromising planes of her face were made to be held between his strong hands, he wanted to put his hands on her cheeks and roughly tilt her head back and kiss the line of her lips, force her mouth open so that he might feast on the honey of her soul . . .

He spoke, and all of his thoughts were present in his few words. "I am not afraid, Milady." He held her eyes as he spoke, and then he deliberately looked down at the curve of her breasts—his hands twitched with the desire to cover them.

"I can not come to the next lesson," Elaine said, and she waited to see the hurt in his eyes, but he was even smiling as he looked up again at her face, and then she could feel him looking at her mouth.

"That's all right," he said, and Elaine thought of how long it had been since she had been properly kissed. She remembered a boy named Carl, back in Firfleet, and how he had kissed her with such desperate desire—finally she had opened her mouth for him and just for an hour thought herself in love, eyes closed, lips locked together, tongues seeking—but then he had tried too much too soon, and she saw herself pregnant and trapped in the poor village of her birth, and she would not let her mother's dream end that way. She had broken up with Carl, she had looked for another man, and so it had gone, until the frenzied priest brought her death before her face—until Arthur rescued her.

Elaine meant to tell Thomas that she would not see him ever again. She looked around—this bare haystrewn floor was just another Firfleet. He was a landless knight, without family or money. He wanted her—but where? Under a tree? Here on the floor? He was blessed with strength and talent for combat. He had no fear of Kings—no fear of her.

Yet he could not take her higher.

He slept on the floor like a pauper.

Why had he not been angry when she had made her statement?

Elaine looked at his face and saw that he was—happy. The hard slate of his eyes had softened as he looked at her—he put out his hand and said, "Come here."

She looked at his hand, at his face, at his mouth: he might hurt her. For a moment she saw clearly in her mind that sweaty wrestler by the rails, and she wanted to say aloud what the serving girl had said to him.

But then that other memory came: "and it is you who will rise again among the nobility of the land."

She looked at the bare floor, at the broken bridle—she thought of the ball to come, of her own beauty—she thought one moment of being a Duchess—she ignored the outstretched hand, and she looked up at the lover's eyes—at the killer's eyes—she shook her head very slightly, an almost imperceptible movement back and forth, yet still quite clear to the watchful Thomas—who refused to accept it.

He smiled and stepped toward Elaine. He took her by the shoulders, but now she was frozen, there was no flow, her body gave him nothing—he leaned down and kissed her cool cheek, and he said, "Another time, then."

The Countess stepped back to say that there would be no other time, but now she did see the pain in his eyes, and she felt on her cheek the mark of his gentle kiss.

There was faith torn by circumstance in his face—she began to understand his belief—for just a moment she felt unworthy and wished that he might love another—and then strength-giving anger swept through her, she wished he would just do better, just do whatever he was put on this Earth to do and God knows his purpose was not at the court.

Elaine wanted to strike him to bring out the greatness she sensed—she could not stay another minute in this stable for landless knights.

"Perhaps there will be another time," she said, and then she turned on her heel and walked away.

The Countess noticed none of the men who stared at her as she walked back to the castle.

She did not hear when their hearts shattered like glass.

Chapter 40

PREPARING FOR THE BALL

Wednesday, June 10, the day of the grand ball . . .

The festivities were not set to start until six by the clock, but Elaine had Sandra come to her bedchamber at noon. The afternoon would be devoted to nothing but beauty.

Soon after Sandra's arrival there sounded a knock on the door. The Countess gave Sandra some instructions, and then took refuge in her dressing room. Sandra let in two burly pages, who carried a huge upright tub between them. They set it down at her direction, and departed—only to return shortly, heavily laden with steaming hot buckets of water. They poured the water into the tub, their minds fired by naked imaginings—but they had not long to muse, for Sandra curtly ordered them out just as soon as they had finished their task.

Once Elaine heard the door close behind them, she stepped back into her bedchamber. She was dressed only in her nightgown. Sandra helped her take it off. Elaine braced herself against her lady in waiting and climbed into the tub. She cried out in shock at the hot water—and then she slowly settled into it until even her breasts were submerged. She leaned her head back so that her hair hung down the outside of the tub. The Countess took no notice of the flushed face of the girl who waited to serve her. She closed her eyes. She let her mind roam.

Elaine remembered her two lessons with Sir Thomas. She pictured him showing her strokes with the sword. She felt again the shock in her wrist as he knocked the sword out of her grip in the rain. She remembered his arms around her—she remembered him from just a few days ago, bathed in light—she remembered how he had looked at her mouth.

She remembered also her anger at the end—and why not?—
he had no position in this world save what he carved out with
his sword—could he keep a woman in his stable?—certainly
not!—he was not invited to this ball, nor would he be to any
other—he was doomed to wander alone—Elaine imagined
Thomas riding around the castle this night on his black stallion,
she imagined him listening to the sounds of merriment coming
from the ballroom, she seemed to see his eyes turning to the
color of a solid frozen pond—she imagined him looking for someone to kill.

Elaine shuddered in the heated water, but then she remembered the sadness in Thomas's eyes after he had killed Gareth.
There was no crude triumph in the man, no pride in his own
violence. His character did not fit together: the silent killer did
not mesh with the sad lover. Elaine did not understand him.
She always thought of being kissed when she was with him—
she wanted him to kiss her, but not—not as the man he was.
She could not come any closer to it than that—he was a double
image to her, and one picture was shadowed—she was suddenly
certain that he was not who he said he was. It was more than a
contradiction of character—he had another identity, she was
sure of it.

Elaine thought of Thomas's magical appearance at the
court—an astonishing warrior under a vow of silence. He was
hiding something—he was hiding himself. He was not the Sir
Thomas that people remembered vaguely—he was someone
else, a man of promise unknown, unarmored, hiding in plain
sight.

Elaine fixed her mind on this false knight, this deceiver who
dared to love her. I could never give myself to a man who is
false even to himself, she thought.

Yet that thought brought on another: she had promised that
she would not dishonor her husband—she had knowingly lied.
She felt her body grow tense—she thought of Arthur, still sleeping in the next room, half a man—she thought of Thomas, doubled and lost—she thought of herself on the eve of betrayal.

They had almost killed her on her nineteenth birthday.

She reached up to touch the white scar—but then she fought
the urge down and put her hand back in the water.

Arthur had saved her once but he could not—would not save
her again.

She needed someone to raise her above the world of mad

priests and blood.

She needed someone to stop the blood that had flowed last week and give her a child.

She needed a man.

She stretched her arms wide in the tub—she felt her breasts taut, burning in the water—she spread her legs and tilted her head back even more, feeling the weight of her long golden hair hanging down.

She wondered what color were the eyes of the Duke of Larraz.

Elaine's own eyes were closed. She opened them now, and looked at Sandra—truly a patient lady, waiting—she looked past Sandra at the stacks of thick towels warming to one side of the fire, warm yet clean, out of the way of any floating ash— Elaine smiled at the dear thoughtful girl who had shared her life for five years.

"Thank you for preparing the towels."

"You're welcome, Milady."

"I don't want you to wash me yet, Sandra. Tell the lads to bring up some more fresh hot water—they can leave it outside the door. After you've brought it in, you can bathe me and then do my hair with the fresh water.

"I'll just soak a bit more while you get everything ready."

"Yes, Milady."

Sandra curtsied and walked away to perform her duties.

Elaine barely heard the girl leave the room. The Countess had closed her eyes again. She was lost again in her dreams—but now she did not think of a man, instead she thought of what a man could give *her*—she thought of the everyday miracle that is the fountainhead of all human existence. She thought of carrying a child, as her mother must have carried her. She thought of her breasts swelling, her belly stretching—she thought of giving birth, and tears found their way from under her closed lids and wandered down her cheeks.

She heard voices at the door. She ducked her face in the water and came up streaming wet. Sandra came in carrying one heavy bucket. She made four trips in all.

"That's all, Milady."

Elaine nodded and gestured toward the bar of fragrant French soap. Sandra picked it up and wetted her fingers.

The Countess abandoned herself to the girl's loving attentions. Every soapy touch was a caress. The girl washed every part of her, as Elaine floated and rose up or down at the urging of gentle hands. The Countess felt her nipples harden as Sandra carefully soaped the softness of her breasts—she felt the tender touch along her inner thighs and she heard her servant's sudden intake of breath as she seized the girl's hand. She stood up in the tub, and guided Sandra's hand where she wanted it, over and under the soft golden fleece—and then she turned around, and made her do the back as well as the front.

Then Elaine sank back down in the water, she kept her eyes closed, or half closed, and she never spoke at all as Sandra rinsed her with love and the softest cloth.

Only then did Elaine fully open her eyes—she looked at her lady in waiting and said, "Do my hair now."

Sandra picked up a heavy bucket.

Elaine smiled at her, and then pushed her hair up from the back of her neck and bent forward so that it fell forward over the top of her head. Elaine quivered like a child as she waited for the deluge.

Sandra looked down at the piled up golden locks, at the submissively offered bare neck, and her hands trembled as she held the bucket high—and then she poured all the warm water in one steady stream and the beautiful light hair went dark.

Sandra brought out some French shampoo—the Countess gave herself up to her lady in waiting's scrubbing fingers. Elaine was a child again, the child she had never been—she closed her eyes and let everything be done for her, wash, rinse, wash, and then the final rinse.

Sandra dried her mistress's face and then helped her out of the tub. Elaine's body was all slick—she slipped once as she stepped out of the high tub—she fell right against Sandra, who caught Elaine in an unexpected embrace. The girl blushed and apologized furiously—Elaine told her not to worry—Sandra recovered somewhat and wrapped her mistress in big warm towels.

The front of Sandra's dress was all damp from her contact with Elaine, but she did not stop to dry herself.

Sandra turned her attention to her mistress's hair. Elaine sat on a low bench, and Sandra stood behind her. The girl took each long strand of hair into her hands, and gently dried it with a succession of warm towels. Sandra's heart was still racing from the shock of feeling Elaine's body against her own—she was glad of this slow quiet time to recover—to stay hidden.

Finally the hair was dry enough for a first combing. Sandra

took a heavy wooden comb and moved it through that long lovely hair. She took great care not to catch any tangles—she
smoothed them apart with light strokes from underneath. She
did well, and her mistress was pleased—Sandra thought that
she might yet get through this day with her heart unbroken.

It was at this point that the door to Elaine's bedchamber
opened without a knock, and there in the doorway stood Arthur
the Assessor.

Elaine did not know about Arthur's game with the gold
sovereign, and thus did not know that he had played it with a
vengeance in this last week—but she could see the effects of
those terrible victories. His skin hung loose and slack on his
face, drooping from his red rimmed eyes—his mouth was thick
with the sludge of gluttony—his hair was thin with the loss of
vitality. It was as though he was selling his soul to the devil bit
by bit—for each broken man in each forgotten village, for each
victory a price had to be paid.

Elaine looked at his dissolution coldly. She remembered that
he had saved her life—she remembered that she had once loved
him—but they had taken different paths now. Arthur was on
his way to death—a moral death, if not a physical one. She was
gong to live—and in time, she would bring new life into the
world.

I can no longer imagine having a child with you, Elaine
thought as she looked at her husband. I must have a lover—
what if it were my lover standing in that doorway? He might
like the sight of pretty Sandra, with her wet dress showing her
body—but then he would look at me, he'd see my nakedness
beneath my towels, I wouldn't be able to keep from moving
under his gaze, I'd lean back toward the bed, my towels falling
loose, he's over me, tearing the last towel from me, lifting me up
and setting me firmly back on the bed, I look up and see Sandra
gasp as he begins to take me . . .

Elaine focused again on Arthur—she smiled, and her smile
was cruel.

Arthur did not say a word. He ducked backward out the door,
and closed it behind him. Elaine and Sandra heard another door
slam, and then they knew he was out in the palace's hallway.
He was gone, at least for now.

Elaine looked at Sandra and smiled lazily. "Get the oil. You
know what I want now."

As Sandra moved to obey, the Countess stood up and

stretched like a cat. The towels fell all about her feet, and she walked naked to her bed and lay on it face down.

Then Sandra was straddling her back, and Elaine felt the first cool touch of the scented oil, as the girl poured it between her shoulderblades. This special oil had been made to soften the skin of harem girls—it had been plundered by Crusaders—now loving fingers massaged it into the delicate skin of the Christian Countess, Elaine the Fair.

Chapter 41

THE APPROACH TO THE BALLROOM

Arthur returned in time to take his wife to the dinner that preceded the ball, only to find that Elaine was not yet dressed. She was sitting before a mirror, wearing only a thin nightgown—her head was tilted back so that Sandra could make up her face.

Sandra, who had been bending over her mistress, jerked upright when she heard the bedroom door open.

Elaine gave no sign that she had noticed someone come in.

Arthur watched her studious disregard for a moment, and then he said cooly, "Get dressed—the Prince expects us."

Elaine still did not look at him. She said evenly, "Please convey my apologies to the Prince and the Duke of Larraz. I will not be able to come to the dinner. You can make up a plausible excuse for me. I know you are quite good at that." Only now did Elaine turn and look at her husband. She smiled at him—a cruel, cruel smile. "Do tell them, however, that it is just possible that I may attend the ball.

"You needn't come back. Sandra will escort me."

Elaine turned away from Arthur without waiting for a response from him. She gestured for Sandra to continue, but the girl was too terrified to work. Sandra stood frozen with a tiny brush in her hand. She could not imagine disobedience of both a husband *and* a Prince. She was afraid for her mistress.

Elaine tilted her head back, waiting, face relaxed.

Arthur's loose jowls twisted—he muttered a curse—he turned and walked away, slamming doors behind him.

Arthur realized that his possession had left his pocket—she sought to live on her own. She thought nothing of him any more.

She planned to betray him.

Arthur had already crossed the line between good and evil—but so far his evil had not encompassed his wife. Now the devil whispered in his ear, and he listened. He felt a thrill—here at last was a worthy foe. This was not some weak willed villager—his next victim would be his wife.

Arthur knew just how he would break her.

He laughed as he walked away down the palace corridor.

The Countess looked at her lady in waiting, and saw that the girl was literally shuddering with terror. Elaine reached out and took Sandra's free hand. She pulled the girl closer—Sandra came reluctantly—Elaine bent down and kissed the tremoring hand that she held.

Sandra looked down in shock as she felt her mistress's tongue run over her knuckles—her hand felt hot in the prison of the Countess's grip—she allowed her hand to be turned over—she wasn't sure that it belonged to her any longer—she felt the second kiss against her palm, she felt Elaine's golden hair brush against her wrist—and then Elaine raised her head, and opened her own hand, and gave Sandra back the use of hers.

Sandra looked down at her own hand as though she had never seen it before. It was no longer trembling. She looked up at Elaine.

The Countess smiled. "You see," she said. "You don't have to be afraid."

Sandra said, 'I love you' in her heart. She said, "Yes, Milady," with her mouth.

Elaine gestured to the brush that Sandra still held in her other hand. "Continue," said the Countess, and it was as though the kisses had never happened.

Sandra allowed herself just a second of voluptuous yearning—and then she dipped the tiny brush into rare Egyptian dye. She leaned forward and resumed her delicate work. She painted the eyelids of her mistress a dark blue—a deep shadow above the pale blue jewels of her eyes.

Then afterwards it was time for the final brushing of the Countess's hair—it was dry now and ready for those long upward strokes that made it fluff out and bounce with a life of its own.

Elaine had had a dress made for this occasion. It was a long simple sheath of delicate pink silk. The Countess was almost ready now—she had Sandra help her with the dress—she had already decided that she would wear nothing under it.

The silk whispered down against skin that had been almost unbearably sensitized by the day's long ritual. Elaine turned— the dress moved as one with her body.

The Countess took out heavy gold earrings, and had Sandra fasten them in each of her ears.

She heard the music begin, faraway, in the ballroom.

Sandra stood close by her side. Elaine turned her whole body to face her lady in waiting—the motion made the silk slide across her stiffened nipples—Elaine caught her breath for a moment—and then she smiled.

"You will come with me to the ball."

"I will escort you there, Milady."

Elaine saw that the girl did not yet understand.

"No, your duties extend further than that, my dear. You will come with me into the ballroom. You will be my guest, you will dance as I will dance."

"O no, Milady, I can not! I have not rank, nor invitation, I have no proper dress—I can not—"

"Stop."

Sandra stopped talking. She looked up at her mistress. The Countess's eyes were a hard furious blue.

"Take off your dress."

Sandra could not face those eyes. She looked down—she remembered someone else who had looked at her like that. She suddenly felt that she understood why her mistress would no longer see Thomas. They were too much alike. If they came together, it would be like touching fire to fire—who could survive such a conflagration?

But what of her own situation?

Sandra did not understand how she could go to the ball. It was not her place. On the other hand, she also knew that she did not dare look up and meet her mistress's gaze. For now, she had to obey.

She reached down and caught the hem of her dress. Like Elaine, she wore nothing beneath it. She lifted the garment off over her head.

Sandra stood naked before her mistress. She kept her eyes downcast—she held her dress in one hand—she shivered in the heat of Elaine's gaze and she dropped her dress on the floor.

She looked down at the crumpled cloth as though that were the only reality in the world.

The Countess took two steps toward her lady in waiting and laid gentle hands on her shoulders. "You are well born," said Elaine. Her voice was caressing, seductive. "Your father was a knight. You have told me that your mother was much admired, as you will be tonight."

Elaine's hands slid down and cupped the girl's plump soft breasts. The nipples felt like little stones. "You need a dress, and you shall have one of mine. You recall the cream dress that was made too short for me and never fixed—it will be perfect for you."

The hands slid lower and spanned Sandra's waist—and then Elaine explored lower still, her thumbs just touching the nest of brown curls as her hands glided over the surface of Sandra's soft quivering thighs and slid in between them and tugged them apart.

Sandra had to shift her feet and spread her legs wider to keep her balance.

Only then did Elaine move her hands back upward. She returned on the same path, and when she cupped the girl's breasts again she said, "You will come with me."

Yet Sandra's eyes were still stubbornly lowered, she was frightened and aroused and confused, and she said, "But Milady . . ."

Sandra could not go on. She felt the swiftly rising storm in her mistress. The hands left her breasts—her chin was cupped as once before—her head was tilted back—Sandra raised her eyes fearfully to those of the lady she loved.

She looked into the full existence of Beauty. It was a beauty that she had helped create, but it was wholly independent of her now. She looked into blue eyes with the dark blue shadow above them. She saw gold gleaming from ears half hidden by the lady's finespun golden hair. She saw the arrogant nose, the red lipped mouth, the high cheekbones of a furious God determined to sow havoc on this world.

She felt the wild force, the unleashed, untamed, barely controlled will of Elaine the Fair.

The Countess could do whatever she liked with her, and in a way it was a relief when, after a long second, her lady turned Sandra around. It was a relief to turn away from that terrible beauty.

When Elaine had turned Sandra, she had caught the girl about the waist with her left arm. Now she put her right hand on Sandra's back and pressed forward and down. Sandra bent over willingly—the certainty of punishment was the antidote to her confusion—she bent over until her offered buttocks were the highest part of her body.

Sandra rested her weight against the strong arm that held her—she felt Elaine caress her upthrust vulnerable softness, and then the hand left her and Sandra knew that the next touch would not be a caress.

"You have vexed me, my dear girl," Elaine said, and then she brought her right hand down with all her force on one soft plump buttock. Indifferent to Sandra's cry, she raised her hand and brought it down with equal force on the other bottom cheek. Sandra cried again. Elaine watched as the perfect pink prints of her hand came up on the girl's tender white skin. Elaine aimed for the marks, and struck twice more.

Then she raised Sandra, and turned her, and brushed away the tears that had just begun to flow.

"You know where the dress is, I believe."

Sandra looked up into her mistress's beautiful face, softer now, and she would have given anything in the world for her lady's kiss—but it didn't come.

She lowered her eyes and said, "Yes, Milady."

Then it was the Countess who helped to dress and make up the lady in waiting—the ball had been in progress for an hour before they were ready.

At last they set off together—they walked down the palace corridor arm in arm.

To get to the ballroom, it was necessary to leave one door of the castle, walk along an outside path (the ballroom was a lavish addition built by Henry II to cater to his love of beauty—it was not part of the castle's original close defensive layout) and then enter through another door which took one right into the pleasure dome. It had been full dark for some time now—but the path was well lit by torches. A pair of armed guards waved Elaine and Sandra along—there was not even a thought of questioning the Countess's guest.

There was someone else without an invitation that the guards *had* stopped earlier—but after a short discussion they had let him pass. That was the knight known as Sir Thomas the Silent.

Sir Thomas had lived on hope, like a desperate hunting dog, all this past week. Just after dark he had come up to the guards and said, "Pass me through. I have no invitation, and I do not intend to enter the ballroom or disrupt the festivities. I wish merely to observe."

"You swear that there will be no violence?" the older guard asked.

"I swear it."

"I am sure that we can trust your honor, Sir—"

"But we have orders from the Prince," the younger guard interrupted. He addressed himself to Thomas. "Sir, we can not let you pass."

Thomas reached casually for the hilt of his sword. "If you refuse me then I shall have to kill you both."

The younger guard looked at Thomas's hand and then jerked around to look at his older comrade. The older man smiled at him. "As I said, it is necessary to trust this gentlemen's honor," he remarked.

The guards stepped back and let Thomas pass.

There was another set of guards at the door to the ballroom. Thomas had stayed out of their sight, but he had a good view of the door.

He had had the same good view for at least an hour now—an hour spent crouched under a spreading yew. He had seen many fine ladies and gentlemen enter the ballroom—and he did not have even a flicker of interest for any of them.

No one had entered the ballroom for a long time now.

Thomas heard the double footsteps.

One stopped. The other went ahead to make a solitary entrance.

Thomas stepped out from his place of concealment. No one would look at him now.

The two guards at the final barrier threw open the massive double doors. Elaine the Fair stood before the entrance to the ballroom.

A thousand torches cast their tongues of fire through the open doorway. Thomas saw Elaine caught in that burst of light, saw her as he had seen no woman on this earth, saw beauty past remembrance and beyond imagining, saw Elaine as she had never been for him—and he felt his heart shatter into a thousand pieces, save only for the hard knot of stubborn belief in the center that he clung to with all his warrior's strength—the crazy stubborn belief that one day she would come to love him.

Thomas began to walk away.

Sandra waited the proper moment, and then followed her mistress into the ballroom. The doors closed behind her.

Thomas walked past the guards he had met earlier.

The older one asked, "Did you see what you needed to see?"

Thomas answered, "Yes," without looking at the man.

He kept walking to where Saladin was waiting, and he got up on the black horse, and he rode off into the black night.

Chapter 42

ELAINE'S ENTRANCE

The ladies of the court had been delighted when Elaine had not come to the dinner that preceded the ball.

Many of these ladies had been kind to Elaine when that country girl had first come to the court. They had helped her dress properly, explained the court etiquette—they had even passed along tips for the boudoir, which the young Countess had made use of during her early days with Arthur.

Yet time passed without Elaine ever becoming one of them. The Countess was as unfailingly polite today as she had been then—but there was always something missing, at least as far as the other ladies were concerned. The fact was that there was no true intimacy: Elaine listened, but she did not confide. She never explained her mysterious scar—never gave a backstage view of her husband—never joined in light-hearted banter about the handsome knights of the court.

The Countess of Anjou remained aloof.

The women stopped trying to bring Elaine into their circle, but the young beauty hardly noticed. She could imagine a woman as a lover—she enjoyed the adoration of her lady in waiting—but she felt no need to be part of a community of women.

Likewise Elaine never encouraged the attentions of men—and for this the ladies were grateful (they knew well that few of their own number showed such restraint). The ladies did not think that Elaine was a danger to them—no one was close enough to see the gradual change in her—no one saw the torment and need in the Countess as her marriage failed—when the break came, it seemed terribly sudden.

Every lady of the court discovered the truth on the day of that terrible duel in which Sir Gareth was killed.

Elaine was looking—their men were not their own.

Sometimes the ladies would try to comfort each other by explaining why Elaine was not beautiful: she was too thin, her face was too sharp, her breasts were too small and so on—but these comforting opinions could never stand up before the reality of the Countess.

The plain truth was that Elaine the Fair could not be rivalled. Which man would she choose?

The ladies fought back in the only way they knew—all dressed carefully for this festive night, and none who had been generously endowed by Nature failed to show themselves off. Decollete dresses were the order of the evening.

The ladies, admiring themselves, admired by their men, had their time of bliss when Elaine did not appear at the dinner. Wine flowed like water as the ladies relaxed—men's glances returned ever more openly to the soft white breasts half exposed for their delectation.

Then the company adjourned to the ballroom, and the ladies' hopes rose even higher, for still Elaine did not appear.

Men and women danced in long lines, and there was no single beauty drawing everyone's attention.

Prince John oversaw the merriment—he lolled on a gilt throne raised at one end of the room. He was attended by a fine featured page and a pretty young maid.

Arthur sat alone—he drank and plotted his wife's downfall.

The Duke of Larraz was the gracious host. He sat at the table nearest the Prince, and received all guests with his customary political charm. Five brave Larrazian knights also sat at his table.

The English ladies looked with interest at these bold warriors—more than a few found reasons to pay their respects to the Duke and his men. And thus it happened that when the music changed, and couples danced close together, there were five English husbands who found themselves without their wives—who saw their wives lost in the embrace of European knights. There were smoldering looks as soft English breasts pressed against manly foreign chests—the Englishmen fondled their swords.

The game was old but always thrilling—the ladies gloried in the attention they received—the attention they deserved—yet each one felt a stray thought come in now and then, perhaps when the music slowed: "Could she—even now, will she . . .?"

Then they would forget their doubts as they changed partners—as whispered words of love found their ears . . .

The doors opened in the middle of a dance, and the music stopped. Everyone's feet froze in place. Men held their partners like forgotten sticks of wood. Every man turned his eyes to the doorway, and most women did as well, though some simply buried their faces against the men's unresponsive chests.

She had arrived.

Elaine the Fair stood alone in the torchlit entrance. She silenced the whole huge room.

The royal crier was the first to regain his presence of mind. His booming voice filled the silent hall as he announced, "The Countess of Anjou, Elaine the Fair!"

Elaine turned and smiled at him, as Sandra came up from behind. The Countess whispered something in the crier's ear. He continued, "And her companion, Lady Sandra of Salisbury."

There was silence again.

Elaine took Sandra's arm and walked toward her destination. She defied etiquette—but etiquette had no part in her plan. She did not pay her respects to the Prince, nor to the Duke of Larraz—she ignored her husband—she simply followed the path that she had set for herself—she had determined her goal following a close inspection of the ballroom a few days before.

The ballroom was a long rectangular space. Elaine had entered midway along the outer wall of one long side. To her right, next to that short wall, rose the throne of Prince John. Just before him, at the head table, was the Duke of Larraz. Coming closer to Elaine, seated at long tables, the nobility descended in tiers of rank. To her left was the dance floor, fairly crowded with staring couples. Beyond them, at the short wall opposite the Prince, the musicians performed (though now they stood becalmed, staring, with their instruments quiet in their arms).

Elaine walked straight across the room between the dance floor and the tables. She did not acknowledge any of the men who tried to greet her. Sandra clung tight to her lady's arm, and walked as she walked, and then they were through the crowd.

There were six loveseats against the far wall, facing out on to the dance floor. Elaine turned left to go to them. None were occupied—usually that would come later in the night. It was the custom for the beginning of a romance to be announced by a couple taking such a seat, there to sit close on a chair just big enough for two. Once a man and woman took that position, etiquette demanded that no other man could approach—save only to issue a challenge.

Never in living memory had two women taken such a chair. Elaine sat down on the comfortable seat, and brought Sandra down with her, and casually put an arm about the girl's shoulders.

Elaine leaned her head against the padded chairback. She felt Sandra's warm body against her own, she loved the light caress of her own dress on her bare skin—she felt the desirous looks of the men, and the jealous stares of the women.

They saw the burnished gold of her hair, and her half closed eyes revealed the novelty of their blued lids. She was a creature from another world—the ordinary rules did not apply to her— they accepted her actions, even the astonishing rudeness of her entrance—but no one dared to approach her.

Elaine relaxed, for all that was difficult had already passed. She had her place, and she had Sandra with her. If she had come with her husband—or even if she had come as she had and then gone to her husband—then all would have been different. Arthur would have taken her arm and presented her to the Prince, and then to the Duke of Larraz. Doubtless the Duke would have invited her to sit down at his table, Arthur would have sat next to her, and there she would be, a tame bird caged between two large men. The wild power she felt now would be muted by the forms of courtesy—she would be in her place, and that she could no longer stand.

She reveled in the fact that she had scorned Prince, Duke, and husband without incurring one word of opposition. She smiled to herself, thinking that she had picked up some of Thomas's rebellious attitudes. She felt like a warrior prince who by a daring maneuver had gained the high ground.

She was just as safe as she wanted to be, on the loveseat with Sandra—she was away from her husband, and (this was the reason she had made Sandra come with her) yet no man could gain her attention simply by sitting next to her.

Any suitor would have to show his mettle and approach her directly from the front. He could not sit, he could only stand and ask.

Elaine luxuriated in her beauty, and waited for the first man.

Chapter 43

THE POLITICS OF THE DANCE

Sir Guy of Sussex was not a foolhardy man. When other knights had rushed to challenge Sir Thomas (and Sir Gareth had met his death), Guy had rather more circumspectly offered his well trained filly for Elaine to ride. Guy had not believed that Elaine would finally choose the landless Thomas—and events had proved him right. *Now* was the time for bold action.

Sir Guy had escorted a pretty young widow, Lady Pamela, to the ball. They sat together at one of the long tables. Now he mumbled an excuse to his lady and stood up. No one noticed Pamela as she turned her head and hid her sudden tears with a soft linen napkin. All eyes were on the gallant knight of Sussex as he began his long walk toward Elaine the Fair.

The only sound in the big room was that of Sir Guy's footsteps.

Finally he stood before the object of his desire.

He bowed and said, "Milady." The single word drifted like smoke through the silence. Elaine gave him her hand to kiss, but she did not answer—she did not make it easier for him.

Sir Guy showed his courage. He spoke in a firm manly voice: "May I have the honor of a dance with you, Milady?"

Elaine did not keep him waiting—her blue eyes were warm as she looked at him—but she shook her head back and forth with sad regret. She said, quietly but firmly, "No, Sir Guy."

The musicians, like everyone else, had been caught up in the drama—but when they heard the Countess refuse, they were reminded of their common bond of manhood. They could not let one of their brethren stand there heartbroken in silence—they struck their instruments with a will. The drums boomed, the hornblower sent a fanfare overhead—but Sir Guy heard only the delicate sorrowing notes of the harp as he walked away in defeat.

He returned to Pamela—she had only lately come through her period of mourning for her husband, dead in the Holy Land— she had set her hopes on this popular young knight who had so surprisingly offered to escort her to the ball—she looked up at Sir Guy, and she smiled bravely, though her eyes still sparkled with tears.

Guy looked down to see two thirds of Pamela's full bosom exposed to his gaze—she looked vulgar and common compared to the delicately covered vision of loveliness that he had just left. His despair turned to anger, and he wanted to strike sweet Pamela—but then he did notice her tears. He took her wrist roughly, pulled her to her feet, and yanked her in the direction of the exit.

Sir Guy hurt Lady Pamela that night. The first time was nearly rape, but somehow not quite—he took her insatiably, over and over—but each time was gentler, and the last one, just before dawn, was almost an act of love. After the sun rose, Guy went to a priest and had the banns posted—he married Pamela in a month.

Never again did Sir Guy ride with Elaine the Fair.

In the ballroom, Guy's departure had been as little noticed as his lady's tears earlier. There was only one focus of attention.

Everyone watched as one brave knight after another approached Elaine the Fair—everyone watched as they walked away in defeat.

Elaine turned down six in a row, giving each the single pleasure of kissing her hand.

Sir Hugo was the seventh. He had waited for a long time, wondering whether he had the right to approach that lady, given the fact that he had already been defeated in battle for her favor. He finally decided that he might, since Elaine had evidently cast aside Sir Thomas—if she had wanted to use her influence, she could surely have obtained an invitation for him.

Hugo walked up to Elaine, and took the hand that she offered with his own mutilated right hand.

Elaine noticed the nervous quickness of Hugo's gesture as he bent to kiss her hand—it was as though he wanted to end the ceremony quickly so that he could let go of her hand—he seemed ashamed of his own wound, ashamed that he had lost two fingers to Thomas's sword. He straightened up and tried to release her hand, but Elaine would not let him go. She curled her hand about his three fingered grip and held him tight.

Hugo looked up to see the compassion in Elaine's eyes, and he asked quickly, "May I have the honor of a dance with you, Milady?"

Hugo had no hope—it was enough that she was kind to him—but she didn't refuse, in fact she didn't say a word—she just squeezed his hand tighter, and it was as though she made him whole. He pulled up, and felt her weight against his fingers, and then she came lightly to her feet. Hugo started to lead her out on to the dance floor, but she stopped him, and looked back over her shoulder at Sandra. The girl stood, and then Elaine caught the eye of a disappointed knight, still lingering after she had lately refused him. A brief gesture made her wish clear—with a shrug, the knight made the best of it and took Sandra's arm.

Elaine danced close with Sir Hugo. She felt the pressure of his wounded hand against her back—felt the phantom pressure of his missing fingers—she remembered the sword blow that had cut them off.

She shivered, and pressed even closer to him—the ever watchful musicians slowed the tempo, and now Hugo held his lady of dreams so tightly that he could feel her body against his, the thin silk no barrier to his senses, and he bent down and kissed her crown of golden hair, and he drank in her flowered perfume, and he felt transported to a Persian palace as he looked down and saw her half closed, blue shadowed eyes.

Then Elaine let her head fall back, blue eyes wide open now, and she looked up into his face and her lips were a parted invitation. Hugo tightened the grip of his three fingered hand, and he spoke with all his soul lost: "I would give all the fingers of both my hands for but one kiss, Milady."

Elaine smiled as she looked up at him. "There is no call for such sacrifice," she said, and then she went up on her toes and kissed him on the mouth.

Sir Hugo froze with fearful joy—the musicians nearly dropped their instruments—and in the sudden silence those close enough could hear Elaine whisper, "I will always cherish your bravery and your love, but you are not the man for me."

Reeling with the blows of her words, but drunk with her kiss, Hugo took the hand Elaine offered him (for she had stepped out of his embrace) and walked with her back to the loveseat. He halfheartedly tried to sit down with her, but Elaine stopped him with a soft hand against his chest.

Sandra broke free of her own partner and hurried over to the loveseat—she sat down next to her mistress.

Elaine, sitting, still held Hugo's wounded hand. She raised it to her lips, and kissed the scarred place, and then she let him go. She whispered, "Good-bye," the word lost in the revived music, and the last thing Hugo saw before he turned away was Elaine's own scar, silent and white, with a story that he would never learn.

Hugo reeled blindly through the crowd—he sat down heavily at the first available table—he found himself opposite a courtier whom he barely knew. That fellow had but one solution for Hugo's condition—he passed over his own nearly full flagon of wine, and Hugo drained it at one go. His three fingered hand tightened around the empty flagon—Sir Hugo stared into the bottom as though seeing his own loss.

So the night went on—Elaine refused dozens of offers, and danced but twice more. Those favored were the two other surviving knights who had dueled for her, but she kissed neither of them, and dismissed each when their single dance was done.

Elaine left broken hearts strewn about the ballroom that night, and there was an air of finality about the way she did it—no man, once dismissed, could ever more approach her.

Arthur the Assessor was a keen observer of the drama. He did not yet see any man who was truly important to Elaine—no one significant enough to kill.

That was the secret to breaking her, he was sure of it: he had to kill the one she loved.

He kept watching.

The Duke of Larraz also kept a close eye on the suitors coming and going. He saw their failures, and he thought that if he could just keep his head, then he might be well on his way to winning Elaine before this night was ended.

He had seen the kiss—and then he *had* nearly lost his head at the sight of the taut arc of Elaine's body, for just a moment the familiar helpless ache came back to him, but then she had stepped away from Hugo, and he had been delivered. He realized—thinking calmly, now—that she had given a kiss, but she had not allowed any man to kiss her.

He intended to be the first.

He admired the way Elaine had chosen her ground. With

Sandra by her side (and the girl only danced when her mistress did) the loveseat was nearly impregnable.

He watched as still more lovesick fools charged and failed—he waited, for he was the Duke of Larraz, a man of wisdom and patience.

He waited until the night was old, until the other loveseats were full, until Sir Hugo slept with his face on a table.

He waited until Prince John's eyes were glazed with drink, until the boy who served him lay half asleep with his head on his master's lap, and the pretty maid (who like the boy had been fed from the Prince's flask all night) knelt half leaning against his side, hardly aware of the royal fingers that had insinuated themselves in her bodice.

He paused even now to reflect that Prince John was one of the few men immune to the Countess's charms—he sought pleasures of much lower value.

He looked once more at Elaine—it had been some time since the last suitor had approached her.

The moment was ripe.

He looked over at the veteran member of his troop, Sir Anton, and summoned him with his eyes. The Duke knew Anton well: the scarred ex-mercenary had never married—he preferred to indulge his taste for wenches half his age.

He was the perfect man for the job at hand.

"Yes, Milord," Sir Anton said, leaning his hands on the Duke's table.

Roland looked up at the grizzled old warrior and smiled. "How do you like Lady Sandra?" he asked.

Chapter 44

THE DANCE OF LOVE

Sir Anton came over to the Countess's loveseat, bowed to Elaine, and then turned to Sandra.

"Lady Sandra," he said with a smile.

The lady in waiting nodded nervously. She didn't know what she should do. She looked up at her mistress—Elaine seemed to be rather amused. The presence of the man was too intense to be denied. Sandra turned her head and looked up at him again.

Anton was still smiling—but his eyes were devouring her body. The dress Sandra was wearing had been cut for the slimmer Countess—it pulled tight against her breasts and thighs and there was really very little that he could not see. His gaze made Sandra feel vulnerable and frightened—and excited.

No one had ever looked at Sandra this way before—they had all been blinded by her glorious mistress. Sandra lowered her eyes but she could not repress a small smile: this one time she was first.

The foreign knight spoke again—he spoke only to her.

"I have been watching you, Lady Sandra. Shall I tell you what I see?" He didn't wait for a reply—he went on, "I see a sweet country bred girl, with the clear white skin that is England's compensation for its terrible weather. I see your happy bouncing curls that tell me you were a child not too long ago. I see that even yesterday you were a girl, but today you stand on the threshold of womanhood. I see that you need a man to help you take those first tentative steps of your new life.

"I watched others maneuver you tonight without thought or care. They were not interested in you.

"I have come for you, Lady Sandra—for the woman in you. I

have come to teach you to dance." Sir Anton put out his hand. "Take my hand, Lady Sandra. I will help you take the first step."

Sandra looked at the hard steady hand and then she looked up at his lined face. She saw the gray in his hair and in his bristly beard—she saw a man of experience. Here was a man who had survived twenty years of war and tourneys and jousts—he had killed and loved, known joy and suffering—yet for all that his dark blue eyes were kind. Her father had been a man like this—and he too late in life had married a pretty young girl. Sandra suddenly blushed—she was taking this far too seriously! He had only asked her to dance—and am I pretty? she wondered—but only for a second, because the knight's answer to that question was only too evident in his eyes.

She understood right then that the look in his eyes was just what she had been wanting—she started to put her hand out to meet his.

The motion of her own hand snapped Sandra out of her romantic dream. She shrank back in a panic and looked wildly at her mistress. She could not desert the Countess! Even without words she knew her duty—she had quickly understood her purpose at the ball—and yet—and yet—she didn't know what to do! Her pretty lips were parted but she could not make a sound—her eyes were big saucers of alarm and budding desire—she was still just a girl.

She let her mistress make the decision for her.

Elaine smiled at Sandra and brushed back a curl from the girl's cheek. Without looking up, she asked the knight, "And you Sir, are . . .?"

"I am Sir Anton, in the service of His Grace, the Duke of Larraz."

Sir Anton bowed again, with a certain overelaborate mockery.

Elaine liked him. She saw that he did truly want Sandra—yet she also knew well that his coming was no accident. She had seen him with the Duke. She would not let Sandra go now—she would not be left alone as a result of some clever manipulation.

Roland could take his chances like all the rest.

Elaine put an arm around Sandra and sank back in the loveseat, pulling the girl close. She sensed more than felt the rapid thudding of the girl's yearning heart.

The Countess smiled at Sir Anton, and he smiled back—until he noticed her eyes. They were pale blue glittering jewels without a speck of warmth in them. They saw through the Duke's plot and they stripped the mockery from Anton's face.

Anton wanted to turn and run—but he held his ground with an effort of will, and he wondered if even his lord could tame Elaine the Fair.

"Come closer," Elaine whispered, in a voice so soft that Anton *had* to take a step toward her if he was to hear—he did not want to take that step, but he showed his courage, and then Elaine's eyes softened, they were soft blue shadowed beauty now and the white scar was tender and vulnerable and her red lips were made to be kissed, red lips whispering to him alone and what she said was this: "Sir Anton, if you love my lady in waiting, then kiss her, and tell her you will be back soon, with your lord, His Grace, the Duke of Larraz."

Anton felt like he was drowning. He turned his head with his last strength, and there was Sandra—a sweet country girl as he had said and God what a relief after the unearthly beauty—he knew now why almost all men including his lord were enslaved by Elaine the Fair—in another moment he himself would have been lost—he counted himself lucky now as he cupped Sandra's face with his tough strong hands and tilted her head back—he saw Elaine release her grip on the girl—he leaned forward and kissed Sandra firmly on her half parted lips, kissed her longer than he had any right to do, and yet he understood already that this girl belonged to him.

He stood up, hands caressing her face as though he could not let her go—but then he did release her, and he said, "As your lady commands, I shall return shortly with my lord. Then indeed we shall dance, and no other man will touch you tonight." Sir Anton turned on his heel, the opposite way from Elaine, just so he would not see the Countess again.

Sandra watched him walk away, and then she turned nervously to her mistress, but Elaine just smiled and hugged her—they were like two sisters playing a game. Sandra leaned her head against Elaine's soft shoulder—she could still feel the rough scrape of Anton's beard against her chin. She dreamed with her eyes wide open—she waited for his return.

Anton made his way to the Duke's table and sat down without waiting for permission. He leaned forward, looked right into Roland's eyes, and said, "She will either kill you or make you the happiest man on earth. It is possible that she will do both, Your Grace."

"And you?"

"Lady Sandra is mine." Sir Anton grinned. "I want nothing more. The Countess, however, requires your presence before I can take her girl away."

"The happiest man on earth?" Roland was grinning also.

"Or death, Your Grace."

"Then let us drink to happiness."

Roland touched cups with the older man, and drank a hearty draught.

"Doubtless it would be better to keep the Countess waiting—but if she is the face of Death, then I must rush to her," Roland said.

He stood up, and Anton followed his lead. Roland looked quickly around the room—and caught the Chancellor of the Exchequer trying to hide behind a drink. For just a moment their eyes met—for just a moment the Duke felt Arthur's drunken jealous hatred—and then Arthur upended his mug and the contact was broken.

Roland had scarcely thought of Elaine's husband since he had been here. He had watched the lady fend off her suitors, but he had never seen her make one move toward her husband—and Arthur had not made one move toward her. No outsider could have guessed their relationship. Now, Roland wondered, do I go over to him and say, 'Excuse me Sir, but I have come all the way from Larraz to steal your wife—do you mind if I try my hand at seducing her out here in front of you?'

Roland laughed to himself and set off vigorously for the fatal loveseat. Anton, following, marveled at the elan of his lord. The knight had known Roland for thirteen years—ever since Charles's untimely death—and he had never seen such lightness and joy in His Grace. It was as though the cares of politics and the weight of family tragedy had finally been tossed aside. Even if it was a mad venture that had brought about the change, Anton was glad to see it.

The two men broke through the loose crowd that blocked their view of Elaine and Sandra—and stopped.

Elaine lay back in the loveseat, with Sandra cradled against her shoulder, and the Countess stroked the girl's soft curls, and ran a hand down her arm. Elaine's eyes were half closed, and her eyelids were a deep bruised blue in the fading torchlight—her lips were barely parted, just a glimpse of white teeth in the beginning of a smile, a smile for herself alone, and then she moved lazily like a cat and kissed Sandra's forehead, and the girl purred.

Roland was shocked by his involuntary erotic reaction to the scene.

He turned his body as though to speak to Anton, and discreetly straightened himself, and then turned back to Elaine. His breath was so short that he did not trust his voice. He swallowed twice, took two steps toward the Countess, and bowed.

He straightened up but the Countess did not look his way—she did not acknowledge his presence.

Seconds passed. The crowd realized that this was the last big drama of the night. Everyone watched.

Roland was disconcerted only momentarily. Now he gained confidence with every second that went by. She did not give him her hand to kiss, as she had done with every other suitor. The fact that she cared to ignore him set him apart.

I have negotiated with Kings, he thought, and never have I gone away empty handed. This dance of love is no different.

He looked at Elaine's "indifferent" profile—he remembered his first view of her, also from that angle. Then he had been lost. Now he was ready.

His voice was steady as a rock when he spoke.

"My dear Countess Elaine," he said, "I have come to meet my death."

Elaine turned faster than she meant to at that last word. She looked up at a big heavy man, built like her husband but not gone to fat, a big burly bear of a man, and the word "death" still hung in the air as she looked at him, and she could think of no repartee to fill the moment until he spoke again.

"My friend here, Sir Anton, tells me that I should never survive even one dance with you. He says that your charm is like a sword, cutting through to a man's heart. He said your eyes fire bolts more deadly than those from a crossbow. He imagines your embrace to be like drowning, a sweet and helpless suffocation."

Elaine looked carefully at the Duke's face. He has brown eyes, she thought to herself, but she was a little uneasy. There were depths in those brown eyes, and she could not read them.

She smiled slightly, and asked, "And you, Your Grace—what do you think?"

"I think that all he says is true," said the Duke, and he extended his hand.

The Countess took it and Roland lifted her to her feet. She

didn't bother signalling to Sandra, for Anton at once took matters into his own hands—took Sandra into his hands—the grizzled knight danced away with the young lady in waiting.

Elaine let Roland guide her out on to the dance floor. He took her left hand. He put his right hand on her silk covered back and it was as though his hand touched her skin. They stood motionless—the music seemed slow and faraway—the smoky burned down torches indicated that this would be the last dance.

Elaine wanted to know this man before he moved her, and Roland understood. He just held her firmly, and she studied his solid, careworn face, and she felt the comforting weight of his body against her, and she felt the strength of his arms around her—and then as she had done once before this night she went up on her toes and kissed her partner's lips.

"And what of my kiss?" she asked.

"Your kiss is the antidote that cancels all the others," Roland replied. "It brings life to me, and banishes death."

Elaine understood at once that this was not mere badinage. The last statement was clearly the simple truth from his heart. She laid her head against his shoulder and let him move her into the dance.

They danced slowly, and sometimes he whispered in her ear, and she answered with her lips against his neck. She let all her body go against him and he took her weight with his hands— she was held gently, firmly, protectively—and when the torches flickered out she was kissed.

It was a long, patient, thorough kiss—it didn't end until Anton and Sandra came up accompanied by a young page with a fresh torch.

Roland whispered a last message to Elaine, and then he looked around in the new light. He saw that Arthur was already gone.

Roland did not try to take advantage of that circumstance. He simply escorted Elaine outside—the page accompanied them— Anton and Sandra followed.

Roland kissed Elaine one more time, as Anton kissed Sandra—good-byes were said—then the two men watched as the beautiful ladies walked away down the path, the page with his torch lighting their way.

The two gentlemen thought only of love—the ladies likewise. Indeed, the whole English court was drunk with the excitement of the ball—it can certainly be said that no one who was at the ballroom that night gave even a fleeting thought to the high seas.

No one imagined that all their lives would soon be affected by a dragon prowed Viking warship that was beating its way across the North Sea even as they danced.

This warship was commanded by Ivar the Heartless. It carried a crew of fifty champions including Sigurd Sigurdsson.

They were coming to seize the most beautiful woman in the world.

They were coming to seize Elaine the Fair.

Chapter 45

HOMECOMING

Norway, June 6, four days before the ball . . .

Sigurd Sigurdsson came home on a late summer's night, past the children's bedtime, though the midnight sun still glowed low on the horizon.

Debbie and Petra had never slept well in this strange land and they woke up right away when they heard the door open. They were frightened—and then they heard their man's voice, and they rushed out to greet him. Sigurd hugged and kissed them both, and the noise of this woke up the children, and all four came toddling out. Their eyes lit up as they saw their father, and they rushed into his embrace with glad cries. Sigurd got down on his knees to hold them—in his left arm he had Stefan, four, and Helga, three, from his union with Petra—his right arm held Inga, also three, and Hans, two, who were his and Debbie's children. No sooner did he have them all gathered in than he heard a loud wail from the back of the house. He looked up with a start only to see both Petra and Debbie grinning at him.

Sigurd felt his own smile stretch his face. "A boy or a girl?" he asked.

"Go see," Debbie said.

Sigurd gave the older children one more big hug and then he rushed back to see Maria and the babe.

Maria stood in her room, wearing a French nightgown that Sigurd had given her, holding the squalling babe in her arms. She looked beautiful but tired—clearly this was not the first time the little one had awakened her in the night.

She offered the babe to his father. "You have a son," she said, in the formal Castilian tones of her heritage.

Sigurd took the little boy, and spoke to him—and the crying stopped almost at once at the novelty of this deep voice. Sigurd was fascinated by the tiny bundled lad—he whispered Viking secrets into the perfect little whorled ear, and Maria, watching, began to cry—but she was very quiet about it, and when Sigurd finally looked up she had already wiped her face clean of tears.

"When was he born?"

"Two weeks ago today."

"He's perfect."

The little boy did not like the fact that his parents were talking over him instead of to him. He started a few low cries to warm up his lungs.

Maria pushed a strap of her low cut nightgown down off her shoulder. One hard full breast came free.

Sigurd handed the boy to his mother. The lad opened his mouth for a big scream—and Maria stuffed a thick brown nipple in it. The boy choked a little and then settled down and started to suck. He put a tiny hand against his mother's breast.

Maria sat down. Sigurd bent down and kissed her, and then went back to rejoin the rest of his family.

It took a while to get all the children back in bed—but finally they all slept.

Sigurd had been away for twenty-three days. His wives had missed him. Petra and Debbie followed Sigurd into the main bedroom and took off their nightgowns—and then they undressed him.

It was an intense reunion. The women vied with each other to give their master pleasure, and once Petra even slapped Debbie—but Sigurd just hauled the Russian girl across his lap and gave her one hard stroke across the buttocks with the short whip he kept by the bed. Petra whimpered, and looked up at Sigurd with those deep, dark, almost Asiatic eyes—he told her to kiss Debbie—she kept looking at him for another long moment, and then she obeyed.

From that moment on there was nothing but pleasure until finally all three slept the sweet sleep of satiation.

Two hours later the sound of his infant son crying woke Sigurd up. Petra and Debbie, used to the noise, remained asleep. Sigurd heard Maria get up—heard her singsong Spanish as she comforted the boy. He would have to give the boy a name and teach him the language of men. He looked out the window and saw that the sun had traveled around the horizon—it was morning—he should go see Ivar.

The thought brought back the memory of Elaine the Fair—for just a second the image of her gorgeous wounded face was before his eyes, and he was blind even to the women he had loved this last night.

Sigurd shook his head. He had looked upon Elaine, and pitied her, for he thought that he was marking her for death—but her image had stayed with him, and now she frightened him. Now he didn't know who was marked for death.

Sigurd got up and quietly dressed. He knew that he did not want to continue with Ivar's mad quest—but he also knew that he had no choice.

It's not a matter of favor or old friendship, he thought, it's the idea of fealty. Each of us swears an oath of fealty to his Chief of Champions at the outset of a raid—there can be only one supreme commander on board ship, or in battle. How many times have I sworn fealty to Ivar? Twenty times? Thirty? At least that. I owe my life to Ivar. He's led me through every scrape without one misjudgment. I don't like him—he's right, I do despise him now—but that has nothing to do with fealty. He is my leader. Without him I would not have these women—I would not be a rich man. He led me to this success. I must follow him, as he searches for his own.

If I were a different sort of man I would have challenged him years ago when he began to kill women without reason. I might have killed him—or I might have died. But I turned the other way, I kept silent, and now I have my wives, and my children, and I'm rich—and I must follow my chief to the end.

Sigurd looked down at Petra and Debbie, each with an arm extended where they had hugged him in sleep. Their hands did not quite touch. He bent down, and moved them gently together, and put their arms about each other. He smiled as they murmured contentedly and settled into a gentle embrace without waking. He traced the mark of his lash on Petra's buttocks, and then he cupped Debbie's unmarked white bottom. He pressed his hands toward each other, as though squeezing together two pieces of clay—he forced the women's loins together, as his hands sank into their softness—the act aroused him but then suddenly he thought of Elaine, he thought of death—and his hands fell away from his women.

He left his house and went to see Ivar the Heartless.

Chapter 46

THE REPORT

Sigurd stood in front of Ivar's ugly shack. He examined the ill-fitting planks of the battered door—and then he knocked. There was no answer. This was normal—Ivar only called out when he didn't want you to enter. Sigurd opened the door.

The place seemed strangely empty. A big fire gave some illumination to the windowless dark room, but it did not seem as though anyone was home. Sigurd could make out the rusty roof supports in the back—no girls were chained to them. The floor seemed all bare, as though someone had swept it clean—all bare except for one shapeless black mass in the center.

Sigurd tried to make out what it was—and then something white rose out of the blackness, and Sigurd stared in horror at the bare skull of Ivar the Heartless.

Sigurd reached for his sword—but then the skull raised itself in the air, and its black eyesockets opened to reveal infernal yellow eyes, and its mouth opened to reveal a carnivore's yellow teeth—and it spoke.

"Greetings, my friend," Ivar said.

Sigurd slowly moved his hand away from his sword. He saw that the Chief of Champions was wrapped in a black cowled robe—and he had shaven his head.

Sigurd wanted only to run—but instead he asked, with a crazed boldness, "Where are your women?"

Ivar smiled, and his yellow teeth gleamed in the firelight. "I killed them the day after you left. They did not interest me any more. I cleaned my house—I did this"—Ivar ran a hand over his smooth shaven scalp—"and I waited for you. I lived only for your return."

Ivar smiled again, a lolling wolf's smile, and Sigurd still wanted to run, wanted to leave this house of murder, but he already
knew there was no place left for him to run. He just stood still,
as erect as possible, and he waited for the question that Ivar
had to be thinking, but Ivar preferred to let him suffer, Ivar
didn't say a word, just grinned and stared with those yellow
eyes and Sigurd couldn't stand it, couldn't stand the wait and
the silence and finally he broke and told Ivar what he wanted to
know.

"I found her," Sigurd said.

The yellow eyes gleamed but Ivar said nothing.

"I asked your question of everyone I met: 'Who is the greatest
beauty in the land?' No matter who I asked, I always received
the same answer. I went to see her, and it was all true and more
than true—she is the most beautiful woman I have ever seen—
she is the most beautiful woman in the world."

Sigurd wanted Ivar to beg for her name but the yellow eyes
just touched him with their reflected fire and it was he who had
to keep talking, he who had to keep giving—

"Her name is Elaine."

He's a murdering beast.

"She is the Countess of Anjou."

He'll have to kill her because she'll never love him and I can't
give her to him but I already have—

"They call her Elaine the Fair."

"You've done well," Ivar said. "Tell me more."

There was a lot more to tell. Harry (the groom at the royal
stables) had been especially talkative once Sigurd had gotten
him drunk. Sigurd told about Elaine's marriage—he knew that
the Countess was seeking a lover. He told about her Wednesday
meetings with Sir Thomas, and suggested that the isolated spot
she went to with Thomas would be ideal for abduction.

"I've always trusted your judgement," Ivar said. "But we have
to consider that her plans might change. But don't worry—I
know how we can handle things . . ."

And so it was that Ivar and Sigurd and a crew of fighting
champions set off on the next day, Monday, June 8. By
Wednesday night, the night of the ball, they had already made
good headway. They had a following wind—they expected to
make landfall on the English shore either Sunday or Monday.

Before Sigurd had left home, he had named his little son Leif,
after the great explorer Eriksson.

Chapter 47

THOMAS ALONE

In the stable for landless knights, Thursday, June 11, the morning after the ball . . .

Sir Thomas the Silent put saddle and bridle upon Saladin and told his old groom, Jim, that he was off to do some hunting. Relations between master and servant had not improved since the day Jim had learned the black stallion's name—the groom grunted at Thomas's words, turned his head, and spat.

Thomas saw the gesture but he could not bring himself to care. He touched heels to Saladin and rode off.

Jim watched with open hatred as his master rode away on that devil horse. Saladin! The evil name burned in his brain whenever he cleaned the animal's muck.

Jim could have already let loose the secret that there was an infidel lover at the English court—but so far he had bided his time. Prince John—that usurping deviant—was hardly the right person to handle this. Everyone said that the true King was coming home soon. Jim could hardly wait. What would the Lionheart do to a man who named his horse for the transgressor of Jerusalem?

Jim smiled as Thomas disappeared into the distance . . .

Thomas did not really do any hunting. He just rode deep into the forest, and when he was lost to all men he leaned down and laid his face against his horse's warm neck and cried.

He remembered Suleka, his dear Arabian girl—he remembered how she had washed his feet every night, how only after that ritual would she kiss him—he remembered how he had found her with the ripping sword wound across her belly that had ended two lives.

Saladin's neck quivered and Thomas slid off the horse. He took off the bridle and saddle, and let the stallion go free to nibble at the forest undergrowth.

It had been almost three years now. Suleka had been killed August 20, 1191.

Why do I think of her now, Thomas wondered—and as he wondered, the image of Elaine from last night came back to him.

He saw her again in the torchlit entrance—he saw her long pink dress and her golden hair—he saw her white scar sparkling and her blue shadowed eyes—and he understood.

Until last night he had never seen a European woman shadow her eyes like that. Elaine had appropriated one of the secrets of the East—unknowingly, she had made the connection that brought back Suleka—sad Suleka with kohl rimmed eyes—he used to stare into those deep shadowed pools and finally kiss her without speaking.

They had never learned more than a few words of each other's language—but Suleka had made it clear when she had known she was pregnant—she had put her hand on her dark, softly swelling belly—he had touched her there—No more!

Thomas began walking stiff-legged, blindly through the trees. Finally he headed straight toward a thick trunked maple. He seized the tree with his two hands and stared at its rough bark as though it were a mirror—he began to talk to the tree.

"Suleka is dead and our child was never born.

"Elaine doesn't love me.

"She picked me to make the break with her husband—she picked me because I am the best at war—but now she's made the break and she doesn't fear any longer and she's looking for love now and she doesn't need me.

"I love Elaine the Fair but she doesn't love me and I will never have her.

"I love Elaine but she doesn't love me.

"I love Elaine."

Thomas stared at the tree with a faint smile on his face, and then he tightened his grip on the sides of the trunk and slammed his forehead into the rough bark. As his head smashed into the tree he cried, "Elaine!" He pulled his head back, and then slammed it forward even harder, the bark breaking and flying loose this time—"Elaine!"

He pulled back again, and looked at the torn up bark and the hard bare wood underneath that he had bared, and he saw the bright red drops of his blood on it, and then he slammed his face right into it a third time—"Elaine!" And now when he pulled away there were three trickles of blood running down his forehead and getting into his eyes but his smile was clear.

Thomas wiped the blood off with one hand and then put that bloody palm over his heart. He felt the hard knot of living belief there, undestroyed: someday she would come to love him.

Thomas turned to look at his horse. "It's all right, Saladin," he said, but the horse did not trust this blood stained vision. The stallion deliberately turned away and paced off a few steps into the forest.

The knight examined the black tail swishing across his horse's strong narrow rump.

"Are you going to kick me?" Thomas asked, but Saladin, of course, refused to answer.

That's just as good an answer as I'd get from any courtier if I asked about Elaine, Thomas thought. Who did she dress up for? Who did she dance with? Who did she kiss? I'm as helpless now as I was three weeks ago when she didn't show for the second lesson. I know nothing of the ways of the court. I can imagine what would happen if I asked some knight about last night—'O, weren't you invited?' he'd ask with a condescending sneer—no I can get nothing from such fellows—and as for the ladies, I have protected them but I know none of them—I did not care to know them—I mourned Suleka and loved Elaine, and that was enough—but now it's not enough, not nearly enough, because I have touched Elaine and I need to truly love her—I need to have her, not dream of her.

I know one honest man who went to the ball—the man who sponsored it. I wonder if the Duke of Larraz would remember me?

Thomas cringed at the hateful memory—hateful not for the Duke, who had been gracious, but hateful because it recalled his own low position of the time.

Five years ago Thomas had been a waiter, and he had had a different name, that being the one given by his parents. The Duke had sought him out before the feast given by the newly crowned King Richard—the Duke had paid him well, and the young waiter had delivered: he had brought the choicest cut of meat directly to the plate of the Duke of Larraz, just so Roland could cut the best bites for Elaine the Fair. Thomas shuddered now, remembering—he had laid the meat down, and smiled at the Duke, and then he had looked at the lady next to him—and the sight of that smiling beauty had nearly ripped his heart in two. There was a woman he could love—there, on the other side of a table, across a thousand miles of class—then and there the waiter had sworn he would become a knight, and he swore that in time he would win that lady.

He had accomplished the first (at least so far as anyone knew), but as for the second . . .

In some ways Elaine the Fair was as remote as ever. He did not know her heart, did not know if she had found love at the ball, or thought she had found love . . .

He had no one to turn to, Roland least of all—he could not risk giving up the secret of his past.

He realized that the only answers possible would come from the lady herself.

"I shall have to follow her," Thomas said.

Chapter 48

THE SHADOWERS

At the ball, Arthur watched as Elaine danced with Roland. He watched as his wife went up on her toes and gave the Duke a kiss, just as she had done with Sir Hugo earlier.

The Assessor had been drinking all night but his mind was clear—he saw through Elaine's feeble attempts at disguise. Here again she tried to divert his attention with a kiss that he was obviously meant to see—he knew who her real lover was—he had guessed it from the start, and this charade only reinforced his opinion. She wanted that landless knight, Thomas—that was the one she kept sneaking out to see—she had been alone with him last week—no public kisses with him! She kept him out of sight! All I need is the final proof, and I know just how I can get that, Arthur thought. And while I gather the proof, I shall set up the awesome machinery of my revenge—ah, it's a beautiful instrument of destruction—it's been such a pleasure tinkering with the details while I have watched my wife insult me—she will never know that the force comes from me until the end—until she sees her lover lying dead at her feet—until I come to claim my reward: the final breaking of her spirit.

Arthur smiled contentedly as the torches burned down—people had started to leave—then he noted that Sir Nigel and Sir Walter were headed for the door. These two were part of his plan. They were profligate fellows who loved the gaming tables quite as much as the brothels. Racked by debts, they had not come close to paying the Saladin Tithe this year (though Arthur had not yet moved against them, for he felt they might sometime be useful) and they were hardly the type to seek expiation in the blazing desert of the Holy Land. They were perfect tools.

Arthur got up and rushed for the exit. He caught up with
Nigel and Walter just as they were going out the door—he got
between them and put his arms around their shoulders and
hustled them outside. He walked them around a dark corner of
the ballroom, and there he made his offer—and being thus
engaged, Arthur did not see Elaine's last kiss—the deep searching kiss that Roland gave her when the flames burned out.

Nigel and Walter were terrified when the tax collector seized
them—but their fear turned to delight when they heard the
easy terms of his offer. They were to discreetly follow Elaine the
Fair, and report to Arthur about anyone she met.

Arthur told them that a good job would weigh heavily in their
favor as regards their unpaid taxes. The two knights thought
that it would be nothing but pleasure to observe the beautiful
Countess of Anjou.

Arthur pressed some gold into their hands, "For horses," he
said—and then as he left he whispered softly, "If anyone should
hear of this . . ." his voice trailing off before he finished the sentence, but the threat of death was so clear that the knights did
not need the words.

They nodded into the darkness, but the fat man was already
gone.

Nigel and Walter stayed up most of the night making their
arrangements, and by the time they were done it was too late to
sleep—so they woke up two friendly maids they knew, and each
man put a hand over his girl's pretty mouth, and pressed fresh
treasury gold into her hand, and nightdresses were pulled up in
the early dawn and the men took their pleasure.

Relaxed then, and cheerful, the chill of death banished, the
knights set up their surveillance. Nigel stayed inside the castle
(Arthur had cleared his presence as a temporary guard) while
Walter was mounted outside, with a fresh horse for Nigel teth-
ered nearby.

They kept tabs on Elaine all day, but nothing untoward
occurred.

Friday was the same, and Saturday was another opportunity
to yawn. They still hadn't caught up on their sleep—but then
those same maids cast inviting smiles at the generous young
knights, and the pleasure seeking fellows could hardly resist—
they did their duty to such effect that they could barely rise and
assume their stations on Sunday morning.

This was the day Elaine always slept late (her lack of attendance at mass was well known) and Nigel wondered if he might take a nap. His eyes were almost closed when Elaine's door opened—the Countess swept by him in the royal purple silk of a queen, she seemed to fly by with a long clean effortless stride, and then there was Lady Sandra, two steps behind, almost running to keep up with her mistress.

Nigel was shocked awake like never before, every limb trembling as the adrenaline surged against his fatigue, and he followed at a safe distance though the Countess did not deign to watch her back. She just stormed down the long hallway and out the door, out the gate, and Nigel barely had time to make the prearranged signal, a red cloth lifted high on the point of a sword, before two horsemen raced up with two more horses in tow, horses already equipped with sidesaddles, and then the ladies mounted and the foursome was off.

Walter almost fell off his horse when he saw the red signal, but then he noticed Elaine and Sandra leaving with two knights, and so he circumspectly drifted back into the trees, he let the foursome go by him down the lawn, and then he followed obliquely, he changed direction often, just a distant knight practicing war, not a shadower at all, and he had time for these maneuvers because the ladies riding sidesaddle slowed the party, he was doing well now, the Assessor would reward him, and now Nigel had caught him up, better and better, they pretended to joust playfully, riding at each other at an angle, the angle always keeping them on the path of Elaine, and Nigel too thought they were doing well, though he wished he had got a better look at the two knights who have picked Elaine up, it had been too fast, he hadn't recognized them, he hadn't seen them very well—and he didn't see Thomas at all until it was too late.

The silent knight closed fast with the reins draped over Saladin's neck, he guided the horse only with his knees, his long lance held crossways in a two handed grip, and he clubbed Nigel to the earth with one mighty blow of that staff, and if Nigel saw nothing before he felt the blow then Walter saw too much, and closing anyway he put spurs to his horse and charged, no lance for such a surveillance job but the sword out, and Thomas couldn't turn his heavy wood in time, but he had noticed the other two shadowers these last four days, and he was prepared, he had looped his shield over his saddle this morning, and he let go of the lance with one hand and grabbed the shield, he got it up just in time, and he felt the swordblow strike it, the blow nearly broke his arm and it drove the steel oval back against his own skull, he saw stars and floated weightlessly as Walter's horse passed him, Thomas was unsure whether he was riding or falling, but Saladin eased his gait for his master, now Thomas felt the beloved horse under him, he tossed the shield down and grabbed the reins and turned Saladin, got him turned right around and kicked the horse forward so that when Walter wheeled his own steed for the kill he saw not the battered warrior he expected, no, Thomas had not been weakened by the blow, Walter saw a ferocious fury charging on his black devil steed, lance implacable at the fore and Walter tried to chop it away with his sword but his blade barely bit into the rushing wood, he could not slow its deadly passage, and Walter looked down as the lance transfixed his chest.

After that everything seemed to move very slowly, there was no pain at all, Walter just floated up into the air, and the blood bubbling up was as bright as a rose a lady once gave him, nay, it was brighter, and he thought of that lady and then he thought of the girl he had kissed this morning, he said her name but no sound came out and his pierced mortal body fell heavily to the earth, he felt that last blow and then he was gone.

It took Thomas a minute or two to work his bloody lance free of Walter's corpse. Nigel had already remounted and now he was racing back toward the castle. By the time Thomas looked around, Nigel was long gone.

The party of four was out of sight as well—but Thomas knew that they couldn't be far ahead. He pointed his lance forward and rode out after Elaine.

This was rolling country—he was in a slight depression now, so it was unlikely that any outsider had seen the small battle. Thomas rode up the slope that Elaine had recently traversed, confident that he would see her when he got to the summit—but she and her party had vanished into the forest ahead.

They had reached the end of the cultivated land that characterized the crown's immediate territory. There were no more formal gardens, ornamental hedges, or carefully spaced young saplings.

There was just the black forest and no sign of Elaine.

Thomas quivered atop his horse, the violence still in him.

With each day following the ball, his anger had grown. Elaine was out of his reach, and yet he was driven to follow her. He had to learn the secrets of her heart—and yet he could discover nothing from her routine activities—activities that had nothing to do with him. He was out of her life, and that fact showed clear every moment that he followed her. He thought obsessively of the night of the ball—he pictured her dressed in all the flames of beauty, and he wondered who that was for—he thought of himself, waiting crouched under a bush, and he raged.

Many times he said, 'I hate you Elaine,' and then hard on every evil desire he said, 'I love you, Elaine,' and Thursday, Friday, and Saturday went by without any serious action, and by Sunday he was ready to kill, and now he had done so, and he felt no ease.

He rode up to the forest, and found the path that Elaine had taken.

Chapter 49

THE TRAIL

The trees swallowed up the sun as Thomas entered the forest. He had to stop Saladin and wait for his eyes to adjust—finally he was able to make out the path torn up by four horses. As always, the English soil was somewhat damp—the churned earth had almost turned to mud.

As he followed the path—slowly, through the dimness— Thomas wondered for a moment who had hired Nigel and Walter. They were not the type to do such a job on their own. Perhaps if he had been more alert he could have kept Nigel from fleeing—but really he hadn't cared—he had only wanted to kill, he had only wanted to remove this obstacle that had got between him and Elaine—now that those English knights were cleared away, he could hardly concentrate on them any longer— only Elaine pulled his thoughts, and he was on her trail.

Thomas knew whom she was going to see.

He had recognized the two who had picked up Elaine and Sandra as Larrazian knights. They had to be taking her to their leader—to Roland, the Duke of Larraz.

Thomas remembered the Duke from five years before: a handsome bearded gentleman, perhaps ten years older than himself. Roland had been gracious—yet even so, there had been no pretense of equality when the Duke dealt with the young waiter.

Things have changed now, Thomas thought. Then I used the money Roland paid me to buy a new sword—and it's the one I still carry. Today I may use that sword to kill the Duke.

Thomas recalled that the two Larrazian knights were armed only with swords, not lances. With the thought, he casually dropped his own soiled lance by the side of the trail. It will be a fair fight, Thomas thought. I'll fight them on even terms before my lady, and I'll kill them, and then I'll challenge their master.

Thomas rode on slowly through the silent forest, keeping his eyes on the muddy trail—the steady motion gradually calmed him, and he began to consider the problem in a new light.

Why would there be any reason to challenge Roland? In fact, if Elaine ran true to form, there would be no reason to fight at all.

Thomas considered Roland's chances. Most would consider you to be far greater than me, the knight thought. You are a Duke, a head of state, you are a fabulously wealthy man with an army at your disposal. You have knights to bring a lady to you at your command, while you need only wait—but when you try to win Elaine the Fair, you are just a man.

You are not greater than me in her eyes. You may love her as I love her, yes, but I watched your dinner with her long ago and she gave you nothing. All she gave was what she gives any man of wealth and accomplishment—but she has given me far more. She has come to me of her own will, she has kissed my cheek, and I have kissed hers, and I have touched her lips, and I have embraced her.

She may amuse herself by coming to see you today—but you should not think there will be anything more. She will fence with you when you try to get close—she will keep her distance. By the time I find you, she will probably be ready to leave—and I will take her home.

Much cheered by this imaginative construction—and perhaps relieved that (at least in his mind) the day's violence was ended—Thomas rode on with a smile on his face.

He did not think of the despair he had felt four days before.

He kept his eyes on the muddy, hoof marked trail—but in the tree covered darkness he never noticed that now he was following three horses—not four.

Somewhere in the forest Elaine had left the party.

Chapter 50

WHAT THOMAS SAW

The silent knight rode on, all unknowing. As he followed the trail his mind was filled with pictures of Elaine. He remembered the young Countess that he had served five years ago (though obviously she did not remember him from that time); he remembered her cool beauty when he had tried to kiss her in his stable; he felt again the gorgeous shock of seeing her torchlit figure before the ballroom.

Thomas thought of seeing Elaine soon again—he dreamed of touching her—and his mind was so colored by desire that he didn't even notice that Saladin had stepped out of the forest until he felt the sun strike his face with blinding force.

Thomas stopped to collect himself and survey the new terrain.

He saw that a small stream cut through the wood—Saladin had just stepped into a meadow that rolled down to meet the stream on either side. The crooked stream looked like a blue snake crawling across a green blanket—and inside a curve of the snake, where the meadow formed a promontory protected on three sides by water, there were three riderless horses. A foreign knight sat on a stump by the horses. He was looking at Sir Thomas.

Thomas felt the tension in his horse almost before he felt it in himself. He patted Saladin's taut neck, and he looked about him for the other two riders, but he saw no one save the single foreign knight.

Everything was wrong. Three horses—why not four? Where was Elaine? For that matter, where was Roland? This did not look like a Duke's encampment.

Thomas looked up at the sun. It was almost noon. He judged

that he had been trailing the party for perhaps two hours since his battle. He had lost time in the forest—these three might well have been here for a half hour or so.

Thomas looked again at the man on the stump. He was a black bearded fellow, about thirty—he wore a light vest of mail and carried a sword. There was no sign of enmity, no fear or tension in the man's face.

Thomas was taut as a bowstring. It was all wrong.

He tightened his legs about Saladin, and the horse moved reluctantly forward down the slope. The stallion did not like the terrain. Thomas noticed that once this land had been forest as well—someone had cut down the trees, leaving half seen stumps all over in the high grass. The idea had been to farm the rich bottom land—but the would be cultivator had evidently defaulted on his dream. This was not unusual. There were patches of fallow land throughout the tax ravaged England of Richard Lionheart.

Saladin scraped a stump with a forefoot. He reared and snorted, eyes rolling—but Thomas brought him down, and talked to him, and guided him around the obstacle and gently urged him forward—and all the while Thomas watched the man on the stump, and he looked all around and checked the meadow, for he still didn't know whether this was trap or mischance.

The bearded one sat calmly until the black horse was only three yards away. Then the Larrazian knight, whose name was Sir Gowan, stood up and spoke in his heavily accented English.

"Please Sir, go no further."

Thomas took the reins in his left hand, and seized the hilt of his sword with the right. As his right hand tightened its grip he felt the rage burn back in him—the killing rage that he had felt this morning. Thomas was almost certain now that he had been tricked. He was barely able to squeeze two words through clenched teeth.

"I must."

"You seek the Countess." It was hardly a question.

"Yes."

"She is not here." Sir Gowan gestured behind him to the semicircle of meadow grass tucked inside the bend of the stream. Perhaps twenty-five yards away, at the point of the promontory, there was a sudden dip to the edge of the water that formed a natural hiding place—yet such a little cul-de-sac could surely hold only two people.

Thomas looked across the stream—there were no hoofprints on the opposite bank.

"Who's hiding under the embankment?"

Sir Gowan smiled, and shrugged. "There is only my friend, and his lady."

"What lady?"

Sir Gowan adopted a conspiratorial tone. "Do you swear to say nothing of this?"

Thomas thought that he might kill this foreigner from sheer impatience before the man ever got to the point.

"I swear on my sword," Thomas said, drawing the weapon a few inches to make his point.

Sir Gowan ignored the display of steel. He continued calmly, "My friend, Sir Anton, and Lady Sandra of your court, are back there." He gestured toward the embankment. "I promised, on my honor, that they would not be disturbed." Sir Gowan looked Thomas in the eye. "I ask you to go in peace, my friend. The Lady Sandra will never again have such a day in all her life."

Just as he said the word 'life' there came a high clear feminine scream from the tip of the promontory. It was a loud unashamed cry of pain, but as it faded, it entered the territory of love, and it ended with acceptance, as though the lady had stopped her voice with her lover's skin.

Thomas looked hard at the bearded knight. "I will not disturb them, if you speak the truth. But I must see."

Sir Gowan nodded and stepped aside. "On your honor then," he said.

Thomas let his sword slide back into its scabbard. He urged his horse slowly forward. When he was close enough, he stopped Saladin and stood up in the stirrups to look over the edge of the bank.

There *was* a little cul-de-sac, just seven feet by three. The couple there had the murmuring brook on one side and the bank on the other to block out any sounds except their own. They had clearly not been disturbed by Thomas and Gowan's conversation. They were totally engaged with each other.

Thomas looked down upon Sir Anton and Lady Sandra—yet without clothes, he saw them as both simpler and greater than their titles. Without clothes they formed a primitive archetype of man and maid.

The maid was a lovely young lass, plump and ripe and happy. Her legs were spread wide for the man who was taking her—she had white legs, soft thighs—her breasts were crushed beneath his chest, her eyes were closed, and there were tears on her cheeks—but her arms held her lover tightly and her lips kissed his neck softly, and the words she whispered, too low for Thomas to hear, could only be words of love.

The man was much older, powerful, gray in his hair but steel in his muscles, his buttocks tight holding himself deep inside his lover, holding still with the wisdom of age, waiting for her to fully accept him there, and Thomas saw the rough white scars on his back, and he watched for another moment until Sandra moved her head and said some words into his ear, and then he began to slowly move, and when he rose up a little Thomas saw the girl's bright virgin blood between her thighs, and he heard her cry out again, but not so loud this time, he saw the maid hug her man tight as once again he drove deep within her.

Thomas looked around the couple for a moment. There was no possible place for Elaine to be hidden. She must have long ago left the trail, somewhere in the forest darkness.

Thomas turned Saladin around very quietly and rode back to the bearded knight.

"You speak the truth."

Sir Gowan smiled and bowed.

"And Elaine?"

"You may cut me to pieces, and I would tell you nothing."

Thomas looked deep into the foreign knight's black eyes. Finally, almost regretfully, he said, "I believe you."

Thomas struck Saladin with the flat of his hand, and rode off the way he had come.

Chapter 51

STORM AND SMILE

Elaine was a cruel mistress in the days following the ball.

Arthur had left her alone again—he had to investigate reports of a tax rebellion in Wales, he said—and so Elaine was left with nothing to do but wait for Sunday.

She was going to see Roland Sunday.

Was she?

Elaine paced.

She thought of Roland's kiss at the end of that last long dance—she burned at the thought, and she raged that even the thought could make her burn. Why had that simple kiss excited her so? It was nothing special really, just the logical end to an ever closer dance, the lights burning down and the two of them alone in near darkness, the music falling away, and she felt his beard first and she thought, Duke of Larraz, I know why you've come here, Duke of Larraz, and she tilted her head back to receive him, she felt his lips on hers, a slow, gradual, insistent pressure, and it excited her that the fate of his whole country hung in the balance, she knew Richard, she had heard the rumors of his return, she knew the magnitude of Roland's risk— 'I have come to meet my death,' he had said—she opened her mouth the way he wanted her to, and then she felt his tongue, entering her, savoring her taste, her texture—she had never been kissed quite like this before, there was something maddening about the way he did it—the kiss made her whole body burn and she pressed herself against him as hard as she could and somehow she expected him to take her outside right then, take her somewhere, but he, aware of the page coming with the fresh torch (as she was not), just broke the kiss, and whispered in her ear that his knights would come for her and Lady Sandra in the courtyard, Sunday morning at ten.

She hadn't had time to protest or press for an explanation. Good-byes had been said, and she had been burning ever since.

Why should I go with this foreign Duke? she asked herself. How can he think that I will allow myself to be borne off by his knights like some tart summoned to her master? He has no right to ask this of me!

The truth is, Elaine thought, he didn't ask me—he told me. The truth is, I think I will go.

It shouldn't be so easy!

Elaine paced, and it was rage that drove her footsteps. She hated the Duke for his luck—how could he have chosen just this time to return?—five years ago she had turned him down without a thought, in fact she had never even let him make a proposal—she wouldn't even have remembered him at all had it not been for the curious circumstances of their first contact . . .

Suddenly it was five years ago, and she was leaving the jousts again: she saw the wrestler, and then the serving girl coming up to him—"Do you want . . .?"

Roland was looking at her.

She wanted . . .

She was back in the present, with only Sandra to keep her company, with nothing to do but wait for Sunday.

The Countess did not take well to waiting.

Thursday Elaine slapped Sandra—because the girl somehow blocked the Countess's heedless pacing.

Friday, Elaine boxed the girl's ears when Sandra dropped a dress.

Saturday Elaine pulled Sandra across her lap and spanked the girl's bare bottom until it was a hot glowing crimson. If there was a reason the Countess didn't give it—afterward she sent the sobbing girl to her room with only a curt reminder that she should come at nine on the morrow.

Saturday night Elaine lay in bed and thought of all the knights whose hopes she had dashed during the ball. She did not regret one bit of the destruction. Then she thought of Thomas, off by himself in her mind as he was always alone in life. He was not the man for her—he was not even the man he said he was—but still she had not closed that door completely as she had done with all the others.

'Perhaps there will be another time.' That is what she had

said at their last meeting.

Perhaps there will be another time.

Elaine slept.

Sunday morning, nine o'clock: Sandra arrived and greeted her mistress with deference. She assisted as always at Elaine's toilette—but this day was rather rushed. The hour of decision was quite literally at hand.

Sandra's hands were nimble as she worked—but her eyes were those of a young doe's, tender melting brown. She was afraid of her mistress, afraid for her mistress—she hardly dared to think of her own dreams, of her own love—but she did think of them—she thought of Sir Anton, more than twice her age, but coming to her as a lover, coming first to her . . .

Elaine saw the look in the girl's eyes and made her decision. Up until this moment she still hadn't been sure she would go. Sandra, even in her naivete, was right. Just the chance of love was worth the world.

Sandra blinked, and jerked guiltily when she felt her mistress's eyes examining her in the mirror. She was frightened at first—but then she saw the Countess's gentle smile, and she realized that the long storm was over.

Elaine turned, and took the hairbrush out of Sandra's hand. "That's enough, dear. We'll go in a few minutes."

Elaine saw the quick relief in the girl's face. The Countess smiled, and brushed back Sandra's unruly curls with the hairbrush, and then she set it down. She looked deep into those doe-like eyes, and then she took the girl's face between her hands and kissed her on the lips. Elaine held her like that until Sandra melted against her, until she felt the girl's mouth open under her own, and then Elaine didn't need to hold the girl's face any more, Sandra was returning the kiss, and the Countess's hands were free to explore.

She stroked down the girl's body, the heels of her hands just touching the sides of Sandra's breasts, the cushiony weight of which Elaine could feel against her body just under her own higher, smaller bosom—her breasts rested on those of her lady in waiting—for a second she wanted to bend down and lay her face just there, but she couldn't break the kiss, her tongue exploring, and then she moved her hands down farther, she spanned Sandra's narrow waist just as she had done—O it seemed so long ago—before the ball, and then with a wicked impulse which excited Elaine deep inside she moved her hands around behind, she took the soft weight of the girl's still sore bottom in her hands—and she squeezed.

Sandra cried out against her mistress's mouth—she struggled against Elaine's grip but the Countess's fingers had bitten deep into her softness, and there was no way she could break that hold, though she could and did break the kiss—she looked up into her mistress's implacable eyes, and then Sandra just moaned, and stopped fighting—she offered her mouth to be kissed again, and Elaine obliged her.

When Elaine was satisfied—at least for the moment—she broke the kiss and bade Sandra sit down on the bed next to her. The Countess turned toward Sandra until their knees were touching—and then she just casually reached out and cupped Sandra's left breast through her dress. She felt the girl's nipple hard against her palm—and then she felt it gradually subside.

The Countess looked into Sandra's eyes, and what she saw pleased her.

If I had wanted to make this girl my slave, Elaine thought, then I have waited too long—for though she loves me, and I can do what I will with her, still her world has grown greater than her service to me. Even now, as I hold her, she thinks of her man—it is to him that she will belong, and I am well pleased, for I do not truly want a slave, and the difference in our stations makes it difficult for us to be true lovers. Perhaps, even so, we can be friends.

Elaine kissed Sandra very gently, and said, "He will take you today."

Sandra looked down. "I know." She looked back up at Elaine. "Will it hurt?"

Elaine smiled and gave the girl's breast one hard squeeze. "Of course it will hurt, silly goose!" Then the Countess got up quickly and stepped into her golden slippers. "Let's go! There's no time to waste!"

With that Elaine rushed to her door and threw it open. Sandra followed as best she could as her mistress took off at full speed down the hallway, racing without a thought past Nigel's astonished eyes.

They flew past guards and gatekeepers, everything blurring for Sandra as she tried to keep up, as she tried to run in her long dress—and then suddenly they were outside in the courtyard, and the sun was upon them, and with dazzled eyes Sandra saw Sir Anton and a blackbearded companion coming for them, each man mounted on a horse and leading another, Anton smiled at Sandra and her heart leaped and then her body leaped as well, he simply caught her under the arms with his strong hands and lifted her right on to her horse, she had to bite back a cry of pain when her bottom settled down on the hard saddle, but then she smiled, and smiled even more when she saw her mistress lifted just like herself, lifted like a child by the black bearded gentleman, and then they were all mounted and they set off without a wasted moment.

Sandra squirmed in the saddle as her horse got up to speed, but she couldn't stop smiling, she was so happy—she looked at her lady, and the Countess seemed happy too.

Chapter 52

A PARTING IN THE FOREST

Sir Anton watched their back as they rode off, and he didn't really relax until they had made it into the forest. He had seen a couple of English knights playfully jousting behind them—for a little while he had worried that that was some kind of pursuit, but then the knights had disappeared into a valley and they had not come out—he supposed they must have turned back toward the castle.

Now his party was in the safe wooded darkness, and as far as he could tell no one was on their trail. He could look ahead now, and concentrate on dear Lady Sandra.

The forest path was narrow, and so they rode in single file: the bearded Sir Gowan led, then Elaine, then Sandra, and finally Anton. They rode like this, without speaking, for nearly an hour. Sandra's sideways perch enabled her to easily turn her head and look back at Sir Anton—but every time she did so, he returned her glance with such power, with such clear proprietary intent, that she would shake with mingled fear and desire. She dared not look at him too often, for she was afraid that she would lose control altogether and fall from her horse.

While Sandra thought only of the man behind her, Elaine looked forward—she strained her eyes in the darkened forest looking for some sign of the Duke. Even so, she was surprised when her well trained horse came to an abrupt stop without any guidance from her—then she realized her mare had to stop because the horse in front had also halted—and only then did she notice the young, dark clad knight (nearly invisible in the shadow) who had stepped on to the path and taken the bridle of the lead horse. The young man said a few quiet words to the bearded fellow in a language that Elaine did not understand, and then he released Gowan's horse and walked back to Elaine.

This lad had been too young to travel with Roland five years before. He had not been included in the lucky few who had attended the state dinner and the ball. This was his first sight of Elaine the Fair, and he made the most of it. He looked up at her queenly features, and all he had read in the English legends came true. He saw his Guinevere, he thought he was her Sir Lancelot—he was eighteen years old—he dived headfirst into hopeless romance.

Elaine said, "Yes?"

The boy stammered, and then managed to come up with his memorized speech. "Good day, Countess. My name is Daniel, and if you please, I will escort you to my Lord, His Grace the Duke of Larraz."

Elaine realized that he meant to take her off alone.

"And what of my friend, Lady Sandra?"

Daniel, lost in his dreams, was the wrong person to ask.

Sandra, looking on, was terribly pleased. 'My friend'—she had never imagined that her mistress would ever say those words— 'My friend'—she clutched the words to her heart like a gift as the silence lengthened, and then Sir Anton stepped into the breach.

Sir Anton said, "Countess," and then waited until Elaine turned to face him. "Lady Sandra will be under my care this day. I swear on my honor that no harm will come to her—and she will be reunited with you this afternoon."

At ten feet it was hard for Elaine to make out his face—but his voice was clear and solid and trustworthy—Elaine could think of no better lover for young Sandra.

"Thank you, Sir Anton," Elaine said.

She handed the reins of her horse to Daniel. "Take me by my friend, so that I may say good-bye."

Daniel turned her mount as she wished, so that now the horses stood head to tail and the sidesaddles, and the ladies, faced each other. When Elaine looked over at Sandra's face she was surprised to see the girl's eyes filled with tears, and even as she watched one drop broke free and began its descent down one blushing cheek.

"Silly goose," said Elaine tenderly, and she leaned forward and kissed the tear away. Sandra impulsively threw both arms about her mistress, and for a moment they had a passionate embrace but then Elaine broke away before they both fell from their horses.

Elaine smiled, but her voice was serious as she said, "God be with you, dear Sandra."

"God be with you, Milady," Sandra replied.

Elaine nodded at Daniel, and he turned her horse away from the path. In just a second, guide, lady, and horse all vanished into the darkness.

Sandra was frightened for a moment, but then Sir Anton rode up next to her, and he took her hand. Sandra felt his strength enfold her, and she knew then that she would remember this day all her life—she would always remember this happy day.

Gowan took off again, leading at a brisk pace. Anton and Sandra followed, pressed close in the narrow path.

They rode until they came out of the forest, until they came to a lazy blue stream that curled like a snake across a green meadow . . .

CHAPTER 53

ROLAND'S REQUEST

If there was a path Elaine couldn't see it. For that matter she could barely see Daniel, just a few feet in front of her, leading her horse. The lad's dark clothes blended into the trees' dark shadows—Elaine craned her neck and tried to see just where in the blackness they were going.

Elaine wished that she didn't have to crane her neck. She wished that she could ride astride like a man, and face what was coming to her. She realized that she did not have any idea where she was, or where she was going—she did not know what Roland had planned for her. She began to feel frightened—and so, to combat the fear, she returned to her earlier thought. She imagined herself riding astride, but out in the open, in the sunlight. She'd ride bareback—she'd feel the strength of the horse between her legs—her purple dress would ride up, she'd be bare to the thigh . . .

She saw a patch of sunlight through the trees. There was a clearing just ahead. Elaine smiled, with the delight of her vision still showing on her face, as Daniel led her blinking into the sunlight.

When Elaine could see clearly again, she saw that there were three Larrazian knights, and Roland, waiting for her.

Roland waved off Daniel with an easy gesture, and the lad released the reins and took his place with the other knights. The Duke stopped Elaine's horse with his own hand. He went alongside and looked up at the Countess.

She wasn't smiling any longer.

"Welcome," said the Duke of Larraz.

Elaine did not give him the courtesy of a reply. She just

looked him over coldly, a long slow stare from crown to toe, for she could still leave, there was as yet no final commitment in her heart. She was relieved that the Duke obviously planned no violence against her—but that wasn't enough. She wanted to know everything about this man who had made her wait—and suffer—these last four days. She wondered if he was the man for her.

She saw his thick brown curly hair, and his soft brown eyes—for the first time she saw his resemblance to Sandra—the Duke might well be her elder brother!—Elaine almost smiled at the thought, but she kept her lips firm, and her eyes were as unreadable as crystal as she followed the path of his curly hair down to the full beard and mustache that surrounded his mouth—she wouldn't look at his mouth yet, she examined first the Roman nose above it—then, yes, his lips, full in an almost Mediterranean way; she could imagine him taking an olive into his mouth, tasting, savoring it, rolling it with his tongue—he had kissed her in just that way—she could look no longer at his mouth—she looked down, and saw some strands of gray in his beard where there had been none in his hair—she tore her eyes from his face altogether, and then she was surprised (for so far she had hardly looked at his clothes) because he was wearing the costume of a country peasant, shirt and trousers instead of the robes of state—but then she looked more carefully, and she saw that the shirt was silk, the trousers the finest linen, and around his neck was a gold chain, the chain supporting a medal of hammered gold that blazed from the breast of his so white shirt, and engraved on the gold was the figure of a unicorn rampant, the symbol of the House of Larraz.

The sun reflected off the one horned beast, and so Elaine shaded her eyes and looked lower—and then the Countess had to drop her hand and cover her mouth to keep from laughing out loud, but still when she moved her hand there was a big irrepressible smile on her face—she still wanted to laugh at the incongruity of it—she looked down again just to make sure, and yes, there they were, Roland's naked toes.

The silk shirted, gold bearing Duke of Larraz was barefoot in the forest.

Elaine never knew that not only the Duke but all his waiting knights had held their breath during her inspection. Now they were all smiling, and Roland had the biggest smile of all.

Elaine looked at Roland's mouth—she still wanted to laugh,

but she wanted to kiss him—she kicked her feet free of her stirrups with a merry gesture, and started to slide down, but the
Duke caught her easily. He held her above him in midair, his
hands just above her waist, and then he brought her right down
to his upturned smiling mouth and he kissed her and she kissed
him back and laughed all at the same time, the kiss dissolved in
laughter, and so Roland let Elaine slide down his body, she was
still giggling as she nestled against him, he put an arm about
her waist, he kissed her again and said, "Come, I have something to show you," and he started to walk her across the clearing, Elaine went willingly, she was sixteen, he was seventeen,
she would see what he had for her, she bumped her hip against
him as they walked along, but then soon, almost too soon, they
traversed the little clearing (it was only thirty feet wide) and
found their way blocked by an enormous evergreen.

They stopped.

Elaine felt the tension in Roland. Whatever it was, it was on
the other side of that tree—but she could not see a thing
through the thickly needled boughs.

Roland turned Elaine to face him and put his hands on her
shoulders. He looked deep into her eyes, and she looked into his,
and now he had only to make his request in order to determine
his fate, but he couldn't manage it, not yet, and anyway he
wanted to give his other knights a few more minutes to do his
will with the flowers, and so for now he just spoke to Elaine in
his mind—

If I had said, 'Tomorrow,' at the ball I think you would have
come, Roland thought, but then I would have been just one more
eager, desirous suitor—Thursday I would have had nothing special to offer you (nothing that you couldn't get from a hundred
other men) and you would have flirted and fenced, and five
years of love would have been wasted on trivialities.

You see I had to find something that you have always wanted
but never imagined—I've had a vague idea brewing for five
years now, ever since I found myself lost in your perfume at the
feast for the Third Crusade—I never forgot the scent of that
flowered perfume, and when I breathed it in again at the ball—
O how it rose from your hair as I danced with you!—I suddenly
knew what I could do, what I was going to do—I knew it would
take a few days to set up, I would have to find a place and so
on—one voice in my mind kept telling me, don't do it, it takes
too long, the Lionheart is due to arrive any day and if he comes

all your plans are ruined—but you see I didn't listen to that voice, I made our date for Sunday, for today—was it hard for you to wait?—I was consumed by terror the whole time, I have ten of my men watching the ports for the King, but praise God no word, praise God you're here, and everything is ready.

Do you know, my love, that I ordered my men to rob the royal gardens this morning? Do you know that I brought the finest silk sheets for the bed? Do you know how much I paid the wood-cutter?

O God how will you answer my strange request?

Elaine had no power to read Roland's thoughts but she saw his love, and his fear, and the courage that restrained his fear—his voice was perfectly calm when he finally made his request.

He said, "Elaine, please take off your slippers."

Elaine understood the meaning behind the request: he was asking for her trust. She had allowed herself to be picked up by two knights, she had ridden through field and forest and dark wood, but this, finally, was the point of decision. She could react lightly, with quip or banter, but that would deny Roland's seriousness, and she would not do that. She looked up at his soft brown eyes, and then she looked at his mouth, and she went up on her toes and kissed him just so she could feel his love for a moment, his lips were firm but not giving, he was waiting, she looked down at his bare feet and smiled a little, and with the smile there came a deeper understanding. He has a gift for me, she thought, but it is a special gift, one that I can only accept with humility and faith. He gives to me not as a Countess, rather he gives to the barefoot girl I once was; he, barefoot himself, gives his nobility to that girl I was—she felt herself smiling as she looked back up at his face—to the girl I am.

Elaine put her left hand against Roland's broad chest and leaned on him. She watched his eyes as she reached down and took the slipper off her right foot. She switched hands and did the same thing with the other foot. She felt the sudden prickle of grass shoots working their way up between her toes.

She kissed Roland again, but this time he returned the kiss, and then he put his arm around her waist as before, and he led her around the enormous evergreen.

CHAPTER 54

THE FLOWERED PATH

Roland had come to England with twenty Larrazian knights. Ten were stationed at various port cities, watching for the arrival of Richard Lionheart. Daniel was in the clearing with the three knights who had waited with Roland. Anton and Gowan escorted Lady Sandra. The four left had been ordered by Roland to set out the flowers (these had been procured this morning—those four knights had run, swords out, through the royal gardens) as soon as the Duke had heard Daniel and Elaine's approach.

The flower knights had completed their task now, and they had hidden themselves in the woods, for Elaine was not to see them at this point. They would come out later to guard the cottage.

Right now they watched eagerly from behind trees—they were pleased by the look of their flowers (they had kept the blooms fresh in buckets of water)—they wanted to see Elaine's reaction to their handiwork.

The three knights in the clearing were also slated for guard duty—they would make sure that no one disturbed Roland and Elaine. Daniel had his own important job—he was supposed to go back to the path and carefully erase all signs of a turnoff.

These were all loyal knights—but they were men, after all. Like their comrades who had laid down the flowers, Daniel and his friends were overwhelmingly curious—they fanned out quietly to the edges of the clearing, so that they could look around the huge pine.

All eight silent watching knights wanted to see Elaine's reaction to their master's gift—they wanted to know if the Duke would succeed with his love.

Elaine did not look up right away. She kept her eyes down as Roland led her around the tree, for her feet felt sensitive and vulnerable and she had to avoid the pine cones that were scattered all about. She didn't look up until she had come all the way to the other side of the tree, until Roland stopped her—and then she did raise her eyes, and she saw it all at once.

They were in another clearing, a narrow meadow that led to a little wooden cottage. There was a path, perhaps fifty feet long, that cut through the high meadow grass and led to the cottage door. Ordinarily this path was no more than short cut grass and clover—but those modest greens were hidden now. Every inch of the path was covered with bunches and bunches of flowers, a carnival of flowers in every color of the rainbow. There were irises, lilies, daisies, marigolds, geraniums, blue veronica, and even the royal purple liatris to match Elaine's dress.

Elaine stared in shock at the array of cut flowers, ankle deep blooms extending the whole length of the path, and there at the end, affixed to the cottage door, was a bright green wreath, a touch of simplicity calling her from the end of the riot of color— Elaine began to shake, she was not held at all now, Roland had let go of her as soon as she looked up, and now she wanted to go to that wreath and open that door more than she had ever wanted anything in her life, and to get there she had to walk over the flowered path.

Elaine took a tentative step forward, she felt the terrible tender softness of the petals beneath her bare foot—she could not put her weight down yet—she reached out blindly for Roland— he took her hand, took some of her weight, and then she did set her foot down softly into the flowers, and the scent of their crushed petals rose up to meet them both—the next step they took together, and when Roland looked at Elaine she was crying, and the tears fell on the flowers that broke under each loving step.

They walked like this to the door, each step tentative, measured, loved and regretted, for each step broke the blooms' fragile beauty and each step transmuted that beauty into glorious scent and subtle caress for the bare destroying feet.

It was pleasure unbearable and it was pain as well—Elaine cried the whole time, tears pouring down her face into two wet tracks, but she did not make a sound. She just held Roland's hand, and she felt the flowers, and she breathed in their scent, and she watched as the green wreath came closer and closer.

Finally they came to the cottage door, and there Roland stopped to brush away Elaine's tears. Then he held her face between his hands, and he bent down and placed his lips right over her silent white scar, he kissed her right there, and Elaine began to tremble again and she reached for the door. Roland finally let her go—Elaine opened the door herself. She opened the door to her new life.

Roland lifted her over the step and into the cottage, and then he closed the door behind them. Eight watching knights could see no more. Even so, they stared at the closed door for a long time before they finally drifted off and assumed their proper posts.

Inside the bright cottage (high windows let in the noontime sun) Elaine looked first at the bed. This was not the woodcutter's cot—no, this was a bed fit for a Queen and Roland's men had had to carry it out here in pieces. The woodcutter *had* been paid well to find alternate lodging for a week—Roland didn't think he would mind the change in decor when he returned. There *were* silk sheets on the bed, but Elaine couldn't see them any better than she could see the clover outside, for every inch of the bed sheet was covered with rose petals.

Elaine started to shake again, it was all too much, too beautiful and she would have cried again had not Roland distracted her by suddenly dropping to one knee. He took the classic pose of the man who begs his lady to marry him, but Roland was far too wise to make that speech now. He just caressed Elaine's ankles, her skin fluttered under his hands, all of her was so sensitive, and then he simply grasped the hem of her purple dress with both his strong hands. He looked up at Elaine for a second, but she did not say anything, she had already said 'Yes' when she had taken her slippers off, so Roland hardly hesitated. He stood up, lifting her dress as he rose—Elaine put her arms up to make it easier as Roland lifted the dress off over her head.

Elaine was naked before the Duke of Larraz.

Roland looked into Elaine's eyes for a long moment, the dress still in one hand, and then he carelessly tossed it aside and put his hands on her. He caressed her shoulders, and then his big hands covered her small breasts—he could feel the tightness of her nipples, the delicate soft skin around them, and he realized that his right hand covered not only her breast, but also her heart—he could feel the thudding pulse of her life under his hand, he could feel the pulse of her life in his hand—the tender touch was suddenly too much to bear, he moved his hands down the exquisite hourglass curve of her body, he paused at her waist with his fingers gripping her sides and his thumbs nearly meeting at her navel—and then he ran one hand behind her and felt the ripe softness of her bottom, and he knew with utter reverence that she was made by God, not man, she was God's beauty on earth, and he moved his hand back up to her waist again and then he lifted her easily and set her on the edge of the bed.

She sat down on the silk blush touch of rose petals.

Roland knelt before her.

He lifted her right foot with his hands, and he kissed the flower imprinted sole—and then he did the same with her left foot. He kissed her ankles where he had caressed her, and Elaine shuddered again—he kissed her knees and she cried out. He kissed the tops of her thighs, for she kept her softness hidden by pressing her legs tight together—he stopped the kissing, and looked up at her face, and put his big hands on her thighs. She looked down at him—their eyes met—he tried to separate her thighs—she resisted—he paused, kneeling before her—his eyes showed his reverence, his gentleness, his love—and then she suddenly understood that she could be free with this man, she could let herself go, she let her own desire sweep over her and she let her upper body fall slowly back on to the bed, she fell into the rose petals and let him spread her legs.

He kissed her inner thighs now, he spread her all the way open but that too was her desire and the flower of her womanhood opened for his mouth. He kissed its petals with a loving, knowing touch, and then he opened her still more with two fingers and bent his head like some giant butterfly feasting on her nectar.

Elaine felt his tongue inside her flower, felt the crushed rose petals under her skin, breathed in the scent of roses—it was all too maddening, tantalizing, she needed something more now—she reached down and grabbed Roland's curly hair and yanked his head violently up and away from her—she looked down into his face with mad eyes but he understood.

Roland knocked her hand loose and stood up. He took off his shirt. It caught his gold chain as he pulled it over his head—the unicorn vanished for a moment, and then swung back as the shirt came free, but if the Duke felt the blow of the heavy gold medal he gave no sign.

He was indifferent to his own body, he just had to touch Elaine, he put out a hand and gripped her soft thigh, while with the other hand he awkwardly pushed his pants down and freed his manhood.

Elaine gasped.

Roland thought that she was frightened—he didn't realize that she had never seen a real man before—the hidden reluctant toy of her husband's was nothing like this—he let go of her thigh, and took her hand instead, and he put it on him, and he said gently, "I will not hurt you."

Elaine held him in her hand, she felt the blood pulsing under the smooth taut skin, she felt the size of him and wondered if she could take him—and then she abandoned herself to her fate, to her own desires—she released Roland, and then she moved back until all of her was on the bed—she lay down on her back and then she deliberately spread her legs—she took the hand that had held him and put it over her left breast, she listened to her own heartbeat, the two stroke beat put two words into her mouth, she watched Roland from beneath half closed lids and then she whispered the words: "Take me."

Roland stopped, pants halfway down his legs—he shook and nearly fell, for her words justified all the pain of the last five years, all that despair flew away on the wings of those two words, and he managed to get his feet untangled, and then he kicked the pants away, and he came toward the bed and all of him was straight and firm.

He got up on the bed and knelt between Elaine's legs—he took her hand from her breast and then he kissed her right there on her beating heart—he guided himself with one hand and eased his manhood inside of her—he was slow, and patient, and gentle, he stretched her but she could take him, he paused and she spread her legs wider and then he was in deeper, sliding in now God yes he was all the way in, all the way in the center of her heat, she was all tight fluttering around him, he rose up on his elbows to get his weight off her but really to look at her face, he looked down into her wide open blue eyes and his unicorn swung down and struck her between her breasts.

Elaine thought that its single horn pierced her heart.

Roland began to move in her—but he was so gentle, so skillful, that it took her a while to realize that she was moving with him, and then she realized he was making her move, he controlled her body, he was playing her like an instrument and she was building toward some crescendo, she tried to fight it and realized she couldn't, he was literally inside her, she moved with his will, he was taking her somewhere, taking her higher, she began to realize that the pleasure she had only given herself was possible to share, and sharing the pleasure somehow expanded it, it was bigger than her, bigger than Roland, they were building toward something that seemed unbearable, it was frightening, it was too intense, but she couldn't get away, she was being brought to it, brought closer and closer to the pain and pleasure of unimaginable beauty, she thought suddenly of the crushed flower petals on the path outside, she had reached blindly for Roland's hand, he had to be with her, she had to know he was with her, she looked up at his face over her, she saw the beads of sweat on his forehead, he was almost there, she felt they were teetering on the edge of this cliff, she would go over O yes but only with him he had to tell her he had to tell her she reached up with both hands and grabbed his face, her fingers were like claws, her face was contorted, she demanded with all the wild strength of her soul: "Tell me that you love me!"

Roland said, "You are the Duchess of Larraz," and it was just the right thing to say, Elaine relaxed and went right over the cliff as his whole body went taut and then he swelled even more inside her and gave her his gift, gave her his gift several times over, and Elaine just held him all the way through, she was spinning, she was whirling, she had gone over the cliff with her lover in her arms and it was all beautiful on the other side.

CHAPTER 55

NIGEL

The shock was the blow from behind by the silent knight.

Nigel struggled to his feet as Thomas fought off Walter's attack—he managed to remount as Thomas turned and charged—he spurred his horse homeward, he was driven by terror, he had no thought of saving Walter, only himself—he looked back once, he saw Thomas's lance drive through Walter's chest—he didn't look back again, and he didn't stop until he reached the castle.

He dropped the reins of his horse near a servant, he ran past the guard at the door and he didn't stop running until he was inside his room and he had locked the door behind him.

He got into his bed and pulled a blanket over his head and shivered in the stifling room.

It was a couple of hours before he could really think straight, and that was when he realized his troubles had just begun.

First of all, he had not paid his taxes (he had meant to—he was always waiting for the big win at the tables that would set him right, but alas it never came) and worse yet he had not paid the Saladin tithe. This meant that he could be conscripted to fight the Holy War—the prospect had terrified him at first when he couldn't pay, but then nothing had happened for months and he had begun to relax. He had thought that he had been overlooked—Walter had felt the same way. Now he knew better—Arthur had been watching the whole time.

Nigel considered his options. He knew that the King was returning soon. He could probably manage to hide out until the King arrived, and then he could go before His Majesty and beg for mercy—and volunteer for foreign service. The King would take him all right—that was not a problem—the Lionheart would need fresh bodies to replace the ones left behind in the desert—he could become a soldier, and that would cancel the Saladin tithe—but all such thoughts were a crazy, meaningless pipe dream. He could not become a soldier—Nigel had learned the truth in just a few seconds this morning. He could not stand combat. He had run after the first blow—he had not even tried to save his friend. He was a coward and the Lionheart would find out and then—no, he could not go to the King.

He could flee—he still had a little of Arthur's gold—he could even take Jillian, the pretty maid that he had enjoyed these last nights—she would go with him, he would bet on it! Yet where could they go? Arthur knew where every penny dropped in the Kingdom—they could never hide from the Assessor. They would be caught—he would be hanged. He could not run.

He shivered as he thought of the third option, because it meant confronting his fear. He could go out again, he could still try to do the job for Arthur. It was true that everything was a mess now—he didn't know who Elaine had gone off with, he had lost Walter, he had lost the track—but Arthur didn't know any of that yet. If he could just find out who Elaine had been with, or who she was meeting now—if he could just figure out Thomas's role—then he could still give a good full report to Arthur, and then the Assessor would reward him and he would be safe.

He felt the bruise on his back from the lance blow and he shivered in his bed for a long time but finally he convinced himself that this was his only chance. Staying here was not an option because Arthur would find out soon. The Assessor (who had moved to another wing of the palace after telling his wife he was in Wales) was too well informed and too powerful to be avoided for long. Nigel decided that he had to bring Arthur *something*.

Nigel crawled fearfully out of bed.

He crouched on the floor until he figured out how he could complete the surveillance in safety.

He would ride out in the most careful, circuitous manner—he would make absolutely sure that no one was following him—he would find a completely hidden spot from where he could watch the edge of the forest.

If Elaine had already come back, then it was over for him any-way—but if she still dallied (and he had the feeling that she was still in the forest) then he would be in position to see her come out.

He would also see who came out with her.

CHAPTER 56

TALES OF MARRIAGE

After their lovemaking Roland and Elaine lay naked, side by side on the shattered rose petals. They both knew that there was one thing to talk of, one thing only, and that was their future life together.

Roland was up on one elbow, looking at Elaine, and she felt blessed by his gaze. She felt that she finally deserved the beauty handed her as a young girl, she felt that every part of her was perfect, and perfectly loved—she felt Roland's seed inside her and she hoped that they had made a child. With the thought, she curled closer and kissed his thick chest over his heart—she squirmed until all her body was against him—she said, "I love you," and then pressed her lips to his skin again—she shuddered with pleasure as his big hand stroked her smooth back and tightened on her soft bottom—he pulled her hard against him for a moment, and Elaine felt his reawakened manhood— and then he released her, he cleared his throat, and when he touched her again it was just to stroke her hair, gently—he began to speak: "My darling," he said, "I love you beyond all reason, and the fact that you love me in return is the first true miracle of my life. I know now that perfect happiness is possible— and I believe that our happiness can endure.

"You are a delight in every imaginable way, dear Elaine—I came to England to win you—I did not come just to steal a moment with you. Our time together shall continue—I have given much thought to our future.

"I am a practical man—I know how society works, and I know how to make the laws and customs of society bend in my favor. You may think I speak of an impossibility, but it *is* true that you will become the Duchess of Larraz."

He leaned down and kissed her hair, and Elaine smiled secretly against his chest, and let him go on.

"I am well regarded by the Church—the Larrazian Archbishop, who owes me much, has considerable influence in Rome. We will go to Larraz, and I will instruct my Archbishop— he in turn will go to Rome, and smooth the way for us. Then we will make a pilgrimage to His Holiness, Pope Celestine III himself, and we will present ourselves humbly—while with the other hand, so to speak, we will bring an absolutely stunning gift for the Papal treasury. I am absolutely convinced that we shall carry the day. The Pope will annul your marriage—"

Roland stopped abruptly because Elaine was laughing.

The laugh had been creeping up on her for some time, she had tried to fight it, she wanted to hear the whole glorious, lovely, needless plan—but when he said 'marriage' the laughter burst free and now she couldn't stop.

Roland was terrified for a moment—was all this only a light romp to her?—and then she started tapping him on the chest, she was trying to talk, he looked at her face, she was so happy in her laughter that he began to relax again, but still when she finally got the words out it was an astonishing shock.

"I'm not married," Elaine said.

With one short sentence Elaine destroyed the 'fact' that had haunted Roland's existence for five years. He sat up—his mouth fell open in surprise.

Elaine wriggled up on her knees until she could put her arms around him, it seemed her whole body was laughing, happy, she pressed her saucy breasts against his chest, she kissed his amazed mouth, she kissed his Roman nose and she kissed his astonished eyes. She kissed his hair, and then she pulled his head right down where she wanted it, she rubbed a bright nipple against his mouth until he caught it, he took most of her creamy hard nippled breast in his mouth and he began to suck, she held him tight to her breast, her beautiful manchild, she cradled his head in her hands, she squirmed until her legs were in a comfortable position, and then she began to tell her story.

Elaine did not tell him everything. She avoided the horror. She did not tell him of the exact circumstances of her father's death, nor that of her mother's. She did not tell him just how she got her scar—she did not tell him of the terror that preceded her flight from Firfleet.

She did tell him of running off with Arthur, and of their audience with King Henry—though in the midst of this narrative she made Roland switch from her right breast to her left, and there he sucked as avidly as before, all the while listening to his love.

Elaine told him of the King's question that had led to their circumvention of the marriage vows. She told him of Arthur's incapacity as a husband. She said, "In all ways, he is no real husband to me."

Roland released Elaine's breast and raised his head. His eyes were shining as he looked at Elaine. "I know now what it means to have received God's grace. I will be your first and only husband, and you will be my first and only wife.

"I love you."

Elaine looked at Roland's kind loving face. "I love you and I will marry you," she said.

Roland felt a surge of strength through his whole body. He reached for Elaine—he was going to press her right down on her back on the bed—he caught her shoulders and her legs began to fall open, she was as ready as he was—Roland put one knee between Elaine's and then before he could go any further there came a knock at the door.

CHAPTER 57

URGENT NEWS

Roland stopped just where he was. He held Elaine tight so that she would not fall back on the bed. He knew that his men would not have interrupted him without good reason.

"What is it?"

"Urgent news, Your Grace. Sir Martin is here. He needs to speak to you at once."

Roland recognized Gunter's voice—he was one of the knights in the clearing. Sir Martin was not part of this group—he had been stationed in Folkestone, watching for the arrival of King Richard—

"One moment."

Roland turned to Elaine, and kissed her, and then got off the bed, holding her there with one hand. He took an edge of the silk sheet, and pulled it up over her body, and kissed her again.

He began to get dressed.

Elaine watched him—the calm leader of men—as he dressed. It was clear that there was a problem—and it was also clear that the problem had not been unanticipated. Roland was obviously working on the solution even as he pulled his pants on— he leaned forward to kiss her again, but his mind was working away from her—So this is what it is like, she thought, to love the ruler of a country. I can feel his love for me—and yet he has blocked it with an effort of will—he's taking care of business, taking care of his nation, taking care of his men, taking care of me—I could never have dreamed that the man I love, a man who loves me, could yet leave me at this moment, but he is doing it—he is so calm, thinking, I realize I am jealous—

Elaine let the sheet fall down below her breasts.

Roland smiled and tucked in his shirt. He pulled the sheet back up and around Elaine's neck. He kissed her once more, and then he said, "I'll be back in a few minutes."

Roland opened the cottage door and went outside.

He saw Gunter with Elaine's golden slippers tucked into his belt—and then he saw Martin standing by his lathered horse.

The Duke went right up to Martin and touched his shoulder. The lad was as sweaty as his horse.

"What is it, my son?"

"The Lionheart has landed, Your Grace!" Martin got that out in one gasping breath. He panted for a second and then raced on. "The King leaped to shore calling for fresh horses. I am ahead of him but he will be coming soon!"

The Duke turned away and spoke to Gunter. "Guard the cottage and keep my lady safe."

"Yes, Your Grace."

Gunter took up a position before the cottage door and thought of the Duke's words: 'My lady'—he had done it! Gunter tried to imagine Elaine, naked on the bed just a few feet away, just behind the door—his knees turned to jelly and he could only keep himself erect by reflecting that now they would surely have to fight the Lionheart.

Roland watched until Gunter took up his position and then he turned back to Martin. "You need to take care of your horse. He must be walked, or else he might founder. Walk him around the edge of this clearing, and I will come with you—I want you to tell me *everything*, from the beginning."

Roland and Martin and the weary horse began their slow promenade.

The watching Larrazian knights felt a double thrill: they knew that their lord had enjoyed the almost unimaginable pleasures of Elaine the Fair—and they were sure (even those too far away to hear Martin's outburst) that the Lionheart had landed. Their blood was fired by images of lust and combat.

Martin led his horse slowly along—the stallion shivered and blew hard through his nostrils, and then he seemed to settle down nicely. Martin didn't look over at the Duke by his side—he went back in his mind to this morning by the sea—he began to speak.

"I was in Folkestone, as you know, Your Grace. I knew you were seeing the Countess today—I had the feeling that the King would come today as well. I paid a farmer for the use of his stable—I hid my horse there, on the outskirts of town, so that I might make a quick and inconspicuous getaway. Then I went down to the beach—it was still early morning—and went out on the jetty, just as I had done for the last few days, and I looked out to sea.

"I was not the only one who felt the excitement in the air—a few other men came out to join me, where there had been none on the previous days. Very soon we saw a ship on the horizon, a ship coming toward us, and I think we all knew right away that it was the one.

"It was beating toward us into the wind, and so it was a long slow approach—but before long we could make out the figure of a tall man standing in the bow.

"I kept my eyes on that figure, and everyone else did the same. I didn't hear anyone give an alarm, but somehow more and more people began to come out to the shore. Soon they lined the docks and piled up on the jetty—I was out on the far tip, and the force of the people climbing on to the jetty behind me nearly pushed me into the sea. The crowd's breathing was one great roar, but no one dared say a word—there was just a straining for position, a straining to see.

"It was an old sailor next to me, a man with a wrinkled face but clear eyes, who finally dared to speak. He said with quiet certainty, 'It is the King. We are saved.'

"I said, 'The Lionheart!' quite loudly, and all who had not heard the sailor heard me, and it was as though I, a foreigner, had somehow confirmed all their hopes. Now they truly believed that the approaching figure was the man they longed for—they began to cheer, rolling chants of 'Long live the King!' and they surged forward even more, and I had to fight still harder to keep my footing. Many did not have my strength—I saw splashes as unlucky citizens were pushed into the water by their exulting comrades. No one helped those unfortunates—no one could even hear their cries over the rolling cheers.

"The boat was closing rapidly now—it was now clear even to those of the weakest eyes that the figure in the bow was the King. I observed him carefully: I saw his red beard and his red uncovered hair—he looked pale from imprisonment but fit—he wore no armor, but he was equipped with two swords, one rather plain and the other dazzling—the latter had a gold scabbard, and a gold, jewel encrusted handle—he took that weapon out now and then and twirled it—he seemed quite skilled.

"I watched him sail past me on the way to the dock—I saw him leap lightly to the shore before the ship was fairly secured. Right in his footsteps leaped a hulking knight—he had been behind King Richard on the ship but I hadn't paid much attention to him then—but now I saw that he was dressed like the King, save for a vest of mail that covered his chest, and I saw that his sandy hair was cut like the King's and his beard was likewise an imitation of his master. I heard some people say 'Brian,' and I realized that this was the King's man at arms, a man who had shared his captivity. To me this Brian seemed a loathsome gargoyle—a bloated, bloodshot eyed caricature of King Richard.

"The King, on the other hand, appeared to be a fine figure of a man—yet there was no joy on his face. He seemed to feel no happiness, either for his homecoming or for his people's adoration. The only emotion that showed on his face was impatience—as soon as his feet hit the dock he called for fresh horses, and he was angry when they weren't brought immediately.

"The people surely expected some ceremony, but he gave them nothing—he demanded only obedience.

"I worked my way back up the jetty, and as I left I saw the horses they gave to him and Brian—and I thanked the Lord for the presentiment that had led me to hide my friend here." Martin affectionately stroked his cooling horse.

"You see, Your Grace, the horses they gave the King were the best in town, but still rather poor—they would surely have taken mine if I had left him in the public stable. The town could not do any better for their King—I noticed that the poverty we all remarked on in the countryside is creeping down into the ports. Besides all that, there are rumors of a coming war with France—trade across the channel has nearly ceased."

"You've done very well, Martin," said the Duke, "but stick to your story and make it quick—I already know the political situation."

"I'm sorry, Your Grace—there's not much more to tell. I got to my horse and rode here just as fast as I could. My estimate, based on the look of the King's horses, is that I am at least an hour ahead of him."

"Maybe less time than that—the King could have switched to a fresh mount on the way. Did anyone follow you?"

"No, but—"

"But what?"

Roland put a hand on Martin's shoulder, turning him—he looked right into the young knight's eyes.

Martin continued, very nervously, "Just before I entered the forest I saw an English knight. He didn't even look at me, and yet he must have seen me. He was sitting absolutely still on a black horse. He seemed to be waiting. I got the feeling that he was willing to wait there all day—there was something very strange about him."

Martin would have found things even stranger if he had not bypassed the castle and thus ridden to the forest on a different course than the shadowers earlier—even so, he hadn't missed seeing Sir Walter's body by that much.

Roland wondered who the waiting knight could be: a suitor, one of Prince John's men, a watcher hired by the Assessor—there was no way to tell. Roland motioned for Martin to start walking again, but now they moved along in silence.

Roland began to line up the pieces. Elaine wasn't married. Richard had returned, impatient as ever, eager to make war yet leading a country that had already been bled white by past taxation. The Assessor's value to the King is the gold he can bring in, Roland thought, but it will be a long time before Arthur can come up with enough gold to finance a war. Richard isn't going to like that—but I know just how to make him happy. Roland smiled because he saw the outline of the deal. He was going to be able to take Elaine with him—without fighting the Lionheart or sacrificing Larraz. I'll pay for Richard's war, Roland thought, I'll give him what he wants right away, I'll shunt Arthur to one side, and I'll make Elaine part of the deal. The King is always pleased to seal his deals with a woman—I've heard about his sister, and I know about the Baroness Pembroke. Richard won't mind offending Arthur if he can have his war—and the clergy can't object because Elaine, being unmarried, is a scandal to them if she stays anyway!

Roland wanted to shout with joy—everything was working out!—but then he remembered the English knight, waiting. That one detail could ruin the whole picture. Richard needed to be approached quietly, humbly, in private. It would be ruinous if the King were met by violent rumors of some foreigner despoiling England's most beautiful lady.

Roland stopped where he was, in front of the evergreen, at the start of the flowered path.

Elaine's reputation had to remain spotless for one more day—

one more day and then Roland could secure an audience with
the King.

As for this English knight, he may know that Elaine came
here to see me, Roland thought. That in itself is not dangerous—she has many suitors, and as far as anyone knows, I am
just one more. I will simply make it look as though I have
failed—as though Elaine has left me broken hearted.

Roland's expression darkened. I don't want to send her off
alone, he thought, but it must be done. We can not be seen
together until after my audience with the King. After that, we
will have the rest of our lives together.

Roland smiled as he thought of Elaine dropping the sheet.
She was a little minx—and she was the overwhelming beauty
crying as she walked down the flowered path. She was all he
had ever wanted. She was the only woman he would ever love.

Yet now they had to move quickly. It would not do for him to
be too late in greeting the King.

Roland called his knights. They came quickly, nervously,
expecting the call to battle—but the first thing Roland said was,
"I don't think we are going to have to fight." Roland smiled at
the men's disappointed faces, and then he told them what they
had to do.

Then he took Elaine's golden slippers from Gunter, and he
walked again, still barefoot, down the flowered path.

He was careful opening the door of the cottage, because he
expected that Elaine would still be naked, and she was.

CHAPTER 58

SALADIN AND THE GRAY MARE

After his conversation with Sir Gowan, Thomas rode back to the forest. Once again he traversed the dark path through the woods, but this time he kept his thoughts on the task at hand. He searched for the turnoff—somewhere in these woods Elaine's horse had left the path. He searched slowly and carefully, and yet he couldn't find the spot, for Daniel had done his work well. After watching Roland's success with Elaine, the youngest Larrazian knight had returned to where he had met the Countess. There he carefully and painstakingly covered the tracks that Elaine's horse had made in turning off toward the cottage. If Thomas had crawled on his knees he might have still been able to see the traces—but on horseback, in the dim light, he didn't have a chance. The only item of interest that Thomas noticed was his own lance—he left it there by the trail, because he felt the frustration of not finding Elaine building again into rage—he might yet find a Larrazian knight to kill, or a Larrazian Duke to kill—but as he had vowed before, it would be a fair fight.

Thomas emerged into the light on the other side of the forest, at just the spot where he had come in, hours before this morning. He had wasted more than half the day—he had killed a man—and he still didn't know just where Elaine was, or what she was doing. Then he reminded himself that really he did know—she had to be with the Duke.

Roland.

You have to come out sometime, Thomas thought. And when you do I'm going to kill you.

Thomas rode Saladin fifty yards down along the edge of the

forest, and then he turned his horse so that he could watch the entrance to the forest path.

Thomas sat unmoving on top of his unmoving horse.

He waited.

He fought his way through every minute.

Every minute that Elaine didn't come brought fresh pain.

She's not coming, he thought. She's run off with the Duke of Larraz and she's not coming back. She loves him. She doesn't love me.

Each thought was a jagged line of pain tearing through his head—but even the worst of those pains could not touch the solid knot of belief in his heart.

Someday she will come to love me.

She isn't coming back.

Thomas felt like he was being torn in two—but he couldn't move. He watched.

He saw a Larrazian knight ride up on an exhausted horse and take the path into the forest.

Message for the Duke, Thomas thought.

He's still there. Elaine is still there.

She'll come back.

Time passed.

Thomas watched.

What did he see through the trees?

A flash of purple.

If she's with the Duke I challenge him to duel here and now.

If she's with the Larrazian escorts from this morning I kill one and send the other to His Grace with my challenge.

Saladin shook all over and took a step.

Thomas tightened his left hand on the reins. His right went to his sword hilt.

More purple.

Saladin's muscles bunched. Thomas's knuckles whitened. His face was as hard as a stone carving.

Elaine's horse came free of the forest. Thomas was fifty yards away to the left. Elaine blinked in the sudden sunlight and then, looking sideways anyway, she saw Thomas and recognized him. She smiled.

She was alone.

Thomas felt the pull in his cheeks and wondered what it was until he realized that his own smile had split his taut face. With that he relaxed altogether: his smile dropped loosely into a grin, his right hand released his sword, his left hand relaxed around the reins—and then he waved to Elaine with his right hand—and that motion was nearly his undoing. Saladin took the wave as a signal to charge—he sprang forward with all the power of his uncoiling muscles, and Thomas felt his seat go right out from under him, he slid back off the saddle and felt himself sitting on Saladin's croup as he dived forward reaching for the horse's mane—he grabbed a thick handful as Saladin rethought his actions and settled into a bone-jarring trot—Thomas was an altogether comical sight as he lay along his horse's back, holding to the mane for dear life as the rough gait bounced him from side to side.

Elaine started to laugh—all of Roland's careful plotting was to avoid this! She laughed harder and stopped her horse, and kicked her feet free of the stirrups—she stretched and relaxed and watched Thomas hang on like a giant caterpillar.

Saladin stopped to sniff noses with Elaine's pretty gray mare. Thomas hauled himself back up into the saddle—his face was three shades redder than his hair.

Thomas directed Saladin around in a little circle so that he came up on the left side of Elaine's horse. Now they were going the same way. Elaine stopped laughing out of politeness but her eyes were unquenchably merry.

Thomas's high color persisted but he managed to speak formally. "Good day, my dear Countess. How are you faring on this lovely afternoon?"

"I could not be happier," Elaine replied, "but are you never going to train that wild beast you ride?"

Thomas felt his grin coming back. "I like him that way!" he replied, with great good cheer.

"But what if you should fall?"

"Then I shall be trampled underfoot, thinking only of you!"

Elaine abruptly turned her head away. Now Thomas wanted to laugh. Any embarrassment in the world was worth it when he could come close to Elaine like this. He felt so happy! He had been a fool to doubt Elaine—he had been a fool to doubt his belief. He had been right at the start—the Duke could get nowhere with Elaine. In fact, it was evident that he had failed miserably—for why else would he let Elaine return unescorted?

It never occurred to Thomas that that was just what the Duke wanted him (or any other English knight) to think. Thomas was unable to penetrate the Duke's ruse—because he himself was incapable of acting that way. Thomas's code was simple: if you loved a woman, and you were in her good graces, then you stayed with her and protected her. In Thomas's view, the Duke had not only failed—he had given up.

Thomas looked at Elaine's body, sheathed in the long purple dress that streamed down the side of her horse. He saw that her golden slippered feet hung loose past her stirrups—he looked up to see her face resolutely turned away from him. He though that he could reach over and pick her right off her horse, but instead he just said, "Countess," softly, and he put out his hand.

Elaine turned toward Thomas and saw his outstretched hand. She needed to be touched. She looked up at his face once, and then back down. She started to put out her own hand.

At that moment Saladin (perhaps in sympathy with his master) decided to make his own amorous attempt. He had quite liked the scent of the pretty gray mare when he had touched noses with her. Now he curled his long neck around and stretched out his big head and gave the mare a loving nip on the cheek.

The prim mare did not approve of the Arabian ruffian's idea of courtship. She whinnied with alarm and jumped away sideways, that is, directly opposite to the way Elaine was sitting in the sidesaddle, directly opposite to the way Elaine was leaning to take Thomas's hand—in short, the mare jumped right out from under the Countess.

Had Elaine had her feet in the stirrups, she might have had just a chance to stay on—without that, there was nothing between her and the ground. She had the eerie feeling of hanging, seemingly motionless, in air—everything seemed to slow down—she watched as she stretched out her hand toward Thomas—she saw his hand enfold hers—now she was falling, falling—she felt his strong grip take hold and now she wasn't falling anymore, it was something different, sweeter, he was swinging her lightly down—she landed on her feet, unhurt, with the strong knight still holding her hand.

"Training?" Thomas asked, and this time they both laughed. They looked over at the mare and saw that she was trotting away. Thomas released Elaine's hand and slipped off Saladin. He took some grain from a saddlebag and told the stallion to behave himself. Thomas walked over to the mare, who had stopped now with her great behind pointed right at him. Her legs were poised to kick, but her head was swung around coquettishly—Thomas sweet-talked her and bribed her with the grain. He grabbed the bridle and brought the horse quietly back to Elaine.

Standing next to Elaine, Thomas realized for the first time how small she was. Before, he had always seen her—even during an embrace—as somehow large than life. Her beauty colored whole vistas—his imagination could not contain her. Yet here she was, the girl who had fallen off her horse—and he, no better, must have been quite a silly sight lying on Saladin's back. He smiled as he looked down—she was tall for a woman, yes, but still half a foot shorter than himself—and she was small boned, thin, and so light that he had been able to hold her weight with one hand—fragile was the word for Elaine. He looked at her face with infinite tenderness, and he did something he had always wanted to do—he brushed back a stray lock of hair from her cheek, he felt the finespun strands against his fingers, he felt the warmth of her cheek as he tucked the errant lock behind her ear—and then he realized that he had exposed her silent white scar.

He put his warm strong hand against her cheek so that he covered the scar—he wanted to protect her—O he just wanted to protect her all his life.

Elaine looked up into his eyes and read his thoughts, she warmed to him in a primitive way, she knew Roland had been right to send her off alone, it was safer in the long run, no bloodshed, no war and everything would work out with the King—but still—God how she needed Roland now, she had opened herself, given herself body and soul, she wished he had come with her, wished he had not left her alone—but she was not alone.

Thomas put his left hand on her other cheek—he held her face between his strong hands—she felt so vulnerable, so lost, all her defenses left somewhere before the flowered path—she didn't resist when Thomas tilted her head back, didn't resist when his lips came down on hers—but she wouldn't let him force her mouth open, and finally she twisted her head to break the kiss, and then she just ducked down under his seeking mouth and buried her face against his chest.

Thomas held her, and stroked her glorious finespun hair. He was shattered by joy. He saw no rival left on the field. He saw no barriers between him and Elaine. He had kissed her. Soon she would belong to him.

"Put me up on my horse," Elaine said.

Thomas deliberately tangled his hand in her hair and pulled her head back. He looked into her eyes and saw that she meant what she said. He thought, she is not ready to go further. Still, he was wildly, recklessly excited. He put his hands on her sides but each of his thumbs touched the softness of her breasts, and he saw that she felt his touch. He lifted her up and set her on her horse. He tucked her feet into her stirrups, right first, then left—he kissed her left foot right on the bare flash of skin that showed between slipper and hem.

The Duke had given her a similar caress—but Thomas gave the gesture none of Roland's reverence—the knight's style was mocking, careless, possessive—Elaine wished yet again that Roland was here.

Thomas mounted. He had never been so happy and confident. He kept Saladin on a tight rein and put out his hand to Elaine as before. Elaine took it because she did not know what else to do. The one thing she couldn't do was tell Thomas about Roland. A public challenge, such as Thomas would surely issue, would ruin all of the Duke's plans.

Thomas folded his fingers around Elaine's small strong hand. "Dear Elaine," he said, quite correctly—whatever the future held, they both knew that the kiss had forever erased titles between them—"Dear Elaine," he repeated, he was trying to gather his thoughts, everything was new, he wasn't even used to his own confidence—and then all of him went stiff as he heard the blazing fanfare floating out from the palace.

Elaine felt Thomas's hand go cold, and then he released her—she looked up at his face and saw his expression change to one of anguish—and then gradually determination stole over his features, and a touch of satisfaction.

"It ends now," Thomas said, though Elaine was not sure that he was talking to her.

"What ends?" she asked gently, as another fanfare started, hard on the heels of the first.

Thomas looked at her. "Do you know why the trumpets are blowing?" he asked.

"Yes. King Richard has returned."

"You do not seem overjoyed."

"I have other things on my mind."

"I don't care very much about that villain either," Thomas said with a cold smile.

Elaine thought that never in her life had she met a man with such a contempt for kings. She was amazed that Thomas had managed to live this long.

"I am concerned about a man called Brian the Brutal," Thomas said, continuing. "He is Richard's personal man at arms—he was imprisoned with the King and I am sure he is returning now. He is an evil man. He killed someone I loved. He killed one vision of my future. His death could never balance the scales—yet still it is the only repayment I can offer to those who were lost.

"I know Richard—he likes homage. I'm sure he'll arrange a big ceremony tomorrow, he'll receive all his admirers. It is there that I will challenge Brian. I will force him to fight me then and there—and it will be a duel to the death. Even if I disarm him, even if he begs mercy, still I will slay him without pity.

"I have been waiting for this day to come for three years. It will close a chapter in the book of my life."

Thomas had been looking at Elaine the whole while he spoke, and his eyes did not waver now.

"I wish to declare my love for you, dear Elaine, but my first true love, dead these three years, must be avenged. I want you to be there tomorrow, on the day that I shall kill Brian.

"Will you come?"

Elaine was stunned by all this rapid flow of information. She remembered Brian from years before at the court: his hulking presence, his air of indifferent cruelty—she knew that Thomas spoke the truth.

She said, as she had said to other brave men before, "I will come, if I can."

That wasn't enough for Thomas. He just looked at her with his eyes of slate, cold chips of stone, and behind them all the fires of his past burning, a past Elaine was just beginning to understand, and he said, "If you can?"

Elaine turned away because she couldn't look at his face any longer. She thought of Thomas in love, the lady dead now, killed by Brian's hand, and then she remembered Thomas's words: 'one vision of my future' and 'those who were lost'—she suddenly realized a child had died too and without warning she began to cry. She thought, I love Roland and I have given him my heart and my body and my future, but it was Thomas who made my own beauty real to me and it is Thomas who needs me now. He tells me how he will kill Brian—he never spoke like that before any other duel, and I can see that part of the reason (though I doubt that he would admit this, even to himself) is that he is afraid. Brian is a master of arms like Thomas is, and Brian is bigger and stronger and perhaps just as adept—Thomas needs me there to give him courage. I will go—this will not disturb Roland's negotiations with the King, and those will take time anyway—I will go—it will be my gift of love to Thomas, and it will be my farewell—I will go, and all debts will be paid, and then my dearest Roland and I will leave this cursed island and start a new life of peace.

Elaine wiped her eyes and turned to face Thomas, expecting to see him as fierce as before—but now it was his eyes that were misty and lost, and he who jerked his head away. Elaine put out her hand—almost unconsciously he put out his own, and their fingers interlaced. Their hands gave each other comfort as the horses walked slowly along, and then Elaine said, "I will be there."

Thomas turned back to her then, but his eyes were lowered. He raised her hand to his lips, and he kissed it.

"Thank you," he said.

He lowered her hand to a more comfortable position, but he did not release her. He needed the reality of Elaine's touch as his mind flew free of his body and raced back to the memory of death and evil. He remembered how Suleka had looked when he turned her over—he felt again the humiliating blows of Brian's lance—he remembered that day of death and flight and then he remembered this morning, eons ago this morning, and he managed to subtly guide the horses into a somewhat circuitous route, he kept Elaine from seeing Walter's body—but he didn't give a thought to Walter's partner.

Thomas never even dreamed he was being watched—but in fact Nigel had managed to creep back into position just in time to see Elaine emerge from the forest.

Nigel had seen the cheerful greeting—he had seen the kiss—he saw them holding hands now.

Nigel felt that he had saved himself—for now he had much to report to the Chancellor of the Exchequer.

CHAPTER 59

DEATH SENTENCE

Prince John had his own watchers at the ports—like Roland, he too had a man at Folkestone. The Prince's messenger was careful not to get boxed in on the jetty—he stayed on the shore and left even earlier than Sir Martin. He rode hard for the Palace of Bermondsey—when he arrived, he told the Prince that Richard Lionheart would be there in an hour.

Prince John did not have much time to make up his mind. He could stay, and beg his brother for mercy—but John sensed that this was the wrong emotional moment. Richard had barely tasted freedom now—he must still rage against the one who tried to keep him imprisoned. He'll kill me if he sees me now, John thought. He has to know of my negotiations with Henry VI—I don't dare hope that he doesn't. I have to flee.

John rode down to the docks by the Thames and commandeered a ship by royal fiat. He ordered the captain to take him to France. John was sure that he would find a safe haven in the court of Richard's enemy, King Philip II.

A knight with a gambling debt brought the news of the Prince's flight to Arthur the Assessor. Arthur accepted the trade of information for money and sent the man on his way.

It amused Arthur that the knight knew where to find him while his wife thought he was in Wales. She was the only one fooled by his deception. She was blinded by desire . . .

Arthur took out a deck of cards and laid it on the table in front of him. He stared at the deck for a moment and then turned over the top card. It was a red king. Richard would be here in minutes. The Lionheart would certainly call for him— and then even Elaine would know that he was still in the palace.

Where were Nigel and Walter?

Where was Elaine?

Arthur cut the deck and lifted out the queen of hearts. He paired it with the knave.

He looked at the pair for as long as he could stand it, and then he put the cards back in the deck and shuffled them.

Who was the knave?

Elaine had left very early this morning—that much Arthur already knew from the palace guards. She must have gone some distance, for no one else had seen her.

She had to be with her lover.

The knave.

Thomas?

Nigel and Walter were on her trail. I will have proof today, Arthur thought.

Everything else was ready for murder.

Arthur smiled and relaxed a little. Every night since the ball he had slipped away from the castle under cover of darkness. He had descended into the netherworld of the city of London. He had found the men he needed in the roughest bars, in the seediest brothels. He had assembled his crew of killers.

They were ready, eager for his gold, just waiting for his command.

Arthur couldn't give that command until he had proof. He hoped that Nigel or Walter would come before the King returned and summoned him. Otherwise he might be out of touch with his shadowers for hours!

Arthur cursed.

He took out the queen of hearts again and stared at the card.

He remembered his orphan classmate from years ago in Firfleet. He remembered their games of 'dress up' and imagination—he remembered their dreams. He remembered the rescue—he remembered the audience with King Henry. He remembered how it felt to stand in royal ceremony with the most beautiful woman in the world on his arm.

He covered the card with one soft hand, so that he could not see the face. He thought of how men looked at him now—the insolent sneers that said they *knew* his wife was seeking a lover—or had a lover.

Elaine thought she was free of him now. She was even so foolish as to think he would leave the city to smooth the way for her infidelity. She would soon learn . . .

Arthur lifted his hand from the card and stared into the face of the queen of hearts. "Unfaithful bitch," he said quietly, "You think you are free of me—you think you do not need to answer to me any more—you think I have no power over you.

"But you're wrong—I do have power over you, and you have given it to me. You are falling in love, I can see it—and being in love, you are easy to destroy.

"All I have to do is kill your lover.

"You are going to watch him die before your eyes.

"You have forced me to this act, and his blood will be on your hands.

"ON YOUR HANDS!" he suddenly screamed, and he slammed the queen back onto the deck and shuffled it madly, shuffled again and again but that still wasn't enough, he covered the deck with his two hands and then raised them—the cards were gone, vanished up his sleeve, he had done the trick perfectly.

He was the magician. He could make anyone vanish. He could transform as well—he took hope and patriotism and bare sustenance and turned those base metals into gold for the royal treasury. He was going to make Elaine vanish—and then he was going to break her—and then transform her into a slave.

Arthur knew he could do all that—he was going to do all that—and yet he realized that in some final way he had already lost Elaine. He might transform her into an obedient slave—but the broken woman he would create could never love him.

No one would ever love him. No one would ever save him. He felt the bullies circling around him again, and he cried like a child, head down, arms loose, and he forgot the deck of cards up his sleeve—the cards slid back down his sleeve and fell to the floor—the deck hit on end and the bright pictures pinwheeled in all directions—the queen of hearts lay on her back—she seemed to be smiling—another card, face down, lay half over her.

Arthur knew the other card was the knave.

He started to wail—but his cry swelled louder and louder, the wail surrounded him, shrieked in his ears even after he had stopped making a sound—and then Arthur realized the trumpeteers were blowing: King Richard had come home.

"That's more work for me," Arthur said to the queen of hearts. "Richard will want gold to fight France, and then Germany. It's a crazy thing to do, of course. The economy is shattered. This country needs only peace and reconstruction. But I must do the

King's will—and I can get the money for him. I'll just squeeze harder. Take crops, livestock—there's no cash to take. Famine, starvation, death—famine imposed from the top. And why not—Richard is God's chosen warrior—so all his actions must be God's will. People dying in the fields—why not? People fleeing the countryside to steal in the city—London one big terrifying slum—why not? God's will. Richard's will. My action. I'll kill people slowly on orders of my King. I'll take away their sustenance, so Richard can win some battles for a change! God's will. And the people will cheer too, I know it. They'll cheer while Richard kills them. While I kill them. I'll kill them. I'll kill them"—Arthur reached out with his foot and turned over the card that lay on the queen of hearts: it *was* the knave—"I'll kill him! I'll kill him! I'll kill him!"

Arthur screamed and sobbed until his head came to rest on the table before him. He stayed like that, with his forehead pressed to the wood, for some endless horror of time—and then a knock at the door alerted all his senses.

He wiped his face on his sleeve and called, "Who is it?"

"Sir Lionel, with orders from the King."

Arthur was cruelly disappointed. He walked slowly across the room, undid the bar, and opened the heavy door.

"Milord, the King wishes to see you at once," said Sir Lionel.

Arthur nodded slowly, and took a step out into the corridor. He took a long slow look to his right, and then another long look to his left. There, at the end of the corridor, half hidden, he saw a knight casually inspecting a red handkerchief. It was Sir Nigel. Arthur checked a winestain on his fine golden cloak. The motion of his fingers might almost have been a wave. Then the Assessor looked up at Sir Lionel.

"Tell the King I'm busy. I'll see him in an hour."

"You can't do that Sir—er, Count"—Sir Lionel was terribly flustered—"the King . . ."

"What can't I do?" interrupted Arthur, smiling his terrible smile, his bloated face a horrible gargoyle before the young knight's eyes. "What can't I do?" Arthur repeated as he stepped back a pace—and then he slammed the heavy door in Sir Lionel's face.

The Assessor sat back in his chair again, looking down at his scattered cards. He was pleased that none were bent or folded, for even in his anger and despair he had avoided stepping on them.

Sir Lionel kept knocking at the door, still trying to do his duty by the King—but Arthur paid no attention. After awhile the knocking ceased. Arthur heard the knight's footsteps walking away.

Not long after came quieter footsteps and a softer knock. Arthur got up and let Sir Nigel come in.

"Sit down," Arthur said, looking at Nigel's white face. "Tell me the bad news."

Nigel said nothing for the moment. The room seemed to have the odor of death. The bright scattered cards on the floor were a madman's dream. He picked his way carefully around the cards and sat down on the opposite side of Arthur's table.

"Milord, may I have some wine?"

Arthur poured him a flagon. Something was very wrong.

"I trust Walter is on the job," Arthur said.

"Walter's dead."

Arthur was still standing. His hands tightened on the back of his chair.

"Who killed him?"

"Sir Thomas."

There it was.

Arthur didn't want Nigel to see his face. He got down on his knees and started picking up the cards—knave first. He congratulated himself—he *had* been right from the start. He had been too wise to impart his suspicions to Nigel or Walter—he had been afraid that they would then tell him what he wanted to hear. But now the proof was coming into his hands—the reconstituted deck was in his hands—he got up and then sat down across from Nigel.

"From the beginning," Arthur said.

Nigel told his tale: this morning's chase down the hallway, the unidentified knights picking up Elaine and Sandra, the battle with Thomas—and here Nigel began to wander from the truth, he said that after he had been knocked down he had tried to follow Thomas but had lost him in the forest—he said that he had then waited all day in a place of concealment, watching for Elaine to come out of the forest—he said he saw Thomas come out, and then a few minutes later Elaine appeared. This is what he believed had happened—for Nigel had come back on watch only minutes before Elaine reappeared, and so of course he had not seen Thomas's painful wait.

From this point on Nigel continued with factual narrative. He told of Elaine's smile upon seeing Thomas—he told of greeting, laughter, kiss—at Arthur's insistence, he described every motion of the kiss that he could recall—he painted a picture of love, and then he told how Elaine had laid her head against Thomas's chest. He told of watching them ride back toward the castle, hand in hand.

The evidence was absolutely damning.

To Arthur it was quite clear what Thomas had done. He had hired two knights to take Elaine into the forest, while he rode behind to eliminate (as he had done) any followers. Then he had met Elaine in the forest, and sent the other knights and Sandra back via some circuitous route. Then he had taken Elaine—Arthur ground his teeth—and then, coming back, he had ridden out in front of her. He had checked to see that the coast was clear, and then he had met her as she came out of the forest, and then the two of them had come back to the castle as though nothing had happened.

It was a good plan, Arthur thought, and it had very nearly succeeded. If Thomas had killed Nigel as well then he might have got away with it. But the knight had been careless—and then even more careless later, kissing Elaine in the open (even if it did appear that no one was watching). Well, someone had been watching—and soon Thomas would find his death.

Arthur did card tricks as he ran through the mechanism of his plot again: kidnapping, the message for Thomas, the amount of lead time allowed, the killing ground, the celebration, the poison—all was in order.

He looked across the table at Nigel.

"May I go now?" the knight asked hopefully.

"No," Arthur said.

Nigel should have run at that moment. He should have fled with Jillian as he had dreamed of doing earlier. They could have used the remnant of Arthur's gold and booked passage to Ireland. There were places in that wild island, especially in the northwest, where the English crown still did not hold sway. Arthur would not have been able to reach him there—perhaps he and Jillian could have made a happy life together.

But Nigel didn't run. He took the easy path of obedience to power. He stayed in his seat—he listened when Arthur told him what he had to do—he listened when Arthur told him of the rewards he would be given.

He agreed to participate in Elaine's kidnapping. He consented out of fear and greed. He feared for his own life—and he believed Arthur when the Assessor promised that after the deed was done successfully, his debts would be forgiven, *and* he would be handsomely rewarded with gold.

Even a poor knight does not make war against women—but by this time in his life Nigel was no knight at all. He had no self respect left—he did not even have the courage to flee—and so he did what he was told.

In less than two days he was dead.

CHAPTER 60

VISIONS OF LARRAZIAN FUTURE

Roland noticed, with a certain well deserved pride, that his plan had worked to perfection. No one paid any special attention to him when he returned to the palace—there were no jealous stares, no challenges, no comments about Elaine. No one knew that he had spent the best part of the day with the Countess of Anjou—no one knew that he had made love with her.

The only concern at the court was the newly returned King. Roland was able to work his way through the crowd around His Majesty and pay his respects. The Lionheart quickly became attentive when Roland hinted that he had gold available to back some royal, Christian expedition—the King told the Duke that there would be a great public ceremony, noontime on the morrow, but after that they could meet in private and discuss Roland's proposal.

It was all Roland could do to keep from skipping as he left the King.

At dinner in the royal dining hall Roland caught Elaine's eye (thought they were far to discreet to speak) and she smiled delightfully. Clearly she had returned home (though this would *not* be her home much longer!) unsuspected. She looked beautiful—as always—Roland just wanted to stare at her, but he contented himself with stolen looks and memories from this afternoon. His heart wanted to burst with happiness! Roland knew that he would prevail with the King—the Lionheart was clearly desperate for gold.

Just one more day, Roland thought, sneaking a peek at his love—just one more day, dear Elaine, and then I can publicly claim you as my lady. We might even be able to sail off down the Thames tomorrow night!

Roland's heart was hammering and he realized he was staring. He looked down at his plate and finished his dinner without noticing what it was.

As Roland left the hall he passed by Elaine's table. She was sitting at one end, with Sandra next to her—the same principle as at the dance—she didn't want any man next to her tonight.

Roland stopped before Elaine and bowed.

"Good evening, Countess."

"Good evening, Your Grace." Elaine was polite, nothing more.

"Will you attend the public ceremony for the King tomorrow, Milady?"

"Of course, Your Grace—all are invited." And I will watch Thomas kill Brian, Elaine thought.

"His Majesty has graciously promised me a private audience after the celebration," Roland said.

"Indeed," Elaine replied. She seemed to be already bored—but under the table she had eased off one slipper. Now she extended her bare foot out from under the narrow table—no one saw her toes come out and press down on Roland's shoe.

The Duke nearly fell to his knees when he felt her touch. He looked down and saw just a flash of pink before the foot was withdrawn.

"Good—Good-bye then, Countess," Roland stammered, and then he took his leave.

One more day!

Roland returned to Lady Smythe's mansion. It was well past nightfall now. He could feel a storm brewing. He knew that his men had been trickling back all day (as the other watchers heard reports that the King had returned) and the Duke was pleased to see now that all twenty were present.

"Good evening, gentlemen," Roland said, looking over his expectant troops, "All goes well. I need to explain a few things. Let's all go to my room."

He meant that he did not want any of Lady Smythe's servants to overhear them.

The knights followed their lord up the stairs. Roland had a big room—but it seemed to shrink before his eyes as twenty large men piled in. Roland sat down on his bed while his men arranged themselves in a semicircle around him.

Roland looked over the faces, from Anton smiling on his left to lusting Gunter in the center to Daniel dreaming on the right.

The Duke smiled and then began to speak.

"Gentlemen, I have told you that all goes well. Now let me explain myself more precisely.

"I have won the heart of Elaine the Fair. The Countess has come to love me as I love her. I have proposed marriage to her, and she has accepted."

The men seemed especially close in the confined room. Their eyes were hot—and yet also concerned. What of the lady's husband? he could hear them silently asking.

"Elaine is not married—her first marriage will be to me."

The Duke smiled as he watched the shock roll through the tight packed room. "Let me explain," he said, and then he told the story as Elaine had told it to him.

When Roland finished that story he paused to accept the smiles and congratulations of his men. Then he went on: "Winning Elaine is but half the battle of course—the other half is bringing her safely home with us. When we set out, we thought that we might have to fight the Lionheart—well, the English King is here, but we do not have to fight him." Roland explained the outline of the deal—his own certainty convinced his men that he would succeed—they looked quite doleful when he finished.

No war! No battles! Return peacefully to peaceful, peaceful Larraz!

Anton chose his moment, and then he asked in a wistful little boy's voice, "Couldn't we have just a *little* war?"

Everyone laughed, even Roland—but then the Duke said, "You will all show the greatest respect to King Richard Lionheart and his troops. I want no incidents. I'm sorry"— Roland smiled slightly—"but I must order you to keep the peace."

There was some good natured grumbling—but the men agreed to follow Roland's lead. In their heart of hearts, they may have been a little relieved. Fighting King Richard might be a grand adventure—but it would be very, very dangerous . . .

Perhaps it was just as well that the Duke could find a diplomatic solution. They would return home with honor—they would *all* return home—and they would bring with them the very real lady of dreams, Elaine the Fair: the next Duchess of Larraz.

Such were the thoughts of the Larrazian knights—visions of a peaceful future. Daniel thought of seeing Elaine every day in the palace of Larraz—Anton reflected that it was really better to eschew battle, for after all, Roland was not the only one who would be returning to Larraz with an English bride!

Each Larrazian knight believed in his Duke—but even the wisest man can not make the world turn to order.

There were forces afoot that were beyond Roland's control.

The men might have done well to remember that whispered inner voice that had spoken to them all when they left Larraz— the voice had said, "You are mortal—you may not come back from this alive."

That voice spoke only truth, though it had been forgotten.

There *were* battles ahead for the Larrazian knights.

In the future, in the near future, death was waiting.

CHAPTER 61

HEAT LIGHTNING AND THUNDER

No one at the English court ever forgot that night, Sunday night, June 14, 1194—for that was the last night that Elaine the Fair ever spent at the Palace of Bermondsey.

As the bells of the city chimed midnight, so did the heavens unleash their portents. Heat lightning flashed jaggedly through the air. Thunder boomed in the distance, hollow crashes at irregular intervals. All over the city, all through the palace, people were jarred from their slumber. They woke up to feel air so thick they could scarcely breathe it—air so charged it fairly crackled with electricity. The people longed for rain to pour down and calm the atmosphere, but all through the long night the rain held off.

There were some who had not been awakened at midnight—some who had never gone to sleep.

Ivar's Vikings rowed hard through the night, trying desperately to make landfall before dawn. They fought their way through the choppy sea, whipped on by Ivar's lashing commands.

Thomas was working through the night as well, but in a quieter manner. He carefully inspected and cleaned all his weapons. When he was finished he allowed himself, just for a moment, to think of Elaine. He recalled the sweet taste of her lips—and then he coldly put the memory aside. He thought of Brian—and Suleka. He knelt to pray, which he hadn't done in years, and then he bowed his head to Mecca, as she had done. He prayed for her soul, he prayed for the soul of their never born child—his thoughts came around, and he prayed for Elaine—then he realized what Elaine had sensed: he was afraid—finally, he prayed for himself.

Arthur the assessor kept moving through the electric night. He traveled from bar to bordello to gaming house—he assembled his dirty force, and gave them their final orders. Then he left his criminals—the situation at the castle had already been arranged, so now all he needed was a messenger. He found the sort of man he sought sleeping off his drunkenness in an alley. He roused the pathetic creature, instructed him, and paid him well with a very special coin. The gambler in Arthur had finally found stakes high enough to interest him: he risked his luck against the chance to break Elaine the Fair.

Roland had enjoyed the love of his life today and he looked forward to his audience with the King tomorrow. All his plans were proceeding with astonishing smoothness. There need be no bloodshed, no war, there was no reason to worry—but he couldn't sleep. The nightmare had come back. It lurked just below the surface of his unconsciousness. Every time he closed his eyes he was struck by the evil omen. He would awaken almost instantly, pouring sweat—all he could see in his mind's eye was the terrifying vision of the floating black cross.

Richard Lionheart clutched the gold sheathed, gold hilted, jewel encrusted sword that Saladin had given him. Every time he touched the weapon it reminded him of his failure—but he could not give it up. It was his only connection to his great enemy—it was proof of his own valor—Saladin *must* have respected him greatly to have given him such a gift. After all, he would have defeated the Moslems had there been better cooperation among his Christian allies—Saladin must have recognized that. So Richard attempted to convince himself, but deep in his heart he felt the terror of the desert heat. The terror kept him awake for hours. It must have been three in the morning before he could force his thoughts round to France. Then he could relax a little—France had no shrieking nomads rising out of sand storms—France had immobile castles, and those he could encircle, and besiege, and starve into submission.

Brian the Brutal drank flagon after flagon of wine, but still slumber would not come. His primitive mind easily forgot the evil he had done—but his soul did not. He had not gone to confession since the day he had killed Prince Henry—the young man who would have been King Henry III—Richard Lionheart's older brother.

Elaine the Fair lay in her bed shaking with every blast of the

thunder. Her skin quivered as though the lightning were caressing her. She was wet between her legs and her nipples were stiff
against her white silk nightgown. She wanted Roland terribly—
she could almost feel him on top of her, inside of her—but sometimes when she looked up at her dream lover's face there was
Thomas coming down to kiss her, and she could not turn away.

Elaine turned over and tried to find roses on her bed, but
there were none.

She would watch Thomas kill Brian in the morning. Then she
would leave with Roland in the evening, regardless of how his
meeting went with the King. Elaine vowed that she would not
spend another night in this bed.

Now she just had to make it through till morning.

Elaine got up and lit a fresh candle from one of the burned
down specimens that still partially brightened her room. She
walked over to the door that led to her lady in waiting's room.
She opened it—she saw Lady Sandra, barely covered by a little
cotton shift, wide eyed and awake on her bed.

"You can't sleep," Elaine said. It was not a question.

Sandra was a little frightened by the sudden intrusion—but
not as frightened as she would have been a day earlier.

"No, I can't, Milady."

Elaine walked over to the bed and put out her hand. Sandra
took it, and the Countess pulled her lady in waiting to her feet.
Elaine led Sandra back to her own bedroom. She shut the connecting door behind them. She walked Sandra over to her bed,
and blew out the bright candle and set it down on her bureau.

Lightning fluttered into the darkened room. The electric glow
illuminated Sandra's face: her soft brown eyes were delicate and
loving as always, but Elaine noticed some subtle changes. There
was something a little different about the way Sandra met her
eyes—there was a resolute courage in the girl's stance as the
lightning flared around her. Elaine smiled—it was clear that Sir
Anton had not just taken Sandra—he had given to her as well.

Still smiling, Elaine stepped closer and took Sandra's face in
her hands. She tilted the girl's head back and deliberately
kissed her on the lips—but this time Sandra did not open her
mouth as she had done in the morning.

Elaine understood and she did not press. She just broke the
kiss and said calmly, "We will sleep together."

Elaine got into bed first, then Sandra. There was no need for
covers. The thunder boomed and shook them both—Elaine gath-

ered Sandra into her arms and pulled her close.

Sandra felt the Countess's understanding and she shared her loneliness—she buried her face against Elaine's neck and hugged her mistress fiercely. Elaine just kept smiling in the dark—she kissed the girl's forehead, and then she pushed Sandra down a little until the girl's head was nestled between her breasts. Then Sandra relaxed, she lay against the heat and softness of her mistress, she felt Elaine's hand gently stroking her hair—she closed her eyes and soon she was asleep.

Elaine looked down at the sleeping girl, she felt her warm comforting weight—now the lightning and thunder seemed far away, the excitement of the day melted into weariness, and the Countess of Anjou fell asleep as well.

By this time the night had exhausted almost everyone. Brian finally drank himself into a stupor. Richard passed out with his sword in hand. Roland, twitching and sweating, finally stayed unconscious long enough for the nightmare to run its course. Arthur returned to his spare room at the castle and collapsed after his unaccustomed exertion. Thomas slept on the hard floor, his head on a doubled blanket, the hilt of his sword in his hand. The Vikings, muscles aching, made landfall on the beach below the monastery that was their first target.

There was one exception to the general exhaustion—there was movement in the stable for landless knights, though Thomas slept on. Jim tiptoed past his master's sleeping form and opened the door silently. He stepped lightly into the sulfurous night. Jim felt happy—he had slept while everyone else had been driven crazy by the heavenly clangor. Now he was bright and alert and ready for his revenge. The true King had returned! Jim walked up to the main gate of the palace, for he knew that sooner or later Richard Lionheart would have to come through there to meet his adoring public.

Jim looked around cheerfully. No one else was waiting yet. A crowd could form behind him but still he would be first. He would be able to tell the King about the black horse named Saladin.

Part III

Battle

Chapter 62

THE KNIFE

Monday, June 15, 1194, an hour before dawn . . .

Elaine the Fair woke up to the sound of screaming. At first she thought it was her own cry, sparked by her familiar nightmare—but then she realized she wasn't dreaming and the voice was not her own—it was external and yet right next to her—she sat up in bed, knowing as she did so that Sandra's warm weight was no longer against her—her eyes opened wide, straining to see in the thin light of burned down candles, in the gray trick light of false dawn—she saw Sandra screaming and struggling on the side of the bed, fighting against two dark men—Elaine opened her mouth to loose her own cry, she reached for her lady in waiting—and then a hard male hand, smelling horribly of liquor, clamped down over her mouth from behind, his other hand came around her body and yanked her back against him— one man had Sandra's arms now, her scream sputtered, the girl gasped for air, struggling, she started to open her mouth and then the second man punched her hard in the stomach, and all the air she had gathered flew from her open mouth in a soundless whoosh.

Elaine stared in shock.

No man hits a woman like that.

This man had.

Evil exists.

She had forgotten, for a few years—but now she knew the truth again: evil exists, not just in dreams, but in reality.

Once a man chooses evil, once he leaves his conscience behind, is there any limit to his actions?

The puncher was not finished yet.

Now came a sibilant whisper as he drew his knife. The gleaming blade appeared to be at least a foot long.

Elaine was sitting up on the side of her bed, pulled back hard against the man who held her, her mouth stoppered, her upper body wrapped tight by the strong rough arm that imprisoned her.

Sandra sat on the opposite side of the bed, facing her mistress, her arms pulled viciously behind her back, her mouth open, gasping for air, her face contorted with pain, her eyes terror-wide as she stared at the knife coming closer.

The puncher insinuated the point of his knife into the neckline of Sandra's shift. Then he jerked downward, and it immediately became evident that the blade was razor sharp—he split the nightdress neatly, straight down between Sandra's breasts, over her navel, down between her legs. There was a little snick as his knife cut through the double sewn hem.

The puncher looked up at Elaine then, as though seeking her approval, and then he carefully folded the ruined nightdress back away from the split so that the Countess could see everything.

The puncher stood to one side of Sandra now. He held his knife with his left hand—he grabbed Sandra's hair with his right hand and pulled the girl's head back.

Evil exists.

Elaine watched with the terror of a helpless child. She remembered her mother in chains . . .

The man brought his knife up before Sandra's eyes, and then he slowly traced her face with the blade, the cutting edge just a fraction of an inch away from the girl's delicate skin, the knife moving in a horrible parody of a lover's caress—and then he aimed the point between Sandra's lips, he moved it closer and closer, he was not stopping—Sandra opened her mouth in terror, but she knew better than to scream—the tip of the blade entered her mouth, just an inch, and then withdrew.

Elaine felt a terrible memory begin to come back . . .

Sandra was afraid to breathe as the man followed the line of her throat with the knife, the blade again just a whisper away.

He followed the path of the cut nightdress as he brought the blade down between Sandra's breasts, and then he twirled the knife with a flamboyant gesture—he was clearly proud of the way he handled the weapon—he spun the blade in a half circle as he brought it up under Sandra's left breast, he brought it right up until he touched her soft skin, and Sandra flinched wildly in terror, though she couldn't break free of the man who held her—she just felt the shivering cold blade and it took her a moment to realize this was the dull top edge of the knife lifting her breast—he still had not cut her.

He used the dull edge of the knife to caress the sensitive underside of Sandra's breast—he followed the beautiful curve forward and up until he lifted her bright pink nipple that was rigid with terror.

He performed the same twisted act of love on her other breast.

Elaine watched as he moved the knife down again. She had seen the blood between her mother's thighs. She hadn't understood then—but over the years, she learned. She had overheard people talk: 'the fit punishment for a witch,' or, 'cleansed her foul loins in blood'—

The knife was between Sandra's thighs now, he was twirling the blade this way and that, threatening to cut, he forced Sandra to spread her legs—

By the time Elaine was twelve, when her own menstrual blood had begun to flow—by that time Elaine had learned what had been done to her mother.

She learned it—but she couldn't live with the knowledge—she had made herself forget.

The point of the knife blade was aimed at the tender, near virginal mouth between Sandra's thighs—

Elaine remembered everything.

She opened her mouth as wide as she could and she got some of the covering hand inside and she bit down on it with all the strength she had.

Her captor howled and struck her face with his other hand—he tore his wounded hand from the clutches of her teeth. The puncher jerked around at the commotion, knife aimed at Elaine—but he hadn't cut Sandra—Elaine would never know how far he would have gone, for now the man who held Sandra spoke up: "There's no time for these games," he said to the puncher, who was clearly the leader. "It's going to be light soon, and we're only supposed to tie this one up anyway. Let's get going and get out of here!"

The puncher looked back at Sandra but the mood was broken. "Right," he said, with anger and frustration in a surprisingly upper class voice—he used his knife viciously to cut Sandra's shift into strips.

Elaine's captor had an arm around her throat now, it was hard to breathe against his choking grip, her cheek throbbed where he had struck her over her old scar, and his vile breath was in her ear as he whispered, "Just try to bite me now, bitch." His free, hurting hand roamed over her silk covered breasts and squeezed them harshly.

All of it was bearable because Sandra was spared.

Elaine watched as they flipped the girl over on her belly on the bed. They tied her, spreadeagled, to the four posts, using the remnants of her shift. The puncher cut a strip off a thick towel—they used that to gag her—they tied it tight behind her head.

The puncher surveyed his handiwork with satisfaction—and then, with a gesture reminiscent of Arthur signing a document, he swooped down with his knife and cut a V into the skin of Sandra's left buttock.

The blood welled up out of the two cuts and Elaine tried to scream but the choker cut off her air. Sandra's scream was lost in her gag.

The puncher laughed and slapped Sandra hard on her unmarked buttock.

"Just something to remember me by," he said.

Evil spoke in a nobleman's voice.

They marched Elaine out of her room and dragged her down the corridor.

There were no guards anywhere.

The puncher led the way confidently, not worried even here in the palace—not just a puncher—a nobleman by birth—Elaine saw again the bloody V and she remembered the scandal from years ago—there was the knight who came to be called the Vulture—V—he used to strike down wounded enemies, already defeated by another knight in a fair fight, and then claim the victories as his own. He had been caught, exposed—he had lost his honor, his title—there had been rumors since that he killed for hire.

Who hired him?

Someone who knew the layout of the palace and could bribe every guard on duty. Someone powerful enough that the royal guards would take his money and obey.

Someone who hates me, Elaine thought.

She thought of the man who had once saved her life.

She remembered turning away from Arthur as Sandra made up her face. She remembered kissing other men in front of him. She remembered the trip to Pembroke that he had forced her to take—she remembered his failure on the inn's single bed.

She pitied her false husband—and she hated him. She knew her enemy, and she relaxed just a little, for she did not think that Arthur would have her killed.

Chapter 63

THE ASSESSOR'S THOUGHTS

The heavens finally opened just before dawn.

The long awaited rain poured down in great sheets—the black thunderclouds blotted out the rising sun.

Arthur the Assessor slipped quietly from one wing of the castle to another. He went into his own bedroom and locked the door behind him.

A chair stood against one wall. He got up on it carefully, and lined up his eye with the peephole near the ceiling—a peephole he had cut long ago to spy on Elaine. Now he checked to see whether his orders had been carried out.

He had told the Vulture and his men to bring Sandra from her adjoining room and tie her to Elaine's bed (not knowing that Elaine would make things easier by bringing the girl over herself) for the lady in waiting had an important, though unwitting, role in Arthur's plot.

Arthur peered through the narrow hole—his eye adjusted to the dim light—and then he started to smile as he saw Sandra's spread, naked, bound and gagged form—but then the smile froze on his face and he had to clamp his teeth together to silence a stream of curses.

Why had the Vulture had to leave his mark?

Arthur stared in disgust at the cuts, each two inches long and crusted with dried blood, that came together to make an unmistakable V.

Stupid.

Arthur got down from his perch and sat down in the chair.

He began to think.

He tried to remember if anyone at the court had seen him

with the Vulture. Gradually he satisfied himself that he was free and clear. He had met the Vulture only twice, both times in the back room of a notorious brothel. The only nobleman who could make the connection was Sir Nigel—and he was marked for death anyway.

Arthur breathed a little easier.

No one could connect him.

The murders would take place far from the court.

He stood up on the chair again, as carefully as before. (It wouldn't do to encourage Sandra by letting her know there was someone in the next room.) He saw that she was awake and struggling—he could tell by the tension in her muscles and the slight mewling noises that escaped the thick gag. He could see that she was not really making any progress towards getting free—her stretched, spreadeagled position kept her from getting any real leverage.

All was well—Arthur sat down again.

The only question now was one of timing.

Once again the Assessor went over the well honed lines of his plot.

Thomas should have received his note by now, Arthur thought, but he won't go yet. He has no proof, no real reason—but he'll be primed, all the same. He'll be like a nocked arrow, pulled back against the tension of the bowstring—one motion will release him into flight.

Sandra will supply that trigger. She'll send him flying, straight to the killing ground.

I need to give the Vulture a good start . . .

Arthur went over the times and distances again. As usual, he settled on noon as the best time to release Sandra.

That meant that the terrified naked girl in the next room would have to struggle helplessly for six more hours.

That fact meant nothing to Arthur. She was just a tool.

He smiled as he contemplated the perfect machinery of his revenge.

In exactly one day's time, he thought, Thomas will be dead.

Arthur never considered the possibility that his vengeance might be aimed at the wrong man.

Chapter 64

THE VAGRANT

Thomas had lived in the stable for landless knights for a year and a half, but he had never bothered to fix the roof. He thought he was lying in a safe spot, but the early morning downpour created a fresh leak. Thomas was awakened by a stream of water striking the back of his head.

The knight jumped up with a curse, drawing his sword—he had never let go of the weapon during the few hours he had slept.

He looked around and saw no enemy—he looked again and saw that even Jim was gone. This he counted as a relief. He did not need sour looks and spitting to precede today's battle.

'I will be there,' Elaine had said.

Thomas felt her hand in his, and he sheathed his sword.

He dressed in dry clothes—he pushed aside the thought of seeing Elaine again—he made himself remember Suleka, he thought of how she had wanted to die—and yet he had given her new life, and even a smile—he remembered how he had left her alone on the one day he should have stayed to protect her . . .

He remembered Brian.

The memories were, surprisingly, not so painful today.

Thomas touched his sword again—vengeance was at hand.

Thomas went over to Saladin's stall and found that the roof there also leaked. The wet horse was in a foul mood. He almost took his master's hand off when Thomas tried to feed him some grain.

Thomas flexed his bitten fingers and watched his horse eat breakfast. Then he put saddle and bridle on, and led the horse out into the rain. Neither the elements nor his impending duel could stop Thomas's morning ride. In any case, he had to eat—it was Thomas's custom to take his breakfast in a quiet inn a couple of miles from the palace. He liked that place because it had none of the trappings of the court—just good plain food and the innkeeper knew to leave him alone.

So Thomas thought of breakfast as he mounted his black horse in the rain—but then his routine was shattered when a muddy vagrant ran up to him and thrust a folded piece of paper into his hand.

Thomas had half drawn his sword as the man ran up—but then he had seen clearly that the ragged creature could not harm him, and he had simply taken the proferred paper. He watched the vagrant run away—the man was frightened—what, or who, had made him wait out here in the rain?

Thomas unfolded the paper. There were three widely spaced words written on it, each one spelled out in crudely drawn capitals. The message looked like this: STONEHENGE TOMORROW DAWN.

That was it. Thomas turned it over to make sure, but there were only those three words—STONEHENGE TOMORROW DAWN—he began to shiver, for all he knew of the famous circle of stones (he had never seen them) was the atmosphere of evil in which they had been cloaked over centuries of Christendom. Generations of priests had defamed the pagan temple (though those priests knew nothing of its origin or purpose) and so one could hardly find an Englishman who did not react to the name Stonehenge with a vague dread. There had always been hints of human sacrifice carried out on those great rocks . . .

He put the paper in his pocket.

Elaine.

Thomas had a sudden moment of pure terror, and then he picked out the fleeing figure of the vagrant again, and he kicked Saladin into a gallop.

The vagrant didn't so much run as stagger—Saladin caught him up easily and Thomas just reached down as they went by and grabbed a handful of the man's wet greasy hair.

Despite the drag, Saladin kept on going for another twenty feet.

Thomas never loosened his grip. By the time the horse stopped, he had nearly broken the messenger's neck.

Thomas tugged the man up on to his toes and looked down into the terrified ruined face.

"Who gave you the paper," the knight asked in a low deadly voice.

"A gentleman, Sir, I don't know . . ."

Thomas, still holding the vagrant up by the hair, now slapped him hard across the face with his other hand. He leaned over until he was nose to nose with this human wreckage—he breathed in the stench of filth and terror and then he asked again, "Who was he?"

The vagrant began to babble. He told everything he knew— Thomas was certain he held nothing back—but all it amounted to was this: the vagrant had been awakened from his slumber in an alley in the middle of the night—or perhaps early morning, he couldn't tell—by a big man who held a knife to his throat. His attacker was a gentleman—he could tell by the way he was dressed—he could also tell that this gentleman would enjoy killing him—there was something terrifying about him. He had not been able to see much beyond the gleam of the knife in the dark—he had been forced into a two man coach, the gentleman had driven himself, and he had sat beside, hardly daring to look at his captor. He had been taken near to Thomas's stable—the gentleman gave him the paper, and told him to put it under his shirt to keep it dry. Then the gentleman had described Thomas—the vagrant had been told to give Thomas the note as soon as he came out. Then the gentleman had explained, in precise horrible terms, just what would happen if the vagrant did not do his bidding—and then, just when the vagrant was most terrified, the gentleman had given him a coin as payment. The gentleman had left then, without another word.

Thomas made the vagrant go over the story again and again but he could get nothing more. The "gentleman" had chosen his messenger well. The vagrant had lived all his life on the streets and he recognized none of the faces of the court. His description—a big man, a killer, someone who could describe Thomas and knew where he lived—was utterly valueless because it could apply to at least fifty knights of the court.

Thomas shook his head with disgust and released his grip on the greasy hair. The vagrant fell on his back in the mud. Thomas drew his sword.

The vagrant was certain that his last second had come. He screamed in profound terror as he struggled in the mud to get up, all the while fishing through his filthy robes. Finally he found what he was searching for, and he made the supreme sacrifice, in a last desperate attempt to save his life.

"Here you can even take the money," he screamed, and he offered up the coin that the gentleman had given him—a coin of such value that it could have kept him drunk for two weeks.

Thomas sheathed his sword and took the coin from the vagrant's trembling fingers. He looked it over, and then he stuffed it into his pocket next to the crumpled message. He touched heels to Saladin, and rode off without looking again at the vagrant.

That poor man rejoiced at first as the knight rode away—he was still alive!—but then he began to shiver in the cold rain, and he thought of how far he had to walk to get back to the city, and he realized that nothing awaited him there—he began to curse, for it seemed that he might just as well be dead, now that he had given up the greatest treasure he had ever possessed.

The coin that he had given Sir Thomas was a gold sovereign.

Chapter 65

ROLAND'S VISION

Roland woke up slowly. It was at least an hour after dawn. He was tired from fighting his black dream all night. He looked out the window (he had put in fresh glass for Lady Smythe, and she had been very pleased) and saw the torrential rain pouring down. It was the kind of rain that would go hard for a while and then abruptly stop. All should be clear by the noontime beginning of the King's outdoor celebration.

Then, afterward, Roland would meet privately with the King.

Everything was perfect.

Roland had wooed and won and made love to Elaine the Fair and she was all that he had ever dreamed of, and more.

If everything was perfect, why wasn't he happy?

He had gone to bed with the feeling of Elaine close to him. He had fought the dream, knowing she was near.

Awake, now, he could not feel her presence.

He tried to imagine her dressing, smiling—no, he could not make an image form.

She was gone.

Had the dream taken her away? No, she was not involved with the floating black cross—not yet.

The black cross was evil and evil was approaching but evil was already here because Elaine was gone.

Should he tell someone of his dream, of his sense of loss? He could tell Anton—he could only tell Anton, who was older than himself—but he had spent all his life avoiding the mystical and living by the rational.

There's no reason to tell Anton, Roland thought. It's just that now I am in love and I have lost my senses, as in every love story every written.

I see dangers where no dangers exist.

I invent a dream to punish my own happiness.

He tried to imagine Elaine in her bedroom, with Sandra brushing her hair.

Nothing.

Nothing.

Then a vision slipped in sideways on a knife edge, a swift brutal vision that lasted only an instant.

He saw a man's harsh face over Elaine, he was kissing her while his hands wandered profanely over her body.

The vision was gone.

No, not altogether gone, there was a sensation of movement—then nothing.

Black nothing vision gone.

He felt dread like a cold snake in his throat, blocking his breath.

Roland believed his vision—but it was nothing that he could tell.

He was a practical man—there were things that he could do.

He would send a message at once to the Countess of Anjou, just to confirm his suspicions—though he was certain that there would be no reply.

He would mobilize his army of English informants—he would have them all brought here, to his headquarters.

He would arrange to provision his men and horses—they would not ride out at random, but given hard information, they would be ready to go in an instant.

He would keep his appointment with Richard, for it was still necessary to negotiate a proper settlement with the King—and he would destroy Arthur's claim to Elaine.

He would keep his wits about him, despite any dreams or visions—after all, nothing proved they were real.

Still, he would act as though Elaine were in danger. He realized that for the first time in his life he would be giving orders based on a mystical tip—if his men asked him why (Why do you want the informants here? Why do you want to provision for a day's journey when your Countess is right here?) he would not be able to give them an answer.

Roland had dressed as he thought and now he stood ready to open his door and greet his men.

He tried to imagine Elaine close to him, soft and safe, well protected in the palace.

He willed himself to see her that way.

Nothing.

The Duke of Larraz pushed open his door.

Chapter 66

DISTANT VOICES

It was noontime now, and the rain had stopped, as Roland had predicted—but the sky was still gray and overcast. Nevertheless, Richard Lionheart had ordered that the celebration should proceed as scheduled. The royal cooks had been busy all morning—the feast was almost ready. The porters had set up long tables on the great lawn below the main gate. Crowds of people struggled to get close to those tables, hoping to get a good vantage point from which they could see the King when he arrived—two rows of soldier with pikes kept the people back. There was another crowd by the main gate—a dozen guards kept that passageway clear—the stubborn ostler, Jim, maintained his position at the front of that crowd.

Thomas, mounted on Saladin, surveyed the scene from the hill that sloped up to the north beyond the great lawn. Behind him lay the city of London—ahead of him, carefully prepared splendor. Thomas watched as the enormous gilt throne of the King was carried out and set on the far side of the head table. The people moaned in rapture.

Thomas shoved his hand in his pocket and crumpled the note around the hard gold sovereign.

When he had drawn his sword over the vagrant this morning, he had hoped to extract one last admission—but all he had received was the gold sovereign, an ordinary coin such as any well off man might carry—no clue at all.

Thomas had ridden to the inn—he had eaten breakfast as usual, but all he thought about was the note.

STONEHENGE TOMORROW DAWN.

Why had he been given this note? What was its meaning?

Who was the "gentleman"?

There were no answers, just an all pervasive feeling of dread, and a terrible fear for Elaine the Fair.

Thomas was certain that the note had something to do with her—no one would go to all that trouble just for him. All knew that he loved Elaine—did someone guess that she loved him? Had someone seen their kiss?

What was the purpose of the note? Thomas knew that he had no friends at the court. The direction could only be a trap—a trap set to close on him at Stonehenge. That thought did not bother Thomas at all. The question that mattered was whether the note was a ruse to lure Thomas away from Elaine—or whether Elaine herself was the bait in the trap. And if Elaine were taken to Stonehenge, what was the meaning of the third word, DAWN. What was to happen at dawn?

Sitting at his breakfast table, Thomas had put the old rumors together with his fresh fears. He began to understand his own terror, for he thought of human sacrifice. He thought of Elaine being killed at dawn.

Thomas had wanted to set out for Stonehenge right away—though he hadn't been there before, he was sure he could find it. He knew the temple stood on the great plain somewhat north of Salisbury. It was a day's ride away—twelve hours on a good horse—but then Thomas had considered further, he had realized that leaving at that moment meant that he would miss the King's welcoming party, and thus he would miss the chance to kill Brian. Besides, what if Elaine was still here? What if his first guess was correct, what if this was all a ruse to get him *away* from Elaine?

Thomas had left his friendly inn—he had ridden aimlessly all through the morning rain, trying to decide: stay or go?

Beset by terror and doubt, he had been unable to make a decision—but then finally he simply listened to the voices of those he loved, and he decided to stay.

In his mind he could still hear Suleka's voice—his dear, dear Arabian girl—and he could hear the formless words of their unborn child. He knew that they would never know peace until he had killed their assassin: Brian the Brutal. Thomas had looked forward to that revenge for all of these last three years—now the time was at hand, and he could not shrink from it.

He had explained this to Elaine yesterday—she had understood, and now he heard her voice too: 'I will be there.'

Thomas believed—he closed his mind to fearful doubt—he made himself believe that Elaine would keep her vow.

Now he looked down from the hilltop at the stage set for a King, and he heard the first fanfare.

He watched the nobles stepping smartly between the lines of soldiers as they headed for their places. He saw the Duke of Larraz sit at the head table across from the King's still empty throne. He saw the older knight who had swived Sandra take his seat beside the Duke. He saw lovely women—many lovely women—but he searched only for hair of purest spun gold, and that he did not see.

Thomas looked down at Saladin, and stroked his neck, and then he heard another fanfare, longer and more artful than the first. Thomas raised his eyes again. He saw the purple robes and the golden sword—he saw the cold face of the red haired, gold crowned King of the English: Richard Lionheart.

One step behind the King walked the royal man at arms: Brian the Brutal.

Thomas looked at Brian's hulking figure and knew his own fear. He knew that one turn of his wrist and one nudge with his heel would start Saladin toward Stonehenge. He could avoid battle for now.

He looked over the noble figures as they rose to greet their imperious King. He watched the bowing, the genuflecting—he watched until Richard sat down on his throne, he watched until all the nobles were seated as well—by then he knew for certain that Elaine was not there.

She had not kept her vow. Was that her choice?

He looked at Brian, six and a half feet tall, with weight to match—the Brutal one stayed on his feet, resting one hand on the back of the King's throne—he kept his other hand curled around the hilt of the sword that had killed Suleka.

He wore a vest of mail to protect his evil heart.

Thomas was frightened—for himself, and even more for the absent Elaine—and yet the essence of courage is to overcome fear.

Thomas knew that he could not help Elaine now. Though she was not here, he still had no proof that she had been taken to Stonehenge.

Without proof he could not race off to the west—but he could end Brian's brutal career right now.

He would stand by his decision.

Thomas touched his heels lightly to Saladin's flanks. He guided the big horse slowly down the hill.

The knight, dressed only in lightweight summer clothes, steadily approached the King's mail clad assassin.

Chapter 67

JIM

Jim was in a good mood when he assumed his position by the main gate early in the morning. Then the rain started to come down, and more and more people crowded up behind him, around him, almost over him—the crowd pushed him forward and the King's guards shoved him back, he was soaked, bruised, and in a foul mood long before the rain stopped.

Once the rain stopped it was worse—for now even more people crowded in, straining to see the King, and Jim's slight body was battered between the impatient populace and the ever more aggressive guards.

Jim began to wonder if even the true King was worth this much discomfort—yet even as he wondered, he prepared his short speech: 'Your Majesty, a knight of your court has named his horse for the infidel Saladin!'

He went over the words again and again as he was battered by his fellow citizens.

Suddenly the gates swung open and King Richard Lionheart appeared in all his purple magnificence.

Jim took a deep breath as the crowd moaned—but then suddenly a farmer burst through the line of guards and knelt at the King's feet.

"Your Majesty—" the man said, but he got no further. Perhaps he wanted to beg for his farm, foreclosed for failing to pay the King's taxes, or perhaps he simply wanted to pay homage to the King he adored, but as it happened his purpose remained unrevealed.

The King simply kept walking. He kicked the farmer out of his way with a booted foot—and then Richard Lionheart continued on along his way, having hardly broken his stride.

Jim let the air out of his lungs and didn't say a word.

Now he knew the truth.

The crowd followed their King, and Jim let himself be carried along—shoved, pushed, pulled, tumbled along.

Jim thought as he bobbled on the human tide—he thought that all of the gentry were alike, from the King on down. All of them put their foot on the working man. The King he had worshipped from afar was no better than the silent knight who had tormented him with his devil horse.

In the end, all the gentry wanted was somebody to clean up their muck.

Jim was elbowed, kicked, and tossed as the crowd carried him down the great lawn, but in the midst of the mob he was utterly alone. His wife was long dead, his children grown and gone who knows where, his life meant nothing, and all that lived in his heart was hate.

He was shoved from behind, he squeezed through the ranks of the already assembled crowd, he looked around a pike-man and saw the King take his seat upon his golden throne.

Jim felt choked by hatred, he felt bile like poison in his throat, he jerked his head away from the sight of the King—and so he was he first man to notice the approach of Sir Thomas the Silent.

Jim looked down and spat on someone's shoe. There was no more happiness for him, no more thoughts of glorious revenge. All he had left was his hatred. He was a proud man who had lived a lifetime of servitude. He had endured a thousand slights, bowed and scraped and fetched and carried for the wellborn, but now he had nothing left to lose.

He had been humiliated for the last time.

He looked over at Sir Thomas, riding confidently on his black devil horse, and he said through clenched teeth, "I will bring you down, even if it costs me my life."

No one heard Jim, for all were cheering their glorious King.

Chapter 68

THE ASSESSOR'S THOUGHTS, CONTINUED

Sandra's moans were getting louder all the time.

Arthur reasoned that she must be laboriously pushing the thick gagging towel forward with her tongue—so as then to work on it with her teeth. She must be gradually cutting through it, though it had to be hard slow work. Arthur wasn't worried, for it was almost noon anyway and it wouldn't matter now if she did cut through the gag and scream. He was going to go in and free her in a few minutes anyway—it would be a nice touch of verisimilitude if the "rescue" appeared to be brought on by her screams.

The first fanfare sounded outside, drowning out Sandra's moans. A moment later the second fanfare announced the King. It was almost time. Every knight of the court must be out there now, thought Arthur. Thomas will be there, watching for the King, nervous, worried by the note, waiting for my wife to appear—and then I'll release Sandra and bring her out and she'll tell everyone that her lady has been kidnapped. Thomas will make the connection—he'll race off to Stonehenge—he'll race to his death.

Every time Arthur thought of his plot he had to smile. It was beautiful—and what made it even more beautiful was the fact that he would eliminate all the witnesses afterward—all of them, that is, except Elaine.

He would allow her to live, as his slave.

Arthur stood up on his chair and peered through his peephole. Sandra was moaning almost constantly now, chewing violently at the towel in her mouth. She had managed to force some play in her bonds as well—she was thrashing and straining to get free. Arthur realized that even without his help, she would probably break free on her own within the hour.

Arthur sat down again. He wouldn't free her yet. Something about her disturbed him.

I find it amazing, the Assessor thought, that she has never ceased to struggle for all these many hours. She's bound and naked, and yet she fights—indeed, as I have noticed, in time she would even succeed in freeing herself. What gives her such strength to struggle? Is it love that drives her? Does she love her mistress? Of course—that's the answer. I'm foolish even to raise the question. *Everyone* loves Elaine—and anyway Sandra made it plain enough when she snuggled in my wife's arms at the ball.

Such a brave loyal girl!

I wonder what Sandra would think if she knew that I have been listening to her torture for hours, if she knew that to me she is just a catspaw, another tool in the plot that will break her lady.

Perhaps she would think of me as the Devil himself . . .

Here the Assessor's thoughts suddenly slued off into confusion. It was not that he feared blasphemy—he willingly worked the fields of evil—it was just that the naked girl next door and the Devil's name brought forth an unavoidable association. He thought of Satan's legendary potency—he thought of Sandra's spread nakedness that offered all her woman's secrets, he thought of the marks on her soft bottom, he thought that he could go in and mount her, helpless as she was, and he *wanted* to feel that evil desire—but he felt nothing, no rising in his loins, he could not even force a tremor of desire, and it seemed that he failed even at evil—he tried to placate his mind with the image of Sir Thomas charging across the empty Salisbury plain, charging through the single entrance of Stonehenge to his doom—he imagined the bold knight being cut down by the Vulture and his henchmen—he pictured the Vulture cutting out Thomas's heart while Elaine watched—he piled visions of blood upon his impotence, but he covered it not, and he was shaking when Sandra cut through the last strip of towel.

Sandra spat out the remnants of her gag and took a mighty breath.

Chapter 69

RAINBOW

The pike-man in front of Jim sensed the armed knight behind him. The soldier jerked around in alarm—but then he froze when he realized exactly which knight it was. He was not about to challenge Sir Thomas the Silent on his own.

The pike-man turning his back was Jim's opportunity—and he seized it with an exultant recklessness. He raced past the distracted soldier and skidded to a stop on the wet grass in front of Saladin. The black Arabian stopped abruptly, hooves cutting into the turf as Jim stretched his arms wide like Christ on the cross and screamed, "Devil!"

This disturbance was more to the pike-man's liking. He grabbed one of Jim's outstretched arms—a fellow soldier grabbed the other arm.

Jim didn't care. His body meant nothing. All he had left was hate, and that he spewed out through his open mouth.

"Blasphemer! Infidel! Warlock!" he screamed, a howl from the pit of his soul, and his wild charges silenced even the cheers for the King.

Heads turned toward the disturbance, and Jim soaked up the attention of a thousand pairs of eyes. At last they see me, he thought, and he howled, "I know what the King does not!"

The crowd went completely silent now. Jim could feel the King's gaze on his back. The old ostler put everything he had into one last cry.

"THIS BLACK DEVIL HORSE IS NAMED SALADIN!"

This was all too much for the first pike-man. He had no love for Sir Thomas, but no groom should be allowed to blasphemously insult a knight. He clubbed Jim over the head with the staff of his pike. The old man slumped under the blow. No more the great accuser, he was once again the beaten old ostler. The two pike-men tossed his limp body back into the crowd.

Sir Thomas, who had waited patiently for the obstruction to be cleared, now touched heels lightly to Saladin, and the black horse proceeded toward the throne at a deliberate walk.

Everyone watched the approach.

Roland was turned all the way around on his seat. He looked up the slope at the black horse silhouetted against the gray sky, for it was still raining over the city to the north. The Duke felt the sun behind him trying to break through—there was fresh light on the face of this knight, he seemed to be familiar, some connection to Elaine from years ago—and then Roland suddenly remembered Martin's report of an English knight on a black horse, waiting—this had to be the same one—who was he?—coming closer, fresh sun on his face, terrible killing face and Roland had to look away, he turned his head just a few degrees, and then he saw that the sun had not just illuminated a face, it had caught the distant raindrops as well, and in the falling rain, the white light broke softly into colors.

Roland let his eyes trace the ethereal beauty of the rainbow from one side to the other.

Then he realized that the Godlike arch made a perfect frame for the black horse and his rider.

Roland caught his breath and said nothing, but others whispered according to their taste, "A rainbow of God," or "Saladin the infidel," or simply "Devil," or simply "Beautiful"—all were affected by the sky's miracle—all, that is, except for ten men who were used to even more spectacular phenomena in their home skies.

These ten had grown up with the aurora borealis—they were ten men of the north, dressed in monk's cassocks. They kept those hooded cassocks pulled up over their heads, so that their lack of the proper tonsure would not give them away—they moved a little uncomfortably inside their unfamiliar clothes, because the bloodstains were getting stiff. This morning these cassocks had been worn by ten prayerful monks—until Ivar and his men had killed them.

Ivar, Sigurd, Fridrikson, and seven others had changed into the clothes of their victims and come to London to seek Elaine. The other forty crew members had been instructed to sail the ship down the coast to a rendezvous point ten miles south of the mouth of the Thames.

Ivar had hoped to return to his ship tonight with the most beautiful woman in the world—but as Sigurd had told him, as he could see for himself, she was not here.

"The knight on the black horse is named Thomas," Sigurd said. He is the one who goes to see her on Wednesdays."

"He looks like someone worth killing," Ivar observed. "Perhaps his actions will give us a clue as to the whereabouts of Elaine the Fair."

Chapter 70

BIRDCALLS

Brian had fought—and survived—for too many years not to notice when someone was coming to kill him. He realized he was the target the moment the ostler threw himself in front of the black horse—and the rider paid no attention. The rider looked only at *him*. Brian had seen that look before—and even with a mind dulled by drink and vice, he remembered the face.

A grin creased the brutal one's countenance.

He bent down and whispered something to the King, and Richard too smiled with the memory.

Thomas rode Saladin right up to the last table before the King. Roland moved to one side, Anton moved the other way. Saladin stood between the Larrazian nobles, his front legs almost against the bench upon which they sat.

Thomas looked across the table at the grinning faces of the men he had hated for years—and then he focused on the one particular murderer who had killed Suleka.

Thomas spoke with the dignity of grief. "I have come to challenge you, Brian, to a duel to the death."

Thomas was ready for any reply save ridicule.

Brian laughed, and then controlled his mirth long enough to say in a simpering voice, "Tweet, tweet, the little birdie's come." Then he laughed even harder and now the King joined in. Most people looked on in shock, but some sought to curry favor with the King, and they followed his lead and also began to laugh. Brian continued, just as though it were all *so* amusing., "You're not a real knight, little birdie, though I don't suppose you've mentioned that fact to these good people." Brian waved vaguely at the crowd. "You have no right to challenge *me*—though I suppose I could knock you on your bottom again, just like I did in Acre!"

Richard laughed again, and then he said to Brian, "Don't dirty your sword. The soldiers can handle this commoner." Then the King looked out at his pike-men and he cried, "Seize this false knight!"

Thomas's mind raced. Soldiers behind him, closing, crowd on either side hemming him in, the table and then Brian and Richard in front of him and he just had one second to act.

If I take the time to kill Brian I'll be dead myself, he thought, and then I'll never see Elaine again and I won't be able to save her, I can feel the danger she's in, but if I live I can save her and kill Brian later and O God the dirty King is laughing—

The first soldiers were one step away on either side—

Thomas saw Richard's golden sword, and he thought it would be a fine weapon to kill Brian with, and he saw the pikes questing for his head and he saw the soldier's hands reaching for Saladin's bridle—

Thomas kicked Saladin savagely in the ribs at the same time as he yanked back hard on the reins. The horse reared high in the air, out of reach of the soldiers, and when he was up Thomas kicked him savagely again, so Saladin's back feet shuffled forward and then his front hooves came down with terrible force on the King's wooden table.

The iron shod hooves struck with two thousand pounds of weight behind them—they smashed the King's table to smithereens.

Wood chips flew everywhere striking Roland and Anton and Brian and the King—Richard tried to go for his sword but Thomas had swung low with his smashing horse and the brave true knight's hand met Richard's on the golden hilt and Thomas yanked the Sultan's gift right out of Richard's grasp.

Thomas kicked Saladin again, and the horse surged through the wreckage, he forced a path between Richard and Brian, a stray hoof knocked Richard's throne to the ground, the King toppled, space opened up, Brian got his sword out but it was too late, Saladin saw daylight and didn't wait for another kick, he leaped forward and hit the ground galloping as Brian cut the air behind him.

Thomas raised the golden sword high as he rode off, racing away from the rainbow.

Richard Lionheart picked himself up and brushed off the

wood chips that clung to his purple robes.

There was a hushed moment as the crowd stared, trying to assimilate what had happened—the rainbow, Thomas accused by both ostler and Brian, the black horse's smashing hooves, Thomas stealing the King's sword—what vengeance would the King call for now?

All eyes turned to their King.

Richard had not been shaken so badly since the day that he faced Guillaume's lance.

He took a moment to recover before speaking.

He waited too long.

The scream came before his words—it was a feminine scream of such high pitched horror that it seemed to enter both ears at once and reverberate in the head.

All turned toward the sound, toward the Palace of Bermondsey.

Richard lost his audience.

The screaming didn't stop.

Chapter 71

SANDRA'S SCREAMS

Sandra had hours and hours of dammed up screams inside her, so when she finally spat the gag out, she was ready to make up for lost time. She howled like the proverbial banshee. She screamed out her own pain and fear and rage, she screamed for her lady, she screamed for Anton to come to her, but mostly she screamed just because she could.

She was hysterical and she knew it and she didn't care. She just screamed, and when she saw the man with the knife come in she just screamed louder, she thought it was her attacker again and she screamed just so someone would hear her before she died.

He cut her bonds, and then she realized it was Arthur, but he was no friend, and not her lady's husband anymore, and she got up as soon as she was free and ran out the door, screaming.

Arthur saw the red V on her bottom as she ran away. He cursed—maybe no one could make the connection but still he'd rather not have that mark seen just now—he pulled a sheet off Elaine's bed and raced after Sandra.

Sandra never gave a thought to her own nakedness, all she knew was that now she could scream and now she could run, she did both, she knew her lover was outside somewhere, she kept screaming, Arthur behind her trying to wrap her up— No!—she would not be imprisoned again, she howled and ran away from him, out the door, down the walk, past the guards and through the main gate, people down there, the King, Anton there somewhere, she couldn't see—

She screamed.

Chapter 72

SANDRA'S TESTIMONY

The fat man, carrying a sheet, chased the pretty nude girl.

It would have been a quite comical sight except for the fact that the girl was screaming.

The howling sound had been too tormented for Anton to make an identification—but as soon as he saw the running girl he recognized his love.

"It's Sandra!" he said to Roland, and then he ran up to greet her.

Sandra ran toward him, mouth open, wild eyes unseeing, breasts bouncing, her dark feminine delta unhidden.

Anton stopped and braced himself and let Sandra run right into his arms.

Arthur pulled up short.

Sandra squirmed and struggled and screamed, but Anton just held her firmly and spoke to her in a deep low voice, the comforting low voice of a father calming a little girl, he said, "Sandra, it's all right, Sandra, my love, I have you now, it's all right Sandra . . ."

Finally the screams faded into gasping whispers. Sandra's eyes cleared, and then she recognized Anton and wrapped her arms around him and hugged him tight.

Arthur said to Anton (but loud enough so that most everyone could hear), "I see you know my wife's lady in waiting—I just found her tied to my wife's bed—and my wife, dear Elaine, is gone!"

Anton tried not to let the shock and fear show on his face. He knew now that Roland (who had given such peculiar orders this morning) had sensed some such calamity. To cover his emotions, and to show that he had no interest in Elaine, Anton said, "The lady should be covered. Please hand me the sheet."

Arthur gladly handed it over. Anton wrapped Sandra up, quite to the Assessor's satisfaction—Anton didn't look around at the girl's backside as he covered her, and now no one could see the V.

Sandra was a soft child now, all swaddled in the sheet— Anton picked her up easily and kissed her and said, "I love you Sandra, it's all right, I'm just going to take you to my lord."

Anton carried Sandra to where Roland was waiting. He sat down on the bench by the shattered table and cuddled the girl on his lap.

The soldiers kept the common people back, but nearly all the court leaned close, straining to hear what had happened to Elaine the Fair.

"What happened, darling?" Anton asked. "Tell me what happened."

Sandra's eyes went wild again for a second, she seemed to see the knife flashing before her again—and then the vision passed—she saw Anton's battered old face, saw his dear lined face, and she remembered looking up at him when he had made her a woman, and now she raised her head and kissed his lips, she felt him, tasted him, he was real, with her, she was safe— but someone else was not safe and her eyes filled with tears.

Sandra's voice was a husky whisper. "They took my lady in the night . . ."

Anton coaxed her through the whole story, while people pressed even closer, straining to hear. Sandra told all that she could remember, save for what had been done to her with the knife, for that she could not tell in front of strangers. She tried to describe the men, but dark and terror had conspired against her eyes, and she could give little.

Sigurd, in his monk's habit, made use of the respect given to a man of the cloth. He successfully pushed his way through the crowd until he was close enough to hear all the useful information that Sandra had to give. On his way in, and on his way out, he noticed that Arthur was standing as though perplexed on the edge of the group surrounding Sandra. He was too far away to hear her whisper—and he was not looking in toward her— rather, he was looking away, looking all around.

Arthur was looking for Thomas, but he could not see him anywhere. It was essential to his plan that Thomas *know* Elaine had been kidnapped—that fact would explain the note—that fact was the trigger that would send him to his death at Stonehenge. Why wasn't he here? Every other knight of the court was here to greet the King, and if that wasn't enough, Thomas had had no way of knowing that Elaine would not be present. Where was he? Arthur had been sure that the note by itself (which did not mention Elaine) would be cryptic enough to keep Thomas around until he had some hard information. Was he crazy enough to have left right away this morning? Then he would only be an hour behind the Vulture's party—then he might have caught them up before they reached Stonehenge—in an open fight, Thomas might have a chance, even at five to one odds.

Thomas might live.

Arthur shivered—he wanted desperately to ask someone if they had seen Thomas about, but it was hardly time for such a question from a worried husband.

He would have to make some grand gesture to show his concern for Elaine—then afterward he might be able to find out where Thomas was.

As Sigurd walked back to rejoin Ivar he looked back over his shoulder once to see that Arthur was still looking everywhere except at Sandra—saw that he was clearly not listening to Sandra's testimony.

"What did you find out?" Ivar asked.

"Elaine has been kidnapped. The girl is her lady in waiting. She doesn't know who did it. The fat man who says he found her—he's the one who was chasing her with the sheet—is Arthur the Assessor, Elaine's husband.

"You remember I told you that the court gossip was that Elaine was seeking a lover. I don't think the husband liked that too much.

"I've noticed—you can see for yourself—that he's paying no attention to what the girl is saying. She's the only lead to his wife's kidnappers and he doesn't care?"

"So what's the answer," Ivar growled softly.

"Arthur arranged the kidnapping himself to punish his wife. He doesn't need to hear the details because he knows them already—and he knows where Elaine is right now."

Sigurd was pleased with his own keen observation and deductive reasoning.

Ivar was pleased too. He smiled—his bloodless lips drew back to expose the yellow teeth of a skull.

All pleasure left Sigurd then—he felt that same horror of the soul that he had felt upon seeing his Chief's shaven head for the first time.

"You have proved your worth again, my friend," Ivar said, and then he patted Sigurd's cheek with a cold hand.

Sigurd wished for a moment that he had kept silent—and then he realized that that would have simply prolonged the quest. This way we'll get Elaine soon, he thought, and then there will be an ending, and I will be able to return to my family.

Ivar dispatched two men to move their closed wagon over near the path to the main gate. When it was in position he turned to the seven remaining champions. "Our target is the fat man, Arthur. He's not a fighting man. Sooner or later he'll head back toward the palace. We'll take him once he gets near the wagon. Should not such a distraught husband seek solace in prayer?"

Chapter 73

CONCEALED SWORDS

Sigurd was the only one present who suspected Arthur. No one else had noticed his disinterest in Sandra's testimony, for the other nobles (save only King Richard and Brian, who were still nursing their injured dignity) were too busy straining to get close to her. Finally it became apparent that Sandra had told all she could. The knights began to disperse.

These brave knights had serious faces, but in their hearts they were overjoyed. Elaine the Fair kidnapped! It was too good to be true! Every brave knight thanked his lucky stars for this opportunity—every brave knight saw himself gloriously rescuing their lady of dreams. She had dismissed her suitors at the ball—but she would certainly welcome her savior with open arms . . .

On a more hidden level, there was also a great sense of relief. Under normal circumstances the knights would have been obliged to avenge the insult to their King—they would have had to go after the deadly Thomas. Now the chivalrous duty to save a damsel in distress took precedence—and every wise knight was glad. Chasing three bestial kidnappers seemed a picnic compared to the first alternative.

The knights had motivation enough, but then Arthur found a way to encourage them even more. He picked up an empty flagon and climbed on top of an unbroken table. He cried, "Knights of the court of King Richard Lionheart!" Everyone looked up at the sound of the big man's booming voice. "I implore you to save my wife—and the brave man who brings her back unharmed will be richly rewarded." He raised the empty flagon high over his head. "I will fill this flagon to the brim with gold, and I will present it to the man who returns Elaine to me."

There were answering cries of "Hear, hear!" and We'll slay the dastardly swine!" and "We will save the Fair One," and so on. Arthur saluted the brave knights with his flagon—the knights marched off to mount their horses.

Roland watched them go.

His men looked at him expectantly. Sandra lay quiet in Anton's arms.

Roland spoke. "Return to your quarters. Do *nothing* until I give you further orders." The Duke looked hard at each man in turn, until finally he met Anton's eyes. "Anton, take Sandra to my room. Stay with her until I return, and let no one else enter. Talk to her. She needs comforting."

Anton understood what Roland hadn't said. He also thought that Sandra was holding something back. "Yes, Your Grace," Anton said.

"I must see King Richard now," The Duke said.

Roland headed toward the monarch whose celebratory homecoming had lost all its thunder—whose sword had been stolen—who had been upstaged by a woman. Richard surely needed an admiring friend now—and Roland was ready to serve.

As the Duke walked toward the King, so Arthur, having made his grand gesture, felt comfortable enough to ask a few discreet questions. He spoke to a young pike-man, and the soldier told the Assessor all about Thomas's exploits.

Arthur thanked the young man, and walked slowly back toward the palace, considering this latest bit of bad news. Well, it wasn't all bad—at least Thomas had not raced off to Stonehenge prematurely. But now he had ridden off to God knows where—would he learn of Elaine's kidnapping? Would he understand the significance of the note? Would the foolish act of assaulting his King somehow save Thomas from death?

The Assessor's path crossed that of the Larrazian knights who were returning to Lady Smythe's mansion. They looked curiously at the rather depressed looking fat man. They wondered how Elaine the Fair could ever have loved such an unprepossessing character.

Arthur, with his head down, barely noticed the foreign knights. He was beginning to think that the whole scheme was too elaborate. He could have had Thomas killed in many other easier ways—but then he realized that he had *wanted* an elaborate plot, he had *wanted* to feel his fingers on all the strings—

mostly he had wanted his wife to *see* her lover die.

Perhaps all is not lost, Arthur thought. The news of Elaine's kidnapping will spread like wildfire all though the countryside. Thomas will certainly hear of it today—and then he will wonder where they have taken her—yes, then he'll understand the note, a ransom note really—he'll know it's a trap, his life for hers, but he's in love, O yes he'll pay . . .

Arthur smiled, imagining—he plunged his right hand into the deep pocket of his robe and fondled the playing cards there, he blindly ran his finger over the knave's throat—and so, distracted by thoughts of murder, he let the "monks" get awfully close before he noticed the danger.

Somehow they were in front of him, around him, behind him—what did they want? They couldn't try anything here, he was less than thirty yards from the guards at the main gate, fifty yards behind were at least a hundred of the King's soldiers, all he had to do was yell, these were false monks surely, closing in on him tighter, he was imprisoned, and then the leader spoke, he said, "Come with us," and Arthur looked into the face of death, looked at empty yellow eyes set deep into the sockets of a skull, looked at yellow teeth in a black hole of a mouth, and he felt the prick of the concealed swords of the other monks as they nudged him through their cassocks, and he knew to yell was to die and he shook all over with fear, his whole body trembling, and yet he could not give in totally, he never surrendered totally to the bullies anymore, he bowed in fearful submission and used that motion to cover a sleight of hand that was faster than the eye could see, he transferred his deck of cards from hand to hand and thence up his sleeve, he clamped the deck in his sweaty left armpit, cards had always been his weapon and they were his secret now, sharp edged cards—he would find a use for them.

One of the monks plucked the knife from Arthur's belt—his only conventional weapon—and felt over his now empty pocket.

Then, head bowed, Arthur allowed himself to be led to their wagon. He climbed in, urged on by more swordpricks, and then they closed the cloth flap behind him and he was in a dark cell with his captors—a moving cell, shortly, for the leader gave some quick orders in a foreign language to his cassock clad driver.

The wagon creaked slowly past King Richard's soldiers. No one questioned the "churchman" who held the reins. That driver, following Ivar's orders, guided his team of horses toward the forest.

They needed a quiet place where they could torture the Assessor undisturbed.

Chapter 74

THE DEAL

The Duke of Larraz bowed low to the King of the English.

The King acknowledged the Duke with a curt nod.

Roland spoke in the honeyed tones of a seducer. "Your Majesty," he said, "I have heard of the French King's criminal thefts of your Continental lands. Though Your Majesty hardly needs the help of my small duchy, nonetheless we would like to do all we can to assist you in regaining what is rightfully yours."

At first it was hard for Richard to think of France, because the memory of the assault was so fresh. That false knight had stolen his sword! And then afterward he had to look upon the defection of his own court, of his own knights! He had seen his men thrill at the prospect of rescuing Elaine the Fair—he had silently cursed as he realized that even his monarchial power could not stop them. Why did they place such value on feminine beauty? And what was that beauty, anyway? He could never see it. He despised love songs with their paeans to womanly form. He was a poet himself, but he composed only poems of war. There was beauty! Men, melded into a common cause by one strong leader—there was the true stirring of the blood! The only woman he loved was his mother.

Richard thought of Eleanor, in her seventy second year—she was still sharp and active—her frequent letters were full of advice for her favorite son. He missed her—at least now he could finally bring hr back from her exile in Aquitaine—but what if her castle was already cut off by Philip's rapacious forces! What might Philip (he was the son of Louis VII and his third wife, Adela of Champagne) do to avenge himself on the woman who had deserted his father?

Richard felt a hot rage sweep over him. It was time to bring France to its knees, time to force Philip into the vassal role in which he belonged—it was time to bring his mother home.

And so his reasoning circled round to the Duke's proposition, and the King asked, "What sort of help do you have in mind?"

"I must confess, Your Majesty, that we in Larraz have profited handsomely from our trade with the Crusaders. We wish to take some of the gold that we have amassed—let us say enough to fully outfit an expeditionary force—and place it in your hands. It will be our gift to the bravest of Christ's soldiers."

Even Richard knew this was too much. He didn't like implied bargains, hints—he wanted the deal plain on the table.

"What do you want in return for this *gift?*"

"If I may beg your indulgence, Your Majesty, I must tell you a long story . . ."

Roland talked of Elaine the Fair. He told the King that she had been carried off at a young age by Arthur, who had taken advantage of her—he explained how Arthur had lied to Richard's father, Henry II, about his "marriage"—he remarked that it was obvious that Arthur had never confessed his sins to the priests of the land—he had never made amends to the lady by sanctifying their union, and therefore he had no true claim on her—he had offended God—perhaps God was angry that money raised by this immoral man had been used for His cause . . .

Roland skillfully slanted the story so that Arthur was at fault at every turn—and the last part was particularly important, because it gave Richard someone else to blame for his own failure in the Holy Land—Roland thought, quite rightly, that Richard would love having such a handy scapegoat.

Richard *was* quite pleased by the story. The King had never liked Arthur anyway, because it seemed to him that the Assessor never showed proper respect—indeed, yesterday the man had taken an *hour* to respond to the royal summons.

Yet still Roland had not properly answered the King's question. Annoyed once again, Richard snapped, "But what do *you* want?"

"I want to marry the Countess of Anjou, Elaine the Fair.

"I made this appointment with you yesterday, Your Majesty, thinking that we might conclude this business today—yet the Devil has had his say, and the beautiful lady I love has been kidnapped. I would truly be in despair, did I not have faith in the bravery of the English knights. I am sure she will be rescued soon—perhaps my men will be able to assist.

"Then, when she has been safely returned, I ask this boon of you, Your Majesty. I ask that she be allowed to make her confession to your Archbishop. I ask that he grant her freedom, so that I may take her with me to Larraz, and make her my wife.

"It may be, Your Majesty, that your Chancellor of the Exchequer will serve you more ably once he is no longer burdened with the sin of false marriage—for my part, I wish only the happiness of love, and the opportunity to serve you, Your Majesty."

Roland bowed nearly to the ground.

Brian, standing by his master as always, looked down at the foreign Duke with disgust. What fool could care so much for a woman?

Richard Lionheart was grinning. It was quite an amusing situation for him. He had been looking for a way to humiliate Arthur anyway—he wanted to cut that insolent fop down to size. Now he had the perfect weapon, handed to him on the proverbial silver platter. To that one could add the favor of the Church. The Archbishop would adore exposing immorality in high places, for then he could demonstrate that God was prepared to smite all, whatever their station in life—not to mention that he would practically trip over his ecclesiastical robes in his eagerness to hear Elaine's confession.

Finally there was the promised gold in such quantity as to finance an expeditionary force—and all together Roland's proposal was the kind of great good fortune a Christian King deserved.

(Richard never concerned himself about Elaine's feelings. For all he knew she still loved Arthur and did not want to go with the Duke—but that was not significant. She would do as she was told. To Richard, she was the least important part of the deal.)

The King saw the deal as vastly favorable to himself—yet it wasn't enough. Roland had planned to give him this much—and so there was no real satisfaction for the King. He needed to force some further concession out of Roland—only such an exercise in power could help to alleviate the pain of his recent humiliation.

Richard thought of the black devil horse named Saladin (the very name a sickening reminder of failure) rearing above him—for a moment he had thought the hooves were going to come down on his head. Then the table had been smashed, he had gone for his golden sword—and he had felt the treasonous varlet's hand against his, struggling to snatch that very weapon! Richard had always been frightened that some man, not recognizing his royal stature, might slay him like an ordinary mortal. It was that fear that loosened his grip—better to let the false knight have his sword rather than risk death. So the thief had ridden off with his prize—but Richard Lionheart had been spared, through God's intervention.

God had saved his life, and given the Duke of Larraz into his hands as the perfect tool. Richard knew what he would do now.

"You are right to have faith in my bold knights," Richard said. "I am certain that they will bring your lady back unharmed."

When Roland heard the Lionheart use the possessive pronoun that way about Elaine, his heart fairly leaped for joy—and yet it was a joy that was still half blocked by his terrible fears for the Countess. He smiled a crooked smile, with half his face pulled taut. He bent one knee as if to run—and he planted the other leg solidly against the ground, as though to show he was not going anywhere.

The Duke, so poised and contained all his life, was desperate, needy, vulnerable now. His weakness showed in his eyes.

Richard took advantage.

"Your gift for our coming French expedition is likewise most welcome," the King said. Now it was he who had adopted a silky tone." I thank you with all my heart, and my people thank you. Yet now I must consider the feelings of these loyal subjects. While I am sure that you would be a fine husband for Elaine the Fair, and while it is clear from your story that Arthur has no claim on her, still we must not forget that this lady is much loved in my country. I could not allow her to leave with a foreigner, even one so illustrious as yourself, unless I knew that my people were convinced of your merit.

"You must pass a test."

Roland nodded humbly. He had counted over a hundred English knights at the celebration today. Even if he and his men could find Elaine without their help, his small band could never hope to fight past such an army. The deal had to go through!

Richard looked into the Duke's worried eyes. The King saw that his inferior was fully in his hands.

Now the King spoke in the flat hard tones of a commander

who expects to be obeyed. "You saw the man who assaulted Brian and myself. He stole the golden sword given me as a gift of respect by the infidel Sultan Saladin. I think you understand that the gift of an enemy can be even more precious than the gift of a friend.

"I want that sword back. I want that thief punished. He poses as a knight, and uses the name 'Thomas'—really he was Sir Thomas's squire in the Holy Land. After his master's death, he went mad—stole his master's equipment and name—wrote up fake tapestries, used my name falsely to ingratiate himself in my brother's court—yes I heard reports of this "Sir Thomas" even in my exile, and I learned the rest of the story last night— I've heard that the imposter has quite a reputation now, and perhaps it is deserved. He is a crazed thief who dares to attack his own King—but as my countrymen know, and as I have learned this morning, he is a most dangerous fighting man.

"You must kill him. You must kill this "Sir Thomas", and bring back my golden sword. That is the mission I give you. Complete it with honor, and you will have proved your worth in my eyes, and in the eyes of my subjects. Then you may have your bride, with my blessing."

Roland looked up at the King, but all he could see was the black horse and rider, and over them both the pale and beautiful arch of the rainbow.

He had thought the rider looked familiar—but that must have been due to the many reports he too had received about the mysterious and powerful "Sir Thomas". Certainly he had never seen the man before. He's not a true knight, Roland thought. He attacked his King. He stole. He deserves to die—I won't think of that rainbow—it's Nature's sign, not God's—we can rescue Elaine from the kidnappers, but we can't fight past Richard's army—only this false knight's death stands between me and the secure possession of Elaine—O Elaine, Elaine, Elaine the Fair— better for one false knight to die rather than have many fall in a hopeless war—Elaine, I will do anything for you . . .

To the King he said, "He will die. When next I see you, I will have your golden sword in my hands."

The Duke of Larraz bowed to the King of England, who returned his gesture.

The conditions of the deal were now complete and agreed upon—there was nothing more to say.

Roland turned and walked away at a measured pace. He

blocked the image of the rainbow. He wondered only what Sandra had told Anton—he hoped that it would be something that would help him find Elaine the Fair.

Chapter 75

TORTURE

The deck of cards was uncomfortable in Arthur's armpit, for the sharp edges cut into his skin. Arthur breathed in the fetid air of the dark closed wagon—he smelled the bodies of men who had not bathed for a week, and through the reek his nostrils detected the fading odor of blood. The Assessor poured sweat—yet he took a grim comfort in the fact that his cards would not warp, even though soaked in his perspiration. He had his cards made to order from the same specially treated paper that he used for the exchequer's censuses. This was tough, all-weather material—he could pour a river of sweat over those cards and their square corners would remain sharp.

He had given his special gold sovereign to the vagrant, but Arthur thought that as long as he still had his cards, he still had his luck.

Ivar the Heartless might not have agreed.

They were almost to the forest before they heard the sound of hounds baying. Ivar guessed correctly that the dogs had been put on the scent of Elaine (helpful knights had plundered her room to find the silk she wore next to her body) and thus there was no specific danger—but he was concerned that the dogs or their handlers might come across them accidentally. He decided that he would have to move quickly to extract the needed information.

Ivar gave some orders, and the driver aimed his horses at the first gap in the forest he saw. He lashed the horses onward until they could go no more. Ivar opened the rear flap of the wagon and looked out. They were perhaps twenty yards into the woods, more or less concealed—it would have to do.

The fat man would not hold out long.

Ivar posted two lookouts to watch at the edge of the forest.

With the flap open there was enough light to see Arthur's terrified face. Ivar stroked the Assessor's thinning hair, as though to comfort him, and then suddenly shoved a torn cloth into his mouth with his other hand. Earlier this day, Ivar had used this cloth to clean his sword after killing two monks—now he tied the bloodstained gag tight behind Arthur's head.

Arthur tasted the blood in his mouth and he tried to scream, but just like Sandra this morning, the only sound he could make was the faint mewling cry of a helpless kitten.

Perhaps it was poetic justice—but Arthur didn't see it that way—Arthur didn't think of Sandra's suffering—only his own terror mattered.

Through all his terror he kept the deck of cards clamped tight in his sweaty armpit.

"Lay him on his back on the floor," Ivar commanded in his own language, "And strip off his leggings."

Two monks slammed Arthur down—then they knelt on his arms to immobilize him, and flipped up his robes. Then they yanked his leggings to his knees—Ivar pulled them off the rest of the way himself.

Arthur's robes were folded up over his belt—below that he was naked. His fat belly puffed up into the air and shook with his fearful breathing—his little manhood contracted and tried to hide, but there was no escape. Ivar sought it out with the tip of his drawn sword—he lifted the male triumvirate on the flat of the blade—the point of the sword pricked Arthur on that tender spot that lies halfway between procreation and elimination.

Arthur stopped breathing.

Ivar held the sword steady and said, "The gag comes out when you're ready to talk."

Arthur had no idea what he was supposed to talk about—he looked up at these strange foreign faces—tried not to breathe—who were they?—what did they want?—*had* to breathe—and then his body expanded with the indrawn breath and the sword pricked worse and all that made him a man trembled on the murderous steel blade.

"Elaine the Fair," said Ivar.

The tax collector stared at his tormentor in disbelief.

"Elaine the Fair," Ivar said again. "Your *wife*." With the last word he pushed his sword forward and the point bit into

Arthur's skin—a small cut really, but terrifyingly placed—
Arthur could feel a rivulet of blood running down between his
buttocks—he was trying to comprehend this madness—

"Where is she?" Ivar snarled, and that question sent Arthur
over the edge—they were mad, the world was mad, they all
wanted her! Only her! My wife! Elaine the Fair! His eyes rolled
in his head, foam escaped his gag and rolled down his cheeks—
Ivar made a gesture and a huge Viking named Thorson tore off
Arthur's gag—and then it was the Vikings' turn to stare in
amazement.

Arthur was laughing. It was a mad, hysterical, somehow defiant cackle. Ivar stood it for a second, and then he yanked his
sword back, spun it in an arc, and drove the point an inch deep
into Arthur's soft belly.

Blood spurted out—Arthur screamed—but then Thorson
slammed a meaty hand down over his mouth, and the scream
shut off like a lifted teakettle.

Ivar kept the point of his sword buried in the Englishman's
body. The Chief of Champions was pleased to see the defiance
ebb from his victim's eyes. There was only pain now, and terror.

Ivar turned the sword, just a touch, and then he spoke. "I see
you care nothing for your manhood—indeed, you would hardly
miss it. But your stomach now, that is a different matter. That
is the part you care about, for I can see you are a man who loves
to eat . . ." Ivar's voice trailed off, and he looked out the back of
the wagon—not seeing anything really, his yellow eyes were
unfocused, he seemed to be recalling some pleasant memory—
then he smiled, showing his yellow teeth, and he began to remi-
nisce: "I used to know a vain, beautiful woman—she was so
proud of her lovely breasts—large, they were, and firm—they
stood straight out from her body and her nipples tilted up—she
thought all who saw her breasts would love her." Ivar turned
back and looked at Arthur. "I tied rough ropes around that
woman's breasts—I attached the rope to a pulley—the ropes cut
into her—I turned the winch—she was lifted off her feet by the
ropes around her proud bosom—a bosom whose shape was being
destroyed by her own weight, destroyed by every turn of the
wheel, every *inch* that she was lifted off the ground." On the
word 'inch' Ivar leaned even harder on the sword, Arthur felt it
cutting into him, entering him, his eyes were bursting from
their sockets trying to tell—

Ivar unbalanced his weight, so that he looked as though he

were about to fall—as though the only support he could lean on was the sword projecting from Arthur's belly—now, with matters arranged to his liking, the Chief of Champions continued. "When that woman's breasts were destroyed, so was she. I killed her soon afterward. When your stomach is pierced, you too will be finished, yet death will not come easily. You will be ripped in half with pain, and you will cry for your death long before it comes.

"I can not hold this position long—in another moment my weight must drive my sword into your guts.

"Tell me where she is."

Thorson jerked his hand from Arthur's mouth, Ivar started to lean and Arthur screamed, "STONEHENGE! She's at Stonehenge!" and he would have screamed it a third time had not Thorson covered his mouth again.

Ivar looked at Sigurd.

Sigurd spoke in Norwegian. "It's an old temple, somewhere in the middle of the country. Debby has told me of it, but I don't know exactly where it is."

Ivar pulled the sword out of Arthur's flesh and smiled down at him. "You'll take us there," the Chief said.

Arthur, whitefaced with pain, weak with relief and terror, nodded his head.

Ivar instructed Thorson to uncover Arthur's mouth. Then Ivar brought his sword back until the point just touched the edge of Arthur's bleeding wound. "You won't scream," Ivar said softly, "Because we have what we need. We can get another guide if we need one—I won't hesitate to kill you right now if you raise your voice." The sword turned and pricked at the fluttering skin of Arthur's belly. "It is, of course, more convenient to keep you alive, since we have you already—so simply answer a few more questions, guide us well, and we will let you go once we have Elaine.

"Some of my comrades will join us by ship. They would prefer a deserted beach. What place on the coast is closest to this Stonehenge?"

The language was Germanic and the faces were fair but the ship was the final clue. Northmen! Now everything began to make sense. The Northmen were famous for their slave raids—and this was clearly the same, if with only one objective—Elaine's fame had evidently spread to quite distant shores—this crazed deadly leader had come to steal the most beautiful woman in the world.

Well, so be it, Arthur thought, as long as I can escape before he gets to her. I know he'll kill me then, promise or no promise, because after that I am no longer useful. For now I must be submissive, and helpful, and truthful. We won't get there today—I'll plan my escape for tonight.

So Arthur thought with the clear part of his mind—he didn't let that calculation show, he showed Ivar an agony he didn't have to fake, and he groaned, "Due south of Stonehenge there is a rough beach just past the Isle of Wight, and before the town of St. Lyons. Your men could land there undisturbed."

"I know the area," Ivar said. "How far is Stonehenge from this beach?"

Arthur gave a sob of pain—through dry lips he whispered, "A man on a fast horse might do it in a day—two days by coach."

Ivar took his sword away, cleaned it and sheathed it. "You'll be a good guide, my fine fat fellow," he said.

Then Ivar took one of his champions aside. He told that young man to take one of the six horses they had pulling the wagon. He ordered the youth to ride the horse to their rendezvous point, and make contact with the ship. He should then instruct the crew to sail down the coast to the beach Arthur had described just past the Isle of Wight. Ivar said that the ship should make sure to stay well away from shore during daylight—but each night they should come in close and look for a signal fire.

That fire would announce the success of their mission—and the presence of a very special captive.

Chapter 76

ROLAND AND ANTON

Two Larrazian knights were on guard in front of Lady Smythe's house when Roland approached. They greeted their lord, hoping for some call to action—but Roland just walked by them and entered the house without a word. The men weren't even sure he had seen them.

The Duke's gaze was turned inward—he was fighting with the thought that kept intruding into his consciousness—the terrible thought that he had committed himself to an evil act.

Roland tried to defeat that thought with logic: this false knight who calls himself Sir Thomas did attack his King—I saw him steal the King's sword. He is a rebel and a thief—any English knight would have a clear duty to kill him. Why then is it wrong for me? I do a favor for the English King, I remove a violent rebel, and for this well justified action I receive safe conduct for Elaine and my men—and furthermore I save my country from reprisal. How can this be wrong?

There was no logical reason for Roland to be wrong—but still he could not drive away the soul searing sense of evil.

He was haunted by the pale and beautiful image of the rainbow—deep in his heart, unmoved by reason, a voice whispered to him—the voice said, 'The rainbow is God's sign, and the knight who rode in its frame is a great man—do not commit the mortal sin that the King demands of you—do not murder this man.'

Roland did not know that both he and Elaine saw greatness in the man known as Sir Thomas.

All the tormented Duke could do was fight with the voice—the rainbow is Nature's sign, he argued, not God's—Thomas is the villain, not I—and Thomas must fall so that I can save Elaine.

The inner voice whispered back, 'But what of your immortal soul?'

Roland opened the door to his room without knocking—he stepped in and slammed the door behind him with unaccustomed violence, as though the noise without could silence the voice within.

Sandra nearly jumped off Sir Anton's lap when she heard the bang, but her lover's strong arms held her. For a moment she fought his embrace, twisting to see who had entered—and then she recognized the Duke of Larraz. She tried to collect herself— she blushed as she thought of what she had promised Anton— and then she turned back to her lover and buried her face against his chest.

Anton stroked her hair and comforted her. "It's all right, my little dove," he murmured.

Roland noticed that now Sandra was wearing a dress—Anton must have sent one of the men to the palace to get it.

Roland could smile a little as he looked down at the forty year old knight and the seventeen year old girl. It seemed to the Duke that Anton had finally come of age after years of fighting and wandering—there was a settled quality about him now, a calm certainty—he had chosen his bride, chosen the future course of his life—Roland could picture the two of them as part of a future family portrait: father, mother, child. Could Sandra be pregnant already? She had the look even now, long before her body would show the evidence.

The Duke dropped to one knee by the couple, and reached out and took Sandra's hand. She turned her face to him—she looked at his caring, troubled face with her huge frightened eyes.

"Lady Sandra," Roland said. "I hope you have not suffered too much. You may rest assured that you are under my protection now, and no harm will come to you—and those who assaulted you will be punished. We will find them, and we will rescue your lady. Look into my eyes, dear girl, and you will see that I love your lady Elaine with all my heart—look into my eyes, and you will see that all I have said is the truth."

Roland watched as the girl's eyes turned trusting and then filled with tears—he went on, "I promise you that we shall bring Elaine back safely.

"Now I believe that you had something more to tell about the men who attacked you—did you tell Anton?"

Sandra blushed, and said, "Yes," very softly.

"Can you tell me?"

Sandra looked up at Anton. Her lover stroked her hair and said, "It's something we have to show you, Your Grace."

Anton looked down at Sandra—he started to move her, but she resisted at first. "Come darling," Anton said firmly, "You have given your word."

Sandra hesitated for just a second more, and then she allowed Anton to arrange her as he wished. He made her lie across his lap with her bottom up—he took the hem of her skirt with one hand and began to pull it up—the image was that of a naughty wench whose master was about to give her a sound spanking— Roland watched intently as Anton drew the skirt up over Sandra's bare thighs—drew it up further to bare her bottom— and then Roland saw the evil that had been done.

He saw that one cheek of her behind was lovely, plump and round and white—and he saw that the other one was wounded, slashed, angry red around the black lines of the cuts—two deep wide cuts made with a heavy knife—two cuts that joined at one end to make a V—the cuts would heal in time, but they would scar as well—the Duke knew that Sandra would carry that V forever.

V.

Roland stared at the letter for a long time as he turned the pages of his marvelous memory. He remembered thousands of bits of information—he remembered a dishonored English knight—he remembered reports of the killer for hire—he whispered the name: "Vulture."

Sandra shuddered when she heard the name of the carrion bird—she was grateful when Roland reached out and pulled her skirt down himself.

Roland stood up and gestured for Sandra to do the same.

Anton helped her to her feet.

"He's a big man," Roland said, "elegant, but it's a twisted gentility overlaid with violence and cowardice. He's the leader of the group, but he's not acting on his own—he's following someone else's orders. Am I right?"

Sandra remembered everything—the description was uncannily apt, even down to being under orders, for that was what the other man had reminded him of—they were 'only supposed to tie this one up.'

Sandra shuddered again. She said, "Yes, but how do you

know . . .?"

"It doesn't matter. The point is that now we know Elaine's abductor is the Vulture, and knowing that we will be able to find him.

"You have been very brave, Lady Sandra, and very helpful. Now I must ask you to wait outside while I discuss our next move with Anton."

Sandra didn't budge when Anton tried to escort her to the door. There was one thing that she had to know.

"Will you kill him—this Vulture?" she asked, looking hard at the Duke.

Roland gave her a cold little smile. "Of course I will kill him," he said, "unless your man gets to him first."

Sandra accepted that answer. She looked at Anton, and he smiled. Sandra embraced him and kissed his mouth. Then she allowed him to lead her to the door. Anton kissed her once more and ushered her out. He closed the door behind her.

Anton turned and faced the Duke. "Sandra told me something else, Your Grace."

"What is it?"

"The knight—or false knight, perhaps—the one who smashed our table—I told Sandra about that and she told me his name is Sir Thomas"—Anton had the Duke's full attention now—"Sandra also told me that on two occasions Thomas met privately with the Countess—he instructed her in the art of swordsmanship, but he seems to have had other ambitions as well—Sandra said that it was evident that he loved her mistress.

"He seems to have been favored by Elaine for a time. He fought four duels for her favor, and won them all, but then he was unable to win the Countess's love.

"I think he must have been severely disappointed when he lost her to you, Your Grace, especially after fighting in all those duels. I think he may be the one who hired those brutal kidnappers."

"Does Sandra think that?"

"No Milord. That last is my own conjecture."

The long ago report about the arrival of the strange and magnificent knight came into Roland's mind. He remembered the tapestries—'fake tapestries', Richard had said, but Roland believed that the sentiments expressed on them were truth: "protection of the ladies of the English court"—the knight had done just that over the years, regardless of his own personal danger. Thomas was a brave man—indeed, crazy brave, as this noontime's incident had shown—he would not hire other men to do corrupt deeds for him. If he knew about me, Roland thought, he would challenge me in a straightforward fashion. Again Roland remembered Sir Martin's report of the English knight on a black horse waiting outside the forest—Thomas!—I fooled him, Roland thought, I fooled him perhaps too well—he doesn't know that Elaine loves me—if I find him should I challenge him for her hand?—and what then if he kills me, as he probably would—all say he is the best—should I give Elaine over to a renegade—no, I should extend no consideration to an imposter, a common thief—I only have to execute him, I don't have to give him a fighting chance . . .

"Sandra is right," Roland said. "Thomas does love Elaine. He must have followed you on Sunday, but apparently he stayed too far back for you to see him—he lost you in the forest—now I remember also what Sir Gowan told me—Thomas is the one who disputed with him while you were busy with Lady Sandra—and it was Thomas again who was waiting outside the forest for Elaine to emerge.

"All his actions have been done on his own. He does not hire people—in any case, from what I know he has neither money nor friends. No, he simply wants to protect Elaine—he wants to love her. He has noble dreams, whether or not he is a nobleman in fact.

"Someone else hired the Vulture.

"As for Thomas, I feel that he may be a great man—but I have to kill him."

Anton had been completely convinced by the Duke's carefully presented argument, and so those last words came as a brutal shock. He stared at the Duke in amazement. "But why, Milord?"

Roland answered in a painful, self-justifying voice that Anton had never heard before. The brave knight listened to the Duke struggling with his honor, and when Roland had finished explaining the deal, Anton did not hesitate.

"We can fight the Lionheart," he said firmly.

Roland gave the older man a heartfelt smile. He put one hand on Anton's shoulder. "There are too many English knights, my friend. No, I have given my word—and anyway, Thomas is not a true knight, and he's a thief besides."

Anton did not bother to observe that it was obvious that the Duke did not believe this.

Roland continued, "Thomas will cross our path again soon, for we both seek the same lady. When that time comes, I will arrange his death. Until then, I ask that you do not repeat this conversation."

Anton looked at the floor. "I won't say anything, Your Grace."

Roland felt a little better now—he had unburdened himself. He knew now that he would sin—knowingly sin—but he would find Elaine and bring her home . . .

The Duke asked sharply, "Did the men bring all the informants in?"

"Daniel's watching them downstairs."

"Haversham?"

"The pickpocket?"

"Yes."

"He's down there."

"Get him."

A few minutes later Anton pushed the nervous pickpocket into the room. The Duke signalled that he wanted Anton to leave—after the knight closed the door, Roland had a little friendly chat with Mr. Haversham.

When the conversation was over, Mr. Haversham left the room, walking a little unsteadily. He had a bloody nose and a gold sovereign clutched in each fist.

Roland had a name and an address.

Anton came back in.

"I'm going out now," Roland said. "I'll take Daniel with me. We should be back in three hours. When we get back I want every man to have a saddled horse ready to go. Put two days worth of grain in the saddlebags."

"We'll be ready, Your Grace," Anton said.

Roland raced down the stairs, pausing only to collect Daniel, and then the two of them went outside and mounted. In moments they were riding hard for the City of London.

The men saw their leader racing and they knew in their souls and in their fluttering nerves that this time there would be no peaceful solution.

Anton came down and told them they had three hours to get ready.

The men groomed their horses, and checked their weapons.

Anton did the same, while Sandra stayed close by his side.

She wondered why he looked so sad.

Chapter 77

DEBT

Thomas stood under a tree, in the darkest part of the forest, and talked to Saladin. "Why wasn't there any pursuit?" he asked softly.

The unfettered horse did not care to reply. He was searching for fresh green shoots at the base of a tall tree—he reacted with annoyance every time Thomas pulled his big head up and whispered in his ear. "Something happened after I left. What was it? Where was Elaine?"

Saladin answered by flattening both ears and nipping Thomas's arm. The knight jerked away. "Go eat then," he said sullenly.

The stallion flicked his ears forward and returned to his nibbling.

Thomas began to walk around in circles. He felt utterly alone.

The knight had dismissed the confrontation with Brian from his mind. Even the insulting "little birdie" could be forgotten like the name he had cast aside long ago. There was no reason to rush fate. He had gone up against Brian twice now with no result—obviously he was destined to engage in the three tests of classical mythology. The third encounter would be decisive—the third encounter would be fatal, for one of them. Suleka would be avenged soon, or he would die in the attempt—but for now he had to concern himself with the living.

Why wasn't Elaine at the celebration? What stopped the knights from pursuing me?

I need a friend to tell me what happened, Thomas thought, and I have no one. I love Elaine, I fear she is in danger, but I know not where she is. What is the significance of the note—has she been taken to Stonehenge?—or did she deliberately come late to the celebration, so as to make a grand entrance—she could be enjoying dinner with her husband right now—or some evil monster could be preparing her for human sacrifice—STONEHENGE TOMORROW DAWN—I don't know!

Then Thomas realized that there was one thing he did know absolutely—he remembered the feel of Elaine's hand in his, and he remembered her words: "I will be there."

Elaine had given her word, and she would not have come late. The only possible reason for her nonappearance was that she had been taken away by force.

To Stonehenge? The day's dilemma flummoxed him anew. Was she there, or was the note a deception that would lead him into a trap away from where Elaine was really kept?

Would going to Stonehenge get him killed for nothing?

Thomas tightened his hands on the hilts of his two swords.

I need more information, Thomas thought. I need a friend and I don't have one.

Thomas drew the golden sword. He admired the pitiless steel of the blade. He remembered severed heads by a stream in May.

I don't need a friend to get information—all I need is someone who owes me—and indeed there is such a person, a Baroness, in fact.

Her debt is quite substantial. She owes me her life.

Thomas smiled coldly and put his new sword away. For now he simply tucked it inside his belt—the naked blade hung down his thigh. He knew that he would have to get a scabbard soon or it would rust—perhaps that was something else the Baroness could provide.

All problems seem easier once one steps toward the solution—Thomas was in his best mood of the day as he put saddle and bridle back on Saladin.

The sly horse took a last bite of leaves as Thomas mounted—the knight realized that there would be ugly green sludge to clean off the bit tonight, but he could not be angry at the horse. He leaned forward along the stallion's neck, and this time Saladin listened to his master.

"We're going to see Baroness Louisa," Thomas said.

Chapter 78

THOMAS AND LOUISA

Baroness Louisa went into the bedroom of the private house she kept for her city pleasures, leaving her young admirer cooling his heels in the living room. She had told him to wait just a moment—she needed to change her elegant, if rather mud spattered, court dress. First there had been Thomas and his wild horse—then Lady Sandra screaming—people climbing over each other, trying to see—the Baroness, who had been sitting at the next table behind the one that got smashed (it was her table that Arthur eventually climbed on) had found herself in the thick of the tumult—she had been pushed and shoved and muddied—she looked into her full length mirror and assessed the damage.

She was a mess, but a very pretty mess.

Louisa's hair, which had been done up in a fancy coronet, was now half undone. She loosened the rest and brushed it out until her russet locks fell in waves to her shoulders.

She kicked off her shoes—she took off her dress, and the chemise she wore underneath. She looked at the reflection of her nude body with pleasure—and then she thought of the man waiting in the next room, and it took her a moment to recall his name.

Sir Andrew.

Not the right man.

She shook her head hard and her hair fell wildly across her face—she had to brush it out again.

Louisa had married the Baron of Nottingham when he was sixty and she was eighteen. She was twenty-two now. She had borne no children. Her husband spent most of his time at his country estate—Louisa spent most of her time in the city. She had committed adultery several times in the last two years. These affairs had started right after Thomas had rescued her from the Picts.

Louisa knew now that she had wanted Thomas to take her on that day. She had also learned of the reality of death—and that knowledge was so terrible that it washed away the absurd technical conventions of courtly love. She had given herself to the next handsome man who wanted her, and she had enjoyed it—and then there had been others.

This Sir Andrew was to be her new lover. She looked at herself in the mirror, looked at her face, looked into her eyes, and she saw the truth: she saw that she didn't love Andrew—she saw that she didn't even want him. Why had she brought him here?

All of the other knights had gone to chase after Elaine the Fair. I thought it was nice that Andrew didn't go, Louisa thought, nice that he paid court to me rather than racing off after the haughty ice princess—it was flattering, but I stand here knowing in my heart that his reason for failing to join the chase was cowardice rather than love for me. Then too, I could tell (but I wouldn't admit it to myself) that he'd heard about me—others must have told him: 'a little sweet talk and you'll have a lady for less than a whore.'

Louisa began to cry.

She did not brush away her tears—she just stared at her blurred image and let herself go back in time. She remembered laying her head against Thomas's thigh, she could recall the feel of his hand stroking her hair, she had been naked then as she was now, O she had wanted him so much—she put one hand over her breast and dreamed on as tears ran down her face—at first she thought she was still dreaming when she heard Thomas's voice.

Two years ago Thomas had been under a vow of silence. This was reality, this was now—Thomas was in the next room.

Louisa got a towel and dried her face. He would come when I'm a mess, she thought—but then she smiled at herself and put on a robe. She belted it carelessly and opened the door—and there was Sir Andrew, white as a sheet, certain his last hour had come. Opposite him was Sir Thomas, wild as ever, a green leaf stuck in his hair, his hands on the hilts of his two swords. One of those had a naked gleaming blade, and a jewel encrusted golden hilt—the King's sword suits you, Louisa thought.

Thomas had been just about to ask "Where is she?" again, but now he turned and saw Louisa—the Baroness was pleased that his eyes did not fail to notice that her robe was half open—he smiled, and said, "Good day, Baroness."

Louisa replied, "Good day, Sir Thomas," and then she turned to Andrew and said, "You may go now."

Andrew edged toward the door. Thomas said, "Before you go, Sir Andrew, please be kind enough to unbuckle your sword and scabbard and give them to me."

Andrew stopped in his tracks. He looked at Thomas's eyes, and then at his hands—he looked at Louisa, but she didn't give him any help—he looked down, and fumbled at his belt—finally he got the sword and scabbard free, but his hands were trembling so much that he dropped the whole works on the floor.

Thomas took a step toward him—Andrew bolted for the door. He flung it open and took off at a run.

Thomas took Andrew's sword out of its scabbard and replaced it with his golden prize. It fit quite well. He buckled his newly covered armament on to his belt.

Louisa closed the outside door and locked it. She was glad that she had given her servants the day off so that they could pay their respects to the King.

Thomas looked at Louisa and he smiled again. The Baroness could hardly breathe. She leaned back against the door and spread her legs slightly. She felt liquid, heavy in the center of her body. She hardly had the strength to stand. She looked at Thomas's powerful hands resting on the hilts of his swords, she let her eyes roam upward over his chest, she looked at his mouth—he wasn't smiling any more. She looked up at his eyes and it was like stepping out of a warm house into the blast of an icy wind.

His slate gray eyes gave her absolutely nothing. He said, "I must ask a favor of you, Baroness Louisa. Please tell me all that you know of the whereabouts of the Countess of Anjou."

Louisa looked at Thomas—he couldn't be serious—but he was—she felt like she was falling, and then the blessed anger ripped through her body and straightened her spine and gave strength to her arm as she walked right up to Thomas and struck him across the face just as hard as she possibly could.

Thomas's head hardly moved with the slap. He just looked down into her face with those cold eyes, and he paid no attention to the fact that her exertions had opened her robe nearly all the way.

Louisa's rage was hardly assuaged. She began to speak in a low deadly voice that she barely recognized as her own.

"You come here because you think I owe you, but you're polite so you say you must 'ask a favor'. Well you are right! You must ask a favor, because it is you who owes me! I was naked and I needed your caresses—your hands on my body, your mouth on mine—I needed that to make the life you saved worth living—and you denied me.

"So now, yes, I will grant your favor—but there is a price."

Louisa shrugged off her robe with an angry gesture. She kicked it away and stood naked before Sir Thomas.

"I can not force your love—that may come or it may not—but I must have your caress, and I must have your kiss. Only then will I tell you what you want to know."

The slate of his eyes was unbroken, but still there was sadness showing, just as she had seen long ago. He cupped her face with his big rough hands, and then he caressed her long russet locks. He pulled her head back with one hand in her hair—his other hand grasped her full left breast and squeezed it and she spread her legs to keep from falling and then his body was against her and he was kissing her open mouth.

He was tight against her now, he moved his hand so that her breasts could press against his chest, her hips felt the cold hardness of his swords, her loins pressed against the hot hardness of his manhood, his right hand was behind her now, she felt his strong hand gripping her soft bottom, his fingers sinking into her flesh, she hoped he would bruise her, she wanted his mark, all of her body was his to do with as he would—and so it was a terrible shock when he broke the kiss and held her away from him with that strong left hand in her hair.

She stared up at him in disbelief—she had felt how much he wanted her—but his eyes seemed even colder now and he said, "I have fulfilled my part of the bargain. Tell me what you know."

Louisa said nothing. Thomas took the hard nipple of her left breast between his thumb and forefinger and squeezed it until she cried out, pain flashing through her hazel eyes.

His eyes were cold, implacable.

He squeezed again. The pain was terrible but it was almost pleasure, it would have been pleasure if he loved her—but he loved Elaine the Fair—he didn't love her.

He squeezed again and really hurt her and Louisa opened her mouth but she couldn't speak for a moment.

Thomas loosened his grip, but still he held her nipple lightly, captive.

Louisa spoke.

"Elaine the Fair was kidnapped early this morning, before dawn. Her lady in waiting was left tied and gagged—when she finally got free she ran out of the palace naked, screaming hysterically—that was right after you attacked the King." (That's why no pursuit, Thomas thought.)

Louisa continued, "There were three men who took the Countess—no one from the court, but strangely, there was no alarm given in the palace. The Assessor has offered a huge reward for the knight who brings his wife back safely—knights have been searching everywhere, all afternoon, but they haven't found her.

"That's all I know."

"Thank you, Baroness," Thomas said. Using her title like that when he could have simply said her name was far more painful to Louisa than even his cruelest pinch. She felt her heart breaking—but Thomas didn't notice—he was thinking: The most beautiful lady in the world and a big reward and every knight around beating the bushes near here and nobody finds her because she's *not* near here—she's been taken to Stonehenge, that's the truth, I know it now, and yes I know too the note means a trap, there's a trap waiting for me, but Elaine is there and she's in danger and I will find a way to save her. I can still get there before dawn.

Thomas kissed Louisa absently, his thoughts far away, and then he released her and walked rapidly toward the door.

Louisa threw a vase at him as he strode away—it missed, and shattered against the wall with a crash, but Thomas hardly noticed. He opened the door and left Louisa's house without a backward glance.

Chapter 79

SALLY

Roland and Daniel had entered the City of London. They were riding past fashionable houses, on their way to an area of far less grace, when they saw a horseman approaching at terrifying speed. There was no time for both of them to move decorously to one side of the narrow city street—they just separated instinctively, and the maddened black steed with his crazed rider barreled by between them, nearly clanging stirrups on either side.

The madman was well past before young Daniel caught his breath and cried, "Your Grace, that's the man who attacked King Richard! The one who stole his sword!"

"I know," Roland said. "He's called Sir Thomas." The Duke paused for a moment, and then he went on. "But let's not worry about him now. We need to find Sally as quickly as possible."

Sally was the Vulture's mistress. Haversham had given Roland her name, and he had described where she lived: in a little house jammed between two brothels on Shaftesbury Avenue.

Roland was not too familiar with London, and so they had to stop and ask directions frequently—and these were often of little help, for the narrow streets twisted and turned without rhyme or reason, and the street names themselves changed arbitrarily almost every block, so finding the sin district of the city proved to be a challenge.

In a way the Duke was pleased by the difficulty of threading the maze—it kept him busy—it kept him from thinking too much about what had just happened.

He smiled, he handed out pennies, he asked his questions and listened to the answers, this street, that street, yes, he had it now—but in the back of his mind he really couldn't stop thinking of the mad horseman.

It had been the perfect chance. Roland had recognized Thomas right away in some primitive visceral way—he had all the time he needed to thrust a sword into the knight's path—Thomas would have impaled himself on the blade—at the speed he was going he wouldn't have had the slightest chance to get out of the way.

I will never get such an easy chance again, Roland thought, but I could not commit that murder. Do I really intend to fulfill Richard's savage condition?

Where was Thomas going? What fired that incredible heedless rush?

Roland knew the answer in his heart, and he whispered the name quietly so that Daniel wouldn't hear: "Elaine the Fair." Thomas must have heard about the kidnapping by now, Roland thought—like me he must have his own sources of information—not Sally, someone in one of those fashionable houses—he swore to protect the ladies of the English court and besides this is the one special lady he loves—I understand him—he has an idea where she is now, he rushes off without a thought to his own personal danger, he's a public renegade whom anyone might kill for profit, and he rides openly through the city streets. I know the woman who inspires such madness. Thomas is going to try to rescue Elaine.

If he helps me save her, can I kill him afterward?

They finally found Shaftesbury Avenue.

Roland checked the hourglass he had tucked upright in his belt. Almost a full hour had passed since they set out from Lady Smythe's mansion.

The Duke and Daniel dismounted and tied their horses before the well kept house of the Vulture's mistress.

Roland walked up to the door, oblivious to the bare breasted slatterns who leaned out of the brothel windows on either side. The women called lewd invitations which Daniel, emulating his master, tried to ignore—but he did sneak a few glances.

Roland knocked.

The door was opened by a stout woman who looked as though she herself had served a long sentence in the flesh trade. She blocked the entrance with her bulk.

"What do you want?"

The Duke of Larraz inclined his head formally and took out a gold sovereign. He put it on his open palm and extended it out in front of him and to his left. The former tart's eyes focused on the treasure—she reached out, turning her body slightly—her fingers curled greedily around the coin, and as she grabbed it the Duke gave her a bump with his hip and pressed his way inside. Thin Daniel scurried in behind him.

"We're friends of Miss Sally," said the Duke, as the big woman turned on them. "No need to announce us—we can hear the lady upstairs, and I'm sure she'll be delighted to see us."

From upstairs came a courteously voiced inquiry.

"Who is it, Peggy?"

Peggy bit the coin and discovered it was genuine. "Friends of yours," she called back. "Gentry, I'd say."

The Duke smiled at Peggy and started up the stairs. Daniel followed him.

Sally, when they found her in her bedroom, was quite formally attired. She liked to play "dress-up" when her lover was away. She would pretend she was a lady of the court—she would look in the mirror and practice her curtsy for the King— she would make herself forget that at sixteen she had already spent a year of her life in a brothel and another year as the kept woman of a murderer.

Roland had noticed the neat house that Sally kept in the midst of squalor—he sensed that she wished to rise above her station—he felt terribly sad as he watched her perfect curtsy, for it was then that he realized how young she was.

The Duke remembered his impressions of the devastated English countryside as they had made their way to London: land wasted and people stripped of their livelihood by their rapacious King. He silently cursed himself for making his deal with Richard, and he bowed his head to this young girl who only wanted a little comfort in her life—and had only her body to sell to get it.

"Milady," he said.

"Who are you, Sir?" she asked, her voice like a little girl's.

"I am the Duke of Larraz, and this is my companion, Sir Daniel."

The girl curtsied again. "I am honored, Your Grace, Sir."

The elegant practiced manners of this damaged girl nearly broke Roland's heart. He had planned twin attacks of threats and bribery to get the information he needed—that was when he still thought of her as the ex-whore Haversham had described. But now he had met her, and here was this little blond child, a rough and simple version of Elaine, a girl dreaming of nobility between two brothels.

One can not negotiate when the heart is touched—Roland had already found this out when he had given too much to Richard. Now he felt himself lost once again—he had lost his detachment, his coolness—he realized that his years of serene political maneuver had been a life lived behind a wall—a wall that kept the world away—a painful hurting world filled with heartbreak and death—his love for Elaine had cut through that wall, and now he had known ecstacy, but also he lived in the midst of pain—he felt this girl's pain, that was Elaine's gift to him—the paradox was that now, in order to save Elaine, he had to hurt the girl more.

He realized that to save Elaine—only to save Elaine—he could do it.

Roland had been staring at Sally for so long that she was becoming quite frightened. Finally the Duke moved. He took out his hourglass, and examined it to see that all the sand had run out. Then he turned it over and set it on Sally's dresser. She watched the grains of sand begin to trickle down.

Then Roland took out a small sack of gold. He opened it to show Sally the contents, and then closed it up again. He laid it down on the dresser next to the hourglass.

Sally began to sense the danger. She sat down slowly on her bed.

Roland began to speak, and his voice was like a tolling bell. "The Countess of Anjou, Elaine the Fair, was kidnapped from the Palace of Bermondsey early this morning. The Countess's lady in waiting, Lady Sandra, was brutally assaulted with a knife during the attack. The man who committed that deed—the man who has taken the Countess away—is a former knight now known as the Vulture."

Sally winced and looked away.

Roland continued. "I think you know the Vulture. I think you know where he's taken the Countess."

Sally was looking at Roland again now. The Duke gestured toward the hourglass. "If you tell me where he's taken her before the sand is gone, you can have the gold."

"And if I don't know? If I can't tell you?" Sally's voice was high, terrified.

Roland wanted to hug her but instead he made his face into a replica of a judge prescribing the gallows. He bowed formally to

Sally—he did not answer her questions. He knew that her own imagination would frighten her more than any threat he could state.

He said, "Your housekeeper, Peggy, seems to be a most charming woman. I'll go downstairs now and enjoy her company. Sir Daniel here will attend to you until you make up your mind—or until the hour is"—a long pause while he looked her over as though contemplating her death—"finished."

Roland turned and walked away. Sally listened to his footsteps on the stairs. She had promised promised promised not to tell.

Daniel was nearly as frightened as Sally, but he covered it with a harsh warlike glare. In his fear he was ready to hurt the girl badly if she tried to escape.

They were children caught in an adult's game.

Downstairs Roland played cards with Peggy. He was waiting for the crying to start.

An hour can seem to last forever. Sally talked and talked to Daniel. She told him more about her life than he ever wanted to know. He could not bear to think of all the men who had stripped and violated her little child's body. He just listened, struggling to keep his face hard as she talked and talked, finally he realized she wasn't even looking at him, she was staring at the hourglass while she went on and on, faster and faster, horror upon horror, racing the sand, he knew he was the first one that she had ever told this to, she just had to tell it all to someone, violation and pain and the scent of death when the Vulture took her but nice things too this house kind too sometimes but then cleaning blood from his clothes still better though better than before four five a day no more no more no more and the last 'more' extended into a keening cry that went on and on and Daniel looked over at the hourglass and he saw that all the sand had run through.

Roland came back up the stairs. He entered the room and walked over to the bed.

Sally sobbed with her face in her hands.

Roland put his hand on her shoulder, and Sally tried to talk through her tears. "He said I must promise not to tell for no one could ever know what he had done and afterward we'd have money, lots of money, we'd leave the city, we'd leave all this"— she gestured weakly toward the windows, the brothels, the streets—"we'd live like a knight and his lady . . ." Her voice just ran down and finally disintegrated into a series of soft choking sobs.

Roland looked down at the shattered girl and her shattered dream. He moved his hand to her head—he stroked her hair gently for a few moments, and then he asked in a rumbling sad voice, "where did he take her?"

Sally whispered the answer, looking down, her voice like a sigh. Roland heard the sibilant whisper but he couldn't make out the word.

He went to one knee by her side—he turned his head and put his ear to her mouth like a father with a shy little girl, and he said, "Again, please."

The Duke felt her breath as she whispered it again. "Stonehenge."

Roland turned and kissed the young girl's forehead. He got up and picked up the hourglass—he left the sack of gold.

The Duke motioned to Daniel and the two of them walked down the stairs. Roland said "Good-bye," to Peggy and then they stepped outside.

They mounted up as the whores hurled insults—they set off at a gallop and didn't look back.

Chapter 80

THE PIERCED HAND

While the men who sought her rushed to and fro, Elaine the Fair endured captivity and struggled to survive.

She had guessed the name of the man who hated her enough to order her kidnapping. She thought of her husband—her false husband—as the three criminals dragged her away from her room, leaving Sandra tied and bleeding. The men dragged her down the long empty hallway and out the door and through the gate and Elaine never saw a single guard. The palace seemed deserted, a ghost fortress, a conspirator in evil. Elaine knew that she would never live there again.

A fine coach and four waited outside for her. A coachman in livery sat up in the driver's seat, whip tilted at the ready. A mounted knight guarded the equipage but Elaine couldn't see who it was, for it was still fairly dark and he kept his face turned away.

The Vulture opened the coach door and his two companions threw Elaine inside. The men piled in after her, the Vulture slammed the door, the coachman cracked his whip, and they were off.

The curtained windows of the coach lit up yellow as lightning flashed all around them—in the glow Elaine saw the silhouette of the knight riding alongside.

So this is my husband's gift to me, she thought: the Vulture, two low criminals, a coachman, and a false knight—five men to punish me because you are not a man . . .

There were two cushioned wooden seats in the coach. Elaine sat facing forward, next to the man who had first covered her mouth—the man who kept his choking arm around her neck.

Facing them on the opposite seat were the Vulture and the third abductor.

It grew a little lighter inside the curtained coach. Dawn was breaking somewhere—and then there came the sound of rain on the roof. The Vulture smiled, and Elaine read his thoughts: in this rain, no one could hear her scream.

She wondered what license her husband had given to these men.

The Vulture made a sign and the choker released his grip. The coach rocked as the two men changed places. The Vulture sat down right next to Elaine. She looked straight ahead as though she couldn't feel his presence, as though she couldn't hear his heavy breathing.

Suddenly he grabbed her face with his vicious animal hands. His grip was so harsh that she was afraid her skin would tear. He yanked her around to face him and he kissed her hard on the mouth.

Elaine fought him with her lips—she kept them closed against his onslaught—she fought to move her head, but she could barely manage a quiver against his strength—she thought of going for his eyes with her fingernails, but with her peripheral vision she could see the other two watching eagerly and she knew that hurting one just meant great pain or worse from the others—the Vulture tilted her head back and she felt soreness in her bent neck, the legacy of the choker's arm—she felt the Vulture's thumb against her fresh struck scar and now pain everywhere was coming up in waves trying to overwhelm her—in the midst of the pain she remembered the knife probing between Sandra's legs and she was sure that Arthur had not ordered her death but she knew too that in one crazed moment their bloodlust could burst the few restraints of Arthur's power—killing a beautiful woman might be all that they had ever wanted—she had to live and preserve her beauty—she thought of her beauty as a separate entity, something valuable, for its delicate power was the only weapon she had—she could not let her face be torn by the Vulture's violent hands . . .

She opened her mouth and the villain's tongue rushed in. It was a rough and brutal kiss, but the pressure of his hands did lesson on her cheeks, and then he abandoned her face altogether as his hands moved down to explore her body.

She hardly felt his hands on her breasts at first, her senses occupied by the invasion of her mouth—she struggled to keep a

mental aloofness when a physical one was no longer possible—
Elaine knew that she had to think, and think clearly, if she was
to survive this day. She had to buy time, as much time as possible, and then Roland would come for her, her Duke, her lover,
her strong man with twenty armed knights under his command—she could feel him missing her even now—she tried to
think only of him, tried to send a message to the Duke of Larraz
even as the Vulture's tongue twisted against her own—and then
it was as though her mind slipped and she suddenly thought of
Thomas and the tapestry he had brought with him to the court:
"the protection of the ladies of the English court"—she remembered his kiss, she remembered the duels he had fought and she
thought that he could kill all of these ruffians single-handedly,
and she knew she wanted to watch him do it.

The thought excited her, and now she was aware of the
Vulture's hands on her breasts, kneading and squeezing them
through her silk nightgown, rubbing his thumbs over her suddenly awakened nipples—the Vulture was nearly driven mad by
her reaction.

He broke the kiss and ducked his head to seek a hard silk covered nipple with his mouth—he bit it in a way that let her know
he could really hurt her—he worried it like a dog and when he
went to the other one he left a wet spot that showed her breast
practically naked. Again he bit and sucked, if anything his frenzy increased, he used one hand to push that breast into his
mouth, and then his other hand went down and grasped the
hem of her nightgown and Elaine knew she had to act soon or
not at all.

She stole a glance at the other two men—she saw them
watching avidly, sweating, tongues moistening their dry
mouths.

There was no rescuer inside this coach—no rescuer in sight.

She had to save herself.

Elaine drew up into herself all her strength, all her love, and
all her heritage—when the Vulture left both bitten breasts and
ducked his head toward the final target, she stopped him. Her
strong left hand shot out and grabbed his hair—she yanked his
head up for just a second and slapped him across the face with
all the strength of her good right hand.

The Vulture reacted more like a snake than a bird. He shook
off Elaine's grip with one twisting, coiling motion—he drew his
knife with a hiss and struck as her face—Elaine saw the blade

in his left hand and she could not allow another scar and her right hand came back to block—the point of the knife went right into her palm.

They froze in dreadful tableau, the only movement being the slow trickle of blood from Elaine's pierced hand, and then the Countess of Anjou began to speak. Her voice was that of a beautiful woman who expects the attention of every man.

"Gentlemen," she said, "I know you are in the pay of my husband." The Vulture started at the last word and jerked the knife out of her hand—fresh blood poured out of her palm and joined the rivulets that painted her wrist, that extended now almost to her elbow—but as she continued to speak the stream slowed, for she was fortunate in that no important veins had been cut. "I know you have orders not to kill me, and not to take me by force." Elaine was certain of the first, not so sure about the second, but if she was wrong it wouldn't matter anyway, and there was a good chance she was right: after several rapes her value as a commodity would greatly decrease, and Arthur wouldn't want that! She continued confidently, "Should you disobey his orders, you will certainly die."

Elaine looked at each of the three faces in turn, and she saw in their eyes that she had divined the truth.

She continued, "I promise that if you try to destroy my honor I shall mark you—with my fingernails, with my teeth, I shall mark your bodies, and the wound I give you will be your mark of Cain. There will be no place on this earth for you to hide—you will have to fear not only my husband, but also every good man who has ever heard of me."

Elaine knew that if she left it there she would finally lose—these crude men could never stand being bested by a woman, and finally their resentment would burst forth in violence—they would rape her, and kill her afterward, thinking in that way to keep themselves safe.

She had to walk a fine line—she must give a little bit, and in so giving, she had to bring them, at least slightly, under her control.

She held up her open hands, one red, one white, and offered her unprotected body for an embrace. "You see, there is really no need for violence. You are gentlemen, and I am a lady. Kiss me, and remember every touch of my lips—one day you will tell your children that you kissed Elaine the Fair, and kept her safe."

The Countess of Anjou had finished with words for the day. She looked at the Vulture, and cast all her beauty on him, and waited for him with parted lips and open arms and one bleeding hand whose pain she ignored.

He did not reach for her.

The Vulture shrank away, as always he had done in the presence of courage—it seemed as though he wanted to find some place in the coach where he could hide.

With a strangled voice he said, "Bart, it's your turn," and so Elaine learned the name of the one who had spoken up about their orders, and thus helped to save Sandra.

Bart did not try to arrange another exchange of seats—he just went to his knees in front of Elaine, and put his hands on her breasts as hers went around behind his head, and then he kissed her quite nicely, he touched her and kissed her for a long time until finally the choker kicked him away, and a new mouth took possession of Elaine's, and so the day passed.

Sometimes they tried to go too far, and Elaine had to slap them (she remembered the boys back in Firfleet, when she was sixteen) but she had struck the right chords with her speech. All men in their hearts want to be gentlemen—and in particular, these men wanted to be *liked* by the most beautiful woman in the world. They were thrilled that she accepted their kisses and their wandering hands—seeking her approval, instead of assaulting her, they accepted the limits she imposed. They treated her honorably, in their fashion—and so Elaine the Fair lived through this day with her beauty unmarred, with only one new scar forming on the palm of her hand.

There was one strange event that took place in the late afternoon. The coach stopped, and only the Vulture stayed inside to guard Elaine. He set her on his lap and made her feel him—but all the while he fondled her she listened to the crack of axes outside. Then she heard the men loading the cut wood on to the roof of the coach—the roof shuddered as the lumber was lashed on—Elaine shuddered inside—what new terror did these logs signify?—she had a sudden nightmare vision of a gallows—the Vulture's face was over her and he was the hangman—she felt his lips and she closed her eyes and opened her mouth for his kiss.

Chapter 81

THE HIDDEN WEAPON

Arthur felt that geography was on his side. There was a thick band of forest before the Salisbury plain, and Stonehenge. Even traveling straight through, with no deception on his part, they would still not reach that forest until well after dark. Surely the Northmen would not try to press through those woods at night. They would make camp—and he would have his chance to escape.

Arthur had to think of escape, for otherwise the day's tortures would have driven him mad.

At first the Northmen made him walk in front of the wagon to give guidance—they whipped him when he could not keep up the pace that Ivar wanted. When finally he fell forward on his aching belly (driven by a whiplash behind) Ivar decided that he could ride in the front seat next to the coachman. Then that driver was able to whip his horses and cuff Arthur indiscriminately—and it also gave Ivar a chance to prick Arthur from behind with his sword.

Ivar interspersed the pricks with questions—Arthur answered truthfully—and so the Chief of Champions learned that there were five men guarding Elaine, and he learned how they were armed.

Ivar never dreamed that Arthur himself carried a hidden weapon.

The Assessor cried out in pain as a sword thrust drew blood— but he kept his deck of cards clamped tight in a sweating armpit.

Chapter 82

THE ENGLISH GUIDE

When Roland and Daniel got back, every Larrazian knight was mounted and ready to go. The Duke had said three hours, and they had taken him at his word—and his word was good. They gave a cheer when they saw their leader—now it was off to save the Fair Lady! They were in the best of spirits—but then Roland came close enough for them to make out his grim visage and they wondered what had gone wrong.

Anton had told their landlady that Sandra was to be his wife. He had arranged for her to sleep in the bed that he had used for these last two weeks. Sandra's happiness would have been unbounded if only her lady were safe. She stayed close to Anton—she could feel his love, and also his anxiety. As she was worried about her lady, so he was worried about his Duke. Sandra stroked Anton's leg as he sat above her, mounted on his horse—she wondered at the excitement she could feel even now. She wished that she could go with him.

Sandra heard Roland ride up on the other side of Anton's horse, and she heard the Duke say, "Elaine's at Stonehenge—we shall have to get an English guide."

Anton understood his leader's gloom. Where could they get a good guide on short notice? They were bound to lose valuable time.

Anton did not know what to reply but Sandra felt a happy thrill because she had the solution.

She slipped under the horse's neck and got between Anton and Roland. She looked right up at the Duke's face—a face that was taut with the fear that he would be too late to save the lady they both loved.

"I am from Salisbury," Sandra said. "When I was a child, I often rode my pony up to the great rocks—until my father found out about it, and told me not to go there any more, for he said it was an evil place. I know the best route to get to Stonehenge. Let me be your guide."

Sandra watched the lines loosen on Roland's face, watched his smile come out like the sun, and she felt the way she had felt when Elaine first kissed her, but this was even better with her man close behind her, and then Roland reached down and took the hand she offered him. He kissed her hand, and said softly, "Yes, you will guide us—and you shall find your lady, and I shall find my love."

The Duke looked up at Anton. "Go get a horse for our English guide—Now!"

Anton rode quickly over to the stables, smiling. Roland addressed his men. "If you could not hear this conversation, let me repeat: My lady is being held at an old pagan temple called Stonehenge. Lady Sandra here knows the way and she will guide us. I count on you men to help rescue the next Duchess of Larraz!"

Everyone could see that the strain had gone from the Duke's face. This time the cheers rattled the new windows that Roland had put up in Lady Smythe's mansion.

Anton came back leading a mount for Sandra. He had decided, with a certain wicked pleasure, that they could not afford to be slowed down by their guide riding sidesaddle. Sandra looked askance at the man's saddle—but Anton just grinned at her and swung lightly down to help her mount. He caught her about the waist before she had a chance to protest and lifted her easily on to the horse. Her skirt pulled up high, baring her legs—her wounded bottom burned as she settled into the saddle—and then Anton squeezed her bare thigh so hard that his fingers left marks, and Sandra felt such excitement that she knew she could bear any pain—she felt the power of the horse between her legs, and she wanted to gallop—Anton vaulted back onto his own horse, and Roland growled, "Let's go."

Sandra tightened her legs around her stallion, and very quickly brought him up to speed.

The Larrazian knights followed their guide as she led them to the west.

Chapter 83

THE UNIMAGINABLE

Thomas rode hard out of the City of London (as Roland observed) and raced to his home stable. There he picked up his longbow and quiver of arrows—but he decided not to take a lance for that would be too heavy over the long journey. Then he remounted Saladin and set off at a high speed towards Stonehenge. He looked neither left nor right—he saw no other knights—and if any other knights saw him, they stayed out of his way.

He pushed Saladin unmercifully, but even the powerful stallion could not keep up such a pace indefinitely. By late afternoon the horse was dragging—the gallop had long since ceased—the stallion alternated between a fast walk and a bone jarring trot that was probably slower than the walk. Finally Thomas pushed too far—he could not stand the rough trot, so he tried to kick Saladin into the smoother canter—but the haughty horse had put up with enough abuse. Saladin curled his long neck around and bit Thomas on the knee.

"Yow!" yelled Thomas, and he smacked the long black neck. Saladin turned his head back straight—he faced forward dutifully—but he planted his feet like stakes in the moist earth—he refused to take a step.

Thomas ran his hand gently over the horse's taut back. Every muscle twitched with fatigue. "I'm sorry," the knight said, "I should never have kicked you that last time."

Thomas dismounted, took the reins, and walked the big stallion until he was calm and cool. Then they were fortunate to come upon a stream—Thomas allowed Saladin to drink a little, but not too much, and then he gave the horse a small ration of grain.

Soon enough it was time to remount and continue the quest—but now Thomas let Saladin walk, both to rest the horse and to allow himself peace to think.

Thomas wanted to know his enemies.

Three men, Louisa had said. No one from the court, no one Sandra knew, no alarm given in the palace.

Thomas thought of all the knights he knew who lived out in the country, mainly veterans that he recalled from Richard's crusading army. There were bad ones aplenty, and yet Thomas was certain that not one of them would steal an English lady by force. There was no end to the horrors they could perpetrate on Saracens—but a lifetime of training would forbid such an attack against a Christian lady of the court.

If the villains weren't knights, how did they get in the palace? How could they have known the layout so well as to avoid detection?

Thomas chewed on the problem as Saladin sauntered along—he found the answer without too much difficulty. The abductors had to be outside criminals, hired by someone who lived *inside* the palace.

Who was the inside man?

That question was much more difficult.

Now Thomas thought of the knights who lived within the walls of Bermondsey, and yes there were a great many who loved Elaine—but who among them would deliver her into criminal hands? Thomas could not think of one suspect.

He reminded himself that there were more than knights residing in Bermondsey—there were various types of courtiers, titled fops of the sycophantic stripe—but Thomas could hardly believe that such a fellow would have both the strength of will and the contacts with the underworld that this job had demanded.

Then a shocking thought hit Thomas: the abduction had occurred immediately following the return of King Richard and his men of arms. Could Brian also be behind this villainy? Was the hulking assassin the "big man," the "gentleman" that the vagrant had encountered? Was Brian some Devil's agent set to destroy any woman Thomas loved?

Thomas felt a swirling madness at the thought, but then he gradually shook off the irrational fears as he recalled Brian's reaction from the day's brief encounter. The man at arms had clearly been surprised to see Thomas. He has not spent his trip to England plotting against me, Thomas thought, for to him I am only worth small insults. He had no time to set this up—he is evil but not supernatural—it is enough that he shall die for the sins that he *has* committed.

Someone else planned the kidnapping.

Who was the inside man?

Thomas tended to discount the possibility of a knight being behind the plot—and so he was left with the unsatisfactory answer of a lovesick courtier with criminal associates. That answer did not seem right to him, yet he could deduce nothing else. He never suspected that Arthur could be the villain of the piece.

Thomas had a blind spot when he looked at the world. He found it hard to imagine actions that were outside the ken of his own character. That is why he fell for Roland's ruse—he simply couldn't imagine that a true lover would send his lady off unprotected. Likewise, he didn't suspect Arthur, because he could not imagine that a man who had the right to make love to Elaine the Fair could ever hate her.

He squeezed with his legs and urged Saladin into a trot.

The rough gait jarred loose another unanswerable question. If a lovesick courtier had had Elaine abducted for his pleasure, why then had he advertised his deed by sending Thomas a note? Why would he give a clue of Elaine's whereabouts to a highly dangerous knight?

The fact was, there was still no solid clue that the note *did* relate to Elaine—just coincidence of timing that felt definitive but on closer inspection was not. Perhaps Elaine had been taken far away in the opposite direction. Perhaps the note was just to lead him astray. Perhaps there were two conspiracies, one against Elaine, one against himself. It was true that he had enough enemies—and yet, and yet, and yet . . .

He could not believe in coincidence. His heart told him of the truth of his first feeling: Elaine the Fair had been taken to Stonehenge—the abduction was part of a trap to kill him.

Someone's pulling the strings, Thomas thought. No weak courtier or true knight conceived this.

Someone hates me enough to kill.

Someone hates Elaine enough to use her as his murderous bait.

If there had only been the former premise then Thomas might

have guessed the answer—but his mind was blocked by his image of Elaine's beauty. He could not imagine knowing that beauty and hating the woman—he could not imagine it, he did not imagine it, he did not suspect Arthur.

He urged Saladin into a canter and rode headlong toward the trap.

Chapter 84

HORSES, AND THEIR PRICE

After Ivar sent his messenger back to his ship, there were only five horses left to pull the wagon—a wagon heavily laden with nine sizeable Vikings and one plump Assessor. Before long the horses began to tire. The Chief of Champions was not happy with their slow progress—and also, thinking ahead to Elaine's capture, he wanted the possibility of a speedy getaway. At that point he intended to abandon the wagon and break for the sea, each man to a horse—with Elaine slung over his own saddle.

In other words, he needed four more horses. No mount was required for Arthur, of course, because Ivar intended to kill the fat Englishman as soon as he sighted Elaine.

In the wet heat of midafternoon the Vikings came upon a noble's estate. This Baron was at the court with his wife—his horses were being looked after by an honest herdsman.

The herdsman tried to defend his charges—Ivar killed him on the grass in front of the stable.

The herdsman's family lived in a little apartment built on to the stable—his wife saw everything, saw the sword tear her husband again and again—she ran out to her man, never thinking of anything save the good man who loved her, and Thorson cut her down with an axe.

There were three children—orphans now—and they did not come out.

Two boys and a girl—too young to really understand—they stood in their open doorway and stared at the strange priests in silent terror.

Sigurd took one of the horses and fitted it with saddle and bridle. He kept his back to Ivar.

Other Vikings outfitted three more horses, and took extra saddles and bridles to use on their coach horses later.

Sigurd stared over his horse's back and he wanted to be sick but he felt Ivar's eyes searing the back of his neck.

All was green, the fresh summer's green that follows a rain—this green should not be stained with blood . . .

Sigurd stared off into the distance until vision became dream: he thought of the Norse settlements in Iceland, and he imagined his children playing there, happy by the hot springs of that remote isle—he saw his wives there too, each one beautiful and he loved them all beyond measure, and then he realized that in his dream he had broken the bonds of fealty—he had imagined a life free from Ivar's shadow—I found Elaine the Fair for you, Sigurd thought. Delivering her pays all debts.

When this trip is over I shall take my family away.

He focused his eyes again and deliberately looked around at the children. He saw their faces stretched by their gaping silent mouths—he saw their enormous fearful eyes—he saw their little fists clenching in terror—no parents would ever again take their hands.

Sigurd looked at the bodies of the herdsman and his wife—and then he looked up and calmly met Ivar's gaze.

As he stared into the sunken yellow eyes, Sigurd promised himself that he would never sail with Ivar again.

Chapter 85

A LAST ACT OF NOBILITY

The Vulture had directed the coachman to take his time—so it was nearly sundown before they reached that last band of forest before the Salisbury plain. The coachman directed the horses to a narrow path—they jolted through the thick woods in near darkness.

Elaine tracked the dying sun through the closed curtains. She felt their vehicle roll onto a smooth plain as the sun turned the curtains red.

The coach proceeded onward in silence. The red faded to gray.

No one had touched Elaine from the moment the coach had entered the plain.

Elaine could feel the emptiness—no people around, no trees, no birds, no sounds, no hills, no valleys—emptiness. Then her skin began to burn as the curtains went black. She could see nothing in the coach.

But there was something, outside—she could feel it.

They stopped.

The men got out. As the Vulture left, he said, "Stay inside, or it will be worse for you."

They had been going west, into the setting sun—through a forest—onto a flat uninhabited plain—a plain with a presence on it, a brooding touch of dead spirits, a huge sullen weight that held the dead to this earth.

Sandra had told her of the hulking masses of rock.

Stonehenge.

Elaine put her head in her hands. Her power was almost gone. All day she had walked the fine line that separated her from rape and death, and now she was exhausted, but no less fearful. She shivered—it was colder now in the night—she still wore only her silk nightgown.

Then she heard the men come back to the coach. They didn't open the door—instead they simply unloaded the wood from the roof. Then she heard the sound of axes again, men cursing as they worked—she smelled a fire—there were light popping noises as they cut more kindling—more curses, heavy lifting—they were building some infernal machine for murder, and she couldn't even push back the curtain and try to see—she hadn't the strength to see—she didn't want to see.

Elaine the Fair covered her eyes in the blackness, but she could not even cry.

Finally the sounds stopped, and the Vulture came for her. He opened the door and pulled her out of the coach. She looked automatically toward the fire, seeking light—but they had stamped it out. The black moonless night enveloped her—she felt more than saw the hulking presence of the stones around her, she realized she was in the midst of that broken damaged circle. She accepted the Vulture's hard grip on her arm without protest—she let him drag her over to the fire's ashes—she ate what he fed her, and drank what he gave her, and then she let him pull her down next to him on a blanket. She struck another man—he cursed, and she recognized Bart—the Vulture cursed back at his assistant—Elaine lay between the two men, and then someone pulled a blanket up over her, and the Vulture put an arm around her and pulled her close.

Elaine didn't fight the embrace but she felt for the face coming toward her in the dark and she put her hand right over his nose, she placed her wound against his nostrils and the Vulture inhaled the odor of Elaine's dried blood, the scent of her courage, the scent of his fear—he shook his head like an animal, he let her go—he turned away.

Then Elaine rolled away onto her back, she lay between the two men and looked up at the black featureless sky, clouds blocking the stars, moon lost and gone, the machinery of death built in darkness, invisible horror of tree trunks and kindling and axes, a death fitted to the awesome brooding rocks, stones of time, thousands of years of death imprisoned within this circle of stones—

One spirit. I would like to speak to one spirit before I die. Can you see me now, dear Mother, dear brave, beautiful Marian?

The stones seemed closer, blacker, menacing—Elaine gave a

little cry and rolled toward Bart—he took her in his arms and drew her against him.

Bart discovered the meaning of the word *beauty*.

His left hand went down behind her, he caressed her smooth back and buttocks through the thin nightgown, he felt her begin to quiver against him, he pulled up the fragile silk so as to bare her bottom, he could hear his own breath as he put his rough hand between her legs from behind, his fingers questing—she resisted not at all, he just felt her upper body shaking where he held her with his right hand, he found her womanhood with his left—and then he discovered that her womanhood was dry and unresponsive, he felt wetness only on his neck and then he suddenly realized that she was crying, she was shaking with silent sobs, not passion, she had only tears to give him this night and anything else he must take by force.

Bart had been a bad man all his life. He had stolen. He had killed.

This night, the last night of his life, was different.

He was noble.

He pulled the silk nightgown back down to cover the lady's femininity—he held her close, he stroked her hair and let her cry quietly, he stayed awake to protect her when finally Elaine the Fair fell asleep in his arms.

He loved, for the first and last time in his life.

Chapter 86

ROLAND MAKES CAMP

Sandra was a very good guide, but also a very tired one by the time they reached that last band of forest before the Salisbury plain. It was a couple of hours after midnight, in Roland's estimation—he asked Sandra, "How much longer?"

Sandra swayed back on her mount—she caught the edge of her saddle with one hand, and barely managed to keep from falling. "Your Grace, in daylight I believe I could lead you through in an hour, and then we would be able to see Stonehenge—but now, in the dark ..." Sandra's voice trailed off. She had been abused and cut and bound, she had been awake almost twenty-four hours and she had ridden for twelve of them, for Roland had allowed only the quickest and most necessary stops. The girl was exhausted.

The Duke considered the problem. Breaking through the woods now would involve a considerable amount of noise—there was probably a path somewhere but they could hardly find it in the dark—they'd just have to push straight on, and so they would hardly be able to avoid crackling branches and binding thornbrushes. The noise they'd make might alert their enemy—they would lose the advantage of surprise. What if Elaine's captors took her off into the night, in some unknown direction? Then too, his men, and the horses, were nearly as exhausted as Sandra. The short sleep available now might make the difference in battle—and in matters of judgment as well. The wise course was to stay here.

Still, Roland felt a mad desire that cried in his mind: Push on! Tear through the trees! he wanted to charge through the hindering forest, sword in hand—he wanted desperately to reach

Elaine.

The Duke's logical mind forbade that madness. An impetuous advance would more likely hurt Elaine than save her.

He gave orders to make camp—quickly, with no fire—he put two men on guard with orders to wake him at the first ray of sunshine.

Roland felt Elaine's presence, close now—he had to fight every second to keep from yelling, "Let's go, now, into the woods!" He held the cry back, he tried to sleep—but the nightmare was waiting for him. He dreamed of the black cross, he woke up quickly, sweating—he heard panting breath close to him and he reached for his sword.

Then the Duke relaxed, relaxed as much as he could—he realized that the heavy breathing was only the sound of love, he made out the shape of the beast with two backs: Anton and Sandra. Tired as Sandra was, her white legs were still wrapped tight around her man—her breathing grew rougher, louder—and then Anton kissed her hard to smother her cry of pleasure.

Roland closed his eyes again, and this time he didn't dream.

Chapter 87

ARTHUR'S STRENGTH

The Viking coachman had made sure that Arthur watched the murders of the herdsman and his wife. Ivar had looked back a moment later (while cleaning his sword) and smiled. The Chief of Champions believed that Arthur was a broken man—this spectacle of death was just a way of showing the prisoner his own future. Ivar wanted the Assessor reduced to helpless blubber by the time they accosted his wife. Then Ivar intended to kill Arthur in front of Elaine—it would be the easiest way to assert his power over her.

Ivar did not imagine that Arthur had something similar in mind for the man he believed to be his wife's lover. The Viking was not aware of the depths of his hostage. Ivar did not know that Arthur (from painful childhood practice) could imitate a broken man without quite being one. He did not realize that Arthur still had strength of purpose and an ego driven will to resist.

Ivar continued to question Arthur throughout the day, trying to get any information that might be useful regarding Elaine. Arthur gave reasonably accurate replies—but he did leave some things out. He did not say a word about his note to Sir Thomas—the Vikings had no idea that that knight was on a similar mission—and of course Arthur said nothing about the death trap prepared for that warrior.

Though Arthur was harried by blows and whiplashes and the burning leaking wound in his belly, still he kept his wits about him. He read his opponent right and tailored his answers to Ivar's character.

He admitted Elaine's infidelity. He told the Northman that he had had Elaine kidnapped, and taken to the distant temple, just so he could punish her as she deserved far from the prying eyes of the court.

This was reasoning Ivar could understand. The death's head smiled at the word, "punish", and then the Norwegian skull came close to the tax collector's ear, and Arthur felt the fetid breath of something dead and buried, and then the voice of death whispered, "I will punish her for you."

The Vikings pressed on into the night, four riding, five plus Arthur in the wagon, and then like Roland (and for the same reasons) they made camp on the near edge of the last forest.

Like Roland, they camped without a fire. They were unaware of the equally blacked out Larrazian bivouac just a mile to the north.

As Arthur got down off the wagon he was careful not to let any relief show on his face.

A young Viking (at Ivar's order) lashed Arthur's wrists together behind his back. He tied the Englishman's ankles together too, and then gave the prisoner a shove just for luck. Arthur crashed heavily to the ground—the young Champion amused himself further by kicking Arthur in the belly, as though accidentally, while stepping over the Assessor's bulk. The Vikings laughed—all save Sigurd laughed—as Arthur bleated and cried and rolled about in agony on the grass.

Ivar told the young Champion that, since he had such energy for amusements, he could mount up and serve as sentry for the rest of the night. The young man hastened to obey.

The other men arranged themselves in a circle around Arthur, with weapons in their hands. Arthur strained his eyes, trying to see their every movement in the darkness—then he listened as they settled into sleep.

Ivar and Sigurd climbed back into the warm wagon for their rest.

The young sentry rode his horse in a circle around the camp, and stood up in the stirrups to peer out into the night.

Arthur felt the blessed weight of his heavy, sharp edged cards—the cards that he had finally loosed from his armpit's grip under cover of his tormented rolling—the specially treated cards of the Chancellor of the Exchequer had slid down along his arm inside his sleeve—they had been stopped by the barrier of the hempen rope that bound his wrists—now with fat, soft, ever so dextrous back twisted fingers, he slipped the tongue of one card under the rope.

Chapter 88

THE KING'S SWORD

Thomas had the best horse of all the men pursuing Elaine, and also the most overworked one. The stallion had been ridden since dawn with only a few short breaks. Saladin had seen action involving a vagrant, a King, and a Baroness—he had bitten his own master, and as day turned to night the horse was ready to bite him again. Thomas was forced to allow the horse another short rest—and then he remounted and rode the testy beast onward through the night.

It was a constant battle for Thomas to keep Saladin going west through the night and unfamiliar terrain. The knight longed for the familiar woods around Nottingham, the forest that he had retreated to after his parents had been killed. He could still recall every tree of that forest—after all, he had lived there for two years.

But now Thomas had to strain to find enough stars in the cloudy night to guide him—and he had to cope with an ever more exhausted and fractious horse.

All things considered, Thomas did not do too badly. He lost the lead that he had had on the other two pursuing forces, and he went a little off course—but he still struck that last forest wall at about the same time as Roland and Ivar's troops, and he was only off line by about three miles—that is, he was three miles north of Sandra's accurate guideline, and he was four miles north of the Vikings.

Unlike the other two parties, Thomas did not even consider stopping when he hit that last wooded barrier. The knight answered only to the certainty of his own love—he cared naught about the risks—he discounted his own exhaustion, and that of his horse. He simply dismounted and led Saladin by the reins—while with his other hand he used his sword to hack a path through the obstructing branches and thorns.

Spiderwebs wrapped his forehead—brushing one off, he encountered a trickle of blood where a thorn had caught him—he didn't care—he wiped the blood away with the back of his sword hand, and then continued to cut away at the under-brush—he was driven by his sense of dwindling hours before dawn—he cut through the last thornbush and came out from under the last tree—he stepped out onto the Salisbury plain, and he saw nothing.

The clouds had completely covered the crescent moon that Thomas had glimpsed earlier in the night. The stars were blotted out. Earth and sky were black, and Thomas had no idea where to go.

He guessed that he was off course. He realized that he could ride out across this dark, featureless plain, and miss Stonehenge altogether.

Thomas took the crumpled note out of his pocket. He couldn't read it in the darkness, but with his mind's eye he saw the word DAWN. He tore up the paper and threw the bits on the ground.

He took off Saladin's bridle and saddle. "Rest as you can, my friend," he said, "for I will be putting them back on you soon enough." Then he rubbed the horse's face and let him walk off, his blackness very quickly swallowed by the night.

Thomas stepped back and leaned against a tree at the edge of the forest. He cleaned off the old sword that he had used to cut through the woods—he sharpened it to erase any imperfections it might have acquired, and he wasn't satisfied until the blade could prick his finger at a touch. Then he put it away and removed his new golden treasure form its scabbard. He could barely see the blade's gleam in the blackness, but he could feel the jewels implanted in the golden hilt.

A King's sword, Thomas thought to himself. Perhaps one day I shall kill Brian with this.

He smiled in the darkness and then suddenly the thought of Elaine came into his mind and then all the world was gone except for that woman he loved. Elaine. Elaine. Elaine the Fair. Thomas touched his finger to the edge of the golden sword. He barely had to touch the blade before it cut through his skin. He carefully cleaned away the blood and then put the weapon back in its scabbard. He was pleased that the royal sword was as

sharp as his newly whetted familiar weapon—the only difference was that the King's sword was heavier, weighed down by
gold and jewels, and then too the blade was thicker, because it
appeared that it had never been used—it had not been thinned
by repeated sharpenings.

I shall use that sword at dawn, Thomas thought.

The knight stepped out onto the plain and then turned
around to look back to the east. He realized that full daylight
would come late because the sun would have to clear those thick
trees. He turned back to the west and tried to make out a shape,
anything, but all he could be certain of was the velvety bulk of
Saladin, quite close now—the horse had either forgiven Thomas
his sins, or else perhaps scented the grain that Thomas had
transferred from saddlebag to pocket.

Thomas gave the horse some grain—he reflected that he
would probably be riding again in an hour, just as soon as a hint
of light revealed the location of the monstrous stones.

Thomas was right. In an hour he would be riding—riding
toward Elaine's screams—riding toward the flames.

Chapter 89

THE THROWN AXE

The skin slowly abraded off Arthur's wrist—and then the slick blood made it easier as he forced card after card between hemp and flesh. When he got about a dozen cards in there, he crumpled them lengthwise. The crude lever lifted the rope off his wrist—but then the strained cord bit deeper on the other side of his arm, and the skin there began to go as well. Arthur was unconcerned. A bit of skin was a small price to pay for his life. He forced another dozen cards into the bloody gap, and when he folded them the pain grew nearly unbearable—Arthur pulled hard and suddenly felt blood sluice over his fingers—then he realized that the flow was no longer blocked by the rope—one hand was free.

He quickly untied the knot—both hands free now—he wiped the blood on his leggings and then untied the rope about his ankles.

Just as he remembered where every card was in a deck, so Arthur remembered the position of each sleeping Northman in the circle that surrounded him. He remembered how they slept with weapons in their hands—he remembered the placement and type of each particular weapon.

These Northmen were all a pack of jokers to the Chancellor of the Exchequer. They had not taken him seriously.

He stretched carefully to get the circulation back in his legs—then he stood up—suddenly he was a huge target—he wished he knew where the sentry was—the moon had gone behind a cloud again and he could see nothing in the blackness—he knew he couldn't stand still forever—he needed a weapon—he took a step toward a Northman who slept with a small battle axe in his right hand, took a step with that lightness of foot that many fat people have and none of the sleepers woke—

The sentry's horse heard Arthur. The horse cocked an ear toward the camp and blew through his nostrils in the cold night air. The sentry had been looking *out* into the night for potential foes—now he picked up Arthur's bulk in the dark and turned his mount in toward the camp.

Arthur heard the hooves—he took two more quick steps and yanked the axe out of the sleeping Northman's hand—Arthur spun toward the approaching sentry and hurled the weapon with all his strength—

The sentry, sword out, was riding in fast now—the last thing he expected of the fat Englishman he had kicked last night was an axe, certainly not a thrown axe—it glinted once in his eyes and then cleaved his skull.

The young sentry fell dead from his horse.

Arthur dashed between two bleary eyed Champions, grabbed the reins, mounted, and took off.

The Assessor hardly needed any time to decide which way to go—west was the way to save Elaine and west was the Northmen's goal and west was the direction that they would search, and so he rode ten yards into the forest that way, crashing through the brush, and then he turned his horse north and finally broke back out of the woods going east, he rode to the east as fast as he could push his horse, he rode toward London, he rode away and left Elaine the Fair to her fate.

Chapter 90

THE VIKINGS PRESS ON

Ivar didn't panic—but he didn't waste time, either. He and Sigurd came out of the wagon, naked swords in their hands, and strode quickly to the spot where Arthur should have been lying in his bonds. No one was there—in fact, the only figure lying down now was the young sentry—Ivar prodded the corpse with his sword and then rolled the body over with his foot—he saw the glint of the axe embedded in the dead man's skull.

"Whose is this?" Ivar asked, in a low, deadly voice.

Fridriksson—who had suffered most at English hands, and who was next in command after Sigurd—stepped forward with his eyes on the ground. He looked once at the buried axe—he feared death for his own unwitting role in the prisoner's escape.

"It's mine, Sir."

"Then take it out and clean it. Prepare for battle, *now*!

As Fridriksson bent to this grisly task, Ivar went on, "We are close enough now. The Englishman means nothing to us." Ivar stopped suddenly, hearing something—he said urgently, "Listen."

The men listened, not even daring to breathe, and then they heard the sound, the only sound in the utterly still night, the sound of hoofbeats, a sound that gradually faded away, the sound of a horse galloping off to the east.

"You see, he means nothing to us," Ivar repeated, and the men looked at their leader in awe (though they could barely make him out in the darkness, his presence had a coldly thrilling majesty). The Heartless One was terrible—but he always seemed to know their foes better than they knew themselves—his expeditions had always been successful, every man here had been enriched by them—it was only right that they should help him seize the one woman he wanted.

Ivar went on, gloating, "He does not care to warn his wife—I think he *does* want me to punish her."

There was a sharp cracking sound as Fridriksson got the axe free. Ivar looked down at him once, casually, and then he continued. "It's just as well that we had this interruption. I see a hint of light in the east—and that means it's time for us to press through the woods. We should get to the other side just as the true dawn breaks.

"Saddle up the wagon horses—we'll leave that monkish conveyance here."

The horses were ready in a few moments. Ivar looked around at his men, and then gave his orders.

"Thorson, you're the biggest of us. You lead the way. Walk your horse behind you. The rest of us will follow in single file—quiet as possible.

"Thorson, the moment you make out the plain, stop. I don't want anyone to break out of the woods until I give the plan of attack."

The Vikings obeyed their orders—no one said a word about the dead comrade they left behind on the ground. Not one of the men even thought to ask their Chief for permission to give the dead man a proper funeral pyre. They knew instinctively that Ivar would refuse such a request—he would never allow their position to be exposed in that way.

The men knew their Chief well—Ivar the Heartless had never allowed sentiment to endanger a mission.

The eight surviving Vikings entered the forest.

A mile away, the Larrazian sentries waited for true dawn—and let their leader sleep.

Chapter 91

TIED TO THE STAKE

A moment before dawn, Tuesday, June 16, inside the sacred circle called Stonehenge . . .

Bart kissed the sleeping lady in his arms. Elaine returned the kiss, for this was the first time in her life that she had been held through the night by a strong man, and in her dream she was on a bed of rose petals . . .

It was the Vulture's cultured snarl that really began to awaken Elaine. She heard the voice of the brutal reality she was living, she felt Bart shake against her—and she didn't understand at first because she was still struggling to hang on to the dream—it was so sweet, she just wanted to keep living in that world—but then the voice snarled again and the powerful instinct of self preservation forced her heavy eyelids open—she saw that the Vulture was beating Bart over the back with the flat of a naked sword.

Elaine stared up in horror at the raised deadly steel—and then she tried to look at Bart, but he avoided her eyes and rolled away from the Vulture's blows, rolled away from her.

The Vulture sheathed his sword—Bart stood up—between the two of them they yanked Elaine to her feet. She looked around wildly in the gray morning light—she saw the gray masses of stone surrounding her—they began to drag her—she saw where they were taking her—she saw the gigantic wooden stake sprouting obscenely above one of the biggest rocks—this was even worse than the gallows she had imagined—she began to scream.

Elaine expected someone to strike her mouth but they just kept dragging her along. She kept screaming, hoping that some rescuer would hear.

Each man had an arm and they had to lift her in the air to counter her dragging feet.

The stake was behind the upright stone nearest to the circle's single entrance. This was one of the best preserved areas of the outer ring. To the left of the chosen stone there were several more upright rocks, and all these were still connected by lintels. Eventually one came upon a stone that had fallen diagonally onto its fellow, and beyond that, the circle degenerated into ruin, with only the odd disconnected stone still standing.

The Vulture's men had built a crude ladder, which they had leaned against the stone by the stake. The two villains did not have an easy time getting Elaine up that ladder. She kicked, she bit, and she howled—but finally strength and numbers overcame her resistance. They got her on top of the rock, and then they tied her to the stake.

She stood with her feet on the stone, facing east—he arms and legs were tied to the sprouting stake behind.

The wood for the bonfire was in front of her.

In the midst of her terror Elaine found time to wonder how Bart could do this to her—how could he prepare her cruel death when he had loved her last night, loved her in the best way that he could—she looked at his face and he was not as tormented as he might have been—and then she looked again at the logs and kindling ready for the bonfire, and suddenly she understood Arthur's trick.

The wood was placed so that the fire would burn in front of her—far enough away so that she would not be harmed by the flames. It was not *her* death that was prepared.

Elaine regretted her screams, for she realized now that she was the bait in her false husband's trap—her cries were the lure, and that was why the Vulture had not covered her mouth—she understood this, but she still didn't know who the intended victim was.

She stared in furious silence at the forest to the east, a forest now pierced by the long rays of the rising sun.

She didn't even deign to look down when one of the men on the ground passed up a smoldering torch—she paid no attention as the Vulture lit the kindling.

She concentrated on the woods. Who would emerge? Roland? Thomas? She wanted to be ready to warn the man who loved her.

But then it seemed that Arthur had thought of that possibility too—she hadn't noticed Bart slipping around behind her—he forced the gag into her mouth before she could resist, and then he tied the cloth tight at the back of her head.

Elaine's screams were no longer required.

Chapter 92

ARTHUR RIDES TO THE EAST

Arthur had gone over every detail of his plot a hundred times in his mind. Even now there was the chance that the trap might slam shut in just the way he had envisioned. He smiled, riding toward safety, and let the little tragedy he had scripted play itself out behind his dreaming eyes.

In imagination, he heard Elaine's screams—yes, the sun had cleared the horizon, she must be howling even now—how he had hated her screams in the night! How helpless, how weak he had felt, expected to give comfort, but having none to give. He closed his eyes to shut out the memories, he let the horse have its head, he let the play go on—yes, first there will be her screams, the sight of the stake alone should be enough to induce her cries, but if she's stubborn the lash can be applied—in any case, they make her cry out, and the brave Sir Thomas will hear her! He's been traveling desperately, knowing he must get to Stonehenge by dawn, but woods and darkness must surely have stopped him—but now he hears her, and soon, peering through the gray light, he sees his screaming love tied to the stake. He sees her gagged, as if to silence her cries once she begins to burn—he charges forward on his great black steed, he watches in horror as a villain lights the fire! He races forward as the flames appear to engulf her beauty. He has no idea that the fire has been set too far forward to harm her—he charges like a madman, straight for the only entrance to the stone circle, sword out to slay the villain and save his lady—but then the black horse breaks his forelegs on the trip rope stretched between the entrance rocks—and then not one, not three, but *five* villains pile on him, they kill him, and the Vulture cuts out his heart while my dear wife watches.

Arthur smirked, dreaming, and he continued the lovely story. Later I come to her, he thought, (imagining what was no longer possible) and this part is especially amusing. The men think I must pay them! There are too many for me to fight, and I can not bring in other soldiers, for fear that my conspirators would tell the whole story. They think I must make them rich, buy their silence—but they are fools. I bring heaps of gold, I bring wine to toast our success. And then I watch as they writhe with poison in their bellies, the poison that Fair Rosamond chose—I watch them die. Elaine watches them die. She'll know then that her life is in my hands. The life of any man she loves is in my hands. I free her on condition of her obedience and her silence. I make her look at her dead lover. I take her home as my slave . . .

Arthur opened his eyes and discovered that his horse was heading off cross country. He pulled on the reins, feeling the pain in his abraded wrists—he got his horse back on the track that led to London, that led to the King.

Arthur thought that it was a pity that the second half of the plot could not work as planned—yet even so, the result might be the same. He considered the possibilities.

If Thomas was ahead of the Northmen, as was likely, he would be killed as planned. Then the Northmen would approach when the Vulture's troop would no longer be expecting danger. Arthur had no illusions about the weak men he had hired. They could never stand up to a Norse force, especially one that outnumbered them eight to five. The Northmen wanted Elaine, not witnesses to spread the alarm. They'd kill the five villains, and that would eliminate any evidence connecting Arthur to his wife's kidnapping.

The Chancellor considered the other possibility: what if the Northmen were ahead of Thomas? Then, with the trap baited and set, it was likely that the Northmen might lose a couple of their Champions—but still, they had eight horsemen—even if they lost the first two to the trip rope, the remaining six would still be more than a match for the Vulture and his men. Once again all of Arthur's conspirators would be killed, again there would be no connection left to their paymaster. So Elaine would end up in Norse hands (as in the first scenario) but this time Thomas would still be at large. Doubtless he would try to rescue Elaine—with any luck, the Northmen would kill him.

Arthur was satisfied—he didn't have perfect control, but still there was no way he could lose, no way he could be connected to his crimes.

Elaine and her lover would be punished.

Arthur kicked his horse, and spoke cheerfully to the animal, "Get going, you old nag, for I intend to demand an audience with the King today! I must tell him that I have discovered that my wife was kidnapped by brutal Northmen. Richard will be thrilled by the chance to be a hero. He might even be able to cut them off—he might defeat the Northmen, and kill their evil leader for me. What will my chastened wife be like after a day with that shaven headed monster? Surely then she will be grateful to me for arranging her rescue.

"And what if Richard is not in time? Well, no matter—a lifetime of slavery might be good for Elaine—at least then I would never more have to hear her cries in the night . . ."

Arthur's voice had run down and it was far from cheerful at the end. He felt tears on his cheeks and he brushed them away angrily—he kicked his horse again but the increased speed was painful—Arthur was not a good rider and every bounce seemed to tear open anew the hole in his belly—he was hungry but afraid to seek food—he raced to the east, driven by terror and self loathing.

His triumph over the Northmen meant nothing in his heart, a heart that knew his own cowardice.

He rode toward the safety of the palace, toward the protection of his King.

Chapter 93

SIX DEAD

There was some gray light for a while, and then the first clear rays of sunshine appeared over the horizon. The Larrazian sentries, following orders, wakened their Duke at that moment.

Too late.

By the time Roland's men cut through the forest the battle was over. They rode up to Stonehenge and found only the stake, and charred wood from the fire atop the rock, and six corpses.

Elaine was gone.

Chapter 94

THE BATTLE OF STONEHENGE

The dull gray bump on the flat surface of the plain had to be Stonehenge, and Thomas rode toward it in the predawn gloom. The first two miles out of four passed quickly enough, but the last two were a seemingly endless agony—though Saladin traveled ever faster—for it was in those last two miles that Thomas was able to make out the small, white clad struggling figure of Elaine—as he came closer he heard her screams, still so faint and far away and yet they burned him like a candle flame against the skin—he saw her dragged up the ladder and onto the big rock—he watched helplessly as they tied her and gagged her and lit the flames—he saw, coming from the north as he was, that the fire was not set to burn her but that was small comfort considering the abuse already meted out—he was closer, closer now, but then he saw the monks coming from his left and he knew he wasn't nearly close enough—he didn't understand what was going on, all he knew was that he had to save Elaine somehow, late or no—he gave no thought to trap or danger—he just charged straight ahead like the lovesick fool he was, charged like a fool from the wrong direction.

If he had been on course, he would have died.

When Ivar heard the screams, and saw the flames—from just inside the western border of the woods—he realized that once again he had underestimated the fat Englishman. The cruel Chief of Champions had thought that Arthur might beat his wife, or even have her raped, but he had never expected that she was to be burned at the stake! Now it looked as though her beauty would be charred in just a few moments—and his own dream of a love that could make him whole would be gone forever.

There was no time for strategy. "Mount up!" Ivar roared. "Attack! Single file behind Thorson." Ivar mounted up himself as he yelled at his men. "Now!"

Thorson and his mount burst out of the woods, Ivar riding close behind, Sigurd and the rest trailing. The charging Vikings stared at the fire and Elaine's white figure, seemingly wreathed in flames. They didn't notice the distant horseman closing from the north.

The Vulture was expecting one man to come at them, and he saw, at first, (looking into the low lying rays of the sun) one man—he turned to Elaine and growled at her in a low gloating voice. "Never more will you dally with Sir Thomas, for you shall watch us kill him now." The Vulture turned his head back to check the distance of the approaching rider—and stared in consternation. This was not a knight—no, it was a huge crazed monk—and there were more behind him! The Vulture scrambled for the ladder and got down from his exposed position on the rock. Bart followed him down.

Elaine understood Arthur's plan fully now. She knew the intended victim (he had always feared the warrior) but she also knew now that something had gone wrong with the plot.

Elaine had the best vantage point of anyone on the field of battle. Even through the haze of the fire before her she could see that there were eight monks charging (not Thomas, as Arthur had intended) and she also knew that these attackers were neither saviors nor true monks—no more than that crazed foaming priest—no she had no time to think of the past now— the monks were closing, she saw them pull swords and axes and bows from beneath their cassocks—she recoiled from their evil, she looked desperately around her and suddenly noticed, quite near, a knight of the English court! It was Sir Nigel, and for just one wild moment she thought she was saved, but then she heard the Vulture say, "Secure the trip rope, Nigel, now!"

She watched Nigel obey—she realized he was the dimly seen escort that she had noticed through the curtains of the coach— the false knight that, until now, she had not seen clearly in the light of day—a false knight like the false monks thundering closer—she felt bitter tears in her eyes, and she could not raise her bound hands to wipe them.

Elaine turned away in despair, turned away from the searing heat of the fire before her, turned away from the charging evil monks, turned away from the cowardly knight and the Vulture and the other criminals—she looked off to the north through her blurred, tear filled eyes, she expected nothing, she only dreamed, she didn't know what that black shape was, something black and big approaching, a horse, a dream horse and auburn haired rider—a dream.

More tears tried to come and Elaine said, "No!" quite loudly, she turned her head when she said it so she looked at the monks, she whipped her head back and forth, she whipped her face with her long hair and shook the tears from her eyes—she turned her head and took one more quick look and then she knew that the black stallion was real and the man on his back was Sir Thomas.

Elaine knew then that her one duty was to make sure no one else noticed the black apparition closing from the north. She stared straight ahead with unfeigned terror—she stared only at the closing monks.

Bart crouched at the base of the rock below the bound Countess. He might instead have slipped between the rocks and crawled through the ditch and made his escape, and in former days he would have, but today he drew his sword to protect Elaine the Fair—he was noble again for the last few minutes of his life.

Thomas did not have to urge Saladin on—the horse had had at least a short rest, and now he was streaking forward with all the excitement of his master, nostrils flaring with the scent of battle, nose extended for the point Thomas aimed for—the brave knight hoped to use the cover of the still connected rocks to Elaine's left, he rode for the diagonally fallen boulder that leaned against the last of that line, he thought they might slip under that leaning boulder and come up behind Elaine, he leaned forward along Saladin's neck to get the last bit of speed out of the horse, he drew the King's golden sword—he looked over at the evil monks—(he had needed no more time than Elaine to scent them as enemies) and he cursed that they would still beat him by a good minute—Saladin was galloping faster than the horse had ever moved before, there was no more speed to be had—Thomas focused on the diagonal boulder—he had no idea that, save for the entrance the monks were approaching, all the rest of Stonehenge was ringed by a ditch—a ditch six feet in depth and width.

The Viking point man, Thorson, had the reins in his teeth and a sword in one hand and an axe in the other. The coach horse he

rode was a big clumsy animal, its gallop was an up and down
seesaw, not smooth at all, and Thorson with no hands to hold on
just squeezed the horse viciously with his powerful thighs—the
trip rope between the entrance rocks was set low for Thomas's
smooth striding Arabian—the ungainly coach horse bounded
right over the rope with its lurching forelegs—the head of the
horse came down, and the strong rear legs of the carriage
pulling horse slammed right into the rope—the rope held, the
horse's legs held, the horse stopped cold and Thorson kept
going. He flew right over his horse's bowed head at the speed of
the gallop—he flew, a two hundred forty pound bird, weightless
for its second of flight, and then he saw the bluestone of the
inner circle coming toward him, he put out his hands to save
himself but he forgot his weapons, the sword tangled with the
axe and he had no time to drop them before his face was
smashed against three thousand year old stone.

Ivar had just time to guide his horse to the right around
Thorson's horse—he saw the rope and kicked his rather better
mount into a leap over it—Sigurd managed the same maneuver
on the left—the next Viking had time to dismount and chop the
rope in twain with his sword.

The rest of the Vikings streamed through the entrance.

The trap was sprung, and Arthur's men were in the trap.

The Vulture tried to run, but Sigurd, mounted, easily caught
him up and plunged a sword through his back. The Vulture
twisted off his impalement, and slid down the side of the ditch.
He collapsed at the bottom and died shortly in great pain.

Nigel fought desperately but ineffectively—the Vikings battled according to no rules of chivalry—they simply set two men
on one and harried Nigel from either side—they poked him and
slashed him as he futilely jerked back and forth—they cut him a
dozen times until he dropped his sword and fell dazed to the
earth—each Viking buried his sword in the helpless knight and
then they stormed off in search of new victims—Nigel lived a little longer, he listened to the faraway sounds of battle—his senses were leaving him, the bright red of his own blood was
blurred—he remembered the afternoon in Arthur's room, the
brightly scattered cards, the madman's dream. "It's all a
dream," he said. "I took Jillian away." He closed his eyes and
died.

The Vulture's coachman had driven his vehicle inside the
third and smallest circle of stones. The horses were all hitched

up—he was waiting for a lull in the battle, and then he intended to drive right out at high speed and make his escape—he crouched low on his seat, but a Viking archer standing up on his stirrups saw the hidden coach—an arrow killed the coachman while he still believed he would get away.

The choker who had tormented Elaine did not try to preserve his life. He had been a criminal all his life, and he had always known this day would come. He had often imagined his own hanging—he had liked to dream that it would take place before the King—but in some ways this death was even better. These armed monks were the judgment of God—he accepted that—he looked up at Elaine, high on her rock—I kissed you, he thought—he smiled, and a passing Viking lopped off his head. The disconnected body jerked in its death agony—but the separated head fell peacefully to the earth, its smile fixed for Roland's men to puzzle over an hour later.

The only conspirator left alive was Bart—he still crouched at the base of Elaine's stone, sword in hand. The Vikings made sure that there were no others—and then they gathered themselves into a group, and looked at the prize and her last guardian. Ivar dismissed the surviving criminal as a threat—he looked up at Elaine and chuckled softly to himself as he came to understand the trick. She was unburnt, unharmed. Would he feel love for her if he looked at her any longer? He turned away, for first there was this man to kill, and killing had long interested him more than love.

Ivar dismounted, as did his comrades. He led his six surviving men slowly toward Bart. The Chief pushed back the hood of his cassock, so the Englishman could see the whole shaven visage of death coming for him.

The other Vikings fanned out behind Ivar.

The Chief of Champions drew his sword. He had not killed anyone yet today.

Bart shook in terror as he watched his death approach. He cringed against the stone that Elaine stood on. All the small bravery he possessed kept him barely upright. He tried, with this last stand, to expiate the sins of a lifetime. He hoped that Elaine would be looking down at him when he died.

Elaine was looking at Bart—and then at the leader of the killer monks, she looked at the gleaming shaven head, she looked at the rest of his infernal crew—she saw one familiar face but she couldn't place him, couldn't concentrate on any-

thing except one thing, and that was what she must not think
of, she must not give any sign or turn of the head, she must look
at the evil monks, look at Bart, she must never allow hope to
show in her face . . .

Thomas and Saladin saw the ditch at the same moment and
they made their decision in an instant because it was the only
decision they could make, there was no time to slow down, certainly no time to stop—they were going too fast to scramble
down the side of the steep drop—the only choice left was to
maintain speed, or even increase it, keep racing—and jump the
ditch. The man's will and the horse's were one. Thomas leaned
forward just a little bit further as Saladin reached for an even
longer stride—Thomas hoped they would land before the angled
boulder—the ditch was almost there—Thomas didn't try to kick
Saladin into the leap for he knew the horse would better pick
the best moment—the knight held the golden sword tight with
his right hand, his other hand loose on the reins, his life gam-
bled freely on the strength of the trusted stallion, and Thomas
hardly felt the leap at first, just another long stride, but then
there was no jarring hoofbeat, they were rising, they were floating forward in the air, still rising O God Thomas suddenly realized the leap was too good, Saladin was too strong, they cleared
the ditch easily, too easily, they were coming down but no they
wouldn't fall short—Saladin's iron shod feet struck the angled
boulder with a crash and an explosion of sparks, they hung in
midair on the edge of a sloping rock and Thomas saw his
chance.

Everyone turned to look, Elaine could look because there was
no secrecy now, even Bart looked—everyone except Ivar
looked—the Chief of Champions was always attentive to the job
at hand. Ivar sighted down his sword and drove its point
straight through Bart's chest—he pierced the heart that learned
too late to love.

Bart's last wish did not come true. He died without a glance
from Elaine. Instead, she watched Thomas turn the horse to
face *up* the rock—she watched him drive the animal, as though
by sheer force of will, until the struggling stallion's forelegs
hooked over the last connected lintel—she saw him give the
horse a brutal kick, saw the horse make a desperate lunge forward and up and somehow gain the top of the rock—the horse's
feet were now level with hers, and the road was paved between
them.

By the time Ivar looked away from his victim, the black stallion was racing again—racing through the sky along the connected lintels toward Elaine, every iron hoofstep marked by an explosion of sparks—Thomas forced the horse to stop right next to the fire, Saladin jerked his forelegs away from the flames and struck a burning log with a rear leg—the log rolled off the rock, and so flame fell from the sky toward Ivar's face—he ducked away and didn't see the golden sword flash twice—Thomas sheathed the sword as the bonds fell away from Elaine—she leaped up to her savior and he caught her with his good right arm, caught her just in time for Saladin drove on forward to get away from the flames, took two leaping strides and came to the end of the lintel and kept going.

The Vikings watched with astonished eyes as horse and man and woman floated through the air and dropped below their line of vision, dropped deep into the ditch, and then they heard the splash and saw the mud come up.

Another time that terrible drop would have broken even Saladin's strong legs—but yesterday's rain had softened the land, and water had collected in the bottom of the ditch— Saladin staggered and righted himself and then Thomas squeezed the mighty horse with his thighs—Saladin scrambled up the steep far side of the ditch, reins loose, mud splashed rider holding Elaine like a roll of carpet under one arm— Thomas kept the horse going south, open country, no time to change direction and anyway the woods would slow them too much, they'd be caught and cut down by the superior force, now Saladin hit his stride as Elaine clawed at Thomas trying to get a grip, she got an arm around him and pulled herself up, she straddled the saddle facing him, he tore the gag from her mouth and threw it away, Elaine ducked her head and embraced Thomas, she wrapped both arms around him and held him tight, he drove the horse south, knowing that the false and terrible monks would soon be on their trail, but still for now he had this moment, he put one arm around Elaine and hugged her as she held him, he was happier than ever before in his life.

Chapter 95

ROLAND EXAMINES THE EVIDENCE

The Duke of Larraz would have rent the air with curses had not Lady Sandra been close by. Since she was there he forced himself to keep quiet but his reproaches tore him apart inside, for the silent horrible curses reverberating in his skull were all directed at himself.

With the perfect hindsight that all men possess, Roland swore that he had *known* Elaine would be in danger at dawn, he *should* have broken through the woods last night as his inner voice had begged him, he was a *fool*, he was *stupid*, and he proceeded from there to far less delicate descriptions. Finally he ran out of names to call himself, and then the only words left were the two that spoke the awful truth: Too late. Too late. Too late! He wanted to scream it but Sandra was behind him, looking wide eyed at sights no lady should see and then too his men had made their search and found all the corpses—everyone was waiting for his command.

Maybe it wasn't too late.

Elaine wasn't here—she must be alive—her abductors couldn't be more than an hour away.

He would examine the evidence—perhaps he could discover the identity of his enemies—perhaps tracks could be found on the grassy plain, for the turf was still wet from yesterday's rain and it would mark easily—there was hope. Roland breathed deeply and then allowed Anton to lead him around on a tour of death.

A few minutes later he called Sandra. The girl came bravely forward. She readily identified the Vulture, and she was reasonably sure about the other two criminals (though the smile on the one's separated head made her quite sick, and Anton had to hold her while she threw up behind a stone). She had never seen any of the other men before. Roland sent her away in Anton's care—he sat down on a fallen boulder and thought. He knew that every moment spent here meant that Elaine was farther away—he also knew that it was vital that he figure out just what had happened.

He laid out the array of puzzle pieces.

The Vulture and his two comrades, dead.

A coachman, (the Vulture's?) dead.

An English knight, dead.

An English monk, dead.

(There were few clues to Thorson's true identity. His weapons had been taken by his fellow Vikings—and his face was gone.)

Roland considered other evidence: there was the fire and the stake, but the fire had not been set to burn anyone. There was a perfectly good coach, but no horses to pull it.

Roland played with the pieces.

Three men kidnap Elaine. They have a coachman to drive them. They tie Elaine to the stake for some mock sacrifice. English knights attack them, one of the knights falls in battle and all of the criminals are killed. Elaine is rescued.

Fine—but it doesn't work. English knights rescuing Elaine would have come back to the east—and we would have met them coming through the forest. Then too, English knights would not have left their comrade to rot on unconsecrated ground—and besides, in none of this is there any explanation for the monk. How did he get here? Who killed him? Why was he left here in this pagan temple? And returning to Elaine, if she had been rescued, why didn't they use the coach to carry her? Where are the coach horses?

What of Sir Thomas? No, not even that amazing knight could have caused this much devastation. Six killed, all by different weapons—no, the attacking force had to number at least six men, and Thomas worked alone.

Roland grimaced as he thought of his terrible bargain with the King.

What if Thomas had saved Elaine?

Thomas was in love with Elaine. He was neither attacker nor defender.

Roland was closing in now.

Six men, maybe more, attack the Vulture and his criminals.

The attackers are not English knights—their behavior is all
wrong. The dead knight must have been in league with the
Vulture. The Vulture used to be a knight himself. Two false
knights, three criminals, attacked by—who was the monk? Was
he a monk?

Roland got up and walked over to Thorson's body. He pulled
back the bloody hood of the cassock. The man had a good head
of blood caked hair. He had not shaved the top of his head to
create the proper monk's tonsure. He was a false monk, a bad
fake.

Roland's mind was racing now. He didn't sit down again—he
paced.

A strong fighting force of at least six men—all disguised as
monks—attack the Vulture and his criminals. The monks prevail in battle, losing only one man. But then do they take Elaine
in the coach? No, they take the coach *horses*. They need speed,
not comfort, because they're still pursuing. One man snatched
Elaine away during the melee.

Only one man in all the world could have come between two
powerful fighting forces and taken away the lady they fought
for—Roland felt admiration in his heart for the man he had
sworn to kill, Sir Thomas the Silent.

There were still loose ends: the true identity of the monks, the
real commander of the kidnappers, the meaning of the stake
and the deceptive fire—but the vital issues were clear now.
Thomas took her off on that amazing stallion—Saladin, the old
ostler had said—for just a second Roland saw horse and rider
again in the rainbow's beautiful frame, and then he remembered the crash as his table was shattered by that horse's front
hooves. The knight that stole the King's sword has now stolen
Elaine—the monks are after him, they outnumber him—which
way would he go?

Open country, Roland thought, he has faith in that great
horse and he won't want to get tangled in the woods—Roland
had walked over past the stake as he thought, past the last
standing lintel, and now he looked down into the ditch—he
wasn't surprised at all to see the waterfilled prints of Saladin's
hooves, deep holes in the moist earth, hooves driven by the double weight on the horse's back: Thomas and Elaine.

Roland saw the muddy hoofprints going off to the south, open
country as far as the eye could see—he saw the marks of a great
number of other horses following.

He called for his men and told them what he had discovered and what he surmised—he said not a word about his promise to kill Thomas.

The tracks were easy to follow at first—the Larrazian troop made good time as they pursued the pursuers of Elaine the Fair.

Chapter 96

ONE CHANCE

Once, long, long ago, a month ago, in another age—Thomas had whispered an endearment to Elaine. It was during the lady's first lesson with the sword—Thomas had said softly, "My love," and Elaine had pretended not to hear—Thomas's soft voice had not demanded a reply. The knight remembered that moment, riding south now—since then he had declared his love a thousand times in imagination, in his mind he had addressed Elaine with every fond endearment—he had practiced enough. Their situation now was not dream, nor proper chivalrous instruction. They were pursued by brutally effective murderers. On the personal level, all false modesty was gone. The Countess clung to him like a woman, not a lady. Her silk nightgown, bunched up between them, was up to the tops of her thighs. Her legs were wrapped around his waist—her arms were tight around his back—her face was buried against his shoulder—and the heat of her barely covered breasts burned his chest.

The fact of Elaine's embrace was the purest happiness that Thomas had ever experienced—and he experienced it in the presence of death. Thomas needed to know where the monkish killers were—it would be hard for him to twist around with Elaine holding him as she was, but it would be easy for her to look back over his shoulder and tell him what he needed to know. All he had to do was ask—but at first he hesitated, for he was afraid of the answer to that question. He drew Elaine even closer to him, he felt the strength in that so narrow, fragile seeming back—he felt the answering pressure of her strong hands—he realized then that this frightened, abused girl was giving him her own strength—he took that precious gift and rose to the occasion.

He spoke clearly to Elaine—his endearment told her that he loved her, his steady voice showed that he was not afraid. "Darling, lift up your head and tell me where the monks are. Tell me how many there are and anything else you notice about them."

Thomas felt Elaine loosen her embrace and raise her head so that she was looking back over his left shoulder—but then she was silent for so long he began to worry about her. Was she still too terrified to talk? What had been done to her?

Thomas wanted to console her, but there wasn't any time.

"Elaine, you're all right," he said rather sharply. "Now tell me, what do you see?"

"Nothing," Elaine said. Her voice was a screamed out, dry harsh whisper.

Thomas wanted to shake her. What was going on? He started to say something and then Elaine continued.

"They're moving around behind the rocks—they're coming now." She swallowed painfully as she counted. "Seven monks, all armed."

"Any idea who they really are?"

"No, but"—Elaine remembered the one familiar face—"I've seen one of them before, I just can't place him."

It was difficult for her to speak. Elaine hadn't had anything to drink since the night before.

"Don't worry about it—just tell me what they're doing."

"They're spreading out—the last man is leading the four coach horses they took from my kidnappers—those four horses are all roped together."

"So that's what took them so long. How close are they now?"

"They're close, they're getting closer, they're coming up on the sides—"

Elaine's voice was getting panicky. Thomas gave his next order in the calmest voice he could manage. "Elaine, duck your head and hold tight—I've got to take a look myself."

Thomas turned his head to the left but he didn't have to look far. One of the monks had come up nearly level with him, just a hundred yards away. Thomas looked the other way and saw another monk at a like distance to his right. He craned his neck to look behind him and saw the other monks spread out like a great letter C—and he was the dot midway along an imaginary line from each endpoint of the letter.

The two monkish point men were armed with bows, and their arrows were nocked.

Thomas had been a poacher, once upon a time. He was a dead shot with the bow. He was sure that he could take out one of the archers—but that would give the other one a clear shot at his back.

If the arrow goes all the way through me, Thomas thought, it could kill Elaine.

Will the monk take that chance?

I have to guess the answer, now.

Why haven't they killed me already? An arrow shower from both sides and I would be dead in seconds—but such action would also, most likely, kill Elaine.

She's the one they're after, and they want to keep her alive—but how important is she to them?

Thomas recalled how the monks had swept into Stonehenge—he had caught glimpses through the rocks of their cold efficiency—they made sure they killed nearly all the English before they turned to Elaine. The one who looks like their leader—the bare skulled killer—he didn't even turn his head when I came riding—he killed instead—for these villains, killing comes first. I cannot risk using my bow—I believe the other archer would shoot.

There has to be another way.

Thomas looked around again—he realized that the monks were keeping up the pace quite easily. Thomas tried to urge Saladin on to greater speed—but to no avail. The stallion was exhausted from yesterday's extraordinary exertions—and then this morning's wonderful sprint and courageous leaps had come on top of that tiredness. The horse had performed nobly in the heat of battle—but Thomas knew now that the assault on Stonehenge had taken his last real strength—and the drop into the ditch had certainly not helped his legs—and now he had another hundred and ten pounds to carry! It was truly amazing that Saladin was moving at all!

Thomas abandoned the thin hope that they could outrun the monks across open country.

The knight did not reproach himself for not choosing the alternate route into the woods—the thick brush would only have been a trap—here at least he had room to maneuver.

Saladin is too tired for anything fancy, Thomas thought. Still, there has to be a way out.

Perhaps there was one chance—for Elaine.

Thomas caught the edge of a plan and began to embroider it. It was a long shot—and he would die—but there *was* one chance for Elaine.

He didn't see any alternative.

He stroked Elaine's hair and then pulled her head back so that he could look at her face.

He spoke calmly, with conviction. "Elaine, listen to me. I love you. I want you to live. I will not let you fall into the hands of killers who hide their evil behind pious robes. I have a plan.

"The monks are trying to tire us out now—they know my horse is exhausted, and the double load doesn't help. We need a fresher horse, and I'm going to get one for you.

"The one thing in our favor is that the monks don't want to use their bows. If they wanted to they could have killed me already—but an arrow might have hit you, and they're trying to keep you alive.

"I think they intend to wait until my horse can hardly walk, and then they'll force the issue with cold steel.

"I don't want to wait that long."

Thomas smiled at Elaine, and kissed her lips just lightly, and then he went on. "I know the town of Salisbury is almost due south of Stonehenge. I'm not sure how far away it is, but we should be seeing it soon. The moment we see the town, I'm going to make my break, I'm going to ride right for it.

"They'll close in to stop me—and that's when you get ready. Slide around behind me I'll need both hands, and you have to be ready to drop off. Wait until the contact starts—don't drop too soon, for then they can go for you without facing me. When you hear my sword strike, you drop. I'll kill one—keep the others busy. You take that dead man's horse and go like hell for Salisbury.

"The townsfolk will help you. Just ride as fast as you can and don't look back."

"Don't die for me," Elaine said.

Thomas just smiled slightly and stroked her cheek. Elaine could see that his mind was made up. She understood that he would be content to die, if only she would live. She couldn't look at his face anymore—she ducked her head and hugged him fiercely again, she pressed her lips against his strong shoulder, she thought of life, whereas before during her ordeal she had only thought of avoiding death. She might truly live. She

thought of the Duke of Larraz covering her on a bed of rose
petals.

"I will do as you order," Elaine said.

Thomas heard the hope in Elaine's voice, and he was pleased
that she believed him, pleased that she thought there was a
chance—for only by believing that could she possibly succeed.
Still, his own thoughts were black. Fear of death bothered him
not at all—no, what worried him was the thought that if the
enemy leader was wise—and the battle of Stonehenge suggested
that he was—then he might *not* commit his whole force to stopping the break. He might send four to block me, Thomas
thought, and leave three in reserve to keep an eye on Elaine.
Elaine drops off while I battle the four—and even if I kill one,
and engage three, there's still *another* three to hunt her down.

My plan only works if he panics and all seven engage me in a
melee—in that confusion, she might well get away, if only I can
keep the battle going long enough.

Thomas stroked Saladin's weary neck. It's a better chance
than we'll have later, Thomas thought.

Then suddenly there was no more time to think. The mildly
sloping ground gave way to a steep declivity falling off at an
angle to the right. There at the bottom of the valley lay the town
of Salisbury.

Farmers were peacefully tilling the land outside of town.
Thomas prayed that even now the local Baron might be riding
out with his knights to inspect his property.

Elaine felt Thomas's tension and took one look. She tightened
her hands around his waist and prepared to slide around
behind.

Thomas waited until he could see the town in the gap
between the second and third monks on his right. One had
crossed the declivity—the other hadn't entered it yet. Thomas
turned Saladin sharply to the right and struck him with both
heels.

The double loaded horse started down the hill.

Chapter 97

IVAR IN COMMAND

Ivar had laughed out loud, after the rescue, when he had seen Thomas and Elaine racing away from Stonehenge to the south. That laugh did much to efface the shock felt by his Champions—the men had stared in shock at the "flying horse," they had seen their prize snatched away—but now they were able to turn to their leader and see that he was only amused.

"Who is this man who has stolen the woman I seek?" Ivar began, looking around at his men. "I will tell you—he is a fool. He thinks he can escape us on a double loaded horse—and furthermore, he rides only in the direction that we desire! We shall let him lead us under his own power to our waiting comrades by the sea—what a pleasant surprise that will be for the English Knight!"

The Vikings could only marvel at their leader's assurance. The most unexpected blows never fazed Ivar—he thought on his feet and never failed to turn surprise into profit. That was why his raids were always so successful—that was why, despite his admittedly repellant character, men vied to sail with him. The Champions obeyed Ivar's orders with alacrity—they lashed together the English coach horses (even in the heat of the chase, the Chief of Champions did not forget that someone might be following *him*—the roped horses were part of a plan to deal with any such pursuit) and set out confidently after Elaine the Fair.

Their confidence in their leader was justified. They easily caught up to the fleeing English. They formed a moving C as Ivar had instructed them—they were able to see for themselves that the "supernatural stallion" was in reality simply an overloaded beast. They were the ones forcing the pace—they drove the horse to the south.

Ivar gave a few more orders once the English were fairly enclosed in the moving trap: he told his archers to shoot at once if the knight went for his bow, but he called the words lightly— he added that he was sure the weak Englishman would not take such a chance. Ivar also said that they must be sure that the English couple was kept away from towns—they must not be allowed to get help.

Ivar saw Salisbury the same time Thomas did—he was ready when the English knight made his break. Ivar rapped out two sharp orders—the first one had consequences for Thomas, the second one called for the release of the English coach horses.

Fridriksson cut the lead that connected him to the four roped together horses—he sent them on their way with a lash across their rumps.

While the Champions moved into the battle array that Ivar commanded, the loosed horses bethought themselves of home.

London animals all, they raced off to the east.

Chapter 98

THE RISING HEAT OF
THE SUMMER SUN

Saladin had trouble going downhill. The extra weight on the front of the saddle threw the horse off—he came down too heavily on his forelegs with each stride, legs already sore from the awful drop into the ditch. Saladin did what any sentient creature would do: he tried to avoid the pain. Long strides increased the pain, since the inclined ground fell away underneath his hooves, thus lengthening the drop—therefore the wise stallion decreased his stride. Thomas tried vainly to urge the horse on, but Saladin ignored his master—the horse knew well that he had already gone beyond the call of duty—he was slowing up, and that was the end of it.

The monks easily cut off the escape route. Four of them blocked the slope: the three from the right side of the C, and their shaven headed leader from behind—the latter grinned at Thomas as Saladin slowed even more.

Thomas looked around behind him and saw the other three monks watching his back—they were carefully staying out of fighting range—but they would be right there if Elaine dropped off the back of his horse.

Everything Thomas had feared had come true—it was as though the evil leader had read his mind.

Thomas acceded to that leader's unspoken desire—he turned Saldin at an angle back up the hill, he continued south as before—for the knight had begun to realize that only in this way would his life be prolonged—and if he stayed alive, then perhaps he could figure out another way to save Elaine.

The monks reformed their great letter C. They made no attempt to charge, they just drove Thomas south, drove him past Salisbury, drove him south along the open plain that extended, with only a few small hills and valleys, all the way to the unseen sea, they drove him, drove Elaine the Fair, drove the horse that carried them both, each step bringing further pain to the exhausted horse, each step agony for horse and master, for every moment Thomas had to be alert for the charge that he was sure would come soon, he could never relax—he held Elaine with one hand, and kept his mind prepared for battle.

Elaine knew that it was not cowardice that had made Thomas decide to turn away from conflict. She had looked back over his shoulder and seen the three trailing monks—she realized then that her brave protector's scheme had failed—she was glad that he had not charged hopelessly.

But was there any hope now? They rode on toward some awful destiny, without water, without food, without rest from fear.

Elaine began to cry, but she had no moisture left to give to the summer's heat. She shook with dry sobs against Thomas's body. He held her tight, and he cursed the burning heat that parched them, he cursed the evil men who drove them, he cursed his own helplessness—but all his curses were silent, held in with the same strength that made his arm around the lady steady and sure—his strong arm was hope, and Elaine's shaking sobs finally stopped.

Thomas brushed back a lock of Elaine's finespun golden hair—he bent down and whispered in her ear, "I love you, Elaine the Fair."

Elaine turned her head and pulled back so that she could look at his face—but the act of pulling back let her see the arc of evil monks, and she shuddered and tried to swallow and then finally spoke. "We shall need more than love," she whispered, her voice cracking on the last word.

It was nearly noon.

Her throat was so dry it just seemed to close up.

She was desperately thirsty—desperately afraid.

Thomas said softly, "No, you're wrong, we need love only—and perhaps also some water from that stream I see up ahead."

Elaine jerked her head around awkwardly and saw the thin flash of blue water—she turned back to Thomas, she smiled, and she kissed him with her dry lips.

Chapter 99

TWO MEN ON THE CHASE

The Larrazian knights followed a heavy track of horses leaving Stonehenge and heading south, but the trail became progressively harder to make out as the morning wore on. The plain was covered with a thick meadow grass—Roland's best trackers kept their eyes on the ground, searching for occasional bits of kicked up mud—the Duke thanked God for yesterday's rain, for without those muddy clues progress would have been almost impossible.

They were able to stay on the track—but it was slow going.

Sir Anton, riding behind the front line with Roland and Sandra, was very worried. He did not want to mention his fears to the Duke unless he also had a solution—as the sun rose higher in the sky, as the trail continued south, he considered the problems and came up with a simple answer.

"Your Grace," Anton said urgently, "we're taking too long. I know you're worried about losing the trail, but remember—Thomas pushed that horse hard all through yesterday. We saw him go at King Richard, and you told me how he galloped out of London. He must have kept up a terrific speed or he wouldn't have beaten us to Stonehenge. Now I don't care what kind of exotic Arab beast he has—if your lady is riding double with him, the other group is going to catch them in a hurry."

Roland had been thinking the same black thoughts. "What do you propose?" he asked.

"Send two men, Your Grace—myself and one other—Sir Gowan can look after Lady Sandra for now." Sandra looked anxiously at her man, but he just reached over and squeezed her hand without looking at her, and continued talking. "We'll ride straight south, fast as we can—we won't even bother to look for a trail, because I have a feeling that Thomas is breaking for the sea, he's not trying any evasive action, he's just pushing straight ahead—if I'm right we'll spot his pursuers fairly soon—we won't engage, we'll just make a quick reconnaissance and then return. If I'm wrong, and they take a turning, then of course we'll miss them—but you won't have committed the main body of our troops. You'll still be on the trail—and if my partner and I don't see anyone for, let's say two hours—you could lend me your hourglass—then we'll simply turn around and head back until we pick up your trail."

Roland's natural caution *had* made him afraid to push ahead fast and possibly lose the trail—Anton's proposal was a perfect solution to the problem. Roland reproached himself for not having come up with the same answer—but at the same time he was very grateful to the old soldier. Roland did not want to deprive himself of Anton's experience.

"A splendid idea, Sir Anton—but I need your good counsel, as you have just shown. I'll send Pierre and Daniel. Pierre has experience, and Daniel speaks English well, just in case they run across any observant citizens."

Anton tried to remonstrate, but the Duke's mind was made up. He dismissed Anton's objections—he called the two knights that he had selected, and they rode over eagerly.

Pierre, at thirty two, (just one year shy of the Duke) was the oldest knight save Anton. He had distinguished himself in Larrazian tournaments for years. He seemed a good balance for Daniel's romantic youthfulness.

The Duke explained Anton's plan. He concluded his orders as follows: "Just try to *see* the Countess. Don't try to rescue her yourselves—just observe the situation, see if Thomas really has her, try to identify her pursuers, count their number and armament, and then report back.

"And remember, if you see nothing for two hours—here, take this"—Roland handed his hourglass to Pierre—"then stop your search and come straight back until you pick up our trail. Understood?"

"Yes, Your Grace," Pierre said. "We will honor your trust."

"Then go, and Godspeed," said the Duke.

The two men lashed their mounts and galloped away from their bunched, envious comrades. Every man there wanted the glory of finding Elaine—tracking bits of mud was hardly inspiring!

Sandra, still holding Anton's hand, watched Pierre and Daniel until they finally disappeared over the horizon. She thought that she should be glad that her lover was still with her, that he had not gone off as he had intended, that the Duke had prevented him from risking his life—but that was not the feeling in her heart. She felt frightened—she felt terribly sad. Her heart fluttered feverishly and she wanted to draw Anton's hand closer and place it over her breast—she couldn't do that with the Duke nearby—she wanted to be comforted but she felt the tension in Anton's hand and realized that he couldn't comfort her now—he had wanted very badly to ride out himself—Sandra wished that the Duke had allowed him to go.

Chapter 100

DEATH'S LAUGHTER

Ivar let them drink.

He waved his men to a halt, half surrounding the English, and watched as the horse drank—watched the lady, Elaine the Fair, the object of his quest, as she slipped off the horse—watched as she went to her knees and drank from her cupped hands—watched Thomas who stayed on his horse, who turned around once and looked back with such intensity that it seemed their eyes met at one hundred yards—Ivar watched as Elaine rose up with water in her cupped hands—he watched Thomas bend his head and drink—he watched as the knight kissed one of the lady's empty hands.

Ivar the Heartless did not wave his men forward until Thomas had lifted Elaine back onto his saddle.

As the English rode off again to the south, the Vikings came up to the stream in turn—Ivar allowed his men to stop and drink, and then the pursuit continued. Once again the letter C formed around Thomas and Elaine.

Nothing remarkable had happened except that Ivar had deliberately missed his chance.

The time when Elaine was on the ground had been the perfect moment for an attack. The four closest Vikings could have charged when Elaine was on her knees. Elaine would have had to stand up and take two steps—and then Thomas would have had to lift her back up on the horse. By the time all that happened, the Viking archers would have been close enough for some precise shooting. They could have filled that black stallion with arrows without hurting Elaine—and once the horse fell, Thomas would have been easy prey. All seven Vikings could have fallen upon him then—by this time he would have been dead, and Elaine captured.

Ivar could have accomplished all that with a single order—he was sure that his men knew that simple truth.

Ivar looked around at the stiff backs of his Champions. He was sure that they also knew that following the black stallion (at its slow, heavily laden pace) was taking much longer than if they simply killed Thomas and carried the lady themselves. Then they could switch Elaine from one mount to another and make good time. This was important, because the men were doubtless also aware that the longer they dallied with this slow pursuit, the more dangerous it was for them. They had left a trail (the massacre in the coastal monastery, the herdsman and his wife, their own dead sentry and Thorson also dead at Stonehenge) *and* there was a messenger alive—the fat man they had tortured must even now be riding hard for the English court. If they took too long, they might be intercepted by an English army of true knights—nothing like Arthur's weak hired criminals—no, a large powerful army that could overwhelm them—and a captured Viking in England was worse than dead. Every Champion here knew the story of Ivar's father.

Ivar looked around to see if his men were watching him—but no, they kept their eyes studiously on the fleeing couple. They tried to give no sign that they knew their Chief had just committed a military blunder—they had sworn fealty, they were completely loyal—but still their tight twisted postures told Ivar all he needed to know. Not even Sigurd, riding fairly close to his left, would meet his gaze.

Ivar wondered what they were thinking—they had been so pleased at first when he had countered the surprise of Thomas's rescue of Elaine. They had liked the idea that the English were simply going their way, that they would drive the couple into a trap, a trap bounded by their familiar sea—but as the day wore on, as it became apparent that they were still far inland (there was not even a breath of sea air, not one gull swooping over these green meadows) they had begun to worry. The horses the champions rode would never be familiar to them like the smooth deck of a dragon prowed ship. They wanted to end this slow chase: kill the man, take the woman, and run to the sea.

Do they wonder why I hesitate? No, Ivar thought, they aren't sneaking looks at me—they aren't talking among themselves—they offer no argument. They don't wonder at all—they think they *know*.

They remember what I said at Stonehenge after Elaine's escape. They think my love of cruelty has twisted my judgment. They think I am getting perverse satisfaction out of driving this brave English knight slowly into my trap. They think I can not bear to curtail the delights of torture. They think that this is my happiness: a half circle of death, constantly threatening, almost enveloping the fearful couple—while the open path to the south tantalizes them with the hope of escape—a hope that I will take away, a false hope that will be struck dead by the waiting presence of my ship.

My men think that this is my way of breaking the Countess— I tease her with false hope, I allow her lover to live—and then, at the sea, I reveal my identity—I produce forty-one more Champions—I demonstrate my omnipotence as I kill her man.

My six unhappy comrades believe that I prolong the pursuit to prolong my pleasure—but they are wrong.

I would never endanger an expedition for pleasure—my own, or anyone else's. Yet I endanger this one, I endanger us all, because I feel my death close, and I am afraid. It is fear—not pleasure's weak cords—that ties my hands.

I have killed many times.

I know Death.

I fear him.

I saw him for the first time—Death with my own face—inside the circle of stones. I had just looked up at Elaine the Fair—she was standing above me, tied to the stake. This was my first clear look at her—and I saw that Sigurd was right in every way. She is indeed the most beautiful woman in the world. I felt her power sweep through every one of my men. I wondered to myself: If I look at her for another second, will I fall in love with her? And then I turned away, I looked instead at that silly Englishman gesturing futilely with his sword, and I killed him. I didn't look at Elaine again until she was being carried off.

I could have kept looking at her in the first instance—one of my men could have taken care of the little Englishman. If I had been watching Elaine I might have been able to prevent her escape—but I looked away because she *is* all that men dream of—I looked away, because when I saw her, I felt nothing.

I knew that another look at her beauty would just have finally brought home the truth of my crippled nature: I can not love—I care for no one.

I saw just the outline of my death over Elaine's shoulder, and he was laughing at me. He reminded me of my promise to Sigurd—and I knew that there was no point in evading it. I can not love—I can not love even the finest of all women—I can not live any longer as a cripple—I must die by my own hand.

I saw so much in that one glance at Elaine—I turned away, and I killed again, and Death laughed.

Sir Thomas came, and took Elaine off, and I was glad, for my death moved a few steps away—but I could still feel him. I feel him now. I do not wish to rush to him.

Now I play out the bitter farce that is the last act of my life. I will let my men think I am basking in evil pleasure. I will put off the moment of reckoning as long as I can. Yet, finally, inevitably, we will reach the sea—and I will have Sir Thomas killed.

Then I will delay my destiny no longer. I will take Elaine the Fair aside, and strip her of that bit of silk. I'll mount her, I'll watch her eyes as I plunge into her, and I know what I'll see. I'll see my death laughing, laughing in her blue eyes. I know even now that I'll feel nothing save fear—I'll see my death laughing as I slit her throat, laughing as her eyes turn to stone.

I'll cut my own wrists, just so I can live long enough to feel my death come—I have never felt life, but surely I will feel every touch of my death—I'll feel his coldness take me over . . .

Ivar felt them coming.

He laughed out loud, with death in his voice, and he snarled, "But my time has not yet come!"

Ivar yanked his horse over so that Sir Pierre's mace missed his head by a foot, and Sigurd dropped flat to his horse when he heard his leader's cry, and therefore Daniel's sword whistled harmlessly over his head, and then the two charging Larrazian knights were carried by their own momentum through the line, they were caught now inside the semicircle of Vikings, Thomas was too far up to help or even profit from the interruption, for after all it happened very fast.

The Larrazian knights were in the killing zone.

Ivar ordered his archers to shoot from either side.

Chapter 101

WISDOM

Pierre and Daniel had just come up over a small hill when they saw Elaine the Fair. They saw her riding double with Thomas on a struggling horse. They saw seven armed monks half surrounding the fleeing couple—the evil monks appeared to be closing with every stride.

Sandra was right to have worried.

Anton would have assessed the situation carefully. He would have observed long enough to see that the monks were *not* really closing the gap. He would not have charged seven with two, for the odds were long and the necessity for action was lacking. He would have turned around and reported back to Roland.

Anton had obtained wisdom in his life—but his wisdom was not a gift, it was the sum total of what he had learned from his experiences.

As a young man Anton had tired of his peaceable homeland—but he was skeptical of the Crusaders' call for faith over reason. He determined to fight only for his own gain. He hired himself out as a mercenary—he fought through the whole boot of squabbling Italian city states. He suffered pain—the scars Thomas had seen on his naked back were proof of that—and he knew pleasure, for many a black haired beauty shared his bed. He saw death—saw the reality of death, and he learned that neither love nor faith swayed the balance on the battlefield, for that balance was weighed in muscle and steel.

He would not have attacked seven with two.

Roland sent the wrong man.

Pierre was a veteran of many, many battles—all of them mock. He had fought successfully in hundreds of tournaments—

but never a war. He had seen death—he had been there when young Charles died—but in a tournament death is a tragic accident, not the merciless design of a superior force.

Pierre looked at Elaine and her pursuers, and it was as though he heard cheers from a thousand invisible spectators. "Save her now!" cried the voices in his head. "Save the Fair One before the evil false monks get to her—only you can save her!"

The imaginary cries fired his blood.

Daniel felt much the same. For this moment he believed he had become his hero Lancelot—and there was his endangered Guinevere! Lancelot would never quail before such odds—all Daniel's youthful impetuosity urged him to charge—he only waited for the older man's word, and he was wildly happy when he heard it.

"There is no time to go back," Pierre said. "We must charge at once!"

Daniel felt the blood pound in his veins, and he nodded his assent—and then they raced down the hill, good Christian knights, invulnerable in their righteous cause—they would save Elaine the Fair from her sacrilegious pursuers, they would be greatly rewarded by their Duke, they would be feted in their homeland . . .

They died.

Sir Pierre didn't know how he missed, the bald headed villain had given no sign he was aware of the attack, but suddenly he jerked away and the mace flew by his head—Pierre was pulled forward by his horse's momentum, he saw that Daniel had missed too—it should have been so easy, kill two and then with Thomas on their side the odds dropped right down to five to three, easy, but now they had both missed, they were inside the seven man pincers, Pierre thought his only hope lay in continuing to charge forward, then he could link up with Thomas and they could fight together, they would fight together to save Elaine, that was his plan but his straight unwavering course simplified the mathematical problem, the Viking archer traversed with his bow and led the moving target, the arrow flew straight and true and the man galloped into its path—the steel arrowhead exploded through Pierre's ear with the sound of a thunderclap—with the sound of a thunderclap, he obtained wisdom, and he died.

Daniel, on the other hand, tried to slow his horse at once so as to turn and fight—and thus the other Viking archer led by too much, and the arrow missed the man and buried itself in his horse's neck. Jerking in convulsions, the horse threw Daniel—he got to his feet, he stood alone, sword in hand—he watched the leader approach, he watched the uncowled death's head approach—all Daniel's dreams of Lancelot were gone, he knew that he was about to die but he was willing to go if he could just take this monstrous embodiment of evil with him, he watched the leader's face and he didn't see Fridriksson dismount and pick up Pierre's fallen mace behind him—Elaine looking back over Thomas's shoulder saw everything—she recognized the youth who had led her horse through the dark forest—she screamed, "Look behind you!" but she was too late, Daniel spun around but Fridriksson was already swinging the mace—the spiked iron ball smashed the boy's head like an eggshell.

Thomas, who had looked once and seen all that mattered, said, "There was nothing you could do," but Elaine kept screaming, or trying to scream, there was no moisture in her mouth or her newly parched throat, she was choking and gasping and bereft even of tears, she remembered the boy's nervous admiring eyes in the wood, she wanted to die but then slowly, slowly, another thought came.

Elaine had seen enough of Roland to know that two of his men would not be wandering off seeking adventure—if these two knights were here, then Roland and the rest of his force must not be far behind, another eighteen men plus the Duke—my lover, she thought, and then she whispered, "I must live," and Thomas heard her and held her tight and said, "Yes," and Elaine felt his strength, she said louder, "I *will* live," and Thomas squeezed her tight with his strong protective arms, he said, "Yes," again, he was pleased with her, she could feel it, and that helped her as she watched the monks reform into their familiar letter C, they seemed hardly disturbed by the skirmish, O she knew she was being driven toward some unimaginable terror, but still, she had hope now, hope dearly supplied by the death of two brave men, but hope nonetheless: Roland was on her trail.

She must not give up—she must fight to survive—her lover was coming.

Chapter 102

LOST

Roland was lost in the woods.

The trail had taken a clear turning to the left opposite the town of Salisbury. Anton saw some farmers working there at the bottom of the long hill (as Thomas had seen them) and he quickly made another request to his Duke. This one was granted. Anton gave Sandra's hand a squeeze and then he let her go—he rode down the hill, hoping one of the farmers had seen something. Sandra stayed with the rest of the Larrazian troop, which had turned east, following the clear track.

It was a long way to the bottom of the hill. By the time Anton reached the farmers his comrades were already out of sight. The wise knight spoke to the first man he saw. "Good day, Sir. I wonder if you might have seen some riders pass by this morning."

The old farmer rested on his rake and looked Anton up and down. Finally he said, "Talk to my son over there. He saw them."

Anton thanked the man and rode over to a young lad who was turning over earth with a pitchfork. The boy looked to be about fifteen.

"Hello, young man," Anton said. "Your father says you saw some riders go by this morning. Can you tell me, was there a lady among them?"

"They were very distant—but I saw a couple riding together, a lady and a gentleman"—the boy looked down and whispered the rest—"she had golden hair."

"On a black horse?" Anton asked gently.

"Yes.

"Who was riding with them?"

"Some monks—I saw their cassocks. They rode a little bit down the valley and then they rode back up again."

"Who rode down first?"

"Well, Sir, it looked like the lady and gent rode down first, but then the monks passed them—like they were racing, see—and then the lady and gent changed direction and the monks followed." The boy gestured, pointing back up the hill.

"How many monks were there?"

"I don't know, seven, maybe eight."

"Were the monks armed?"

"What!" The boy had answered the questions in a sort of dreaming reverie, most of the time forgetting to call Anton 'Sir', just dreaming of the distant lady whose exciting bare legs he hadn't mentioned—and now he was shocked awake, the picture in his mind suddenly sharpened, there had been something wrong about those monks but he hadn't really wanted to see— "O God! They were carrying something, carrying things on the other side of their bodies, blocking my view but I should have seen—what is going on?"

Anton took out a gold piece and handed it to the boy. "Thank you, my son. You have helped me very much, and you have helped my comrades, the knights of Larraz. We are on the trail of those evil false monks—and we are going to rescue the lady— you may know her name—she is called Elaine the Fair."

"I'll come with you," the lad said, in a clear steadfast voice.

"No," Anton said kindly, "Your duty is here with your father, but you will always remember that your words helped save the fairest lady in the land. Thank you again—and good-bye."

Anton turned his horse and rode back up the hill at a gallop. He caught up with Roland a few minutes later, as the Duke and his men followed the trail to the east. The Vikings had ridden far apart, so their individual mounts left few traces—but the four roped together coach horses had managed to kick up a good amount of mud. Roland was sure that he was following the main body of Elaine's pursuers. Anton rode up next to the Duke and told him what he had learned.

"You were right about everything Your Grace. Seven or eight villains disguised as monks (they're all armed) are chasing Elaine. She's riding double on a black stallion with an English gentleman."

"Thomas."

"Yes, Your Grace. They tried to make a break for Salisbury, but the monks cut them off—they doubled back, and judging from these tracks we're following, they decided to take their chances in the woods."

"Do they have a chance?"

Anton heard the desperation in his Duke's voice, in his friend's voice, but also he knew there was no true comfort save the truth.

"He has no chance, Your Grace. She does. They haven't killed Thomas yet because they are afraid to hurt Elaine. The boy I talked to said the monks easily cut off the double-loaded horse—but they didn't use their weapons. I think they are going to tire Thomas out and then cut him down—but your lady will live."

Roland accepted the truth of all that his friend said—but there was a darker thought that even Anton was afraid to express. The evil monks wanted Elaine alive—they wanted *her*. Roland thought of his beautiful lady—his tender fragile lady—he imagined her being raped by rough men—his face seemed to split with the pain of the thought, he felt that his skin wanted to peel back from his skull—he could no longer stay in the back with Anton, he rode up to the front line, and as he passed his men he told them quietly what Anton had discovered, explained that his surmises were correct, and encouraged his soldiers by telling them that they outnumbered the enemy force at least two to one.

The tracks led to the wood—they entered the forest, and now they were lost.

It was too dark in there to follow a trail—it was hard even to keep on a straight heading in view of the dappled, distorted sunlight that drifted vaguely through the leaves—Roland finally gave up any pretense of tracking and simply ordered his men to press on—they could cut the trail by searching up and down on the far side of the woods.

Still, it was a good hour before they fought their way through the forest—and then more time was lost as they had quite some difficulty finding the trail again, for as it happened the London horses they were following had angled north through the forest. Those horses had then returned to the last Viking campsight—then, frightened by the smell of death—but pleased to be on the familiar path toward home—the four had set off again to the east.

The Larrazian knights followed blindly. They saw the monks'

deserted wagon.

Gunter rode up ahead and gave a cry. All the Larrazian knights came forward excitedly—and looked down at the dead monk with the gaping hole in his forehead.

"Pull back his hood," Roland said.

Gunter dismounted and pulled it back—the dead man had a full head of hair.

"They've lost two," Roland said. "They can be beaten. Let's keep on the track—stay quiet and keep your eyes open."

They rode on—but visibility was not nearly as good here as on the Salisbury plain. This was rolling country like that around London—down in the dales one could scarcely see one hundred yards ahead, and even up on the hills one's view was blocked by the trees and thickets that seemed to line every cultivated field.

The enemy could be behind any hill—behind any tree—somewhere, just out of sight, Elaine might be struggling . . .

The Larrazian knights followed the trail with nervous care, and it was behind a group of trees that they discovered what had led them so far astray.

There was a rich green meadow behind those trees, and a stream, and the four London horses were no longer in much of a hurry. They munched contentedly on the long grass by the side of the running water.

Roland followed the track with his eyes as it led up to the four linked together, riderless horses. There were no evil monks in sight—no Thomas—no Elaine the Fair.

The Duke stared—it was the longest minute of his life—and then in one brutal flash of enlightenment he realized that he had been tricked. He threw back his head and howled—he cursed with a foulness totally appropriate to the situation—he cared not at all that Sandra could hear him—he screamed unGodly words toward heaven, words no one present had ever heard him use before—his voice reverberated with rage and pain and despair.

The London horses, unmoved, continued to graze peacefully by the bright running stream.

Chapter 103

CLOSED CIRCLE

Noontime, by a stream south of Stonehenge, an hour before the Larrazian knights were killed . . .

When Elaine gave Thomas water to drink, he noticed her pierced hand for the first time. He knew the water had to be burning the wound, and so he drank quickly. When he finished he kissed the red cut (as Ivar watched) and then he lifted the girl back up on his horse. Once she was in his arms again, once they were moving again, he asked, "What happened?"

She said, "Later, I can't tell you now."

Not now, she thought, not with this evil around us, perhaps not ever for how can I live again through that day? I was kissed by three dead men.

Elaine shuddered and embraced Thomas, but she could not relax against him. He had kissed her. Was he going to die?

Elaine could find no comfortable position on the rising front of the saddle. She squirmed, she pressed against Thomas, she broke away—and then she saw the Larrazian knights coming, and she did not say a word for fear of ruining their surprise attack—and then she saw that attack fail, and she cried out to Daniel—too late.

She went crazy then for a moment—she screamed until there was nothing left of her voice save a dry hurting whisper—and then, in that pit of desperation, hope came back to her, and she told Thomas that she would live.

Thomas held her with all the strength of his brave loving heart, and Elaine finally allowed herself to relax. She was hot and thirsty—her dry throat hurt while her face and hair were wet with sweat—she was being driven by murderers—and yet she had hope, and the will to survive, and a man to protect her, and a lover coming to rescue her—I will live, she thought. I will live.

Thomas bent down and kissed her wet hair. "You're beautiful," he said.

Elaine raised her head to show Thomas her sweatsoaked face. She ran one hand over her lank wet hair.

"Like this?" she asked.

"Yes."

"You're crazy."

Thomas lifted Elaine's chin a little further with one finger, and then he kissed her lips.

"I'm not crazy," Thomas said.

Elaine smiled slightly at that, and then she gently brushed his hand away and let herself fall dreamily against his chest. She felt the strength of his arm encircle her, hold her close. She rubbed her face against his shirt, and she whispered, "Yes, I'm beautiful," and then she closed her eyes. She let no evil come behind her eyelids—she filled her mind with honor, hope, and beauty—she let the motion of the horse rock her, she gave in to her own exhaustion—for the second time in her life she fell asleep in the arms of a strong man—but this time her protector was of much finer quality.

Thomas had to use more of his strength to hold Elaine now—her limp form tended to slip, and he had to constantly balance her—but he was happy. She trusted him.

Thomas was proud that Elaine believed in him as her protector—and with the pride came desire. He looked down at the vulnerable sleeping beauty he held—he felt her warmth against him, and he answered with his own heat. He felt a powerful erotic desire rise up in him—a desire that easily brushed aside trivial concerns like heat, hunger, and thirst. For just a moment he thrust forward so as to press against his lady and feel her softness through their few clothes—and then he smiled at himself, and relaxed a little, for there was no need to hurry. All he had to do was save Elaine—and survive himself—and all his dreams would come true.

Thomas looked around at the monks. They kept their distance—they drove him—but they didn't press. Saladin plodded stolidly along—they didn't try to frighten the horse into a gallop. They didn't seem to be in any hurry. Thomas sensed that they would not make a move if he did not force them—or at least, they wouldn't move until they had driven him where they wanted him to go.

Thomas had been desperately pessimistic before, with good reason. He knew quite well that they could have killed him—and taken Elaine—when he had stopped by the stream. They could kill him now if they were willing to charge and risk losing a couple of men. Thomas had no illusions about seven to one odds—and he knew these men were good fighters.

But they've made a big mistake, Thomas thought. They've waited too long—they've given me back my confidence. Elaine believes in her life—I have come to believe in mine. I am going to survive—I am going to outthink these monks—and I am going to defeat them.

I know that all the English knights are out looking for Elaine—judging by those last two unfortunates, the Larrazian men have also joined the hunt. The longer the monks wait, the more vulnerable they are to such an attack—though I hope the next one is better planned and carried out in force. I feel that these monks are going to wait too long—with just a little help, I can turn on them.

I'd like to kill them all.

Thomas held Elaine and rode on through the afternoon sun. He chewed the reins to get moisture for his mouth—he sucked the leather dry and was left with a terrible taste in his mouth. He tried to ignore it—he closed his lips, and held Elaine, and held to his resolve. He was glad that she slept through the worst of the heat.

He saw the monks tilt their heads back and drink from some kind of flask they carried. In his hurry, he hadn't even brought a flask with him. He couldn't remember when he had last eaten.

The sun was going down when he saw the river.

Thomas tried to force Saladin to run for it, but the horse had nothing left. Thomas kicked the stallion, and slapped him, and cursed him as Elaine began to stir in his arms—but nothing worked. He watched in horror as the enemy point men began to converge in front of him. He looked around him—he saw the other monks speed up and close the gaps—he saw the two monks ahead stop by the shallow river and turn—they were about twenty yards apart, and they had their bows out—he slowed Saladin—the other monks were much closer now—they stopped just twenty-five yards away—they were all twenty-five yards away—Thomas stopped Saladin—he was a prisoner inside a closed circle. The gaps were only about twenty yards between each monk—some had throwing axes in their hands. Not enough room even if Saladin could gallop—not even a prayer for a breakout at a walk or a trot.

Thomas turned all the way around and looked back at the gleaming skull that housed incarnate evil—the death's head creased into a smile, and then that leader dismounted. Thomas saw the other monks follow suit.

The sun turned Elaine's hair red and then it sank beneath the horizon. The monks took turns going to the river to drink. They evened up the gaps when one was so engaged.

They didn't kill Thomas.

I suppose we spend the night here, Thomas thought.

Elaine was moving in his arms but she was still asleep. Thomas touched her cheek gently to wake her—without thinking he touched her scar.

Elaine woke up, mouth open, trying to scream—a painful dry whistle came from her dry aching throat—her eyes were black and wild in the near darkness—Thomas put his hand over her mouth and said, "You're safe."

Elaine shook her head under his hand, she saw the surrounding monks, present fear joined with the past terror of the dream—she kept trying to shake her head but Thomas just stopped her mouth and held her face still—"You're safe with me," he said.

Elaine stared up at Thomas in the near darkness, she fought the remnants of the dream and the present horror—she looked at her knight's face, and she realized that not to believe him was to die. Thomas was the man who stood between her and death. Thomas had protected and held her through her slumber. Because of Thomas, Roland had a chance to rescue her. Because of Thomas, the two brave Larrazian knights had not died in vain. She was going to live—she pushed Thomas's hand away— she raised her head and kissed Thomas with dry hurting lips, and that was all the belief he needed.

Thomas kissed her back with a grave gentleness, and then he helped her dismount, and got down himself. Saladin shook with grateful relief. Thomas took off the horse's bridle and saddle. Saladin put his head down, but for a while he was too tired to graze.

Arthur the Assessor had said that a man on a good horse could get from Stonehenge to the sea in a single day. Saladin, with his double burden, had covered three quarters of that distance.

Tomorrow morning, both hunters and hunted would begin to smell the sea.

Chapter 104

BACKTRACK

Early afternoon, in a lush green meadow, by four riderless horses . . .

There was not one sound in the Larrazian ranks after Roland's outburst. They all knew too well what this disaster meant.

Sandra began to cry quietly, tears streaming down her face as she thought of her mistress—cruel sometimes, yes, but so much more often kind. She thought of their parting in the forest, before they had separated to go with their lovers—she remembered Elaine calling her "friend". She remembered a kiss, a long time ago—she remembered the Countess slipping as she stepped out of her bath, and she remembered the shocking pleasure of the brief, accidental embrace that followed, Elaine naked in her arms—she remembered looking up into the full existence of Beauty. It was unbearable to think of that beauty being abused—unbearable, unthinkable, and Sandra kept crying, knowing that everyone around her was thinking of the same horror.

They had lost hours—how could Thomas hold back the blood-thirsty monks on his own?

What would happen to Elaine after Thomas fell?

Anton dismounted and walked over to the London horses. He caught the rope that bound them together, and stroked their well kept coats. "These are quality horses, Your Grace," Anton said calmly, just as though that quality was the only concern here. "They haven't been ridden today. We might do well to change mounts."

The Duke gave his assent, and dismounted. A few knights

worked together to quickly switch the tack—and then Roland, Anton, Gowan, and Gunter mounted up on the horses that had led them astray.

Anton was the first one up. He rode quickly over to Sandra and put a tough worn hand on her shoulder. She felt his strength all through her body.

"We're not giving up," he said. "We're going to make time now, so keep your horse as close to me as you can. We'll backtrack—we should run into Pierre and Daniel somewhere on the way—I'm sure they'll have valuable information for us."

He handed Sandra a handkerchief. "Keep this—I have another. I can't help your lady if you are going to fall back because you're crying too much."

Sandra wiped her eyes and blew her nose. She tried to smile at Anton, but then they had no more time because Roland rode past. He neither stopped nor spoke. His face was terrible to look at. Sandra was glad when he got out in front, because then she only had to see his back.

The Larrazian knights fell in behind their leader—once again, they rode off to the west. They rode past the dead monk again, they fought their way through the forest again, and finally, in late afternoon, they found themselves opposite Salisbury, at the initial point of their wrong turn.

Their trail was easy to follow—Pierre and Daniel should have met them somewhere on the way back, but there was no sign of them.

With every bitter step of the return Roland thought of how he had been duped. The monks had obviously expected someone to come after them, and they had sent off the roped together horses as a decoy. They had gained hours of time for their evil intentions—no! Roland shied away from his terrible fears for Elaine, but he could not forget Anton's words: "He has no chance . . . They are going to tire Thomas out and then cut him down."

If Anton was right, then the monks must have Elaine now. Roland's mind tried to veer away again, but there was no brighter subject. Where were Pierre and Daniel? And now, now that they were finally back at the place of error, what were they to do? How could they follow an old trail left by a deceptive enemy riding well apart?

Roland turned to look at his men. He saw that they too knew the questions. They hoped—even now they hoped—that he would have some answers.

The Duke did his best. He addressed his men without a trace of the panic he had shown earlier. "All we know is that Thomas was riding to the south. We will assume that he continued in that direction. He's riding double with my lady—I don't know how long he stayed ahead of those monks. He may be dead now. Elaine may be a prisoner. That is probably the most likely possibility, and with that in mind we must be careful not to come up on them too fast. In such a case we will need surprise in order to rescue Elaine while insuring her safety.

"On the other hand, one must keep in mind that Thomas is the most esteemed knight in this land. He may yet have eluded his pursuers. If that is the case, if the monks are *not* holding Elaine, then we can attack them at once without mercy—and we will destroy them. Than I will reward Thomas greatly for taking care of Elaine."

A look passed between Roland and Anton. The knight saw that his lord meant exactly what he said. It was plain that the Duke had changed his mind about honoring his ugly promise to King Richard.

"If we rescue Elaine in this manner, then we'll go directly to the sea, and hire the first boat we find to take us across the Channel."

You're not going to report back to London, Anton thought with approval. A big smile creased the knight's face.

Sandra wondered why her lover looked so happy.

"We hope Thomas has kept Elaine out of the monks' hands— but we expect the other. For now, I want you to spread out into a wide straight line, all level with me at the center. Separate as widely as you can, so we can cover a lot of terrain—but make sure you can see your comrade on your right and on your left. If you see a sign of the monks, put up a white handkerchief, and each man who sees that signal will wave his fellows into an approach—we'll converge silently, and I'll give you the plan of attack."

Roland surveyed his troops. "No one attacks on his own."

The Duke turned his horse and started off to the south.

The men arranged themselves as ordered, a long line of knights stretching across the horizon. This time, setting out, there was not even a whisper of a cheer. Anton and Sandra were closest to the Duke on his right. Gunter rode to his left. No one spoke. Their eyes swept the empty plain.

This was the afternoon of the second day of the chase. There was still some grain for the horses, but the men were as starved and parched as Thomas and Elaine.

They rode south guided by nothing but hope. The ground had hardened through this long hot day—there was no disturbed mud, and any hoofprints that existed were covered by the high meadow grass. There were no signs at all—plants pressed down earlier had had time to spring up—there was no way of telling that Elaine was still in front of them.

The falling sun had turned red by the time they came upon the stream where Thomas and Elaine had refreshed themselves. The Larrazian knights drank quickly and pressed on. There was still no sign of Elaine or her pursuers. There wasn't much daylight left. Everyone wondered if they were once again on a false path.

It was almost dusk when Anton saw Roland himself raise a white handkerchief. Anton waved emphatically to the man on his right, as Gunter waved to the man on his left. The knights began to converge in the near dark. They were nervous, eager, they quietly drew their swords from their scabbards—and when they reached Roland, they learned definitely that they *were* on the right track.

On the meadow before the Duke's horse lay Sir Pierre and Sir Daniel—dead.

Chapter 105

A NEW PRAYER

Also at sundown, many miles away, Arthur the Assessor arrived at the gates of the Palace of Bermondsey. The guards took a moment to recognize the battered tax collector—and then they opened the gates. Arthur rode his horse into the royal courtyard, tossed the reins to a page, and dismounted.

Arthur was wounded and weary—but his mind was as sharp as ever. He needed to see the King—but a private audience with Richard would be dangerous. Arthur knew that he was in no shape to withstand interrogation. It would be far better to come to the King riding a tide of acclamation that would stave off critical questions—a rising tide that would glorify both the King and himself—a purifying tide that would certify Arthur's version of the facts.

The Assessor knew just how to accomplish this.

He saw dejected knights in the courtyard, singly or in small groups, and more returning. They talked quietly among themselves. They had searched all this day for Elaine the Fair, but their dreams of heroism had come to naught. The only clue they had discovered was Walter's body—Arthur gathered that that death was attributed to Elaine's kidnappers. Better and better, thought the Assessor.

Arthur ran his hands over his blood encrusted robe. He looked around him through the long red streaks of faded light. He willed the tired knights to look at him—and they did so. With a sudden quickening of interest they recognized his disheveled figure—here was the husband of the lady they sought—a husband who had been missing almost as long as his wife. They stared at the wide irregular bloodstain that had spread out on the golden robe that covered his broad belly. They saw hints of blood on his wrists. A silence spread through the darkening courtyard, as every man there waited for Arthur to speak.

The Assessor's body was damaged, but he still possessed the solid booming voice that had saved Elaine long ago. There was weight and power in that voice—he said, "I know who has taken Elaine."

No one breathed.

"The question for you"—Arthur gestured to include them all—"is this: Who among you has the courage to fight the Northmen?"

There was a chilling pause, for everyone knew and feared those ferocious raiders, and then Sir Hugo stepped forward. This knight had already given two fingers for his love—now he showed that he was prepared to give his life. "I am ready," he said clearly.

This declaration shamed the other knights into action. There came a veritable storm of vows and martial boasts—every knight present shouted his willingness to engage the Northmen under any circumstances—they would kill those swine, and save Elaine the Fair!

The tumult brought more folk from the palace, more knights pledged their honor, and the news of kidnapping Northmen set off at once on the fast beating wings of rumor.

Only one name could quiet the crowd now, and Arthur used it.

"Silence, my friends, silence in the name of the King! In the name of His Majesty Richard Lionheart, we shall destroy these vicious beasts and save my lady—let us go to the King now, so that he may lead us!"

With this one brilliant stroke Arthur gained a roaring mob at his back. The knights cried their approval as they shoved Arthur before them—the mass of armed knights swept over astonished guards, there was no stopping the human wave—until Arthur was thrown up against the locked door of the King's private chamber.

Arthur knocked on the door with the force of thunder—his voice was a clarion call to his King.

A page opened the door—the Assessor was catapulted into the room by the force of the eager crowd pressing behind. Arthur stopped, halfway into the large room—behind him the knights stepped in quietly, their boisterousness suddenly gone. Arthur looked over at the King of the English. Richard Lionheart, wearing only his nightshirt, was playing checkers with his similarly attired man at arms, Brian the Brutal.

Richard jumped a checker, put the captured piece aside, and then looked right at Arthur. "What is the meaning of this intrusion?" the King asked in a low deadly voice.

Arthur met Richard's eyes. The Assessor's voice was steady—the story he told was terrifying.

"Northmen have penetrated even into this castle, Your Majesty," Arthur said. He noticed that even Brian was looking at him now. There was dead silence in the room. "They were disguised as English monks. They took my wife, the Countess of Anjou. They killed Sir Walter as they were escaping.

"With Sir Nigel I followed their track to Stonehenge"—an icy shiver rippled through the tense audience—"and we saw—that was this morning—that the blasphemous barbarians had tied Elaine to a stake. I don't know if they planned to kill my lady there at that heathen temple—I couldn't wait, I charged them, Nigel and I charged them, and we broke up whatever strange ceremony they were conducting—but Nigel was killed, and I was left for dead—they took off riding, carrying Elaine.

"When I realized I was still alive, I saw there were other corpses around too—they had killed some English party, just as on their trail we saw other traces of their bloody work. I saw that Nigel was dead—but I saw that one of the Northmen was still alive. I made him talk before he died."

A low growl came from the men behind Arthur. He looked into the King's emotionless eyes and continued his story.

"This Northman spoke English—he said he learned it from an English woman he had enslaved"—the growl behind became more of a snarl—"he was arrogant—I had to hurt him badly before he would tell me anything about Elaine—he wouldn't explain anything about the ritual, but finally he said they would probably keep her alive now—'to enjoy her,' he said—I nearly killed him then—he said their ship was waiting by the rocky beach just past the Isle of Wight—he said there was nothing I could do, but I thought he was wrong.

"I killed him, and I rode as fast as I could to you, Your Majesty."

The impatient knights ceased their eager rumblings. They stared at the King and waited for his word.

Arthur was pleased—with all this tension in the room, Richard had to make a decision at once—the King had no time to poke holes in his story.

Richard had watched Arthur carefully all though the performance. He knew that the Assessor was lying about some parts of the story—but most of it had to be true, else he could not go public with it in this way. Besides, all in all, it was a marvelous opportunity. There was a chance here to destroy all memory of yesterday's humiliation. He could play the gallant for the whole English nation—he *would* save their beloved lady—he would kill the vile interlopers who dared enter his own castle—he would be *King* in word and deed—this triumph would echo throughout the land.

Richard stood up.

The King had made up his mind. He stopped looking at Arthur—he addressed the room at large. "In our churches we pray like this: 'God save us from the fury of the Northmen.'

"I say that we offend God with the weakness of our prayers!

"From now on we should say this: God save the Northmen from *our* fury!"

A savage little answering cheer came from the knights' throats. They were in the King's thrall now—they were exalted, inspired, and ready to kill.

Richard silenced the men with a wave of his hand. He continued calmly. "There is no time to intercept the Northmen on land—but we can move on the sea at night, following the coast.

"I toured the docks today—the captain of the warship Lionheart offered his services to me—he had outfitted the vessel in preparation for my return, and it is ready to sail. It is the biggest ship at the dock—you will find it easily. At midnight I expect to find one hundred brave English knights on board, armed and ready!

"We will show the Northmen who owns the English seas!"

The cheers were deafening.

"Now go, and prepare yourselves." The knights could not hear their King over their own shouts, but they understood his gestures, and in a few moments the room was clear save for Richard, Brian, Arthur, and the King's page.

"You'll come with us," Richard said to Arthur. The King smiled, remembering his deal with the Duke of Larraz—this was also a perfect opportunity to pay back the Assessor for his lack of respect.

"Yes, Your Majesty," Arthur replied in his humblest voice—though in truth he was none too pleased, for he would have preferred staying at the palace, awaiting results in comfort.

Richard told the page to bring fighting clothes for himself and Brian.

The King was quite cheerful as he thought of battle, victory, and the breaking of the Chancellor of the Exchequer. It will be a pleasure to rescue his wife, Richard thought, and then give her to another man. Arthur will learn then the true meaning of royal power! Of course, I won't give Elaine to Roland right away—unless he has fulfilled his conditions. Still, I am confident the Duke will do the job I prescribed—after all, he's *hopelessly* in love (Richard's expression had changed to a sneer) and he'll do anything to have her—kill, pay me her weight in gold . . .

A worry suddenly creased Richard's brow. What if the Northmen did decide to sacrifice Elaine? What if they killed her before she could be rescued? The Duke could hardly be expected to pay for her dead body.

That would be a terrible shame, Richard thought, for then, due to lack of funds, I might have to postpone the invasion of France.

Chapter 106

IVAR'S PLAN

An hour after sundown, in the Viking circle . . .

One of the Champions got lucky when it came his turn to drink from the river. As he bent down over the water, he saw a silvery, serpentine form just under the surface—he drove his sword into the apparition without pausing for thought—and discovered that he had impaled a twisting, five feet long, seagoing eel. The creature was surprisingly heavy, but he was able to slip it out onto the bank. Then he cut off its head, and blocked the body's wriggles with his feet.

Ivar, once apprised of the windfall, permitted a small fire. The eel was cut into chunks, and the fat greasy portions were heated over the flames.

Again the Vikings took turns—they came up one at a time for their dinner. After the last man was fed, Ivar ordered the fire doused. Blackness settled over the scene once again—the crescent moon barely illuminated Elaine's white nightgown.

Ivar stared at that bit of silk and considered the mood of his men.

The Champions had not had much of a chance to talk to each other today, spread out as they were—but there were a number of low conversations as each man came up to take his chunk of eel. Not so much conversation, really, Ivar thought—the men were grumbling. They were unhappy with the delay—they wanted to take Elaine *now*, they had been ready all *day*—they were far from mutinous, but they were unhappy.

And why shouldn't they be? The futile attack of the two foolish knights could be considered a harbinger of some overwhelming force to come—the Champions were justifiably uncomfortable, on land in a foreign country, never knowing when some monstrous army might attack. Of course they wanted to snatch Elaine and run.

But all I need is one more day, Ivar thought.

I see hope for myself. I see a way out.

The closer I have come to my own death the more I dislike the prospect. I could have let that charging knight kill me and end my troubles—but I fought to live—I want to live—I prefer my life, empty as it is, to the certain nothingness of death. I believe in no heaven, no Valhalla, no living hell—after death I shall just be a husk, fit only for worms, and soon not even them.

And yet I know I will choose death, I will kill myself, should I fail with Elaine the Fair. If this woman of unparalleled beauty can not touch in me what other men call the soul, then that knowledge will indeed be so terrible that I will be forced to take my own life.

I wish to be protected from that knowledge.

I can not kill her myself before I know her. My position would be forfeit should my men discover my cowardice before this woman.

Her death must be induced—I must keep my distance—my hand must stay hidden.

I will drive them all day tomorrow, drive them to the waiting dragon of my ship, and there on the shore I will take away the Englishman's last hope.

I will tell him what I propose to do to his lady—I will paint the horror brightly in his language—I will give him a last chance to save Elaine from what his countrymen call a "fate worse than death."

I'll give him a last chance to save her body from torment and her soul from shame—I'll give him a chance to kill her, and if he does, no one will be able to blame me—and I will never have to confront her naked beauty in my arms.

I will live then, without having to face the final knowledge she would have given me—I will live to kill again, and so extend my days.

Chapter 107

SONG IN THE NIGHT

Sundown, in the presence of the dead . . .

Roland knew there was no point in going on into the gathering darkness, for then they could easily miss their foes altogether—or even worse, fall into an ambush and end up the same as Pierre and Daniel.

I should have sent Anton, the Duke thought—I can not think of even one thing I have done right today—if there was ever a place for a man to cry, this is it, a cluster of grieving men, a desperate woman, all of us gathered around the dead on a dark open plain—my errors haunt me, the night closes in on me—but I can't cry, I can't show weakness while Elaine lives and depends on me to come for her—depends on me *not* to chase riderless horses . . .

Roland lashed himself with his misdeeds, but he did not cry, and finally he pulled himself together enough to order a proper burial for the two brave but foolish knights.

There was not much to dig with—swords and a couple of axes—but the men worked hard and finally the graves were ready. The bodies were handed down into the holes, and then Roland suddenly came to understand the value of religion. He needed some way to bridge the unknowable—but he had avoided the Church all his adult life, and he did not know the words that might ease the pain of this moment—finally he recalled a simple, sad phrase—he said, "Ashes to ashes, and dust to dust," and his words, themselves as insubstantial as dust, drifted through the haunted night.

The men filled in the graves.

They fashioned two crosses from Daniel's sword and a broken

wagon stave they found nearby. They placed Christ's symbols firmly in the English earth. They waited in the silent black night.

They did not know just what they were waiting for until Sandra began to sing.

It was an old English folksong about lost love, and she had a sweet quavery voice. The men gave Sandra their attention—they listened in warm silence as Anton put his arm loosely around her waist. As Sandra sang, the men took her home in their hearts—she became one of them. Elaine was the Goddess, the Holy Grail they sought—but Sandra was a comrade. She grieved, as they grieved, for their friends who had fallen.

The song ended—in listening to the song, the men had managed to say good-bye to Pierre and Daniel.

Now it was time to turn again to the future, and where Sandra had calmed the scene, now it was Anton's place to light a low fire.

He spoke with calm certainty. "We shall avenge our comrades."

There was a low murmur of assent, no wild cheers, just a slight quickening of the pulse.

Gunter said, "They will not escape us."

It was personal now, Roland realized. His knights would save Elaine, yes—but what drove them now was revenge. The thought did not displease him—in fact it helped him throw off the coils of depression that threatened to envelop him. Nothing would stop his knights tomorrow.

"I commend your spirit," the Duke said. "Now let us get some rest."

Roland assigned sentry duty—he gave orders that he was to be awakened before dawn.

The Duke of Larraz lay down on his blanket and stared up at the stars.

If there is a God, he thought, then these men may not have died in vain. We may not be too late to save Elaine.

There is still hope.

Chapter 108

THOMAS BEGINS HIS STORY

After dark, inside the closed circle . . .

The smell of the cooking eel was torture for Thomas and Elaine. It was a heavy, greasy scent—and heaven, for all that. Thomas was reminded of his youthful days in the forest—often he had enjoyed similar feasts. He felt his nose twitching, his mouth watered painfully—he looked at Elaine and saw that she was in no better shape.

Thomas pulled her close. "Perhaps we can live on the smell," he whispered.

Elaine tried to smile, but her dry lips hurt.

Thomas pushed her soft hair back from her ear and whispered very low against it, "When they stop moving around I'll get water for us."

Elaine turned toward Thomas—there was worry, a question in her face—but then she chose not to ask it. She eased herself into his embrace and lay her head against his shoulder. She waited.

Saladin stayed close, but his black bulk could scarcely be seen in the thin light of the crescent moon.

Thomas was pleased that his horse had started to graze. He listened to the chewing sounds and thought of escape. He tried to imagine bursting through the circle—but the odds were not good at all. They were watching—they never stopped watching him. Thomas sat very still and held Elaine—he never felt the monks' vigilance slacken. They watched him while they ate and drank. They watched him now, after extinguishing their fire. He couldn't break out on his own—he would have to let them drive him a little farther—he had to hope that someone else would come along and create a diversion.

What if no one comes?

What if the diversion is as ineffective as the charge of the Larrazian knights? It was frightening to see how easily those knights had been handled. Who were these assassins? They wore the brown cassocks that are the uniform of English monks—they must have killed some poor clergymen to get their clothes.

Who could do such a thing?

Thomas remembered the savage Picts who had attacked Lady Louisa—perhaps these were more of the same, a robber band come down from Scotland to pray on the English. Hating all things English (many an English army had tried to conquer their land) such a group might well kill monks and soldiers alike—suddenly Thomas remembered that Elaine had said she had seen one of them before.

"Where did you see him before, dear Elaine?"

Elaine said, "What?" almost too loud, for his voice was a shocking intrusion and his 'dear Elaine' was all wrong. She had been resting against Thomas's shoulder—but the present reality was so terrible that she had allowed herself to dream of another man, of a happier time—in her thoughts she had been lying on a rose covered bed, and her heart was pierced by Roland's hammered gold unicorn.

She struggled to come back to the man who protected her now—she heard him say, "One of our pursuers—you said you saw one of them before."

Elaine understood the question this time but she could not answer right away. All she wanted to think of was Roland—Roland loving her—Roland coming to rescue her—two of his men had died, he *must* be coming—she was ready to give her love only to the Duke, and so she needed to create some distance between herself and Thomas, be he ever so brave and true.

Elaine said, avoiding the question and speaking with difficulty through her dry throat, "Is it true that you can get water?"

"Yes, said Thomas. He drew his old sword carefully, mindful that it didn't glint in the faint moonlight—he put the sword between their bodies—hunching over, he drove the point straight down into the earth. "With the river this close, there must be water near the surface of the ground."

It was hard muddy labor—harder still, because he had to do it very quietly—but finally Thomas found a wet seepage at the bottom of his square cut hole. Thomas leaned over to check it with his hand—and then a dark shape banged powerfully into his shoulder—Thomas nearly panicked, but then he realized it was only Saladin shoving him out of the way with his big head.

The horse stuffed his head down into the hole and drank first—then Thomas got water in his cupped hands for Elaine—finally Thomas drank some of the muddy brew himself.

Elaine hadn't minded the flavor—she felt much better now with her mouth and throat soothed by the cool wetness. She looked up at Thomas and kissed him with moistened lips.

"I'm sorry that I didn't answer your question right away—I was dreaming. I do remember that man—but I just can not place him. I will try to think. If I can remember, I will tell you."

Thomas nodded, and then looked around at the dark circle of enemies.

"Are you going to stay up all night?" Elaine asked.

"I must. I think that their leader—the one with the shaved head—is insane. They could attack at any time."

"Then I will stay up with you," Elaine said, for she had an idea how long Thomas had gone without sleep. At least she had rested this afternoon and last night.

Thomas was wonderfully pleased by her gesture, and he reached for her to kiss her again, but she put a hand on his chest to stop him.

"You mustn't, for you do not know me so well, Sir Thomas."

"Then tell me, Elaine, tell me all about yourself, for I love all of you, I wish to love your past and your present and your future—please tell me of your life, so I may love you better." He took her right hand, and kissed the line of the wound. "Tell me who did this, so I may avenge you."

Elaine took her hand away from Thomas. "That monster is dead," she said, "and I can not speak more of it now. But tell me of *your* life, Thomas—you are a mystery to all the ladies of the court who love you. On this night we have together, I would truly like to learn of your history."

When Elaine spoke of the ladies who loved him, Thomas naturally included her in their number. He was happy and flattered—what man can resist a beautiful lady's request that he talk about himself?

Thomas paid no attention to the sadness in Elaine's tone—he thought she was only concerned about their desperate situation—in his optimism now, he was certain that situation would change. He had confidence in himself—confidence in himself as Elaine's lover—he was absolutely certain that she loved him—and so, inevitably, they must be able to find a way out—he would defeat their enemies—they would be free soon, and he would prove to her that happiness was possible.

It never occurred to Thomas that Elaine's vision of happiness might include the embrace of a different lover—not him.

"I need to touch you," Thomas said.

Elaine hesitated, and then once again she offered her wounded hand.

Thomas smiled—he took her hand between both of his. He held her gently, and said, "You trust me, and I trust you. I will tell you no lies—I will begin at the beginning."

Thomas looked around at their foes once more, and then he took a deep breath and began his story. "I was not born into the nobility, and my given name is not Thomas." He looked at Elaine and smiled slightly. "My parents gave me a silly name, one that I didn't like then or now, and there is no reason to mention it to you. In time I earned the name Thomas, and the knighthood that goes with it, as you will see . . ."

Chapter 109

ROLAND'S PRAYER

After dark, in the Larrazian encampment . . .

Roland was afraid to close his eyes. He had closed them—he had slept, for just a moment, it seemed—and then he had been violently awakened—he had been struck by a blow inside his head—a phantom blow with real force—the arm of evil encapsulated in a vision of a floating black cross.

Roland knew that if he closed his eyes he would see it again.

What was it? What was the meaning of this horror?

The Duke's face was covered with sweat in the hot still night. The air was charged with that special stillness that presages a violent storm. No sound—O yes, that sound—they seemed to seize every opportunity with an almost desperate hunger.

Roland listened for a while to Sandra's held in moans and Anton's harsh breathing. He was taking her almost brutally—her bottom must be hurting where she had been slashed—there was pain in her voice as she moaned and yet at the same time an achingly sweet pleasure. Why was Anton so rough with her? Did he want to mark her in some way, mark her because he didn't have that much time left—

It was a horrible thought. It was so dreadful that it even drove the image of the black cross from Roland's mind.

Anton: his one true friend among the men, his advisor, his confidant—the one man he had told about Richard and the ugly deal, the man whose respect he had regained when he had decided to renege on that evil bargain—Anton, the one man that he had trusted to approach Elaine at the ball—and how had he come back? Roland knew that he would never forget those words: "She will either kill you or make you the happiest man on earth. It is possible that she will do both, Your Grace."

So Anton had seen death from the beginning. Could it be his own death that he had seen?

Already two brave knights had died. I sent the wrong men, Roland thought with bitter guilt. Now we are in a desperate position—Elaine is terribly menaced, because of *my* errors in judgment. I was the fool who was misled—how many more of my men must die to rectify my errors?

Must Anton die to save my lady? Must he die, Lord?

Roland had not prayed in years—but he prayed now with a terrible silent intensity.

Spare my lady, he prayed, his silent words touching the silence of God's ear—spare my lady, and spare my friend—spare them Lord, take me if you must, but spare my lady, spare my friend . . .

Roland prayed into the night—prayed with his eyes open lest the dream return—prayed while Anton made love to Sandra—prayed while the sentries looked out into ever blacker darkness—prayed while the moon and stars were finally winked out by black low hanging clouds—he was praying when the wind whipped up and the rain started to come down.

Chapter 110

THE BLACK KNIGHTS

Thomas speaking . . .

"As I said, I was not born into the nobility. I came into this world on the twenty-seventh of January, in the year of Our Lord eleven hundred and seventy. My father was a tenant farmer. My mother was a seamstress. We lived in a little thatched roofed cottage on the great estate of the Baron of Nottingham.

"I was an only child who came late into my parents' lives—I was indulged by both of them.

"My father had been an archer in the service of King Henry II. He fought at Malmesbury, where the usurper Stephen was defeated—one of my earliest memories is of my father telling me the story of that battle—they fought in a howling winter storm, but God Himself directed the sleet straight into the eyes of their foes—the good King triumphed, and my father played his part well—he was still an excellent archer seventeen years later, when I was born—he taught me to use a bow just as soon as I grew big enough to hold one.

"Of course, most of the time my father had to work in the fields—while he farmed, my mother did fancy sewing and fine embroidery for the Baroness. As a young lad I used to sit on my mother's lap and watch her stitch—she taught me how to use a needle—but when I got a little older I discovered that other boys did not consider this a manly pursuit, and so I gave up my career in embroidery, and took up hunting and fishing instead."

Thomas felt Elaine smiling in the dark. He searched for her face with his hand, and touched her cheek. He drew her close, and kissed her lightly on the lips, and this time she did not stop him.

"I played in the woods like a young nobleman, and indeed, we were a privileged family. The Baron marked well my father's early service to the King—the Baroness, a kind but plain lady, was much pleased by the flattering gowns my mother sewed for her. We were given the most fertile section of the estate to farm—each year my father gave the Baron ten percent of the harvest, and we lived in comfort and amity.

"My education was not neglected—there was an old scribe who wrote the Baron's letters—my mother prevailed upon him to teach me to read and write.

"All went well until the summer of 1186, when I was sixteen years old. The old Baron died at the age of sixty-three, and his wife followed him just a week later. They were survived by two children: a daughter who lived on the Continent—she was well married to the Count of Poitou—and a son, Wesley, a middle aged roue who had never married. We had scarcely ever seen this heir—he had preferred to live in London, pursuing vice on his father's income—actually, on a lot more than his father's income, as we would soon discover.

"Wesley (I was never able to really think of him as a Baron) came up to the estate to claim his inheritance. His first act was to send a messenger around to all his tenant farmers (Wesley was not a man to do things himself). The message that was read to us said that due to "special circumstances" the Baron would have to take a higher percentage of our harvest: not ten percent any more, but *fifty* percent."

Elaine felt the shudder of rage in Thomas's voice as he said the number. She put her hand on his arm as he went on.

"We soon found out that the "special circumstances" referred to gaming debts, brothel debts, tax debts, and all Wesley's personal borrowings that he had failed to repay. Our job was to starve in order to relieve Wesley of the consequences of his sins.

"Some of the farmers simply left that first day. They gathered their tools and their families, and they walked.

"We stayed. First of all my father hardly believed that Wesley was serious. He tried again and again to see the new Baron (believing that he could reason with the man, if he could just meet him face to face) but he was always rebuffed.

"Summer was changing to fall—harvest time was approaching. It appeared that Wesley was serious. My father was a stubborn man. He couldn't leave, and admit defeat—he couldn't stay, and knuckle under to injustice.

"He chose a third course of action. He worked to unite all those men who had stayed. He told them that if they all stood fast for the traditional tithe, the new Baron could hardly deal with them all. The men fell in behind my father—but that was exactly the problem. They were no stronger than their leader.

"Wesley hired two mercenary knights who came up from London. We heard news of this on the last night I saw my parents alive. My friend Johnny, who was about my age and lived in a nearby cottage, came over and told us he had seen them: powerful knights, in black armor. The news didn't frighten us as much as it should have—perhaps only my mother truly understood.

"The next morning she *insisted* that I go out and get her a duck for dinner.

"I went out into the forest with my bow, and I was lucky—I bagged a brace of fine drakes with ease. I headed home—I saw the smoke before I was even halfway there.

"Johnny was waiting for me at the end of the path that led back to my house, a house that no longer existed. All that was left of it were charred beams and ash. Between Johnny and the burned out wreckage lay the bodies of my parents. They had been horribly mutilated by swords.

"I went back to look at them—I knelt by each—and then I came back to Johnny. I saw that he was crying, but I knew my own face was set and hard.

"He told me that his family was waiting for us down the road. They were leaving, going to London. He said that no one had any thought of opposing Wesley any longer. Those who could not leave were prepared to give any amount of their harvest rather than risk death. He said that he would help me bury my parents, and then I could go with his family.

"I realized that his parents were keeping their distance because they did not want to show any involvement with my family. Who knew when the black knights would come back? It could be dangerous to be seen showing sympathy—they just wanted to leave. I understood their attitude—and I did not reproach them for it. This was not their fight.

"I thanked Johnny, but I told him that I would bury Father and Mother myself. I told him that I also had to refuse the offer of the trip to London. I told him that I would stay—I said that he could go, just as soon as he answered a few questions. I asked him about the horses the black knights rode, and about the tack they wore. I asked him about their weapons, I asked him about their armor, I even checked as to whether the knights rode with their visors open or closed. Johnny answered all my questions as well as he could—when his recollection faltered, I just asked the question again until I was certain that I had learned all that he knew.

"I found a shovel with a handle that was only half burned, and I set to work. I saw that Johnny stayed where he was, watching me. I realized that he wanted to help me—but he was frightened of me at the same time. I put him out of my mind.

"I dug the graves. I buried my parents, and I fashioned two crosses for them out of what was left of our home. Sometime after that I looked up and saw that Johnny was gone.

"That night I crept up to the Baron's mansion, and I tacked a note to the door. It said, 'You left one alive.'

"The next morning the two knights came for me, as I waited by my parents' graves. I wore a loose shirt, trousers—no armor, no visible weapons, but I had a long knife concealed in each sleeve—the sheaths were tied to my forearms—the hilts were toward my hands.

"The knights wore full black armor, as Johnny had said, and their visors were closed—my friend had been very accurate.

"They came at me, seemingly invincible in their head to toe mail. They hadn't brought lances for a foot soldier's son like me—but their swords were out.

"I called to them—I told them that I wished to speak before I died, and they slowed down, I supposed to sport with me, for I posed no threat. I caught the bridles of their mounts—I stood between their powerful warhorses. I looked up at the steel clad murderers.

"'Which of your killed my father,' I asked, but they gave no answer. I could barely see their glittering eyes through the narrow slits of their closed visors.

"'Which of you,' I began again, as if to ask of my mother—knowing they would kill me when I completed the question—but I never completed it—as I said 'you' my hands crossed and I drew my knives—if you stroke up under a horse's chin, you'll find a soft spot just beyond the protection of the skull, just forward of the arch where neck joins head—I drove the points of my knives into those soft spots, I drove upward with all my strength, and the poor horses died in less time than it takes me to tell of it. The animals' knees buckled, they crashed to the

ground—their riders fell with them, and once fallen, they were
as helpless as turtles turned upon their backs. One, in fact, was
half pinned under his dead steed—I had heard his leg snap as
the horse fell down on him. The other had rolled clear but otherwise he was not in much better shape. The heavy mail he
wore—his 'protection'—made it impossible for him to get up on
his own.

"I plucked my knives free. I chose the pinned one first. I
picked an eye, defenseless behind the narrow slit, and I drove
my knife through it and into his brain.

"The second one was a little harder because of the way he
thrashed around, fruitlessly swinging his heavy sword at my
legs. I couldn't get close enough to use my knife, so I took the
dead one's sword and swung it at the survivor's wrist. The blow
was only intended to disarm, but as it happened I stuck the
metal joint just right, struck it with all my strength behind the
blow—I took his hand off at the wrist, and blood fountained out
of the black casing.

"There was no need to strike again. I watched until he bled
dry, and then I took the two swords—plus my bow which I had
leaned against my father's cross—and I walked away. I left
their bodies as they were.

"I was sad about the horses, but you know Elaine, I learned
something that day"—Thomas's voice was like a whisper from
an ancient grave—the arm that Elaine held was like ice—"I
learned never to wear full armor. It's not true protection, it's a
trap, it's really just a trap . . ."

Thomas hesitated, as though he was not sure of where he was
going with the story—as though he was not even sure of where
he was—his eyes were lost in the moonlight—they shined
because they were full of tears.

Elaine took his face between her two hands. She felt the wetness on his cheeks—she felt the presence of the watchers
around them—she needed Thomas back, *with* her—she kissed
his lips once—a second time—he returned the third kiss, and
then he broke away. He looked out at the enemy circle. With
quiet care, he turned his body so that he could check the position of each shadowy foe.

Elaine was much relieved by his renewed vigilance.

Thomas turned back to her. When he spoke again, his voice
was that of a small boy who wants something desperately—and
isn't at all sure that his wish will be granted.

"Shall I go on?" he asked.

Elaine looked at Thomas—she was reminded somehow of Roland's request that she take off her slippers—this too was a critical question, a question from the heart—she saw Thomas as a boy, burying his parents—she saw how manhood had been thrust upon him—she was suddenly confident that Thomas the man would always be with her, even if the boy should get lost in the past—he was not frozen in adolescence, rather, he was both boy *and* man—he was one person who had suffered, and yet he had come so far from the house of ashes—he was the knight who had found her, he had saved her, he had protected her and he protected her still—how had the lost boy come so far? How much farther did he have to go?

Elaine reached out for Thomas and hugged him fiercely. She knew that this was a night for secrets that would never again be revealed. She whispered, "Please continue."

Chapter 111

IN THE ROYAL COACH

London, a half hour before midnight . . .

Hubert Walter, the Archbishop of Canterbury, rode with Richard and Arthur as they headed for the docks and the warship Lionheart.

The Archbishop had come to London to bless the newly returned King, and honor him for his brave battle against the infidels. Hubert Walter was very pleased that there was no strain between him and the King, so unlike the tragic gulf that had opened up between Henry II and his predecessor, Thomas Becket. Hubert saw King Richard (in contrast to the impetuous Henry) as a devout selfless ruler, a deeply religious man who was willing to lay his life down for the cross.

This evening the King had asked Hubert to accompany him on his expedition against the Northmen. The Archbishop, despite his admiration for the King, was not that eager to go at first. He had planned to personally conduct a mass at the court on the morrow—but then the King told him of the dead monks. A wandering peddler had come across the massacre—the distraught fellow had just reached the palace with the bloody news.

The Archbishop's duty was clear. He said he would go with the King. He asked God's blessing upon this noble expedition.

Now he rode in the royal coach with his two companions, and he thought of the wickedness of the world: ten monks dead, murdered in cold blood, stripped of their clothes. He shuddered and made the sign of the cross.

Richard asked Arthur to run through his story again.

Arthur was happy to oblige. The peddler's appearance had

been a stroke of luck for him: a solid, outside confirmation of his story. Richard would never doubt him now—and besides, Arthur had had time to weave together a seamless blend of fact and fiction.

He started with the basic premise that he was trailing the Northmen (rather than their prisoner). He told of finding the bodies of the herdsmen and his wife—he described the faces of the little children, and wrung tears from the eyes of the Archbishop—even Richard showed concern—he spoke sincerely about how he and Nigel had comforted the children, though duty soon forced them to move on—he alternated flattering lies and brutal truths—he painted a terrifying portrait of Elaine tied to the stake in the midst of bloodstained Northmen—he gave Nigel a gallant death—he described the Norse flight with Elaine—he described in savage detail his mythical interrogation of the wounded Northman.

The story was so good that he wanted to believe it—perhaps he could believe it—perhaps he had trailed the Northmen—perhaps he had comforted the children—perhaps he had fought bravely to save Elaine . . .

Then again, perhaps it doesn't matter, Arthur thought. The Archbishop and the King believe me. What more do I need?

The coach came to a stop before the good ship Lionheart.

The hundred armed knights Richard had requested were already on board.

The church bells chimed midnight.

Chapter 112

THOMAS CONTINUES HIS STORY

Thomas was greatly relieved when Elaine asked him to continue his story. He kissed her. "Thank you," he said. He looked away from her—he cleared his throat and returned to the past.

"I went into the woods to live among the animals. I thought of killing Wesley, but I did not, for three reasons. One, though he had certainly ordered the murder of my parents, he had not carried it out. The two black knights had done the killing—the stain of the act was on their souls. If they had been men of honor—true knights such as I had heard of in the legends of King Arthur and his Round Table—then they would have refused the corrupt Baron, no matter what payment he offered. A second reason was that I was leaving the company of men— but I was not ready to die. I knew there would be a price put on my head after killing the knights—but still the local people would know what had happened—justice had been served, eye for eye, death for death. No one would look for me very hard. But killing the Baron would bring the King's soldiers down on me—alone in the woods, without even a horse, I would have no chance. Finally, the last reason was a simple one: I had had my fill of revenge. I had seen more death in two days than I had seen so far in all my life. I had lost the two who had been with me every day of that life—I needed quiet, solitude—I needed time to mourn."

Elaine laid her head against Thomas's chest. He stroked her hair gently as he went on.

"I lived off the fish and animals of the forest. I found trout and eels in the streams—I slew rabbits, squirrels, and occasionally deer with my bow. I knew, of course, that the latter were

the 'King's deer'—but being often hungry I chose myself to execute the royal prerogative."

Elaine laughed softly against his chest. Thomas raised her
chin with one hand—he tried to read her face in the dark.

"Am I a fool?"

"Yes," Elaine answered—and then she smiled. "And you are
very brave. Now go on with your story."

Thomas looked around at the circled watchers. Then he continued. "I became an expert marksman with my bow. It is amazing how keen one's aim can become when one's dinner depends
on it. Also I practiced with the swords I had taken, and in time I
became a tolerable swordsman.

"I saw no reason to return to the world of men—a world
where because of my 'low' birth (though I knew my father and
mother were of the finest of God's creatures) I could never be a
knight, never own land like a noble, never command men like a
king. I was sure that if I returned to the world I would attempt
all those things—I would attempt to rise above what was
ordained as my station—and then, like my father standing firm
for justice, I would be slain.

"I preferred to live with the animals.

"Speaking to no one, I began weaving wild fantasies of my
own royalty—it took me a long time to realize that I was only
pitying myself—and then once I realized that I was able to step
away from myself, I thought of the brave lives of my parents,
and then finally, all alone, I cried for them as I had not done on
the day of their deaths. I cried for hours—and then I prayed for
the souls of those who had given me life, and then finally I was
able to accept their death—and then too, I was able to accept
my own life.

"This was after a year of solitude. I realized then that I was
perhaps *capable* of returning to society—but still I had no desire
to come back yet. It was another full year before I returned—I
spent two years without addressing another human being.

"I was facing another winter (this was the fall of 1188) when I
decided to leave the forest. It was not fear of the cold that drove
me. Instead it was another basic desire: I wanted a woman—I
needed a woman, with all the desperate hunger of any eighteen
year old boy." Thomas felt Elaine stiffen in his arms, for gentlemen did not talk like this to a lady—but Thomas felt that his
love for Elaine was such that he could never disguise or ignore
the truth in his dealings with her—she had asked for his story

and he would tell it, the truth as he knew it—and he knew that she could accept truth, for she was an exceptional woman—she would come to understand him, and perhaps tonight she would return his love.

He loosened his arms to give Elaine a bit more freedom, but he did not let her go, and he went on without censorship.

"I came out of the forest, and I sold the carcass of a deer I had killed to a poor family who still lived on the Nottingham estate. They bade me bathe in a nearby stream, for I had the smell of an animal—afterward, when I was a bit more presentable, they gave me some old clothes. Then they told me of the events of the past two years. Most surprising was this: Wesley had died just a month after the murder of my parents. He had been found slumped over a spilled tankard of port. Some said that the Hand of God could be seen in his shortened life—others said that he had killed himself with his own dissipation.

"In any case, the estate had changed hands once again. Wesley had left no heir, and his sister was content with her husband in Poitou. Therefore the title had reverted back to the old Baron's younger brother—he was a widower, fifty-eight years old when I emerged—my new friends said that he was a kindly man. The standard ten percent tithe had been reinstated.

"As a side note, you may know this Baron—two years later he married Lady Louisa of the court."

"Yes—Alfred of Nottingham—I met him once," Elaine said. "I don't believe he comes to London very often."

Thomas gave Elaine a slight smile. "No, he doesn't.

"To return to the story, the people told me that all charges against me had died with the unlamented Wesley.

"I was a free man.

"I could have stayed on the estate, but I chose not to live my father's life. I made my way to London.

"I needed money—and so, like any other fellow with quick hands and good manners, I learned to wait upon the gentry. I made enough to live on—and a little extra to indulge myself—I discovered the women of Shaftesbury Avenue—I satisfied my body, though my soul was unawakened.

"In such a way I lived happily enough for another year. King Henry II died, and Richard took his place, bringing ever more pomp and circumstance in his wake. There was a need for more waiters at the court—I succeeded in securing a position.

"I did my work well—I was privileged to wait upon knights

and ladies—several times I waited on a Countess."

Elaine looked sharply at Thomas. It was her turn to try to read his face.

"Yes, I waited on you, dear Elaine. I know you don't remember me, and it matters not to me that you don't." Elaine frantically *tried* to remember Thomas in such an incarnation, but he was right—she could not recall him that way. "I saw you, from close at hand, and I fell in love with you. The first day I saw you I swore that I would become a knight—on that day I swore that in time I would win your heart."

Elaine looked up at Thomas, amazed by the enormity of his devotion, of his effort. Was he mad? And how could she have inspired all this without being aware of it? How had he managed to come this far? She had to admit that he had very nearly succeeded in his quest.

"Tell me how you became a knight," she said.

Thomas smiled. "The short answer is that I changed my name and put a Sir in front of it—but we have time, and I will tell you the long version."

The smile had faded and there was only sadness in Thomas's voice when he finished that sentence. He went on. "I knew that battle was my only chance. If I distinguished myself enough, I thought that I might be able to leap the barriers of class. I joined the Third Crusade. I fantasized that in the coming conflict I would somehow save King Richard from beastly Saracens, and then of course he would knight me on the spot—and then I'd come home a hero . . ."

Thomas smiled again. "I won't tell you the rest of that youthful dream. Anyway, I found a knight without a squire, for he had no money to pay one. He was the last scion of a noble but impoverished family. They had lost their land as well as their money.

"I offered my services to this gentleman, and he explained about his finances. I told him that I would serve for the experience only, and he took me on.

"We became friends.

"His name was Sir Thomas."

As he said that name, now his own, the heavens were split by a bolt of lightning.

Thunder boomed a second later.

Thomas had not noticed the darkening of the sky, the blotting of the moon.

He pulled Elaine close as rain began to come down.

Chapter 113

ANTON AND SANDRA

In the Larrazian camp . . .

There was thunder and lightning and rain. The rain was cold on Sir Anton's back, but all the front of him was warm, even hot, for Sandra lay naked beneath him. Anton was up on his elbows so that Sandra did not have to take his whole weight— but he was close enough to feel the whole length of her body—he teased her swollen nipples with the rough gray hair of his chest—he inhaled her sweet breath, and touched her lips with his tongue.

They had already shared the supreme pleasure of love twice this night. Anton could not remember any other woman who had joined with him so easily and completely. He moved lazily on top of his love, and thought of a day nine months in the future: Sandra was going to give birth. He did not know about tomorrow—he did not know whether or not they would save Elaine—but he knew with an iron certainty that Sandra had conceived. His spirit had mingled with hers and made a child.

He would love Sandra forever.

Anton thought of that: forever. He felt the purest love for his bride to be, the expectant mother of his chid—and then with the perversity that is endemic in human nature, he deliberately turned his thoughts to the beautiful Italian whores he had known. He thought of what he had done with them—he thought of what he had made them do to serve him.

He teased Sandra's mouth open with his tongue—and then he came down on her. He kissed her brutally—he forced her mouth to open even wider—he sought her throat with his tongue, and then he suddenly moved away, leaving Sandra gasping and frightened.

He sat back—he leaned against his saddle and spread his legs—with his hands he pulled Sandra to the position he desired, between his legs—on her knees.

He took her hair in his strong right hand and forced her down until she kissed his rigid manhood—and then he pressed down harder until she took him in her mouth. He pressed harder still, he made her take more and more—finally she began to fight him, fight his hand—her own small hands came up and clasped his arm—and then she felt his muscles like steel there as he held her to his will, and in her heart too she felt a final shifting, an acceptance of this man as her master, a knowledge that there was nothing of her he did not own, and then she relaxed, she took him even deeper, as he desired, and then he was gentler with her, he let her go up and down, he taught her the shape of him, and he was only cruel again at the end, his arm tightened once more into a bar of steel and he held her down until she swallowed all of his very essence.

Then he let her come off, but he still held her hair—he hunched forward to protect her from the rain, and he tilted her head back so that he was looking right down into her shadowy face—he wanted to see her expression, he wanted to see her reaction to his violence—and then the lightning flashed again, her face was illuminated for a second, and in that second Anton was shocked to his soul.

He saw Sandra's big brown eyes looking up at him with a calm and loving devotion—he saw that he owned her in a more absolute way than even an emperor can own a slave—and yet he saw too that that ownership had been won at a dear price. He saw in her eyes that she knew he had given her his heart. No more could he roam free. He would have a wife, and soon enough, a child. He might yet go to war again, be separated from them for months—yet he knew that his thoughts would never be separate from the family he had begun. He would think of Sandra every day. He would think of their child, alive already in her womb. This was his fate.

He loved Sandra. He had given his freedom for love.

He felt a sudden rage against this loss of freedom—and the rage reignited his desire.

He pulled Sandra roughly across his lap—he raised his thighs so her buttocks were offered to the night—he watched for the next flash of lightning, and when it came his right hand was up and ready—he waited the proper second and then brought his hand down with the force of a seasoned warrior—he struck the unmarked cheek of her behind, struck it harder than the Vulture had done, ten times harder than her mistress had ever spanked her—the crack of the blow and her cry alike were drowned in nature's thunderclap.

Sandra was still moaning a minute later when Anton had pressed her face down on his blanket and spread her legs. He entered her from behind—and then he took her hands, both her hands, and he led them back to her buttocks, he made her spread herself open, and then he was gone for just a second, only to come back to that other tighter orifice she was opening for him—she stood it for as long as she could, she held herself open for him as he possessed her, and then she let go and her hands shot forward, she wanted to grab the blanket and stuff it into her mouth to stop the scream she couldn't hold back, but then she found that Anton had anticipated her, his hand covered her mouth—she bit into his hand with all her strength and screamed into his trapped flesh, screamed silently again and again but then finally some of the pain went away—she opened her mouth wide to take a deep breath, she freed Anton's hand but he did not take it away—she felt his manhood, big and implacable, spreading her, stretching her—she discovered that when he moved, all of her moved—she was owned by this man she loved—she kissed the hand she had bitten, she ran her tongue over the bite marks she had made, and she felt her master come deep inside of her, and she gloried in the feeling.

Anton's rage was gone. He pulled out slowly, carefully, and Sandra turned to wash his manhood gently in the falling rain. Then she took it all, soft as it was, in her mouth, and so she showed Anton that she loved all of him, she accepted him, she accepted all he had done to her—Anton understood, and he freed Sandra from her submission, he raised her up and kissed her lips.

Anton realized that his lover was tired past exhaustion. He cuddled her tenderly in his arms, and Sandra gratefully ducked her head under his chin and lay against his warm chest. She closed her eyes, and soon fell asleep.

Anton flipped the blanket over with one hand so he could pull the drier side up over Sandra's back. He held her, he protected her from the rain, and he thought about forever.

Chapter 114

THE GIRL IN THE ROAD

Thomas and Elaine tried to find shelter under Saladin's bulk, but still the rain pelted them. Water—a desperate need just a few hours before—now lashed them with its cold spray. They shivered as they held each other—they stared at the brown cassocked watching monks illumined by every lightning flash.

The night was a horror—and yet there was good in it, there was good in telling the story so long hidden. Thomas put his lips against Elaine's wet ear. "Shall I go on?" he asked.

"Yes, please," Elaine replied. "Take me away from here."

Thomas continued with the tale of his life.

"Thomas and I, and all our comrades under the command of Richard Lionheart, set sail from England on March 3, 1190. We were bound for Acre, in the Holy Land, where Christian forces had trapped a Moslem garrison led by Karakush. I expected that we would make the trip as rapidly as possible, but instead Richard led us on an aimless course. We wandered here and there, conquering small kingdoms at will—more for sport than for any other reason, or so it seemed to me—and so more than a year passed, and we still had not come to the Holy Land. Finally, after conquering the island of Cyprus in the summer of 1191, Richard decided that we should at last sail for Acre. Amazingly enough, the Moslem defenders were still hanging on. The Christian siege had lasted for two years—and still the infidels (we all called them by that name, never thinking that in their land *we* were the infidels) refused to surrender. No one knew how they had managed to survive for so long with no new supplies of food—perhaps they lived on prayer, or on the hope that Saladin with the main Moslem army would come to their rescue. The prudent Saladin, however, had no intention of engaging our massed forces at a fixed point—he left the garrison to its fate, though I'm sure he never dreamed how terrible that fate would be.

"I must add that not all the suffering was on the Moslem side. The besiegers did not have it easy either. They were dependent on ships, expeditions like ours to resupply them—we heard that when the intervals between ships grew too long, then good Christian knights were forced to kill and eat their own horses.

"Richard, now that he was at last committed to true battle, believed that the coming of our troops would decisively tip the balance. He was the one who was destined to break through the walls and take Acre.

"And so we sailed from Cyprus, but it was a difficult passage. Our fleet was separated by storm—my ship was driven so far off course that we lost sight of Richard's flagship—we wandered for days in the trackless sea, and then finally a hard following wind drove us headlong toward the Holy Land, and we ran aground on the sandy shore somewhere south of Acre.

"The ship was too badly damaged to be repaired. We disembarked gladly—we felt the hot sand under our feet. We were young men, eager for adventure—we rejoiced in our Christian power—we marched to the north, following the seacoast. Before long we came upon another errant ship from our fleet—this one was somewhat less mangled by wind and weather, and the captain and crew were repairing it. This captain was quite experienced and knowledgeable—he told us that Acre was just two days march to the north—the soldiers he had carried had disembarked the day before, and we could follow their track. He warned us to be alert for Saladin's cavalry, and he wished us Godspeed.

"We set off again with light hearts.

"Most of us were on foot—only the knights, like Thomas, were mounted.

"The journey was uneventful at first, save for the extraordinary heat. Those knights who had put on full armor began almost literally to roast. We had to pause while their squires helped remove the burning mail. I did not have to perform this service for Thomas—as I said, we had become friends, and we had spent a long time talking on our long journey to this place— I had told him of my parents, and the black knights—you see, Elaine, you are the second person I have told that story to—anyway, Thomas agreed with me that full armor is often only a trap, one becomes dependent on one's horse and other men, and so he was only burdened by a light protective vest.

"How can I describe Thomas? Physically he looked a lot like me, but his character was really quite different. He was truly *humble*—perhaps that is the best word for him. He was willing to listen to advice from a commoner like me—he offered friendship and never demanded homage. He felt no competition with his fellow knights—he rode at the rear of the column—when others paused to take off their armor he did not use that chance for self advancement. He had no dreams of glory.

"He had something else in mind—something I could not share with him at all. He had a zealous religious faith—he truly believed that this Crusade was the will of God. As a humble servant of the Lord, he wished to do his part.

"So though I had told Thomas I wished to become a knight, I did not tell him that my reason had nothing to do with the Holy Cause. I did not tell him that my desire for that title was linked to my desire for a certain, beautiful lady."

Elaine smiled at Thomas, and he touched her rainwashed cheek, and then he went on.

"You must understand, Thomas was a Believer. He believed in God and His Holy Cause—he believed in his King—he believed in his own essential goodness.

"In the coming months, all those beliefs would be shattered.

"The first blow awaited us just over the horizon, where we could see smoke drifting into the sky. Thomas mentioned food cooking—I thought of my charred home in Nottingham, and I said nothing. As we came closer we gradually made out the remnants of a small village. The little huts had been burned. Old women and children hid in the shade of sparse bushes. Bodies cluttered what had been the main street.

"It seemed to take a long time to approach, for we could see much—too much—in that clear desert air.

"We knew who had caused this devastation—our comrades from the other ship had done this—it was the fire of the Cross that had purified"—Thomas choked on the word—"this poor Moslem village.

"I felt my friend recoil in horror as we got closer to the scene. I believed that right then the first crack appeared in his faith.

"There was dead silence as we entered the little village. I could see the squires in front of me trying to lead their knights' horses around and between the dead bodies. Not one of us wanted to stop for even a second—and then some horse missed his step, and put an iron shoe on the back of one of the dead—and the body came alive with a horrible shriek—it jerked free of the panicked horse, and then it fell sideways and tightened into a fetal position—now we saw it was a woman, beaten on her face and other places—she clung to herself while her open mouth kept shrieking.

"One by one our men passed her, going by as quickly as possible, squires wanting to run, knights wishing to kick their horses into a gallop—they were afraid of this half naked abused woman, and ashamed of what their countrymen had done to her, but there was no thought of stopping to help—our men hurried by, until only Thomas and I were left.

"I said, 'Just a minute,' and then I walked over to the girl and picked her up.

"She shrieked even louder when I touched her. Her body was rigid in its curled up posture, and so I had to hold her like a big awkward ball in front of me. Holding her like that, I walked over to the bushes where the surviving elders of the village watched. I just wanted to give her to them, to be sure that someone would care for her. I headed for a group of two old women and one old man—but as I approached I saw their eyes narrow with hatred, a hatred not just for me but for the girl too. The old people began to yell at me in their own language—and the girl in my arms understood. From being tight and rigid she suddenly collapsed as though her will was gone—she started sobbing— I didn't understand until the two women began to spit at the girl with hatefilled faces, and the man indicated with violent gestures that they wanted no parts of her.

"Then I too understood: the girl had been raped by the Crusaders, and now her own people believed her to be unclean. They would not take her back. It was no wonder that she had lain in the road like the dead—she wanted to be dead, but she was young and strong—and with the bruises gone I thought she would be beautiful—I put her over my shoulder and walked back to Thomas. We moved on at a brisk pace, we caught up with the end of the column, I walked along by my friend's horse, and I carried the damaged girl.

"We walked along in silence for a while.

"Thomas seemed to be wrestling with his belief. How could God have allowed this to happen? he must have wondered. How could men sworn to defend Christ do this? What was his duty under God? Should he succor this infidel? Was that opposed to his mission to bring Christ to this land?

"He must have thought of all those things, seeking guidance from the good Lord, and when he finally spoke it was with the voice of Christian charity. He said, 'You must be tired carrying the young lady for so long. Pass her up to me, so that way my horse can share our burden.'

"We had been friends before, but this act of charity brought me even closer to Thomas—I gratefully handed the girl up to him (she was limp and unconscious now) and he took her and held her like I held you this afternoon. We took turns carrying her that day, and when we camped that night we were able to get her to eat with us.

"Some of the other men made jokes to the effect that we had already appropriated an Arab bed slave, but we ignored them, and the talk did not get too rough for the other men were still ashamed that they had done nothing.

"We slept with the girl between us, and then on the next day she could walk some on her own—and that night, June 8, 1191, we finally came upon the huge Christian encampment that surrounded the doomed city of Acre.

"For two years the siege had gone on, a long dance of death, a carnival of madness—we heard every language of Europe as we approached in the darkness, we saw jugglers twirling fiery clubs, we heard peddlers hawking their wares, we saw ladies of the evening plying their trade—thousands of men sought one last thrill, knowing they might die tomorrow—thousands had died already, thousands on either side—and still the spectral defenders of Acre continued to resist.

"We had come to finally break that resistance. I was caught up in the excitement of the camp, but I saw that Thomas looked sad, older far than his years—it was as though he knew that victory would bring only evil.

"Thomas gave me some of his small store of money to purchase a tent for us, while he went off to report to the King (we had heard coming in that the Lionheart had already arrived). The girl stayed with me—I bought a tent from one of the many peddlers who clustered around us new arrivals, and I set it up for the three of us.

"Thomas came back soon: he told me that we would be in the attack at dawn.

"I was too excited to sleep. I saw that the girl, whose name I still did not know, was also awake. She was terrified, cut of from her own people—and she was near the very men who had raped her (our comrades had greeted us cheerfully in the darkness, but none of them had recognized their victim—had she even been a person, an individual to them?) She had no place to run to—in desperation she opened her arms to me. I embraced her and pulled her close—I looked past her at Thomas, lying quietly on his side of the tent—he said, 'Do with her as you will, my friend. As for myself, I must rest for tomorrow's battle.'

Then he turned away to sleep. I understood that he wanted no claim on the girl, and I was greatly relieved that I did not have to share her. I took off the girl's few garments as gently as I could, and then she gave me willingly what had lately been taken from her by force. When it was over I kissed very gently all the bruises on her face, and I felt her shudder in my arms. I turned sideways, I held her loosely—but she suddenly embraced me with a kind of desperation, she clung to me with a strength too soon exhausted—and then finally she relaxed all over, and I realized that she had fallen asleep.

"I closed my eyes as well, I slept the night with my girl in my arms."

Chapter 115

SULEKA'S SMILE

"Was she the mother of your child?" Elaine asked.

"She would have been," Thomas said.

Elaine put her head on his shoulder. She waited for him to tell her the next act of the tragedy.

Thomas was silent for a long time—and this gave Elaine a chance to think of her own past. She recalled the deaths of her parents—yes, she and Thomas had things in common. She remembered the horror of her nineteenth birthday, a horror from which Arthur had saved her—and yet a horror she could never leave behind, for she carried its mark on her face. She could tell Thomas about that. Elaine realized then that she would respond to Thomas's request. When he was finished she would tell him all about her past—she wanted to break her own silence and share her pain, as he shared his own. They would ease each other's burdens—and then if they could only survive . . .

Thomas began to speak again, in the voice of his past.

"I learned that her name was Suleka. She added a woman's touch to the rough soldierly lives that Thomas and I led. She washed our clothes and cooked our food for us—we bought her needle and thread, and she mended our well worn clothes.

"She stayed in our tent most of the time—she was afraid to go out when other knights were around. The effects of the attack stayed with her—she only knew some kind of happiness when she was actually touching me.

"Our comrades simply assumed that Thomas and I shared her as our bed slave. Thomas did not deny this, but in fact he never touched her. He concerned himself only with righteous battle—

he flung himself into combat with such eagerness that his valor was noted by the King. Richard gave Thomas a few gold pieces as a reward for bravery—my selfless friend used the money to buy a horse for me.

"Thomas taught me how to fight on horseback—we practiced in the evenings, and when he judged me ready, we went into battle together. We fought like fellow knights, not as master and squire.

"Acre began to crumble. Every day we made breaches in the walls, though the haggard defenders poured burning naptha on our men. I saw men burned alive—I saw death in all its forms.

"I gave death myself—I killed many, when we crashed through the walls—I was often nearly killed in turn, when the desperate defenders would drive us out.

"Then I would come back to Suleka, and she would be sitting, rigid, waiting for me—when she saw me her whole body would relax, and then she would wash my feet as was the custom of the land. Only then would she wait on Thomas—and then she would cook our dinner.

"Richard had been right about one thing. The coming of the English troops did tip the balance. The siege only lasted five more weeks after our arrival.

"On the night before Acre fell, Suleka told me she was pregnant. She put my hand on her belly and said, 'You!' I didn't understand at first, and then she made a curving motion of her hand, indicating that her belly would swell like the full moon. I understood then, and I laughed, and Suleka smiled for the first time since I had known her.

"The smile changed her face—the bruises were almost gone—she was beautiful.

"Do you know, Elaine, when I remember this I can not ever recall even *thinking* that the child could actually have been from one of the men who raped her. The timing was too close—there was no way she could have told—but we both simply accepted on faith that it was mine, and to this day I am certain we were right.

"I lay there thinking about my future that night. The fact of the child and the beauty of Suleka's smile changed things for me. Suleka's head nestled in the hollow of my shoulder—I caressed her as she slept, and I felt contented. I wondered if the love I had felt for you was just a boy's fantasy. You were, after all, a married woman. You did not know me. I thought that perhaps I had stumbled into some Divine plan—my love for you had sent me to the Holy Land, and so I came to rescue the wounded girl who slept now in my arms. I had helped her heal—I had given her love, and new life within her, and she loved me in return.

"I thought that after we took Acre, I could perhaps take part of the town as my share of the conquest. Title or no, I could live there like a prince. Suleka would bear my children, and they would grow up like the bright green shoots of spring that signal the end of winter. Our children would be God's blessing on this land that had been struck by horror—I dreamed on . . ."

Thomas smiled at Elaine—a dreadful smile. He went on. "Acre fell the next day—that was July 12, 1191. Richard Lionheart rode proudly into the conquered city. His first official act laid the groundwork for the massacre to come."

Chapter 116

THE TERMS OF SURRENDER

"What did the King do?" Elaine asked.

There was another long pause.

Finally Thomas spoke. "Richard took Karakush and his top generals aside. He forced them to sign the articles of surrender that he dictated. Richard wanted three things: 200,000 gold pieces, as ransom for the 3,000 Moslem prisoners taken; the release by Saladin of 1,600 Christian captives; and, most important of all, the return of the True Cross.

"Karakush tried to argue. He said he could not sign such an agreement, for he could not honor it. Only Saladin himself had the wealth and power to honor such terms—and Karakush went on to say that Saladin would never agree to such a capitulation.

"Richard said, 'Sign it—or die now.'

"You see, Elaine, I know all this because Thomas was there. As I said before, the King had noticed his valor—and likewise his piety had made a good impression—and so Richard commanded him to come along and witness the surrender. This was meant to be a special treat for Thomas—but the actual result was that another of his beliefs began to crack.

"Thomas had thought of Richard as God's chosen warrior— but up close he was able to see the falsity in the image. Richard did not want to *fight* Saladin—instead, he hoped to *extort* the trappings of victory.

"Richard was a bully who liked to threaten helpless men— yes, Karakush signed, for he could see that Richard was ready to carry out his threat—but Thomas and I agreed, as we discussed the situation that night, that Saladin could not be coerced in this manner. If Saladin had not committed his forces to rescue the garrison before, why then would he ransom them now? And why should he honor an extorted agreement anyway? *Saladin* had not been defeated in battle.

"Thomas and I saw that nothing good could come of this—but we were alone in so thinking.

"The men were flushed with victory. They believed in their leader, the Lionheart—the man whose mere arrival had caused the walls of Acre to crumble. They believed that as Karakush had capitulated, so Saladin would follow suit—and so every time an Arab emissary appeared, the shout would go up: 'The True Cross is coming! The True Cross is coming!'

"Of course the True Cross never appeared. Saladin simply asked for delay after delay, or else he proposed new conditions, such as that the Christians give him an equal number of hostages, or he asked that the Moslem prisoners be released first as a mark of good faith, or he simply invented new and varied excuses as to why he could not meet the demands . . .

"In the Eastern manner, Saladin never abruptly refused Richard's terms—he just slid away from them in a most frustrating manner. Saladin knew well that time was on his side—this desert was his home, while the Europeans would never be comfortable there. I think the leader of the Moslems just intended to keep the negotiations going as long as possible—I don't think that he ever intended to accept Richard's extortionate demands.

"I had to keep silent about my thoughts. Emotions ran high on the Christian side. Now every time an emissary of Saladin's appeared—without the True Cross—the men cursed him and his master. They swore at Saladin for not honoring the terms he had not signed. The feeling of easy triumph slipped away from the men—and rage took its place.

"Even Thomas was affected. His doubts about Richard—indeed about the Cause itself—were still as nothing compared to his longing for the True Cross. 'If we could just get the Cross,' he told me, 'then we could forgive all the rest.' He too began to rail at Saladin. 'What good is the Cross to him,' he would cry, 'when he believes in Mohammed? He is worse than Aesop's dog in the manger. It is true that infidels are evil . . .'

"And he would go on in this manner, while I prayed that Suleka could not understand him.

"Every week the rage rose higher in our ranks—a rage that might be directed at *any* Moslem. I was worried about Suleka.

The three of us shared a house in the conquered city now, but no longer could I dream of a secure future there. There were ugly incidents in the streets—I forbade Suleka to leave the house—I had food sent in.

"Suleka's breasts had begun to fill and harden. I never thought of her as an infidel. She was my woman. The child she carried was part of me.

"I don't think Thomas ever really understood my love for this Moslem woman—likewise I could not share his religious fervor. Our friendship was deep, but it was strained by the tension one could feel in the air. The negotiations dragged on, day after nervous day—until finally Richard showed his hand.

"One morning—it was August 20, a little more than a month after Acre's surrender—Thomas said to me, 'One hundred knights including myself have been summoned to the plain below the mountains to the east of the city. You are not to come.'

"Naturally I was curious. After he left I kissed Suleka, and made her promise again to stay inside. I mounted my horse—I rode out to see what I could see.

"I wish I had never gone that day."

He took Elaine's face in his hands.

"You do not need to know what I saw."

Chapter 117

THE ENCLOSURE

Elaine felt herself caught by Thomas's strength, a strength that held her away instead of drawing her close—but she could not be shut out now. She reached up and took his powerful wrists in her own strong hands—she looked into his eyes—she wondered for a moment at the fact that she could see him, and then she realized that sometime during the story the rain had stopped—neither of them had noticed the storm's ending—now his face was visible in the thin light of the crescent moon that had reappeared—there were even a few stars sparkling in his gray eyes—Elaine looked into those eyes and pushed outward against his holding arms, and she broke his grip.

She said quietly, "There are no secrets tonight. No secrets for you, and no secrets for me. You must tell me everything."

Thomas looked at her with a sudden quickening of interest—she *would* tell him of her life. Like him, she would tell of things never before disclosed—she would tell *him*.

She loves me, Thomas thought, and I love her, and I can give her strength to bear the truth.

"Very well then," Thomas said, "just give me your hand, and I will tell you of evil."

The little warfare of hands and arms ceased. In a moment Thomas held Elaine's right hand in both of his. He held her tenderly, he looked out into the past, and he continued his story.

"I rode out to the east, following Thomas as I have said, but there was no sign of him nor of the hundred knights he had mentioned. There was only a huge rectangular enclosure, a strange sort of stockade that had not been there the day before. The thing was crudely built—the framework was a series of

wooden stakes about six feet apart—each stake was connected
to the next by a single cord that stretched horizontally about
eight feet off the ground—and over the cord, between each set of
stakes, blankets had been draped.

"It looked like all the washing in Acre had been set out to dry.

"The distance was deceptive, as so often in the desert. I had to
ride a considerable ways out into the plain before I was close
enough to see movement behind the blankets. The enclosure
had been set up really quite close to the Moslem controlled hills
to the east.

"I rode still closer, trying to understand the movement that I
could see through the gaps between the blankets—and then a
wind came up, and lifted the feeble covering, and blew some
blankets off completely—and then I saw the knights, Christian
knights in full armor, and I saw the Moslem prisoners of Acre,
thousands of them—I would learn later that the exact number
was 2,600. Of his three thousand prisoners, Richard spared only
the four hundred of highest rank.

"But still at this point I did not know those men were doomed.
I looked for Thomas, but the wind died down and most of the
blankets settled back like a veil—I did not see him. I wondered
why all the knights I saw wore full armor—the day was hot, and
the Moslem prisoners, with hands bound behind their backs,
were certainly no threat.

"I said I did not know about the prisoners' fate—I should really say that I knew, but my mind would not accept it at first—
there was something else that I should have noticed right away,
but my brain rejected the knowledge of my eyes—until finally I
had come so close that I could no longer deny the existence of
this instrument of murder: a wooden cross projected up above
the tight drawn cord—the unholy cross of a gibbet. I saw the
rope hanging down from one end, and I didn't need to see the
noose hidden behind a blanket—I *knew*.

"It was a hot day, as I have said, but I began to shake with a
cold horror. I spurred my horse around the enclosure—I rode up
a foothill on the other side. This was Moslem country, but I did
not care. Now I could look down into the enclosure. I knew that
I alone could not stop this evil—but I had to *see*.

"Do you know, Elaine, later on I realized that the whole set up
was quite deliberate on Richard's part. The crude fence with
gaps in it, the gibbet projecting above the line, the fact that the
enclosure was set up so close to Moslem territory—all this was

planned so that Saladin's sentries in the foothills would see the massacre—Richard did not hide his sin—he was proud of this action.

"I watched as my fellow Christians began to hang the unarmed prisoners, one by one. I saw that Thomas *was* there, easy to distinguish because he was the only one not wearing full armor—and if he was not participating yet, then he was not protesting or leaving either. I saw King Richard Lionheart directing the murders—like all his knights save Thomas, he too wore full armor, and this was most uncharacteristic of him.

"I saw the prisoners watch as their comrades died, slowly, horribly, only to be brusquely cut down while another was selected. I could tell the moment that the prisoners suddenly understood that they *all* were doomed—they began to resist, even in their bonds they fought with feet, shoulders, teeth—I heard Richard Lionheart give the order and I saw his man at arms Brian lead the charge—Brian rode, sword out, straight into the terrified mass of prisoners—he began to slash in every direction—Christian knights followed his bloody wake, they chopped into heads and arms and torsos—Thomas joined in with the rest, as eager as the rest, he slashed and he killed like every Christian there—blood coated the knights' mail, blood coated Thomas's clothes—I heard howls of outrage and hoof-beats behind me—brave Moslem sentries, unable to bear the sight of the carnage, raced down past me in a forlorn attempt to aid their fellows—they charged into the swirling knights, and they were cut down—I hoped they had sent at least one messenger back to Saladin—I watched as the slaughter continued—I rode back down the hill—I swung wide around the enclosure. I was sure there was nothing more to see. The knights, caught in blood lust, would not stop until every prisoner was dead.

"I rode slowly back toward Acre, for I was not eager to see Suleka after seeing what my people had done to hers. I was numb, so sick at heart I could not think—I could not see—my eyes had been blinded by blood—I felt my clothes, expecting my fingers to come away sticky with blood—I was clean but I kept seeing Thomas in the frenzy of murder—I dreamed myself in his place—who was my friend?

"Who was I?

"I couldn't go forward to Suleka—I was afraid to look back, and then I thought it all might be a nightmare, perhaps I dreamed the killing just as I dreamed of blood on my clothes, perhaps none of it was real—and so I looked back, and there was the enclosure, half the blankets blown awry, I could see the gibbet, and a body dangling from it, and I realized I had been shutting out the sounds of the screams, and now with my senses alive I heard men crying for mercy that would never come—bodies in piles now—and then suddenly a knight burst out of the left side of the enclosure, unarmored, it had to be Thomas—he rode like a madman to the north, then changed his mind and turned his horse to the east—he galloped toward the Moslem hills, he rode up some rocky slope—and then he vanished from my sight.

"He was my friend—and so I turned my horse around, and I followed him.

"I never once thought that Suleka could be in danger because of Thomas's action—if I had thought of that possibility, I would have gone to her right away—and I suppose I would have died too.

"I should have gone to her."

Chapter 118

THOMAS CONCLUDES HIS STORY

Thomas had spoken very quickly when he told of the massacre, but once he rode down the hill (in his story) his voice began to fade. He barely managed to whisper. 'I should have gone to her,' and then his voice just stopped altogether.

There was no light in his lowered eyes now. Elaine looked at his pale face and saw that he was silently crying. Two silvery tracks of tears ran down his cheeks. Thomas unclasped Elaine's hand—he turned his head sharply to the left, and then when he looked back at Elaine his tears were gone.

He continued his story.

"I picked up Thomas's trail where he turned to the east. It was easy to follow him. Blood stained every sandy hoofprint. His horse must have been wading through it.

"Thomas had a good lead on me—I still could not see him anywhere—I could tell he had been whipping his mount by the distance between the prints—I thought, it is not your horse's fault that blood follows you everywhere—right then I hated Sir Thomas—a man who had given me nothing but kindness—a murderer—I thought nothing could atone for his part in the massacre."

Thomas's voice had faded again, and with the word 'massacre' he stopped completely and stared off into the night. He didn't seem to know how to go on. Elaine thought she understood: the real Thomas had been a good man, a good friend to this man by her side—yet that same Thomas was also a murderer, a participant in the most vile horror. She realized that even now her companion had trouble coming to grips with this. How could evil exist inside a good man? If it existed, was he ever good? And if even good men have this capacity for evil, is anyone good?

"You took his name," Elaine said. "He must have atoned."

"Yes," Thomas said. "He killed himself."

There was a long pause.

"I followed the trail of blood up a rocky hill—I knew that it was only a matter of time before I found Thomas—his horse could not keep up this driven pace—the tracks led around to the eastern side of the hill, and there I found my friend—he had stopped running.

"He was sitting on a flat rock. He had made no attempt to clean himself. His face, his clothes, everything was stained with blood.

"'I've been waiting for you,' he said.

"I nodded. I didn't trust myself to speak.

"'Did you see?'

"'Yes.'

"'I thought you were watching—that's why I turned this way instead of riding back towards town.' He looked over at the higher mountains to the east. 'I learned something today— you're not always right, my friend.' He looked back at me and smiled. 'Full armor has its uses. Blood can be taken off with the mail. The wearer is not touched. Steel can be cleaned.'

"He dropped his eyes. 'I can never be cleaned.'

"'I don't think you can,' I said.

"'I didn't know what was going to happen. I was probably the last to understand it. I thought we would just make a demonstration, hang a few infidels . . .'

"'A few infidels helpless as women,' I said.

"He looked down at the rock he sat on. 'I had visions of the True Cross being brought down from the hills'—he stopped, and then everything came out in a rush—'I hated them so much! They took our Holy City—they took the True Cross upon which our Savior was crucified—they command Christ's sepulcher— they hold these things without belief or honor—their very touch is profane—they have no humanity—they would not give up the Cross even to save their own people—I hated them as though they were animals without reason, and when Richard's order came I waded in with the rest, slashing, killing, these were the heretics who trampled on Jerusalem, I felt no remorse, I even liked it, O God I liked it, I was Divine spirit, I gave death and the field of our Lord ran red with blood—and then some of that hot red blood splashed upon my face, living human blood from a dying man, a slap in the face from the true God—I suddenly knew in my heart that this was wrong, horribly wrong—did not Jesus say that only he that is without sin should cast the first stone? We were all sinners here—and with every swing of the sword, the mortal sin of murder was added to our souls.

"'I stood up in the stirrups and shouted, "Stop it! This is enough! Stop!" I was screaming and I didn't see Brian coming from behind. He smashed the sword from my hand, and then wheeled his horse around and stopped in front of me. He flipped his visor up and said, "If you're not man enough to do your duty, if you can not obey your King and your God, then get out of here and run to your Moslem whore!" He was gesturing wildly with his sword and foaming at the mouth—I was unarmed and at that moment I feared death—I took off, I rode through a gap where a blanket had blown away, I rode up this mountain, knowing somehow that you would follow me.

"'I have had time to think, waiting for you. I know my destiny. I fear death no longer. I embrace it.

"'I know that you would not have taken part in the massacre. You were the only one of us who extended Christian charity to Suleka when she lay in the road. I am not worthy of you, my friend.

"'I am not worthy of life.

"'When I die, all that I own shall be yours.

"'I must ask you for one last favor. Please give me your sword.'

"I unsheathed my weapon and handed it to him.

"Thomas wedged the hilt of my sword between two heavy rocks, so the blade pointed straight up. He stood up, and tilted his head back, and closed his eyes before the light of the sun. Like that, he said a long silent prayer. His lips moved, but I couldn't hear the words. Then he looked down, eyes wide open now, and he gauged the angle. He let himself go—he fell perfectly onto the blade. He abandoned his soul to God.

"The sword transfixed his body, entering his chest and coming out his back—he hung there like that, and I realized that body and sword together had made the shape of a cross, and I felt the touch of a merciful God on my friend."

Elaine saw tears on her brave protector's face again. She reached up and brushed them away with her warm hands—and then she took Thomas's right hand in both of hers, as he had held her before, and she gave him the strength to go on, for she knew that the tragedy was not yet complete.

Thomas raised his eyes as though to look at his beautiful companion—but Elaine knew he didn't see her, couldn't see her, he saw his dead friend, and he saw another death coming.

He went on with a breaking voice. "I couldn't touch my friend right away. First I took the bridle and saddle off his horse, and I gave the animal a light swat to send it home. The poor beast had been through enough—it trotted away quickly.

"Then I did have to turn to Thomas. I lowered him gently to the ground, and I took my sword out. I cleaned the weapon and put it back in my scabbard—and then I took it out again, when I realized that was the only digging tool I had. I managed to cut a shallow grave into the rocky earth, but it took a long time. Finally I was able to bury Thomas. I laid stones in the shape of a cross on the grave.

"You understand, Elaine, that I could have taken Thomas back to Acre and had him buried with the full rights of the Church. I would not have needed to explain his suicide—I could have said that he had been killed in battle, and no one would have been able to contradict me. I did not take that course, because I had already begun to think of changing my identity. Thomas had given me all that he owned—so be it—I would take his name, which I preferred so to my own, and his title. I knew now that I would never be given such a title by King Richard—I did not want a title from that King—indeed, to me Richard was only a cowardly murderer—I could not imagine lowering myself to seek his favor. I thought, yes, Thomas has atoned, Thomas has give me all that was best in him—now I shall make his name one to respect and honor.

"I was an arrogant, self righteous young man—I fear that I smiled as I rode toward Acre—I knew now that Suleka would never be safe in the Holy Land, but I had a dream future ready for her—I thought we could go to some unsettled corner of England, or even some free county in Ireland—we could establish ourselves as an English knight and his Arabian princess (for if I was a knight then Suleka surely was a princess)—I dreamed but I didn't think—I didn't understand the significance of Brian's cry 'run to your Moslem whore'.

"I never thought that vengeance would be taken against her—I never thought of the consequences of publicly disobeying England's brutal King.

"There was a hush in the city when I returned. The knowledge of horror hung over the place like a suffocating cloud.

"I rode slowly through the deserted streets—and then fear struck my heart, and I made my tired horse run faster—my heart froze with dread and the chill penetrated my soul—I *knew* but I refused to believe—I kicked my horse into a mad gallop—I knew but I fought against the knowledge—I rode faster still as though speed could help—but finally nothing could spare me from the truth.

"I had left Suleka alone on the one day that I should have stayed to protect her. I reached our house, and I saw that the door was smashed in, and then I saw that they had thrown her body out into the dust of the road.

"I felt a sudden surge of hope. Once before she had feigned death—I leaped from my horse and ran to her—she lay face down, her back unmarked—and then I turned her over, and I saw how she had put both hands to her belly to protect our baby from the sword, but the slashing steel had cut through her hands and into her womb—she was dead, and my future was dead, and I lay my face on her cold breasts and cried.

"I heard hoofbeats behind me, but I didn't turn. I heard a voice say, 'So the little birdie's come back,' and I knew it was Brian, for such did he always call me, but still I didn't turn, for life meant nothing at all to me then, and I suppose my passivity must have angered Brian—I felt a violent pain in my side as he struck me with his lance—the blow knocked me over onto my back—I lay limp next to my dead love—I looked up at Brian, and at the several knights with him.

"I noticed that they had all found time to take off their armor.

"'Where's your master?' Brian asked.

"'He's doing penance before God,' I said.

"'That's a ripe one,' Brian said, laughing with his men. 'He fails to do his Christian duty, he disobeys his King, and now he hides in church.' Brian laughed again. 'When he comes back, tell him what we did to his infidel whore. We know how much he loves these people.'

"With more laughter they prepared to leave, but now I had strength to rise—a strength fueled by a bottomless hate. I got to my feet and screamed, 'Brian!' He turned to look at me, and I said, 'Someday I will kill you.'

"He just laughed and said, 'Why not today, little birdie,' and then he knocked me to the ground again with his lance. I got up and he knocked me down again, I got up and he knocked me down, the other knights were laughing uncontrollably, I got up and Brian swung again but I was ready and I dropped under the blow, I ran before he could strike again, I leaped onto my horse and touched him with my heels as Brian struck one more time—the blow missed me but caught my weary horse on the rump—my stallion let out a whinny of dismay and burst forward into a gallop—I raced away on a frightened horse, and there was no pursuit.

"A mere squire, I was hardly important enough to chase.

"I left the city. I thought of Suleka, lying unattended in the dust of the road.

"I think of her still.

"I have often wondered if someone gave her proper burial."

Thomas's voice was calm but the hand Elaine held was covered with cold sweat. He forced himself to continue the story.

"I rode north from Acre, and before long I encountered a Moslem warrior who rode the best horse I had ever seen. I killed the man, and I took his horse—that is the horse that shelters us even now. I rode this mighty beast for months before I gave him a name—but I did start calling myself Sir Thomas. I headed for England. When it was necessary to cross water I paid my way with money earned as a mercenary knight. I fought other people's battles all the way across Europe. I was numb to the world.

"Finally I reached the coast of France in the middle of the winter. I had to wait a week for a boat. I made the acquaintance of a minstrel who lodged with me at the local inn. He had entertained the troops at Acre—he had left the city a few weeks after the massacre. He told me that everyone had expected Saladin to retaliate by killing the Christian captives in his charge—but he had spared their lives.

"I thought how strange it was—the Moslem had showed mercy—the Moslem had turned the other cheek—and then suddenly I realized that I had found the right name for my beautiful Arabian horse. I named him Saladin, in honor of the distinguished Moslem leader—this was a gesture of respect, and then too it was a living remembrance of my dear lost Suleka—my horse and I were one, we lived and fought together—and then we were Moslem and Christian, joined together without prejudice or fear or hate."

Thomas was crying again but it didn't matter, he was finishing now, he had told of the worst and it made no difference that Elaine saw his tears—he brushed them away with his free hand, and continued.

"So I had a new name, and a new horse—but I also needed a story to tell when I reached England—or not to tell, as it were, and so I got an idea—I made good use of that last week in France—I bought embroidery supplies, and I set to work as my mother had taught me. I made the tapestries that I displayed for Prince John.

"Of course I had not been silent in recent months, but no one in England knew that—I dated the 'vow of silence' from August 20, 1191—the date of Suleka's death.

"The vow might as well have been real. I had no desire to speak to anyone—it was easy to remain silent. I hoped that my image would take the place of the ill remembered Thomas, and my plan succeeded. By the time I spoke, in 1192, no one could recall his voice. I was accepted in his place, I lived as a knight—and finally I began to heal.

"Two years went by, and then one day a beautiful lady once loved spoke to me, and her words and her look brought me all the way back to the world. I fell in love with her—not the youth's infatuation I had known before, but the true strong love of a man.

"I love you, Elaine," Sir Thomas said, and with those words he concluded his story.

He lived in the present now—he stroked his fair companion's face with his free hand, and then that hand went around behind her head, and he pulled her close. He kissed her mouth, and she kissed him back, gravely, firmly, and beautifully—but she did not surrender to him.

She broke the kiss. She thought, I will break your heart.

But she said nothing, and Thomas was quiet too. He felt so much lighter—it seemed as though he had pushed an enormous weight off his chest—he was exhausted from the pushing and yet exhilarated by his freedom—truly anything was possible now.

He looked around at the circled watchers, and he thought, I will defeat you, and the thought was a certainty in his soul.

He was content. He held Elaine's hand. He had told his story and declared his love. It was her place to speak now.

While he waited he looked up at the sky. It seemed that such a story should have taken the whole night—yet he could see by the stars that only a few hours had passed. There were still perhaps three hours left before dawn.

He felt Elaine's hand tighten against his own.

"I too have a story to tell," she said.

"Yes," said Thomas. "I want to hear it."

Chapter 119

THE DRUNKEN CAPTAIN

On the good ship Lionheart, in the dark hours of the morning of a new day, Wednesday, June 17, 1194 . . .

Arthur the Assessor was seasick and his stomach ached unbearably. Once on the ship, the Archbishop had personally seen to his wound—now his belly was swaddled in cloth but it still felt like it was leaking.

Arthur had tried to eat—but he had pitched all that over the side when the storm hit shortly after they had got underway. Then he had tried to drink, hoping to knock himself out—but the liquor had not tasted good going down, and it was even fouler coming back up. He didn't know what his stomach would hold—it just hurt.

Most of the knights had gone below when the storm hit—Arthur had followed them, only to find that belowdecks there was no way to anticipate the motion of the ship—he came back topside, sicker than ever.

Now he stood on the nearly deserted deck. He leaned against the rail—every so often dry heaves shook his body. He was on the right side of the ship—the sea was palely lit by the crescent moon—when he suddenly realized that he could not make out the shape of land to the west.

They were supposed to hug the shore until they came to the Northmen's landing place—where were they now?

Arthur staggered across the deck until he found the Captain, who was drunk.

"Where are we?" demanded the Chancellor of the Exchequer.

"I expect we've been driven out to sea a bit," said the Captain, taking a pull at his flask. "Can't rightly tell till daybreak."

"What about the stars?" Arthur asked.

"Too many clouds," the Captain said agreeably. He waved his hand upward to include all the heavens. "Clouds," he muttered again, and then he took another drink.

Arthur staggered away. He barely made it to the rail before he heaved again.

If my stomach didn't hurt so much, I'd have to laugh, Arthur thought. The King of the English and one hundred gallant knights rush out to save my dear Elaine the Fair—but then they let their quest be directed by an incompetent drunk! It was so typical of Richard—the grandiose scheme undone by the King's trusting faith—this venture will probably be just as successful as the Third Crusade.

Arthur grimaced at the thought. Richard never took Jerusalem—he'll never save Elaine either. I'll never see my wife again.

Arthur thought of crying but in fact he did not weep—the few tears he had shed the day before had already marked the end of whatever love he had felt for Elaine the Fair.

The ship drifted out to sea.

Belowdecks, Richard Lionheart slept peacefully, convinced that all his actions were guided by God.

Chapter 120

ELAINE BEGINS HER STORY

Elaine let go of Thomas's hand. She sat back—she created a little distance between them—and then she began to speak.

"We were both born in the same year, but I am just slightly the younger. I first drew breath on March 1, 1170, in the small village of Firfleet. I had noble blood in my veins from my mother, and a heritage of courage from my father.

"My father was not there to see me born. Two months before, some louts had besmirched my mother's name in the vilest of terms—discounting their numbers, and the fact that he was alone, he fought them—he would not give up, and so they kept beating him, and he died with my mother's name on his lips."

Thomas reached for Elaine's right hand. He found that it was clenched into a fist.

She went on, "We were always outsiders in that village . . ."

She told Thomas of her heritage—she told him of the Countess Elaine from Normandy, she told the story that her mother had passed on, and then she continued, "And so you see, even from birth I was different from all the other children in the village.

"My mother encouraged me—or perhaps didn't discourage me is more accurate—she allowed me my freedom, but she was always there fore me to lean on—it was so hard for her, for she had no husband to love and protect her—she was alone in the face of constant threats and taunts from the other villagers, but she managed to keep the ugliness away from me.

"So my early childhood was quite happy—but I *was* different. I never learned to crawl like a normal baby—instead, I got around on my hands and feet, like a rabbit." Suddenly Elaine freed herself from Thomas's grip—she dropped down onto her hands, her feet were under her but her knees didn't touch the ground, her bottom was cocked right up in the air, with the silk clinging to it—and then just as fast she bounced back into a normal sitting position as before. "Just like that. I got around very quickly that way too, my mother told me. I always loved her name, she was called Marian." Elaine's hands were fists again—Thomas could barely keep up with her moods. "Anyway, I got around like a little bunny, and then I learned to walk, and I learned to talk. The only problem was that I didn't speak English. Shunned by the children around me, I had developed my own language. I spoke this way with full confidence, and Mama always understood me."

Elaine looked down at her clenched fists and then uncurled them a little bit. "I had to piece a lot of things together, much later—I finally figured out that at first the uncultured villagers thought I was speaking the High French of my aristocratic ancestors—but actually my mother had forgotten that language.

"My mother drank a little too much.

"I ran around, happy in my own world, my four year old world—I didn't know anything about the blight that had struck the beautiful fir trees that gave our village its name—trees that were so valuable for shipbuilding that the crown sent a royal team for their wood each year—I didn't know that the needles were turning brown in midsummer—didn't know that there were dark murmurs of Devil's influence—I was joyful, careless, and so when the old scholar came out from the court to examine the trees, I ran right up to him, for he was a stranger, an interesting stranger who did not shrink from me—I looked up at his kindly face and talked to him at length in my own language.

"He was a true gentleman, and so he listened patiently. He patted me on the head when I was through, and he told me I was a beautiful child—and then he asked me where I had learned that language.

"I just stuck my tongue out at him, and ran away. It was only much later that I learned that one of the villagers had then said to him: 'The child speaks French.'

"The old scholar replied, 'I know all the dialects of French, and that is not one of them. I have never heard that language before. I daresay the child made it up on her own.'

"I'm sure the kindly old man never dreamed that with those words he had signed my mother's death warrant.

"The villagers quickly decided that they did not need any Oxford educated court scholar to discover the reason for the blighted trees. They had found the answer they wanted to find. They shipped the old man back to London, and then early the next morning they came for the outsider they had always hated—they took my mother away.

"They tortured her. They wanted her to admit that she was a witch, that she had poisoned the fir trees out of some satanic malevolence—they were certain in their righteousness, for I had spoken a language no one knew, a language that I could only have learned from my mother—a language that, being unknown, must certainly have come from the Devil.

"Such was their logic, but no matter what they did to her, my mother refused to tell them what they wanted to hear, for she feared that to do so would cost me my life.

"Finally, that evening, they dragged me to where my mother was chained. They told me to speak. My own words were to be the proof of the Devil's influence. I looked at my mother's pleading eyes, and I knew that it was very important that these horrible people should understand me. I decided to speak in their language (I had learned English, but I had never felt the necessity to use it before—I liked being different) and so I said, very clearly, 'Let my Mama go.'

"They were shocked, and they let her go."

Elaine told Thomas of the last night of her mother's life. She explained that it was then that Marian had passed on the story of her family's history. Elaine told of waking up by her cold still mother—she told him about the sunflower, and the gold, and the priest.

Elaine did not cry as she told this story. Her body was taut, fists clenched—the memories were alive and painful in her heart—yet even as she relived that pain, Elaine was careful— she left out one line of her mother's story, one line that she had been turning over and over in her mind for years and years, one line that still affected her life—even now she could hear the whispered prophecy: "And it is you who will rise again among the nobility of the land . . ."

Chapter 121

BEAUTY

"So you listened to everyone as you grew up, and finally you put the whole story together?" Thomas asked.

"Yes, mostly listened. I also asked a few discreet questions, and sometimes they would answer frankly. Just as you explained about Richard Lionheart, they were proud of their sins—they had won, you see—evil had been uprooted, the outsider (whether witch or not) had been punished—even their blessed fir trees grew again, but to be sure that was only after the blighted ones had been cut down and burned—they could have done that right away and there would have been no need for murder—but then, as I grew older, I realized that the fir trees had only been an excuse—a Godsent excuse, you might say—look at the good that was done—I ended up in the care of a priest—it was thought that just maybe I might be saved from the Devil.

"Anyway, by the time I was twelve I knew the whole story.

"I have spent the last twelve years trying to forget it."

Thomas looked at her clenched fists. He reached out and covered them with his big hands.

"You should not forget it," Thomas said. "Honor your parents who gave you life and strength. Honor them, remember them—but let them rest. Let yourself rest."

Elaine loosened her fists, but then took her hands away from Thomas when he tried to hold them.

She made no reply to Thomas's remark. She continued her story. "I found a friend, a playmate who was an outsider like me. He was an odd little boy—enormous intelligence combined with a high squeaky voice and a fat round body—he was despised by the boys as I was shunned by the girls. He was a cardplayer—a wonderful gambler even as a child—he won many unusual treasures—he also won money, but his father took that—this boy and I studied together under Father Ashendon—we both dreamed of a bright future at the court.

"Some of our dreams came true. You know this boy now as Arthur the Assessor, Chancellor of the Exchequer."

Thomas felt a thrill of pleasure. She had not referred to Arthur as her husband. Clearly I have no rivals, Thomas thought.

Elaine told Thomas of her slow blossoming adolescence, of Father Ashendon's death when she was sixteen—and then she looked defiantly at her knight's face and said, "I became beautiful."

"I am not arguing with you," Thomas said.

Elaine smiled slightly. "Perhaps it is because of you that I can see my own beauty now. I couldn't see it then—I used to peer into the small looking glass I had—I'd examine my face from every angle, but I could never see anything special—well, I did see a lot of flaws."

Thomas smiled—but then he saw Elaine's expression turn melancholy as she remembered . . .

"Yet I had only to leave my little cottage," she said, "and I saw what was called 'Beauty' reflected in the eyes of every man who looked at me. I see it in your eyes."

"Why do you say that so sadly?" Thomas asked.

Elaine didn't answer. Suddenly Thomas noticed that she was shivering. He reached out to embrace her but she pushed him away.

She spoke this time almost cheerfully. "One day this beauty will be gone."

Thomas shook his head slowly. "No."

Elaine smiled. She had smiled like that at Thomas on the first day she had spoken to him, when she had asked him to teach her how to use weapons. He had given her his heart that day. Now he just wanted to touch her. He stared at her face in the pale moonlight. Her beauty was shattering—and she knew it.

He held his hands by his sides with a supreme effort of will.

Elaine seemed amused. "I have come to believe in you, Sir Thomas," she said. "I believe that we shall survive tomorrow—and thus I shall grow old, and my time of beauty shall pass. Finally I will move men not at all, save perhaps only to pity."

"No." Thomas shook his head again. "You will always be beautiful to me."

Elaine thought at first that he simply couldn't imagine her old, stooped, lined, the golden hair gone white—but no, he was not so simple. It was his love that made him see her beauty as permanent. Because he would always love her, she would always be beautiful to him.

And I will break your heart, she thought.

She reached out for one of his tautly held hands and took it between both of hers. She raised his hand to her lips, and kissed it, and then she said, "I know that I will always be beautiful to you. Yet even for you, in the future, it will be memory. My face will have lines, this hair will be white—if you know me then, if you should touch my face, then you must know that the old wrinkled flesh beneath your fingers will be me—not the memory of this beauty that you recall—I will *be* that old woman."

"You will be that old woman—and you will be beautiful to me," Thomas said.

Elaine looked at Thomas's stubborn face for a long moment, and then she released his hand. She spoke clearly about a matter that lay close to her heart. "I am young—and I am beautiful. Whatever you say, those gifts will soon pass—but while I have them, I wish to bear a child. That is my desire, my hope, and my dream. When I was with Arthur, I thought once that I would have a son—but that was a false dream, and I know now there will never be a child with him—when I imagine my future now, I see my firstborn as a daughter—a daughter to whom I can pass on this heritage of beauty, a heritage that for her must only be a blessing, and not a curse as I have so often known it— I would like to give to my daughter all those things my mother would have given me, had only she lived . . ."

Elaine was crying, and now she didn't resist at all when Thomas gathered her into a gentle embrace. She just laid her head against his chest, and let her tears flow. Thomas stroked her trembling back, and he felt the heat of her beneath the thin silk, and he thought of how she had put her husband behind her, and he thought of giving her a child, he thought of making a child, and he trembled too, he wanted her and he loved her and he listened to her cry, and he stroked her very gently until finally she raised her head.

Then he looked down at her wet blue shining eyes, and he stroked the dark gold of her hair, still damp from the rain, and he kissed her mouth.

Elaine didn't return the kiss—she accepted it, and then she pushed him away with a quiet authority, and she surprised Thomas by going right back to her story.

"I was kissed for the first time when I was sixteen, and I liked it. Then I was kissed many more times—various young men kissed me—I liked all of it—I liked the kisses and the caresses, and I forgot my one real friend, the fat boy with the high squeaky voice.

"I liked being adored—but I would not give myself, and I refused to choose a husband from the men of my village—I set myself above them all."

Elaine looked up at Thomas cooly, and as he looked down at her he saw her as she must have been then—all the arrogance of youth combined with that unearthly beauty—and she the daughter of an outsider, a supposed witch—he shook his head. "They must have come to hate you."

Elaine's arms were around Thomas. He felt her hands close into fists again—he felt their hardness against his back.

"Yes," she said. "I should have been plain, or if not plain, at least humble. But I was neither, I walked with the knowledge of nobility in my step—I was in love with myself in the simple manner of youth—I had no regard for other's feelings—I walked with my blood aflame from the last night's kisses and yet my eyes were fixed above the heads of the men who desired me—I saw only my own glorious future."

Elaine drew her hands back away from Thomas, and shifted a little to break his embrace. Then she continued her story.

"I did not realize my beauty was an affront to them—and I did not understand my own power. I could not see my own beauty—and so I never thought to check it, or control it—I sowed desire indiscriminately—not just the young men wanted me, but also the solid married citizens were driven mad when I smiled—I didn't realize that the elderly men who stared at me were cursing their own devil's desire—there were even women who stopped talking to me because they wanted to touch me—I didn't understand any of it then. I thought my world was bright, exciting—but if my mother had lived, I know she would have sensed the mounting hysteria—she would have taken me off to London in time, and indeed I should have gone there on my own.

"But I was flushed with the attention I was receiving, and I thought that I would not have to move myself, I thought that a man would come for me. I didn't think clearly, and I had no one to guide me. I didn't know that desire had turned to hatred.

"I learned the truth on my nineteenth birthday.

"They came to kill me, my own neighbors came to kill me, and when they showed me the manner of my death, I understood everything. They wished to destroy my beauty, as though the Devil himself lived in my countenance. They wished to destroy my face, and cover it, so that they would no longer be tempted.

"They might have been successful, except that a man did come to rescue me—he stopped them in time, but the murderers left their mark"—she touched her face—"this scar that I will always carry."

Chapter 122

THE DEMON MASK

A long moment passed.

Elaine stayed still, silent and far away, one hand at her face. Thomas put out his right hand, open, palm up—he held it steady, and he repeated Elaine's own words.

"There are no secrets tonight," he said.

Finally Elaine lowered her hand—she bared the silent white scar—she placed her hand in his. He held it gently. "Tell me the rest," he said.

Elaine nodded slowly, and gathered herself—he felt her hand jump once in his grasp, but he didn't let her go—she moistened her lips, and then she began to speak—and she didn't stop until she had come to the end of her nightmare.

"A priest came to Firfleet a few days before my nineteenth birthday—a strange itinerant priest who called himself Peter, after the Hermit—he wore ragged black robes—the light of madness glowed in his eyes.

"I shunned him—I did not know that his coming was the 'divine' sanction needed for my death.

"My birthday fell on a Sunday that year. Since Father Ashendon had died three years before, there had been no weekly services. Once a month a priest from the nearest city came around to hear our confessions. There was no scheduled visit for this Sunday—instead, I heard that the strange Peter was going to perform Mass in our long neglected chapel.

"I had no intention of going, for I had decided to give myself a birthday present.

"I lived often in dreams then. I decided to imagine that a rich handsome nobleman of the court—a Count at least, or a Duke—

was coming for me. Even if I could not see my beauty, I vowed that I would so accentuate my looks that he, my imaginary lover, would come to cherish me above all women. I lost myself in fantasies—and so I bathed that morning, and then spent an hour on my hair, brushing and combing it till it shone, and I brightened my lips with berries I had long hoarded—I used all the small store of perfume I had, I put it on my throat, and between my breasts, and my own touch filled me with desire for my imaginary lover.

"I put on my best dress—really just a simple white cotton shift, but when I belted it tight it showed the curves of my body, for I wore nothing underneath it—the thin fabric pulled taut over my breasts, and I imagined my lover looking at me—my nipples scraped stiffly against the cotton—I picked up my looking glass and I saw my eyes wild with yearning—I wondered if this look was Beauty, and if it was, would it somehow bring my lover to me? I thought that it might, and I smiled, and the girl in the mirror smiled back, and then there came a mighty crash as my door was smashed open.

"I looked around in terror and saw the priest—Peter with his mad eyes and foam on his lips—and behind him a mob of villagers, both men and women—people I had known all my life— men I had kissed—women who had bathed next to me in the stream—their faces showed a strange gloating mixture of hatred and desire—I barely heard Peter's screaming denunciation, I just saw the flecks of spittle flying from his mouth—I stood there numb, with my looking glass in hand, and I caught a phrase now and then: 'Witch with her secret arts—Whore of Babylon—Red stain of sin on her lips'—always returning to 'Witch—Witch—Witch—The evil one who practices her Black Arts while the Godfearing go to church—The evil seductress'— they stared at my mouth and at my breasts and then suddenly Peter cried, 'Take her to the church' and hands seized me all over, pulling, tearing at me, and they dragged me through the village, all of them screaming now, 'Witch! Witch! Witch!' at the top of their lungs—then I was inside the church, and they tied me to the cross. My arms were spread out and tied, and my ankles were tied to the base so I was helpless—my dress had been torn to the waist by their violent hands so my breasts were bare. The crowd surged about me, buzzing with hatred—and then a woman burst out of the group and seized my breasts with her hands—she squeezed and twisted them with such strength that the pain literally took my breath away—I could not scream, and it seemed as if my soul removed itself from my body. I found I could look down dispassionately as this woman tormented me—I could see her clenched teeth and the terror that lay behind the hatred in her eyes. I understood her then—I understood how much she wanted to love me—she wanted to kiss me, and run her hands lovingly over my body—it was fear that impelled her to torture—I wanted to tell her that it was all right, that she need not be ashamed of her desires, she could kiss my lips, my breasts, and I would stroke her hair—but I was far away from my bound body, and I could not speak or move—I just looked down at my neighbors, I saw the twisted desire on their faces—hatred and fear had twisted them, and now the only way they could reach satisfaction was with my death.

"One of the men pulled the woman away from me. He cleared a path for the priest. Peter was carrying the implement of my death. It was a demon mask, a horrible disfigured gargoyle face, its rusted iron countenance studded with nail heads. He showed this face to me—and then he turned it around so that I could see the inside—all the sharp nails projected through—he held it up, level with my face, the nails coming for me—I understood that he meant to force the demon mask onto my face, drive the nails through my skin.

"I looked around for a savior, and I saw the man who had cleared the way for the priest waiting his turn with a hammer in his hand. He was going to hammer the mask down once it was fitted to my face—he would drive the nails into my skull. I understood then that this was what my neighbors wanted—they wanted to see my beauty destroyed, ripped through with nails—they wanted to see the mask hammered down on my face so that my beauty would be covered forever—it would be covered by the mask of the demon, the demon of their own imaginings.

"I never screamed then. Countless times since I have screamed till my throat was raw as I remembered this scene in my dreams—but then I just watched, my soul outside my body, waiting for death.

"The nails came closer, until finally the blackness of the mask blotted out the crowd, and then I felt the first prick just below my left eye—I felt the thin ribbon of blood run down my face, and then I heard a deep powerful voice roar, 'Stop in the name of the King!'

"Peter spun around, yanking the mask away from me in the

process—and I suddenly felt pain everywhere as my soul returned to my body.

"There was a big heavy man in the doorway of the church. He was clad in court robes, and he carried a scroll. He had a plumed hat on his head, and a good knight's sword hung from his belt. He pointed at me and his voice boomed out again—a commanding voice that no one, including me, could recognize. 'Is this woman Elaine of Firfleet, daughter of Marian?'

"There were a few murmured assents.

"'Then hear this,' he cried, 'And know I come from the King!'

"Then he opened his scroll, and read from it. 'By order of His Majesty Henry the Second . . .' and so on, 'the presence of Elaine of Firfleet required at the court . . .' and so on, and beneath the fancy verbiage it became quite clear that my attractiveness had been noted by some royal messenger—I was being summoned to the King's bed.

"Now this was hardly an unprecedented act for our good King Henry II, whose desires were well known, and by and large there was relief in the church. The villagers were rid of me without the stain of murder on their souls. As the deep voice went on, reading the proclamation, I could feel the madness leave the room—the mob lost its force and cohesion—the people became ordinary citizens again. The strange priest stood there foolishly, holding the heavy mask.

"The King's messenger finished his speech and strode up to me, roughly shoving the priest aside as he did so. Peter opened his mouth to speak—the madness started to light in his eyes again—but the messenger put his hand on his sword, and said, 'Remember the fate of Thomas Becket,' and the priest shut his mouth like a clam. Peter turned away, but no one in the crowd was on his side any more—I saw him bend down and lay the mask on the floor—he stood up then as though he had nothing to do with that dreadful implement.

"The messenger untied me, and when I felt his touch I realized at once that it was Arthur, my childhood friend. His face and body were transformed by the court trappings, but now that I recognized him I recognized the clothes as well—over the years he had won them from various traveling noblemen—and yes, a King's messenger had also been one of his victims—we had played with some of those clothes long ago, long before Arthur could fit into them—but it wasn't just the size of him that had changed, no the big change was the voice—the rock solid voice of a man had finally supplanted the high squeak that had distinguished him as a boy—it was the new voice that had defied recognition and assured belief.

"I gave no sign that I knew him—I just pulled my dress up as best I could, and I followed him out of the church—he helped me mount the horse that was waiting for me.

"He said, 'I'm sorry I took so long, but I had to write that whole proclamation.'

"I couldn't even smile, much less speak, but I tried to show that I loved him with my eyes, and I know that he understood me.

"He mounted in turn, and then we rode off together toward London, toward the court of the King."

Chapter 123

THE BRAVEST ACT OF HIS LIFE

Thomas let go of Elaine's hand.

Elaine kept talking. Nothing could stop her now.

She told Thomas of her first night of love with Arthur. She told him of their presentation at court. She explained the gifts of titles and fortune handed out by King Henry II—she explained how she and Arthur came to be "married" without benefit of clergy.

She told the story of her life with Arthur—happy beginnings that gradually turned sour—desires kindled in her that were never assuaged—her own longing for a child, and the gradual realization that there would never be a child with Arthur.

Elaine told Thomas far more than she had told Roland, more than she had ever confided in Sandra—but Thomas could barely pay attention to the new revelations, so shattered was he by the story of the demon mask. He kept seeing those nails coming for her beautiful face, and now it was his big hands that kept curling into fists—he wanted to lay waste to Firfleet—he wanted to smash the face of the false priest . . .

Elaine told of her first steps toward seeking a lover—though she never once mentioned Roland—and then suddenly there was fresh horror, the knife in her bedroom before dawn, the Vulture and his confederates—Thomas was destroyed again, he was listening with all his powers and at the same time almost wishing that she would stop—it was too much horror to be borne, it was unbearable to think of Elaine confined to a carriage with those men—but she had borne it—and when she told how she had preserved her honor, at the cost of the knife piercing her hand, then Thomas's heart just went out to her—if it were possible he came to love her even more than formerly—he just loved her, loved her, loved her, loved this dear brave girl—and then she told him of the fire and the stake, and she told him what the Vulture had said when the trap was set: " 'Never more will you dally with Sir Thomas, for you shall watch us kill him now.' "

Thomas suddenly looked very sharply at Elaine. He remembered the vagrant's description of a large gentleman—and he had figured out himself that it had to be a man of the court. A gentleman who wanted to punish his wife—Arthur the Assessor. Thomas remembered the shadowers—Arthur's men of course—the one who survived must have sneaked back, Thomas thought—he must have seen me kiss Elaine for the first time.

Arthur must think we are lovers, Thomas thought, and he wanted to smile—but instead he said very seriously, "Arthur hired the criminals."

Elaine lowered her eyes. "I know," she said. With those words she concluded her story.

If Elaine was sad, Thomas was almost jubilant. He thought that if they were accused of being lovers anyway, then they certainly had the right to become guilty in fact. It was as though they had already paid for their pleasure. He had been marked for death—Elaine had suffered greatly—and yet they had come through! Surely love should be their just reward.

Thomas dismissed the monks from his equation—they were an outside force, and he would defeat them on the morrow—surely anything was possible now! He looked around at the silent watchers. He had to admit that he owed them a debt of gratitude—their attack had ruined Arthur's trap—but still they were fools—they had waited too long—they were still waiting—they wouldn't start driving him again until dawn, and so for now he had the night—he had Elaine—dear, sweet, brave, O so beautiful Elaine—the *unmarried* lady who had suffered so from her false husband's false accusations—well, they will be false no longer, Thomas thought.

He looked over at Elaine and his voice came out in a low powerful growl. "Come here."

He had said the same words to her in the stable, long ago—but then he had been asking—now he was telling.

Elaine didn't move.

He spoke again, he could feel his voice rumbling from his chest, he said, "Come here."

Still she didn't move.

Thomas, facing Elaine, now slipped around until he sat by her left side. He put his arm around her just above her waist. Her body was as rigid as a block of wood. He tightened his grip around her—he could not believe that she was not feeling the same charged desire that he felt—and then he realized that all her stiffness was of her own making, she was holding herself taut by the exertion of enormous effort—she was holding herself, in some way, away from him—he tried to pull her closer but she wouldn't move, he felt the tension in the muscles of her back, her right side was tensed against his holding hand, there was no give to her—he leaned over and kissed her golden hair— he found that it was almost dry now—he pressed his lips against that finespun glory, he let his mouth linger there, and still she didn't move, just all that tightness in every inch of her body—he looked over her shoulder and he saw the slight but perfect swellings of her breasts, barely covered by her silk nightgown, and he understood that this was the moment.

Thomas had fought black knights and Saracens and the toughest mercenaries of Europe—and he would have more battles to come—but until he died he would still always consider this next moment to be the bravest act of his life. He understood right then that courage is sometimes measured in seconds—he understood that he had to act at this moment in time, holding Elaine in her stiffness, with no encouragement from her—he had to act now, with kisses in the past but never that unalterable leap towards intimacy or failure—he had to act right now in the face of her silence and his own fear, for if he waited the value of the moment would be gone—he would be reduced to asking once again.

He didn't wait and he didn't ask—he acted.

With a smooth steady motion Thomas placed his left hand over Elaine's left breast. Half a handful—his big hand covered it completely, a dizzying softness surrounding a nipple as rigid as the rest of her.

And then he watched, holding her like that, as her right hand came up from her lap, slowly, slowly, almost reluctantly moving upward toward his hand, he watched, he held his breath, he felt only her soft breast with its hard nipple against his palm, he watched that right hand come up to his to push him away—her fingers just touched his hand—and then her hand fluttered open and fell away, and all of her relaxed in his arms, and the sudden knowledge of her acceptance was like a dam giving way in his body, clearing the path for the rush of blood—Thomas felt his blood rushing, sluicing toward his inflamed manhood until he felt himself grow to proportions it seemed could hardly be imagined—he couldn't stand his clothes and at the same time his hands and his mouth were all over Elaine—her head was back and he was kissing her mouth and his hands had gone down her body and up under her nightgown, he pushed the fragile silk up to her waist, he held the ripe softness of her naked buttocks, his tongue invaded her mouth, and finally he broke the kiss only so he could back off for a second and get his pants down, he was going to push her right down on her back on the grass and spread her and take her right there, his mind raced ahead of his actions as he fumbled with his pants—and so when he heard the quiet "No. No. No." it was like a voice from another world, not a message for him, he freed his enormous swollen manhood, he wanted to be *in* her, he reached for her but she caught his hands, "No. No. No." He pressed forward but she held him with all her strength, she wasn't fighting him, she wasn't screaming, she wasn't alerting their enemies—she just stopped him, she just repeated the word, "No" over and over—he didn't want to look up at her face, he looked down at her body, the nightgown up to her waist concealed nothing, she wanted him—but she held him, and she said "No" and he could have broken her strength, but it was her voice that was stopping him—he could have forced her but instead he listened to her— "No. No. No." There was something certain in her voice. He looked up and he saw that her face was tortured by desire and need, but still something certain beneath all that, and her voice spoke from that certainty, and so he stopped pressing, he stared at her face—his own showed the wild savage pain of thwarted desire but still he had stopped—when *she* realized that he had stopped, when she knew that he could truly hear her, she said, "I can not be unfaithful to my lover," and she broke his heart.

Thomas didn't move for a long time. He felt the blood flow away from his manhood, felt the little jerky nods it made as it gave up its power, and then he covered himself.

Elaine pushed her nightgown down.

Thomas didn't react. He could barely breathe.

Elaine was somehow more relaxed. For her the worst was over. She had remained true to her lover, and to her mother's prophecy. If she lived, she would rise among the nobility.

Thomas might save her or kill her now—it was out of her hands. She did believe in him, as she had said earlier. She believed that he would defeat the monks, despite the great odds against him, for he was her ideal knight. If she lived it would be because of him. If she died it would be by his hand.

She spoke carefully to his silence.

"My lover is Roland, Duke of Larraz. We made love in a cabin in the forest the day before I was abducted. I was returning from being with Roland when you met me at the edge of the woods."

"I kissed you," Thomas said. His tongue was thick in his mouth.

"I was wrong to let you kiss me. I was wrong to let you touch me tonight. I am sorry."

Thomas brushed away her apology with an awkward gesture. He looked at her, and he saw that she understood his pain—and he also saw that she would do nothing to ease it.

Elaine looked back at him. She did not know whether she saw her life or her death in his eyes.

Then he said, "I love you, Elaine," and she knew that she saw her life.

"I will always cherish your love," Elaine replied, and that was the truth.

Another truth was that she did not love him.

Elaine offered her wounded right hand—Thomas saw the hand that had fluttered away and allowed him to hold her—but in his mind he heard her voice again, saying 'No.'

He didn't take her hand. He turned away, and if he cried for the rest of that night until dawn, then Elaine never saw his tears, for he kept his face averted from hers—and if there was sobbing then that also could not be heard over the sound of his whetstone sharpening his two swords.

Finally morning came in the form of gray light fighting its way through fog. Elaine saw his face then, indistinct but unmarked, and yet something terrible about it—he was ready to ride, a bow over his shoulder, a sharpened sword on each hip— he put the bridle and saddle on Saladin, and then he boosted her up, facing forward this time—he mounted behind her and as they set off he put his left arm around her to steady her—she was acutely aware of her vulnerable breasts but his arm just encircled her firmly just below their rise, he was protecting her, nothing more—the monks were mounting around them, there were shouted orders in a foreign language—a path opened in front of them as the familiar formation fanned out on three sides—they were driven into and across the shallow river, driven on to the south—Elaine summoned her courage and turned around to look into her knight's face—there was enough light now to see clearly—enough light to look into his eyes—and what she saw scared her so much that she recoiled as from the sight of evil—she jerked around and looked forward, looked away from him, away from his eyes—but she could feel them observing behind her, observing everything with a cold, impersonal, implacable stare—she knew if she never looked at him again today she would still never be able to forget those eyes that had looked at her without recognition, eyes drained of all feeling, cold, emotionless, murderous eyes, and she knew that it would not be long before Thomas would kill.

Chapter 124

IVAR'S MISCONCEPTIONS

It is terrible to have no heart and always long for one. It is terrible to live outside every definition of human society and always long to come in.

It is less terrible when the longing stops.

Such were Ivar's thoughts this last night. He had stayed awake just like Elaine and Thomas.

As they had played out their drama, as they came to know the truths each of them could express, so Ivar felt that he had finally come to the truth about himself.

He would never love. He would never care for another human being.

He realized that the very qualities that inspired other men to love Elaine the Fair were for him repellant. Her staggering beauty was for him a target to smash. Her sensuality, so evident in her every motion, seemed like a trap to him—he feared her warm embrace—he wanted to fend her off with cold steel.

He would induce Thomas to murder her.

In thinking these thoughts, the cold pragmatic planner of many successful raids went seriously astray. Ivar was lost in this unfamiliar emotional terrain—indeed there were two gaping holes in his plot.

In the first place, he underestimated the optimism of a man in love. Whether Elaine loved him or not, Thomas believed that his love for her gave him strength. In his own way Thomas was as foolish as Pierre and Daniel, though his foolishness was tempered by skill and experience. He would never give in to despair, and thus he would never do Ivar's bidding, for in his heart of hearts he truly believed that he would prevail, despite the odds against him.

The second error in Ivar's thinking was even more important. He believed that he knew himself now—he believed that he was as heartless as his name indicated—but he was wrong.

He did have a heart, like any other man, and he did have the capacity to care for someone besides himself.

His discovery of this fact, one day hence, would cost him his life.

Chapter 125

THE MEANING OF A DREAM

Roland woke to the image of the black cross smashing his brain. He staggered to his feet in the dim predawn light—he was awake but he couldn't shake the image inside his head—he could barely make out Anton and Sandra, who had stood up to greet him. Those two were fully dressed and cheerful—Sandra looked sweet and innocent and lovely, she showed no traces of the fact that she had been taken in every way a woman can be taken this last night—and Anton also seemed only invigorated from his exertions, he was smiling, he was eager to face the new day.

"Good morning, Your Grace," Anton said.

The Duke twisted his face to look at his friend—the black cross struck again—Roland's body jerked away, so his head fell sideways on his shoulder—he looked like some misshapen hunchback—his eyes were wild and his face was slashed with lines of pain, though nothing was touching him.

The smile left Anton's face. What was the cause of this agony? What vision was Roland seeing with his wild eyes? It was clear that the Duke could not shake it off himself—he had started to walk in a tottering circle, with his head leaning in—so Anton stepped in front of him and placed two firm hands on Roland's shoulders. He stopped the younger man, and straightened him, and then he looked into the nearly mad face and asked, "Your Grace, what do you see?"

Roland said, "I see a black cross."

Their faces were but a foot apart—but the Duke still could not see his friend.

"Where is this cross, Your Grace?"

"It's striking me in my head, it has followed me ever since we began our journey, it floats, it has no base on earth, it floats —"

Anton let go of the Duke's shoulders and turned and walked away. He stopped with his back to the Duke, five paces distant.

The last piece of the puzzle had fallen into place.

"You should have told me sooner, Your Grace," Anton said.

Something in the tone of Anton's voice penetrated into Roland's rational brain. The Duke snapped fully erect. The dream was banished now.

"What do you know?"

Anton didn't turn around—he also dropped the Duke's title.

"You know the raiders who call themselves Vikings—here in England they are known as Northmen."

Roland felt the sickening realization sweep over him as he looked at Anton's back—at Sandra's white face. The outside fighting force disguised as monks—

Anton went on: "Their ships fly one big square sail. The center of the sail is marked by a huge black cross. It sways above the sea—that's why you saw it floating."

Like everyone else Roland had heard tales of these ferocious raiders—but he had lived all his life inland, in a safe landlocked duchy—he had not studied the Vikings as well as he might have—he hadn't known a simple fact like the manner in which they decorated their sails—

"I encountered them once in Italy. I was based in a little town called Caravenna. I had gone out into the field that day to pursue a bandit gang, on the orders of my employer, the local lord. When I came back that night Caravenna was nothing but smoking ruins. The church had been ransacked. My lord was dead. His daughter, a beautiful eighteen year old virgin, was gone. My mistress, a lovely young courtesan, was gone. The most beautiful daughters of the town—all of them—were gone. Dead men lay in the streets.

"It had all happened so fast that none of the survivors could give me a clear account—but everyone remembered the black cross rising above the dragon prowed ship.

"Then whenever I traveled by the sea I asked people about the Vikings—I learned they live on plunder and they trade in flesh—women who are less than perfect they sell in the slave markets of the East—they keep the best for themselves."

Sandra put a comforting hand on Anton's arm. Her lover had given his whole long speech with his back to the Duke. All the rest of the men were awake and listening. No one had ever heard Anton say so much at one time before.

Roland's mind was whirling frantically. Anton had described the typical coastal raid for which the Vikings were famous— what were they doing so far inland, on horseback no less?

"This can't be an ordinary raid," Roland said.

Anton shook off Sandra's hand and turned around.

The two men began to work together.

"They're not looking for women to sell this time," Anton said. "They're only after Elaine."

"They would pursue her this far?" Roland asked.

"The Viking leader is called the Chief of Champions. Only he would have the power to keep his men in line and abjure plunder while they go after this one lady. He must want her for himself."

"That's why he's been so careful not to engage Thomas too soon. He's making sure she lives."

"He's driving them," Anton said.

"What?"

"I've often thought you have second sight, Your Grace—the floating black cross that terrifies you—that's what he's driving them to—his ship, waiting at sea."

"Due south, he's spread out, keeps them moving forward—"

"Because of the monkish disguise, Thomas doesn't know who they really are—"

"He'll make a stand when he sees the ship—"

"We'll get there, Your Grace."

The Duke suddenly realized that every Larrazian knight had pressed close enough to hear the rapid conversation. That was good. Now he didn't have to repeat anything. He asked Anton one more question. "How many men on a Viking ship?"

"Fifty."

"They lost two, perhaps eight left in the raiding party—forty on the ship."

The Duke looked around at his men and he smiled for the first time since they had begun the pursuit. "We know the name of our enemies now," he said, "so all I need to add is this: Death by sword is almost too merciful for slave raiders like these—and a quick death is the *only* mercy we'll show. We're going to run down that raiding party *before* they get on that ship—before they take Elaine away—we'll kill this 'Chief of Champions' "— there was a deliberate sneer in Roland's voice—"and all his

men—we'll avenge the deaths of Pierre and Daniel—we go now
to rescue the next Duchess of Larraz!"

Roland could see that every man was with him now—the
formless enemy had taken shape, and the known is always easier to fight—every Larrazian knight was ready to battle eight
Vikings or forty eight if they had to—they wanted nothing more
than this: a beautiful lady to save, and an evil villain to slay.

One man growled, "Have faith in us, Your Grace. The Vikings
will never take your lady."

The Duke looked down into the young man's determined face,
and he said, "I believe you." Then he cast his eyes over the
group at large, and he ordered, "Now mount up, and spread out
like before. We ride due south, fast as we can—I'll call a break
only when the horses need it. Signal if you see the Vikings—
don't attack until I give the order. Let's go."

The zealous knights got ready in a hurry—the line strung out
across the horizon, everyone mounted now, widely spaced (only
Anton and Sandra riding close together)—the Duke waved once
and they surged forward into the clear morning air, they
smelled the sweetness of the rainwashed meadow grass, they
looked out over the bright wet green and they saw clinging
droplets lit like crystals by the rising sun.

It was a morning of new knowledge, a morning of hope—so
the Duke wondered why he kept thinking of that one thing
Anton had said: 'You should have told me sooner.'

Another mistake in judgment! He had followed the wrong
horses, sent the wrong men, and now this! The memory of
Anton's mournful voice sounded like a death knell in his head:
'You should have told me sooner.' Had he been ashamed to confess his fears to his friend? Had he been afraid to admit to being
frightened by a dream? Whatever the reason it wasn't good
enough. His proud (or foolish) silence had left them without
information on their enemies, information that could have
helped a great deal. If he had known they were Vikings he
would have known they were pushing toward the sea—he would
not have been misled by their lure—he would have saved Elaine
already!

Was it too late now?

No, not too late, it can not be too late—

'The Vikings will never take your lady.' So said the brave
young knight, and he spoke the truth. It was not possible that
Elaine could be taken away to be enslaved by barbarians.

She would be saved.

Last night Roland had fought with a dreadful presentiment of death.

Now he remembered his prayer.

Yes, Elaine would be saved.

At what price?

Chapter 126

THE FOG AT SEA

Captain Barnes of the good ship Lionheart was in serious trouble.

Richard Lionheart would certainly have killed the hungover Captain that morning had the King known aught of navigation—but for right now the drunk was protected by his monarch's ignorance.

They were in the midst of a fog so thick that the Captain had no idea of the location of his ship—nor did he know which way it was facing—east or west, north or south—it was impossible to tell. Nothing could be discerned inside the cushiony cloud that enveloped them.

The King had to put his face a foot from the Captain's in order to see him—two feet away and he might just as well have been yelling into some formless gray soup.

Richard threatened the Captain with every manner of torture if he did not get the ship back on track toward the Northmen's rendezvous—but the King's brutal words were, at least for now, just a venting of spleen without a serious intent. Even Richard could see there was nothing to be done now—and when the sky cleared, as Barnes prayed it would soon, then Richard would need the Captain's knowledge to make up for lost time.

Both men knew that fact, though the knowledge hardly checked Richard's rage.

Knights grumbled and stomped on the wooden deck—Arthur clung to the rail and saw nothing—the Archbishop prayed—Brian pulled at his flask—and Richard kept cursing the Captain, and the Captain quivered, and wished he had a drink.

THE BOY AT SEA

Chapter 127

THE RABBIT

If Thomas had not once been a poacher himself, he might never have seen the old man—but he caught a whiff of the cooking rabbit, and a glimpse of smoke, and then he spotted the crouching old fellow preparing his meal. The poacher's fire was concealed under a mud bank, just as Thomas had done it in the old days—the knight felt a kinship and a sympathy for this old man who lived by his wits and his good aim—a free man in the country—but for all that, hunger was greater than kinship.

Thomas snapped, "Hold on," to Elaine—she grabbed a double handful of Saladin's mane—Thomas booted the horse into a gallop—Saladin had had his rest, now it was time to earn his keep! They charged straight toward the old man—the poacher dived into some bushes and disappeared, dragging his bow behind him—Thomas reached all the way down, he held on only with right foot and right hand, his left hand smashed through the bank and came up with mud, ashes, and yes, a nearly cooked rabbit.

Thomas allowed a grin to crease his features as he righted himself—they continued on to the south—the monks following didn't know what was going on—he didn't think they had even seen the old man—Elaine probably hadn't seen him either—Thomas snapped off a juicy rabbit leg and stuffed it into Elaine's mouth—she fought his hand for a moment, and then sucked greedily on the hot morsel—Thomas took a bite for himself, and it was wonderful—Elaine unselfconsciously spat out the bones—Thomas gave her another leg and then took two more big bites for himself—they finished the meat before they had gone another three hundred yards—Thomas threw the remaining bones away and then put his greasy fingers against Elaine's lips—she licked them clean and laughed—then he put his hands over her breasts and she stopped laughing.

Thomas pulled his hands away. Then he cautiously put his left arm around her tense figure—he held her properly as before, and she relaxed slightly, and so they rode on.

Thomas felt the hot food settle in his stomach, giving him strength for battle—his face set again in the killing mode.

Chapter 128

THE FOG ON LAND

The fog that plagued Richard Lionheart gradually unfurled itself like a huge wet blanket. It rolled over the southern coast of England and climbed the cliffs there—and then it gradually spread northward over the Salisbury plain, an expansion that slowly weakened the low lying cloud—Thomas rode into a haze, rather than the soup the sailors faced—but still he was forced to slow Saladin to a walk, and the Vikings were forced to close within twenty yards of him, for beyond that distance vision vanished into chimera.

The Vikings had grumbled, last night and this morning, when Ivar had once again let their quarry go. But now the fog brought with it the scent of the sea, and this raised their spirits. Perhaps our leader is right, they thought. We can drive our prey to the sea without any risk, for no English army will find us in this fog. Then tomorrow we shall be on our ship, we'll be safe on the high seas with our prize.

Roland was about eight hours behind Thomas and Elaine. To begin with the Larrazian force gained some time, for they were all fired by enthusiasm and their new knowledge of the enemy— but then by noontime they too were delicately entangled in the fog's misty grip. They had to close up their line so they could see each other—they had to slow to a walk, for the horses simply refused to go any faster—they would not run toward what they could not see, and Roland was forced to accept that fact—he cursed but he accepted it—he cursed himself, he thought of Elaine, and he rode on into the mist, guided only by the salty smell of the sea.

Thomas liked the fog. It gave him time to think.

He did not concern himself with his broken heart. He considered the question of life or death: How do one knight and one lady with two lessons in swordsmanship defeat seven tough fighting men?

As the afternoon progressed, he gradually came up with some answers. He needed the advantage of surprise—he needed deception, some kind of trap. He needed first of all to be in a desperate situation—something terrible and hopeless that would give credence to a false capitulation. Only then might the enemy lower their guard.

Thomas knew by now that they were driving him to the sea. The monks evidently believed that only then would he be completely in their power. Thomas knew that he would have to find a way to use their own confidence against them.

The fog was his friend. At this slow pace, they would not reach the sea before nightfall. With any luck he and Elaine would have one more night—one more hopeless night with their backs to the wall.

Thomas laughed.

Elaine froze, for the sound she heard was the mad cackle of a murderer.

Chapter 129

THE GALLOWS TREE

The fog got worse as Thomas and Elaine approached the sea. The sun became an ever vaguer glimmer in the west—and then vanished. Thomas heard the monks around them—had they moved closer? He urged Saladin onward toward the heavy briny scent of the sea—the horse responded and took a long stride forward into the darkness—one stride too many—the right front hoof came down on nothing—the great horse skidded to a stop on three hooves and whinnied with a near human cry of terror—Thomas felt the sweat burst out on his horse's back and turned him violently to the left—Saladin pulled his dangling hoof back and planted it, with relief, on the edge of the land.

The horse stood now on the edge of a sheer drop to the sea.

Thomas realized that the monks had stopped in their tracks when they heard Saladin's cry. He heard the sound of waves raking the stony beach that seemed to be directly beneath him. He dismounted, and helped Elaine down, and told her to stay where she was, on the landward side of the horse. Then he maneuvered around the still trembling stallion, he got down on his hands and knees, and he reached out until he felt the edge of the cliff. He pulled himself closer and looked down. In the fog and dark he could just make out the white surf below—he heard the turmoil of water polished stone as it was spun by the waves—had Saladin not held up, they would have dropped fifty feet straight down—a sheer fifty foot drop to their deaths.

Thomas heard the orders in the foreign language—the monks had found the cliff edge as well—they were settling in for the night, twenty yards away in every direction except south—the opening of the letter C was sealed off by the drop—they had him in their killing zone now.

It was just where he wanted to be.

Thomas felt a shape nearby—he moved over a few feet and felt the gnarled trunk of an old oak—a tree that had perversely chosen to anchor itself in the last bit of earth before the rock of the cliff edge. It was an old strong tree—Thomas felt a thick branch stretching out over his head, parallel to the edge of the cliff—he reached up and ran his hand along that branch—and then he jerked away when he felt the cylindrical coil—his primitive senses screamed 'snake!' but then his mind intervened and recalled the lifeless feel of old rope—he reached up again, yes, it was only a coil of rope, old, nearly rotted—it was looped around the branch and then it hung down to the ground—Thomas laughed again, that same mad cackle, for now he knew that everything was perfect.

They had come to the end, the last stand, the killing zone—and there to greet them was a gallows tree.

Chapter 130

THE ENGLISH LANGUAGE

Richard Lionheart was lost in the fog at sea.

Roland's force slogged through the fog on land—no vision at all in the darkness now, but no thought of stopping—they followed their noses toward the sea.

Ivar the Heartless, the culmination of his life at hand, dispatched Sigurd on a detour around the cliff and down to the shore. Sigurd's mission was to light a signal fire to guide in the waiting Viking warship. He was to tell the crew that the prize would be picked up at first light.

Only when Sigurd was out of earshot did Ivar approach the English pair. He stopped halfway to the cliff, thirty feet away, invisible even at that distance, and he called to them in his heavily accented English—a language that none of his men (with the exception of the absent Sigurd) could understand.

Chapter 131

THE LORD'S PRAYER

"Englishman!"

Thomas and Elaine both jerked with alarm when they heard the harsh voice in the night. Thomas very carefully and quietly drew both his swords. He gave his own to Elaine—he kept the jewel hilted royal sword for himself.

"Do you hear me, Englishman?"

Thomas was certain that the voice belonged to the shaven headed leader.

"Yes," Thomas replied quietly.

"We are not monks."

"I know."

"You want to know who we are."

The voice was not asking a question.

Thomas didn't reply. He just stared into the darkness from whence the voice came. He wanted to see the man, but he couldn't make out a shape. He did desperately want to know the true identity of his pursuers—but he had no intention of admitting that fact to their evil leader.

The voice lashed out once again. "Look out to sea, Englishman."

Thomas turned his head slowly, warily, his eyes constantly flicking backward toward the voice, his hand tight on his sword. He chanced one hard look down past the cliff edge. He saw the white breaking waves in close but only blackness beyond.

He looked back at his tormentor as the voice asked, "What do you see, Englishman?"

Elaine felt the weight of the sword in her hand. She feared that something terrible was about to happen. She moved closer to Thomas and touched his sword arm with her free hand—she felt his extreme tension.

"I see nothing," Thomas replied.

"Use your imagination," the voice advised.

There was a pause—and then Thomas suddenly realized that he had figured his enemy wrong from the start—he had thought of the monks as one complete unit, seven men that he could somehow deal with—but now he thought of an enemy coming from the sea, the band that had pursued him as just one part of that enemy—he guessed the answer and he couldn't repress the shudder that rippled through his body—Elaine with her hand on him felt that spasm—she knew now that Thomas, the bravest knight in England, was afraid.

That knowledge terrified Elaine even more than their unseen interrogator—but then she felt Thomas draw up his courage, she felt the strength of him, and when he spoke there was no tremor in his voice.

"You're Northmen and you have a ship coming."

"Excellent!" replied the voice. "Picture a dragon prowed long-ship with forty-one fine champions aboard, coming close to the signal light—look down again, Englishman!"

Thomas looked, and yes, he saw the fire now—he looked back into the darkness at the voice and he wanted to charge forward and kill the man who was trying to destroy his hope—but he felt Elaine trembling, clinging to him and he knew that charging was suicide, they would all come in on him, charging meant death for him and slavery for Elaine, his only hope was the plan he was beginning to work on, the trap—but even then they would have no chance if Norse reinforcements came up to join these seven. How confident was the leader? Thomas wondered. Does he still think seven to two is enough? Has he been lulled by the submissive way I have allowed him to drive us for these last two long days? Is he absolutely sure that we are helpless, jammed in between his sea and land forces? If he thinks that way, then he won't call for any more men—and we still have a chance.

"I see the fire," Thomas said with sad resignation.

"Good!" the voice replied. "But do you see your future?"

The voice went on without waiting for a reply. "This is the time the masks come off. I know who you are. You are Sir Thomas, and your lady is Elaine the Fair. I am Ivar the Heartless—I am the one who destroyed Marvelsville fifteen years ago."

Ivar allowed his victims a moment to recall that famous massacre, and then he went on. "The folly of the English is that you pray to God for deliverance from us—but you don't know that there is no such deliverance. We strike whenever we care to—I have only kept you alive this long in anticipation of this moment.

"I want to tell you what I'm like—why they call me the Heartless.

"You see, I'm different from my brethren. I don't keep slaves—I don't make children—I don't love. My only pleasure is the taking of life. I'm not going to take Elaine back with me tomorrow, Thomas. I'm going to kill her.

"There is no escape for her.

"You can't protect her.

"God won't protect her.

"Let me tell you how it's going to be."

Elaine had been trembling ever since Thomas had said the word 'Northmen'—now her fingers bit into Thomas's arm with the unconscious strength of terror.

Ivar continued. "At first light we'll come for you, Thomas, seven to your one—your woman can watch while we cut you—I hope you don't die right away, because if you're still alive you can watch me strip Elaine—I'll be the first one to rape her—"

Without conscious thought Elaine began to pray. She sounded like a child repeating her lessons—the holy words came out in a choked halting whisper. "Our Father, who art in heaven—"

"Then you'll see my men, sporting with her, between her legs, in her mouth—"

"Hallowed be thy name—"

"Turning her over, spreading her buttocks—"

"Thy kingdom come—"

"Then after pleasure, the pain: We have good English horsewhips—"

"Thy will be done—" Thomas had joined with Elaine now, he added his child's whisper to hers—

"To lash her flesh until the blood flows—"

"On earth as it is in heaven—"

"Then it will be the turn of the knives—"

"Give us this day our daily bread—"

"I hope you live to see as we cut into each piece of her—"

"And forgive us our trespasses—"

"Split her nipples before your eyes—"

"As we forgive those who trespass against us . . ."

Elaine held Thomas in her terror, and his, and they prayed together.

Ivar continued, a hideous snarl in the night.

The surrounding Vikings thought correctly that Ivar was tormenting the couple—they knew that such was his pleasure—but even those hardened men would have been shocked by their leader's depravity had they understood his words. In truth Ivar's men were not prepared to carry out his most vicious threats (though of course Thomas did not know this). The Vikings were prepared to kill Thomas, yes—but the pointless torture of women had no charms for them—and indeed, so far as they knew, the whole reason for this expedition was to take Elaine alive.

The Champions did not realize that Ivar was fighting for his life—fighting to remove the test of love that he was certain he would fail—fighting for Elaine's death, so that he might live.

Finally Ivar (and Thomas and Elaine as well) heard Norse voices on the shore. The longship had come in. Ivar knew that Sigurd would report back soon.

He stopped his horrific recital.

Thomas and Elaine stopped praying. Now the silence in front of them was magnified by the foreign voices below and behind.

Then Ivar spoke again. "Kill her before dawn, Thomas. Spare her what I have promised, and her soul will be grateful to you—and then I will give you too a quick and honorable death."

Thomas heard the footsteps as Ivar walked away.

He and Elaine were left alone, shuddering beneath the gallows tree—but there *was* hope. 'Seven to your one' Ivar had said—he wasn't going to bring up reinforcements—and he did not know that Elaine could handle a sword.

Chapter 132

SETUP

Elaine stepped around in front of Thomas. She handed his sword back to him. He took it, and returned it to his scabbard—he also sheathed the royal sword that he had been holding. Elaine put her hands on his shoulders. Thomas reached out and caught her at the waist with his big hands. Neither one of them was trembling now.

Elaine had heard the worst. She knew exactly what she was risking. She tilted her head back and looked right at Thomas's mist-blurred face. She said, "I have to live," and her words came out with a perfect clarity.

Thomas tightened his grip on her waist a little, and then he leaned forward until their noses were almost touching. Elaine could feel his breath on her lips. He said, "You will live, my darling, I will see to that." There was an enormous ferocity under his quiet words.

Elaine opened her mouth to be kissed, but Thomas refused the invitation. He stepped away from her and then caught her hand. He led her over to the gallows tree. He sat down first, with his back to the oak, and then he drew Elaine down with him. "I must plan for a while," Thomas said, "so I do not want you to speak to me until I tell you that you can."

Elaine gave a little nod, and then she curled up on her side like a little bunny, and she laid her head on Thomas's lap. Thomas pulled her nightgown down so that it covered her feet. Elaine closed her eyes, and then she felt Thomas's hand gently stroking her hair. She found that she could not sleep, but she was able to rest, and feel safe, if only for an hour.

Thomas used that hour to devise a plan for murder—he composed a deadly trap with a beautiful bait.

Thomas stroked Elaine's hair back from her cheek—he tucked the long strands behind her ear. He leaned down and whispered, "Elaine"—just her name, nothing more.

Elaine was instantly alert. Her whole body tensed—she curled even tighter into a ball. "Tell me the plan," she whispered.

Thomas told her, as Elaine listened in disbelief and horror. She interrupted him before he had gone too far—"You can't do that," she said.

Thomas slapped her bared cheek, hard. He left his hand there—he felt her tears roll down her skin as he told her the rest. Elaine did not interrupt again.

When he was finished he eased her off his lap and stood up. He left her curled up on the ground. He walked over to Saladin. The weary horse had been waiting patiently, head down, for his master to take his tack off. Now he raised his head as Thomas approached. Thomas took the horse's bridle and led him about five yards to the right (as one faced the cliff) of the gallows tree. There he stopped the horse, still about fifteen yards from the nearest Northman, and about four feet from the edge of the cliff.

Thomas looked back at Elaine. All he could see was a faint blur of white. He couldn't see the Northmen at all. He felt the weight of the damp fog on him as he drew the golden sword.

Elaine heard the hoofsteps stop. She held her breath. She wrapped her arms around her own head, as a child tries to cover both eyes and ears.

Thomas let Saladin sniff his left hand, and then he stroked the horse up under his chin, up towards the neck—he found the soft spot—he thought of the black knights—his right hand tightened on the jeweled hilt—and then he moved his left hand out of the way and drove the sword upward with all his strength.

Thomas's aim was true—it was a perfect killing thrust, and another horse would have dropped like a stone.

Not Saladin.

The brave stallion reared up from the sudden horrible pain, his forelegs cleared the ground for one magnificent moment— and then his back legs buckled, and he twisted a little coming down, he crashed back to earth on a right foreleg that wouldn't support him, he fell over on his right side and jerked all four legs in a last wild run—and then finally the mighty Arabian gave in to death.

Thomas knew that the Northmen had heard the thud. There was some conversation in their ranks, then a command, then silence. They didn't move in—there was no reason for them to risk that in the dark. They knew he was in their killing zone. He couldn't get out. They didn't think he could do anything to harm them. Perhaps Ivar thought that he had just killed Elaine.

Thomas pulled the sword free and cleaned it with his shirt—then he returned it to his scabbard. He reflected that from now on he would have to be very quiet. He let his bow slide off his left shoulder and into his hand. He took an arrow from his quiver and fitted it to his bowstring—then he drew back, aimed downward, and let fly. The arrow penetrated to half its length. The point buried itself in Saladin's silent heart. The feathered shaft protruded obscenely from the horse's dead body.

The first part of the setup was now in place, but there was still more work to be done before dawn.

Thomas set to—very quietly.

Chapter 133

EAST OR WEST?

Thursday, June 18, 1194, shortly before dawn . . .

Roland feared the sunrise.

His mind was whirling with vague images of horror, but one thing he knew for certain—he had to get to Elaine by first light.

They reached the sea while darkness still reigned—yet this was not the black pitch they had wrestled through before. The fog was thinning out. There was a hint of gray lightness in the east. Dawn was coming—and in the night they had veered off the track.

They stood at the edge of the sea. Which way was Elaine: east or west?

Roland looked right—he looked left—he saw nothing. He could feel the grains of sand of Elaine's life trickling away. He could feel the sun rising under the curve of the earth, ready to spread its rays on some terrible tableau. He was frozen in indecision.

It was Anton who saved the day.

He spoke sharply to the Duke. "Your Grace: Help Sandra get up on my shoulders."

Roland understood at once and rode over. He grasped Sandra under her arms and lifted her as though she were no heavier than a feather pillow—he stood up in his stirrups, the leather straps straining under the stress of the double weight, and then he set her on Anton's shoulders. Anton was blinded by her skirt for a moment—he pushed it up and behind his head—he felt his lover's hot womanhood pressed against the back of his neck—he held her bare thighs to steady her, and then, using just the strength of his legs, he stood up in the stirrups—again the sound of creaking leather—he forced his legs to straighten while he balanced the whole double weight on the two thin strips of steel beneath his feet—and then finally Sandra was raised on a man who was raised on a horse. High in the air she was—she looked west with her keen youthful eyes and saw nothing—she turned, Anton's legs quivering now with the strain but still holding firm, his upper body solid, Sandra looking to the east now, searching, she was raised above men to see farther than they could—and there in the distance of the east she saw the faint wavering glow of a fire.

Chapter 134

MARKED FOR DEATH

The Vikings had left their usual skeleton crew of twenty Champions on the ship. The other twenty-one were on shore, weapons ready. They had been met by Sigurd when they had splashed ashore. He had explained the situation and relayed Ivar's orders: they were to guard the cliff (not that anyone really expected the English couple to come flying over) and also the twisting path to the west that Sigurd himself had come down (this track was the only reasonably quick way up and around to the killing zone). The Champions were *not* to come up and assist in the final capture, unless Ivar specifically called them.

There was some snickering about this last order. The men assumed that Ivar would take his pleasure at least once (and that was why he wanted a certain privacy) before he brought Elaine down to board the ship.

The Champions asked Sigurd to describe the fair lady, but he felt reluctant to speak of her. There was sadness in his voice as he said, "She is indeed the most beautiful woman in the world. You will see for yourselves soon."

Sigurd took his leave. He walked back up the twisting path (the footworn track snaked this way and that around lumps of rock) and he tried not to think of what the morning would bring. He thought of his wives, of his children—he wanted to go home, and yet there was still this last test of fealty to endure. He made his way back to the Viking circle—he reported to Ivar, and then he took his place as a watcher.

Down below, the twenty-one Champions grew ever more irritated and impatient as the night slowly passed. They were unhappy that they would not have a share in the glory of killing

Sir Thomas, and likewise they would have no part in the actual capture of Elaine. There was no chance for one of them to actually touch her.

They grumbled a little, and their unhappiness made their physical discomforts seem worse. They were struck by the cold spray from the sea—they breathed in the fog's wet chill—they cursed as they warmed their hands over Sigurd's signal fire, but not one of them guessed the truth.

They were unaware that a young girl's searching eyes had marked them all for death.

Chapter 135

A BREEZE AT THEIR BACK

On the sea, just before dawn . . .

Captain Barnes had a religious experience when the fog finally began to thin out as the sky lightened in the east. The Captain looked to his right—and he saw land—he looked to his left—and he saw land—and then he realized that his ship, guided only by the sure hand of God, was passing through the strait between the Isle of Wight and the mainland. There was even a light following wind pushing them in the correct direction. The Captain stared with rapture in his eyes—and then he said, "We're almost there, Your Majesty," in the most assured voice he could manage.

Richard Lionheart looked about him and saw the truth of the Captain's words. The King accepted the miracle as his due. "Quite right, Captain," he said, and then he added, "I suppose I shall let you live."

The Captain bowed his head to hide his deep sigh of relief—he swore to himself that he would never touch a drop again.

Richard called for all of his knights to come up on deck. The excitement in the King's voice brought all the warriors on the double. They looked to their leader—but before he could say a word there came a cry from the lookout above them.

"I see a sail, Your Majesty!" The young sailor could barely contain himself. "A black cross on it! I see the dragon head! Northmen! Northmen, Your Majesty, straight ahead and to the starboard!"

Richard shouldered his men aside as he strode to the bow. He peered into the vanishing mist—and yes, he could just make out the sail. He smiled. The breeze at their back would blow them in on the Northmen without a sound. This was the best part of war: a sudden attack with massive force on an unsuspecting enemy—lovely!

Richard turned and gave his orders to the Captain. "Slide in as close to the longship as you can—and tell your crew to have their grappling irons ready." Richard observed his knights. He could almost feel their hearts thumping with anticipation—the King was thrilled to be able to direct this masculine power. He held up his hand and said, "Quiet men, quiet. You'll have your chance to roar in a minute." The King smiled. "We're going to board that dragon ship—and we're going to drink its blood."

The English knights clenched their teeth and felt for their weapons.

The huge English warship drifted silently through the rising mist like some deadly specter closing in on its prey.

Chapter 136

THE LURE

With the fog thinning out, and some light filtering in from the east, the Vikings were able to see many things before they were ready to believe their eyes.

Ivar quietly directed his men to take cover, for he suspected some kind of trap. The Vikings crouched down behind bushes and rocks, weapons at ready. They stared into the dimness— stared in disbelief and amazement—and then the first clear rays of the sun illuminated the scene while destroying the last remnants of the mist.

The Vikings were forced to confront the truth of their own vision.

Thomas was gone.

The black horse was dead.

Elaine was naked and bound.

The English Countess stood on the edge of the cliff, beneath the first great horizontal branch of the gallows tree. She stood where many a condemned man had waited with a noose around his neck—waited for the push that would send him out into the void—and then the drop, the rope yanked taut, and death by strangulation.

The rope that had carried a man's weight unto death had been cut in twain and used to bind Elaine the Fair.

She stood on the lip of death with the morning's light on her strained body. She faced the Vikings. She did not struggle or scream.

Her arms were pulled high and bent backwards slightly by the ropes that encircled her wrists—ropes that were then tied together and coiled around the branch above her. Her hair wreathed her face with wild golden ringlets. Her eyes were a fierce blue, and there was no fear in them. Her mouth was a thin proud line that did not beg for mercy. Her breasts were taut, pulled upward by the tension on her raised arms—her bright pink nipples were hard, brazen, and unashamed. Her waist dipped in, punctuated by the small firm depression of her navel—her hips blossomed out and then extended downward into firm thighs and beautifully shaped, parted legs.

She was standing up on her toes to ease the tension on her wrists.

The point of a king's sword had been driven into the dirt between her feet. The steel blade rose upward between her legs until, just forward of the arch of her body, it was crowned by the golden, jewel encrusted hilt. This ornamented handle blocked the Vikings' view of Elaine's mount of Venus.

She stood there, tense from toes to wrists, naked and proud, shielded only by the hilt of a deadly weapon.

She was the most beautiful woman in the world.

It was a painful duty to drag one's eyes away from her, but the Vikings, fighting men all, finally did so. They saw Elaine's white nightgown lying on the ground a few feet to her right. They stared again at the macabre sight of the dead horse to her left—they looked at the arrow driven into it—they saw how the horse's jumbled legs, projecting nearly to the cliff, were frozen in an attitude of flight.

They did not see Thomas, but they looked for him. They searched and searched with their eyes, they looked everywhere within their killing zone, they even looked up into the tree—but they could see no sign of the English knight.

Minutes went by and there was still no clue. They looked everywhere, and everywhere again—but he had vanished. There came a moment when they could look for him no longer—each Champion felt his eyes drawn by the overpowering force of Elaine's beauty.

They stared as one man at her arched nakedness. They stared with sweating palms and racing hearts and swooning souls, and their one desire was only this: they wanted to touch her.

Every man shared this desire—every man, that is, save Ivar the Heartless.

Chapter 137

IVAR'S WARNING

Ivar broke the worshipful silence with a harsh command.

"Sigurd, take the sword from between her legs—I want to see all of her."

Sigurd stood up slowly.

The rest of the Champions looked longingly from Elaine to their Chief and then back again.

Ivar snapped, "The rest of you stay put and watch for the Englishman—maybe he crammed himself in behind the sword!"

There was some scattered laughter at the coarse joke, but not as much as Ivar would have liked—they love her, he thought, they love her.

Sigurd drew his sword and took a step forward.

The men stared spellbound at Elaine the Fair.

Ivar saw that his last chance was gone. He had failed to convert Thomas into a murderer.

Now he was all alone—with his death.

Ivar could no longer see his death—for it was so close now that it had become a part of him. Its claws strummed his heart. Its foul breath rattled in his throat.

Sigurd took two steps and then stopped at some tiny noise.

Ivar remembered his last words to Sigurd before sending him out on this quest: 'I may discover that I can not love—I may discover that I am fated always to be a cripple. If such is the truth, then I will kill myself—but I will kill her, first.'

Ivar knew in his soul that he meant those words. He could not love her—he would die—but he would take her with him.

He stared at Elaine with hatred.

Sigurd satisfied himself that the noise had only been a bird.

Now he started forward again—but he changed direction. He was headed for the horse now, not the woman.

Ivar realized that Sigurd was looking for the vanished Englishman—but what did he matter? Elaine was the one who had to die.

Sigurd, sword out, moved cautiously toward the horse.

Why is he so afraid? Ivar wondered. He looks almost as though he too can feel his own death.

That possibility jolted Ivar. He had thought once before of Sigurd dying, and he had imagined that he would feel nothing. Now he knew that he had been wrong. He was terrified that he might lose his friend. Sigurd is my friend, Ivar thought. Sigurd might really die.

Ivar was shaking as he watched Sigurd examine the horse—he sensed that something was terribly wrong.

(The hole was practically under the dead horse's belly. Thomas had taken all the dirt from the hole and dropped it silently, a handful at a time, over the cliff. Then he had arranged Elaine just right—and then he had gone back to his hole and crawled in. He had had to unbuckle his two scabbards, for he found that his cramped quarters did not allow for their stiff length—he had stuffed them into the dirt at his feet. He had pulled the piece of turf that he had cut very neatly with his sword back over the mouth of the hole. He had crouched and waited—now he still crouched in the black darkness of his own pit—he listened to the near footsteps reverberating through the earth—he tightened his hands on his bow and nocked arrow. The waiting was almost over.)

Sigurd looked the horse over but he suspected nothing—and everything—he looked up in the tree but nothing nothing nothing—no English knight anywhere—he circled around until he stood directly in front of Elaine the Fair—four paces in front of her—he looked at her face, and then he was lost.

All the men watched as Sigurd slowly sheathed his sword.

Ivar wanted to scream, No—No—No—Danger! Save Yourself! But there was no danger to see—just a tied, naked woman.

Sigurd took one step.

Ivar thought furiously. Something wrong—something—if he could just think of it he could save—

Sigurd took another step.

Two more steps to go and then he could take that royal sword. Two swords!

Thomas wore two swords! Ivar had noticed that when he had cut Elaine loose at Stonehenge—the golden one in his hand, yes, but also a plainer one swinging in its scabbard—*if he has escaped why didn't he take both swords? Why leave one that Elaine can't reach?*

Sigurd took a third step.

One more!

It's a trap, it's a trap, Thomas wants her to look helpless the golden sword is a decoy—

Sigurd took the fourth step and reached for the weapon's sparkling hilt—

Ivar stood up and screamed, "SIGURD! SHE HAS ANOTHER SWORD!"

(Elaine was not really tied to the tree branch above her—that was just an artful illusion, an illusion that she contributed to by standing up on her toes as though she were being dragged upward by the taut ropes. In truth, the tension on the ropes above her head was supplied only by the light weight of Thomas's sword on the other side of the branch—Elaine had to keep herself tense and still so that she would not pull that sword into view before she was ready.)

She was ready the instant Sigurd reached for the golden decoy.

She was coming down on her heels even as Ivar shouted his warning. The whole arch of her body snapped forward like an uncoiling spring—the motion yanked on the ropes and the hilt of Thomas's sword flew into her right hand—she grasped it firmly and swung with all her strength but Sigurd had heard his Chief and he was already leaping backwards—

Elaine had intended to cut off the Northman's head but his backward leap foiled that plan—she only caught his throat with the last two inches at the tip of the sword—but the only real difference that made to Sigurd was that it took him a minute to die.

Chapter 138

THE TRAP SPRUNG

The trap was supposed to work as follows: the Northmen, seeing no sign of Thomas, only the extraordinarily alluring Elaine, would smell some kind of deception. They wouldn't risk more than one man to check out Elaine—and besides, Thomas thought, they would certainly assume that any one man of theirs could handle a tied naked woman.

Elaine would kill that man with the concealed sword. With any luck this would provoke the rest of the Northmen to charge forward heedlessly, furious for revenge. Once they broke cover, Elaine would toss the King's sword toward the dead horse and cry, "Spare me!"

That was to be Thomas's signal. He would burst out of the hole by the horse (it had been sadly necessary to kill Saladin for various reasons—the living horse would have sniffed out Thomas's hiding place, while the dead horse concealed it—then too, the dead horse, deliberately marked with the arrow, was a perfect symbol of hopelessness and defeat) with bow in hand. He would shoot rapidly—one, two, three. "We need to kill four right away," Thomas had explained. "That leaves three to fight with the sword, for then they will be too close for me to use the bow any longer. I'll pick up the royal sword you tossed and take on two—you keep the other one busy. I'll kill my two and then finish off the one you're holding. Then we take two of their horses and ride away from the sea."

It was a beautiful plan and it might have worked had not Ivar shouted his warning. The Chief of Champions had yelled in English because he only wanted his friend to hear and understand. Even in his panic he made sure that the other

Champions would not see any crack in his heartless facade. If he were wrong they would never know what he had yelled.

Sigurd understood the cry but it didn't help him.

Thomas, under the turf, understood as well and he had no way of knowing that the warning came too late. He had to make a snap decision—and right away he realized that if Elaine failed to kill that first man it was all over. That Champion could take her hostage and end the battle before it could start. Thomas decided in a flash that his first duty was to protect Elaine—he couldn't wait—he couldn't let her be captured—he would take out the first man himself.

That was the wrong decision—and thus the trap sprung too soon.

Thomas burst out of his hole like a malignant toadstool, turf flopping crazily off his head, bow and arrow ready—he looked at Elaine and saw she was fine, saw the blood fountaining from Sigurd's cut throat—he realized that he had exposed himself too early but there was no turning back now—he spun towards the center of the Norse line—none of his lesser foes had broken cover but there was the leader on his feet—*there* was the torturing voice from the night—*there* was the death's head visage of incarnate evil—Thomas drew back his arrow and released it in the space of a heartbeat.

Ivar was staring in shock at his dying friend, the man he had tried in vain to save—he didn't think at all of how vulnerable he was, standing alone—he didn't think of his own life, or of his death—he felt one pure moment of love for Sigurd Sigurdsson, and that was the only such moment of his life.

Thomas had sent the whistling shaft on a straight true course—now the steel arrowhead ripped through the heart of Ivar the Heartless.

Ivar clutched the embedded shaft—and his own bright blood from his own human heart colored his hands red. Was he evil incarnate? He died like any ordinary man.

The fact that their Chief could die at all panicked the Vikings so badly that none of their number could react quickly, with the sole exception of one young archer on the wing. He shot an arrow at Thomas—a wobbly, desperate effort, nothing like the Englishman's well aimed bolt—indeed, the Viking shaft missed Thomas's body completely, though something twanged as the arrow flew by.

Thomas saw that archer break cover for his shot and he

reached for another arrow—he tried to fit it to his bowstring—
and that's when he realized that the Northman's errant missile
had cut it in two.

He was disarmed—and as he realized that Thomas felt the
worst moment of pure terror in his life. He felt more naked than
Elaine—and then the thought of her shocked him into action—
he threw his bow down and ran toward her, ran four giant
strides and then he dived for the golden sword that still stood in
the dirt between her feet—

Elaine knew why Thomas had jumped up—there had been no
way to stop him, but he should have trusted in her, he should
have waited—then she saw him take out the leader and she had
hope for a second—then the arrow snapped his bowstring and
she realized it was all hopeless—everything slowed down for
her—Thomas running toward her—she turned away because
what chance did he have—she looked without emotion at the
dying young man she had slashed—he lay on the ground on his
side now—his mouth was opening and closing though no sound
came out—she recognized him now as the "groom" who had
stared at her before her second lesson—you pitied me, she
thought, remembering—you knew the fate planned for me—you
joined with evil and yet as I watch you die I see you trying to
send a message to those you love—

Sigurd's mouth opened one last time and stayed that way as
his eyes glazed over—

You're dead, Elaine thought. I killed you. Am I dying too?

She turned back to look at Thomas—he was flying through
the air—a long slow dive—everything seemed so slow to her—he
was a beautiful man, flying like that, though his head was going
to hit the dirt before his outstretched hand reached the sword
hilt—I love you, Sir Thomas, Elaine thought—

That same Viking archer had a moment to collect himself for
the second shot. He knew what the Englishman was aiming for,
so it was just a question of timing. The archer released his
arrow, and it flew straight and true this time—his calculations
were perfect—

Thomas's face struck earth and skidded—his big right hand
wrapped itself around the jeweled hilt—and then Elaine
watched as the enemy arrow tore through that right hand. She
heard the bones snap. The arrowhead went through his hand
and came out the other side and smashed against a jewel in the
sword hilt. The jewel was a ruby and it was harder than

Thomas's bones—the steel arrowhead broke off, but the length of the shaft stayed embedded in Thomas's broken hand—a hand that suddenly refused to grip—it slid down the naked blade of Saladin's gift, pouring blood and cutting itself anew on the razorsharp sword edge—Thomas gave one short cry as his body finally skidded to a stop, as his flayed hand finally struck earth—a cry, not of pain, but of frustration and helplessness—and it was that cry that pierced Elaine's reverie and brought her back to life.

She didn't want to die.

She didn't want Thomas to die.

She pulled him to his feet with one hand (she still clutched Thomas's older sword with her own sore right hand) and then as soon as he was up she picked up the royal sword. She offered the bloody hilt to Thomas—she saw that his momentary despair had ended with her touch—he was smiling—and then he yanked the arrowshaft out of his right hand and threw it away. He ignored the fresh spurting blood—he reached out and took the royal sword with his left hand—but Elaine saw the cost of that movement—as Thomas moved so his dangling hand seemed to shriek its pain—Elaine couldn't bear it and she didn't see how Thomas could—she did the only thing she could think of, she reached out with her left hand and gently grasped Thomas's wounded right.

Thomas swung Elaine around so that they stood side by side, facing the still concealed Northmen. "It's perfect this way," he said. "Swinging from either side, we can control all the space in front of us."

Elaine looked up at his face. The smile that he had shown when she had pulled him up had deepened into a maniacal grin. He was crazy—but he was also quite correct. She could swing her sword from the right, without interfering with his swing from the left.

She grinned back at him, even though she knew the hidden Northmen could finish them any time they wanted with two more well aimed arrows.

Why didn't they shoot?

The Vikings had recovered from their initial shock. They had suffered terrible humiliation. Their leader had been killed. One of their best men had been struck down by a woman.

They had been tricked by Thomas.

They felt betrayed by Elaine. They had started to love her—

and she had turned out to be a deceptive murderous witch.

They could not even the slate with simple killing. Only an awesome revenge could satisfy them now.

Fridriksson took command. He saw how awkwardly the Englishman held the sword with his left hand. There was no more to fear from him—and of course the woman would be easy.

Fridriksson ordered the young archer to drop his bow.

The new leader of the Vikings waited until he was obeyed, and then he stood up. He drew his sword and pointed it at Thomas. "For him, the Blood Red Eagle!" he screamed. There was a gutteral roar of approbation from his men. Fridriksson went on: "I shall cut him open myself—and we'll make *her* watch. Then afterward it will be time for pleasure—and not one of our number shall fail to know Elaine the Fair!"

There was another gutteral roar as all of the Vikings came to their feet. Each Champion had his sword in hand.

Fridriksson beckoned to his four comrades, and so they closed the gaps between them until each man was but a sword length from his neighbor. The English could never break through that line—and if they tried to run around, they could be easily taken from behind.

The Vikings began their advance.

Elaine and Thomas, hand in bloody hand, sword right, sword left, walked slowly forward to meet them.

Chapter 139

ROLAND'S DECISION

Both during this campaign and after, Roland would often savagely criticize himself for the mistakes in judgment that he made.

No one else viewed his leadership so harshly.

The truth was that Roland did the best he could under adverse conditions—he made some mistakes, yes, but on the whole he did quite well.

Nothing showed his good and patient generalship better than the decision he made after Sandra saw the fire.

Every one of his men wanted to race along the narrow beach until they came upon the Vikings—but Roland only let them have their way until he was close enough to see the fire himself and judge its distance. Then he ordered his men to follow him back up the hill away from the sea. He led them in a deep half circle—he ignored his own terror when he was struck by the first long rays of the dawning sun. He calculated the turning point precisely—he drew his sword and urged his horse into a gallop toward the sea. Every knight followed his lead—Sandra dropped back to the rear at Anton's terse command.

The Larrazian force came up on Fridriksson's party from behind.

Had Roland charged straight along the beach, he would have run into the largest Viking force. He would have had to engage those twenty-one Champions in useless battle—and thus he would have been far too late to help Elaine.

The decision he actually made saved her life—for Elaine would have fought unto death, sword in hand, before she would have submitted to Viking rape.

Chapter 140

ROLAND ARRIVES

Thomas heard the horses first, and he laughed.

"Stop," he said to Elaine. "Your lover is coming. Call him."

Elaine stopped in her tracks. She saw the menacing Northmen in front of her, gradually closing—she saw no sign of any rescuer—but then she, like Thomas, heard the distant thunder of the gallop—she felt the earth vibrating beneath her bare feet—she felt the justification of Thomas's mad confidence—she felt the proof of her own love, and she screamed, "ROLAND!"

Before she had even finished crying his name the Larrazian leader burst into view over the top of the rise just fifty yards away—a whole stream of knights galloping behind him—and Sandra bringing up the rear!

All the Vikings heard the horses now. Four of them turned around to face the new enemy.

Fridriksson remembered the arrow shower at Marvelsville—he had been trapped then and he was trapped now—he knew by the sound that there were far too many knights coming from behind for his small group of five to have any chance—he knew that he was about to die—with that knowledge in his heart he charged straight at the English couple in front of him—the hated English! He would die, but he would take these two with him.

The Viking swung his sword at Thomas with all his strength and the impetus of his run—and yes, Thomas was awkward with the left hand, and weaker, but still he managed to get the royal sword up to block—steel rang on steel, and the force of Fridriksson's blow nearly drove Thomas's weapon backward into his own body—Thomas's arm was numbed to the shoulder—the next stroke would have killed him but it never came for Thomas's defensive action had gained one crucial second—Elaine lunged forward and drove her sword right through her foe's heart—the lunge carried her right up against the Viking as her sword passed through his body—his eyes turned to her in disbelief—his outraged heart pumped a jet of blood that splattered on Elaine's breasts—she jerked back in horror—she left her sword in the tottering, dying man—she looked down at herself and she began to scream.

Roland lopped off the head of the first Viking he came to and the horses behind him ran over the headless corpse.

The other Vikings didn't fare any better.

Elaine was still screaming—

Thomas tried to hold her with his broken hand—

Roland saw the blood on his lady's naked body. He leaped from his horse and ran to her—but then he saw with enormous relief that the blood was not her own. He tried to touch her to comfort her but she recoiled, howling, seeing nothing save her own bloody front—

Sandra had dismounted as well and now she came up and put her womanly arm around Elaine's waist—the Countess recognized the familiar touch—she let go of Thomas's hand and allowed herself to be led away from the dead—

Anton had counted five Vikings killed in the quick battle—then he saw two more dead on the ground—he wondered where the rest were—if that had been a signal fire then perhaps twenty more could be on land—he saw a path that disappeared down the hill to the west and he rode over to investigate—he never saw the battle axe, just a gleam in the morning sunlight—and then he heard his horse's agonized whinny as the thrown axe broke the poor beast's right front leg—the horse's shoulder collapsed—Anton kicked free of his stirrups and leaped clear as his horse went down—he landed on his feet at the top of the path—he stood there alone by his fallen horse, sword in hand—in front of him were twenty-one maddened Vikings, charging.

Chapter 141

ANTON'S GALLANT STAND

The Vikings down by the fire had heard Ivar's desperate warning, and right away they had begun to head upward along the path to the battle zone. As they negotiated the twisting track, they heard Fridriksson's call for the Blood Red Eagle, and they began to fear the worst—then they heard the horses and they began to run.

The lead Viking threw his axe at the first horse he saw, and he brought it down.

Anton had perhaps a second when he could have run, but he knew in his old soldier's heart that he was the balance between victory and defeat. His fellow knights—cavalry against the Viking foot soldiers—should in general have the advantage but that advantage could be negated by surprise. If he let the Vikings pour by him, then they could wreak havok in seconds—they'd strike down other horses as they had destroyed his, they'd cut down half the Larrazian force before those knights knew what hit them—and then the Viking superiority in numbers might well prevail.

If the Vikings won the battle they could seize Sandra.

That could not be allowed.

Anton blocked the path with his body. He thrust his sword out before him, and he roared, "You shall not pass!"

Sandra heard her lover's voice. She jerked around toward him and she let go of Elaine—she would have run to her man had not Elaine grabbed her—the women struggled—Elaine was only now shaking off the horror of her own ordeal but she knew she couldn't let Sandra go—

Roland had been trying to assimilate the unexpected images

of Elaine: naked, hand in hand with Thomas, blood on her breasts, hysterical—she had called for him but she had hardly fallen into his arms when he had rescued her—but then he knew he *hadn't* rescued her yet when he heard Anton's courageous declaration—the Duke ran back to his horse and caught the reins and mounted—

Thomas knew about the Northmen below but in the confusion of the Larrazian attack, fending off Fridriksson, Elaine screaming, he had not had a moment to mention them—but when he heard Anton he knew at once what was happening and he knew also that his left arm was not nearly good enough for blade work—he let the golden sword fall from his hand as he raced to where the young Norse archer had dropped his bow—

It took all of Elaine's strength to restrain Sandra. The Countess had come back to reality and she was quite aware of the situation—she would not let her friend run toward the attacking Northmen—

The path was so narrow that only three Vikings could attack Anton at once—three were still too many but it took them a while to overcome him—long enough—

Anton parried the blows—one, two, three, he was happy, one, two, three, he was holding them—then the two wing men attacked at once and Anton blocked beautifully, one long swing that clanged off both their swords—but the middle Viking, a lefthander, seized his chance as Anton's sword flashed past the center of its arc—the middle Viking thrust at that moment and drove his sword through the right side of Anton's chest—

Anton's sword arm abruptly lost its strength—he couldn't fight back but he refused to fall—

The middle Viking yanked his sword out and shoved the wobbling knight out of the way—the pressing warriors behind let out a howl of triumph as the impediment was removed—the twenty-one Champions surged forward on to the cliff bound plain.

Anton's gallant stand had lasted half a minute—and those thirty seconds made all the difference. The Vikings did not wreak havok on disorganized, surprised horsemen—instead they discovered a disciplined fighting cavalry—

Roland had been barking orders as he mounted and turned his horse—his men had fallen in behind him—now he led his knights in a swooping charge along the edge of the hill—he circled behind the Vikings as they rushed forward—he cut off their retreat as he cut off the heads of their stragglers—the Vikings were in the killing zone—

Thomas discovered that the two middle fingers of his right hand didn't work, but he nocked an arrow with just thumb and forefinger—he ignored the pain in his hand and drew the arrow back—he grinned as he watched Roland's maneuver—he aimed at one of Anton's attackers, he let fly, and his aim was true—Thomas nocked another arrow as his first victim fell—

Sandra had seen Anton's chest pierced, she had seen him flung aside, she had seen him spin and slowly fall. She tried to get to him but someone held her—

The Vikings didn't know what to do. They were no match for the swirling knights, and those who tried to run were cut down by some bloody handed archer. The Champions slashed wildly in their confusion, but to no avail. They did succeed in killing three Larrazian knights—but not one of their own number escaped his mark of doom.

When there were only a few wounded Vikings still standing—and those clearly on their way to death—Elaine let Sandra go.

The girl ran across the bloody field, looking only at her fallen man—

Elaine might have let her go too early, for one of the wounded Vikings still had a sword in his hand and rage in his dying heart—he slashed at Sandra as she went by, but the blow lost its force when a timely arrow from Thomas's bow shattered his wrist—the sword tumbled loose of his hand and ripped through Sandra's skirt, but her skin was untouched—

Sandra heard the fabric tear but she didn't stop for such a trifle—

She ran in a straight line, and if corpses blocked her way she jumped over them—

She reached her man.

Sandra threw herself to her knees beside Anton. She looked at his face—and she stared in disbelief. His dark blue eyes were clear and he was smiling at her—and then understanding came as she realized that he was in shock, that right now he was feeling no pain—she looked down and saw the foamy blood from his pierced lung decorating his chest—she heard the awful sucking sound that the wound made with each breath he took—she looked again at his unmarked face, at his brave smile, and then suddenly she couldn't stand it any longer, she began to cry, she bent down and let her tears fall on her lover's face, she gathered his head in her arms and held him tenderly—she looked at her man through blurred eyes and then she bent down farther and kissed his lips.

The kiss was sweet but Anton turned his thoughts away—he didn't have much time and he had to think of the future that Sandra would face after he was gone.

Chapter 142

RICHARD'S TRIUMPH

As Ivar was killed on the shore, so another attack was silently prepared on the sea. Richard's warship was almost close enough . . .

The Vikings on their longship heard the clamor on shore when their Chief was killed. They saw their comrades leave the beach and race up the narrow path to the west. They watched their friends overcome a lone knight—and then the Champions disappeared over the top of the hill.

Then there was only sound to tell the tale of battle—and what the sailors heard were the death screams of their friends.

The Norse sailors, staring sorrowfully at the shore, feared the worst.

There was always this danger when a quest took too long. On hostile land a Viking force could always be cut off from their great mother the sea.

That was why the quick hit and run raid was always the best.

Ivar's plan had been too slow and elaborate, and now he was paying the price.

The son, like his father, would never leave England alive.

Such were the thoughts of the Viking seamen. Some of their number were among the twenty-one survivors who had piloted Ragnar's ship home from Marvelsville fifteen years previously.

They thought that they might have to take this ship home the same way.

They thought that they would be *able* to take this ship home.

They thought that they had nothing to fear from the sea—they had no one looking in that direction, and so they had no warning—the first blow, utterly unexpected, shattered their illusion of safety.

The grappling irons bit into the skin of the longship like crunching metal teeth.

The Vikings spun around and saw that their ship was caught by a monster—a monstrous warship that seemed to have come up like a leviathan from the deep—and then an enormous red haired Englishman leaped onto their deck and drew his sword. He howled some command in his barbarous tongue—and then a hundred armed knights followed his lead, they leaped upon the longship, and as they drew their swords they opened their mouths and bayed for blood—

That's what the Vikings saw, and at five to one odds they didn't live to see much more.

The Vikings painted their deck with their blood.

The English took no prisoners and left no survivors.

When the short battle was over, King Richard took time out to survey the carnage. The sight pleased him—he smiled—and then he vaulted lightly over the ship's rail and splashed into the chest high sea. He held his bloody sword up above his head—he waded through the surf toward the rocky beach—he heard the splashes behind as his men followed him.

Richard had seen the Northmen on shore run up the hill—he guessed quite correctly that if he followed their trail he would find Elaine the Fair.

Chapter 143

THE DRINKING HORN

Elaine saw that Sandra had reached Anton safely. Then the Countess looked back down at herself—and the red horror she saw shocked her mind back toward the paralyzing hysteria she had felt earlier—she could think of one thing only: she had to get rid of the blood.

Gunter had dismounted to finish off the last dying Viking. He used a savage two handed sword blow for the coup de grace— the Viking toppled from his knees to the ground, and as he went down a drinking horn fell out of his monk's cassock. Gunter had barely had water for the last hectic day of the chase and he didn't pause to examine his good fortune—he just picked up the horn, unstoppered it, and took a long draught. The Larrazian knight enjoyed the good hard liquor—it burned all the way down—and then he felt guilty, he felt that he should share his find—

Elaine felt the alien touch of blood on her breasts, blood dripping down her belly and congealing on her skin—blood to remind her that she had just killed two men—

Gunter looked around and saw the naked Countess of Anjou, the future Duchess of Larraz. She was all alone and she looked like she needed a drink. Gunter could hardly believe his good fortune.

Elaine stood, frightened and very still—she hardly recognized herself and she didn't know what to do—

Gunter saw the blood on her body as he approached but like Roland earlier he saw it was not her own. The touch of red did not disturb the knight—he saw only beauty. He remembered how he had tried to picture Elaine when he had guarded the cabin at the end of the flowered path—he had conjured some naked visions, but he saw now they fell far short of reality—she was far more beautiful than he had ever imagined.

Elaine felt a man's shadow come over her but she couldn't talk to him when she was like this. She didn't raise her eyes.

Gunter was right in front of her—he saw that she didn't notice him—something was wrong—he didn't think anyone, including himself, should see her like this—he wanted to protect her—he would give her a drink to cheer her up, and his shirt, so she could cover herself.

"Milady."

Elaine jerked as though she had been struck. She looked fearfully at the man in front of her—and then she relaxed a little when she saw that his eyes were kind.

"I have brought you a drink, Milady—please hold it," Gunter said, and Elaine automatically reached out and took the proferred drinking horn. "There you go—now let me give you my shirt, so you can cover yourself."

Gunter turned away as he started to remove his shirt, so that the Countess would not be embarrassed by his gaze.

Elaine held the half full drinking horn in her hand—and then she suddenly realized that her problem was solved. Her mind cleared—she gave a silent prayer of thanksgiving—she said, "Kind Sir"—but Gunter's shirt was about his ears and she realized he couldn't hear her—now he had it off, and Elaine started again, "Kind Sir, thank you"—Elaine took the shirt that he held out to her but she made no move to cover herself—she went on, "I have left my white nightgown over by that oak"—she gestured toward the gallows tree—"Would you please get it for me?"

"Of course, right away, Milady," Gunter said—he turned past her, and even though he thought he shouldn't, he took one last look so that he would remember her forever—and then he set off at a trot to fetch the bit of silk.

Once he was on his way Elaine unstoppered the drinking horn. She poured the liquor carefully, a few drops at a time, over her breasts and down over her belly. The alcohol burned wonderfully on her skin—and then she scrubbed herself clean with Gunter's rough shirt—when the liquor was gone so too was Elaine cleansed of all the blood.

When Gunter came back, she smiled at him, for she recognized him now—she handed his shirt back to him, and if he had looked twice before he looked a third time now—he looked at the white and pink perfection of her body, and then he handed her the silk nightgown—he kept looking with wondering eyes as she pulled the nightgown over her head—he watched as it fluttered down her body, and then he looked up at her face, at her smile, at Elaine the Fair in the full consciousness of her beauty, and he slowly went to his knees.

She gave him her hand to kiss.

He touched her with his lips—and so took another memory for a lifetime.

Then Gunter stood up on legs that threatened to fail—he said, "I must see His Grace now," because that was all he could think of to say—he walked away like a drunk—he saw Roland riding over near the path that the Vikings had come up—and then Thomas yelled a warning, the short lull ended, and Gunter ran for his horse.

Chapter 144

A CALL FOR A PRIEST

Thomas had seen the glint of a high held sword.

"Duke of Larraz," he cried, "there's more coming up the path!"

Roland had been looking back over the battlefield, making sure that all of the enemy were dead—but when he heard Thomas's cry he suddenly thought of the twenty Vikings left on their ship—they must have come to aid their friends—the Duke spun in the saddle as he thought, his sword already in motion—with the quickness of thought his sword described an arc—the blade flashed down toward the face of Richard Lionheart, and if the King had not had such distinctive red hair, his royal countenance would have been forever ruined.

Roland recognized that famous hair and slowed the stroke that he could no longer stop—that slowing gave Richard the second he needed to parry the blow.

The two bloodstained swords clanged together and stopped before the King's face.

Roland looked down through the crossed swords and said, "Welcome, Your Majesty."

"Your Grace," Richard replied formally.

The two men withdrew their weapons.

Roland looked quickly around him at the Larrazian knights who were racing to his aid. "Halt, halt!" he cried. "Friends!"

Richard likewise spread his arms to stop the rushing English knights behind him.

"What of the Northmen we saw climbing this hill?" Richard asked.

"All vanquished, Your Majesty," Roland answered. "And what of the Northmen on board their ship?"

"We came by sea," Richard replied with a smile. "We boarded their ship and slew them all. Then we came up here to search for your Countess—how is she?"

"She's here, Your Majesty," Roland replied, gesturing behind him (he had noticed Gunter's kindness). "She's perfectly safe now."

The Duke had taken a position that blocked the path. Now he began to move his horse out of the way, so that Richard and his men could come up onto the plain. In the confusion of battle and suddenly encountering Richard the Duke had not thought of his deal with the King—but as Richard began his next question he remembered all in a rush.

"And have you—"

Richard is going to ask me about Thomas, Roland thought, and I have no answer but I did see the golden sword lying on the ground somewhere—

A small figure scampered in front of the King and interrupted him in midquery.

Roland was greatly relieved. I can use this little time, he thought.

Richard was thoroughly annoyed. He scowled down at the young woman who had come so close for her curtsy that she practically banged his knees.

"What is this?" he snapped.

The girl—Sandra—straightened up and met his angry gaze. "Your Majesty, my lover is gravely wounded," she said urgently. "He needs a priest now! By the grace of God, do you have a good Father with you?"

Richard decided that the simplest way to get rid of this feminine irritant was to grant her wish. He turned to Brian, who was as always close at hand. "There is no danger here," said the King. "Fetch the Archbishop."

Brian gave a surly grunt and started back down the path.

Richard spoke to Sandra. "God is with you, young lady. Wait with your man. The prelate will be with you shortly."

Then the King, ignoring Sandra's fervent, "Thank you Your Majesty!" brusquely pushed past the girl and strode on to the battlefield.

Sandra looked at the King's back for a moment, and then she ran back to Anton. She knelt and took his head in her arms again—she cried again when she saw the pain in his eyes—the shock was wearing off—his death was coming but he was fighting it—she saw him trying to frame a question so she quickly answered it before he wasted energy on words—she said, "Yes, a priest is coming soon," and then she made herself smile. "Not an ordinary priest either—'tis the Archbishop himself!"

Anton tried to smile in return, and Sandra kissed his brave face.

Meanwhile Roland had dismounted and walked over to where he had seen the golden sword. He picked it up and took it over to the King, who was contemplating the dead body of Saladin with satisfaction.

"Your Majesty," Roland said, "I promised that when I saw you again, I would have your golden sword in my hands." Roland offered the weapon to the King. "I now fulfill my promise."

Richard's eyes lit up as he took the sword. Roland pressed his advantage—he continued quickly before the King would think of asking about Thomas's fate.

"Now you must excuse me, Your Majesty, for the Countess has suffered grave shocks and I must comfort her for a minute." Roland turned away before the King could reply. The Duke was thinking quickly and accurately as he walked away. He looked once at Anton and saw that Sandra was still ministering to him. It was good that his friend was still alive—but Roland had seen the sword thrust and he knew that Anton couldn't last much longer. Roland needed to go to him—but love and justice were his first priorities.

He had to go to Elaine, and comfort her, as he had told the King.

He had to talk to Thomas, and try to save his life.

Roland walked straight toward the lady he had loved for so many years. He saw her in all her beauty, dressed now in her white silk nightgown—and Thomas was beside her, and as before she had taken his hand.

Chapter 145

DECISION POSTPONED

Thomas recognized the King of the English the same moment Roland did—Thomas was a little disappointed when Roland slowed his swordstroke.

The knight watched as the Duke and King reverted to friendly terms—and then Thomas saw someone else and he realized that his battles today were not yet finished.

Thomas dropped the Norse bow that he held and walked over to Elaine. He held out his bleeding, broken right hand and said, "I can't fight like this. Will you bandage it for me?"

Why do you need to fight more now? Elaine thought, but she didn't ask the question for she noticed that Thomas was looking past her, he was staring at someone with great intensity—she turned and looked herself—she saw, partially blocked by Richard Lionheart's tall form, the hulking figure of Brian the Brutal.

She remembered Thomas's story—she felt the pain of Suleka, dying as she tried to protect her unborn child—she knew the answer to her silent question.

She took his broken hand between both of hers.

"I will do what I can to help you," Elaine said.

"Do you remember when I first kissed you?" Thomas asked.

"Yes."

"I told you a little about Brian then. You promised that you would come to watch me fight him—and so, when you didn't appear that next day, I knew for certain that evil had befallen you. I might have killed Brian that day, at the cost of my own life—but I stole the King's sword instead, and lived to rescue you.

"Now you're safe. You're here with me. I shall challenge Brian soon. You shall watch me fight him, as you have promised."

"Yes."

Thomas had still more to say. He continued, using every moment of this private time that he knew would be brief. "You told me, the night before last, of your lover. I met him once before—I knew him as a man of courtesy, and I know him now as a man of courage. In short he is a fine man—yet much has happened in this last day and I do not accept your decision in his favor as final."

Thomas's slate gray eyes bored into Elaine's, bored into her soul—she felt her hands suddenly wet with sweat as she held his—she had a sudden fear that he had somehow divined her thoughts from this morning—she had watched him dive for the King's sword and in her mind she had said, 'I love you Sir Thomas'—Elaine had to force herself to keep meeting Thomas's ferocious eyes.

"I ask that you make your final decision *after* I fight Brian. If I die, then your choice will have been made for you. Go in peace, marry Roland, have children with him, live a long and happy life.

"But if I live, then you will have to make a real choice. Go to Larraz with Roland, or stay here in England with me.

"I believe that I will succeed in killing Brian. When the battle is over, I shall need to know your final decision."

Elaine had gathered her own courage, and she had been thinking rapidly as she listened to Thomas. Now she looked straight at his savage face and spoke firmly. "I will postpone my decision—on one condition. If you survive, and if I choose Roland, I ask that you do not challenge him."

"I would kill him."

"If you fought him, yes, you would—but you would also kill any love that I feel for you."

Thomas saw that Elaine spoke the truth. "I accept your condition," he said.

"Thank you," Elaine replied. "I can now agree to your request. I shall postpone my decision until after your duel with Brian."

Thomas's heart had been broken when Elaine had told him about Roland—the pain had been enormous, and yet still he had not been shattered. He had held himself together to rescue her, and he had done his job well. Now he was being rewarded with the gift of hope. Perhaps the broken halves of his heart could come together again.

Perhaps he could yet know happiness—Thomas felt the hard knot of his sundered but undestroyed belief quivering again in his heart—she would choose him, he thought, and so he hardly minded when Roland came up to them.

"Elaine," said the Duke. "Are you all right?"

Elaine let go of Thomas's hand with one of hers—she put that free right hand around Roland's neck and drew him to her—she kissed his mouth, and said, "Yes"—she kissed him again and said, "I'm fine"—she kissed him a third time, and a fourth, but all the while she kept a firm grip on Thomas's wounded hand with her own left, she held him steady so that his pain would not grow worse.

Chapter 146

THE VOICE OF GOD

When Roland could finally draw breath after Elaine's kisses, he said, "I love you, my dear, and I am overjoyed that you are safe, but I must talk to your brave knight for a moment."

The Duke turned and looked at Thomas—immediately he felt that shock of recognition that had disturbed him beneath the rainbow—some connection to Elaine, he had thought, and then suddenly his marvelous memory came up with the answer. He remembered a young waiter at the English court—at that time the young man went by a different name.

Thomas saw the Duke react. "So you remember me," Thomas said, rudely omitting the Duke's title.

"Yes," Roland replied kindly, "but I see no reason to speak of the past. I have observed you and I have followed you these last four days—and what I have seen tells me that you are a true knight. God bless you for keeping Elaine safe."

"God bless you for coming when you did," Thomas replied.

"Thank you," Roland said. He looked down. "May I see your hand?"

Thomas let Elaine raise his hand, palm up, for the Duke's inspection. Roland touched the wound gently with his fingertips.

Elaine looked, not at the wound, but at Thomas's eyes. She saw them flicker with pain as the Duke found each of the broken bones.

"Hold his hand steady," Roland said to Elaine. The Duke tore off two long strips of cloth from his own fine robe, and then he gave the makeshift bandages to Elaine. She took them with her free hand.

Roland addressed Thomas: "You have two broken bones—the ones that extend up to your two middle fingers. You can't move them, can you?"

"No I can't."

"I'm sorry—but at least it was a good clean snap—I can't feel any loose fragments.

"This is what we're going to do: I'm going to fit your bones together as well as I can, and then Elaine is going to bandage you just as tight as possible—there's a good chance that they'll heal back together then. Are you ready?"

"Yes—and thank you."

"You won't thank me when I bring your bones together—it's going to hurt like hell. I could probably scrounge up some whisky for you if we had time—but we don't have time."

Roland looked over at Elaine. "Let go of his hand. I have it now."

Elaine obeyed. She tossed one of the torn pieces of Roland's robe over her shoulder—she held the other one ready. She watched as Roland's gentle fingers guided the loose bones under Thomas's skin.

"The King wants to have you killed, Thomas," Roland said as he worked. "I gained a little time by returning his golden sword, but I know that won't be enough to mollify him. I know him, you see—I know you frightened him when you took that sword, and he'll never forgive you for that"—there was a slight audible snick as the two halves of the first bone came together. Roland held the bones like that with strong fingers, while Thomas fought against the waves of sharp searing pain that made him want to tear his hand loose—but he kept his hand still. Roland kept talking as he sought the second break. "The King hasn't recognized you yet but as soon as he does you're a dead man—you can't fight a hundred English knights—and so that's why I'm doing this now—you've got to be able to ride"—there was another snick and the second bone came together.

"Wrap him as tight as you can, Elaine," Roland ordered.

Elaine laid the makeshift bandage over the wounded hand—and then she swiftly wrapped it around and around and pulled it tight. She performed her task well—she fixed the bones in their proper position—she kept her eyes on her work, so that she wouldn't see Thomas's pain racked face.

After she tied the knot, Roland said, "Now the other one—come over the thumb this time and overlap on an angle."

Once again Elaine performed as well as any nurse.

Roland began to talk again, rushing his words. "I saw the Vikings got your horse—I'm sorry—a magnificent animal—but don't worry—I'll bring my own horse over—you mount him and take off—as far as Richard knows you'll be dead—he's seen your horse too—I'll tell him the Vikings must have killed you—you'll be free!"

Thomas had been watching Elaine work over his hand, but now he slowly straightened up and looked at Roland. The knight's eyes were a frighteningly empty slate gray, as though he had willed them clear of any pain.

"No," Thomas said.

The single word was an absolute refusal.

Roland had no reply. Thomas went on: "I thank you again for your help with my hand. I had asked Elaine to bandage it even before you came over—but I did not need it bandaged in order to flee—I needed it fixed so as to be able to fight.

"I am going to challenge Brian the Brutal to a duel to the death."

For one terrifying moment Roland thought that Thomas was going to challenge him—but then he heard the name of the real foe and he wondered if Thomas had gone mad. How could the knight challenge a much feared man at arms with a useless sword hand? Even assuming the King would allow a fair duel— a large assumption—it was still suicide.

"Why?" Roland asked.

"He killed the first woman I loved. Her name was Suleka, and when she died, she was carrying my child."

Roland nodded slowly—he understood but he saw no hope for Thomas—he could not force the man to save himself—there would be more death this day.

As Thomas explained his refusal, so Brian returned with the Archbishop. Behind them walked Arthur the Assessor.

The Archbishop stepped out on to the battlefield. He heard Sandra's call from a few paces away—he went over and knelt by her wounded knight. He found a man who was clinging to life by sheer force of will—a man who refused the last rites—a man who suggested, instead, rites of a different order.

Meanwhile the Assessor stopped at the edge of the battlefield and looked for his wife (for so he still thought of her). He spotted her quickly—he also noticed that she was with Thomas and the Duke of Larraz—he decided that it was best not to go over to her just yet.

Brian noticed the direction of the Assessor's gaze, and he immediately picked out the figure of Thomas with a bandaged right hand.

Brian took a moment to recall that Thomas was righthanded, and then he smiled and yelled, "Your Majesty! Look over by the Countess!"

No one else could have given the King that kind of direct instruction.

All conversation stopped on the field of battle.

Richard and everyone else looked in the direction that Brian pointed.

The man at arms spoke again, just as loud as before. "The one with the bandaged hand, Your Majesty—that's the little birdie who flew away from the Holy Land—the thief who stole your sword—shall I kill him now?"

Richard smiled as he looked upon Thomas.

This day was turning out to be quite pleasant for the King. A lovely victory first thing, his sword returned, and now this opportunity for revenge. This time the evil commoner had no horse, no tricks, not even a right hand. His death was assured—only the manner of his execution had to be ordained. Richard savored his choices. He could let Brian do the job; he could do it himself; or perhaps it would be even more fun if he made Roland fulfill his pledge! Yes, that was it! He'd make that smooth politician dirty his hands and pay the price agreed—

Roland saw the King looking at him and he didn't wait. He stepped forward and his voice boomed just as loud as Brian's.

"Your Majesty: The man next to me has earned knighthood by any standard in the world. Outnumbered by Northmen seven to one, he nonetheless kept our beloved Countess alive and safe. Without him Elaine the Fair would be dead! He deserves—"

"He deserves nothing!" Richard roared. "The man is a commoner who only poses as a knight. He is a thief without respect for his superiors. He must die now!"

All Roland knew was that he couldn't kill Thomas. If he drew his sword now, it would be to fight the King. He reached over and touched the hilt of his weapon—

Larrazian knights, watching, followed their Duke's lead—

English knights did the same—

Elaine didn't have to count heads to see that the odds were at least six to one against the Larrazian force—she could see the

tension in the men—she knew that a sound, a careless movement, almost anything could trigger a massacre—

Given Richard's anger and Brian's bloodlust, that something
would have come very soon—had not a new voice suddenly filled
the air.

Brian, Roland, and Richard had all yelled to make themselves
heard across the battlefield. This fourth voice was quieter, and
yet somehow far more penetrating.

If it is true that God can speak through man, then it is certain
that that day God spoke in the voice of the Archbishop of
Canterbury.

"Your Majesty," the Archbishop said, rising to his feet by
Anton's recumbent form, "Gentlemen: I have just received the
last wish of a dying man. I am about to grant that wish—I am
going to preside over vows of holy matrimony. I believe that it is
self evident that such vows can not be given while the climate is
stirred by violence. I ask for a little respect."

The Archbishop looked over the crowd, until finally his eyes
rested on Richard Lionheart. "As for this man you accuse, Your
Majesty, I see no need for a summary execution. I see that the
gentleman is unarmed—likewise he has defenders who should
be heard. I believe that the simple solution is for Your Majesty
to take him into custody. Then later, when tempers have cooled,
you may deal with him as the law requires.

"For now, let me minister in peace to the brave spirit who is
about to leave us."

Not even Henry II would have argued with that voice.
Richard said, "As you wish," quietly to the Archbishop, and then
he turned to Brian. "Take the villain over to that tree and tie
him up—we'll deal with him later."

Thomas whispered urgently to Roland: "You see that
Northman on his back with the sword through his heart—that's
my sword—take it out and keep it ready for me."

The Duke nodded.

Brian came up with a length of rope from an untended
Larrazian horse. He was eager for a fight—but he was disappointed.

Thomas made no protest as Brian seized him by the right
arm—he marched as directed to the gallows tree—he didn't say
a word when his back was slammed against the trunk—he submitted patiently as he was bound—he didn't cry out at Brian's
parting kick to the kneecap.

Thomas thought only of the Archbishop's Godly presence and calming words—words that even the King was constrained to obey. In his head he heard again, 'deal with him as the law requires'—he put aside the fresh pain in his knee and the throbbing in his hand—he thought of his chance for justice, coming soon.

He almost smiled as he realized that for the first time in his life the law was on his side.

Chapter 147

A WALK ACROSS A BATTLEFIELD

Elaine watched as Thomas was dragged away—and then she went up on her toes and kissed her lover on the cheek.

"Thank you for standing up for Thomas," she said.

"It was nothing," Roland replied quietly.

Elaine smiled and kissed his lips. "More than nothing," she said. She touched his hand. "Will you go with me to Sandra and Anton now?"

"In a moment my dear—you go ahead—I'll join you shortly."

Elaine kissed Roland once more and then she set off across the field of battle. She walked slowly, gracefully, clad in white silk—she stepped carefully around the corpses—knights stepped back to open a path for her—Elaine could not help remembering her ancestor the Countess Elaine of St. Valery—that lady had found a friend on the battlefield of Hastings, a proud mistress who had lost her lover—and now Elaine thought of Sandra, her dear friend and lover of Anton—'a dying man', the Archbishop had said—another brave lady was about to lose her lover.

Again, just like at Hastings long ago, there was a pure intense silence as all the soldiers watched the progress of the beautiful Countess.

Roland took advantage of the mass distraction. He went over to the Viking corpse that Thomas had pointed out, and discreetly removed the knight's sword. He cleaned the blade on the dead man's woolen trousers, and then he slipped the weapon inside his own belt.

Elaine came up behind Sandra. The girl sat on the grass, Anton's long body stretched out on his back to one side, his head cradled in her lap.

Elaine knelt by her friend's other side.

Sandra looked up from Anton and tried to smile.

Elaine put her arms around the girl and kissed each tear wet cheek—and then she just hugged Sandra for a long moment, but as she held the girl she looked down at Anton. She saw his proud face, lined with age and experience and pain—she saw how hard he was struggling to live—she gently broke the embrace, and when Sandra moved back, then Elaine could see all of Anton—she could see that the whole right side of his chest was covered with bright foamy aerated blood—she saw more bubble up with each sucking breath he took.

The sight was unbearable. Elaine turned back to Sandra and blurted out a question without thinking. "Is this your wish?"

She meant: Do you really want to marry this man, and become a widow in moments?

Sandra's face firmed immediately. She looked straight into her mistress's eyes. "It is our wish," she said calmly.

Elaine was embarrassed. "I'm sorry," she said to Sandra, and then she remembered her mother's words: 'she showed courage and did not shrink from the face of death'. She forced herself to look at Anton again. She saw that he bore her no ill will—she saw that he was long past being hurt by words.

Elaine bent down and lightly kissed Anton's lips—when she straightened up she had to fight to keep from crying.

"Is there anything I can do for you before your marriage?" Elaine managed to ask.

"Get the Duke," Anton said. The three words came at great cost—a cost that he really hadn't needed to pay, for before Elaine could react she felt Roland kneel down next to her.

The Duke reached out and touched Anton's better shoulder. "I am here, my friend," Roland said.

Chapter 148

SACRAMENT

The Archbishop had discreetly held back while the couples got together—but after a few minutes he stepped forward to organize the ceremony. Very quickly he received a big surprise.

"You are the *maid* of honor?" he asked Elaine.

"Yes, Archbishop," the Countess replied. "I must and I will make full confession after the ceremony—but for now I can only say, as God is my witness, I have never married."

The Archbishop considered saying, 'But I have known you as Arthur the Assessor's wife for five years!'—but then he looked at Anton's bloody shirt and he decided that this was no time to argue. He turned to Roland.

"And you Sir are the best man?"

"Yes, Archbishop."

The prelate looked at Anton and Sandra. "Are you quite sure that this is what you both desire?"

"Yes," they said together.

"So be it," the Archbishop said. He looked out at the crowd of soldiers beyond the bridal party. "Gentlemen: We are about to begin the ceremony. All those who wish to witness may gather round, but do not crowd the bride and groom."

There was a certain amount of shuffling as knights pressed closer. Everyone wanted to see this strange wedding.

The Archbishop looked down at the bride and groom. They were sitting next to each other now—Roland had his strong arm behind Anton's back, holding him up. The groom's shirt was a red mess—the bride's dress, since she had hugged her man, was not much better.

The Archbishop doubted that he would ever perform a more

unusual ceremony—but unusual or no, the prelate was certain of one thing: this couple truly loved each other.

The Archbishop cleared his throat—he looked up at the sky and let the spirit of the Lord fill him. Silence descended on the gathering—and then into that silence the Archbishop spoke the gorgeous words of God's sacrament.

"Dearly beloved, we are gathered together here in the sight of God, and in the face of this company, to join together this man and this woman in holy matrimony. . ."

Chapter 149

THE DEATH OF SIR ANTON

After the wedding was over—after Anton had kissed Sandra—the Larrazian knights marched off to the far end of the battlefield. They began to dig graves for their fallen comrades.

English knights wandered off to take souvenirs from the Norse corpses.

Richard drew Roland aside—the King had a new idea—the two leaders began to negotiate a fresh deal for their mutual advantage.

The Archbishop took Elaine's arm and led her to an isolated spot where he could hear her confession in private.

Thomas remained silent in his bonds.

All present acted with the utmost courtesy. They left the married couple alone with their love.

Sandra sat now, as before, with Anton's head in her lap, and she stroked his hair. She saw how shallowly he was breathing, his lungs no longer fighting to keep him alive, all of his battles over, his eyes closed—she thought of how beautiful the ceremony had been—all had felt the presence of God—she remembered how painfully Anton had struggled just to say, "I do"—now she was pleased to see how peacefully his life was ending—she watched as his breath just faded away—his pained chest ceased to rise—and then it seemed that her own heart seemed to stop, a gasp stuck in her throat and she couldn't breathe—then she gave a little choking cry, her heart began to beat again, she began to breathe again—she told herself again that she was glad, it had been a gentle passing without pain—and then suddenly his eyes popped open, bright blue, alive and happy—she would have screamed but the shock had stolen her breath again—Anton smiled, as though to reassure her, and then he spoke, with no strain in his voice now. "Promise that you'll name the boy after me," he said. Sandra gasped once and then she got her lungs working again—she looked into those bright clear eyes, and then she said "O of course I will, my love, of course I will!" She bent down and kissed Anton, she hugged him—but then she realized he was cold—she looked and saw that his eyes were closed again—he was O so heavy now—he wasn't breathing—he was gone.

She touched his face, serene in death. She knew now that he had truly given her all that was best in him. He had touched her soul, and she had conceived.

A child was forming in her womb.

Chapter 150

ABSOLUTION AND PARTING

Elaine confessed everything to the Archbishop.

When she was finished, he said, "I cannot order any penance for you, Countess, for you are truly a lady who has suffered more than enough for your sins. I must say that if you wish, I will accompany you to the King—you could tell him what you have told me, and I am sure that he would punish Arthur for his crimes."

"I do not want that, Good Father," Elaine said. "I only wish to leave him in peace—I wish to start a new life."

The Archbishop put his hand on her head, and blessed her, and then he said, "Go forth, my child, and sin no more. I will announce the annulment of your marriage."

Elaine took his hand in both of hers—she drew it down to her lips, and kissed it, and then she said, "Thank you again, Archbishop, but please say nothing until I have told him good-bye."

The Archbishop nodded his assent.

Elaine stood up straight and tall—she gave the Archbishop a smile, a dazzling smile—and then she turned and set off toward her false husband. She recalled the many faces of Arthur as she approached him: her childhood companion, her savior, her first lover—and then later, the man who could not love her, the man who had her kidnapped, the man whose distant fingers had tied her to the stake—

Elaine stopped right in front of Arthur the Assessor.

"I know everything and I have confessed all," she said. "I know you hired the Vulture to kidnap me. I know you planned to kill Sir Thomas."

Elaine saw that Arthur's eyes were cold and empty—there was nothing between them any more. Suddenly she wanted to hurt him very badly.

She moved even closer to him, she advanced until she was stopped by his swaddled belly—she put her hands on his shoulders—she leaned forward so that her breasts were almost touching his chest—her mouth was just inches from his, and then she whispered, "The Archbishop has given me absolution. I am free of you."

This struck home. Arthur hated to lose a possession. Elaine saw pain in his eyes—but then she understood that his pain was only for himself—he cared not at all that she had suffered—understanding that, Elaine felt her anger turn to black hatred—and then suddenly that harsh emotion brought back the terrible memory of the demon mask—she remembered the big heavy man with the commanding voice who had saved her—Elaine moved her hands to Arthur's face, she touched him gently—she started to kiss him good-bye but then she felt in the tightness of his features that he didn't want her kiss—even her touch was repugnant to him—she learned now at the end that he had never truly wanted her touch—she stopped herself, she released him—she said softly, "In some way I shall always love you," and then she turned and walked away. She looked over at the Archbishop and waved once.

The Archbishop spoke, and as before his quiet voice stopped all activity on the battlefield.

"I speak to His Majesty the King, to the knights of the English court, foreign warriors, and all others who are concerned—I speak for the one true Church. I have found that the Countess of Anjou, Elaine the Fair, has never been married in the eyes of God. I have annulled her union with the Count of Anjou, Arthur the Assessor.

"The Countess is a free woman. The Church stands ready to bless any true marriage she might make in the future."

This was indeed a joyful announcement! English knights felt fresh hope—Roland and Thomas were well pleased that their road was clear to unencumbered happiness (each discounted the chances of his rival)—Richard savored Arthur's humiliation.

Elaine turned away from the ever more desirous looks. She saw someone who needed help—someone who had loved her for many years. She walked over to Sandra and sat down beside her—she embraced the weeping girl—she did what she could to comfort her friend.

Chapter 151

THOMAS'S COMMAND

As Elaine comforted Sandra, Thomas came to the decision that he had waited long enough.

He had seen the wedding, and then he had watched as: the Larrazian knights dug four graves; Elaine made her confession; Richard and Roland came to some sort of agreement; Elaine said good-bye to Arthur; Anton died; and Elaine was set free by the Archbishop.

That last announcement was sweet but Thomas turned his thoughts away from future happiness. He made himself look at Brian—he saw his enemy, sitting on a large flat rock, pouring liquor down his throat from a captured drinking horn.

Thomas let his last memory of Suleka come back: he saw again her broken bloody hands pressed to her wounded belly—her last act in life had been an attempt to protect their unborn babe.

He let the steaming lust for revenge grow in him until he could barely control it—he knew that if he kept looking at Brian he wouldn't be able to control it—he looked for the man who had given him a chance for justice—he saw the Archbishop walking toward the graves to prepare for the coming funeral—he felt the rage choking him but he fought it down—he ignored the ropes that bound him—he fixed his eyes on the man of God, and his words came out as a precise command.

"Archbishop! Cease your steps!"

The Archbishop stopped in his tracks and turned to look at Thomas.

Everyone turned to look at Thomas.

The prisoner looked only at the Archbishop. "It is not yet time for burial," Thomas said. "There is one more grave yet to be dug."

The Archbishop had no answer for this, but he didn't have to come up with one, for a huge man began to move in the stillness and silence—Brian the Brutal stood up, took a last pull at the drinking horn, and threw it away.

"The little birdie's ready to die," he said.

Chapter 152

THE TRIAL

The knights had formed into a big circle that enclosed most of the battlefield. The area inside the circle had been cleared of corpses: the fallen Larrazian knights awaited burial by their graves on the landward side of the circle—the dead Vikings had been stacked up near the cliff edge.

In the center of the circle, about fifty feet from any spectator, were four men: Thomas (unbound now), Roland, Brian, and Richard.

Richard spoke to Thomas, but his voice was loud enough for all to hear. The King came straight to the point. "You are accused of impersonating a knight—you are accused of assaulting your King—you are accused of theft.

"I have seen with my own eyes that all these charges are true—but before I pronounce judgment on you, I will allow you, in accordance with the law, the chance to speak.

"Do you have anything to say?"

"Yes, Your Majesty," Thomas said. "I do." Thomas looked straight into the King's eyes. "Your father, His Majesty Henry II, gave our people the right to a fair trial by jury. Yet I do not request that—I appeal to an earlier law—an ancient law that stretches back to the days of King Arthur and the Knights of the Round Table.

"I speak of the ancient privilege of trial by battle.

"Under this law, which has never been repealed, I have the right to challenge Your Majesty's representative, and so argue my case in combat—for it is well known that God strengthens the arm of the righteous.

"I challenge Brian, your man at arms—I challenge him, not

just to prove my innocence, but also to right an old wrong. On August 20, 1191, Brian killed my lady Suleka—she was at that time pregnant with my child."

The crowd had been quiet before but there was a special quality to the silence now—it seemed that no one was even breathing.

Thomas went on, "For my part, Your Majesty, I do not raise my sword against helpless women. I say that I am the true knight, and Brian is the false one.

"By your leave, Your Majesty, let me engage Brian in a duel to the death. The victor, by our traditional law, will have proved his case."

Richard sensed that the crowd was with Thomas—at least they'd rather see a fight than an execution. The King looked at Thomas's bandaged sword hand and decided to be magnanimous.

"The right of trial by battle," the King said, "belongs only to knights—and you, 'Sir Thomas'"—the King's voice dripped with sarcasm—"have a most doubtful claim. Nevertheless, as a merciful King, I shall grant you this chance to prove yourself."

The King turned to the Duke of Larraz. "Roland, I see that you carry two swords—I trust one is for the challenger."

"Yes, Your Majesty."

"Give it to him."

Roland obeyed. Thomas took the weapon with his left hand.

"Brian, are you ready to accept this challenge?"

"I'm ready, Your Majesty." The man at arms grinned eagerly. He looked like a bullmastiff just before feeding time.

Richard spread his arms to include all the spectators. "Archbishop, Gentlemen, Ladies: We are about to witness an honorable duel to the death. Let neither of the combatants escape the circle until one has met his fate."

The King began to retreat from the center of the ring—Roland did the same—the two combatants were left alone.

"I commend you warriors to the hands of God," Richard said, as a place was made for him in the circle. "Let the true knight prevail. Let the battle begin."

Chapter 153

THE DUEL

Richard stood, watching, between two English knights.

Roland, Elaine, and Sandra formed another group in a different part of the circle. Roland had put a strong right arm around Elaine's waist—the Countess held Sandra in the same manner.

Roland put his mouth next to Elaine's ear and whispered, "King Richard has given us his ship—we will be able to sail to Europe just as soon as our tasks are finished here."

Elaine listened to her lover but she didn't take her eyes off the combatants.

She saw that Thomas lacked authority with the sword in his left hand. He made no move to attack Brian, who stood motionless for the moment, about six feet away.

Elaine observed that Brian wore a heavy vest of mail that protected him from throat to waist—Thomas had no armor of any kind.

Brian was bigger than Thomas.

Now Brian moved, with an executioner's sense of theater. He drew his sword slowly—the gleaming blade seemed to go on forever—finally it was free of the scabbard, and Brian held it out straight in front of him. All could see that it was a foot longer than Thomas's uncertainly held weapon.

Elaine looked at Thomas—he looked so frail and thin—his face was chalk white—how long had it been since he had slept?—she knew he hadn't eaten for a full day—he was wounded, he was crazy, he couldn't win, he was going to die—

Brian bellowed like a savage best and charged, sword first—

Elaine lost Thomas behind Brian's bulk for a second and for one moment of pure horror she thought her brave protector was dead—

Thomas barely managed to jump out of the way—

Before Elaine could get used to the idea that Thomas was still alive she saw Brian spin and aim a sweeping slash at Thomas's head—

Thomas ducked under it—he didn't try to parry because he had already discovered against Fridriksson that his left arm was not nearly good enough—one arm numbing shock like before and he'd be helpless—

Brian noticed that Thomas didn't dare cross swords with him. He began to slash, wide sweeping chest high strokes—Thomas couldn't parry them, and couldn't duck under them, so all he could do was give ground—

Elaine watched as Brian stalked Thomas. Each slash forced Thomas to jerk back—each retreat lessened the area of the circle that Thomas could maneuver in—

I'm not that quick with the left hand, Thomas thought, and not that strong either so I'm going to have to get close and I'm only going to get one chance—

Elaine watched as Thomas was driven relentlessly backward toward the far side of the circle—she felt herself shaking her head, she said, "No, No," but nothing got better, she could see Thomas was exhausted, he didn't even have the strength to hold his sword up, he just hopped backward at each stroke—and there was a sturdy line of English knights that he was going to bang against in another ten feet—they'd stop his retreat and the horrible sword would tear open his chest—

I move in the second just before the killing stroke, Thomas thought—

Elaine's hand, no longer a comfort, shook against Sandra's body—the young widow covered it with her own hand—the two friends laced their fearful fingers together—

Roland tightened his grip about Elaine's waist—he stepped forward a little in an attempt to shield her from what would be too painful to see—but Elaine shuffled forward herself, bringing Sandra with her—she *had* to see—

Brian slashed, sweating and grinning—the little birdie had room for maybe two more hops—

The third stroke kills me, Thomas thought, so I strike after the second—

Elaine saw Thomas hop back one more time, he didn't have any more space that she could see and then Brian's gleaming sword came slashing back—

The English knights in that portion of the circle had braced themselves to cut off Thomas's retreat—

Thomas leaped back away from Brian's whistling sword—he slammed into a knight who stood as solid as a brick wall—and then he kicked off that wall and flung himself forward as Brian came back with the killing stroke—

Elaine saw Thomas slam into the knight behind him—and suddenly her fear fell away—she knew Thomas by now—she had been hunted with him—she knew he was most dangerous at just this moment: when his back hit the wall. She felt herself start to smile as he flung himself forward—she remembered his duel with Sir Gareth, when he had guided his narrow bodied steed inside of the driving lance—she saw Brian's sword come around in what would have been the killing stroke—but Thomas, flying forward, was already inside the arc—

Brian corrected at the last second—his sword was going *around* Thomas—Thomas was inside his guard—too close! Brian yanked his sword back toward himself, his blade cut through Thomas's shirt and tore into the flesh of his back, but that was not nearly enough—

As Thomas felt the searing pain across his back he tilted up his low held sword and plunged it into Brian below the vest of mail, the thrust driven by the momentum of his short rush, driven even more by the pain behind—he forced his sword up through the drinking man's belly—forced it up through Brian's body until the point found the assassin's heart—

Elaine saw the two men embracing in a grotesque bearhug. Thomas had got his right arm around Brian's neck—he was clamping Brian down on the embedded sword—Brian was mortally wounded but he refused to die—he kept sawing with his sword at Thomas's back—each man kept pulling his foe closer—they swayed together like drunken dancers—they spun all the way around, so now Elaine was looking at Thomas's back—a sheet of blood pouring down it from the gash that Brian was working deeper—Elaine could see Brian's gargoyle face now, his wide open mouth—and then a convulsion shook the assassin, his sword beat hard against Thomas's back and then dropped from his fingers, his arms flopped loose to his sides, and a torrent of blood shot forth from his open mouth and splashed over Thomas's face.

Thomas was blinded. He screamed in primal terror—he let go of his sword, let go of Brian's neck—he stepped back, scrabbling at his face, trying to clear his eyes—

Brian rocked back on his heels and then rocked forward—but he didn't fall. A strange otherwordly determination spread over his countenance. He gained control of his hands with a monstrous will—he slowly moved them to the hilt of the sword that was killing him—he began to draw it from his guts—he would take the little birdie with him—

Thomas scrubbed frantically at his eyes with his bandaged hand and finally one sticky lid popped open—he saw what he could barely believe—he saw Brian pull the last inch of blood red sword out of his stomach—saw the monster start to come for him—Thomas screamed again as Brian pointed the bloody blade at his heart—he couldn't fight death itself without a weapon—and then he remembered Brian's sword dropping down his back—he reached down and seized the weapon with his left hand as Brian lurched forward—as Thomas stood up, Brian thrust at his heart, but the blade never got there for Thomas extended his left arm and poked the point of the monster's own sword into Brian's right eye—the widening blade caught in the socket of the skull and stopped Brian's charge—the shorter sword ripped Thomas's shirt but didn't touch his skin—

Thomas stared down the length of the long sword at the beast at bay—Brian couldn't reach him—Brian didn't have the strength to raise the shorter sword and cut at Thomas's extended arm—Thomas looked down at Brian's ever feebler slashes and then he looked with his one open eye at the one eye Brian had left. He said, "You're dead, Brian. I killed you."

Brian felt the sword scraping inside his skull and he didn't know why it didn't hurt. He felt his vision blur and then vanish from his remaining eye. He didn't feel his heart stop—for his last second of life was filled with pure terror for his immortal soul.

Thomas pulled the sword loose of the dead man's eye. The corpse dropped to its knees and then fell sideways onto the ground.

Thomas looked down at the dead body. He remembered someone else, dead on a dusty road—he remembered a smiling girl who drew the shape of a moon over her swelling belly.

"Rest in peace, Suleka," Thomas said, and then he dropped the long sword by the dead assassin.

He turned then to face his future—he looked at his lady of dreams, the lady he was now free to love—he started to walk toward her—

Elaine saw a specter with one gray eye alive in a blood smeared face—

Thomas said, "Elaine," and then he smiled and fell face down on the ground.

His hands didn't even move to break his fall.

Chapter 154

ANOTHER BANDAGE

Elaine freed herself of her lover and her friend—she ran to the true knight who had called her name.

She knelt beside Thomas. She saw that he was breathing steadily—the gash across his back was ugly but hardly fatal—he was going to live.

Elaine guessed that his fall had been caused by simple exhaustion—he had pushed beyond any natural limits of fatigue to do the tasks he had set himself—once those were completed, he relaxed, and then his overworked body just collapsed.

The Countess looked again at the twelve inch bleeding gash—clearly she needed to make another bandage for Thomas.

Elaine pulled Thomas's shirt off over his head and down his limp arms—once she got it off, she tore it into pieces. She discarded the bloody back of the shirt—the front she tore into handcloth sized squares—she tied the sleeves together to make a long bandage.

Preparations complete, Elaine called for alcohol, and an English knight brought her a flask. She poured some of the whisky over Thomas's wound—the burning pain snapped his eyes open—he tried to rise, but Elaine just told him to stay still, she spoke soothingly to him as she cleaned the cut with a piece of shirt. When she was finished she laid the cloth aside and placed the bandage over the wound—she did tell Thomas to raise up then—she brought the bandage around under his chest, and tied the free ends together against his side.

Then Thomas sat up to look at his love—Elaine took one look at his ghastly face and wet another cloth with whisky—she gently cleaned all the blood from his face, she even delicately cleaned his stuck eyelashes—finally Thomas showed two clear open eyes in a clean face.

"I love you, Elaine," Thomas said.

Elaine put her hands on his stubbled cheeks, leaned down and kissed his lips.

The kiss was heaven for as long as it lasted—Thomas couldn't understand why she broke it—there was sadness in her eyes as she backed away—she seemed to be receding as in a dream—Thomas wanted to reach for her but he had no strength to move—there was a shadow across her form—she moved back farther as someone else stepped forward and blocked her from view.

Thomas raised his eyes to the face of his King.

Chapter 155

RICHARD'S SPEECH

When King Richard looked down at Thomas, he saw the man who threatened his good cheer. This *had* been such a wonderful day—indeed, *before* the duel, the King had thought this might be one of the best days of his life.

One reason for the King's happiness (besides his victory and the return of his sword) was the great idea that he had come up with during the wedding. He had been thinking that he did not want to put to sea again with the drunken and fortunate Captain Barnes (who might as likely steer their ship to France as to London)—and then the King realized that he had a far superior alternative. He could return to London on land—he'd stop in every village on the way so that the people could admire their victorious King! He'd have the Northmen's heads cut off and mounted on pikes so that all could see the proof of his heroism. The people would bless him for protecting them from the evil raiders—and they would be happy (especially when confronted with one hundred armed knights) to pay any tribute that he would order the Assessor to obtain.

Then, too, Richard figured that he could also be paid on the other side of the slate. Roland had to want to get to Europe quickly with his lady—surely the Duke would pay handsomely to rent the good ship Lionheart.

After the wedding, the King had made his proposal to the Duke—and Roland had been just as eager as the King had expected. The Duke only asked for one boon—he wanted to be absolved of any responsibility regarding the killing of Thomas.

The King was in an expansive mood (the sum Roland offered for the boat rental was quite handsome indeed) and he was sure

that Brian could take care of the villain. The King graciously
acceded to Roland's request.

Then the perfect happy day was marred by Thomas's victory
in the duel.

Richard didn't mourn Brian (servants can always be
replaced)—but he was quite bothered by the reaction of the
Countess of Anjou. The way she rushed to Thomas afterward
was not a good sign. The King did not want all his good arrangements with the Duke to be ruined by some fickle woman's infatuation. After all the essential deal was this: Roland would
receive Elaine, with the King's blessing—in return, the Duke
would finance the King's coming invasion of France. Clearly the
deal could not go through if the lady threw herself away on this
disrespectful commoner turned knight.

The King decided that it was time for him to destroy this villain before the lady's eyes. She had no husband any longer—he
would leave her no alternative save Roland.

Richard smiled now as he looked down on Thomas—then just
for a moment he recalled the hard hand yanking his sword from
his grasp—his expression hardened, but he spoke—at first—in a
conciliatory manner.

"Sir Thomas, I congratulate you on your victory. You have
indeed proved yourself in battle.

"But I remember your master"—the King's tone of voice had
hardened now to match his face—"whose name you took, disobeying my orders due to his love of the infidels. I recall that
you joined him in that sacrilegious love.

"I remember your assault against my person—a capital crime
under any less merciful monarch.

"I see now that you have triumphed over my good servant, a
man who should have been your brother in arms.

"It is clear that you are not one of us, Sir Thomas, and you
never will be.

"I now pronounce my verdict: You may keep the name you
have chosen, and the title of knight—but you will remain forever landless, for never would I give even one acre to a man who
shares no common cause with his fellows. Likewise, you will
never serve again at court, for the court of the King is my property, and your disrespect is not welcome there. Finally, you will
never serve again in my army, for you do not honor the cross
that I stand behind.

"Go, Sir Thomas, go in peace—but after this day do not let

mine eyes fall upon you ever again."

Richard turned away, well pleased with his own efforts. He looked for Elaine, to gauge her reaction to the banishment—but all he could see of her was her back.

The Countess was walking away—she was headed for the edge of the cliff.

Chapter 156

HORIZON

Elaine had not been able to stand the look on Thomas's face as the King lashed him with each vicious word. It hurt too much to see his rage and helplessness and fear—she knew that he wanted to stand up and fight the King, but he was clearly well aware that if he tried he'd be cut down before he even made it to his feet. He stayed in place, sitting on the ground, while the purple robed bully warped his past and ripped at his future.

Elaine turned away—but she listened to the end. As soon as she heard the final banishment, she started to walk toward the cliff edge. She went to the left of the gallows tree (Saladin and the Norse corpses were on the other side)—she stopped with her bare toes just six inches from the precipice.

She looked down at the rocky beach. She felt no fear and her eyes were dry.

She looked out a little farther—she saw the dragon prowed ship with its red deck and collection of bodies.

She looked out farther still—she saw the King's ship waiting to take her to a new life—she saw a drunken man onboard, waving at her—she didn't respond, having no idea that he was the captain.

She looked out past the ships, far out to where the dark blue sea shaded into the lighter sky—she looked at that shimmering line where the elements of air and water met—she looked at that unknowable horizon, and then she tried to look beyond it— she tried to see her future—she sought some clue that would help her make her decision.

She knew that she had to make her decision now.

I love you Thomas, Elaine thought, I love your bravery and

your mad happiness and your stubborn confidence in the face of any odds—I know you as the cold killer too and I understand you that way and I love you that way too—I understand that if you were not that killer I would not be alive now—I've seen all sides of you, I've seen your gentleness and understanding as well—you could have raped me two nights ago, and few would have blamed you, but still you held back, you were a true gentleman while I hurt you with my confusion—I do love you, Sir Thomas, but how can I live with you? What will you do? The King was horribly cruel to you—he twisted your life—and yet he *has* that power. You have always acted as though you were above him—but that attitude has led only to this banishment. What will you become? A mercenary, as before: 'I fought other people's battles all the way across Europe,' you told me. Is that what you want to do, become a killer for hire? Is that to be your fame, your accomplishment? Am I to follow your trail of blood? Am I to bear children who will grow up with that heritage? Where is the greatness I used to see in you? I thought once that your name might come to be better known than that of Richard Lionheart himself—but now the King banishes you and I *can't* see a future for you. I see only a wanderer—O yes you would give me love—and I could love you—

But I love Roland. Roland, I love you for your wisdom and your patience. I love you for giving me this time now—no reproaches when I kissed Thomas, no move toward me as I walked over here—I love you for knowing what I want before I even know it myself—I love you for waiting five years until I was ready—I love you most for giving me the dream come true of the flowered path—I had not truly dared to dream of such a thing, yet you knew somehow that the desire existed in my secret heart—and you fulfilled that desire, yes you did, you gave me pleasure beyond imagining, you gave me your heart, you told me that I was your Duchess—

Elaine looked far out to sea, and in the distance of past and future she heard the gentle tones of her dear mother's voice: 'And all our children have been dark, until you, my dearest one, and it is you who will rise again among the nobility. . .'

Elaine's eyes filled with tears.

She turned around and started the long walk back.

Chapter 157

ELAINE'S DECISION

Thomas managed to get up after Elaine—and the King—had walked away. He found his longbow—he fixed it with a spare string from his quiver. Once he was satisfied with the pull, he slung the weaponry over his bare shoulder. He tightened the two leather straps that held bow and quiver—he thought that he was ready to ride off with Elaine, but then he realized that the little effort he had just expended was too much—his legs buckled and he sat down hard on the ground.

Thomas let the sky circle round for a while. He felt the throbbing pain in his back and in his hand. His head felt like a heavy rock—it wanted to fall forward onto his chest, but then he saw Elaine coming back to him, and that vision snapped his head right up—standing was another matter, but he put everything he had into the effort, and he made it to his feet on the second try.

Thomas dug in with his toes to keep the earth in one place. He looked at the approaching Countess and saw that she was crying.

Elaine walked straight up to Thomas and buried her face against his chest above the line of the bandage. She put her arms around him lower down—she slid her hands under his bow and quiver and embraced him with all her strength.

Thomas felt the gift of her body pressed hard against him—he felt her tears trickling down his skin and catching against the bandage—he put his left hand in the center of her taut back and held her gently—he used the thumb and forefinger of his right hand to smooth back one golden lock of hair.

"It's all right, Elaine," Thomas said, but the Countess just shook her head. A convulsive sob racked her body—and then she tilted her head back to look up at his face, but it was hard to tell what she could see, for her eyes were swimming with tears.

Thomas used his bandaged right hand to carefully dry her eyes.

Elaine began to shudder as Thomas did his delicate work—she didn't want his tenderness—she had to fight to stop fresh tears from forming—she tried to speak when he was done but she was shaking too much, she couldn't form words—and then Thomas reminded her of a rainy day long ago—he placed one finger across her lips, he stopped her panic—she looked up with clear eyes at his face, and she knew that she loved him.

Thomas took his finger from her lips, and he smiled.

Elaine told him her decision.

"I love you Thomas, I will always love you, and I will always cherish your love for me.

"But I love Roland too, I love him as much as I love you—and King Richard has given us his ship, we shall sail for Europe in an hour—I will go with Roland to Larraz. I will marry him and be his wife."

Elaine went up on he toes and kissed Thomas hard. Her left hand went behind his head, her right hand found his solid shoulder—she felt his strength, she imprinted the shape of his lips on her memory so that she would never forget him—and then she came back down, and she said, "I will love you forever—but I must go now."

Even as she said those last words Elaine saw the change in Thomas. He had been numb at first—he had let her kiss him, he hadn't responded—but now he knew the truth—he could see in her face that she had spoken the truth—he didn't argue or fight.

He accepted her decision.

Elaine watched him crumble.

Everything of his face that had been proud and strong seemed to topple inward—he had been broken before, but never destroyed, shattered like this—his nose looked as though it had been punched, his mouth had fallen loosely open, but his eyes were the worst—the hard slate had been broken down into a thousand bits of silt—he showed droopy wet gray eyes with tears flowing from them—and then he must have seen the horror in her face, he turned away, he shook and almost fell—and then he suddenly screamed like a wild beast, a cry from the depths of his soul, he walked away from Elaine, screaming, and then his feet turned and he came around in a circle, still screaming, he couldn't see her, he was just trying to fling the pain from him, he screamed louder as everyone stared—and no one dared move, save for Elaine: she walked carefully over to the Duke of Larraz, and he put a strong protective arm around her and held her close—Thomas kept howling, kept circling in tighter and tighter rings—he was spinning like a whirling dervish now, his scream had a birdlike pitch of terror—and then, just as suddenly as he had started, he stopped his cry.

Thomas took a moment to regain his balance—he shook off his self induced dizziness—and then he looked for Elaine, and he found her, but his eyes did not linger on his love. He looked instead at the man who held her.

Thomas walked up to Roland and the two men locked eyes.

Elaine could see that the hard slate was unbroken again—she wondered what it cost Thomas to look like that now.

Thomas spoke only to the Duke.

"If you do not treat her right," Thomas said, "I'll kill you."

Roland didn't flinch—he held Elaine with a steady arm—he calmly returned Thomas's stare.

"I'll treat her right," the Duke said.

"Then get me a horse! Your best horse!" Thomas screamed, and then he furiously turned his head to hide the flow of fresh tears.

Roland gave a quiet order—moments later a Larrazian knight walked the Duke's horse up next to Sir Thomas.

Thomas wiped his eyes and mounted. His face was still turned away—and then Elaine saw every muscle in his body go taut—he won some terrible victory, and then he turned back to face the lady he loved.

His face was composed and his eyes were clear.

He rode his horse up next to Elaine.

He put out his left hand.

Elaine reached out and touched his fingertips with hers—she looked up into his eyes, she hid nothing of her love—and then she said, "Good-bye, Sir Thomas," and she took her hand away.

Thomas snapped his hand back—he struck his horse a sharp blow on the flank. The animal jumped forward—Thomas leaned into the leap, and his demanding heels quickly pushed the beast into a gallop.

He rode away from the sea—he didn't look back.

Elaine could still feel his touch on her fingertips when he disappeared down the hill that Roland had ridden up so magically hours earlier.

'Your lover is coming,' Thomas had said, 'Call him.'

Elaine turned toward Roland—he wrapped her up in his big arms and pulled her close.

They embraced until they could no longer hear the racing hoofbeats of the vanished horse—until the Archbishop reminded everyone that there were somber duties still to be performed. "It is time for us to bury our dead," the prelate said.

Elaine thought of someone who had suffered more than herself—she turned away from Roland and saw Sandra, close by and utterly alone.

Elaine took Sandra's hand—Roland took Elaine's other hand. So linked, the three followed the Archbishop to the freshly dug graves.

Far beyond the funeral party, Thomas rode on towards nothing.

Chapter 158

THE EMPTY ROOM

Thomas kept rhythm with his horse as he rode—a four beat rhythm, four hooves, four words repeating in his head: I want to die, I want to die, I want to die. . .

He rode for an hour, heading nowhere with nothing but death in his mind—and then he suddenly remembered what Elaine had told him: 'We shall sail for Europe in an hour.' Thomas could picture them climbing aboard, Roland first, then he'd turn and help Elaine up over the rail—she'd fall into his arms and he'd kiss her, she would cling to him as the ship sailed away—

I love you Elaine and I want to die because I know that my vision is true—

You say that you will love me forever but that means nothing because you have left me for another man—

You love another man—

Thomas felt that he could look inside of himself. He watched as the last hard knot of his belief unraveled. He saw that sacred certain truth—that Elaine would come to love him—fly out an open window. He saw an enormous empty room that had once been filled with love—a room that stood now barer than a monk's cell—he wondered how he could ever fill that room—and then as he rode the answer came to him in waves of agony: pain fills the room when love has gone.

I want to die—

Thomas kicked free of his stirrups.

This isn't my horse—my horse is dead—I want to die—

The horse ran right out from under him. Thomas fell backward—a rock waited to smash his spine, but the quiver that hung down his back saved Thomas from that fate—he heard the cracking sound of breaking wood and then felt the thump as his head struck earth—he rolled over, and looked at the rock that should have killed him—and then he unbuckled a strap and took a look at his quiver. It was smashed, and all but two of the arrows inside were broken. His bow had slipped to one side, so it was all right.

He looked at the rock again—he looked at the splintered arrows that had saved his life—he looked at the two good ones he had left.

One more than I need, Thomas thought. If I can make the pull, drawing away from my body, then I need not depend on nature—I will be able to kill myself.

Chapter 159

THE DUCHESS OF LARRAZ

Roland and Elaine, Sandra, and the fourteen surviving Larrazian knights set sail for Europe on the good ship Lionheart.

Captain Barnes was drunk (his morning's vow of sobriety had lasted only until King Richard had left his ship) as was his crew—the ship yawed through the waves, but Europe proved hard to miss. They made landfall at sundown of the second day—they landed at a small town with a famous history: St. Valery.

So it came to pass that Elaine the Fair spent her first night in Europe in the town of her heritage—she dreamed of her great great great grandmother—she dreamed of an archer, and a garland of flowers—she dreamed of a daughter.

The next day Roland bought horses while Elaine bought clothes. After shopping and lunch the seventeen member party rode out of town—they rode past the castle where the first Countess Elaine had lived—they rode east, and they hardly stopped for fourteen days.

On July fourth they arrived at the Palace of Larraz—and they found what seemed to be every last citizen of the duchy waiting to greet them.

Rumor had flown faster than their horses—tales of Roland's quest had been filtering back for a month—the people identified with their good Duke, and they were thrilled to hear that he had succeeded, for his triumph was theirs—but still, what really brought the populace to the palace gates was the chance to see the most beautiful woman in the world.

Elaine did not disappoint.

Roland announced that he would marry the Countess in one month's time.

The month passed swiftly in a frenzied whirl of social activity. A thousand toasts were drunk to Elaine—a thousand times the Duke was congratulated—and then suddenly the day of the wedding arrived.

It was August 4, 1194.

The Archbishop of Larraz presided over the ceremony; Sandra, of course, was the maid of honor; Gunter was the best man; and all the people of Larraz were witnesses as Roland married Elaine.

A month and a half before, on a rose covered bed at the end of a flowered path, Roland had said, "You are the Duchess of Larraz."

His words then had the truth of prophecy—now his words had become reality.

The Duke kissed his Duchess.

The citizens cheered.

A marriage began.

Chapter 160

FEVER

Thomas was not able to kill himself.

He *was* able to bend his bow back, drawing away from his body—he aimed one of his two good arrows at his face, his eyes, he opened his mouth and let the steel point enter, he tasted death with his tongue—but then the presence of death brought back the living memory of Elaine. I love you Elaine, he thought—a mad thought really, she loved another, she had left him, still it was a true thought—I love you, I love you, I love you Elaine—that thought was stronger than death.

Thomas pulled the arrow away from his face and loosened the bowstring. He kept that arrow nocked, and he tucked the other one in his belt. He lay down on the ground. He closed his eyes and dreamed of Elaine.

When he woke up he cried for her, but she was gone—he stared at the enormous empty room in his heart, and he knew that he would never be able to find enough pain to fill that room—he wanted to die, and he couldn't kill himself.

Thomas wandered without thought or plan. He killed small game now and then (being careful to retrieve his arrows)—he ate without pleasure, wanting only to die—he slept often and happily, for then he could dream of Elaine—he always dreamed of Elaine, and he always woke up, and then again he would want to die.

Days passed, weeks passed, he lost all sense of time. His wounds healed well enough (though he still could not bend the two middle fingers of his right hand)—he could go where he liked, but there was nowhere on earth he wanted to go—his wandering described a slow circle over many days—he never strayed that far from where he had fallen from his horse—that was where he had called for death, that was where he still called for death—he wandered, and waited for it to come.

One night he was awakened by a cold summer shower. Thomas, who had no shirt (and his bandage had long since fallen off) was chilled to the bone—but he didn't seek shelter. He lay there in the wet grass and took the rain's beating—he called for death all night, and he heard the answer in his own burning throat the next morning.

Thomas was grateful at first as the fever took him down—but then he discovered that Nature is not a kind murderer. He had to endure the slow sapping of his great strength—the ugly clammy cold sweat of midday—the wasting heat of night fever—the demons of delirium.

He wanted it to end long before he had fallen all the way to the bottom—he was finally ready to kill himself, but he found he no longer had the strength to draw back his bow—he tried, he tried again, but he could not do it—he got to his feet, he staggered a few steps, he thought that if he were erect he might somehow be able to use his weight to draw back the nocked arrow—but then he tripped, he fell face down—he fell into the pit of unconsciousness.

He would surely have died soon had not Arthur sent men to kill him.

Chapter 161

ARTHUR'S INSTRUCTIONS

Arthur was back in the Palace of Bermondsey, stroking his own hatred.

He hated Elaine—the duplicitous bitch had had *two* lovers (Arthur would never believe that he had been wrong about Thomas) and then she had left him in full view of the King and the knights of the court.

Arthur hated Roland—not only had the treacherous Duke taken Elaine away, he had also undermined Arthur with the King.

Arthur hated Richard—the vicious bully had presided over and approved all of his humiliation.

But most of all, Arthur hated Thomas. Thomas was the vile seducer who started Elaine on the path to adultery. Thomas was the one who ruined their perfect marriage. Thomas was the one who saved Elaine from just punishment by the Northmen. If only she had died, Arthur thought, then I would have received such an outpouring of sympathy! But instead, Thomas saved her, kept her alive so she could humiliate me—and so I was exposed as a cuckold and left behind like a second or third choice—all of this is Thomas's fault, and he must pay.

Arthur's mood was foul, and the constant pain in his pierced stomach did nothing to improve his disposition. He found that he could no longer tolerate the good food and wine that he had formerly enjoyed—any decent meal caused him to retch horribly. He was forced to live on milk and mashed children's food—he hated it, and the fat assessor grew thinner every day.

Arthur could not even play his "game" any longer—his lucky gold sovereign was gone and anyway traveling was not good for his stomach.

Knights treated him with contempt—they refused to undertake any tax raids for him.

The King ordered Arthur to use any means available to bring in more gold.

This order finally gave Arthur something he could turn to his advantage. At Arthur's urging, the King signed some writs authorizing deputy tax collectors—the Assessor took the writs into the city and did some recruiting.

The first two men that Arthur hired were a pair of hardened criminals, associates of the late Vulture. Arthur showed them the writs—he explained their duties, and assured them that they would have the full backing of the crown.

Arthur marked the town of St. Lyons for destruction. This choice was no accident—St. Lyons was the nearest town to the battlefield that had marked the end of his marriage (the gallows tree to which Thomas had been tied was the traditional place of execution for the few miscreants St. Lyons produced). On the way back to London with Richard, Arthur had noticed a riderless horse join their caravan—even though a knight quickly mounted it as though it was his own, Arthur was sure that it had been Thomas's horse.

Thomas, wounded and on foot, was probably still in the same area.

There was a chance for perfect revenge—but of course the King had to be satisfied first, for Arthur had no intention of losing his position.

With those facts in mind, Arthur gave his instructions. He told his deputies that they would sail to St. Lyons on one of the King's warships (Richard had been sending his ships around the country to impress young men into his army—he was preparing for the invasion of France). They would be let off at the dock with an appropriate show of force. Then they had carte blanche to sack the town. The Assessor recommended that they confiscate a wagon to carry their plunder—or taxable goods, he should say. They were then to proceed overland back to London.

Arthur promised the criminals a generous share of the loot— the two thieves were delighted with their new commission. This was a real treat! They could steal in the King's name, with utter impunity.

When they were fairly hooked, Arthur whispered his special request. He described Sir Thomas precisely—he noted the wounds that marked the knight's body—he said that it would please him greatly if this man were killed—and he promised a rich reward. If they brought back Thomas's head, he would present *each* of them with a flagon full of gold.

Arthur had formerly offered one such reward for Elaine, alive—now he doubled the price for Thomas, dead.

The criminals grinned at each other.

They told Arthur that they would do their best to please him.

Chapter 162

TAX COLLECTION

Arthur's deputy collectors arrived at St. Lyons at noon on a summer's day. All the strong young men of the town were out on their fishing boats. Old men, women, and children stared in terror as the giant warship glided up to their dock.

The two criminals leaped ashore, grinning and carrying writs signed by the King—they stepped into the town, and they looted it.

They confiscated a wagon and loaded it first with all the wine and spirits they could find. Then they took hundreds of yards of nets that the women were mending—the pleading cries of these wives and daughters went unheeded, for the criminals were having too good a time. They thought next of ripping apart people's homes in a search for coin—they found little money, so they compensated by stealing any handmade treasure they could find.

The warship had sailed away by now—the people might have resisted, but the collectors each carried a sword and an axe—should a woman die to protect her property? And if they all fell on these men, and killed them, would not the King's forces come and raze the town?

One man only protested, when the criminals began to profanely handle his daughter—he ran to his daughter's cries, disregarding his sixty-three years—he saved his child from anything worse, and he lost his life.

After the murder, the two collectors decided they had enough. They hitched up two stolen horses to the stolen wagon and drove it out of town.

They headed for London, quite pleased with themselves.

An old man watched them go. He had been the Mayor of the town for so long that the people called him by his title instead of his name. He looked around at the destruction of the town that he had lived in for all of his seventy-five years.

The reserve nets were gone—that meant that any damage to the nets now being used would idle the fishermen—a blow the town's fragile economy could hardly stand. Another blow was the loss of their wine and spirits—the brackish local waters were far from pure—what would his people drink? Then too, there were the ravaged houses, treasures and savings stolen—but even that was not the worst.

The Mayor had only to turn his head—there was a brave citizen, dead in the street—his weeping daughter knelt beside his body.

The Mayor knew that he had to say something to his people—they would come to him soon for comfort and guidance—but all he could think of was the signature at the bottom of the looters' writs.

If I say what's in my heart, the Mayor thought, I will say this: God Damn Richard Lionheart!

Chapter 163

RAGE

The criminals had driven perhaps eight miles from St. Lyons when they saw the half naked body of a man. The still figure lay face down in the meadow by the cart track they followed. There was a dark line across his bare back.

The criminals felt a sudden quickening of interest—they stopped their horses, and then jumped down off the wagon.

They walked over and took a close look—and there it was: the twelve inch fresh scar across his back, just as Arthur had described it.

"That's Thomas," said one collector, almost dazed by his good fortune.

"Looks like he's croaked already," said the other one.

"Let's prick him and see," the first one said. He drew his sword and stuck the point into Thomas's side.

Thomas had been lying there for hours, waiting for his death. His head was full of fevered hallucinations, so when he heard the men he thought at first that the Grim Reaper was finally coming. Then he heard them talking and he realized with disappointment that they were just men—and then he felt the sword pierce his skin and it all became too much to bear. He had been waiting for death for too long—he simply refused to die by inches. He felt another prick—why didn't they kill him—he couldn't stand this—he felt an enormous rage pour through his body, a rage that gave him an insane strength—he rolled over violently—

The criminals had thought that Thomas was dead and unarmed—now they stared in horror as he came alive with a weapon in his hands—he had been lying on his bow and an arrow was already nocked—as he rolled the arrow came up—

Thomas got up on his feet as he drew the arrow back, he shifted it back and forth, aimed at the first one, then at the second, back and forth, and then Thomas asked, "Why didn't you kill me?" and he looked hard at the first one as though expecting an answer, and he released the arrow and the first one jerked away but he wasn't the target, Thomas had shifted and the arrow flashed through four feet of sunlight and tore through the second one's black heart, Thomas nocked his remaining arrow in the blink of an eyelash, he drew the shaft back, he aimed carefully at the first criminal and this time he screamed, "WHY DIDN'T YOU KILL ME?"

The villain had no answer, he would not have been able to speak even if he had an answer, he had never felt such terror, this knight was mad, inhuman, he had to get away—he turned and ran but Thomas was quite beyond chivalry, he released his bolt and the arrow drilled through the fleeing criminal's back.

Then Thomas staggered over to the wagon, he threw his bow inside—he hung on to the side, reeling, and then he saw an axe lying by the driver's seat, and suddenly he had a wonderful idea, he picked up the axe and weaved over to the first criminal, he raised the weapon high and brought it down in a great sweeping arc, then he pulled the blade out of the dirt and reeled over to the second criminal, he performed the same act, this seemed funny now, he laughed and laughed as he dropped the axe and picked up the two heads he had separated from their bodies—he carried the two heads over to the wagon, and tossed them in—he climbed in himself, and loosened the horses' reins—he twisted and half fell backward, he lay back on his side, he looked back at the staring eyes of the separated heads, his laughter was gone, he couldn't remember what was so funny, he felt so sad now as he looked at the staring dead eyes, "Why didn't you kill me?" he asked plaintively, and then his head fell against the wagon floor and just before he closed his eyes he said, "I love you Elaine."

Chapter 164

THE DEATH OF SIR THOMAS

The wagon horses, given no guidance, saw no reason to continue on to London. They thought of the good food they received in their home stables—they circled around and headed back toward St. Lyons. The load they were pulling was heavy, so they stopped often to munch grass—only to pull a little more when they remembered the much tastier grain they were missing. Their progress was sure, but very slow—the dreaming Thomas did not enter St. Lyons till well after sundown.

The fishermen of St. Lyons had returned as usual before dark—by now they had had hours to cry out in helpless fury.

Few citizens slept in the ravaged town—many were frightened when they heard the ghostly hoofbeats and the heavy scraping of laden wagon wheels.

One brave young fisherman named Paul seized a lit torch and went outside to investigate—and then he gave a glad cry, and another man ran out, and he too gave a cheer, more men came out, the women followed, and soon the whole town was out there in the street, they surrounded the wagon, they held their torches high, the sky lit up like carnival night—they stared in amazement at God's mercy, and God's justice.

They laughed as bold fellows held the heads of the looters up in the air—they drank toasts with their recovered wine—they cried over the nets that had been restored to them, but most of all they praised and blessed the sleeping unknown hero who stayed unconscious in the midst of all the excitement.

The Mayor made his way through the crowd. He saw what others, in their rejoicing, had missed. He saw the fresh dried blood under the man's side—he saw the marks of other recent wounds—he touched the man's forehead and was almost burned by the heat there.

"Clear the road!" the Mayor shouted urgently. "Can't you see this man's hurt? Clear the road!" The Mayor turned to Paul, who was standing close by. "Drive the wagon to my house," he ordered.

The young man climbed into the driver's seat and touched the horses with the reins to start them forward. The crowd parted to let them through. The Mayor walked in the wagon's wake. The men of the town fell back, a little ashamed of their boisterousness now—the ladies pushed forward to cluster around the Mayor. "What's wrong?" they asked, and "How bad is he hurt?" and "What can we do to help?"

The Mayor silenced them with a gesture—he replied to them all as he kept walking. "He's been wounded in a few places, one's very fresh, he's sick too—he must have the hottest fever I've ever felt—I need some fresh bandages right away, and some clear soup or thin broth as soon as you can make it—he's burning up, he has to drink something."

There was a quick chorus of "Yes, Mayor," and then the women hurried off to their houses to do his bidding. They felt their hearts fluttering with concern and excitement—they vowed to nurse the mighty stranger back to health.

Paul stopped the wagon by the Mayor's house. The Mayor opened his door—he held it open while Paul turned around and picked up the stranger. "Carry him inside and lay him on my bed," the Mayor commanded.

Paul carried his unconscious burden past the Mayor. The Mayor refused to let anyone else inside. When Paul came back from the bedroom, the Mayor said, "My servant is off visiting his mother in the country, so I'll need your help. Stay here by the door. If the ladies come with something useful, let them in—nobody else."

Paul nodded and took his position.

The Mayor went inside and sat on the edge of his bed. He looked down at the young hero. He saw a stranger's face, eyes closed but hardly relaxed, a man balanced between life and death.

The Mayor wondered whether King Richard and the Assessor would now try to punish St. Lyons. He didn't think so—judging from the state of those heads, the collectors had been killed far outside of town. Their bodies would be found—the blame would fall on some unknown bandit—they'll think the bandit took the goods—they'd never dream that he would take them back to us—they'll think that there's nothing left to steal here—it's doubtful that they'll risk more men to take less than nothing.

Some other town would be struck next.

The Mayor smiled sadly as he looked at the wounded warrior. "At least you saved us, young man," he said.

The man on the bed began to moan as if to answer—his feet kicked at the sheet to drive it further down the bed—his eyelids began to quiver—he was clearly about to wake up.

The Mayor placed gentle fingers on the fevered forehead. "Don't fret, young man," he said. "You are among friends, and we will take care of you. I am the Mayor of St. Lyons. Our town is in your debt.

"I would just like to know who saved us. What is your name, my son?"

The sick man heard the kind, calming words as a distant rumble through his delirium—nothing was clear until the final question.

He heard that—he wanted to answer—if he was alive he had a name, but there was simply too much pain associated with being Sir Thomas, a name taken from a dead man, the name now of a man dying of lost love, Sir Thomas was dying, dying—the sick man struggled with his soul to live—he no longer had the strength to bear up under a falsehood—once he had watched as a sinner named Sir Thomas died—now he watched as the false part of himself called Sir Thomas died—the Mayor's question still waited for its answer—he turned to the past, he went back in time to his happy childhood, he remembered his mother and father—the Mayor's gentle touch reminded him of his father—he thought of the name his father had chosen for him—he had never liked that name, he had tossed it aside, he had not used it for three years—but still, it was his only true name—it had been given to him with love at his birth.

He opened his eyes and said clearly, "My name is Robin Hood."

Then he squirmed after he said it, for there had been so many insults over the years—in some mad way he expected the Mayor to make some joke about a "little birdie" but of course the Mayor did no such thing—in fact, no one in the world would ever again make fun of Robin's name, for he would shortly become, as Elaine has predicted, as famous as the King—indeed, in the distant future, it would be Robin Hood who would be remembered better than Richard Lionheart.

But on this day, in that little house in St. Lyons, there was no thought of the future. The Mayor just smiled down at the hero he knew, the man who had saved his town.

He said, "We honor you, Master Hood, and we welcome you, and we thank you with all our hearts. Stay with us for as long as you wish."

Robin heard, with a certain surprise, the respect in the Mayor's voice—he felt a deep gratitude—he felt that he could live with this name that was his birthright—and then he heard a woman's voice at the door, he felt a crazed moment of hope—and then he heard the voice again—it wasn't Elaine's voice—and then he realized that whatever identity he chose, he would still love Elaine as long as he breathed—the pain of that knowledge drove him back into unconsciousness—but it didn't kill him.

Only Sir Thomas was dead.

Robin Hood would live forever.

Part IV

Legend

Chapter 165

NORTHERN CLIMES

On the morning of June 18, 1194, the morning that Elaine appeared as the beautiful lure, the morning that Thomas buried himself beneath a dead horse, the morning that Elaine slashed the throat of Sigurd Sigurdsson—on that morning Sigurd's three wives were sitting close to one another, chatting, enjoying the new baby in their midst. Little Leif was nursing at Maria's breast—Debbie and Petra's children were playing outside under a clear Norwegian sky.

Debbie put her hand under Maria's full heavy breast—she let the weight of it settle into her hand, she could feel the pull of the little boy's sucking—she felt an answering throb in her own breasts, for a moment she wished to be pregnant again—and then suddenly she saw the bloody vision. She jerked her hand away from Maria—her mouth opened and closed but no scream came out, no more than Sigurd could make a sound through his slashed throat, she looked and saw Petra with a hand to her own throat, she saw Maria choking, all of them breaking down—and then they all froze, listening, as the dying words of their man sounded in their ears: "I love you Petra, I love you Debbie, I love you Maria, and I love I love I love all our children, Stefan, Helga, Inga, Hans, Leif—I love you all, I love . . ."

The fountain of blood slowed and stopped. Debbie could not understand at first why they were not all marked with it—then water covered her eyes, she could not see—she wept.

Sigurd's spirit was gone.

Ivar had asked Sigurd, "If you were killed, would your women weep?"

Sigurd had replied, "Yes, I believe they would," and now he

was proved correct.

All the women wept—but then they could not cry too long, for their tears alerted the baby that something was terribly wrong in his world—he pulled his mouth off Maria's nipple and he began to scream with all the power in his sturdy lungs. Maria got up and walked around the room with her little boy—she tried to stop her sobs so that she could sing to him, but her voice cracked and Leif was not comforted—Petra put out her arms for the child and Maria handed him over—Petra tried to rock him, but hidden sobs kept jerking her body, the boy kept crying— Debbie took a turn next, but she was no more successful than the others—finally Maria took her child back, she sat down again and just held him close while he cried, she whispered that she loved him all the while—finally the boy cried himself to sleep—the evil of the world had touched him, but then he was still safe in his mother's arms.

After a while Maria laid him down in his little bed. She looked for a moment to make sure he would stay asleep—and then she returned to the other two women. They gathered her into an awkward triple embrace, they all hugged one another— and then each woman wanted to know what the others had seen and heard.

All the stories were the same: the slashed throat, the fountain of blood, the declarations of love—and the departing of Sigurd's spirit.

There could be no doubt that he was dead—yet the women vowed to keep this fact from the older children for now—likewise they would keep their sorrow a secret from the other people in the village.

They would mourn quietly—but already there was a feeling among them that this life, without Sigurd, was intolerable.

As days went by they noticed other women with haunted faces—they saw men give cheerful reassurances to one another—yet underneath there was a sense of tragedy. There was an unspoken but deeply felt fear that *no one* would return from Ivar's so uncharacteristic quest.

Every night, after their children were asleep, Petra, Debbie, and Maria got together to talk about their future.

If Sigurd's death were proven, their nominal status as wives would fall away—they would be mere slaves, subject to be sold—and they *would* be sold, for Sigurd had no other family to claim them. They could be separated—a real but intolerable possibility, for they were sisters now, closer even than if they shared the same blood.

If they were sold, and separated, then too the children would be broken apart from one another—that possibility too was intolerable, for the children knew their brothers and sisters as one family—the mothers could barely think of the heartbreak of their children.

The future was a yawning pit of despair—as she faced that despair, Debbie found the strength to tell her sisters a bitter truth.

"I have been thinking of our husband," she said, in the midst of one strangely lit night. "Sigurd was a good man in his way. He loved us, and we all loved him. And yet that does not change the fact that he took each of us by force in the beginning—he tore us from our homes and families—we had no choice for our love. I fear for our sons. They will grow up to believe that it is right to kidnap a girl for love—that it is right to pillage her father's property, and kill him if he resists, or even if he doesn't—they will live in a society that extols the code of the criminal—and they will become criminals themselves, like their father.

"Sigurd deserved to die. If our sons grow up to be like him, they too will deserve to be killed."

There were gasps from the other two women, and harsh looks, but Debbie pressed on, for the last thing she had to say was the most important: "I love my little Hans—but I do not want him to grow up to be a thief, a kidnapper, a rapist—for that is his destiny as a Viking warrior—I would prefer to see him die now, rather than become a man who sows sorrow across the world."

Maria looked over at her sleeping baby—she thought of the unimaginable sorrow her parents must have known when she was taken away—she wondered if her sweet little boy would ever cause such pain—and she knew, if he grew up here, that one day he would.

Maria put her hand over Debbie's, and she said, "You are right. You are brave, and you speak only truth."

Then the two of them looked at Petra, and the Russian girl said, "Yes, you are right, Debbie. I too can not bear the future that you have so clearly drawn—and likewise, I fear the more immediate possibility that we will be sold and split up one from the other.

"I did not know how to fight that fate—but you have given me the answer, Debbie, and I thank you." Petra's eyes seemed to look far away, as though she were staring down the long steppes of her homeland—a soulful Russian fatalism crept into her voice. "You see, my sisters, as Debbie has shown us, there is no future worth living for us here—and having no future, there is no reason for us to fear death, for ourselves, or even for our children. In the absence of fear, we can escape." Petra's lips curved into a distant smile. "We have no way of making the sea voyage to either of your countries—but my country, the Grand Principality of Muscovy, can be reached by land, though no one would expect us to attempt that journey. If we succeed we will be welcomed—and if the Grand Prince Dimitri still rules, I have no doubt that he will still desire me. I am more beautiful, and wiser than when I was taken away—when I was seventeen, and a virgin, I turned the Prince down—he will not have forgotten that.

"So let us go, my sisters—let us travel as a family. We may die, but we will die together—we will pass on no heritage of sorrow and pain."

Maria looked over at Petra with black shining eyes. "If we live it will be a miracle—but I am ready to pick up Leif and leave now."

Debbie said, "I am ready as well, but let us prepare tomorrow and leave tomorrow night."

The next day the three women discreetly loaded Sigurd's wagon with blankets and foodstuffs—they waited until the village slumbered through the sunlit night before they hitched up the horses—and then they woke up their children, and told them that they were leaving on a great adventure—a secret adventure—the little ones would have to be as quiet as tiny mice.

The mothers played whisper games with their children as they slowly drove out of town—and no one stopped them.

The next day they were missed—their escape to the east was noted—but the men of the town had more important things to worry about. Their concern was with the sea—they strained their eyes as they searched for some sign of Ivar's boat—the fate of fifty men and their Chief of Champions was far more weighty than the life or death of slave women and their children.

In any case, they thought there was little chance that the family could still be alive, for those sailors thought that overland travel in the north was absurd during any season—and overland travel without a man was simply suicide.

That was their view of the family's flight—they thought the women must have been overcome by grief when their master did not return—they viewed the escape as a mad rush to death, just as a woman might throw herself on her husband's funeral pyre.

They saw no reason to pursue—they kept their eyes on the sea—they left the family to their fate.

Their fate was terrible struggle, terrible hardship—but they did not fear death, and so the three young mothers simply pressed on—they carried their children toward some unknown but honorable future.

And then, too, though they did not fear death, they did not embrace it either—they fought to live, they fought to keep their children alive—and as they fought, they always kept moving.

They traveled through Norway and Sweden—then they proceeded south through Lapland, and finally crossed into Russia—Petra rejoiced when she could speak her native language again, she sang with the boatman when he ferried them across the Volga—and then finally they reached her home city of Moscow, the city she had not seen for five years.

Petra drove the wagon to the door of her old family home, as servants stared at her in disbelief. She opened the door herself—her parents looked out and saw their daughter standing in the lighted doorway—they froze, thinking she was a wraith, a shadow—but then she entered, holding the hands of two small children who hid behind her back—and then two more women entered, and they had children as well—all were hushed, until suddenly the baby that one of the other women carried began to cry.

This piercing cry was reality, life itself—the baby's cry freed Vassily and Alexandra Romanov (for such were the names of Petra's parents)—they ran forward and embraced their daughter, they hugged her and kissed her, they touched her over and over just so they could be sure she was real—then Alexandra hugged her grandchildren, and then Petra introduced Debbie and Maria and their children, everyone was embraced, Vassily became more exuberant by the moment, his heart burst free from its five year prison of sorrow, he declared that the women were all his daughters, the children all his grandchildren, he loved them all, he looked up to heaven and roared, "It is a miracle!"—Maria suddenly smiled, remembering her own words—it *was* a miracle, their journey was over—they had all survived—

and now Vassily knew just how to celebrate such a gift of God, he called for vodka and music and food, and the children fell asleep long before the dancing and feasting were finished.

Somewhere around dawn the three sisters fell asleep—but only after they saw that their children, sleeping peacefully, were all being looked after by trusted servants.

Around noon Alexandra gently woke Maria up, and gave her her son to nurse—Leif cried a little, at first, and that woke Debbie and Petra—they asked of their children, and they were told that they were still sleeping—and then Alexandra whispered the very special news. She told her daughter that the Grand Prince Dimitri had already heard of her miraculous return—he wanted to see her at the palace at three o'clock.

Petra smiled and hugged her mother.

Three ladies bathed and perfumed themselves—they discovered that Alexandra had not had the heart to throw away her daughter's dresses—the three sisters slipped into five year old finery, and kissed their children and told them they would be back soon—the grandparents surrounded the children with hugs—the ladies went to visit their Prince.

Soon the three beauties were ushered into Dimitri's presence (somehow, perhaps just by chance, the Prince had failed to mention this visit to his wife, the Princess Tatiana, and so that good lady was nowhere to be seen)—the Grand Prince looked at Petra, and he did remember that rare failure from his past—he saw that she was, as she knew herself, even more beautiful now than when she had spurned him. The Prince threw himself into the challenge.

He jumped from his throne with an utter abandonment of decorum—he embraced Petra, he kissed her on both cheeks, he thanked God for her safe return from the Vikings—and almost in the same breath he offered to set her up for life as his mistress.

Petra smiled at the Prince's impassioned torrent—she stepped back away from him, and then she put her left arm around Debbie's waist, and her right arm curled around and encircled Maria—she said, "These ladies, Your Highness, are Debbie and Maria—they are my sisters, and I love them so much that we can never be parted. Look at them, Your Highness, and you will see that either of them could please you more than you could imagine—but I wonder, are you the man I imagine? Are you the man who could please all three of us together?"

Petra's dark eyes challenged the Prince—but there was a joyful flirtation in her smile, a kind of lightness and pleasure that she had never felt during her helpless submission and desperate desire for Sigurd—she was teasing and she was being courted—she could surrender but only on her own terms—she would never be a slave again—she was a woman, she was home, and she was happy.

The Grand Prince made a comic business of looking left, looking right—and then he looked back at Petra, and dropped his hands in an exaggerated gesture of defeat.

"So be it," Dimitri said. "I shall have a house built large enough for all of you—and I will set aside a fund so that you, your sisters, and your children can live in comfort. You will not dispute these terms." The Prince was looking very fierce now. He went on, "Likewise, Petra, you will no longer ask foolish questions." The Prince looked even more fierce. "After all, what makes you think that only three of you could satisfy me?"

Debbie and Maria did not understand all the words, but they had practiced each other's languages through the long winter nights, and they got most of it, they started to giggle, Petra started to laugh—the Prince was having trouble maintaining his fierce face, first he smiled, then he just let go altogether, he burst into the booming confident laugh of a Russian Prince utterly secure in his manhood, the girls fell against him, all laughing helplessly now, they couldn't remember when there had been such freedom to laugh, the Prince embraced them all with his big arms, he kissed the fresh washed shining hair of each lovely lady, and then he whispered something in Petra's ear.

The something was an address—that night the three ladies went to the apartment that the Prince kept for his assignations, and he enjoyed them one after another, and then finally they all rolled into one taut circle of kisses.

Then in time the house was built, a glorious edifice overlooking the Moscow River—at first it seemed far too large for three ladies and five children, but then it gradually filled up with more children and nannies and tutors, a joyful place for the Prince to rest from the cares of state, though he sometimes complained when all his mistresses were pregnant at the same time—still, the women knew him now, they saw the laughter behind his scowls, and they teased him and laughed with him.

And so the children grew up with love and laughter, Dimitri

never favored his own over Sigurd's, they were all gifts of the ladies he soon realized he loved and would always love—yes the children grew, girls brave and beautiful like their mothers, boys handsome and accomplished who became stalwart young men, men who never needed nor wanted to take someone's daughter by force—they conquered their women only with charm.

So mothers looked on with pride—years passed and mothers became grandmothers—they lost their man when the Prince died after loving them for thirty years—they cried with the whole principality as their ruler was buried—Petra and Maria followed him soon after, but Debbie lived on for another dozen years.

One thing that pleased the English lady in her old age was the slow spreading legend of Robin Hood. This legend finally made its way to Moscow around the time of the death of the Grand Prince. Debbie loved hearing about the magical green archer (never dreaming that the hero had anything to do with the killing of Sigurd) though she wasn't certain that all the fanciful tales were true. Regardless, she liked the idea of a man of compassionate greatness in England—when she gathered her grandchildren together in those last years, she often told them stories about Robin Hood.

She was one of many who passed the legend on, around the world and down through the generations.

Chapter 166

THE ARCHER AT CHALUZ

Richard Lionheart received the huge gold shipment from Roland on the same day that the Duke married Elaine the Fair.

Richard stared at the glowing coins and saw no legend save his own.

The King quickly put the money to work.

Richard had returned to a debt ridden, impoverished country, desperate for hard capital to invest—England had been bled white by the expense of the Third Crusade and the exigencies of paying Richard's own ransom—and so the King, using his best judgment, applied every ounce of gold he received to assembling and equipping a great army for another foreign war.

One month later, on September 4, 1194, Richard sailed for France with his magnificent army. He landed without opposition—he rode out in front of his foot soldiers, and slowly pressed forward, as fleet messengers raced to Paris to give the news to King Philip II.

The French King thought the reports of the English strength had to be grossly exaggerated. He decided to see for himself—he invited Prince John (who had been living at the French court ever since his flight from England) to accompany him.

Philip proved to be an able scout. He led John (after a few days hard riding) to a vantage point from which they could observe the English from concealment. This was a hill overgrown with thickets—the King and the Prince peered through the bushes, and they saw the whole of the English army. Nothing had been exaggerated.

Philip was shocked. He knew England was fiscally in tatters and he knew that the English loss of life in the Holy Land had been severe—never in his worst nightmares had Philip dreamed that the Lionheart could raise an invading force like this—but there it was, the truth of his own eyes could not be denied.

The King knew that he had to get back to Paris at once and try to work out some sort of strategy—he could never match Richard's force—he mounted and rode away without a thought for John—only after he had gone at least a mile did he realize that John was no longer with him—he said a quiet "Good riddance" to the fickle Prince, and he rode on.

John had been equally impressed by Richard's army. He knew that his brother would be in a good mood, with such a fine troop at his command—John decided that his future lay in England.

As Philip raced for Paris, John rode over to the English line. He dismounted—he prostrated himself before his brother—he begged forgiveness for his sins.

Richard, who could always be touched by homage—and who needed someone anyway to watch over the English court—decided to forgive his brother. He sent John back to England to rule in his place as before.

So the English people were fortunate once again to have the despised Prince to blame for their troubles.

As John sat lightly on a dubious throne, the great Lionheart continued his majestic progress on the other side of the Channel. Richard defeated whatever opposition he encountered—but he didn't run into much, because Philip *had* come up with a strategy: Stay out of Richard's way!

Under no pressure, Richard took time to fortify each castle that he captured. He did not advance rapidly along a narrow line that could be cut—instead, he moved slowly on a broad front, he secured his position to the north, and to the south. He reasserted his control over his Continental possessions (Philip had been nibbling at these while Richard was imprisoned, but there was no sign of the French King now). Richard accepted the homage due him in Gascony, Poitou, Anjou, and Aquitane—and once in that last province, he took time to visit his mother, Eleanor. He was pleased to see that she had never been threatened by Philip's troops—he admired her vigor in her seventy third year. Eleanor likewise was full of praise for her favorite son—this boy was never unfaithful to her.

Richard went back to the "fray"—but even when he invaded France proper he still couldn't find anyone to fight. He conquered burned fields and empty castles—he had to pay great sums to traveling suppliers just to feed his army.

Richard used up the Duke's money in a year.

The familiar refrain began again—Richard sent messages to John: send gold, send more gold, send more . . .

As Richard's demands increased, so the flow from England decreased. There was little that the English people could do for their hero. They had no more to give.

Besides, as John wrote to his demanding brother, when the tax agents were able to seize something valuable, more often than not they were ambushed by the bandit Robin Hood—the valuables were then redistributed among the people—the collectors often failed to return.

This information sent Richard into a violent rage. He remembered the "little birdie"—he cursed himself for showing mercy.

Richard sent a murderous reply to John—he ordered the Prince to use whatever force necessary to kill Robin Hood—but then years went by, and somehow, someway, the bandit always escaped.

By the spring of 1199, Richard's prospects looked bleak. Since crossing the Channel five years earlier, he had never been defeated in battle—he had by now conquered half of France—and yet he had nothing to show for it. His once magnificent army had become a hungry ragged collection of scavengers—he was the lord of a wasteland.

His position was unbearable! He was the King of the English, Richard Lionheart—and yet he was a beggar to his younger brother. His sword cast its sway over two nations—and yet he couldn't eliminate a common bandit who dared challenge his authority.

He couldn't return to England as a failure—and yet every victory in France made him poorer.

Suddenly a ray of light pierced Richard's awful gloom. He learned that a vassal in the service of the Count of Chaluz had dug up an amazing find. This was a set of statuary, buried probably for hundreds of years—the set included an emperor, and his wife, and two sons and two daughters, all seated around a table. Each molded statue was made of pure solid gold.

The value of the set could hardly be measured.

The dutiful vassal reported the discovery to his master—and the Count of Chaluz blessed the honest farmer, and rewarded him well. Then the Count took the gold statuary to his castle—he had it cleaned and set out in state—now all who entered the castle stared in amazement at the golden glowing vision.

Richard was determined to steal that gold.

The King of the English decided to advance at night so that no alarm would be given—he drove his ghostly force across moonlit fields—he hid his army in forests in the daytime—he gave death to any travelers unfortunate enough to cross his path, for he *had* to have surprise—he could not let the gold get away.

The King was overjoyed when he reached the Count's castle just before dawn a week later—there were the normal complement of guards at the gate—this was no abandoned fortress—this would not be an empty victory.

Richard directed his army into the form of a coiling snake—he surrounded the castle of the Count of Chaluz—the King was prepared to squeeze the life out of every person inside those walls if the Count did not give up his seven gold statues.

The Count woke up to the sight of his besiegers.

Richard conveyed his demands.

The Count refused to surrender the beautiful statuary.

Richard tightened the siege. He ordered his men to make sure that no supplies reached the trapped inhabitants of the castle.

Now he only had to wait for starvation.

The Count would come around when he got hungry enough.

As far as his own troops were concerned, Richard was in luck. His surprise night marches had given the French no chance to leave with their goods—there were many farms and markets in the area, all ripe for plundering—Richard sent out a detachment to do just that.

The King was quite cheerful. He went for a ride around the castle, just so he could gloat over the trapped victims within. They were in his power—there was no escape, no hope for them—in time they would beg him to take their gold, if only he would spare their lives . . .

Richard was so blinded by his powerful fantasies that he never noticed the young French archer who stared down at him from the parapet of the Count's castle.

The archer was armed with a new and deadly crossbow.

Richard rode on, unconcerned, without armor as usual.

The archer sighted down the shaft of his drawn back arrow. He spoke softly to the King who would never hear him: "I see you Richard Lionheart—I see that you have come to steal from us—I tell you now that I stand in your way."

The young man touched the trigger of his crossbow, and the arrow flew.

The English King would not have been surprised if a dove had flown in front of him and intercepted the bolt. He would have accepted that divine intervention as his due—but this time God did not raise His hand.

The arrow struck King Richard Lionheart—and it killed him.

Chapter 167

KING JOHN

Prince John endured the last five years of Richard's reign by praying daily for his brother's death.

John could barely stand the wait—for he was despised by everyone from Barons to servants. He was the weak Prince who lied about his brother and then fled to an enemy nation. He ruled only by Richard's sufferance. His orders were obeyed reluctantly—if at all—unless he could prove they came from the King.

John thought all this would change when Richard died. He thought that, as King, he would at least have the people's fear (even John knew he would never have their respect). He thought that the people would obey him then—he thought that he would be able to do whatever he liked.

Richard Lionheart died on April 6, 1199. The late King had loved only one woman in his life: his mother, Eleanor. He left behind no son, no heir save his younger brother.

John was crowned King of England—but also, and unfortunately for him, he was named Lord of Gascony, Poitou, Anjou, and Aquitane. And that was not all—he was also expected to assume control of Normandy and all the other French districts that Richard had seized in the past five years.

John inherited this restored and expanded empire—plus a leaderless army on a rebellious battlefront. The word from France was that Philip (greatly cheered by the death of the Lionheart) was massing his forces for a counterattack.

The new King found that the monarchial freedom he had imagined did not exist. He was essentially forced (because all cried for him to fulfill his obligations to empire and soldiers) to cross the Channel and ride through half of France so as to take command of the English army.

This was just about the last thing John wanted to do (John liked secret personal revenge, quiet assassination—he hated full scale, open war, where even he could be killed). The King took comfort in the fact that even though he was forced to lead, he was not forced to fight.

When Philip arrived, full of new courage and leading well rested troops, John fell back at once.

Philip advanced further—John ordered retreat.

The French King, who already was acquainted with John, now knew the best strategy to adopt. He pushed forward steadily—but he made no attempt to encircle John or corner him in any way. Philip did not want to force John to fight—he just wanted to push the English off French soil.

The strategy worked. John fell back before the pressure—he retreated to the southwest—he backpedaled through Aquitaine, where he picked up his mother—he continued to fall back until he reached the sea.

At this point Philip made slow elaborate gestures presaging an attack—but he gave John all the time he needed to confiscate enough boats to get his troops away.

Only at that point did Philip start his deliberate attack—John took to the sea, leaving all Continental possessions behind.

John returned to England with his mother and his troops. He had saved an English army and ended a draining foreign war—but he was not welcomed. The King's arrival in London was marked by shouts of "Coward!" and "Traitor!" He was blamed for losing the war. He was cursed for failing to hold the territory gained by the sainted Richard.

John learned some valuable lessons from this affair. He knew now that his status as King would not save him from revilement—but nonetheless, he had avoided war and he had made it home safely. He could not do everything that he wanted, but still his personal power was very great. He decided to use that power for the sort of private revenge he enjoyed—he picked out two victims: the lovely Isabella of Angouleme and her fiance, Hugh de Lusignan.

Hugh was—or had been—a wealthy nobleman. His fortune was based on the land he owned in Poitou. Now that land had been swallowed up by France, confiscated by Philip II. Hugh had reason to be angry at John, and he was a brave and intemperate man. He called the King a coward to his face.

That indiscretion would cost his fiance dear.

John had Isabella dragged from her bedchamber one night, just one week before she was to marry Hugh. She was taken to the King and left alone with him. John examined the thinly clad maiden with lascivious pleasure. The King's excitement was increased by the thought that he was denying Hugh his bridegroom's rights—that twisted revengeful thought drove John forward.

He raped Isabella of Angouleme.

Still, John's triumph was not complete. Isabella showed a surprising strength of character. She submitted when she realized she had no choice—she gave up her physical virginity—but she kept part of herself inviolate.

John determined to crush that resistance and also flaunt his power publicly over Hugh. He forced Isabella to marry him.

The mean spirited marriage pleased no one, not even John. Hugh became an enemy for life—he rallied other noblemen in opposition to the crown—his actions were the seeds of the Baronial revolt that would plague John in later years. Likewise Isabella refused to be broken—she submitted coldly to John, unmoved either by blows or caresses.

John got his wife with child, but even pregnant she defied him with her indifference. He went to beat her one night, but Isabella never thought of showing the fear he wanted. She just put one hand on her swollen belly and said calmly, "Do what you like, kill me, kill the child—it matters nothing, for I will always love Hugh."

John looked at her serene face, at the shape of the living child within her—and he found he could not raise his hand.

John left her bedchamber, and gave orders that kept Isabella a prisoner in the palace for the rest of his life. After that day the King was only seen with his Queen—and the child she bore, a son named Henry—on formal occasions. He never again tested his power against Isabella in private, because he knew that he would lose.

There were other problems for the weak willed King. He had inherited a devastated treasury from Richard—and there seemed no way to fill it. Tax collections were meager—tax collectors went in fear of their lives, for they never knew when they might suddenly meet Robin Hood.

John tried for years—first at Richard's request, and then on his own account—to kill Robin Hood, but the outlaw seemed to have a magical ability to escape capture. The people loved him—he was the hero of song and story, and none would betray him. Even the powerful Barons were afraid of him, for all too many had felt the outlaw's wrath. Country society quickly learned that a landowner should not charge his tenants more than the customary ten percent of the harvest. Those Barons who tried to gouge with higher duties tended to suddenly find their guardian knights killed, or their mansions robbed—sometimes there was a green feathered arrow left at the scene like a signature.

All would know that Robin Hood had visited—all trouble stopped when the fee dropped back down to ten percent.

Barons found that it was easier to make do with ten percent than to try and fight the mysterious bandit.

John cursed Robin Hood and the Barons who gave in to him—he raged even more because there was not enough gold in the treasury to pay for his pleasures. The King sent for Arthur the Assessor—he *demanded* gold.

Arthur, as usual, had his answer ready—he had had his answer ready for a long time—he had been waiting for the King to reach this point of desperation.

"The churches," Arthur said.

"What about the churches?"

The churches are rich. We tax the churches, and we are rich as well."

John hated the way Arthur used the royal we as though he were an equal—but he decided to overlook the Assessor's hubris, given the sheer brilliance of the idea. This was literally manna from heaven! John enthusiastically agreed to Arthur's plan.

Soon Arthur's practiced extortionists descended on the churches of England.

The results were wonderful! John had hardly imagined that there were so many riches hidden—but not protected—behind religious cloth.

Of course Robin Hood intercepted a number of collectors, but given that there were so many ripe targets for the tax agents, the outlaw's depredations had little effect—indeed they were a source of cynical amusement for the King. John noticed that Robin, like himself, did not seem to have any real religious feeling. The outlaw recaptured many holy treasures—but he never returned them to the churches from which they had been taken. Instead, he bypassed the priests and distributed the loot among the poor—he also, according to John's calculations, seemed to be keeping a bit for himself.

So perhaps Robin made a profit—but the King was doing even better.

The money poured in to the royal treasury, and John was overjoyed. He could now spend freely on his pleasures—he hired the finest whores—he paid for some quiet assassinations, just to feel the thrill of murder without risk.

For a short time John was happy, but his happiness didn't last.

Pope Innocent III heard of the royal pillaging of England's churches—the Pope's pen flashed—he excommunicated the King of the English.

John, of course, was outraged by this unfair sentence of damnation—after all, it hadn't been *his* idea to tax the churches!

The King sent two knights to arrest Arthur. John planned to have the Assessor stretched on the rack until he made a full confession—then the King would offer Innocent a broken scapegoat, plus his own humble confession: John was prepared to admit that he had been led astray by a devil's minion.

Arthur refused to oblige the King—he had long been ready for this moment. The Assessor had been siphoning gold off for his personal treasure since the days of Henry II. Arthur bribed the knights that came for him—he paid them sums that they could never earn in a lifetime of service to the King—but to the Assessor, the money was just a trifle.

Arthur quietly left London and reclaimed his treasure from his various hiding placed around the country—and then he made his way to Firfleet, the village of his birth. He bought the largest house in that impoverished hamlet—he settled down to live out the rest of his days. He became known as a sort of usurer—but he demanded homage, not financial repayment. He would "give" money away—but only after the supplicant had begged, and crawled, and kissed his boots.

Many engaged in such humiliating trials, for times were hard, and getting harder—Arthur felt wondrous thrills when the village's erstwhile bullies crawled at his feet.

Arthur had come home—he lived on revenge and baby's mush until he was eighty-two years old.

But King John knew none of this. Few people were still loyal
to their hellbound King. John could not trust his informants or
his messengers. All he knew was that another enemy had
escaped—and without Arthur, he had no scapegoat the Pope
would accept.

John was desperate, bereft of any good counsel, damned and
alone. Arthur's departure had effectively stopped the taxing of
the churches—the King knew that he would run out of money
again soon.

He was running out of time.

John had scoffed at religion before—but now he felt the terror
of hell closing in—he found he could not bear the sentence of
excommunication. He begged Innocent for terms—he got them,
and they were harsh, but John agreed.

The King surrendered England as a fief to Rome.

John sold his country to save his soul.

Innocent lifted the excommunication—but now, at least theo-
retically, England was not even an independent nation.

The King had no friends left. Open rebellion began against
the crown.

John called on the Barons of England, the last stable force
existent, to rally to his side. The King demanded that they put
themselves and their knights into his service—he declared that
if they fought together, they could crush the rebellions that
were springing up everywhere like mushrooms.

The Barons refused. They had not needed the Pope to tell
them that the King's soul was damned—likewise they accepted
neither John's rehabilitation nor his surrender of England.

The Barons armed themselves against the King—they presented John with their demands.

All his life John preferred accommodation to uncertain fight.
Here too he followed his characteristic path. He was afraid to
battle the Barons—so he allowed himself to be humiliated like
no other previous English monarch. He voluntarily came before
the assembled Barons in the midst of the great meadow at
Runnymede—he signed the document they set before him:
Magna Carta.

An historic principle was established: even the King is not
above the law.

There were no more pleasures left for King John.

He lived one more desperate year. Then he contracted the dis-
ease—dysentary—most suited to his character, and he died on

October 19, 1216.

As John's soul was judged, Robin Hood disappeared.

Many looked for their green hero as England sank into anarchy and civil war (there was no one to lead the devastated country, for John's son Henry was but nine years old) but Robin Hood could not be found. His reality was gradually replaced by legends that would live forever—his corporeal body was never seen again in England after the death of King John.

Chapter 168

THE SUIT OF GREEN

Long before the death of King John, long before the death of King Richard, before there could be an evergreen legend, Robin Hood had first to survive.

He lay on the bed of the Mayor of St. Lyons, he shook with fever, and he called for his lost love Elaine. He threw off the sweated sheets that oppressed him—he called for blankets on hot summer days—he wondered why the townsfolk put up with him—he wondered why they treated him as though he were a hero.

He just wanted to give up—but the ladies forced their soup down his throat—they nursed him day and night—they refused to let him die.

The problem was that he didn't really want to live—there was too much pain in life—living meant acknowledging the loss of Elaine, and every thought of her was like a whiplash laid right on his shattered heart. He wanted just to dream about her, when he slept he always dreamed happily of her—if he slept forever he would never have to wake up to the agony of loss—was death a neverending sleep?

The ladies were always waking him up to feed him.

He cursed them, and they answered respectfully and firmly, and they made him drink his soup.

Simple curiosity moved Robin a little bit from the abyss of death. He wanted to find out what heroic deed he had done that so endeared him to this town. Since he didn't want to admit his ignorance, he was forced to listen to the talk around him. He had to show a little interest in the world.

He caught fragments of conversation: "the Assessor's scum—

poor Mary's father—taking our life's blood in taxes—even our
nets, our nets, mind you"—he started to put the story together,
and then suddenly one day he slipped into a dream state, he
saw himself killing the two men, he saw again the heads in the
packed wagon—he came awake, he realized that he had saved
St. Lyons from the Crown's brutal taxation—he smiled just
slightly when he realized that he had done it all in delirium,
that his "heroism" was a crazed man's act of chance violence—
he decided not to tell his hosts of the real circumstances of his
great deeds.

As he fell asleep again, he began to wonder if he might just
have stumbled on his destiny.

He woke up with *her* name on his lips: Elaine, Elaine, Elaine
the Fair—he woke up to familiar agony—but now in the back of
his mind there was a small but growing reason to live.

Robin began to get better. He was more polite to the ladies
who served him. He sat up in bed, and ate some solid food.

One Sunday, when the boats were idle, Robin heard a great
hubbub in the street. People were talking rapidly to one another
with excited voices—they were coming his way. Robin felt a
moment of fear. He looked around the room that had hardly
concerned him during this last month and a half of fever, delirium, and convalescence. Now he saw that his bow was leaning in
a corner. He saw that a new quiver had been made for him, and
it was full of arrows.

The voices were closer—Robin heard the cheery voice of the
Mayor leading all the rest. Robin relaxed—he put a pillow
behind himself and sat up as the door opened.

The Mayor and an exceptionally tall young man entered.
Robin could see what looked like the whole town surging up
against the open door. Obviously they expected the Mayor to say
something very important—they went dead silent the moment
he started to speak.

"Hello, my friend," the Mayor said.

Robin didn't answer. He was wondering why the Mayor
hadn't called him by name.

The Mayor smiled broadly and went on. "We have all wondered who you truly are. I have not been alone in imagining
that you must be a knight—but now that I know the truth, it is
brighter than anything we could have imagined."

The Mayor was so happy with his story that he didn't notice
Robin's growing anger.

"This tall fellow by my side is a son of this town," the Mayor continued. "He went away to serve as a knight's squire—now that he has returned, he has told us the whole story. We have learned that Northmen attacked our most beautiful Countess—and now we know that it was you, a knight of the realm, who saved her from those barbarians. Your heroism was without measure—and then we know that you did not rest on your laurels—you saved our town from the excesses of the King who so falsely tried to drive you away. We have not honored you enough, Sir—"

"Stop!" Robin snapped. His eyes were a hard cold slate gray—his countenance showed a ferocity that no one in the town had ever seen before.

The Mayor's smile crumbled. The town held its collective breath.

Robin spoke: "It is true that I saved Elaine the Fair from the Northmen—and also from her perverse husband, Arthur the Assessor, who oppresses us all. I set Elaine free—I love her, as all you who have heard my lamentations know—but as a free woman, she had the right to make her own choice, and she chose another man. She has gone to Europe with the Duke of Larraz.

"As for myself, I am of good plain stock. There is no noble blood in my veins. I clawed my way to knighthood in an attempt to win Elaine's love—with her gone from my life, I have no title, nor do I wish for one.

"I do not wish to represent the King who is raping this country. I am proud that I was able to intercept his minions and save this town—I am prouder of that act than of anything I did while I was a knight—I have found my destiny, and I will act in my own name.

"That name is Robin Hood."

Robin noticed that the Mayor's smile was starting to come back.

"I want to thank all of you, and especially the ladies, for keeping me alive when I wanted to die. I saw only my own problems then—I saw no reason to live—but now I have found that reason—I have chosen life, but I see battles ahead in my future."

Robin looked at the tall man. "Squire, get my bow and quiver—I need to go outside to practice."

The squire moved obediently at Robin's order.

Robin got out of bed and stood up. For the first time in many weeks he put all his weight on his feet.

He fell down.

The tall one rushed over to help, but the look on Robin's face was so terrible that the squire stopped in his tracks. Slowly, painfully, Robin got up unaided. The Mayor stood aside—the townsfolk opened up a path—the squire followed, as Robin Hood walked out of the house.

The bright summer sun was blinding. Robin swayed in the street—he looked like he was going to fall again, but then he just managed to catch himself. He stood there squinting for a long moment, and then he put out a hand, and the squire handed him his bow. Once he had that securely, the squire handed over a single arrow.

Robin nocked it, and as he tested the bowstring's tension, he experimented a little with the movement of his right hand. The thumb, the first finger, and the littlest one worked. The two middle fingers stuck out, rigid, unbendable. The bones in his hand had fused, but the cut tendons had not repaired themselves. The stiff fingers could not answer his brain's directives.

"So be it," Thomas said quietly, seizing the base of the arrow-shaft, "I only need thumb and first finger." Then he spoke much louder: "I need a target."

Two small boys had been scurrying frantically, anticipating their hero's wishes. Now they picked up the bale of hay they had been dragging and set it, with great effort, at a child's distance (about fifteen feet) in front of Robin. One of the boys took his shirt off and draped it over the bale.

Robin rewarded the boys with a smile.

Their mothers removed them from the line of fire.

Robin tried to draw back his arrow, but the bow seemed stiffer than iron. Sweat poured off his face as he struggled in the pitiless heat. The bow wouldn't bend. Robin began to sway—he swayed forward—he rocked backward, and as he went back he put all his weight in the service of those two fingers that were drawing back the arrow—he bent the bow at last, and then he seemed to fall forward, he aimed the arrow down at the bale, and he let fly.

The arrow pinned the boy's shirt neatly to the wrapped hay.

The young lad would soon outgrow that shirt—but he would never throw it away.

Robin Hood kept falling forward—he really was going down this time, he was holding his bow, he had no way to block his fall—

The squire caught him before he hit the earth. This young man proved to be amazingly strong as well as tall. He picked Robin up with no apparent effort.

Robin whispered, "Tomorrow tell them to move the target back," and then he passed out in the squire's arms.

So after that Robin practiced archery every day. The tall squire assisted him faithfully.

Robin had another faithful companion, a girl who visited him in the evenings. Her name was Dorothy, and she was eighteen years old—for the last three of those years, she had known that she was the most beautiful girl in the town.

The Mayor, playing matchmaker, let Dorothy have an hour alone with Robin every night—he hoped that Robin would marry into their town.

Dorothy always took special pains with her hair and her face before she visited Robin—she wore low cut peasant blouses that showed off her proud young breasts—she would lean over Robin's bed (the Mayor had never tried to reclaim it—he slept on a cot in the kitchen) and bring him choice food that she had cooked, a welcome change from the ubiquitous soup—she combed his hair for him, before he had the strength to do it himself—she talked to him, and he listened.

Dorothy watched Robin in the daytime too. She watched as every day he had the target moved back—and every day it became smaller: first a shirt, then a square cut cloth, then the square halved—farther away, farther away, farther away—a month after Robin first stood up, the target was a shilling at fifty paces—and he made it ring.

No one in the town had ever seen archery like that.

Dorothy watched Robin's growing strength as he drew back his bow, and her whole body shuddered with desire.

In her own bed at night she would remember his magnificent speech, renouncing knighthood—and she would cry, "I love you, I love you, I love you," into her pillow.

Robin rarely spoke to her when she visited him in the evenings.

He never once kissed her.

Dorothy became ever more frightened as Robin grew steadily stronger. She sensed that he was preparing to go away.

Dorothy's parents saw their daughter's desire—in general they approved, her father said that Robin would make a fine son in law—but her mother was cautious. She said, "Dorothy, you must wait for him to come to you. He has lost a love—you must not rush him."

Dorothy didn't listen to her mother—but she gathered other information. She talked to sailors down on the docks—she picked up news from Europe that gladdened her heart. She was close enough to overhear when Robin told his squire to get two horses ready for the morrow.

Dorothy listened mostly to her own yearning heart. This was no time to wait—she had to make him take her with him!

So Dorothy came to Robin on this fateful night. He was not lying on his bed—rather, he was sitting on the edge, thinking. He said, "Hello, Dorothy," quietly when she came in.

She said, "Hello, Robin,"—her voice sounded strange even to herself—her heart was pounding so loud she felt sure that he could hear it—she knelt before Robin, and put her arms around his knees. She looked up at the man she loved, and smiled with all her courage.

Robin looked down at the girl before him, nearly all of her firm breasts exposed to his gaze, her soft flesh rising and falling with her breathing—he looked upward along a lovely curved throat that led to a determined chin and then parted, ripely desirous lips that were just waiting for his kiss—he saw a fine straight nose and yearning brown eyes—he looked up past her white forehead to her brushed back brown hair that flowed smoothly down her back—he looked again at her yearning eyes, and he said, "You're beautiful, Dorothy."

Dorothy shuddered with pleasure, her whole body moved forward to touch this man she wanted so, she crushed her breasts against his knees and buried her face against his thigh—she said, "I love you Robin, I love you, I love you—"

Robin stopped her. He put his left hand in her hair and pulled her head back so that she had to look at him—his cold gray eyes frightened her—he said, "I am honored that you love me, and it would be a blessing if I could love you—but I can not ever love you Dorothy, for I love another."

Dorothy looked up at Robin with eyes filled with tears—and then with all her woman's warmth she tried to bring his love to her. She took his right hand and led it down into her blouse—she pressed his hand against her hot trembling breast, and she said, "Elaine is gone—I am here, I am yours, touch me, love me, please love me . . ."

Robin cupped her hot breast very gently, he brushed his stiff fingers over her equally rigid nipple—he moved to her other breast, and caressed it in the same, too gentle way—and then he took his hand away.

He spoke with a great sadness. "Your breasts are beautiful, Dorothy, all of you is beautiful, but still I must leave tomorrow, for I can not love you. I will always love Elaine the Fair."

Suddenly Dorothy got to her feet. All her emotions burst free in a screaming rush of rage. "You can't go to her! I've learned from the sailors that she has married! She has already married the Duke of Larraz! You can't go!"

Dorothy stopped, panting.

Robin said calmly, "Your news does not surprise me. I knew she would marry the Duke. I was not intending to go to her, and I will not go to her now. I understand that my love is hopeless—but I also know that I can love no one else.

"When I leave St. Lyons tomorrow, I will not go in search of love—I will go to fulfill my destiny."

Dorothy searched Robin's face for her place in that destiny—but he gave her nothing.

She began to cry but he didn't move toward her.

She turned and walked blindly from the room.

The next morning, before Robin had even dressed, a delegation of the town ladies (not including Dorothy) came into his room to see him. They brought a large wrapped parcel—this they laid on his bed. The oldest lady, Beryl, (she was the Mayor's sister and the leader of the group) said, "Open this before you dress—we will wait outside for you."

They filed out.

Robin opened his present—and there were all the new clothes he needed, beautifully made. There were leggings, shirts, trousers, a leather jerkin, fine robes and even a hat—and everything was a pure shining green.

Robin tried everything on—each garment fit perfectly. Robin didn't know that the ladies (with a fair amount of giggling) had often measured his unclad body while he slept.

Robin put on a suit of green to wear this day—he packed the rest of the new garments to take with him—he threw away the few clothes he had worn when he came to St. Lyons.

He picked up his bow and quiver and stepped outside. He posed a little, resplendent in his new finery—the watching ladies were thrilled—they admired their own work—they admired the hero who filled out the clothes they had made.

Robin broke the silence. "I thank you from the bottom of my heart—this was just what I needed, and never have I owned finer clothes—but tell me, please, what is the reason for the color?"

"You brought hope to our town," Beryl replied simply, "and green, the color of spring, is the color of hope."

Robin embraced her, and kissed her cheek, and then he did the same with each of the other ladies.

The Mayor, who had been waiting discreetly in the background, now stepped forward and wished Robin a good morning.

Robin replied in kind.

The Mayor said, "I see that my sister has already presented you with an excellent gift—I also have something to give you. This is not something you can wear or carry—but I believe it will prove useful, nonetheless.

"I offer you hospitality, now and in the future.

"I think I know what you are planning to do—I know that you will face grave dangers. I give you my word that you will always have a home here in St. Lyons—or a refuge, if you need one— you can come here to hide or celebrate—you will always be safe here."

"Thank you," Robin said.

He shook hands formally with the Mayor, and then that just wasn't enough—he embraced the old man, they held each other for a long moment—and then they heard the sound of horses.

Robin stepped back and saw the tall squire riding up on a solid bay—he was leading a thin chestnut that was all saddled and ready to go.

Robin mounted the horse he was given.

He could leave now—but he kept his horse still. He looked all over the town—he didn't know where Dorothy lived and he saw no sign of her—he nudged his horse and started away at a walk.

The squire rode next to him.

Robin waved to the Mayor and to the ladies—he left them behind but he kept his horse to a slow speed—he felt a great sadness as he reached the edge of the town—he could have had a simple life, a simple love here—and then he heard the sound of rapid footsteps.

He looked around and there was Dorothy, hair wild, tears on her face—and a bouquet of flowers in her hand.

He stopped his horse as she ran up to him. He took the offered flowers—he looked down as before at her loving, yearning face—

but this time he did bend down farther and kiss her lips.

Then he straightened up—he touched heels to his horse—he left Dorothy alone, for his only companion on this quest would be the tall squire who rode by his side.

After they had traveled some miles in silence, Robin took a good look at his faithful companion. He was struck, as always, by the sheer size of the fellow—even on horseback he seemed a good head taller.

It occurred to Robin that he didn't even know the man's name.

"What do they call you, my friend?" Robin asked.

"John," the squire replied.

"Like the Prince?"

The squire grimaced. "Certainly not like the Prince!"

"Then I shall have to call you something else."

The squire shook his head. "As you know yourself, Robin, one must finally answer to the name one was given."

Robin smiled. "The John can stay, but I must improve it." He looked up and down the enormous length of his friend's figure. "'Little John' should fit just right," Robin said seriously.

The squire was taken aback for a second—but then he saw the glint in Robin's eye and he began to laugh, "Yes, yes," he said, and then he began to laugh harder, and Robin joined him—and so, laughing, Robin Hood and Little John set off to find their destiny.

Part V

Marriage

Chapter 169

HEALING

Elaine and Roland honeymooned in the Duke's vacation cottage high up in the foothills of Larraz.

It was a time of healing for the new Duchess. While she was physically recovered (the skin of her wounded hand had come together nicely, leaving only a near invisible hairline scar) the mental wounds were still fresh. She had had no time to deal with that pain during the month of frenzied social activity that had preceded her marriage. Now she was alone with Roland (and two discreet servants) and there was time and quiet.

She let the memories come back.

She told Roland every detail of her violent journey from London to Stonehenge to the sea.

Roland listened, and caressed his lady, and comforted her.

Elaine told him about the knife in her bedroom—the Vulture's brutal kisses—the flames crackling before her as she was tied to the stake—the awful confirmation of Arthur's role in the plot—Thomas's wonderful rescue and Daniel's shattered head—Thomas's overtures and her refusal—Ivar's threats on that last night—the horror of Thomas killing Saladin—even though he had done it for her it was still one of her most terrible memories—she cried when she told the story of the poor brave overburdened horse—she talked of the horse more than she talked of the blood on her breasts—she said very little about killing two men—she seemed to go away from Roland, though she lay in his arms—but then slowly, slowly, with infinite patience, he brought her back.

Roland was the perfect lover for Elaine. He eased her mind—and he tenderly awakened her body.

He always took her with patience and gentleness. As days went by in the small cottage—and then weeks—she began to respond more and more easily, until finally just the sight of her husband brought joy to Elaine. In bed she referred to him affectionately as "my big bear"—she loved being enfolded, sheltered by his big warm hairy body—she played with his beard and the mat of hair on his chest—they both made jokes about a bear's love for honey, because Roland loved to search out the sweetest source . . .

One day Elaine woke peacefully before her husband. She realized that the terrible nightmare that had plagued her for years was gone. She had not dreamed of the demon mask once since she had told the story to Thomas.

She had never told her husband the whole story of how she had received her most famous scar—she wondered if she should tell him now, but then she decided there was no reason to bring up that distant past again. It was enough that Roland helped her deal with more recent terrors. She felt confident that she could eventually leave all past horrors behind her.

She could think now of the future—she could think of her new life.

Elaine held up her left hand so that she could admire her golden wedding band in the clear morning light. She gazed at the endless circle of perfection—she remembered a perfect day, she remembered the flowered path. She thought of that path leading her to this wonderful honeymoon, leading her onward to the future, a path of beauty without end like the ring's golden circle.

She thought of her own body, scarred but whole, ready for the next adventure—she was ready to bear a child—she looked forward to that happiness.

She pressed all of her nude body against Roland and whispered in his awakening ear, "It's time to get up, you big bear."

Chapter 170

LITTLE ANTON

When Roland and Elaine returned to the Palace of Larraz following their four week honeymoon, they found good news awaiting them. Sandra was now clearly pregnant, and that knowledge had taken much of the sorrow from her features.

Lady Sandra had become very popular at the court. Everyone in Larraz had heard about Anton's gallant stand—the widow of such a great man was much honored—and Sandra's modest demeanor only added to her charm.

Roland discovered that Anton had died owing money. The Duke quietly paid off his debts and he settled a certain income on Sandra. This gave her enough money to live comfortably.

The Duke also offered to buy Sandra her own cottage—but she asked to remain in the palace, so that she could be close to Elaine.

The Duke gave his consent. He gave Sandra two rooms, one large one for herself and the babe to come, and another for a servant.

This last was strange for Sandra—she still thought of herself as Elaine's servant (though of course she no longer had such duties—Elaine now had a pretty Larrazian girl named Valerie as her lady in waiting). Sandra did not believe in her heart that she was Elaine's equal, and in a way she liked that. Elaine was the great lady who took her in when she came to London, a little girl all alone—Elaine would take care of her now, as she journeyed through her pregnancy without her loving man.

Months passed—Sandra's body changed to accommodate the growing child in her womb. Her breasts were full and heavy—her belly grew so big that she could only lie comfortably on her side, and so it was in that position that she would visit with Elaine in the afternoons.

The two ladies, one slim and golden, the other dark and soft and full, would lie on their sides, facing each other, on Roland and Elaine's bed (unlike in London, now Elaine slept *with* her husband). Elaine would slip a hand up under Sandra's loose dress and place her palm on the taut swollen belly—only to jump when the active baby inside would kick with great power. Then Elaine would say, "Little Anton, you are such a strong boy," and Sandra would smile, but there would be sadness in her eyes too, for her husband would never see his son. Elaine would see that sadness—she would embrace Sandra, and hold her as close as she could—she gave comfort to the young girl, and in those moments the Duchess knew her own pain.

Elaine would feel the full proof of her dearest friend's pregnancy pressed against her own flat stomach—she would stroke Sandra's curly hair while hiding her own feelings—she was saddened, and frightened, by her own emptiness. She wanted to be like Sandra—she wondered why she didn't conceive.

Even *since* her honeymoon she still made love with Roland at least once a day—often twice! Why then was she not fruitful?

Roland seemed unconcerned—Sandra, caught up in her own drama, never noticed her friend's hidden worries—Elaine told no one of her fears.

Sandra was eight months pregnant when Roland arranged for a special midwife for her. Roland explained his choice to Sandra one day while Elaine listened (the two ladies had just finished having lunch together).

"She is the best, Sandra," Roland said. "She is a wise old Gypsy woman, name of Davila, who got tired of traveling and settled in the country near here. She has assisted at the childbearing of many of the ladies of the court, but now that she is very old, she only comes down here by special request. I have made that request, and she will live here at the palace and attend you until the baby is born. I trust, Sandra, that all this meets with your approval."

"Thank you, Your Grace," Sandra replied, "but I must meet this woman before I can give my approval."

The Duke was a little taken aback by this spunky reply, but he just smiled and said, "That's an easy condition to meet," and then he waved a hand at his page and the lad left the room, only to return a moment later with a small bent over old woman who walked with the aid of a cane.

Sandra wondered how such an ancient person could possibly help her. Davila's approach seemed to take an age. Sandra watched the painful little steps, the gnarled hand gripping the cane—she wanted to tell the Duke to send the woman away— she didn't want a feeble old stranger to touch her baby—but then Davila finally reached her, finally stopped right in front of her—this little old woman, standing no taller than the seated Sandra—this old woman looked at her, and she seemed to know everything—perhaps she had known Anton before—suddenly Sandra was sure that she had—Sandra trusted her from the moment their eyes met.

Davila put a tiny strong hand on Sandra's swollen belly—a strong comforting hand that didn't flinch from the baby's kicks—despite her age, this woman was *not* feeble—Davila looked at Sandra with compassionate, knowing black eyes, and she said, "He will be the image of his father, but he will have your goodness of spirit too."

Sandra said, "Yes, O yes," to Davila—and then she turned to the Duke and said, "I'm sorry I questioned your judgment, Your Grace—you made the right choice."

Elaine, looking on, could hardly bear to watch the now convivial and cheerful scene—she just wanted so badly to be in Sandra's place.

After that day there was not much to do besides wait. Weeks went by, Sandra still got bigger—finally it was March 14, 1195, nine months to the day since Anton had taken her maidenhead—Sandra was as ready to have his baby as she was ever going to be—the whole court waited for the blessed arrival— Roland felt the tension in the air—he felt the tension in himself, for on this day he had just been told some rather special English news.

Elaine knew her husband's methods now. She had learned that there was no fixed schedule for his mornings—he might travel about his domain (the duchy was small enough that one could ride from border to border in a day), he might deal with petitions, or proclaim laws—indeed, some mornings Roland abandoned government altogether and enjoyed his wife instead.

On the other hand, the afternoons were inviolate. That was when Roland gathered his information—when he listened to passing travelers, his informants. Whether a visitor was expected or not, the Duke was *always* available, every afternoon. He learned about the changing world. Elaine was amazed by the range of Roland's interests: he wanted to know about rainfall in Sicily, rebellion in Alsace, adultery in Paris—he listened to all his travelers, and rewarded them well, and he remembered all they told him.

Elaine often listened with her husband during the early months of her marriage—but most of the news seemed rather boring to her—Elaine realized that she preferred the personal to the political. Once she realized that, she began to spend almost every afternoon with Sandra.

So Elaine had not been present today when the English monk, on his way to Rome, told his story to Roland.

The Duke wondered at first if he should keep this new information secret—and then he realized that would be a mistake— this was something he *had* to tell Elaine—but he delayed for a while, he waited until nighttime, waited till after they had made love.

Roland kissed Elaine and then he said, "Darling, I have news of England."

Elaine snuggled against Roland and laid her head on his chest. "Tell me," she said.

"First of all, I must say that all I predicted has come true. King Richard did attack France—he's made effective use of the gold I sent him, he's driven the French back steadily—indeed, he has retaken all the old English provinces, including your Anjou, my dear."

Elaine laughed against his skin and said, "I don't need a province when I have a duchy!"

Roland stroked her hair affectionately and continued: "Prince John rules in England, unpopular as ever—the Chancellor of the Exchequer continues to tax at unGodly rates."

Elaine noticed that Roland, diplomatic as ever, had avoided saying Arthur's name. She shivered even now, remembering Arthur's plot against her—she held her dear husband tighter.

"Now we come to the most interesting part," Roland said. "These last few months something strange and amazing has been occurring in England, something I have never heard of before—Prince John has tried to keep it quiet, but the monk I spoke to today tells me the whole country knows anyway—the fact is that someone, an outlaw all dressed in green, has been attacking the tax collectors. He attacks them when they are loaded with spoils for the Exchequer—he takes, not for himself, but rather for the people whose goods and money were confiscated by the state. He steals what the crown claims—and gives it back to the people.

"I am told that he has saved whole towns from starvation by returning necessary goods that were pillaged by the Exchequer's agents—and not only that—he has attacked wealthy landowners who demand too high a percentage of their tenant's crops—what he steals from greedy Barons goes back to the humble tenant farmers—he is loved by common folk throughout the land, he is their champion, their bright green hope.

"Barons have hired knights to kill him, the Prince has already sent a whole army after him—but somehow he always escapes. He is said to be a fabulous archer, capable of near unbelievable feats—he doesn't carry a sword."

Elaine, who had been so relaxed and satisfied a few minutes previously, now felt her whole body tense. Her heart was pounding—she felt hot and feverish—she thought of the broken sword hand that must never have totally healed—she thought of the powerful thumb and forefinger that could still draw back an arrow—she hoped Roland didn't notice that her nipples were hard, that her thighs were drenched with new wetness—she asked, and she barely had the strength to whisper, "What's his name?"

"His name is Robin Hood."

Elaine froze—that was not the name she had expected—yet no one else could do such feats—then suddenly the memories came back to her: 'My parents gave me a silly name . . .'—she recalled how Brian had addressed him, and everything fell into place. "The little birdie," she said.

"Yes," Roland answered, studying his wife in the candlelight, "Robin Hood is his real name."

Roland didn't have to say who the "his" referred to.

The Duke watched his wife and waited for her to speak.

Elaine took a deep breath to calm herself, and then she said, "I always expected greatness from Thomas—from Robin Hood—and I am pleased to see him come into his own. His destiny was never at the court—now I am sure that soon the whole world will know of him. I am honored that I knew him once." Elaine looked up at her husband. "But Roland, it's you I love, I love you my husband, I love you, hold me, just hold me tight . . ."

And Roland held her, but not for long, for within moments

there came a pounding at the door, and then a page cried, "Lady Sandra is in labor. She requests the presence of Her Grace at her earliest possible convenience."

Elaine said, "Tell her I'll be right there," and then she got up and began to dress—she wondered why babies always seemed to come at night.

She kissed Roland on her way out—she said, "Thank you for telling me what you learned—I love you, don't ever doubt that— but now I must go, and you should sleep, because I don't know when I'll get back." She kissed Roland again, and opened the door, and walked to Lady Sandra's room.

Davila was already in attendance, looking sprightly despite her age. Her cane leaned unneeded against a wall.

Sandra was lying down.

Elaine sat on the edge of her friend's bed. She took Sandra's hand in hers, and did not move from that position for the next eight hours.

Elaine felt every contraction of Sandra's labor through the grip on her hand—she saw every pain in her friend's brown eyes—in those same eyes she saw joy beyond imagining when Davila held up a healthy baby boy just as dawn's first light entered the room—she felt tears on her own face when she heard the lad's first proud cry—she let go of Sandra's hand so that the new mother could gently take her child, as Davila handed him to her—Elaine watched as Sandra cradled the boy to her breast—she watched as the baby found his mother's nipple and began to suck—she watched the indivisible bond form between mother and child as Sandra held him there, eyes only for her new miracle—Sandra said, "Anton, little Anton, Anton I love you so"—Elaine wiped her eyes and just looked at the little boy—he was so tiny, so perfect—she felt her tears coming again—she bent down and kissed the baby's lovely soft skin— she moved over and kissed Sandra on the forehead—Sandra smiled but she just stared at her babe—Elaine looked at Davila—the Gypsy said, "Get some sleep, Your Grace, every-thing is fine now."

Elaine nodded—she looked once more at the babe, and then she quietly left the room.

Chapter 171

FIRST ANNIVERSARY

Little Anton was nearly five months old and learning to roll over when Elaine and Roland celebrated their first wedding anniversary. The occasion was marvelously festive. Roland gave a great ball, to which all the ladies and gentlemen of the court were invited—and no invitations were refused. The ladies all dressed in their best, though none tried to rival the Duchess— no woman *could* compete with the Duchess—Elaine the Fair was above them all, as was right and proper. The women just longed to possess a little of her magic.

The men admired their Duchess from afar—and if some brave knights had seen her naked on an English battlefield, they kept those memories to themselves. They saw her as she was now, as she was meant to be, resplendent in silk and gold. They loved her without thought of personal desire, for Elaine belonged to their lord, and that too was right and proper.

All eyes were upon the Duke and Duchess when they danced together—the love they felt for each other was plain to see.

Roland and Elaine felt their subjects' adoration, a swelling force that seemed to lift them up into their own special world— they danced, never feeling the floor . . .

The guests began to quietly leave around midnight—finally Roland and Elaine noticed that they were all alone save for musicians and servants—they danced one more slow dance, and then Roland dismissed all the workers save his personal page.

Roland took Elaine's arm—they followed the page's torch as he lit their way down the long corridors of the palace. The lad led them to their bedroom without instruction—there he lit some candles and then quickly withdrew.

Elaine and Roland were alone, wrapped in the special glow of this night—they embraced.

Elaine felt free to speak from the depths of her heart. She said, "Dear Roland, I want so very much to have a baby."

Roland kissed her and said, "I too want to have a child—I do wish we could have a son."

Elaine almost said, 'But what if we have a daughter?' but then she realized that there had been something deep and somber in Roland's tone—she decided not to answer lightly. She looked into his eyes and asked seriously, "Why do you want to have a son?"

Roland took Elaine over to their bed. He sat her down on the side, and sat himself down next to her. He looked away—and then slowly, with great difficulty, and crying sometimes, he told the story of Charles's short and tragic life.

Elaine had not even known that Roland had had a brother—she put her arm around her husband as she listened—she knew that he was giving her a secret key to his heart.

Finally Roland finished the story. He wiped his eyes and turned to his wife. "If we have a son," he asked, "would you mind if we named him Charles?"

Elaine did not even think of opposing her husband. She replied, "Of course, dear love, our first son will be named Charles—but I must tell you, sad bear, that in my imaginings now I always see my first born as a girl, so what shall we call our daughter?"

"You are not planning to have only one child, are you, my dear?"

Elaine bowed submissively—but she smiled underneath—and she replied, "As many as you wish, Your Grace."

"Then let us not worry over names, my darling," Roland said. "We shall have a son in time—and we shall have nine months from today to think of a beautiful name for a beautiful daughter."

Elaine looked up at Roland's face—a dear face that was full of confidence now—she felt a wonderful hope in her heart—they had shared each other's pain, now they were free to bring life into the world—she kissed her husband, and he kissed her back, he did something while he kissed her, and suddenly her dress fell from her body, he pushed her back on the bed, he followed her down, kissing her, he freed himself and took her the first time that night with his clothes still on—afterward Elaine undressed him, slowly, lovingly—by the time she was finished he was ready again—their lovemaking did not cease until dawn.

Roland did nothing that morning save sleep—but he woke at twelve, and he received visitors as usual in the afternoon.

Chapter 172

THE FULL MOON

The full moon nearly broke Elaine's heart when it appeared two weeks after her anniversary. In all the years of her womanhood, the full moon had always drawn the blood from her empty womb—each month of her marriage to Roland she had looked at that moon in sadness, but this month—this month, she had been sure that her fortunes would change.

The flow of blood mocked her—the pain of emptiness was unbearable—Elaine took to her bed and cried for two days. Roland could not console her. On the third day Elaine went to see Sandra and young Anton, but that only made things worse. The Duchess took to her bed again and coldly waited for her week of misfortune to pass.

Elaine spent the time thinking of all the mothers she knew. She thought of Sandra, who had had only a week with her man—and she had gotten pregnant. She thought of the many wives, both in London and Larraz, who had become pregnant during their honeymoons. She thought of many other wives who at least conceived sometime during the first year of marriage.

But not me, Elaine thought, not me. Not with Arthur—and looking back I'm glad I didn't have a child with him but still I would have loved the little boy I imagined—but no, no child—we made love so seldom, I always thought that was the reason, but now with Roland that doesn't apply—O I love my dear sweet bear so much, I love him and I want a baby with him—and he wants a baby as much as I and we make love so often, at the end of our honeymoon we were joined day and night alike, and now every day and extra in the mornings sometimes—(Elaine calculated for a moment) we've made love more than five hundred times, five hundred times and nothing nothing nothing—

Elaine began to cry on this day, the sixth day of her menses— she was still crying when Roland found her an hour later, but she would not let him touch her.

She was totally preoccupied with a single dreadful fear: she feared that her stunning surface beauty was just a sham, a cover up for lifelessness within—she feared that she was barren.

She could not let Roland touch her until she knew the truth.

All day Elaine had been thinking that there was one person who would be able to tell her the truth of her condition—Elaine knew now that she would have to go to her—even the most terrible knowledge was preferable to this uncertainty.

Chapter 173

MOTHER'S MILK

Lying awake that night, Elaine found that her flow had ceased. She got up and looked out the window—she saw that a crow had bitten off a sliver of the full moon. She went back to bed, and slept, for she knew that she would get her answer on the morrow.

The next morning, after Roland went off to receive his travelers, Elaine went to visit Sandra. The Duchess opened her friend's door without knocking—Sandra looked around from the chair she was sitting in. Elaine started to speak—but Sandra quickly shushed her and pointed to the bed. There was little Anton, sound asleep on the middle of his mother's bed, a fine, content, handsome boy—Elaine looked back to Sandra, and saw the circles under her soft loving eyes, and she understood the reason for the shushing.

"He kept me awake all last night," Sandra whispered. "I should sleep now but I love to watch him."

Elaine came over and put her hand on Sandra's shoulder—the younger woman was only wearing a loose robe, carelessly belted—looking down Elaine could see most of Sandra's full taut breasts, swollen with milk—the Duchess slipped her hand down inside the robe and cupped Sandra's left breast—it was so much bigger than she remembered from past days in London, so hard and heavy—the nipple was swollen too, it was hard against her palm—Elaine was afraid to squeeze for fear that milk would come out on her hand—she just held Sandra gently, and then she said, "I have a fear that I have not even confided to my husband. I am afraid that I am barren."

Sandra didn't look up at Elaine. She kept her eyes on her

child—she said quietly, "No, that can't be."

"Still, I am afraid," Elaine said. "I must know the truth or falseness of my fear. The Gypsy, Davila, will be able to tell me."

Sandra put her hand over Elaine's and held it tighter to her breast. "Yes," Sandra said, "she will know."

"You took little Anton to her home when he was four months old, didn't you?"

"Yes," replied Sandra. She was breathing more heavily now.

"You'll tell me how to get there—and if Roland asks later, you will not tell him where I am."

"Yes."

Elaine opened Sandra's robe completely, revealing both her breasts. The Duchess went around in front of Sandra and knelt down. She placed both her hands on the breast that she had already caressed. She leaned forward—

"Please be gentle," Sandra said. "My nipples are very sore."

Elaine took the hard thick nipple in her mouth—she still held the firm breast with both her hands.

Sandra had moved her hands away when Elaine had opened her robe. She had that feeling again that her body did not belong to her—she felt the hot mouth of her mistress claiming her—she did not dare to stroke Elaine's golden hair—she just held tight to the arms of her chair and stared at her sleeping son.

Elaine ran her tongue again and again over the throbbing nipple—and then she did squeeze the swollen breast with both hands, and she bit down hard with sudden, deliberate cruelty—she heard Sandra's gasping struggle not to cry out and wake her babe—she felt the hot jet of milk in her mouth, so much sweeter than she would have guessed—she sucked hard for a long moment before she let Sandra go.

Elaine stood up and looked down into Sandra's frightened eyes. The girl was still panting—but she hadn't cried out. Elaine pulled Sandra's robe together so that her breasts were covered again.

Elaine's voice was coldly formal as she said, "You'll tell me the way now."

Sandra gave directions with the exactitude of one who had once guided Larrazian knights.

When she was finished Elaine leaned down and kissed her hard on the mouth, just a little tenderness at the end of the kiss, and then the Duchess straightened up again—she looked quickly at the sleeping Anton, and then she took her leave.

Chapter 174

THE RIDE TO THE CABIN

Elaine rode with the horse between her legs. The groom had been shocked when she had ordered a man's saddle—but then he had looked at the Duchess's cold glittering blue eyes and he had obeyed.

The palace of Larraz was no fortress. There was a ceremonial gate to the north, which opened up to the prosperous part of the capital city—and there was an unguarded road to the south which led first to the city's poorest district, and then continued onward into the country.

Elaine took that road to the south. The people stared at her as though unsure whether she was their Duchess or an angel—she was too beautiful to be anything else—but what Duchess or angel rides astride with her dress fluttering around the tops of her bare thighs?

The Duchess ignored the stares, and no one dared approach her.

Finally Elaine left the city behind. She continued to follow the road for a few miles, until she spotted the discreet turnoff to the left. Elaine made the turn and found herself on a narrow but well worn path—this led, Sandra had told her with a smile, to the duchy's most famous brothel. Elaine had not heard of Madame Genevieve's establishment before—she reflected as she rode that Sandra seemed to know more about their adopted country than she did—or perhaps certain topics were just not considered fit for a Duchess's ears.

Anyway, she rode along until she saw the quite imposing structure of the house of pleasure (evidently business was good) and then she continued on past it and now suddenly there was r.o more path.

This was where Sandra's information was most valuable—
Elaine would never have been able to find her way had it not
been for her friend's precise enumeration of the landmarks—
and even with that help, Elaine got lost several times. Then she
had to painstakingly backtrack and search again for the next
landmark.

It was slow hot work—it was nearly dusk before Elaine suddenly saw the cabin looming in front of her, just as though some
dark shadow of the woods had magically acquired substance.

Elaine stopped her horse. She strained her eyes in the fading
light—and then she saw that another shadow was actually the
old woman. Davila, leaning on her cane, was wrapped in dark
robes as though she were fighting the cold—Elaine herself felt
hot in just her thin dress.

Elaine dismounted and walked over to the Gypsy. Davila
looked up at her with black knowing eyes.

"I have been expecting you," she said. "Take care of your horse
and then come inside."

The old woman turned away from the Duchess and vanished
into her cabin.

Elaine felt no anger at the curt way she had been addressed—
she felt only relief that she had been expected—she felt certain
now that soon she would know the answer to her fearful question.

Chapter 175

DAVILA

Elaine, after dealing with her horse, had trouble with the cabin's heavy wooden door. She could not understand how the frail old woman had slipped inside so easily. Finally, exerting all her strength, Elaine forced the door open.

The Duchess stepped into the cabin—the door shut with a solid thunk behind her.

The day had been hot—but it was hotter still inside the cabin's single room. The Duchess looked first at the fire burning to her right—she observed that nothing was cooking. In front of her she saw a table with some strange shaped jars on it, the jars filled with unidentifiable substances. Davila's cane leaned against the table.

Elaine looked to her left—there Davila stood, unaided, just in front of a low wide bed.

"You fear that you are barren," Davila said. She was not asking a question.

"Yes." Elaine felt that she should be frightened by this strange woman who knew so much—but she wasn't. As before, when Davila announced that she had been expected, she felt relieved. Now she didn't have to state her problem—the burden had been taken from her shoulders.

She was in Davila's hands now—like Sandra, she trusted this very special old woman—and then with sudden fear, she wondered what answer Davila would give.

The Gypsy read her thoughts. "You have come to me to learn the truth about yourself. You want to know if you can have children."

"Yes."

"I will tell you"—Davila's voice became stern—"but you must pay me first."

"Of course," Elaine said. She was somewhat disappointed that magic seemed to be giving way to commerce. She fumbled with the purse, heavily laden with gold, that she had brought for just this eventuality.

"Not with that," Davila snapped.

Elaine's finger froze on the clasp of the purse—she felt the little hairs rising on her bare tingling arms—the power of magic was back in the room.

"I don't want your gold," Davila said softly. She looked straight into Elaine's eyes. "I want something far more precious." Davila dropped her eyes slightly and looked at Elaine's mouth. "I want one kiss."

Elaine ran her tongue over her suddenly dry lips. "Yes," she whispered.

The Duchess walked slowly over to the Gypsy. Up close, the little old woman only came up to her breasts. Elaine put her hands gently on Davila's frail shoulders, and tried to bend down—it was awkward, and Davila did not help at all, she did not look up—Elaine could not reach her lips.

"How can I do this?" Elaine asked.

"You get on your knees," Davila replied simply.

There was a long pause, and then the Duchess of Larraz knelt on the hard wooden floor of the Gypsy's cabin.

Now their faces were on the same level. Elaine looked into Davila's black eyes—and then she put her hands on the old wrinkled cheeks. The Gypsy's skin was loose but very soft—Elaine shuffled forward a little and then slowly brought her face toward Davila's—Elaine kept looking into those black eyes as she approached—and then suddenly she saw a vision of a young Gypsy girl dancing around a fire, shining black hair wild as she leaped and spun, big gold hoop earrings flashing like lightning, a scarlet blouse carelessly torn so that her young breasts nearly bounced free, a black skirt whirling high with each pirouette, firm shapely legs revealed underneath—and now a young man joined her dance, a young man as dark and handsome as she was beautiful—his dance mirrored hers, until with a savage grace he reached out and captured one of her hands—the Gypsy girl danced away, only to be swung back into his embrace—her breasts against his chest, her hand held, the girl surrendered to his kiss—Elaine kissed Davila—

The vision gradually faded.

Elaine gently ended the kiss. Slowly, almost reluctantly, she took her hands from the old woman's face.

"You understand now," Davila said. "I was beautiful once."

"Yes," Elaine replied, "I saw."

Davila nodded slowly as though Elaine had passed a test. She walked over to the table with the jars, and said over her shoulder to Elaine, "Take off all your clothes and lie facedown on the bed."

Elaine did as she was told.

Davila came back with one of the jars in her hand. She used her other hand to push Elaine's legs apart, and then she knelt between them. She opened the jar, revealing a thick pale green liquid with a pungent smell—she leaned forward and poured a healthy measure of the potion between Elaine's shoulderblades. Elaine flinched from the cold of it, but then she gradually relaxed as the Gypsy's small strong hands massaged the liquid into her back. A warmth began to pervade her skin—Elaine felt comforted, cared for—Davila worked all over her back, skirted her soft buttocks and then followed her legs to her toes, came slowly back up and this time deliberately lingered over the sweet behind, caressing, massaging the softness there—and then suddenly Davila spread the cheeks and thrust one lubricated finger up where Elaine had never been entered before.

Elaine cried out and tried to struggle, but Davila's other strong hand pressed down against the center of her back—she could not escape—Davila forced another finger in to join the first.

Elaine tightened her muscles to try to expel the intruders but she couldn't—she felt the insidious heat of the potion inside her—she felt her nipples scrape stiffly over the bedspread—she heard her own helpless moans—finally she resigned herself, she gave herself physically to Davila as she had already submitted in her mind, she relaxed—Davila began to move her fingers, in and out—she forced Elaine beyond submission into complicity—Elaine felt hot all over her body now, she could not help herself, she started to push back—

Davila withdrew her fingers and slapped Elaine hard on the right buttock.

Elaine cried out at the sudden pain—and then she just lay still, feeling the tingling imprint of the blow, picturing the red mark on her white skin.

Davila moved back and deliberately wiped her fingers on a towel—and then she said, "Roll over and spread your legs again."

Elaine obeyed.

Davila moved forward until her knees were pressing Elaine's widespread thighs. The Gypsy picked up her jar and poured another good measure between Elaine's breasts. She didn't tease this time—she massaged the potion right away into the soft, tender breasts—she worked the liquid into the rigid nipples, she squeezed them and rolled them between her fingers until they were hot and tight and unbearably sensitive—only then did she work her way downward, she pressed hard against Elaine's flat stomach, a finger bored into her navel—and then finally she came to the fine blond fleece that failed to guard Elaine's womanhood—there were the little pink lips, open like a mouth about to be kissed.

"Close your eyes," Davila said.

Elaine obeyed. Vision gone, every other sense was heightened. She heard the jar being opened again, smelled the liquid emerging, heard the splashing sound as it was poured—but she felt nothing on her own body, and then she realized that Davila had simply annointed her fingers, she felt those wet fingers caressing her, knowing fingers opening her, entering her, moving slowly inside her, gradually filling her more and more, working their way deeper, the fullness growing, stretching her, almost too much, she spread her legs wider, too much, something big in her and Elaine raised her head and opened her eyes and saw that Davila had her whole hand buried to the wrist in her, tiny hand yes, but all of it inside her was big, bigger than—and then she felt the fingers move in her, fingers probing in, entering her womb and the shock of being *known* that way broke Elaine, she gave Davila her final submission, her body shuddered and released, shuddered and released, she clamped down on the hand within her, she screamed once as the fingers moved again and then she just lay back and closed her eyes again and quivered helplessly until her terrible pleasure was over.

Elaine kept her eyes closed as Davila slowly retreated her hand and finally removed it—then there was an aching sensation of emptiness—Elaine covered her tender womanhood with a hand and listened to Davila.

She heard the Gypsy pick up the jar and stand up—she listened to the footsteps as Davila walked away, slow painful footsteps, the walk of a very old and very tired woman—Elaine opened her eyes.

She watched Davila shuffle to her table and then lean heavily upon it as she set the jar down—saw her feel for her cane and finally reach it—saw her shuffle a few more steps with the cane's aid until she got to a chair by the fire—saw her sit down heavily and pull her robes tighter around her small exhausted form.

Her face was in profile to Elaine. She did not seem to want to look at the Duchess.

Elaine stood up and put her dress on, and her shoes, and picked up her purse. She looked over at Davila and said, "Tell me the truth."

Davila spoke in a very sad voice. "You are fertile. Your beauty is meant to bring many children into the world."

Elaine took a long deep breath. She felt an amazing rush of happiness.

Why was Davila so sad?

Elaine looked over at the Gypsy—her black eyes were bright in the firelight—were they bright with tears?

"The man who wishes to fill you will do so," Davila said.

This didn't make sense. Roland wanted a child as much as she did—he wanted to fill her—then why . . .?

"I don't understand," Elaine said.

"It's time for you to go," Davila answered.

Elaine wanted to ask again for an explanation, but another look at the exhausted old woman convinced her not to.

"Is there anything I can do for you?" Elaine asked.

"Just go," Davila said harshly.

Elaine walked over and laid her purse on the edge of Davila's table.

"It's a gift, not a payment."

Davila nodded.

Elaine wanted to say something more—but it was clear that she couldn't stay. She opened the heavy wooden door with the same difficulty as before and stepped out into the night.

She could see her horse in the moonlight.

She knew Roland must be searching for her—and since he hadn't found her yet, she knew that Sandra must have kept her secret.

Chapter 176

THE LEAST LIKELY PLACE

When Roland finished his afternoon conversations, he would always come straight back to his bedchamber. Elaine was always there waiting for him. This was not something they had formally agreed upon—just a custom they had slipped into, as married folk do in all strata of society.

So Elaine had always been there waiting—sometimes they made love right then before dinner.

She had always been there waiting—until today.

Her absence was absolutely terrifying. Roland thought that he had left that kind of fear behind in England—but now it came back with a vengeance.

The Duke made a big effort to calm himself. There was really no reason to suppose that this was another case of abduction. He found his page and asked him where the Duchess was. The lad replied that Her Grace had gone to visit Lady Sandra, many hours before, and she had not yet returned.

Roland allowed himself a small sigh of relief—he thought that the two ladies must simply have lost track of time.

He walked quickly down the long corridors of the palace, knocked on Lady Sandra's door, and entered.

Sandra was asleep on her bed. Her robe had come undone—she cradled her sleeping babe against her full breasts.

Elaine was not in the room.

"Lady Sandra."

She slept on.

Roland stepped forward and put a hand on her bare shoulder. "Sandra, wake up," The Duke said urgently.

Sandra opened her eyes and saw a man—she was frightened

but then she realized he was her Duke—she also realized that she was uncovered, but because of the way she was holding her son, she could not close her robe.

"Just a moment, Your Grace," she said.

Anton's head was against her breast. Sandra let his head slide down onto the support of her hand, and then she gently laid the babe on the bed. She started to close her robe—but then Anton made it clear that he didn't approve of the loss of his mother's warmth—he woke up and started to cry.

Sandra left her robe open (Roland remembered how embarrassed Sandra had been in England when she had had to show her wounded bottom—she had clearly become far less modest since becoming a mother) and picked up her son. She offered him a breast.

He didn't want it. Anton's little belly was already full. He had just finished nursing ten minutes ago and then he had fallen into a contented sleep with his mother. He was very annoyed now that his nap had been interrupted.

His cries escalated into howls of indignation.

Sandra got up and began walking around the room. She bounced her boy, and cajoled him, but nothing helped. She said a quick, "I'm sorry, Your Grace," as she went by Roland—but she gave most of her attention to her son, who continued to demonstrate that he had very healthy lungs.

Roland couldn't wait for the baby to calm down. He tried to make himself heard over the noise. "Did Elaine visit you today?"

"Yes, Your Grace, this afternoon," Sandra replied, and then she bent her head and continued to speak to her son, "There's a good boy, Mama's got you, it's alright—"

"When did she leave?"

"Later on this afternoon, Your Grace, not too long ago." As soon as she made her reply, Sandra looked back down at her boy with concern—Anton seemed to be getting louder.

"Where did she go?"

Sandra didn't look up.

Roland grabbed Sandra's shoulders and forced her to face him. Between the two adults, the baby screamed.

"Where did she go?"

Sandra didn't try to lie. "I promised not to tell, Your Grace."

Roland looked into Sandra's loyal brown eyes. The baby continued his unnerving howls. The Duke realized that his own unfamiliar presence was part of the reason for the boy's continued agitation.

Roland's thoughts whirled. What am I to do? Should I slap the answer out of her as she holds her screaming babe in her arms?

Roland rejected that idea as soon as he thought it—he just wanted to leave but he didn't know where to go—his confusion and pain showed on his face.

Sandra had to give him something. "Your Grace, don't worry. She'll be back soon enough and no harm done—but you might check the stables and see if she took a horse."

"Thank you, Lady Sandra," Roland said, glad to have some direction. He hurried away, followed by the fading screams of little Anton.

The groom told Roland about the man's saddle. "With all due respect, Your Grace, she was a fiery sight."

"Indeed," Roland said, giving the groom a cold look. "Which way did she go?"

"South."

"Wake up the trumpet player," Roland ordered, (this fine musician was notorious for his nighttime drunkenness and daytime slumber) "and tell him to blow like his life depends on it. I want him to summon every knight in the duchy."

"Yes, Your Grace," the groom said, and he ran off.

Before long the fanfare was drifting high into the air over Larraz—every knight who heard it made haste to the stables behind the palace where Roland was waiting.

It was getting dark. 'Back soon enough and no harm done'— Roland didn't trust that. There were dangers in the dark, even in peaceful Larraz. Elaine could be seized, taken away as before—and this time he might not get her back.

The fear screamed in Roland's mind.

Where had she gone?

Roland had seen Elaine crying this last week but still he did not know the depth of her pain. He could not share her deep seated need to feel life inside her, to nourish that life, to give birth—and so he could not comprehend the horror she felt for her own emptiness—he could not feel her desperation, and so he did not know where that desperation had sent her.

Roland thought of Davila as someone to be summoned only *after* the fact of pregnancy—her name did not cross his mind in connection with his wife.

The knights were ready now, mounted, impatient to be off— Roland didn't know where to send them.

He remembered following the false path, tracking down the grazing horses—

He spoke with all the confidence he could manage. "You all know why you're here. My wife is as brave as she is beautiful, gentlemen, yet sometimes her bravery takes her to the point of foolishness.

"She has gone out riding alone through the south end of town. Most likely she has merely become lost in the countryside beyond the city. I doubt there is any highwayman unwise enough to seize my lady, but if there is such a one"—Roland paused and looked hard at his men—"kill him."

The knights growled their assent.

"Go now, and find her, and bring her back safely," Roland said, and then he waved one hand to send them on their way.

The knights took off with a thunder of hoofbeats in the gathering dark. Though their faces didn't show it, they were all happy. They thought how blessed they were to have a fiery beautiful Duchess who got herself into such trouble—each man fantasized that he would be the one to save Elaine the Fair from some dastardly highwayman—a brief clash of swords, victory, and then perhaps she would reward her hero with a kiss . . .

Roland stood alone by the horse the groom had made ready for him. He stood there silently for a long time, thinking, thinking, trying to guess where Elaine had gone. He could not come up with an answer—and he couldn't face Sandra and her child again.

Finally, as a joke on himself, he decided to think of what place Elaine would be least likely to go to. Right away he thought of Madame Genevieve's brothel—not only would that be the least likely place for Elaine to visit, it would also be the last place in the world that his men would search. Roland mounted and set off for the house of pleasure with a smile—he reflected that even an absurd destination is better than none at all—and after all, the brothel did lie to the south.

As he rode Roland recalled his first and only visit to Madame Genevieve's. His father, as was customary, had taken him there following his first public joust at age sixteen. "A boy proves his courage on the field of battle before he has the right to a man's pleasure," his father had said. Roland had been terrified during the joust—he was frightened later too, but the woman had been understanding, the memory was sweet—but now Roland felt a sudden spasm of pain seize his body—tears flowed freely down his cheeks before he could stop them—all the other memories came back, the memories of the visit that didn't take place—he had arranged to take Charles to the brothel following his younger brother's first joust—but Charles was killed—Charles died without ever knowing a woman . . .

Roland had never wanted to visit Madame Genevieve again.

Now a fool's errand was taking him there—but he had nowhere else to go.

He rode on until the nightwind dried his tears—he rode until he came to the torchlit mansion that housed Madame Genevieve's pretty charges.

He stopped his horse—he heard laughter coming from within the building and he knew that Elaine wasn't in there—he decided there was no reason to make a greater fool of himself by knocking—he thought ruefully that he had wanted an absurd destination and he had certainly found one—he hoped that his men had done better—he tried to turn his horse to go back but the animal wouldn't budge.

Roland pulled on one rein to turn the horse's head—the horse rolled his eye and pulled back the other way.

"What do you do if I let you have your head?" Roland asked quietly as he loosened the reins.

The horse answered by stretching out his neck and sniffing the air.

Roland felt a sudden excitement.

He listened—he heard faint hoofbeats, crackling noises— hooves breaking through underbrush—a horse at a walk, coming through the woods—coming closer—his own horse gave a soft whinny as he recognized a stablemate—a black shape appeared at the other end of the clearing that surrounded the brothel—hooves silent now on the soft grass, the horse stepped into the light—Madame Genevieve's torches lit up half the horse, half the rider—what shined the most was one gorgeous bare leg of Elaine the Fair.

Roland felt a sense of relief such as he had never known before. This time he had not followed the false trail—this time he had trusted his crazy heart and found his true love. He was so faint with happiness that he nearly fell off his horse—and then he thought, Why not? He jumped down, he ran to Elaine and caught her horse's bridle—he barely had time to set himself before Elaine, her dress flying perilously high, vaulted off her mount—he let go of the bridle and caught his wife, caught her

bare thighs as her legs scissored around his waist—her arms
came around his neck, and her mouth came down on his, and
they kissed until they just absolutely had to stop to breathe.

They took a couple of panting breaths, staring into each
other's eyes, and then Roland slowly let Elaine's legs slide down
until her feet were on the ground.

She kept her arms around his neck—she pulled him down and
he kissed her again, slower this time, in the searching way he
liked—finally he raised his head and said, "Thank God you're
safe. I was so worried. Where were you?"

Elaine gave her husband a saucy grin. "I've been to see
Davila."

"Davila? But you're not—"

"Silly bear, I wanted to see if I *could* become pregnant."

Elaine was positively bubbling over with good cheer.

"What did she say?"

"She said that I could have many, many children—as many as
you wish, Your Grace," Elaine said, deliberately repeating the
phrase from their anniversary night.

This time Roland pulled her hard to him and kissed her and
kissed her again.

Finally he said, "That's wonderful news, darling, wonderful
news—still you should never have left without a word. Your dis-
appearance terrified us all. I had to call in all my knights."
Roland waved a hand to indicate the surrounding countryside.
"Every knight of Larraz is out there somewhere, searching for
you."

Elaine smiled slightly.

Roland tried to look stern. "After all the trouble you've
caused, I really ought to spank you."

Elaine looked up at her husband with smoldering eyes. She
felt again the sting of Davila's striking palm—she remembered
spanking Sandra, the day before the flowered path, until the
girl was sobbing—until her bottom was crimson. She wondered
what it would be like to have that happen to her—she felt
strange tremors of fear mingled with desire—when she tried to
speak she could barely get the words out.

"If you think I deserve it," she whispered, "you certainly
should."

But by the time Roland had escorted Elaine back to the
palace, he was too happy to even think of punishing her—and so
he just made love to her three times, he filled her three times—

but perhaps three times wasn't enough, for when the full moon came again in a few weeks it once again brought Elaine's unwanted flow of blood.

She cried, but quietly, only in the afternoons so Roland wouldn't see—she thought often of what the Gypsy had said: "The man who wishes to fill you will do so."

She could not understand.

Chapter 177

THE FUTURE SEEN WITH A COLD EYE

The months passed slowly in the second year of Elaine's marriage. Every month followed the same pattern. First there was the joy of loving and being loved—hours spent in bed with Roland, lovemaking passionate and tender; then a rising anticipation as the month wore on—lovemaking sharp and intense—the feeling that *this* time her wish would come true; then a growing nervousness toward the end of her cycle, fear and desperation creeping in—she could only make love if Roland coaxed her with long patient kisses; then finally the full moon with its cold light on the world—the hot tormenting blood of failure—black depression to be hidden from Roland—bitter tears in the afternoon that Valerie, Elaine's lady in waiting, learned to carefully wash away; finally smiles for Roland as a new month started—he loved her so, he wanted to fill her—and so there would be love once again in the big bed . . .

The cycle continued.

Elaine thought at first that she might get used to it—but instead the pain just got worse—each proof of her emptiness became harder to bear.

The Duchess found that she could no longer stand Sandra's company. Her former lady in waiting was as sweet as ever—but she was also wonderfully happy with her little Anton. That happiness engendered an evil jealousy that Elaine did not want to show—but she was afraid she could not overcome it, and so she stopped the visits with her friend.

This did not mean that she did not often see Sandra and Anton around the palace—that was unavoidable—she also saw many other ladies of the court with their children—the loving sight of a mother kissing her child was like an arrow piercing Elaine's heart.

Elaine's one comfort was Roland, her big gentle steadfast bear. She spent as much time as possible with him, except during those weeks marked by the full moon.

So once again she received visitors with the Duke—and while Elaine still had no interest in Sicily's rainfall or the musical beds of the Paris court, she always listened intently when there was news of her homeland.

There were more and more reports about Robin Hood, but all were hearsay—none could be confirmed. Still, these reports agreed on many details. Robin was said to command a group of Merry Men; he had an encampment in Sherwood Forest near Nottingham; (Elaine started when she heard this—Robin's parents had served the Baron of Nottingham! And after his revenge on the black knights, Robin had gone to live in the forest for two years—he just didn't tell me the name of the forest, Elaine thought—he's finally gone home) his most trusted lieutenant was a giant called Little John—these two were rarely seen apart; and finally, despite his base in Nottingham, Robin seemed to have a magical ability to strike anywhere in the country—some thought that he had more than one group of Merry Men who answered to his call.

Tax collectors walked in fear, Barons cursed and held the line on their fees, and Prince John fumed.

Balladeers sang the praises of Robin Hood.

No one could catch him—not the Baron's hired knights, not the Prince's soldiers, certainly not the Sheriff of Nottingham. This last fellow—a fat sycophant who had been appointed by Prince John—had vowed to capture and hang Robin Hood, which had the effect of setting the Sheriff himself up as the butt of endless jokes. The Sheriff's corpulence and incompetence had become the symbol of corrupt official England.

There was a touch of wistful romance in the reports too— Elaine learned that all over England, women were sewing green clothes for Robin, just hoping for a visit . . .

Meanwhile, closer to Larraz, there was news of King Richard. He was still winning victories and gaining territory in France— but he was also said to be running short of cash.

One summer afternoon, (it was July, 1196) after listening to a long report about King Richard's finances, Roland shocked Elaine with a simple matter of fact statement. "The Lionheart is going to fall soon," he said.

Elaine's surprise showed on her face—Roland continued, delighted to have his wife's interest. "King Richard's problem is his own success—the more victories he wins, the further his army is overextended. He can't live on the land forever, for the French simply flee before him, taking their valuables as they go. The King can't get satisfactory coin or supplies from England, because Robin Hood has cut off the tax base. If I know Prince John, and I do, he will take care of his own pleasures first, and think about Richard later. He'll send his brother as little gold as he can get away with, and blame the low shipments (with some truth) on Robin Hood's attacks.

"If King Richard were wise, he'd go home and straighten up the situation in England (Elaine wondered if such a 'straightening' would include killing Robin—but she didn't interrupt) but the Lionheart is not the sort to think of retreat—certainly not when he is winning on the battlefield.

"So you see, my dear, the King's position worsens every day — others will notice his weakness—he will rush to his death.

"I give him no more than two or three years—it's not too early for me to begin some rather delicate negotiations with King Philip II.

"In the long run, of course, France is a better ally for us than England, since we share a common border. I shall send an emissary to King Philip, and if he is open to suggestion, I will tell him that we will be ready to throw our support to him the moment Richard begins to fall. I have no doubt that we can manage to get some valuable trading agreements in return for our help."

Roland beamed at Elaine.

Elaine looked at the brilliant politician who had just cooly dismissed a man's life. She knew that such accurate, unsentimental foresight was the basis for Larraz's peace and security—she knew that those "valuable trading agreements" were the coin that paid for her own luxury—she knew too that Richard was an evil man who deserved to die—still, he had been an ally—it had been Larrazian gold that had initially sent Richard to France—it was strange to see Roland's pride as he prepared to secretly switch sides.

Elaine looked at her smiling husband—she tossed a smile back to him, but inside she felt a chill as though her heart had been touched by an icy ray of moonlight.

And yet in bed that night Roland was once again her warm loving gentle bear—he lay next to her and hugged her, and she hid her face against his chest—she listened to the comforting beat of his heart while he stroked her body—she felt the kindling of her own desire—she slowly moved her face upward, kissing as she went—she brushed his beard away and found his mouth, she kissed him and let him kiss her—she wanted more than his kisses now, she rolled away from him, onto her back— she opened her legs for him and heard his breathing change— she saw his eyes light up with an almost worshipful look of love—she closed her own eyes—she felt him positioning himself over her—she felt his chest hair tickling the tips of her breasts—she felt his strong manhood begin to enter her, and she just reached up blindly and wrapped her arms around him and pulled him down, she wanted him all the way in her, she wanted to feel his weight—she wanted her senses to be overwhelmed, she lost herself in the heat of the moment, and so she banished the chill of the moon—she came swiftly to her own pleasure, she abandoned herself to that pleasure—and then she felt Roland's answer, she felt him come deep inside of her, her husband filled her loving cup to overflowing—Elaine soon fell asleep, contented, satisfied, full of hope in the middle of her cycle.

By the time of her second wedding anniversary, coming in just a few weeks, she would know that once again she hadn't conceived.

Part VI

Decision

Chapter 178

THE NOTE

Friday afternoon, August 4, 1196, the day of the second anniversary of the Duke and Duchess of Larraz . . .

All the court was aflutter, as men and women prepared for the evening's gala ball.

Elaine also prepared for the show—at this moment she was taking a bath, assisted by Valerie, her lady in waiting.

The Duchess laid her head back over the edge of the tub—her golden hair cascaded nearly to the floor. She closed her eyes as Valerie began to gently soap her breasts—she let herself slide into a sensual reverie—but then her pleasure was sharply interrupted by a quite discourteous knock at the door.

Elaine opened her eyes. Valerie stood still with the soap in her hand.

Elaine said, "Just open the door a crack, darling, and see who it is."

Valerie did as she was told.

Elaine heard a page's voice from the other side of the door.

"A thousand apologies for disturbing Her Grace on this special day, but I have been charged to deliver this note." A white sheet of paper appeared—it had been folded once and sealed at the open end. "Please give it to Her Grace right away. The lady who wrote it says that it is very important."

Valerie took the paper. "I'll give it to Her Grace right now," she said, and then she shut the door.

She walked over and handed the note to Elaine.

Elaine cracked the seal and unfolded the paper. The message read like this:

Dearest Elaine,

I beg you to do a favor for me.

I must see you tomorrow afternoon.

Please come to *my* room as soon as His Grace is engaged.

I love you.

Sandra

Elaine read the message twice, then three times, until she knew it by heart.

Valerie was wise enough to back off and give her mistress privacy.

When Elaine was certain that she could remember every word, she stood up and got out of the tub. She walked across the room, heedless both of her nudity and of the water she dripped on the carpet. She stopped in front of a lit sconce and plunged the paper into the flame. She held the note by a corner until it had burned right up to her wet fingers—then she flicked the ash away and walked back to the tub.

Valerie hurried over to assist the Duchess as she climbed back in.

The bath continued, but Elaine's thoughts were far away.

Chapter 179

PROMISE

The second anniversary ball was splendid—Roland was handsome, Elaine astonishingly beautiful, and their lovemaking afterwards was as wonderful as ever.

And why shouldn't it be, Elaine thought as she lay awake by her contented, sleeping husband. There's new hope—this is the beginning of my cycle—my week of moonlit misfortune ended just three days ago. Surely this month—Elaine's thoughts faltered—surely this month—she tried to maintain her mood of cynical assurance but she couldn't go on—she couldn't even *think* the words of hope—she just broke down on her marriage bed—well loved, on a night of celebration, she began to cry—but she let her tears fall silently, so as not to awaken her husband.

Elaine cried out of a dreadful sense of emptiness, an emptiness made bitter by the failing of hope—she felt no new life inside her, she was sure that this month would be no different than any other—she pictured years of beautiful empty anniversaries—she felt an utter revulsion towards such a future—she looked at Roland sleeping next to her and she couldn't—

She forced her thoughts away.

She thought of Sandra's note.

She let the words run back through her mind. "I love you," the sweet girl had written.

I love you too, Elaine thought. It's been wrong of me to avoid you—I shouldn't be jealous of you—you saw your man die in your arms—you have known great sorrow and you have given me only love—you have never asked me for anything before—I will gladly do you a favor.

I will visit you tomorrow—I will give you whatever you desire.

Elaine felt much better after making her promise.
She closed her eyes, and soon fell asleep.

Chapter 180

SANDRA'S REQUEST

The Duke of Larraz had begun to greet his first afternoon visitor when Elaine knocked on Sandra's door.

Sandra opened the door, ushered Elaine in, and then locked it behind her.

Elaine looked over the room. Little Anton was nowhere to be seen.

"I have a maidservant now," Sandra said from behind Elaine. "That's strange for me. She is also a widow—she has two daughters. She's often offered to take care of Anton for me—to give me time—but time for what?" Sandra strode nervously past Elaine. "I always wanted him with me—I took care of him myself all the time that I could—but then Anton—you see I don't call him little Anton any more—he's a big boy, over a year old now—he walks well—he talks, calls me Mama, wants to know what a Daddy is"—Sandra was pacing back and forth in front of Elaine now—"and now do you know what—do you know what my boy has done?" Sandra stopped her pacing and looked hard at Elaine.

Elaine shook her head.

"I'll show you," Sandra said.

Sandra was only wearing the loose robe that both Elaine and the Duke had seen her in and out of—now she pulled at it, almost angrily, as she approached Elaine—she finally got it off—she tossed it on a chair as she came to stand right in front of the Duchess.

Sandra was completely nude now—her full breasts curved pleasantly against her chest, her soft round belly showed off its prominent navel, a sight that drew the eye down further to the soft brown curls at the juncture of her thighs . . .

Elaine let her eyes deliberately sweep Sandra's body and then come back up to her face. Sandra seemed calmer now. She took Elaine's hand and guided it to her left breast—Elaine held her just as she had done nearly a year before. Elaine felt the weight of the soft, luxuriant womanly breast in her hand, felt the nipple coming to life against her palm, felt the soft flesh give as she squeezed it with her fingers—and then she understood.

"He stopped nursing," Elaine said. She put her other hand on Sandra's shoulder—and then she slid it down the girl's smooth back, she pulled Sandra closer to her, but she still held Sandra's soft breast with her right hand.

"Yes, he did," Sandra replied. "A month ago. I wasn't ready. I wasn't trying to wean him. He just weaned himself. He knows his own mind. Quite the little man, just like his father. He eats in the dining room with me now—he gets food all over, but he eats—he likes to sit on the men's laps—he likes their deep voices.

"He's with Christina now, my maidservant. She'll take care of him all afternoon."

Sandra moved closer. Elaine released the soft breast that she held and put both arms around the girl. Sandra embraced Elaine likewise—they held each other tight, the shorter girl fitting under Elaine's chin—looking past her friend, Elaine saw a red towel neatly folded on the bed—but there was a lump near the fold—something was wrapped in that towel—what did Sandra want?—Elaine looked further—she saw a flask of whisky sitting on the dresser, but Elaine had never seen Sandra drink anything stronger than wine.

Sandra pulled her head back and looked up at Elaine—she saw that the Duchess was puzzled—she smiled, and then she went up on her toes and kissed her former mistress on the lips.

In all their long relationship, Sandra had never before initiated a kiss.

Now Sandra came down from her toes, she kissed her way down to Elaine's throat—she nuzzled there, and Elaine just held the sweet girl in her arms, a girl who seemed to have changed a lot in some ways—Elaine stroked the girl's soft curls, pressing her face even closer, and then the Duchess could look down past the smooth soft back, she looked at the ripe round buttocks, fearing what she might see—and it was there, the white scar was very prominent on the left cheek and it was clearly not going away—there was the white scar in the shape of a V, a permanent reminder of the Vulture and his knife.

Elaine shuddered and held Sandra even tighter—Sandra whispered against Elaine's throat, and the words seemed to come to her through her skin. "What's wrong, Milady?"

"I remember the night they took me away—I see what that man did to you—"

"Don't be sad, Milady. I can change my past. You can help me—that's why I asked you to come here."

Sandra looked up into Elaine's eyes. "But first I must tell you of something else."

"First you have to help me get this dress off," Elaine said, and they both laughed.

Then when they were both equally nude, Elaine took Sandra in her arms again, and kissed her, a cruel selfish kiss but terribly exciting for all that, her tongue deep in the girl's mouth and Sandra was gasping when Elaine finally let her go.

"Now tell me," Elaine said.

Sandra looked up at Elaine's cold blue eyes and she bowed her head. She kissed Elaine softly between her breasts—she felt Elaine's heartbeat through her lips.

"I need a man," Sandra whispered. "I didn't know how much I needed a man until after Anton stopped nursing. I learned even more from kissing you just now.

"I love my child, and I will love him until I die—I received a great sensual pleasure from his nursing, but that is past now.

"I love you, Milady, and I will do anything for you, and you may do whatever you like with me—the pleasures of your kisses are enormous—I love you, dear, dear Elaine—I love you, but still finally I need a man.

"And there is a final consideration, greater than all the others. My son needs a father—a living man who will guide my boy surely along the path to manhood. I can not do that myself—but I know that I can find a good man who can.

"I will always love Sir Anton. He made me a woman, he loved me and he gave me a son. Yet now it has been more than two years since his death—the time of mourning has passed.

"It is time for me to look for a husband.

"And so I thought of all this, this last month—I thought of loving a man, and finally making love with him. I thought of him undressing me, seeing me nude—and I thought of the V that had been cut into my flesh, and I could not imagine displaying that memory.

"I also wondered what sort of man I should look for—I thought that he would have to understand that Sir Anton was my first true love and that I would never forget him—he would have to realize that in some way Sir Anton had marked me forever—he would have to accept a son from another man—I realized that I could only love a man who accepted those things about me.

"And then it came to me that my own thoughts had given me the solution—Sir Anton had marked me with his love—why not also my flesh? This would be a test for my new man: if he could love me, with the mark of my late husband on my body, then I would know that he could accept both my past and my future."

Sandra walked over to her bed—the white V clear behind— and unfolded the red towel. She stepped aside so that Elaine could see the deadly looking knife that was revealed—it gleamed against the red background.

Sandra picked it up carefully—she held it with the blade pointing toward herself—she walked back to Elaine and offered the hilt of the weapon to the Duchess.

"This was Sir Anton's," Sandra said. "I've been sharpening it these past few days—you must be careful. I want you to cut a crossbar from one side of the V to the other—I want you to turn that V into an A—I want you to destroy the mark of evil, and leave me with a mark of love.

"When the wound has healed I will begin my search for a husband.

"Please do it, dearest Elaine. You are the only one I could possibly ask—there is no one else."

Elaine heard Sandra's every word, though for the last minute she had only been staring in horror at the razor sharp knife. Now she looked up at Sandra's face, she saw her friend's pleading brown eyes, and she remembered her promise in the night.

She reached out and took the knife.

"I'll do it," Elaine said.

Chapter 181

SANDRA'S REQUEST GRANTED

Elaine sat on the edge of the bed, the red towel spread over her lap—and Sandra lay across the towel with her bottom up. Her legs were to Elaine's left—Elaine forced those legs apart with her own left hand, and then she quested down and underneath. She cupped the girl's womanhood, and found it already moist. Elaine used one finger of her right hand to trace the bright whiteness of the V shaped scar.

Elaine had put the knife back on the bed—it was behind her and to her right, within easy reach of her right hand. The capped flask of whiskey lay just beyond the knife—ready, not for drinking, but to cleanse the wound that the Duchess would soon inflict.

Now Elaine let her right hand roam all over the plump offered buttocks—she caressed, and squeezed, and then she said, "The last time I had you in this position I spanked your bottom until it looked like a sunset."

Sandra squirmed over Elaine's cupping left hand and spread her legs wider. "I remember," she said in a husky whisper, "but I don't remember why you did it."

"I'll tell you why," Elaine said. She placed her right hand across the crease of Sandra's behind, and she pressed down hard. The effect was like crushing a peach—Sandra's womanhood seemed to burst on the cupping hand below, a hand that was now drenched with sweet juices. Holding Sandra like that, Elaine completed her answer: "I did it for my own pleasure."

Sandra moaned, a moan of surrender, a gift of self—she spread her legs as wide as she could and let her weight rest on the hand that held her.

Elaine knew that Sandra could even stand the knife now, but she wanted to take the girl further—

"Tell me of Sir Anton," the Duchess demanded.

Sandra just moaned again, she seemed unable to answer—

Elaine raised her right hand and smacked the girl hard, right on the scarred place—she left red fingermarks interrupted by the white bars of the V—"Tell me how he made love to you," the Duchess said.

Sandra quivered all over, and then she just started to rock gently against Elaine's cupping hand. Her voice was surprisingly calm when she began to speak. "I can tell you this: On the first day he took me, on the second day he loved me, and on the third day he used me for his pleasure. I learned that day that I belonged to him, that my body was meant to be used by him— but also he discovered"—Sandra was starting to shake with a mixture of sadness and excitement—"my husband discovered that he also belonged to me."

Sandra began to cry.

Elaine moved her left hand out from under Sandra—she took the girl's weight on her thighs, and then she extended two juicy fingers and thrust them right up inside the girl's hot wet cave. The velvety walls within caressed her fingers, and welcomed them—Elaine's right hand slowly caressed the vulnerable buttocks—she guided the girl into the motions of love.

The Duchess paid no attention to Sandra's falling tears.

"Tell me more of the third day," Elaine said.

Sandra felt the fingers inside of her moving slightly, spreading her, keeping her open—

"It was night really, we had been searching for you—but as dark fell we found the bodies of two of our brave knights who had perished at the Northmen's hands—we buried them in the darkness, and then we could go no further. Sir Anton took me aside and made me get undressed for him—I was ashamed of my nakedness at first, but then he undressed as well, and laid me down on a blanket—he covered me with his body, and I played with the scars on his back that I was coming to know, and he took me long and gently that first time."

Sandra's whole body was undulating slowly now, like the sea, Elaine thought, the waves surge in and flow back out—

"The second time he was rougher with me, faster, and I was still sore from the first but his tongue filled my mouth so I couldn't cry out, I just held him tight and dug my nails into his back—"

The sea was rising steadily now, the power of the waves building—Elaine felt the pull of the tide in her buried fingers—

"It began to rain and it was in the rain that Anton drew away from me—he let the cold drops fall on me as he sat back against a saddle and spread his legs. Then he forced me to kneel before him—he forced my mouth down upon him—I tried to shy away, but he gave me to understand that I had no choice—his strength was far greater than mine—I bowed to his will and took his manhood into my mouth. Thus he used me—his hand in my hair guided my head—but then when I felt him swell enormously in my mouth I tried again to escape, but his powerful hand held me to my task. I could not move against his strength—and then I simply stopped fighting, I accepted this man as my lord, and when his seed came pumping forth I swallowed all of it, I *knew* him that way—"

The sea was building to a fury, a feminine fury of hidden currents and whirlpools and whitecapped waves on top, all that power rushing toward the shore—

"When the deed was done and he had freed me, I looked up into his eyes and he looked into mine—and he saw something that frightened him, I think—he suddenly understood that in the very moment of proving his mastery over me he had also come to belong to me—this discovery made him angry, but it did not turn him away from me—he chose to accept his fate, he chose to accept his love for me, and my love for him—but he also moved to prove his mastery over me in the final way—"

Choppy, shuddering waves raised and broke in the tormented sea—there were huge hard rocks on the shore waiting to receive them—

"He took me over his lap and spanked me, terribly hard, and then he laid me face down on the blanket—"

Elaine herself began to shake but she willed control—she remembered the painful exciting way Davila had entered her—she deliberately wet her thumb in Sandra's abundant juices—she kept her two fingers buried deep as she quested upward with her thumb—she forced a path between the clenching buttocks and found the tender orifice—Sandra felt the touch and gave one desperate sob—Elaine reached back for the knife—

"He wet his staff in my quim and then he drew it out—he made me—he made me do this"—Sandra could hardly talk any more—her face was soaked with tears—still she reached back and spread her buttocks for Elaine just as she had done for Sir Anton—Elaine forced her thumb into the tight tender hole and Sandra sobbed again and then in a pain choked voice she said—

"He thrust in and he hurt me and I bit his hand, but when he was all the way in I thought, now he has filled me in every way—"

"He loved you, Sandra," Elaine said.

The waves seemed to hang suspended, high over the rocks—and then Sandra said, "Yes," and all of her femininity broke on that truth, broke on that knowledge of love and death, she flung the waves of her power onto the rocks, and shattered in a huge crashing climax of body and soul—and as that crashing wave struck Elaine dug the point of Sir Anton's knife into the side of the V scar, drove it deep enough into the flesh so that this cut would scar too—and then she drew the knife straight across in one bleeding line until she reached the other side of the V, and so the A was formed, in white and red.

Sandra screamed, one piercing shriek of pain—and then pain itself was subsumed in the crashing waves of her pleasure, the waves broke one after another, and Sandra just cried now, cried as her body spasmed again and again, cried with pain and joy and finally peace, cried because she knew Elaine had made the cut, cried because the A was complete, and now she had only to heal.

Sandra was almost still when Elaine poured the whisky over the fresh wound—the girl gasped once but she didn't scream again, she just accepted the burning, cleansing pain—she felt free now, not free of the past but free to live her future—she felt so so grateful to Elaine—she felt her mistress gently patting her rump with the ends of the red towel—she felt so well loved—the towel was pulled out from under her and put away somewhere—Sandra could feel the heat of Elaine's thighs under her now—she felt Elaine's hands directing her and she understood at once what was desired—she went to her knees, she knelt between Elaine's widespread legs—she wiped her eyes and smiled as she looked at the honey soaked womanhood of her mistress. Elaine had never demanded this caress before but now it was only her due—Sandra felt Elaine's hand in her hair but she didn't need to be forced—she bent forward willingly and pressed her lips to Elaine's womanhood—she kissed, and then she licked—Elaine's hand tightened demandingly in her hair—Sandra remembered Sir Anton in the rain, and fresh tears rolled down her cheeks as she lovingly and gratefully gave pleasure to the Duchess of Larraz.

Chapter 182

SADNESS

Elaine was impatient with Roland that night when he wanted to kiss her between her thighs—she had enjoyed that caress already today and now she just wanted her husband's hard manhood—she wanted to feel his strength deep inside her—she made her desires plain. So soon Roland was over her, his hardness was knocking at her portal—Roland never rushed in—now Elaine felt just a slight penetration—somehow that took her back to the wild events of the afternoon—Roland slid inside a little more—there was something she had to remember, something important that she hadn't noticed at the time—Roland thrust deeper—she could almost grasp it—Roland abandoned his control and drove all the way in, he filled her, and Elaine remembered—she remembered what Sandra had said: "Now he has filled me in every way."

Roland has never done that, Elaine thought.

Roland began to move in a gentle rhythm—Elaine moved with him, but her thoughts turned (as so often this past year) to Davila's cryptic pronouncement: "The man who wishes to fill you will do so."

Elaine wondered for the first time whether she had misunderstood the Gypsy's meaning. She had always thought that the phrase "wishes to fill you" had referred to the man's desire to make her pregnant. And Roland did want to make her pregnant, he did want to fill her in that way.

But now there was another way to look at Davila's words—one need only recall Sandra's adventure with Anton—one could think of a man's desire to fill a woman for pleasure and conquest, regardless of procreation—Elaine imagined a hard shaft filling not only her womanhood, but her mouth as well, and even her—

Elaine came with a sudden burst of pleasure that was almost as much of a surprise to her as to her husband.

Roland had not been nearly ready, but the sight of his wife's abandonment spurred him on—

Elaine held him tight as he reached his completion—she felt his seed pouring into her and she wondered, does Roland want to fill me? Or does he only love me?

When Roland finished, he looked down at his wife, expecting her smile—he intended to ask what had excited her so much— but he found that she had turned her face to one side and there was nothing but sadness in her expression.

She showed no sign of the pleasure that she had so obviously experienced just moments before—Roland could no longer ask her about that—instead he asked her what was wrong, but she gave no answer.

Roland moved off Elaine and lay down beside her—he embraced her and stroked her hair and she seemed to like that—finally she fell asleep in his arms—she fell asleep without revealing the secret of her sadness.

Chapter 183

ANOTHER EMPTY ROOM

Elaine went to see Sandra again the next day. She was expected—Sandra had already sent Anton off with Christina.

Elaine and Sandra spent thirteen afternoons in a row together.

Sandra was a sweet lover for the Duchess—as the girl proved over and over during their first week together—but Elaine was rather cruel. In bed they were always mistress and servant: Elaine commanded, Sandra obeyed. Sandra knelt frequently to pay homage to the Duchess's womanhood—but Elaine never reciprocated.

It pleased the Duchess to see her power over Sandra—she liked to excite the girl, and then leave her that way. The Duchess developed a little ritual good-bye, which went like this: Elaine would make Sandra lie down on her back on her bed—she'd make the naked girl spread her legs and offer all her charms—Elaine would observe the honey soaked thighs, the swollen nipples, the parted lips that silently begged for kisses—and then she'd quietly tell the girl not to move. Then Elaine would calmly get dressed—she'd take her time with her hair—she'd check her appearance in Sandra's looking glass—and only then would she come back to the obedient, needy girl. Elaine would smile down at her—and then she'd take Sandra's right hand and guide it down to her mount of Venus—she'd cover that hand with her own and press down until Sandra had begun, helplessly, to caress herself. Then Elaine would bend down and kiss Sandra once on the mouth, far too briefly—after that the Duchess would go—she'd leave Sandra to whatever pleasure she could give herself.

Elaine was always waiting for Roland when he came back from his afternoon conversations.

In bed with Roland Elaine was soft, languorous—she wanted to lie between his legs and take his manhood in her mouth and just suck until she felt his seed—but Roland pushed her away in a moment, for he did not think she should serve him, he much preferred to kiss *her*—Elaine moved then, bonelessly, she draped herself over his sturdy thigh, she arched her back and raised her bottom, hoping for and fearing the resounding smack that didn't come—she let him turn her onto her back, she accepted his mouth and then his hard shaft—she felt him inside her, so big and yet so gentle—and all the while he loved her she kept thinking of Davila's pronouncement: "The man who wishes to fill you will do so"—she felt unfilled, unfulfilled, she felt a great and growing emptiness inside her—an empty room like her legacy to Robin—a room she wanted to fill with love and children and the big gentle bear atop her did not touch that room, gave her pleasure but did not fill her, and she blocked her mind against the thought of the man who would—she let sensation take her over, she let herself come, but that wasn't enough—

The next day Elaine was back with Sandra, she took her pleasure cruelly from the sweet girl who loved her, but that wasn't enough—

Elaine was doubly loved for six days and still never truly satisfied—on the seventh day she sought something new—this day Elaine dressed to be seen.

The Duchess went to Sandra's room as usual—she found the lovely young widow already naked and waiting—Elaine smiled, she turned Sandra around and told her how well the A was healing—she patted her lover there—and then she gave the girl a rather harder smack, and followed with a brisk command: "Get dressed—we're going out."

Chapter 184

AT THE JOUSTS

Elaine took Sandra to watch the jousts.

Since coming to Larraz with Roland, Elaine had not once been a spectator at this sort of entertainment (though jousts and tournaments were held regularly in the capital city). Roland had made it plain that he disliked those stylized battles (Elaine had learned why on the night of her first anniversary, when Roland had told her the story of his brother Charles) and so Elaine had never thought of going alone, or with a friend.

This was the first time, in a little over two years of marriage, that Elaine had gone out to a public function without the Duke.

She felt that she had no choice. She was driven by the emptiness, the lifelessness within her—she was called by the theater of combat and the real possibility of violent death.

At the stadium, Elaine and Sandra were conducted with great ceremony to the Duke's private box (which hadn't been used in years). The steward who guided them babbled on and on about what a great honor it was to have Her Grace and Lady Sandra—Elaine was relieved when she could finally slip the man a coin and send him off. The two ladies sat down, close to the rail that separated them from the jousting field—they were as close as Elaine had been when Thomas (Robin!) had fought his duels for her favor.

Elaine closed her mind to those memories, and waited for the first joust to begin.

There was a delay—longer than she expected, and then the first two mounted knights appeared. Their squires led the horses straight toward Elaine. The Duchess realized then that the knights must have been told that she was in attendance—they were clearly coming to present themselves before combat.

As they came closer Elaine recognized one of them—he was the black bearded fellow who, with Sir Anton, had guided Sandra and herself from Bermondsey to their parting in the forest.

Sandra recognized him too. After Elaine had gone off with Daniel, he had accompanied her and Sir Anton to the bend in the stream. He had stood guard—he must have heard her scream when Anton took her virginity. As he stopped before her, Sandra saw that same memory on his face—she turned away, blushing, wishing that she knew his name.

The knights bowed to the Duchess, and she wished them both good luck with perfect impartiality.

The men were about to ride off when Sandra suddenly stood up and called impetuously, "Wait! Wait!" Both knights stopped their horses. Sandra looked only at the black bearded fellow—he looked back at her through his open visor. Sandra undid the green scarf that she was wearing against the wind. The knight maneuvered his horse closer, and put out a gloved hand. Sandra handed him the scarf—she felt the grip of his leather covered fingers for a second—and then she said, "Good luck, Sir . . .?"

"Sir Gowan," he replied clearly, and he handed the scarf to his squire. That worthy tied the banner to his master's unsharpened lance—and all the while he was engaged, Gowan and Sandra looked into each other's eyes—Sandra could feel her face blushing hotter, but she could not turn away.

Finally the scarf was secure—it fluttered boldly in the breeze—Gowan gave Sandra an equally bold smile, and then he bowed formally one more time to the Duchess. The other knight did the same—and then the two combatants rode off towards the opposite ends of the jousting field.

Now Sandra was almost afraid to look at Elaine, she was afraid of the anger she was sure she would see in her lady's eyes, but then she had to know what Elaine thought—she did turn, she looked bravely up at the Duchess—but there was no anger to be seen, there was only a tender expression of love and sadness and intimation of loss—and then Elaine smiled slightly and brought a single finger to her lips—she kissed it and then she touched that finger lightly to Sandra's lips—Sandra thought it was the sweetest kiss that she had ever received from her dear lady.

As Elaine took her hand away Sandra reached over and

caught it with her own—she squeezed it gently—and then they
turned as one to watch the combat.

Sir Gowan charged from the right, the other knight from the
left—Sandra held Elaine's hand even tighter and forgot to
breathe—the other knight tried to sweep Sir Gowan from his
saddle, but the swinging lance never completed its arc, for Sir
Gowan's straight held weapon struck first—the sleek green
scarf blown back along the shaft seemed to guide it—the dull
point struck the foe dead on in the center of his chest—the loser
was driven straight back off his horse—he struck the earth with
a thunderous crash of metal and lay still—Sir Gowan raced
by—Sandra took a gasping breath—the fallen knight's squire
rushed out to help his master—Sandra gave a sigh of relief
when she saw that the knight was shaken but not seriously
hurt—she looked around then for Sir Gowan, and she saw him
with his visor open again, looking at her—she stared mesmerized at his face as he rode up for the second time and stopped
before the Duke's box.

Sir Gowan turned to the Duchess and bowed to her once
again—and then he looked at Sandra with black eyes that
seemed to know all her secrets, and he said, "I will send my
man with a message for you tomorrow."

He rode off before Sandra could think of a reply.

Elaine held tight to the girl's trembling hand.

There were many more jousts that day, many other knights
came up to the Duke's box to pay their respects, but Sandra
noticed none of them. She thought about tomorrow—she wondered how long it would be before her A completely healed.

Meanwhile, Elaine was wishing that she had not come here
today. Every knight, every battle, even Sandra's scarf reminded
her of one man—one silent knight—one green hero who had
raised himself above King and Prince to champion the
oppressed people of England—one man of brutal power who had
wanted her—

She would not think of that man.

And yet she couldn't think of Sandra either, she could feel
Sandra going away from her, Sandra the young mother who
would be a mother again, her sweet gentle lover who would soon
find a new husband—that thought brought Elaine around to
Roland, her sweet gentle bear—and then suddenly she realized
that she had thought of Roland and Sandra in the same way:
sweet, gentle—she did not want to think of her man that way

but she did, she did think of him that way, and the emptiness inside ripped and tore at her soul, she saw no love in the empty room in her heart, Roland didn't fill her, no future, no children and then a savage hateful thought crackled through her mind—Roland is no more capable of giving me a child than Sandra is, she thought—but then she jerked away from that bitterness, she knew that was her frustration speaking, she knew too that she could easily fill the empty room in her heart with hate—she shook her head violently, she should never have come here, she looked into the crowd so as not to look at the knights, she did not want to think and she did not want to remember—she was immensely relieved when she finally saw someone in the crowd who was unusual enough to command her attention.

This person she saw was an elderly woman—her face testified that she was at least sixty, but she had the bright red hair of a twenty year old country girl—and even as Elaine watched, a knight made his way to the strange lady and paid his respects quite formally indeed. Elaine kept watching—she saw that the knight was just one of a continuous stream of admirers. The lady sat in the section allocated to the common folk—why did so many young noblemen come to honor her?

Elaine pointed the woman out to Sandra, and then she asked, "Who is that? And what has she done with her hair?"

It took Sandra a moment to rise out of her romantic reverie, but then she had to laugh when she recognized the object of Elaine's curiosity.

"That's Madame Genevieve," Sandra said. "Remember when I gave you directions to Davila's cabin, I told you that you would go past the best brothel in Larraz—well, there is the lady who runs it."

"Evidently she has many satisfied customers," Elaine observed. "But how do you know all these things, you little minx? And what about that hair?"

"The hair is a wig—she has all kinds. The last time I saw her she was blonde like you.

"Do you remember the great summer picnic His Grace gave about three weeks ago?"

Elaine nodded.

"Nobles, commoners, everyone was there. You were still not speaking to me then—Anton had just stopped nursing and Christina was taking care of him while I amused myself—except I wasn't amused—I was at loose ends until Madame

Genevieve took me aside. She introduced herself and I liked her right away—we went for a little walk, and while we walked she talked to me quite frankly about her business—then we stopped in a quiet place and she told me that she knew I would soon be seeking a man.

"I was shocked, of course—I was just beginning to figure that fact out for myself—I could not understand how a stranger could guess so much about me, but then I considered her long experience with women (she had already told me that she had run her brothel for thirty years) and I had to admit that she was right.

"My admission pleased her—she smiled and asked me if I wanted to work for her, just part time, now and then. She told me that I would be surprised by the number of court ladies who found occasional excitement and gold at her house. She told me there was no danger of discovery—she had wigs and makeup enough to make me an African princess if I so desired—I laughed when she said that, and she laughed with me, but I noticed that she watched me while she laughed—I still had not answered her basic question.

"I thought of making love for money—and then my answer came very quickly from my heart, and I said, 'Thank you for your offer, but I can only give myself for love.' Then she studied me for a moment, and finally she smiled again and told me I was a sweet girl—and she added that if I ever changed my mind I should not hesitate to contact her."

Sandra paused and looked up at Elaine, but the Duchess was still staring across the way. "And so you see—that's how I know these things, Your Grace," Sandra concluded with a certain arch formality.

Elaine felt the new confidence in the girl—she squeezed Sandra's hand and answered without turning her head. "You *are* a sweet girl, Sandra."

Chapter 185

A LONELY EXPERIENCE

Roland heard about Elaine's attendance at the jousts, of course, but that did not bother him nearly as much as the way she was in bed that night. He was shocked by the realization that something was very wrong with his marriage.

Elaine had been sad after lovemaking last week—and even though she hadn't told him the reason why, he still had been able to comfort her. Elaine had been frightened often during their honeymoon—she had had nightmares—but he had always been able to sooth her and gentle her with his touch. Likewise he had always been able to arouse her with his knowing hands and seeking lips—she had always come to return his passion, and so when they made love, each time they made love, it became something they truly did together: that was a truth of their marriage.

Tonight it was false.

Elaine lay naked on the big bed as though she wanted to make love—her body was utterly available to Roland—but her spirit was somewhere else, untouched by his caresses.

Roland tried to please her. He kissed her from the crown of her head down to her perfect pink toes—he loved every inch of his Duchess, but still she did not respond—he did not know that all the while he was caressing his wife, she was wrestling with questions that she could not answer.

Leaving the joust today, hand in hand with Sandra, Elaine had happened to notice a pretty country girl as the lass went up on her toes to kiss a handsome young soldier. The incident was really nothing like the one she had seen at that fateful joust a week after Richard Lionheart's coronation, but the circumstances were similar, and the memory had come right back: the summer heat, the wrestler sweaty from his bouts, the serving girl coming up to him, standing before him, spreading her legs—and asking her question . . .

Then, seven years ago, she had first seen the man who had become her husband. Roland must have seen her watching that young couple—should she ask him the same question that the serving girl had asked her wrestler? What would Roland's answer be? The girl had used that crude English word—but was that not the Gypsy's meaning? Does my husband wish to fill me? Does he want to—

Roland was helplessly aroused by his wife's beauty. He entered her, slowly and gently—he made love to her, but never with her—he tried and tried to bring her to him, but she was lost, blocked by the questions she couldn't ask—and so finally all his persistence was wasted.

Roland came alone, a release that was far from pleasure—it was such a lonely experience that he wished he had not come at all.

Chapter 186

LAUGHTER AND GRAPES

Sandra, fully dressed, was pacing nervously around her room when Elaine arrived the next afternoon.

Elaine didn't have to ask the reason for her friend's agitation.

"He hasn't come yet," the Duchess said.

"Do you think he will come?" Sandra asked in a frightened voice as she continued to pace.

Elaine caught Sandra's arm firmly and stopped the girl in her tracks. Then the Duchess marched Sandra over to the full length mirror that stood in one corner of the room.

"Look at yourself, you silly goose. See how pretty you are. Sir Gowan will send his man, just as he said he would.

"Now stop worrying and don't move. I have something to show you."

Elaine had been carrying a bag, which she now put down on the bed. She opened it and took out a small hand mirror.

"Pull your dress up to your waist," the Duchess ordered.

Sandra obeyed.

Elaine came up behind and to one side of Sandra. She held the hand mirror near the A—she adjusted mirror and girl until the image was reflected back in the large standing mirror.

Sandra stared in wonderment at the tall looking glass. There was her A, the mark of her husband.

The crossbar of the A was now a thin black scab lined with red, but it was definitely healing. Sandra was certain that when the blackness fell away she'd be left with a perfect pure white remembrance.

Given that remembrance, she allowed herself to think of the future—

There came a knock at the door and Sandra jumped and shoved her dress down in a hurry. She wanted to run to the door but Elaine restrained her.

Elaine led Sandra over to her bed. "Sit down, my dear," the Duchess said. "I'll handle this."

Elaine walked over and opened the door.

Sir Gowan's young squire was quite shocked to see the Duchess—he stammered for a moment, and then bowed low—he used the time with his head down to regain his composure.

Finally he looked up again.

"Your Grace, I am honored," the squire said. "I have a message from my master, Sir Gowan, that I have been entrusted to deliver to Lady Sandra.

"May I ask, Your Grace, if she is here?"

"She is here. Give me the message, and I will take it to her."

"By your leave, Your Grace, I must also wait for a reply."

"And you shall have it, young man. Give me the message and wait outside for a moment. When Lady Sandra has written her reply, I will return the letter to you."

"Thank you, Your Grace," said the squire, and he handed a sealed envelope to Elaine.

The Duchess stepped back and shut the door without giving the squire a glimpse of Lady Sandra.

Elaine walked over and handed the note to Sandra. She watched as the girl's trembling fingers fumbled over the envelope. Sandra's nails got stuck in the wax seal—then finally she cracked it open, slit the envelope, and drew the letter out.

Elaine turned away to give Sandra privacy.

Suddenly the Duchess jerked around at the sound of Sandra exploding in peals of laughter.

Elaine stared in amazement. Sandra was laughing without restraint—the Duchess hadn't heard Sandra laugh since—who knows when? The girl was waving the letter helplessly, still laughing—finally she extended a hand and offered the letter to her lady.

Elaine took it and read:

> My dearest Lady Sandra,
>> Your inspiration was a great tool,
>> It made my foe look like a fool,
>> To me it's quite a boon,
>> Though you drive me crazy as a loon,

> If I don't see you soon,
> I'll surely meet my doom,
> The stadium, tomorrow, noon?
> > Very truly yours,
> > Sir Gowan

Elaine looked over at Sandra. The girl had stopped laughing, but she was still smiling a wide private smile.

I am not included in that smile, Elaine thought. The Duchess turned her mind to Sandra's suitor. Who would have guessed that such a silly man lives inside that black bearded countenance? Then again, perhaps he is a wise man—he knows that it is time for the widow to stop mourning—it's time for her to laugh.

In some ways Sandra has been very lucky with her men.

Sandra broke into Elaine's thoughts. "What shall I reply?" the girl asked.

Elaine paused for a moment to collect herself, and then she gave her answer. "You musn't be too eager. Tell him you will see him in one week's time."

Sandra's face fell. "A week?"

Elaine looked down at Sandra with cold, opaque blue eyes. Sandra could see no feeling at all in those eyes.

"One week," the Duchess said, very distinctly.

Sandra knew that she was not being given a suggestion—this was an order.

She took the letter that Elaine handed back to her. She read it over again and couldn't keep from smiling—she thought, Yes, it will be fun to make you wait.

She took a quill pen and wrote under Sir Gowan's signature:

> I will see you in one week's time.
> > Sandra

She put the letter back in the envelope and handed it to Elaine.

The Duchess took it across the room and opened the door. She gave the letter to the squire—he thanked her and rushed off.

Elaine turned around and saw that Sandra was still sitting on her bed. The girl looked up at her without fear.

"Do you want me to serve you, Your Grace?"

Elaine put out her hands and gestured for Sandra to come to her. The girl came over—the Duchess embraced her, and kissed her—it was a long, thorough kiss—and then Elaine said, "I thought we'd go for a walk."

And so they did, they walked through the palace gardens, they put flowers in each other's hair, and then they went to the vineyards, the grapes were ripe and bursting, they put the sweet fruit in each other's mouths, they stained fingers and faces purple, they kissed often in the shade of the vines, and they giggled like careless young maids.

They stayed out for hours—finally they skipped back to the palace, hand in sticky hand.

Sandra said, "I have to go get Anton now."

Elaine kissed the girl's stained cheek—she watched Sandra's happy walk as the young mother went off to pick up her child.

Then Elaine looked over at the setting sun. It was late—Roland was probably just finishing up with his last informant of the day. Elaine knew that she would have to hurry to get back to her bedchamber before Roland—but she did not want to rush.

She had no child to go to.

Did she have a man?

Chapter 187

ONE OF SIX

Nighttime, sleeptime, time to go to bed . . .

Roland entered his familiar bedchamber—but it seemed different to him. The room seemed larger—the bed seemed even bigger than usual—Elaine, who was already on it, seemed very far away.

The Duchess was naked. Roland had seen her put a nightgown on earlier, but she must have thrown it off because of the heat. The dog days of August were holding Larraz in their sweltering grip—the nights did not even begin to cool off until well after midnight.

Roland looked at Elaine, but she gave no sign that she was aware of his presence. She lay on her back with her eyes closed. Roland could tell from her breathing that she was awake.

She offered her nude body—she was just as available as she had been last night—just that and nothing more.

Roland remembered the terrible loneliness—he stood still by the side of his bed.

The Duke was wearing an Oriental sleeping jacket that he had bought from a passing trader—he didn't know whether he should take it off and lie down next to Elaine—or whether he should keep it on and lie down as far over on his side of the bed as possible.

He knew that he couldn't just stand there and look at his wife.

Roland decided to get rid of the light. He walked around the bed and blew out every candle save one.

He thought it would be easier then when he looked back at the bed—but it was worse. Elaine's white form had lost definition in the near darkness—she had become a pale ghostlike shape—gone when the candle flickered—now back again—

Roland was frightened.

He could not go near that shape.

He did not even dare speak to the woman he loved.

He climbed onto the bed—he lay on the edge, far away from his lady—he kept his back to her, but he could feel her, still wide awake.

Hours went by before Roland fell asleep—but he thought, next morning, that Elaine had still been awake when he had finally dropped off.

Six nights in a row were like that.

In a way it was a relief when the explosion came on the seventh night.

Chapter 188

THE WHEATFIELD

Every afternoon Sandra received a comical note from Sir Gowan—usually these predicted his imminent demise from heartsickness—and Sandra would send them back with her signature and a number: 6, then 5, then 4 . . .

Then after the ritual of the note, Sandra would go for a walk with her Duchess.

Sometimes they would walk for hours, hand in hand, hardly speaking—other days they brought wine and a blanket—they'd sit on the blanket between the rows of grapevines—they'd pass the wineskin back and forth, and hold the wine in their mouths, and kiss until they didn't know whether it was the wine or the kisses that made them drunk—finally they'd wander back to the palace, weaving a little, arms around each other's waists now— then a proper kiss on the cheek, and one happy girl would go off to find her son—one beautiful lady would force herself to walk to her empty bedchamber.

Elaine was always cold sober by the time Roland returned.

At night Elaine lay awake—she closed her eyes and bathed in the cold rays of the waxing moon—she listened to the emptiness within herself.

Sandra wrote cheerful numerals on Sir Gowan's letters: 3, then 2—

That day Elaine and Sandra walked straight east from the palace until they entered some farming country. They stopped at the beginning of a long shimmering stand of wheat.

Elaine squeezed Sandra's hand tightly and said, without looking at her friend, "I won't come see you tomorrow."

She said it almost as if she was going away forever.

Sandra turned toward her lady. "Please come. I want you to come."

Elaine didn't turn her head. She gazed at the bright green of the wheatfield—she let her eyes run to the end of the green, she looked out and up to foothills, mountains, blue sky—

"I can't come," Elaine said.

Elaine turned around, still holding Sandra's hand, and the girl came with her. They walked straight back to the palace—they got back early this once.

Elaine kissed Sandra on the cheek as she did every day at this point. Sandra walked off, not fast and happy as usual, no, today the girl had a slow, sad, wondering walk—but even so each step brought her closer to her bright handsome boy—each step took her farther away from the distant figure of Elaine the Fair—her thoughts changed course—she allowed herself to think of tomorrow: she would write a 1 on Sir Gowan's note—she tried to think of the day after that but her heart started to flutter so badly she couldn't—

She shook her head, she smiled, and she stepped into the courtyard where Christina was playing with Anton.

She stared at her little boy with a heart full of love.

Meanwhile, the Duchess was still standing where she had kissed her friend good-bye.

Elaine could not seem to find the strength to move her feet.

Chapter 189

"MAKE ME BEAUTIFUL . . ."

The next day was Friday, August 18, 1196—it was exactly two weeks after the second anniversary of the Duke and Duchess of Larraz.

Elaine lay alone on her conjugal bed, drenched in the heat of early afternoon. She was thinking.

Roland was greeting the day's first visitor.

Sandra was signing Sir Gowan's letter with a trembling hand.

Elaine thought of neither husband nor friend.

She thought of the man she had left behind—she thought of the man he had become.

She thought of Robin Hood.

I must call you Robin now, Elaine began, for that is your true name. I used to see greatness in you—but I knew it would not come at the court—you were never suited for that life. When I heard your contempt for the King, I knew that you would need to become greater than he—I thought you might well succeed—and you have. You have found your destiny—not as a knight of the court, nor even as a protector of noble ladies—no, you have gone home to the countryside, home to the forest—you have reclaimed your true name, and you have become a hero of the English people—you are their bright green hope in the midst of oppression. You fight the King, the Prince, the Sheriff—you set yourself above them, and answer only to God. Your arrows fly like the bolts of Zeus that the Greeks told us of—already you have become more than man—you are Legend.

I know that your name will live, when Kings and Princes have been trod into dust. You are hope and justice for those who have never had either. You are there for the farmer who loses such a percentage of his crop that he can't feed his family—you are there for the fisherman whose nets are confiscated—you are there for every poor man whose pockets have been picked clean by the state.

This is what you were meant to do.

I used to think that you were holding yourself back—but you weren't ready then. You had to be finally disillusioned with the life of a knight of the court—you needed your own King to order your death—you needed to lose the love of your life: you needed to lose me.

Those things would have killed anyone else—but not you.

Elaine was breathing harshly as she whipped herself with her thoughts. She got up off the bed—she was hot in her dress—she went over to the window but there wasn't even a hint of a breeze—she backed away from the cut in the stone and tore her dress off—she heard it rip at least twice and she didn't care at all—she kicked it away from her when it fell to the floor—that motion sent a slipper flying—she kicked the other one off as well—she took her earrings off and hurled them at a tapestried wall—she stalked around the room like a naked savage—she got back on the bed and lay stiff on her back, every muscle tense, her mind racing, raging—

Nothing kills you—not the Northmen, not Brian, not the Prince's soldiers now—and so you are seen as some superhuman, godlike figure—but I know you, and you're just a man.

You're a great man—but you can be hurt, just like all the rest of us.

Why don't you carry a sword anymore?

I know—because you took an arrow through your right hand. Your bones crack as well as anyone's. Roland and I did our best to fix the break—but I suppose only God could have truly restored your full powers—and you don't receive any special dispensation from Heaven—you're just a man.

What kind of man are you? Do you let those girls who sew your green garments see you naked? They must adore you—do you take the prettiest one from each village? You could—O I hope you do, I hope they run their fingers along the scar on your back as you swive them, O God I hope you are taking your pleasure—

But I know, damn you, I know that you are not.

You still love me and I can feel it and I wish I couldn't feel it. You were the first man to make me see my own beauty. The night after my first lesson with the sword, I made love to myself—I held tight to the image of me that you gave. I've always been beautiful—but you made me see it, made me love it, and I gave you nothing.

I hate you.

I would have given myself any time—under the pine tree, in the stable, on the grass surrounded by Northmen—if only you had been Robin Hood.

I could never give myself to Sir Thomas, the fraud. Sir Thomas was a dead man. I'm glad he's gone.

Who was it who saved Suleka and gave her new life? Not Sir Thomas—the true hero was the squire Robin Hood.

Robin, I'm sorry. I know the pain of emptiness—but what is that next to your loss? Your lover was killed with the child she carried. God grant that you shall have another love, another child.

O Lord, tell me what to do.

Elaine lay still for a long time.

Then finally she put two fingers in her mouth and sucked them slowly, almost reflectively. She spread her legs as wide as she could, and then she moved her hand down and thrust the wet fingers deep inside her womanhood. She tried to possess herself—but she could not control that most secret part of her body—she was shocked by the absence of pleasure. She took her fingers out and brought them back up to her mouth—she licked them clean, and what she tasted was a longing emptiness that wanted—that needed to be filled, and she began to cry with her fingers in her mouth, she cried like a little girl, eyes flowing, nose running, mouth sucking—and then she yanked her fingers free and rolled over, she rubbed her face against the bedspread until the wetness was gone—but then her position—naked, face-down—brought back memories of Davila—memories of being entered *that* way, and then the slap, and turning, entered again, known all the way to her womb—a fruitful womb, but empty and unused.

"The man who wishes to fill you will do so."

She remembered Robin, shoving her nightgown up, ready to push her back on the grass and take her—fill her—No, No, No, I said No, I was in love—I am in love—with Roland.

Roland made me a Duchess—but Robin gave up his sword hand for me.

Roland put flowers beneath my feet—but Robin killed his

horse to give me a chance to live.

Roland loves me loves me loves me—but what did that serving girl say to the sweaty wrestler she admired? "Do you want to—?"

That question was ringing in my ears when Roland saw me for the first time—that question, and the wrestler's answer.

Roland fell in love with me at that moment.

I'm going to take him back to that moment tonight.

I'm going to ask that question tonight—I'm going to say all the words, even the one that I don't dare think—I'll ask the question just like the girl did, with my legs spread and my body offered—and if my husband says yes, I'll never leave him.

Elaine rang the bell for Valerie, and then she got up off the bed. She was very calm now.

The young lady in waiting came in—and then stopped at once at the sight of her naked mistress. Valerie had bathed her lady often enough before—but somehow this was different. She looked down and saw the torn dress on the floor—she felt her heart pounding in her chest—she forced herself to look up and speak clearly as she had been taught. "Yes, Your Grace?" she asked.

"Come here," Elaine said.

Valerie moved a few steps.

"Closer."

This time the girl stepped forward until she was only a half pace in front of her mistress.

She stood there, trembling—she looked up at Elaine's face because she was afraid to look down at her body.

Elaine put her hands on the girl's shoulders. She felt the trembling and she read all the girl's thoughts—she raised one hand and gently stroked Valerie's cheek.

"Don't be afraid, darling—I don't want that." Elaine smiled slightly. "Perhaps some other time." Elaine touched the girl's cheek again. "For now we must think of my husband. He will be coming back in a few hours. I want you to make me beautiful for him—I want you to make me more beautiful than I have ever been before."

Valerie felt relieved at first—and then perhaps just a little disappointed—but by the time Elaine had finished she was frightened again—she did not see how she could make the Duchess any more beautiful than she already was.

Still, Valerie did her best—and her best was very good indeed.

She let her own fear guide her—she accented the savagery in Elaine's beauty—she was terrified when she was finished.

Elaine was very pleased.

She kissed Valerie and sent her away.

She gathered her powers and waited for her husband.

Chapter 190

FLAGRANT

Roland was dazzled.

Like a man looking at the sun, he could only glance at his wife for a few seconds at a time.

He stole quick looks at her as he walked her to the dining hall—he glanced between bites of untasted food—he looked back at her to smile once as he summoned his court musicians (Elaine's beauty demanded celebration)—he dared to look down at her face now and then when they danced later in the near empty ballroom.

Only the Duke and Duchess danced. There were no other nobility in attendance. The musicians played, and a single page waited.

Elaine lit up the room.

Roland could recall only one time when Elaine had looked something like this—that was in another ballroom, back in England.

He remembered Anton's words from that night: "She will either kill you or make you the happiest man on earth."

He remembered how he had 'rushed to meet his death'—only to find that Elaine accepted him—he had danced with her, he had kissed her, he had told her that he would send for her—

She had been amazing then, she was like that now—but this time the violence that Anton had sensed was much more evident. At that long ago ball she had worn pale pink—tonight her dress was brazen scarlet. The gold earrings and the blue eye shadow were the same—but the eyes beneath those blued lids were much harder now—they blazed like blue steel caught by the sun. There had been a touch of demure purity then—but tonight she wore a heavy gold necklace that hung down between her breasts—the weight of it pressed the thin silk down against her skin in the hollow there—and so each breast was defined against the fabric—her hard nipples were flagrant. And Elaine hadn't stopped there—no, she also wore a chain belt of gold links, pulled cruelly tight around her narrow waist—she flaunted the shape of her body as she made one think of a prisoner chained—she moved like she might rip the blazing links from her body at any moment—she was beauty animated by rage and she would not be denied the confrontation she sought.

Roland danced with her for a while but she grew wilder as the night wore on, and finally he couldn't hold her. She spun away—she whirled like a Gypsy, scarlet dress flying—she made him chase her, and then finally she stopped and let him run into her—she gave him her breasts, she let him feel her hard nipples that seemed to want to tear through her dress, and when she knew he felt her heat she went up on her toes and kissed his lips—kissed him and then bit him, hard, and Roland had to yank her away with one hand in her hair—he looked down into her blazing eyes, and he waved his free hand, and the musicians stopped playing.

Chapter 191

THE QUESTION

The page who had waited in the ballroom lighted the way for Elaine and Roland. He preceded them down the long corridors with torch in hand—he led them into their private domain—he opened the door of their bedchamber and stood aside.

Light from a few candles came from within the room.

"Be a good lad," Elaine said, "and go in and light every candle we have, and also the torches on the walls—we need to see."

"Yes, Your Grace," the page said, and he walked first into the room.

Roland looked sideways at Elaine as they followed the boy. Her face was hard and set. He could get no clue from her features, save that this business was obviously part of her plan—a plan that began with her spectacular dressing for what would otherwise have been an ordinary Friday night—a plan with an unknown objective. He rubbed his lower lip where she had bitten him—he would have to wait and see where Elaine was taking him.

The page made the room blaze with light. Elaine's gold adornments sparkled—her dress (muted in the dim corridor) caught fire again.

The Duchess was ready. "Go on now," she said to the page.

The lad left the room hurriedly and closed the door behind him.

Roland stared at his wife and rubbed his lip again.

Elaine came up to Roland and touched her lips to the bitten place—then she turned around and walked ten short steps away. She stopped there, about halfway to the bed. She made a deliberate half turn to her left—she showed Roland her profile.

The Duke could just see the tiny white scar under her left eye.

Elaine started to smile, and then stopped—she held the pose, she seemed to be staring at something—or someone.

Roland knew where she was taking him now: back into the past.

"Our first meeting," he said.

Elaine turned and faced her husband.

"Yes. Did you never wonder what I was looking at?"

"I have wondered. I looked over right then, but I saw nothing special—I don't know why I've never asked you about this. What did you see?"

As soon as he said those words Roland felt a thrill of fear shoot through him. He felt as though he should never have asked that question—he was afraid her answer would reveal something terrible, something best hidden—but then he scoffed at his own fear, he made himself recall the scene: there had been nothing evil, nothing strange—and Elaine had been smiling . . .

"I'll tell you," Elaine said.

She took a step toward her husband.

"The royal jousts were held in the King's great stadium that day—you and I both witnessed them. But King Richard wanted a greater spectacle than just the jousts—and so the area around the stadium was one great open air carnival. This carnival had its own kind of sporting events, of a sort less attractive to the nobility. There was bear baiting for the most vulgar, and boxing, and"—Elaine paused—"wrestling."

Elaine took another step toward Roland. She stared into his eyes with a ferocious intensity that didn't seem to go with her accurate but (at least so far) unexciting account.

"When I arrived that day I took a walk around the stadium. I looked at some of the less noble activities. I was younger then, not far removed from the rough pursuits of country life—I paused at the wrestling arena. There I saw a rough, long haired country fellow—a proud man with powerful muscles—I thought that if I were a gambler, I would surely bet on him. I was tempted to stay and watch his bouts—but then I remembered my new position as a proper lady of the court—I went inside the stadium, and I watched the jousts.

"Some hours later, when the knights had ceased to pound each other, I left with the crowd. I was seeking Arthur, for he had said he would meet me—I was walking along slowly, looking all around, when suddenly I saw the wrestler I had admired earlier. I stopped and looked at him.

"He was tired now—he was leaning against a fence. I saw that he was covered with sweat—his hair dripped with it (the greasy man, Roland thought) and his shirt was plastered to his body. I noticed then that a gold medal hung from a ribbon around his neck—I was very pleased that he *had* won, and I smiled. I might have gone on then in another second—but my eyes were drawn by an approaching figure, and so I stayed there a little longer.

"A girl was coming toward the wrestler. I saw that she was a serving girl, probably from the palace staff. Her face was fairly pretty, though only exceptional for the look of intensity that she directed toward the wrestler. She must have watched his bouts all afternoon—her expression showed that he was a hero to her.

"The wrestler realized right away that she was coming to him, though I could tell from his face that he didn't know her. I saw him look her over—she had a nice plump figure, and she walked slowly to show it off—her hips swayed, her shoulders were back to thrust her breasts out—"

Elaine walked toward Roland in just that way—

"The wrestler smiled at the girl—I could see the strength come back into his body—he stopped leaning on the fence—he stood calmly, poised and confident—the girl came right up to him and then she stopped."

Elaine was right in front of Roland now. "She looked up at the wrestler's face, and then she spread her legs like this"—Elaine did it, a slow deliberate parting, her womanhood offered beneath the stretched dress—"I watched her do it, and it was the most erotic thing I had ever seen—she stood like that for a second, with her back arched, her breasts offered and her legs spread, and then she asked, 'Do you want to fuck me?' "

Roland seemed frozen by his wife's words. He stood perfectly still—he stared down into Elaine's blazing blue eyes.

"The wrestler smiled even wider when he heard the girl's question—he just looked at her for a long second, with that smile on his face, and then he said, 'Sure,' with a certain arrogant casualness—I saw the girl start to relax—he put an arm around her and pulled her close, and she just melted against him—I knew how she felt, she had put herself on the line and now she felt blessed by his desire—she was safe, relieved, and happy—I wondered if I would ever have the courage to ask such

a question—and then I felt someone watching me, and I turned
and looked, and there you were.

"And now we are here, seven years later, and there is only one
question that I want to ask you."

Elaine's legs were already parted, but now she widened her
stance even more—she arched her back as the girl had done and
thrust her breasts forward for Roland's appreciation—she
looked up at her husband's face and she asked the question.

"Do you want to fuck me?"

Even though she had prepared him, even though he knew
exactly what she was going to say, Roland was still shocked.
This time she was not quoting some anonymous serving girl—
this time she was saying it on her own—the coarse word hurt
him like a low kick—when she had made ready to ask the question he had told himself that he was going to answer 'Sure' like
the man in her story—but now he felt sick, he didn't have the
confidence to give that kind of answer—he didn't even want to
give that kind of answer—he didn't want Elaine like this—

"I just want to love you," he said.

Elaine looked into her husband's soft brown wounded eyes,
and she realized that he spoke the truth, the only truth that he
could give her.

Elaine turned away from him. She walked quickly to her
dressing table—she picked up the hand mirror that she had
lately used to show Sandra her healing A—she turned around
suddenly and threw that mirror with all her strength at
Roland's head.

He ducked—the mirror shattered against the door—a thousand pieces of glass showered down onto the rug behind him—
the jagged shards lay still there, glistening with reflected light.

There was dead silence in the room.

Elaine remembered Davila's sadness. She understood that
now, just as she understood the meaning of the Gypsy's words.

She was sad herself, not angry any more—but she didn't have
any choice at all.

"We will never have a child together," she said to Roland, and
then she headed toward the door with a determined stride.

The Duke could have reached out and caught her as she went
by—but he made no move.

His head was still lowered in reaction to the flung mirror—he
looked at the floor as she passed him—he heard her slippers
crunching over the broken glass—he heard her open the door

and close it again—he heard her speak to the page on duty in the next room: "Give me a candle—thank you, there's a good lad—I'm off to see Lady Sandra—don't worry, I'll find my own way."

The Duke heard Elaine's footsteps going away.

He went to his knees and started picking up the broken glass.

Chapter 192

KISSES

Sandra's door was not locked, so Elaine just slipped in quietly. A few candles flickered in the room—Elaine blew out the one she was holding and put it down on Sandra's dresser. Sandra was asleep in her bed—Elaine walked over to look at young Anton. The boy slept peacefully in his nightshirt on his own small bed—Elaine could see his bare feet, as well as his serene face, because he had kicked off his sheet sometime during the hot night.

The Duchess felt an awesome longing in her heart—she bent down and kissed the boy's sleeping forehead.

Elaine had hardly made any noise at all—but still a mother always knows when there is a presence near her child.

"Who is it?"

Elaine heard the alarm in Sandra's voice, but as she turned her head to answer there came a second question in a less worried tone, "Is that you, Elaine?"

"Yes, it's me."

Elaine walked over to Sandra's bed and knelt down beside it. She leaned over and kissed Sandra—the Duchess seems very sad, Sandra thought—and then Elaine spoke again.

"Will you do a favor for me, Sandra?"

"Of course, Your Grace." Sandra was more awake now, and she used the title.

Elaine kissed Sandra again, very lightly on the lips.

"Just call me Elaine tonight."

"Yes—Elaine."

Elaine smiled—the saddest smile Sandra had ever seen.

"I want you to take Anton to Christina and have her watch

him for the rest of the night. I need to talk to you—actually, I
need for you to talk to me and I am afraid we would wake him."

Sandra looked up into Elaine's sad, needy eyes and she said,
"Don't worry—I'll take him over. He's a good sleeper—he probably won't even wake up."

Elaine moved aside to let Sandra get out of bed—the young
mother went over to her son and looked down at him with love.
Then she leaned down and kissed him, just as Elaine had
done—then she picked him up easily—the boy continued to
sleep peacefully.

Elaine opened the connecting door to Christina's room—
Sandra went in and Elaine followed her. Sandra stopped by the
side of Christina's bed and handed Anton to the Duchess. Elaine
felt the unexpected weight—she felt her own heart racing as she
held the boy's warm little body in her arms. She looked down at
his sleeping, trusting face—she kissed each of his round cheeks
as she heard Sandra whispering to Christina—the maidservant
gradually woke up—she glanced over, saw the Duchess, and
tried to curtsy while still in bed. Sandra calmed her and
explained what she wanted. Christina assented at once—she got
up and made a space between her two daughters—the older girl
woke up—she was disturbed by all the people in the room, but
Christina held her and kissed her, and explained that she would
have little Anton to sleep with this night. The girl accepted this,
but she didn't go back to sleep—she watched all the proceedings
with bright alert eyes.

Elaine handed Anton back to his mother. Sandra gave her boy
a few last kisses, and then she laid him down between the two
young girls. The awake one put a protective arm around the little boy—Sandra smiled.

Anton slept through it all.

Sandra bent down and whispered, "I'll see you in the morning,
my love," and then she thanked Christina.

The maidservant managed a proper curtsy this time.

Sandra led the way back to her room—Elaine closed the door
behind them.

Sandra waited for instructions.

Elaine didn't say anything. She walked past Sandra to the
bed—she stood there with her back to her friend. She unfastened her tightly drawn belt—she tossed the heavy golden chain
onto the bed. She pulled the scarlet dress off over her head and
dropped it by the belt. She kicked off her slippers.

Then, naked save for earrings and necklace, she walked over to the head of the bed and took Sandra's two pillows. She came back a step—she set the pillows down, one atop the other, the long side of the pillows parallel to the long side of the bed. There was just enough space to sit down on the edge of the bed in front of the pillows.

Elaine turned around and looked at Sandra.

"Take off your nightgown," the Duchess ordered.

Sandra obeyed—then she folded it and placed it on a chair.

"Come here."

Sandra walked slowly over to her former mistress, mesmerized by the sad, sweet smile on Elaine's face.

They embraced, and as always Elaine's high small breasts rested on top of Sandra's heavier, fuller bosom—but this time Sandra could feel the hard gold of Elaine's necklace between them—it seemed to be holding them apart—Sandra didn't want to think of what she had already guessed—she felt her tears come and she looked up blindly to be kissed—Elaine did kiss her, a wonderful, giving, loving, so so sad kiss—Elaine was crying too—their tears mingled as they kissed and nuzzled and hugged and kissed again, but still the sadness broke through their kisses—Elaine let her hair fall forward, and she used the fine strands to dry Sandra's face and her own, and then she said softly, "I'm going away."

Sandra said, "I know," and then her eyes fluttered and she tried to turn away—but Elaine's strong hands were cupping her cheeks, and she held the girl where she was.

"Sandra, before I go, I have to know the truth. Is it worth it?"

"Is what . . . ?"

"I can't have a child with Roland. I love a man who loves me, a man who can fill me, a man who will give me a child—I want to go to him—"

"Robin Hood."

"How do you know?"

"Everyone has heard the legends—but I know what he was formerly called—and I know you, my dearest, dearest Elaine. I remember delivering your message to him—you know, the one where you said you wouldn't meet him—he terrified me"— Sandra managed a small smile—"he's a lot like you, dear lady."

Elaine kissed her.

"Am I really so frightening?"

"Sometimes—but—O Milady, must you go?"

Sandra's tears were starting again. Elaine kissed them away. "Not just yet, sweet girl, not just yet. I haven't told you exactly what favor I desire."

Sandra looked up at Elaine with a touch of faint hope in her eyes.

"I asked you if it was worth it—what I mean is, I want to know about having a child—I want you to tell me about having little Anton, tell me of all your pains and pleasures—it is the lack of a child that sends me, and yet I know nothing of the experience—please tell me, dear Sandra, tell me everything."

Sandra tried another smile. "And if I tell you it's terrible, you'll stay?"

Elaine's eyes were sad and serious. She shook her head slightly. "You won't lie to me, Sandra."

"No—but just hold me, hold me tight."

Elaine hugged Sandra, hugged her fiercely until the hard necklace dug into the girl's tender skin—and then she walked Sandra over to her bed and made her sit down on the edge, with her back to the pillows.

Elaine knelt before her former lady in waiting. She put her hands on the girl's knees and quite firmly pushed them apart—and then the Duchess of Larraz bowed her golden head to give a caress she had never given before: she pressed her lips to Sandra's sweet womanhood.

Sandra was shocked—she kept her hands by her sides—she didn't know what to do.

Elaine kept her face where it was, she kissed, and then she extended her tongue and licked delicately upward along the line of the split peach.

Sandra heard a moan and then she realized it was her own—she felt a slow sliding, a heaviness of moisture within, she spread her legs wider and offered herself more fully to Elaine's mouth—

The caress stopped. The Duchess tilted her head back—she looked right into Sandra's eyes and said, "Tell me everything."

Sandra looked down at Elaine, and then she reached out with one hand and ran her fingers through that finespun golden hair. She stroked Elaine like that for a moment—and then she tightened her grip—she had a whole handful of hair now—she knew she was pulling but she couldn't let go—she felt a raging excitement tear through her, a rush of power such as she had never known before—she looked down into Elaine's blue eyes and then she suddenly forced the blonde head back down—she forced Elaine's face into the gap of her spread thighs, and she held her there until she felt the Duchess's tongue again, serving her, and then she relaxed her cruel grip just a little, but she still kept control, and then she said, "Yes, kiss me, kiss me just like that and I will tell you all that you wish to know."

Chapter 193

SANDRA'S STORY

"I told you already how Sir Anton discovered that he belonged to me—but I knew the first day that I belonged to him. I gave myself on the grassy bank of a small stream, naked on my back before the summer sun. He spread me wide, and mounted me— he broke through my maidenhead, and I screamed, but even in my pain I clung to him, for he was mine, and I was his. Our souls met that day—I felt his seed come deep inside of me, and I knew that I would conceive."

Sandra had released the thick clump of hair that she had held. Now she was stroking Elaine's blond locks lovingly, caressingly.

Elaine's mouth was adoring, not really seeking, just kissing and licking the spilled honey.

"He died, you know." Sandra's voice seemed to have drifted far away, and her fingers became only a faint ghostly presence in Elaine's hair. "His was a hero's passing. He fought the Northmen, and saved all our lives—and then he fought Death itself, until he had lived long enough to marry me. With that last act, he took care of our son, gave him legitimacy and honor—and then he told me—he told me—" Elaine buried her face deeper, so as not to look up and see Sandra's tears—"he told me to name the boy after him, and I promised I would, and he died.

"He died but he didn't leave me. I must thank you, Elaine—" the Duchess felt the stronger touch of Sandra's fingers, she allowed her head to be guided for the girl's pleasure— "for completing the A, for that is the mark in flesh of what I know in spirit: my husband's soul and mine will always be intermingled, and the proof is in the sturdy growing boy who is blessed with his father's name."

Sandra pulled Elaine's head back by the hair, pulled her up from the bent over posture of the supplicant, and then urged her forward. Elaine shuffled awkwardly closer, on her knees between Sandra's spread legs—and then Sandra looked down into her eyes and asked, "Do you really want to know everything?"

"Yes," Elaine answered.

Sandra smiled—then she bent down and kissed Elaine's mouth, a long, probing kiss—Sandra tasted herself on Elaine's tongue, she felt her nipples aching—she broke the kiss and pulled Elaine's head down to her left breast—Elaine kissed the nipple and sucked it into her mouth, sucked as much of the soft breast as she could and Sandra stroked her hair approvingly—Sandra looked down at the slim lines of Elaine's body, she felt the sweet pull of the sucking mouth at her breast, and then she went on.

"That's where you feel it first—there is a fullness right there, in your breasts. They swell, they ache—" Sandra guided Elaine to her other breast, and made her suck that one as well—"they hurt, but it's a good hurt, going straight to the heart—they are growing for your child.

"Now I was lucky—" Sandra pulled Elaine away from her right breast, and guided the Duchess's face down her soft belly—Elaine, directed by the firm hand in her hair, kissed whatever she was offered—"for though many women told me of their morning sickness, told me of waking up to pain and nausea, I had none of those problems. I ate with pleasure, my face filled out, my hair got thicker—and you go down now, my dearest Elaine, go down and taste the truth of my body, yes, there, yes—" Sandra leaned back against the two pillows Elaine had set up for her, leaned back and gave herself to the pleasure of her loving friend's mouth, and then finally she spoke again, from time past but never to be forgotten—"I became beautiful, beautiful with the life growing in my body—I never knew before what it was like to be you, but then for a while I gained some knowledge—everywhere I went people told me I was beautiful—I could see the change in my own mirror: my swollen breasts stood out perfectly, my face glowed, I stared at myself and brushed and brushed my thick shining hair—O yes, I became a little vain—but then I realized all this was a gift from God, a gift that came with my blessed babe—and then suddenly I forgot myself in my new concern for the child—I wished that I could truly feel him—I wanted a sign that he was well and healthy—I watched my belly swell, watched my perfect figure pass away like any fleeting vanity, and I did not care at all, I just wanted to know the truth about my child—" Sandra's fingers were tight in Elaine's hair now—"and then, O thank God, in the fifth month I felt him, I wasn't sure at first, I directed all my attention to the miracle inside my own body, and then yes, I felt him again, alive in my womb, and then I relaxed, I rejoiced, and I started visiting you in the afternoons.

"Anton got stronger and stronger. I remember how you used to jump when he kicked at your hand on my stretched belly. Sometimes I'd smile at you then—but more often I'd cry, thinking of my husband—but you would always kiss me, and embrace me, and your kindness brought me back from sorrow and toward the joy of that birth that would come soon.

"I was an awkward lady by now. I carried my boy slowly before me—I waddled, craving fresh fruits—in the winter! Yet I was fortunate again, His Grace let me in the palace root cellar, and I don't know what he was saving those apples for, but I took them all and ate them in a week.

"My belly was so big and swollen. My breasts were big too, my nipples had even grown and there was often moisture on their tips—they were ready to be sucked, I was ready to give birth, and then I met Davila, and I knew indeed that my time was close at hand.

"I spent the last month dreaming and waiting—and then, on the night of March fourteenth, I felt this great tightening—it wasn't really pain, just a hard squeeze all through my belly—I called Davila and she came in and felt me, and waited with me for the next one, and that one hurt a little bit, and she waited for the one after that, I had no sense of time but she said they were coming slowly, she said that I should rest and relax, not much would happen for a while, but she said she would stay with me, and so I lay on my side on the bed, and I spoke to my brave son, I tried to give him courage for his journey, the pains kept getting stronger, hours went by—and then suddenly my water broke. I didn't know what it was, a great gush of liquid between my thighs, I was frightened but Davila told me I was fine, this was normal—she said my boy had decided it was time to come out—I smiled and told her to send for you, because I love you and I needed you there—I knew that this was the hard part coming but when I remember it now it doesn't seem so hard.

"You helped me—I remember you sitting on my bed, holding my hand—you never moved, never left, never closed your eyes—the pains got worse and worse, yes, stronger and stronger, but I would look into your blue eyes, and lose myself there, and sometimes I saw us in your eyes, and sometimes I saw Sir Anton, but mostly I saw my brave little boy, each pain another step of his journey, and then I could feel Davila's hands opening me, measuring me, making sure I was ready, her touch gentle, knowing, my focus in your eyes, in your eyes I saw him coming down, getting ready to be born, my pain was nothing, it was just what I had to give, what I gladly gave so that he might live, and then Davila told me that I was ready, she told me to push, and I did and O what a glorious feeling that was, I was helping now, I was giving birth, I pushed and pushed, I could feel such a stretching, burning pain but I could feel my son being born and that was worth so much more to me, Davila told me she could see just the top of his head, I wanted to use all my strength then but she stopped me, it was hard to wait, I felt Davila's hands again, she was adjusting my baby, showing him the way, and I waited, anxiously, I saw the first rays of morning light enter the room, I saw the light reflected in your eyes and then Davila finally gave me the command I was waiting for: 'Push!'—there was urgency in her voice now and I pushed and I felt him move and I had been tired but I forgot that now—I pushed and pushed again and then I felt him come free of me, I could feel his soul as it was born into the world, and then I heard his cry and I knew joy beyond imagining, beyond existence, my whole life was joy, I saw only colors—Davila must have taken care of the cord then, for when my eyes worked again, there was my boy, alive and on his own, resting on my belly—I cradled his tiny form with my arms, I felt his perfection, and I brought him to my breast, I felt him take my nipple and begin to suck, I felt the tug of his tiny mouth and I said, 'Anton, little Anton, Anton I love you so'—O I love you so, I love you, I love you—" Sandra put both hands in Elaine's hair and cried of love all through her pleasure.

Chapter 194

GOOD-BYE

Fifteen minutes had passed since Sandra had reached the summit of pleasure.

Elaine was fully dressed once again.

Sandra had put her nightgown back on.

They stood close, facing each other, but they did not touch.

"Is there nothing that will make you stay?" Sandra asked.

"I hurt Roland in his manhood tonight," Elaine replied. "If I stay, I must accept him as half a man—I must accept life without a child—I must accept the knowledge that of the two of us, I am the stronger.

"He can accept that—but I can not."

"So you will go to Robin Hood?"

"Yes."

Elaine looked down at Sandra and gave her a sad, loving smile—then she put her hands on the girl's shoulders and drew her close and kissed her.

This kiss had a meaning that was unmistakable—this kiss said good-bye.

They broke apart just slightly and looked into one another's eyes.

"I will never forget you, Sandra. I will always love you."

"I love you Elaine."

"Good luck with Sir Gowan."

"And to you with Robin Hood."

Sandra had spoken bravely but now she felt her tears coming—she said quickly, while she could still get the words out, "Elaine, if you don't go now I'm going to get down on the floor and grab your knees and hold you so you can't get away!"

Elaine ruffled Sandra's brown curls affectionately. "Silly goose," she said, but she also felt her vision blurring.

Elaine released Sandra and turned abruptly. She walked purposefully to the door. She opened it—she looked back once, and blew Sandra a last kiss—and then she was gone.

Chapter 195

LEAVING THE PALACE

The night groom did not like the idea of rousing one of his horses in the middle of the night. He thought also that the demand for a man's saddle—for a woman—was outrageous. He wanted to protest—but then he raised his torch, and got a good look at the Duchess's eyes, and he found that he could not say a word. He went off and did as he was told, cursing silently all the while.

Elaine knew that she had no chance to do what she had to do before dawn if she were riding sidesaddle—she needed speed, she needed to see where she was going in the night—she looked up at the sky, and saw her old adversary the moon, almost full—she thought, You are my friend now, you will guide me as I begin my journey to my love.

The groom brought the horse over. He gained a measure of satisfaction by allowing his hands to wander as he helped the Duchess mount.

Elaine thanked him kindly nonetheless.

She touched heels to her horse, and left the palace of the Duke of Larraz.

She would never return.

Chapter 196

ANGEL

Elaine rode beneath the moon toward Madame Genevieve's house of pleasure.

She knew in her heart that she had answered all the arguments against her journey—save one. Even as she rode, she could still hear her mother's dear voice: "And it is you who will rise again among the nobility of the land, and that is why I gave you the name Elaine."

I have done all you asked, Mama, Elaine thought. I left Firfleet, I became a Countess, and then a Duchess. If titles are the measure of nobility, then I have risen as high as it is possible for me to rise. My appearance shows my class—my clothes are silk, and my jewelry is gold.

Yet when I think of your prophecy, I think of more than titles and wealth. I remember that you charged me with passing on the story of our heritage to my own child—I remember you saying that in your heart you believed that true love was cherished by God.

I know my true love, Mama. I know that he will give me a child—many children.

He has no title—just his name. Yet he has a nobility of spirit that makes him greater than all those who claim higher birth. His character has been formed in the hell of war and loss—and yet he has not become hard. He has learned compassion—he gives of his strength to help others, and yet he stands alone in his pride.

I am certain that he is noble in the eyes of God.

His name is Robin Hood.

I love him.

Elaine seemed to feel a swirling presence near her—she could almost hear the beating of angel wings, almost feel the loving touch of weightless fingers caressing her face.

She heard a voice that was like a thought inside her head: My child, my only child—I love you so and I worry about you. How will you live?

Elaine gave her own silent answer: I used to wonder myself, Mama. I thought, does he wish me to live in a stable, or under a pine tree? But he has changed now. He has become a man, and he will provide for me, and for our children. I believe this—I go, trusting in this belief.

Elaine heard no reply. She felt fearful, like she was a child again—but then she made herself continue: I've made up my mind, Mama, I'm going to go—O Mama, I love you so, and please listen, for there is something else. You gave me a beautiful name and I thank you—but that name is too well known, and using it, in the future I see for myself, would bring too much danger to me and the man I love.

For a time I must take a new name.

You should know, Mama, that there is only one other name that I could answer to—one other name that shares my spirit—and that is your name, dear Mama, for you gave me life, and died so that I could live.

You have a beautiful name, and God grant that I have your blessing. I shall call myself Marian.

I love you Mama, I love you, I love you—

Then Elaine heard someone crying, someone crying close at hand—but then perhaps the only sobs she heard were her own.

Chapter 197

BARGAIN

Elaine knocked at the heavy barred door of the brothel.

She waited a moment, and then knocked again.

Finally she heard the sound of footsteps—and then a young woman asked, in a very cross voice, "Who is it at this time of night?"

"I am the Duchess of Larraz."

"And I'm the Queen of France. You'll have to do better than that, my dear."

Elaine took several deep breaths. She thought, as long as I stand on Larrazian soil, I still have my title. She said again, "I am the Duchess of Larraz," and this time there was enough ice in her tone to freeze the blood of anyone who heard her.

The girl on the other side of the door was suddenly and absolutely terrified.

She scraped her hand as she unbarred the door, but she didn't even notice the slight pain. She threw the door open in a panic.

"Please come in, please please forgive me, Your Grace."

Elaine stepped inside without comment. The girl nervously shut the door behind her.

"I must see Madame Genevieve at once," Elaine said.

"I will wake her—please wait here, Your Grace."

The girl ran up a flight of stairs and disappeared.

Elaine paced.

It took a while for Madame Genevieve to dress and select a wig. When she came down the stairs, Elaine noticed that Madame had become a brunette for this serious occasion.

The elderly lady greeted Elaine with formal propriety. "Good morning, Your Grace," she said.

Elaine nodded but she didn't reply. She simply unfastened her belt and handed the heavy golden chain to the old business woman.

Madame Genevieve lifted the gold links up into the light of a bank of candles. She weighed it carefully (much to Elaine's ill concealed annoyance) with hands that had a long experience of judging value.

Finally Madame was satisfied. "It's genuine," she said. "What do you want to buy, Your Grace?"

Elaine told her.

"Your Grace, that's far too much," Madame said with a smile.

Elaine's eyes glittered savagely in the candle light. "The belt is worth far more than your costs—but that's not the main point. If you don't give me what I ask this will be the last night you ever do business in Larraz."

Madame Genevieve made a conciliatory face. She had calmed many an angry customer in her time—and she also knew when one was serious. She decided that this was no time to bargain.

"Do not fret, Your Grace. You are quite right, of course—I simply forgot myself for a moment. Your payment is more than adequate—all will be done as you have commanded."

And so, an hour later, Elaine left the house driving a fine little coach. This 'love carriage', as Madame had called it, came equipped with heavy curtains and a square bed instead of seats. Elaine hadn't bothered to ask what it had been used for—she had simply supervised the loading of provisions and clothing.

Now the Duchess, sitting up on the driver's seat, cracked her whip over the matched pair of gray mares in front of her. The lively horses moved obediently into a trot—Elaine bounced along, under the moonlit sky.

Elaine still wore her red dress, but all her blond hair was covered by a wig of midnight black. A delicate beauty mark on her cheek hid her scar. Her lips were painted a crimson that was even brighter than her dress.

She remembered how she had smiled when she had looked at herself in Madame Genevieve's mirror.

She looked like the most expensive courtesan in the world.

Chapter 198

THE SECOND COACH

Once the Duchess was out of sight, a second coach left Madame Genevieve's house. By the time this coach had got onto the main road, Elaine had already turned off, heading to the west.

The second coach went straight north to the palace. The driver did not try to sneak in via the south entrance—he circled around, and came in properly to the north gate.

The two guards there recognized the vehicle—but the good Madame's coach had never come to the palace this late before. Stranger still, a horse was running behind the coach, attached by a long lead.

"I think that's one of the Duke's personal horses," the first guard said to the second.

"Who goes there?" boomed the second guard.

"As if you didn't know," said Madame Genevieve's coachman, still surly at having been wakened out of a sound sleep. "Madame is kind enough to return one of His Grace's horses—and there's something else . . ."

The first guard went around back and unfastened the lead from the coach.

The coachman got down and opened the passenger door. He put out a hand and drew out a frightened young girl—the same girl who had answered Elaine's knock.

The second guard looked her over appreciatively. She was dressed and made up for love—her fear seemed to make her even more attractive.

"This is Bridget," the coachman said—and then he leaned over and put his mouth right against the second guard's ear.

"She is to be delivered to the Duke's bedroom—the Duchess herself commands this."

The second guard grinned widely. "I'll take her in myself," he said.

He took Bridget's arm with a firm grip and called to the first guard, "Hold your post here—we'll take care of the horse later. I'll be right back."

He turned and escorted Bridget into the palace.

The first guard watched them go with a scowl on his face. Such is always my luck, he thought. He gets the lass—I'm left holding the horse.

The coachman watched until the palace door closed behind Bridget and the second guard. Then he climbed up onto the driver's seat again. He turned his horses around—he set off towards his home, a little cottage tucked in behind the brothel.

He hoped that when he got there he would be able to get back to sleep.

Chapter 199

A WELL TRAINED GIRL

Elaine understood her husband: Roland blamed himself for his wife's anger. He accepted her strength—he cursed his own weakness, but he did not overcome it. He just agonized over his faulty reply to Elaine's question, just as he still agonized over his mistakes in leadership during the pursuit of Elaine across England. He blamed himself for all the deaths among his men—never mind that he had succeeded in an extremely difficult mission, he still cursed himself for following those riderless horses—and besides all that, he still blamed himself for Charles's death, even though quite rationally he knew that there was nothing he could have done to have prevented that tragedy.

He had tried to be good to them all, and he had failed.

After Elaine had left, he had picked up all the little shards of glass himself, and put them in a couple of empty flagons. Then he had undressed—he had put on his bed jacket, and lain down on his big empty bed. There he allowed his thoughts to run over a catalog of never forgotten mistakes (his manifest successes never entered his mind)—he followed this mental trail to the inevitability of death, and indeed that seemed rather comforting.

In some ways he would rather face death than Elaine. He was sure that she would come back from Sandra's room in the morning. How should he apologize to her? He didn't have an answer—he didn't know what he had done wrong except love her—he only knew that he had not pleased her—he wished that he could give his life to make her happy.

He fell asleep with that thought in his mind—but he awoke to voluptuous pleasure. At first he thought he was dreaming, but

then the sensation became too real for fantasy: his hard manhood was buried deep in a girl's adoring mouth, she was licking
him, sucking him—he reached out and touched a smooth leg
near his face—he blinked three times and opened his eyes. He
saw a nude, full figured girl, not Elaine, lying reversed on the
bed next to him as he lay on his back. Her red hair was fluffed
out, hiding what she was doing, what he could feel so well—ah,
she sensed him stirring, she redoubled her efforts, she slid down
and offered him her throat, she was taking him all, her hands
were questing underneath his buttocks—he fought the new sensations, he forced his analytical mind to work—this was no lady,
and she was young—too young to know all this on her own—a
well trained girl—one of Madame Genevieve's girls, yes, she had
to be—Elaine had to have sent her, no one else would dare—

Elaine was going away.

She was buying time.

Roland knew that he had a choice to make, now, this second,
with his blood boiling: he could shove this girl away, and call his
knights, and ride out in pursuit of Elaine—or—or—he saw
Elaine's hard blue eyes, he saw her hurling the mirror—

He did not challenge his wife's power.

He reached down, he used his heavy masculine hand to hold
the girl where she was—he felt his manhood swelling—he gave
himself to this girl he had never seen before—he came in
Bridget's mouth, something he had never done with Elaine.

Chapter 200

LEAVETAKING

Roland enjoyed Bridget in many ways that morning—it was almost noon before he told her to dress.

The Duke put his own clothes on, and then he handed Bridget a small stack of gold coins. She thanked him graciously, not mentioning that the cost of her services had already been covered.

Bridget waited to be dismissed, but Roland obviously had something on his mind—suddenly he let it out.

"What did my wife say to you?"

Bridget looked into the Duke's eyes—she saw right away that she could not even think of lying to him.

"She told me what to do."

"Everything?"

"Yes."

"And what else?" He meant, was there a message, any message for me?

"She told me I would be punished if I didn't please you."

"And . . .?"

"She kissed me."

"And . . .?"

"She left."

"She left?"

"Yes."

"You may go now. My coachman will take you back to Madame Genevieve's."

"Thank you"—Bridget suddenly blushed—she realized that she had forgotten to use the Duke's title all through their conversation—"Your Grace."

Roland turned his back.

Bridget hesitated for a moment, and then she suddenly felt that she just had to get out of there. She turned to go, but she wasn't quite fast enough—as she turned she saw his shoulders sag—the terrible sound of a man sobbing followed her as she walked to the door—she threw it open and almost ran into the page on duty in the next room—he asked her where she was going, and she said, "To the coachman, now!"—the page heard the Duke and he hustled Bridget out of there—the door to the Duke's bedchamber remained open.

Roland waited until he could no longer hear the hurrying foot-steps of Bridget and the page. Then he shuffled slowly to the door and shoved it shut with his body, for there was no strength in his hands—none in his arms—none in his legs—he collapsed to his knees, his forehead sliding down the door—he looked down at the carpet and saw a bright shard of glass that he had missed—he saw his teardrops falling next to it, each one shining like the glass as it fell.

He thought, no message—a leavetaking as final as death.

Roland did not call for any pursuit of Elaine.

Instead he announced the Duchess's death. He explained that in his grief he had buried her secretly in the night.

He didn't care whether or not anyone believed him.

He went into mourning.

He wore black until the day he died.

The people of Larraz thought the whole affair was very strange—and perhaps the strangest thing of all was that even that day the Duke received his traveling informants as usual.

All dressed in black, he listened, he rewarded, and he remem-bered.

Chapter 201

CROSSING THE BORDER

Peaceful, peaceful Larraz . . .

There were no guards at the border between Larraz and France—only a cairn of stones by the side of the road to mark the end of the Duke's territory.

Elaine stopped her horses. She stood up in the driver's seat so she could look over the coach behind her, back to the east. Dawn had broken a half hour before, so she was looking into the rising sun. She put up her left hand to block the most intense light. Now she could see the road behind her clearly—there were no pursuers in sight—the only trace of her husband was the wedding ring that gleamed brightly just inches before her eyes.

Elaine brought her left hand down to her mouth, and ran her tongue over her third finger. Then she pulled on the ring—it came off quite easily. She looked at it for a moment—and then she tossed it onto the empty road behind the coach.

She turned around and sat down on the driver's seat again—she touched her horses with her whip, and drove across the border on this morning of August 19, 1196.

She left all titles behind her.

Now she was only Elaine the Fair, daughter of Marian.

In the near future she would use only her mother's name—she thought that later on she might be able to reclaim her own.

She was very tired now, after staying up all night. She drove slowly into France, until finally she had to stop and rest. She directed her horses off the road. The August sun was hot now, and she was thirsty. She reached back into the coach for a wine-skin and took a drink. She thought of sweet Sandra's lips, all stained purple. She looked at her fine gray horses, and she thought of gray eyes, and she imagined the tall proud figure of Robin Hood, all dressed in green.

Part VII

Love

Chapter 202

"GOOD MORNING"

A morning in England, September 1196 . . .

Little John was used to the way Robin woke up by now—after two years he was *very* used to it—indeed, the ritual had become quite tiresome.

This morning began the same as ever. Little John woke up to the sound of his friend saying, in a love drenched voice, "Elaine, Elaine, Elaine the Fair." The big man saw Robin's smile in the gray morning light—saw the brightness in his friend's wide open, dreaming eyes—saw those eyes gradually focus on himself—saw Robin's consternation, then the slow dawning of comprehension, the even slower acceptance of reality (this from a man famed for split second decisions in battle)—John said wearily, as so often, "It's just me, Robin, she's not here."

Robin turned away—when he looked back his whole face had changed. All trace of the lover was gone now—he showed only the hard face of the outlaw—his cold gray eyes were ready to stare down any man.

But there was only Little John.

Robin made an effort—he tried to smile—he said, "Good morning."

Little John smiled back—this was a first!

Was Robin recovering from his obsession?

Chapter 203

EXPLOITS

The sorrow Robin felt upon awakening did not prevent him from accomplishing great deeds at other times of day. The last two years had been full of heroic exploits—Robin had found a destiny big enough for his talents.

Now the Prince, the Assessor, the Barons, and the Sheriffs lived in fear of him.

The common folk loved him—they sang about him, and they told stories which became tall tales which became legends.

Robin enjoyed his fame—he used it like a magician's cloak— he tossed it gaily in people's eyes, and then disappeared behind it. He did not, in fact, wear green every day.

He also did not live in Sherwood Forest—and because he didn't, this was Robin's favorite of all the legends about him. The Prince's soldiers had searched that wood so many times! The royal hunting dogs had even been put to work—they sniffed and they barked, but they never found an outlaw, or even a trace of an encampment. And even though they found nothing, the rumors were so insistent (and Robin made sure never to deny them) that the soldiers kept coming back, time after time.

It was true that Robin spent a lot of time near Nottingham— but he had comfortable quarters there—he never once had to sleep in the forest.

Likewise he never had any band of Merry Men—Little John was his only companion. When young men asked to join his band (this happened often) Robin always put them off—he would say that he had all the men he needed.

Little John did not understand this at first. One day he said to Robin, "We really could use a few more men."

Robin looked back at him as though his friend understood nothing—and then he said, "We live with a price on our heads, and yet we are not afraid, for we are only two. I trust you absolutely, and you trust me absolutely. If we added a third man, it is unlikely that each of us could trust both of his companions that perfectly. If we added a fourth man, the seeds of betrayal would certainly be sown—and instead of adding a fifth man, we could save time by going straight to the Prince's hangman ourselves!"

Little John never again suggested that they should increase their number.

Meanwhile, many of the men whom Robin had rebuffed (yet also inspired) found themselves unable to go back to lives of submission. Why should they allow the Assessor's agents into their homes? Why should they give up their property to pay for a Prince's debauchery and a King's foreign war? Robin's example gave them an alternative—many chose to fight back.

Tax collectors, press gangs, and sheriffs were assailed throughout the length and breadth of the land. Robin Hood seemed to be everywhere—and nowhere.

From time to time brave rebels were captured, much to Prince John's sinister delight. He thought that these unfortunates possessed the key that would lead him to Robin Hood—and so each time he would go himself to the Tower—he watched as ancient instruments of torture were applied to their bodies—he savored their cries of pain, their desperate confessions—and yet in the end he was always frustrated, for even when they told all they knew, they still did not betray Robin Hood—they could not betray Robin Hood, for Robin kept his secrets to himself.

Robin knew about the torture. He was seldom inclined to show mercy when he met up with representatives of the crown.

Two weeks ago, near the small village of Langly, Robin had come upon four of the Assessor's men. Robin had heard that they had been running roughshod over that rural area, looting and raping—he killed them all with arrows from long range, arrows that seemed to come out of the trees, out of the sky—the villains died without ever seeing their slayer.

Afterwards Robin and Little John took a small portion of gold from the bodies as their pay (they did not intend to be poor in their old age)—and then they returned the rest of the confiscated funds to the grateful village—and rode off again before they could even be properly thanked.

Robin liked to keep moving—he stopped in here or there, listened to the news, and moved on.

Messages were left for him, for Robin had become a last resort in matters of justice. There was one case from about a year ago that Robin remembered well—it concerned a foul old Baron who believed that he had the right of *droit de seigneur* over all the maidens who lived on his estate. As the Baron aged, his ways had become ever crueller—girls went to him virgins, but they left crying with pain and shame, bearing on their bodies the marks of his perversities.

A mother's cry reached Robin: her daughter was sixteen, engaged to be married—the girl's stalwart fiance had disputed the Baron's prerogative, but now the brave young man had been clapped in irons—the innocent girl was to be delivered to the Baron this very night.

Robin and Little John rode thirty miles in an afternoon—they arrived at dusk at the Baron's mansion. Little John smote the Baron's guards and cracked the shackles that imprisoned the brave young lover—Robin rode around the side of the mansion, and then he stood up on his horse's saddle—he looked through an open window into the Baron's well lit bedchamber, and beheld a scene of horror. A young girl wearing only a nightgown was backing toward the window—in front of her the aged Baron shuffled, pointing his cane at her face. A sharp steel blade projected from the end of the cane. The Baron said, "I just want to prick you, my dear," in a strange falsetto voice and then he giggled insanely, but that was his very last laugh—Robin's arrow flashed through the open window and found its target in the Baron's open mouth—the point came out the back of his neck— the old ogre's teeth clicked down on the wooden shaft—his eyes crossed as he tried to focus on the instrument of his death— blood poured out and turned the green feathered shaft red—the girl, who had been silent in terror, suddenly began to scream— the door burst open and Little John and her fiance came rushing in—the Baron toppled over and crashed to the floor—the girl's scream stopped in mid note—she stared numbly, she started to fall herself but her lover got to her in time—she fell into her man's arms.

Robin rode around to the front of the mansion—he caught Little John's horse on the way, and slew a mounted guard who tried to stop him—he took the dead man's horse—he met the young lovers and his friend just as they were coming out the front door—the youth carried a bloodstained sword as well as his girl now—later, when they had a moment to talk, Little John told Robin that the young man had acquitted himself very well indeed.

But they had no time to rest for a while. They rode hard (the lovers rode double) first to the girl's mother's cottage—by then the girl had recovered enough from her fright to kiss her mother and assure her that she was all right—the good mother embraced her daughter and blessed Robin Hood—Robin announced that they had dallied enough, for if there was pursuit, this would be the first place that the Baron's men at arms would look.

Robin and Little John led the couple to a safe house they knew, and left the young lovers alone.

The girl gave her virginity that night to the man who loved her.

No one who was at the Baron's estate that night would ever forget Robin Hood.

People talked, and so this exploit became story, and finally legend—one of many.

Women heard these legends, and sewed green garments, hoping, hoping . . .

Robin could have had any number of adoring girls—but as Elaine correctly guessed, he refused them all.

He learned to say no as quickly and gracefully as possible. He refused even to see Dorothy alone again. He was determined that he would not sleep with a woman until he was sure that he would awaken with her name on his lips—he did not want to cry for Elaine with another woman in his arms.

Little John had no such problems. Many women that Robin rejected sought solace with the tall squire. Little John did his very best to cheer them—such good deeds kept him nearly always in a genial mood.

Little John wondered if Robin would ever find the woman who would make him forget Elaine. If there was such a person, the squire thought, then she must surely be the lady they were going to visit today.

Was it the thought of this lady that had motivated Robin to say "Good morning"?

Chapter 204

ELAINE'S JOURNEY

Roland had considered passage to the west impossible when England and France were at war—but Elaine did not have that much trouble. Roland's knightly force would have been seen as a threat, and thus a potential enemy of either great army—but Elaine aroused emotions of a different order.

Elaine's guise as a courtesan excited men's lust—but then they came close to her, and in her eyes they discovered the true depths of her shattering beauty—a beauty that demanded their protection. Elaine told the soldiers she encountered that her coachman had been killed—and yet even as a woman alone, she had to press on. She said at first that she was bound for King Philip—and she was believed, for her beauty was truly fit only for a King—French soldiers insisted upon escorting her—they spent many nights with her on the road, but they were gentlemen (and they feared the wrath of their King)—they reached the outskirts of Paris one evening—in the morning when they awoke, planning to take Elaine into the city, they found that she and her coach were gone . . .

Elaine encountered English soldiers to the west of Paris—she amused herself by saying she was bound for Prince John, a gift of the Duke of Larraz—the men took unauthorized leave to guide her to the seacoast—they were gentlemen (and they feared the wrath of their revengeful Prince)—one morning when they could smell the sea they woke up and found the lady and her coach missing . . .

At the seacoast Elaine found the captain of a fishing boat, and she promised him a kiss if he would take her and her coach and horses across the Channel—he agreed with pleasure, and

Elaine fulfilled her part of the bargain—when they docked on the English side that afternoon she gave him a kiss that he would remember for the rest of his life—while he was recovering she drove her coach across the gangplank—when he opened his eyes again she had already disappeared into the English fog . . .

Elaine was back in her homeland.

Roland, pushing straight through, had traversed this same distance in two weeks. Elaine, dependent on her escorts, had taken almost twice as long. The date was now September 14, 1196—the red blur of the sun through the fog indicated that it would be full dark soon—Elaine was alone in an English port town whose name she did not know—she did not know where Robin was either, but she was confident that she would find him.

She would just have to ask the right people.

Elaine saw the torchlit sign of a tavern, and she stopped her coach.

She went inside—and smiled when she saw four ladies of the evening leaning against the bar. She had hoped to find such professionals in this coastal town—she went up to the ladies, and graciously invited them to join her at a table in the corner.

They assented at once, for her voice was that of a lady of quality, regardless of her costume—and they also saw the gold at her throat and ears.

Elaine and her four new acquaintances sat down around a round table as men stared—Elaine ordered good wine all around, and after it was served she took off her golden necklace and laid it on the table in front of her.

"For that, you can have us all, Milady," the oldest of the waterfront courtesans said.

"But what would you charge Robin Hood?" Elaine asked.

The youngest one's face softened. "There is not one of us who would charge him a penny, Milady," she said.

There were murmurs of agreement all around—then the eldest one said, "I would pay him!" and they all laughed, even Elaine.

After the mirth died down, Elaine made her proposal.

"I know that ladies such as yourselves must hear a great many things," she said. "I have been away from this country for two years—I have been away while Robin Hood has come to fame. Tell me all you know of the great outlaw—tell me truthfully, and my necklace is yours, to be divided equally among you."

One lady who hadn't spoken yet now examined Elaine with suspicious eyes. "Do you come from the Prince?" she asked.

Elaine looked openly at her questioner—she allowed her own heart's desire to show. "I do not come from the Prince," she said simply. "I am here only for myself, for I love Robin Hood. I wish to find him, so that I may give myself."

"Do you think if we knew where he was we'd still be here?" the fourth one asked. "He and his Merry Men must be in sore need of comfort after all their battles—and we'd be comforting them right now if we knew where they were—but *no one* knows how to find Robin Hood.

"People have seen him—he drops in here and there—but you never know when he's going to come back—he allows no one to come to him—and that's why he's still alive.

"Take your necklace, Milady. Go home and dream like all the rest of us—we have nothing to offer you—we can't help you find him."

Elaine smiled at the honest courtesan, and then she pushed the necklace a little further distance from herself.

"You can help, my friends," she said. "Just talk to me."

Once they got started they couldn't stop.

It took hours and Lord knows how much wine, but the ladies managed to regale Elaine with every story, tale, legend, or anecdote they had ever heard about Robin Hood. They spoke with awe of their green hero—and they gave due consideration to his huge friend Little John, and all of the brave Merry Men.

One common thread surfaced in their tales—while Robin might appear anywhere in England, the only place he repeatedly showed up was in the area around Nottingham. Elaine remembered Roland's reports—Nottingham again, always Nottingham—he *had* to have some safe place there—

"In Sherwood Forest, he lives in Sherwood Forest with his Merry Men!" declaimed one with drunken conviction.

He lived in the forest as a youth, Elaine thought, but would that be safe for him now? Elaine's mind whirled with wine—she had the feeling she knew something, she should remember something—

"The Prince invaded that forest with a hundred knights and a thousand foot soldiers," argued another. "They beat every bush and they didn't find him, because he's not there! He just puts out that story to hide where he really lives!"

"But where does he really live?"

"He does so live in Sherwood Forest, but he can make himself invisible!"

"Can he make his Merry Men invisible too?" Elaine asked.

"He can do anything," that one replied with some heat. "Anyone who can make Barons knuckle under can do anything!"

Suddenly Elaine got it. She remembered the story of the Picts, and the flying heads, and one lady who owed Robin her life—one lady named Louisa, Baroness of Nottingham.

Elaine remembered another bit of Roland's information: Louisa's husband, the aged Baron, had died about a month after Elaine had married.

So Robin, Elaine thought, you are the scourge of Barons—but not of one particular Baroness.

Does she love you?

Of course she does—

The tavern keeper came over and asked them to leave. Everyone else was gone and he wanted to close.

Elaine didn't mind at all—she had all she needed. She thanked all the ladies and stood up—then she had to hold her chair to keep her balance.

The other ladies weren't about to leave yet. They refused to budge until the tavern keeper applied his biggest cleaver to the golden necklace. He managed to chop it into four equal pieces. Now the ladies were happy—they each took a piece and swayed to the door.

The tavern keeper remembered to demand payment for his wine.

Elaine took off her earrings and handed them to him. He bowed low and asked if there was anything more he could do for her.

Elaine asked directions to Nottingham.

The tavern keeper knew the route well—he gave her clear instructions.

Elaine thanked him, and then she went out the door that had been left open for her.

The tavern keeper locked it behind her.

The youngest and prettiest of the courtesans was waiting just outside. She pressed her body against Elaine. "Come home with me, Milady," she said. "You've already paid me far too much just for conversation. Stay the night, and I'll please you—you'll see."

Elaine looked down at the lass—under the make-up she saw a girl of no more than sixteen. "You're sweet, and thank you, but I must go," Elaine said softly. She gently disengaged herself from the girl and started toward her coach—and then she looked back at the other three ladies, who were still lingering. "Goodbye, and many thanks!" Elaine called cheerfully.

They wondered why the lady looked so happy when they had only told her what everyone knew. Could she really find Robin Hood?

As Elaine sat down on the driver's seat, the eldest one called out to her. "Before you go, Milady who loves Robin Hood, tell us your name!"

"Marian," Elaine said, and then she touched her horses with her whip and moved off down the road.

Elaine had a three quarter moon to guide herself this Thursday night. She drove her horses until dawn—then she took a short nap, and drove on through most of Friday. She slept in the coach Friday night, and woke up before dawn on Saturday. She gave her horses the last grain she had, and then she pushed them hard through the morning until she reached the Baronial estate that covered thousands of acres outside of Nottingham. She asked directions of a tenant farmer—she tried to calm herself without success—she got even more upset when a sudden downpour drenched her to the skin—she arrived at the front door of the Baroness Louisa's mansion about two hours before noon.

Elaine got down off her coach and walked up onto the porch. She was grateful for the porch roof that protected her from the rain. She was hungry and cold—she wore a soaked courtesan's dress that she had taken from Madame Genevieve's. Her black wig was matted down on her head. She had no jewelry left.

She knocked on the door.

A maid opened it, took one look, and told her to go around to the service entrance.

Chapter 205

CHILL

Baroness Louisa, assisted by her lady in waiting, was dressing carefully in her finest evening wear—though it was only ten o'clock in the morning—because she expected Robin Hood for lunch.

She was not happy at all when her preparations were interrupted.

"Just send her away," she snapped.

"Milady, I tried, but she won't go," the maid said. "She insists that she must see you. I told her that wouldn't be possible, but she just looked at me with these strange eyes—a chill they gave me, Milady, I've never seen eyes like that in my life."

It can't be.

Louisa shivered as though she had been touched with ice.

The thought banged through her head again: It can't be.

Not after two years.

Not, dear God, not with Robin coming today.

Not when he is coming to me, when I know he is finally coming to me.

Not now!

It can't be her. It's just some crazed woman with wild eyes.

It can't be her.

Louisa gestured to her lady in waiting. The girl quickly fastened up the Baroness's dress.

There were finishing touches yet to do—but even now Louisa looked both lovely and elegant.

"All right, Jenny," Louisa said to her maid, "I'll go down and send her away myself."

The Baroness, followed by her maid, walked down the stairs

and through the foyer to the front door. She opened the heavy door and looked with relief and pity at the bedraggled creature there. The black hair of course took away any fear—and then just to make sure Louisa looked an inch below the woman's left eye—she saw a brown beauty mark there—Louisa started to smile, but then a gesture froze her blood. The woman's hand was going up to her face with evident purpose—one delicate finger went to that beauty mark—Louisa watched that finger with all her concentration so that she wouldn't have to meet the woman's eyes—she concentrated now on the tip of the woman's fingernail as it quested underneath the edge of the beauty mark—the false beauty mark—the woman peeled off the little deceiving patch, and flicked it away.

Louisa's whole body began to tremble—she looked up into the clear blue eyes of Elaine the Fair.

"I prayed you wouldn't come," Louisa said.

"I'm sorry," Elaine said. She stood quietly on the porch in her soaked dress.

The trembling reached Louisa's face and then she began to cry. She turned away and started walking back to the stairs—and as she walked she spoke through her sobs to the maid: "Jenny, we have a guest—have her horses looked after—get her some hot food—fix her a hot bath—"

Louisa bumped into the first step.

She shook her head to clear her eyes—and then she suddenly ran right up the stairs and into her dressing room, slamming the door behind her.

Elaine still stood on the porch.

"Please come in, Milady," Jenny said.

Chapter 206

LOUISA'S LOVE

An hour later Elaine, full of hot biscuits, was relaxing in the tub upstairs while Jenny attended her.

Louisa entered the room. She was wearing the same dress as before—yellow silk, decollete—but now her russet locks had been brushed until they shone, her make-up was perfect, and jewels sparkled at her throat and wrists. She walked over to the tub where Elaine was naked in the water.

Louisa looked at Elaine—but she spoke to her maid. "Jenny, go out for a while. I have to talk to Her—"

"Please just call me Marian," interrupted Elaine.

"Yes, my friend Marian here. I'll call you when I need you."

"Yes, Milady," Jenny said. She left the room.

Louisa followed her to the door and locked it behind her. Then she turned around and looked at Elaine again.

"Marian, Your Grace?"

"I am no longer married to the Duke of Larraz. Our union has dissolved in my heart, and I have left my title behind—likewise I no longer wish to be known as a Countess.

"I can not use my own name, for news of my presence would arouse great ire on the part of the Chancellor of the Exchequer—this unwelcome attention might well endanger the man I have come to see: Robin Hood."

The mention of his name was like a blow across Louisa's heart—but this time the Baroness didn't cry—she got mad.

The brazen bitch didn't even try to hide her intentions!

Louisa's face twisted with rage and her fists clenched. She stalked over to the tub and looked down at her insolent, unwanted guest.

"What makes you think you can do this?" Louisa snarled. "You throw a man over, and go away for two years—and now you come back and expect him to love you? You're a fool! He'll spit in your eye! Why do you think you even have a chance? What do you have that any other woman does not? What do you have that *I* do not? Nothing! Nothing!"

Louisa had grabbed both sides of the wooden tub by now—she was leaning over Elaine—their faces were less than a foot apart.

"Well, let us see," Louisa continued in a somewhat calmer voice. "We'll start at the top."

Louisa plucked off Elaine's black wig—she threw the wet hairpiece aside with a gesture of distaste. Then she unpinned Elaine's natural hair—she put the pins aside more carefully, and she watched as the golden locks tumbled down.

Louisa stroked that finespun hair. "Yes, I must admit your hair is pretty—but certainly no prettier than my gleaming russet locks." Louisa did a half turn—a curtain of her perfumed hair brushed across Elaine's face—the Baroness was quite right in her comparison.

Now Louisa turned back and cupped Elaine's face with her hands. She examined the woman she held, and then she said, "Your face is thinner than mine, and your nose is too long, which makes your features far too sharp—combine that with your cold blue eyes, and you look as though you were born to hold a whip—not to love. Look at my face, Elaine—you are naked, and I must call you by your true name—look at my face, yes, you see—I have a loving face, softer than yours, and my hazel eyes are far more intriguing than your icy blue orbs. You see too that my face is unblemished—but you have a scar, Elaine." Louisa touched it with a fingertip—and then she brought the finger down in a caress until she touched Elaine's lips. "Your mouth is adequate, I suppose—" Louisa probed with her finger, forcing Elaine's lips to part—"there is succulent potential in the lower lip, but then yours can hardly compare to my full 'bee-stung lips', as the poetry I receive describes them."

Louisa slid her hands down Elaine's neck, and paused there, as though considering strangling her rival—but then she moved her hands down lower, down into the water, and she cupped each of Elaine's breasts.

"Your breasts are well shaped and soft, and your nipples are sensitive and easily aroused—as they are now, as everyone at the court used to see when you wore your dresses without a chemise underneath—but one must note that they are quite small—" Louisa leaned low over the tub—her full breasts flirted perilously with her low cut bodice—"mine are much larger, as you can see—and mine are just as soft, and just as sensitive."

Louisa flicked her thumbs over Elaine's hard nipples and then she moved her hands lower. She spanned Elaine's narrow waist.

"You do have a lovely figure—a perfect hourglass—and yet no more perfect than mine."

Louisa brought her face to within inches of Elaine's—she kept her left hand at Elaine's waist while she brought her right hand around to the front of Elaine's belly—she bored into her rival's navel with a thumb, and then she slid that right hand down until she found the slick wet golden fleece. Elaine's legs were already spread. Louisa found the place she was searching for—she thrust one finger roughly up inside Elaine's womanhood.

Elaine's eyes flickered, and her mouth opened, but she made no sound. She could feel the Baroness's hot breath on her tongue.

Louisa thrust deeper with her finger, and then she spoke in a harsh whisper. "You are made there just like any other woman—just like me."

Louisa could go no further.

Elaine felt completely calm now. She leaned back against the edge of the tub, the motion forcing her womanhood harder against Louisa's hand—her swollen nipples broke the surface of the water as though begging to be caressed—her lips were parted still, ready to be kissed—but her eyes were as cold as panes of blue glass.

Louisa looked into those eyes for nearly a minute before she broke.

Then the tears came—no sobs—just tears filling up her eyes and then sliding slowly down her face.

"What is it? What do you have? Why do I, who has never desired a woman before in my life—why do I want to kiss you? Why do all men love you? Why does Robin love you?"

The tears kept rolling down.

"Let me love you. I'll dry you and take you to my bed. I'll kiss you all over—please let me."

Louisa's hazel eyes were begging through their veil of tears.

Elaine reached down into the water and gently pushed Louisa's hand back until the finger came free.

The slight rebuff caused Louisa to straighten up. She stood there lost before Elaine, hands, arms, face all wet.

"I'm going to take away the man that you love," Elaine said. "That is enough reason for you to hate me. I will not steal your love as well."

Louisa reached for a towel and dried herself mechanically. When she was done she let the towel fall to the floor.

She looked at Elaine and said, "Robin is coming soon."

"I guessed—from your dress."

"We call him Sir Myles here."

Elaine nodded.

"I'll call you Marian."

"Thank you."

"I'll send Jenny in with fresh towels and a dress for you."

"Thank you."

Louisa wanted to bend down again and this time really kiss Elaine—but she couldn't now. The gulf was too wide.

She didn't want to go—but she knew that if she stayed any longer she would only cry again.

"I've always loved Robin," Louisa said, "even long ago when he had another name."

"I know," Elaine said.

Louisa looked into those blue eyes that hadn't changed at all—'a chill they gave me, Milady,' her maid had said—Louisa tried to smile but instead she did suddenly begin to cry—she turned and ran from the room, leaving the door flung open behind her.

Elaine wondered if she should get out of the tub and retrieve her wig—but then she thought, I have been away from England for more than two years—no one knows me here in the countryside save Louisa and the man I will soon meet again—those who have heard of me think me well gone—so, yes, I shall simply appear as I am—but I will continue to use my mother's beautiful name.

Chapter 207

THE SABLE COAT

Elaine did not expect Louisa to remember to speak to her maid after she ran out—but in fact, when Jenny reappeared she did bring fresh towels and one of Louisa's dresses.

Meanwhile Robin Hood and Little John—or Sir Myles and Squire Greg, as they called themselves this morning—were riding hard through the rain. They reached the Baroness's estate just before noon. They went to the stables first—Little John took care of the horses and then helped Robin get out of his armor (Robin's prejudices against armor had vanished when he realized what an excellent disguise it was). The two friends then walked quickly through the rain to the mansion—they saw that Louisa already had the door open for them.

The Baroness stood back in the doorway, beckoning them in— her face was in shadow, but Robin smiled at the bright sunshine of her yellow dress—he walked even faster as his eyes danced over the white expanse of bosom that she offered to his gaze—a merry step over the threshold, and he was inside the house, smiling—and then he looked closely at Louisa's face and he saw why she had stayed back away from the light. Her eyes were puffy and swollen—her nose was red from blowing—her cheeks had clearly just been scrubbed free of tears.

Robin stopped. Little John came up behind him and looked over his friend's shoulder at the Baroness—then he turned away almost at once because he just hated to see anyone hurting like that. Little John shut the door behind him—he knew somehow that Louisa's hurt was tied to her love for Robin.

Robin stepped forward now and took her in his arms. "What's wrong, my dear?" he asked.

Louisa just whimpered and laid her head against his chest. Robin stroked her hair—and then he noticed a movement at the top of the stairs. Due to the angle (he was several feet from the base of the stairs) he could only see one foot—in a golden slipper—and an ankle, but still he knew right away, and Louisa knew that he knew in the same moment. His whole body stiffened while his heart beat wildly against her breasts—but he didn't break the embrace, and after a moment he pulled Louisa even closer to him.

He did not lower his eyes.

The lady above began to make her way down the stairs.

Robin could see both feet now, and the curve of a knee behind silk.

As a boy he might have left Louisa and run up the stairs to Elaine. As a man now, he held Louisa, and stroked her hair, and made Elaine come to him.

He saw Elaine's thighs now, sliding under the white silk—the white dress of a bride, he thought suddenly—his heart began to pound again.

The white dress, cut for Louisa's abundance, billowed around Elaine's upper body—she seemed lost in it, fragile—

Robin didn't know it but he was holding his breath—

Louisa hugged him with all her strength—

Little John had felt the extraordinary tension from the first moment. He observed from behind Robin, not daring to say a word—

Elaine took another step, and her face came into view.

Her eyes found Robin's—he met her gaze for a second—and then he took a deep breath and deliberately broke the connection. He looked down at Louisa—he pulled her head back by the hair and deliberately kissed her lips.

When he finally looked up from the kiss, Elaine was still on the same step—her face showed neither anger nor sadness. She simply asked, "Where will we live, Sir Myles?"

Robin realized that for the first time since he had known her, Elaine lived nowhere. He thought of all that she had given up to come to him—he saw all her love—he understood that she was his, and with that understanding he realized that he had to do more than take her, more than protect her—he had to cherish her, and give her a house to live in, a shelter not just for her but for the children they would bring into the world . . .

Robin looked into Elaine's eyes and saw his future there—and for the first time in his life he felt that his future truly mattered.

"Your question is unexpected, Milady," he said. "Let all of us take a walk, and I will answer it."

Louisa understood. She looked around and saw Jenny peeking down one side of the stairs, and Susan, her lady in waiting, was peeking down the other side. There was not a sound from the kitchen—evidently the cooks preferred listening to preparing lunch.

There was no doubt that every soul in the house felt the charged emotional currents.

It will be better outside in the rain, Louisa thought. We will have privacy in the realm of nature—and these two are forces of nature in themselves. They are made for each other—I know now that I can no more keep them apart than I can keep the rain from coming down.

"Jenny," the Baroness called, "bring down two coats: the new sable for Lady Marian and my usual mink for myself."

"Right away, Milady," Jenny said, and she was very quick.

In a moment she came down the stairs, and stopped by Elaine (who hadn't moved—she still stood on the middle step) and helped her with the coat. Elaine put her arms through the sleeves and pulled the luxurious garment partway around her—she left it open in the front, and she thanked Jenny—and meanwhile the three watchers below had their collective breath taken away. They stared in silence at the vision that had been created before their eyes.

The coat that had changed things was ankle length black sable—a recent indulgence of Louisa's—and it covered most of the billowing white dress, leaving just a pure white panel from neckline to hem. The black slashed at the white all the way down—and all the way up, until one's eyes were drawn to Elaine's serene face: the face of a woman in love. But then, as one looked at her face, one could not help but notice her scar—the mark of violence. The serenity had been dearly won from evil—look down again and black continued to threaten the frail strip of white—Elaine defended that purity and yet she embraced the blackness as well . . .

Louisa began to see the answer to her question: here before her was the cruelty and the tenderness, the savage beauty and the pure heart—

Robin remembered Elaine's story of the battle of Hastings,

and he saw the final synthesis here of Edith the Swan-necked and the Countess Elaine: it seemed as though the spirits of the proud mistress and the sweet bride had joined to create Elaine the Fair.

Little John realized as soon as she put on the coat that this lady's name was not Marian—he understood now why Robin had called for her for so long—for himself, he was simply thrilled to be looking at the most beautiful woman in the world.

Jenny held the mink coat for her mistress, and Louisa slipped it on easily—but she kept looking at Elaine.

Finally the Baroness extended her hand to her guest.

Elaine came down the stairs, and took Louisa's hand. Little John opened the heavy door. The two ladies stepped out onto the porch, followed by the two men. Little John closed the door behind them while Robin came up and took Elaine's right hand—Louisa still held her left. Little John came forward and boldly took the Baroness's left hand—then the foursome set off into the rain.

They walked briskly until they were far away from the great house. The power of the storm slackened as they covered the distance. Louisa thought of what she had seen on the stairs— she stopped the march when she knew that no one in the house could see or hear them anymore.

Louisa disengaged herself from Little John and swung around in front of Elaine. She retained her grip on the former Duchess's hand, and she said, "Elaine, I do not know if you will ever marry Robin in church—but I can see in your eyes, and I have seen in Robin's eyes, that you are married in spirit already. The sable coat is my wedding gift to you. Keep it, and wear it in good health."

Elaine let go of Robin's hand. She looked long into Louisa's sad but honest eyes, and then she said simply, "Thank you. I shall treasure it always." She put her free hand on the Baroness's shoulder and drew her closer. She looked again for an answer in Louisa's eyes—and then Elaine bent down and kissed her on the left cheek, and then on the right, and finally on the lips.

When she stood up straight again both of the ladies' eyes were wet from more than the rain.

The gentlemen took the ladies' hands again—Robin led them to the shelter of a solitary elm.

Elaine could see that he had been thinking of her first question—but he spoke to Louisa.

"Louisa, did you find out about that gold shipment?"

Elaine suddenly understood how Robin kept informed about court business.

"Yes, but you can't do it Robin," Louisa answered rather casually—but then she heard no quick answer, and she looked past Elaine at Robin's face—she saw his eyes, and she shivered and said urgently, "You *can't* do it, Robin."

Elaine heard the panic in Louisa's voice and then she too looked up at Robin. She had seen him look like that once before—when he had told her that he was going to kill Saladin. She turned to Louisa. "He has already decided," she said softly. "You can't make him change his mind now. But tell me what is going on, for I have a right to know."

Louisa took a deep breath and then she answered Elaine. "You know what Robin has been doing. He's been fighting back against the Exchequer, and returning seized goods to the people. When he cuts off revenue, he also hurts the war effort in France, where King Richard grows poorer with every victory.

"There are a lot of legends about Robin—I'm sure you've heard them"—Elaine nodded—"and some of them are even true. But they tend to give a false picture. One might think from those tales that the government has come to a halt, but that is not correct. Robin and Little John are just two men—there are a few kindred spirits here and there, but there are no Merry Men, as you may have already guessed. Anyway, Robin can not be everywhere at once—and the crown can hire a lot of men, especially when one considers the low criminals who work for the Exchequer now. A lot of what they loot from the people *does* get through—and Prince John has been converting it into gold. He hasn't sent any to his brother in a long time—I heard last month that King Richard threatened to come back and chastise John personally if he did not send some funds soon—I told Robin, and he asked me to find out when the shipment was going out."

Louisa turned and looked up at Robin. "Now listen to me, and don't be stubborn. You *can* change your mind."

"Just tell me what you know," Robin said sharply.

The color came up in Louisa's face, but her voice was dead calm as she laid out the situation. "The gold is kept in a vault in the Palace of Bermondsey. It's guarded night and day, and even if you get past the palace guards, and the vault guards, you still won't be able to open it because Prince John has the only key.

"The shipment goes out next Saturday, a week from today. The Prince has already separated out King Richard's share of the treasure—that portion of the gold is locked in a chest inside the vault. I am told that it takes two very strong men to lift that chest—four to move it."

Robin looked over Louisa's head and caught Little John's eye. He smiled slightly at the squire.

Louisa thought he was smiling at her. "Are you listening to me?" she snapped.

Little John grinned.

Robin looked straight into Louisa's eyes and said, "Yes," very seriously.

Louisa continued: "So on Saturday they are going to clear the streets. A row of pike men will line each side of the route. The chest will go in a coach—the coach will go down the middle of the street between the pike men—*and* it will be guarded by fifty armed, mounted knights. They will escort it straight to the wharf on the Thames where the Lionheart's warship will be waiting. Many of King Richard's most trusted knights will be on board to oversee the transaction. The chest will be loaded onto the ship—the ship will sail away.

"You see, Robin—it's impossible! Don't get yourself killed!"

Robin might not have heard Louisa's last warning. He said, "Thank you, my dear, you've been very helpful as always. Now please excuse me, ladies, for I must speak to Little John for a moment."

Louisa stared in disbelief as the men walked off—Robin put his arm around Little John's massive shoulders.

Louisa turned back to Elaine—but neither woman had words for the fears they both shared. They just held hands, and waited, and it really wasn't very long before the men came back.

Robin stopped right in front of Elaine and looked into her eyes. "It's all set," he said. "I know how to take that gold, and I'm going to do it."

Elaine let go of Louisa and put her hands on his shoulders.

"Why?" she asked.

In that one word she put all the anguish of every woman who has seen her man go off to war.

"I have helped our people much in these past two years," Robin replied. "I have battled a corrupt government—I have fought injustice. I will do those things again, but this venture is

for myself alone. You asked, 'Where will we live?'—I promised
you an answer and here it is: I shall seize this gold, and use it to
buy us a grand estate, a place suited for you to live as my wife—
a place suited for one whose rank truly is superior to that of
Duchess and Countess as you have received. You shall be my
Queen—our home will be equal to your station, and just as
important, it will be a secure haven where we can raise our children."

Robin smiled at Elaine. "I feel in my heart that we will have
many children."

Elaine tried to smile but she kept thinking of fifty armed
knights against two.

Robin finished calmly. "My venture is dangerous, of course,
but the prize as I have described is worth it. Anyway, as you
have said yourself, I have already made up my mind."

Fifty against two.

Elaine shivered, and then she looked up into Robin's eyes.
She opened her mouth—she didn't know what she was going to
say, and she never got to say it, because Robin kissed her. He
held her to him with one hand in her hair for as long as he
wanted, and when he finished Elaine knew there was nothing
more to say.

The foursome walked slowly back, but they veered away from
the house and went to the stable.

Robin said, "Louisa, you can't be connected to this in any way.
Stay here for at least two weeks. Little John will go off to
London now. Elaine and I will head for St. Lyons—and that's all
you need to know.

"Elaine, I saw your coach. We can take that, but how are your
horses?"

Elaine thought of her good gray mares. "I've been pushing
them Robin—I really wouldn't want to race them now."

"Can we trade them for two of yours, Louisa?"

"Of course, Robin, you don't need to ask."

"Thank you. I'm sorry we can't stay for lunch, but it's best if
we go now." Robin looked carefully at the Baroness. "Louisa,
you're soaked. You better go back inside now—think of a good
excuse for us."

"I will," Louisa said.

Elaine and Little John felt her tension and they let go of her
hands. The Baroness walked over to Robin. She reached up and
put her hands behind his head—she pulled him down almost

desperately and kissed him hard on the mouth. Finally she broke away—she looked down at the ground for a long moment to compose herself, and then she looked up at Robin again and said, "Be careful Robin—please be careful."

"I will be," he said.

Then Louisa turned to Elaine, and this was somehow easier. They hugged each other like sisters, and then like gentle lovers, they kissed and then they had to stop to wipe their eyes.

"I wish you all happiness with Robin," Louisa said.

"Thank you," Elaine replied. "And thank you again for the lovely sable."

Chapter 208

TEASE

The 'love carriage' rolled toward St. Lyons . . .

Elaine sat next to Robin on the driver's seat. Before, walking outside Louisa's house, she had taken his left hand—but now he sat to her left, the reins were in his left hand, and so she took his right hand with both of hers—she felt the stiff middle fingers—she remembered hearing his bones snap—she raised his hand to her lips and kissed the scar at the center of his palm.

'Let me see yours," Robin said after a moment. Elaine allowed him to bring her right hand over—he looked for where the knife had gone in, but the thin line was almost invisible now—still, he pressed his lips to the memory of her wound, and then he put her hand down on his thigh.

He looked down the road—he kept the horses moving along—and he reached out and tangled his right hand in Elaine's golden hair. He pulled her toward him—and when he turned his head she was right there, utterly willing—he kissed her mouth hard—then he pulled away and looked down the road, he urged the horses onward—he turned back to Elaine and kissed her again—pulled away—kissed her—pain had vanished from Robin's heart at the first sight of Elaine's foot at the top of the stairs—now love surged into the empty room in his heart with each kiss—he pulled away with a sure confidence that he could come back—Elaine never got as much as she wanted—she drove herself at his mouth more avidly with every kiss—she wanted to be devoured—she wanted to devour him—the room in Robin's heart filled and then the walls burst—he kissed Elaine with all the love in his soul—then he pulled away—Elaine grabbed at his hand in a frenzy—she yanked it loose of her hair and pulled it down under the sable coat—she placed his hand right over her left breast—she made him feel how hard her nipple was, how hot her breast was—she made Robin remember the night inside the Northmen's circle—she told him without words that she was his now, she was ready now, she wanted him to take her in any way he chose—Robin's hand curled and he caught her nipple between thumb and forefinger—he rolled it through the silk, he pinched it hard enough to make her gasp—and then he shocked her: he took his hand away, and said, "Not now."

He looked down the road, and flicked the horses with the reins.

Elaine sat up straight in disbelief—and then she swung her right hand hard at Robin's face, but the blow never got there. Robin caught her wrist with his right hand—his powerful thumb and forefinger encircled that most delicate part of her arm—she struggled, jerking and yanking, but she could do nothing against his archer's strength.

Elaine looked at Robin's profile with her eyes blazing—she realized that he had caught her wrist without even bothering to turn his head—he wouldn't even look at her now—she struck with her left hand like a cat—she raked her fingernails over the back of the hand that held her.

Robin turned his head and looked at her with his cold gray eyes—Elaine tried to meet his gaze but she couldn't—she lowered her eyes—her whole body seemed to soften—Robin released her wrist and she let her hands fall limply to her lap—she wanted nothing more in the world than to be naked with this man.

Robin pulled her coat more open and put his right hand on her thigh. He pressed down on her softness with the calm certainty of possession.

He looked down the road and said, "Deeds count, not words, dear Elaine. You have proven your love for me by leaving your husband and coming to me—and I know too that you can not have had a child, for you would not have left a babe without his mother."

"You're right, Robin, I couldn't have done that," Elaine said. She looked down at his hand on her thigh. The white streaks that she had scored into his flesh were slowly fading. "I have no children, no marriage, no title—I bring nothing to you but myself—I love you Robin."

Robin kept looking down the road, but the three fingers that worked tightened, digging into the flesh of her thigh.

"And I love you, Elaine—but that isn't enough. I have not proved my love as you have proved yours." Robin felt Elaine start to speak but he dug his fingers even harder into her thigh to forestall her. He went on, "Until I come back from London, with the gold, I will not truly have won you. Only then will I be able to give to you and provide for you. Only then will I take you."

Robin eased his grip.

Elaine looked down at the two stiff fingers that projected out from the hand that held her. She stroked those fingers with two of her own.

"Do you have feeling in these?" she asked.

"Yes, I just can't move them."

Elaine gathered Robin's relaxed hand with both of hers, and lifted it from her thigh.

"I'm glad you'll be able to feel this, Robin," Elaine said, and with that she bent her head down over his captive hand. She ran her tongue over the first of his stiffened fingers, and then she took it in her mouth. She bowed her head until all of the hard digit was imprisoned—she caressed it with her tongue, and then she tightened her mouth around him and sucked hard and Robin felt his body react with such force that he very nearly broke his word within seconds of giving it—he was as hard as he'd ever been in his life, as hard as he'd been in the Norse circle—

But he could wait.

"If you're that hungry, my dear," he said, "there's a country inn up ahead."

Elaine was startled by his calm voice.

Robin freed his finger.

His voice was calm but Elaine remembered the way she had felt his body leap—she looked down at his lap and smiled, but then she *was* hungry.

She decided she wouldn't tease him any more till after lunch.

Chapter 209

BESS

A few minutes later Robin stopped the coach at the inn he had mentioned. He unharnessed the horses and attached them to the hitching rope that was provided. There did not seem to be any other customers. Robin helped Elaine step down from her seat—he held her hand as they walked toward the door.

This was a first visit for Robin—because of the inn's proximity to Baroness Louisa's, he had never had a reason to stop before.

Inside, the innkeeper was counting his troubles—until Elaine came in, wearing her sable coat. He stared in amazement at the noble lady—the first such customer he had had in years. If her coat is any clue, he thought, she will surely be able to pay any amount I choose to charge. He smiled at that thought—but then he took a quick look at her escort, and the tumbling coins in his mind went instantly silent. He had never seen this man before, but he recognized him, for he had heard him described a hundred times. The innkeeper decided that *this* customer—and his lady—would dine free.

"As I live and breathe," he said, " 'tis Robin Hood. Welcome, Robin, welcome to you and your beautiful lady—whatever we can provide is yours, and never a charge."

"Thank you," said Robin. "But how do you know me?"

"All know of you," replied the innkeeper.

This was not welcome news to Robin—he was becoming far too recognizable. He thought that after the London raid he was either going to have to wear disguise all the time—or he would have to find an entirely different way to operate. For now he let none of his worry show on his face—he smiled, and spoke of the business at hand. "If we could prevail on your generosity then, we'd like a good dinner—whatever's fresh."

"Of course, Robin—and now if I might seat you and Lady—"

Robin remembered the name that Louisa had called up the stairs—he remembered that that had been Elaine's mother's name.

"Lady Marian."

"I am honored," the innkeeper said, bowing low. He held out a chair for Elaine, and offered another to Robin—then he said, "I'll sent out some wine in a moment, after I confer with the cook—that's the Missus—she's going to be thrilled!"

The innkeeper dashed off to the kitchen.

Elaine put her hand on Robin's thigh under the table. "If that's what the men are like," she asked in a teasing tone, "how are the women?"

Robin put his hand over hers, and looked into her merry eyes. "Guess," he said.

The innkeeper came back out with the wine—but this time his wife followed him. There was something very wrong about her—Robin and Elaine could see that right away—but it took them a minute to figure out what it was. This woman had once had the plump figure and ruddy cheeks that are the right of any good country cook—but there was no color in her cheeks now— her skin hung loosely—she looked empty rather than thin—she had obviously just lost a great deal of weight, and yet she did not look like a victim of illness. Her eyes were bright as she walked, with timid eagerness, straight toward Robin. She came up to his side and knelt, utterly unselfconsciously. She took his free hand in hers, and kissed it—then she looked up and said, "Thank you, Robin."

"You are truly welcome, good woman," Robin replied, looking down into her shining eyes. "But what have I done for you?"

The woman cast a quick glance at her husband, and then she got up awkwardly and scurried back to the kitchen.

Robin looked over at the innkeeper—there was certainly more here than generalized gratitude—Robin wanted to know what was hidden.

The innkeeper's grand welcoming style had faded. In a very subdued voice, he asked, "May I share some wine with you, Robin?"

Robin gestured toward the third seat at the round table.

The innkeeper sat down and poured them each a flagon of wine. He drank half of his own with one gulp.

"I snared some rabbits this morning. Bess—that's my wife—has a rabbit stew already going. She told me it will be ready soon—will that be satisfactory?"

"Perfect," Robin said. "Now tell me your story."

"What story?" the innkeeper asked.

Robin just looked at him.

The innkeeper became extremely nervous. He glanced quickly at Elaine and then looked down at the table in front of him.

"I would tell you, Robin—but your lady . . ."

"My lady knows of many things, both good and evil. Tell us the story."

The innkeeper finished his wine.

Elaine lowered her eyes and sipped hers.

The innkeeper wiped his mouth and began: "A month ago, the Assessor's men came—"

Elaine's hand jerked in Robin's grasp, but he wouldn't let her take it away.

"Scum they were, low criminals, four of 'em. They had a writ that said they were taxing me in the name of the King. They said they were going to count my money, and take the King's share.

"Now it's rare enough that I get a paying customer." He looked up and managed a brief smile at Elaine. "When I saw your coat, Milady, I thought that I had found the first one in a long time. Most of the people around here pay me in game—maybe it's poached, but I don't ask any questions—I'll give 'em a room for the night, or some wine—we get along.

"So I told the swine I didn't have any gold—and they slammed me against the wall, and hit me a few times, and then they tied me up. They tore the whole place up, looking for gold—but they couldn't find any, because there wasn't any to be found. All this time Bess was here, terrified—she was afraid to leave me alone—and I couldn't tell her to run because they'd stuffed a gag in my mouth. One of them watched me all the time so she couldn't get me loose—and then the other three came back—they were disappointed and they were in an evil mood—they looked at me and then they looked at Bess—I knew what they were going to do, and I couldn't stop it.

"They raped her right in front of me, and they made me watch. All four of them did it, and she screamed the whole time.

"I can still hear those screams . . ."

The innkeeper stared blankly at his empty flagon—and then

he continued: "They left when they couldn't do any more.

"Bess got up after a while and cut me loose. I tried to comfort her as well as I could, but she wouldn't say anything. It was as though she had screamed away all the language she knew. She had no words left—or maybe she just had no words to tell me how she felt.

"For two weeks she didn't make a sound—and then one day a boy came running in here, all excited, and he said that Robin Hood had surprised four of the Assessor's men down by Langly."

The innkeeper looked up at Robin, who nodded and said, "Yes, that was me."

"Well, of course you know all about it then, but anyway the boy said you had killed them all, and that's when Bess called from the kitchen, 'Let's go have a look.' Those were her first words: 'Let's go have a look.'

"So naturally I hitched up our old coach, and we went down to Langly. You were long gone by then, of course, and the villagers had already been at the bodies—they had mounted the heads on pikes. Bess got out of the coach, bold as you please—she walked around and looked into each dead face—she wanted to make sure that you had got them all, and indeed you had.

"That was two weeks ago today. She's been much better since then—she talks to me now, and I try to be cheerful for both of us—but she used to love to eat, and she's hardly touched her food since the day of the attack—even knowing they're dead hasn't changed her in that way—O Robin there's nothing more to say—I couldn't help her then, and I can't help her now."

At this point Bess came back, bearing two steaming platters of rabbit stew.

Robin and Elaine both thanked her—she curtsied and then rushed back to the kitchen.

The innkeeper went back behind the bar, though there were no customers there.

Robin and Elaine stared at their food.

Robin had been very hungry when he had come to the inn. Now he didn't see how he could eat a bite.

After a long moment Elaine suddenly broke the tableau. She squeezed Robin's thigh very hard, and then took her hand away and placed it on the table. She picked up a fork with her other hand—she held it like a weapon—she turned to Robin and spoke in a savage whisper: "Start eating, Robin—and you better down every morsel, or I'm going to run you through with this fork."

She was dead serious. Robin was shocked at first, but then he understood—he picked up his fork and set to with a will.

About halfway through they even began to taste their food—they discovered that Bess was indeed a fine cook. They kept going—they didn't speak or stop eating until their plates were clean.

Then they relaxed a little, and drank their wine. When her flagon was empty, Elaine stood up. "I'm going to see Bess now," she said. She walked over to the kitchen and pushed past the swinging door.

She came up behind Bess, who was washing some pots. Elaine did not want to startle the woman with a touch—she just said softly, "Bess—Bess."

The woman turned around, eyes frightened—but then she relaxed a little when she saw it was only Robin's lady.

"Your stew was excellent," Elaine said, "the best I've ever tasted. There's not a bit left."

"There's more here—I can bring some out—"

"No thank you—we're full now—but there is another way you can help."

"I will do anything for you and Robin," Bess said.

"Good. You see, Robin and I will be married next week—married in the eyes of God. Yet I have learned, from traveling through the land, that he belongs not just to me, but also to all the English people. We cannot invite every citizen to our wedding—but we would like to spread the word, and share the good news."

Elaine took a step forward and put a hand on Bess's arm.

Bess had never been touched by a noble lady before. She didn't know what to do.

"I want you, Bess, to tell our story. Tell all the people who come to the inn, tell your friends and acquaintances and family, tell everyone you know that you saw Robin and Marian. Tell them how you kissed Robin's hand—tell them of the rabbit stew you cooked for us—tell them what he looked like on this day. And look now at my face, so that you will never forget it—tell the people of my beauty—tell them of the love between Robin and his bride.

"Will you do these things for me?"

"Yes, Milady," Bess breathed.

Elaine tightened her grip just slightly on Bess's arm. "Then you must live and be strong," Elaine said, "to tell our story through the many years to come."

"Yes, Milady."

Elaine smiled. "I must go with Robin in a moment—but first I shall kiss you—and remember, where I kiss, roses will bloom."

Elaine bent forward and deliberately kissed each of Bess's slack cheeks.

The woman stood still in silent wonderment.

Elaine turned and started to walk away, but then Bess recovered herself—

"Milady—"

Elaine looked back over her shoulder.

"Thank you, Milady."

Elaine nodded, and then she turned away again and walked back to Robin.

Robin stood up and took her arm—the innkeeper escorted them out.

Robin hitched up the horses again as Elaine climbed up onto the driver's seat. Bess came out and stood shyly by her husband.

Robin climbed up, and spoke to the horses, and they were off. The outlaw and his lady waved good-bye to the innkeeper and his wife.

Elaine saw Bess put an arm around her husband, and she smiled to herself.

Robin and Elaine traveled onward. That night they stopped at another inn to sleep, and Robin was once again recognized— Elaine was introduced as Lady Marian—and so it went for each of the four days of their journey to St. Lyons.

Elaine never traveled through England again—but Bess talked about her, and the courtesans talked about her, and innkeepers and servants talked about her—they called her Marian, the name she had chosen—she became a legend: beautiful, mysterious, the perfect consort for the great outlaw.

Down through the centuries these two names would be forever intertwined: Robin and Marian.

Chapter 210

THE THIRD FINGER
OF HER LEFT HAND

After hearing Bess's story, Elaine did not tease Robin quite so flagrantly anymore while they were traveling. At night though, she insisted upon going to bed naked. She said that she could not sleep in a dress—and she pointed out correctly that she had no nightgown. Each night she made Robin hold her tight and kiss her for a long time before she would go to sleep.

They got to St. Lyons on Tuesday evening. Robin found them a room at the town's best (and only) inn. He made arrangements to stable their horses, and he ordered a good dinner to be sent up to their room.

They settled in—the food arrived—they ate in silence.

When the plates were clear Elaine spoke. "You're going away tomorrow."

"Yes."

"Take me with you."

"I can't."

"Take me with you."

"No."

"I can't stay here."

"You can. It's the safest place for you . . ." Robin told Elaine then what he had done after she left with Roland. He told of killing Arthur's men in his fever, and of coming unconscious into St. Lyons. He told of his hero's welcome, and how he had reclaimed his true name. He told of the Mayor, and Little John, and the little boy who gave his shirt for a target. He told of Beryl and the ladies, and the suit of green. He told her that it was here that he had finally discovered his destiny—he explained that this was the only place in England where he felt completely safe.

He did not mention Dorothy.

He did not even imagine that it would be in this town of St. Lyons that he would be betrayed for the first time.

Elaine listened politely to the end.

"So I'll be safe here," she said.

"Yes."

"Do you think that is what concerns me?"

Robin didn't answer.

"I'm worried about you!" She reached out and seized his right hand. She touched his two stiff fingers tenderly. "You might have need of my good sword arm," she said softly.

Robin smiled, but there was no doubt in his voice when he spoke. "There are no swords in my plan—and no women—not even you, my darling. You'll stay here, Elaine—I won't take you."

Elaine looked up at her man, and she saw that his face was set as firmly as his words. She knew that she could not dissuade him.

She felt almost faint as she looked at him. She could hear her own breathing. She felt the weight of desire in the center of her body—a desire that slowly spread through all her limbs—her arms seemed to move very slowly as she started to take her dress off.

Robin stopped her, not with violence, but with a gentle hand on her arm. "No darling," he said, "wait—listen to me. If we make love now, it will be because we are afraid. Let us wait just a few more days. I'll sail tomorrow morning—I'll probably be back next Tuesday. Just one more week, dear Elaine, and then we will make love in triumph! Then the future will be as clear as blue sky before us. We'll make love then—we'll make a child then—we'll come together in happiness, not in fear.

"Don't worry about me, darling. I'm going away—but I'll come back. I'm going to live."

He kissed her. He stroked her soft hair, and her tense back, and then he said, "I have to go see the Mayor now—and then probably a few other people—I'll be back late—try to sleep, darling."

He kissed her again—she looked up at him with the eyes of a needy child—he knew that she would still be awake when he returned.

Robin left the room.

He saw the Mayor, and then he visited the Mayor's grandson

Duncan (who owned a good fishing boat). He made certain arrangements, and then he stopped in at different houses around town, until he had spoken individually with each of the five men of Duncan's crew. Finally he went to see the Mayor's sister, Beryl—a new suit of green was waiting for him.

He carried the clothes back to the inn.

Elaine was awake, as he had expected. She shivered at the sight of the famous green of the outlaw.

Robin put the clothes down and took her in his arms. He hugged her, and then he undressed her completely. He took his own shirt off—they got in bed under the covers.

He held her tight, and kissed her for a long time, and finally she fell asleep in his arms.

Robin waited until she was sleeping soundly. Then he quietly tore a bit of yarn from the bedspread—he used it to carefully measure the circumference of the third finger of her left hand.

Chapter 211

ELAINE AND THE MAYOR

Robin sailed away at dawn on Duncan's boat. He wore the striped jersey and fish oil slick trousers of any fisherman—no one could see that under his rough togs he wore his new suit of shining green.

Elaine stood on the dock with the Mayor. She waved good-bye to Robin like any fisherman's wife—she watched him wave back—she blew him a kiss for luck, and then she turned and walked back into the town with the Mayor.

The Mayor took her to his house—he told his servant to make breakfast for two.

Elaine and the Mayor sat across from each other at his simple table.

The breakfast when it came was quite good—but the Mayor preferred looking at Elaine to eating. Elaine did not let his gaze interfere with her enjoyment of the meal—only when she finished did she look up at his wise old face. "What do you see?" she asked.

"One moment" the Mayor replied, gesturing toward the kitchen. He called his servant out, and thanked him for the fine meal—then he ordered the lad to go out and buy some fresh bread. Only when the servant was well gone did the Mayor turn back to Elaine.

"In my position I hear many things," he began. "I remember, years ago, I heard of a young lady who came to the court—this was in the last year of the reign of the good King Henry—a young lady who shocked everyone, including the King, with her astonishing beauty. She had golden hair and blue eyes—she was of noble blood, so it was said—quite rightly the King gave her the title of Countess of Anjou."

The Mayor looked searchingly at Elaine. "This lady was also distinguished by a mysterious scar an inch below her left eye"—involuntarily Elaine raised a hand and covered it with a finger—"she was called Elaine, or as the King himself named her, Elaine the Fair."

Elaine put her hand down. There was no point in hiding.

"You know about Robin's previous visits here, yes?"

Elaine nodded.

"Robin recovered from his fever in my own bed." The Mayor gestured toward the next room and continued, "All through his delirium he called for his love, Elaine the Fair."

Elaine looked down at the table.

"Robin was unhappy because his love had gone off with another man. She married the Duke of Larraz.

"Just last week I learned something interesting from one of the fishermen who has family across the Channel. He said that Elaine the Fair, the Duchess of Larraz, was dead.

"Indeed, she is supposed to have died about a month ago—although when I look at you now, Lady Marian, I find that hard to believe."

Yes, Elaine thought to herself, that is how Roland would react. He prefers sorrow and mourning to the harshness of life—I'm glad I left him.

She looked up at the Mayor and smiled. "You know all my secrets, Milord."

The Mayor smiled back at her. He waved a hand as though to indicate the town. "You left England behind—married a foreigner—died as a result of that misjudgment—no one could imagine that you would come back from all that." The Mayor was grinning like a happy leprechaun now—obviously his 'no one' did not include himself—he quite evidently enjoyed knowing just a bit more than his fellows.

"Is this our secret?" Elaine asked.

"What secret, Lady Marian?" the Mayor asked mischievously, grinning even more.

Elaine stood up. Her own smile was quite gone. She walked around the table and looked down into the Mayor's eyes—stared down into his eyes for so long that he began to get frightened—his mouth slowly straightened out of its grin—Elaine leaned down then and kissed his lips.

Elaine raised her head after a minute—the Mayor took double

that time to recover. "Young lady, you ought not to do that," he said. "Consider my heart—I do not want to die before my time!"

Elaine refused to smile. She asked again, "Is this our secret?"

The Mayor looked up at her face and said, "Yes," very quietly.

Elaine smiled brightly and extended a hand. "I feel in the mood for a walk after that good breakfast, Lord Mayor. Would you like to show me around your town?"

The mayor took her hand and stood up. "It would be an honor, Lady Marian," he said.

Chapter 212

LONGING

That first day wasn't too bad. Elaine had told herself that she wouldn't worry. Robin was off on his adventure—he would be back in a week. The Mayor was a congenial companion for her.

No problems at all—until she found herself alone that night in her small room at the inn. Now there was no place to go and no one to talk to. She stalked around the tiny room—so much smaller than her palatial Larrazian quarters—she thought of the last four nights.

After I search for Robin, she thought, after I find him, he rejects me and then leaves me like this!

This is how my true love treats me!

Elaine felt a dark emotion building as she sent her thoughts directly to her absent man: I was naked in your arms and I felt you want me but NO—

The emotion was rage, blind hateful rage and she wanted to hurt Robin—she struck the door with her fist and hurt her hand and woke up the innkeeper.

She backed away and ran into another wall—no room no room no room—

She kicked that wall and howled like a trapped beast—

Nothing nothing nothing for me, no life inside me—I needed you, I need you, and you're gone. You left me with nothing. How could you do it? How could you hurt me so? And how could I have let you?

That was the worst. She remembered herself obeying Robin, being soft and submissive in his arms, waiting for him to come to her, always waiting for him, now waiting alone—

She screamed and beat on the door with her fists until the

innkeeper came upstairs and opened it.

For one frightening moment he didn't recognize the wild creature inside—and then he realized that this was indeed Robin's lady—but she was rather upset—

"Lady Marian," the innkeeper said in his calmest voice, "is there anything I can do for you?"

Elaine let her hands fall to her sides. She spoke perfectly calmly. "Thank you for opening the door," she said, just as if the innkeeper had done her a great favor—as though she had not realized that she could have opened the door herself.

She picked up her sable coat from where it lay on the bed and folded it neatly over one arm. She walked past the astonished innkeeper and down the stairs. She put the coat on there, before the front door, and stood waiting. The innkeeper hurried down the stairs and opened that door for her as well. Elaine the Fair stepped out into the cold fall wind that blew off the sea.

The sun had set hours before but Elaine could see, for this was the first night of the full moon. She looked up at the golden glowing orb—and then she set off toward the jetty that thrust its rocks out into the sea.

She walked carelessly out over those slippery rocks—she was alone in the night, with no one to save her if she slipped and fell into the cold sea.

She cared nothing for her own safety.

She made her way to the last rock—she spread her legs slightly and balanced herself on its slick surface.

The sea foamed over her golden slippers, and its coldness numbed her toes—the spray wetted her sable coat—the wind whipped her golden hair.

She cared for none of those things.

She stared out over the moonlit sea.

She longed for Robin so much that she felt her body ache with the pain of it.

She hated him for leaving her like this.

She loved him.

The pain started again, but it changed this time, it became a real physical pain, a cramp in her lower belly—

Elaine was happy for once to feel the beginning of her monthly flow.

By the time Robin got back she would be renewed, ready for him to fill her.

Chapter 213

MEASURING A LADY

Elaine slept late the next day. She had breakfast in the inn—soon after she finished she had a visitor. This was Beryl, the Mayor's sister. After introducing herself, Beryl said, "I have some friends over at my house who would love to meet you, Lady Marian. If you wish to be alone I'll leave you in peace—but I thought you might prefer some company."

"Perhaps," Elaine said.

Beryl didn't know whether that was acceptance or rejection. She looked at this still young lady before her. Beryl could remember when she herself had been called beautiful—she had seen lovely girls come and go through the seventy years of her life—but she had never seen anything like this Lady Marian.

She had never seen anyone so beautiful—or so lost.

She reached out, as to a daughter, and took the young woman's hand. "Come with me, my child," she said firmly.

Elaine rose obediently at the older woman's urging—she allowed Beryl to lead her—some ten minutes later she found herself in Beryl's home.

Several ladies were waiting there to greet the honored guest of their town—they were all very effusive (save for one, the youngest woman there—she seemed to become suddenly sick when she saw Elaine, and had to run home right away—but then no one paid much attention to her), they did their best to make Elaine feel welcome—Elaine accepted their attentions, but she didn't say a word.

Her mind was with Robin.

Beryl got her seated on a sofa—she brought tea and cookies, but Elaine neither drank nor ate.

The ladies tried to carry a conversation without Elaine, but that did not work well, and finally an uncomfortable silence descended on the company.

Trying desperately to reach her guest, Beryl said, "You know, Lady Marian, it was my friends and I who made Robin's first suit of green. Is there something we could make for you?"

To the surprise of everyone Elaine answered, for the question had touched on the path down which her thoughts were wandering. "Something to wear to bed with Robin," she said simply.

The strained formal atmosphere of the room cracked in an instant as the ladies cut loose with cheerful ribald laughter.

"Of course, my dear, of course!" Beryl said, and she and her friends took Elaine back to her bedroom. There they undressed their lovely guest, and told her a hundred times that she was beautiful, and they touched her body tenderly as they measured her with great care. They all noticed the cloth between her legs, of course, and they all made the same calculation that Elaine herself had made earlier: she will be ready when Robin comes back, they thought, and they smiled to themselves.

When they had all the measurements they needed they dressed Elaine again and brought her back to the living room—but this time Elaine refused to sit down. She simply pushed past the ladies as though she couldn't see them anymore—before they knew it she was out the door.

They crowded into the doorway, uncertain as to whether they should follow—they watched her walk to the sea—they watched as she stepped onto the slippery jetty—they watched as she strode out over the rocks—they saw her stop at the last rock, and they breathed a communal sigh of relief, because for a moment all of them had worried that she was just going to keep walking into the sea—she was still now, the sun touched her golden hair—they watched as she stared out over the unknown ocean.

Chapter 214

VOLUNTEERS

The days didn't get any better for Elaine and the nights got worse.

The innkeeper didn't know what to do. He tried sending his wife up when Elaine started banging in the night (while he himself observed from downstairs). The first few times his wife was able to calm their wild guest, but even her feminine sympathy lost its effect as the week wore on. Elaine would storm down the stairs and look at him with her strange demanding eyes—he would look up at his wife and she would shrug—he'd open the outside door, and Elaine would take off into the night.

She always walked out onto the jetty—each time she stayed out there for at least an hour, regardless of the weather.

Had she not had the gift of the sable coat, she would never have been able to defy the elements in this way.

The whole town became familiar with Elaine's habits—and so it came to pass that day or night there were always a few stalwart young men lounging in the vicinity of the jetty. Neither fishing nor sleep could compete with the chance of catching a glimpse of the lady they knew as Marian—and each brave young man was ready to plunge into the icy waters of the sea to save this lady, if ever she should slip off the rocks.

Elaine never seemed to notice her volunteer protectors.

She never slipped.

Chapter 215

THE STONE COTTAGE

While each day seemed an eternity for Elaine, time passed almost too quickly for the Mayor. He was very busy with a task Robin had given him—he hoped that he could complete it by Tuesday.

Robin had explained that he wanted a house for his honeymoon. He wanted privacy that the inn could not provide. Later on he intended to build or buy a suitable mansion for Elaine—but he was not about to wait that long to have her.

A simple house in St. Lyons would do for now.

Robin had asked for the Mayor's help, and the Mayor had replied like this: "I'm sorry, Robin, but housing is scarce here—there's nothing vacant, unless—"

"Unless what?"

"Well, I mean, unless you count the tumble down place near the waterfront that no one has bothered with for years. It was a nice stone cottage once—but it was badly neglected by the old drunken couple who lived there—when they died, the cottage was too far gone for anyone else to want it."

"Can you fix it up?"

"Robin, it needs a roof—I know one wall with a window is standing, but I can't guarantee anything else—"

Robin had emptied a small sack of gold on the table between them. "Get everything ready by the time I get back—but don't let my lady know what you're up to—I want it to be a surprise for her."

The Mayor had looked down at the spilled gold. "Robin, I don't need all this money."

"You don't—but the workmen do. Pay them double, triple,

whatever it takes—and one more thing—I'll need a big bed."

With that, Robin had gone off to see Duncan.

The Mayor had gone out to round up some tradesmen (actually fishermen who doubled at a second occupation).

He had been persistent—and he had Robin's gold—so work had started the next day. Elaine had displayed no interest in the construction when he had shown her around town—and he had offered no explanation—but he had taken a long look, just the same, and he had not been pleased with the speed of the workers.

So after that day he let his sister try to amuse Elaine—he spent every daylight moment overseeing the job—he wanted to make sure that the house would be ready in time.

He had his doubts for a while, but then by Monday morning it began to look like they were going to succeed. The outside was done, the roof was on—they even moved the bed in (a huge bed, at that—it took up a good half of the one room cottage). The Mayor relaxed. He told the workers to put on a good door, because Robin would want his privacy—he told them not to worry about finishing the interior walls, since the couple would likely spent all their time in bed anyway.

There was a lot of laughter that Monday as the men enjoyed their accomplishment, and imagined honeymoon delights, and anticipated being paid in gold.

They got the door on by late afternoon. They discussed the window, a problem because there were no glassmakers in town—the Mayor decided to leave it open. He reasoned that Robin would want all the light he could get to see his love— boarding the window up would make the interior far too gloomy. Anyway, it was fairly small and high up—it shouldn't let in that much cold air, and it could always be covered with a blanket at night.

They checked the fireplace and it worked.

It was nearly night now.

The Mayor paid the men, and they went off whistling.

The Mayor stayed where he was. He looked fondly at the completed cottage. He thought of Robin and Elaine coming together there on the morrow.

Chapter 216

...FOR A WEDDING NIGHT

Elaine proved impossible to amuse or even divert that week—so Beryl and her friends concentrated on the one project that would make her happy.

Beryl had managed to secure a bolt of the finest, sheerest white silk.

While Elaine looked out to sea, the ladies sewed. They touched their needles to the delicate fabric—they pierced it, wishing to be pierced themselves—they thought of Elaine and Robin in bed together—there was not one of them who was not wet between her thighs the whole week they worked on that garment.

Dorothy was not among them.

They made a nightgown for Elaine, a fragile beautiful nightgown for a wedding night.

Chapter 217

GIFT

The ladies of the sewing circle came to visit Elaine bright and early Tuesday morning. Beryl carried a cloth bundle—she knocked on Elaine's door with her free hand.

Elaine, who was already up and dressed, opened the door very quickly. She did not really expect Robin so early—but even so she was disappointed when she saw seven ladies before her— and no man.

She turned around without a word and walked back into her room. Beryl and the ladies followed—the small room was barely able to hold all of them.

"Lady Marian," Beryl said.

Elaine looked around.

Beryl held out the bundle of cloth that she carried—it was brightly wrapped with green ribbon.

"We have a gift for you, dear lady."

Elaine took the bundle and unfastened the ribbon. She unfolded several pieces of cloth without result—until suddenly she came to the core of the bundle, and there was what she had asked for—

Something to wear to bed with Robin.

Something beautiful.

Elaine picked it up carefully by the thin straps and let the protecting cloth fall to the floor. She held the nightgown up to her body. It seemed to shimmer in the morning light—one could nearly see through it—it was so delicate—

Robin's going to tear it, Elaine thought.

She was suddenly so short of breath that she feared she would faint.

She made herself recover. She turned and draped the night-gown over the bed. Then she turned back and stepped into Beryl's arms. She embraced and kissed that old lady on each cheek—and then she moved to the next member of the sewing circle. When she had embraced them all, she said, "Your gift is beautiful, thank you, I thank all you ladies—thank you."

The ladies replied in a friendly chorus: "You're welcome," and "God bless you," and "All happiness to you today," and so on, and then finally there was nothing more to say.

The ladies filed out—all but Beryl, who lingered in the door-way. She looked into Elaine's faraway blue eyes, and she asked, "Are you going to wait here for him?"

Elaine trembled slightly—in her mind's eye she saw a vision of a distant ship on blue water—she had to get out and see—

"I think I'll go out to the jetty in a little while."

Beryl said, "Be careful, my child, be careful."

Elaine didn't answer.

Beryl touched the young woman's cool cheek, and then she turned and followed her friends down the stairs.

Chapter 218

ON WATCH

A half hour after receiving her gift, Elaine left the inn and walked to her lookout place at the tip of the jetty.

She wore her black sable coat over the red dress that she had worn when she left Larraz. She wore nothing under her dress—her flow had stopped last night on schedule—she was ready to be loved.

She looked out over the ocean and imagined seeing Duncan's boat—she imagined opening her coat so that Robin could see the scarlet flash of her dress like a beacon—she imagined Robin coming toward her, coming closer and closer . . .

There were no boats on the horizon. The sea—at low tide—was barely disturbed by waves.

Elaine looked out over the empty ocean, dreamed, and looked again . . .

The fishing boats of St. Lyons had not put to sea this morning. The whole town was waiting.

Young men clustered around the base of the jetty. They talked to each other, and passed around a wineskin, and watched for Duncan's boat—but mostly they kept their eyes on Elaine the Fair.

The ladies of the town were busy in their kitchens—when Robin returned there was going to be a festival to end all festivals—naturally a lot of food would be needed for the celebration.

The Mayor and his servant went to the inn. The Mayor spoke to the innkeeper and gained access to Elaine's room. The servant packed all of Elaine's things, save for the exquisite nightgown—the Mayor noticed that right away, and he carefully picked it up himself.

The two of them then moved all of Elaine's possessions to the stone cottage. There was a point where Elaine could have easily looked back and seen them—the Mayor got a little nervous—but Elaine only had eyes for the sea.

Inside the cottage the servant laid out Elaine's belongings as they had been in the inn. The Mayor laid the beautiful night-gown over the bed.

They left the cottage and walked by the jetty on the way back to the Mayor's house. The Mayor noticed that the tide was rising.

In his house he kept thinking about that rising water. After a time he got up and went back alone to the jetty. Elaine was still out there on the last rock. How many hours had she been standing there? He saw that the watching young men were standing now as well—there was concern on their faces, but they seemed indecisive. They didn't know if they should try to rescue a lady who was not asking for help.

The Mayor came closer and he saw the reason for the lads' concern: waves were starting to break over the jetty. Elaine's feet must already be soaked—but she wasn't moving to come back.

The Mayor didn't hesitate. He tapped Paul (who had helped him before with Robin) and another young man standing near-by. "Paul, Roger," he snapped. "Bring the lady in *now*. Tell her your orders come from me."

"Yes Sir," the young men said together. They walked out along the rocks, fighting the waves that tried to sweep their feet out from under them.

They stopped, side by side, on the last rock behind Elaine.

She gave no sign that she had heard their splashing approach. The seawater rolled over her feet, but she did not seem to feel it.

"Milady," Paul said, "we have come to bring you back to the shore."

Elaine didn't turn around. "I must stay here and keep watch," she said.

"The Mayor has *ordered* us to bring you in," Roger said. When she didn't reply he added, "He's concerned for your safety—we all are."

"I must stay here," Elaine said.

Suddenly a much stronger wave broke over Elaine's ankles—for just a second she lost her balance, and then she got her feet planted again—but by now the two young men had seen enough. They leaned forward—each one caught her under an arm—they lifted her right up out of the water.

Elaine screamed.

It was an unearthly, animal like scream—it shocked Paul and Roger so much they nearly dropped her—but then she just went totally limp, she didn't resist as they pulled her toward them— Paul, the larger of the two, said, "I'll take her"—Roger helped drape her over Paul's shoulder—the two men accomplished the delicate maneuver of turning around on the slippery surface— Roger led the way back—Paul held Elaine with one hand and clutched Roger's shirt for balance and guidance—after a few intense minutes they reached the shore safely.

The Mayor said, "Paul, please carry Lady Marian to my house—I'll warm her feet and my man will make a hot meal for her."

"Yes Sir."

Paul turned to go—and so Elaine, who was draped over his shoulder, was now looking at the Mayor. She stopped Paul by digging her fingers into his arm. She couldn't seem to speak— but her eyes were desperate, pleading—

The Mayor understood. He looked at Elaine, but he spoke to the other young man. "Roger, you stay here," he said. "The *moment* you see a boat, you come right to my house with the news."

"Of course, Sir," Roger said, and then he looked at Elaine. "Don't worry, Milady," he said kindly. "I'll keep watch—at the first sign of him I'll let you know, don't worry."

Elaine tried to smile—she let go of Paul's arm—he carried her to the Mayor's house.

Elaine's feet were soon wrapped in warm heavy towels—the Mayor's servant began cooking some fish for lunch.

The Mayor sat next to Elaine but he didn't know what to say to her.

After a time the servant served the meal. Elaine surprised the Mayor by eating, though he doubted that she even tasted the good haddock.

When she finished she laid her fork down, and touched her lips with her napkin, and said calmly, "He's not coming back, is he?"

"Of course he is!" The Mayor said rather too heartily—and then he couldn't think of anything else to say, so he said it again. "Of course he is!"

"Perhaps I might have some wine," Elaine said.

The Mayor raised his hand and the servant brought her some.

Elaine drank fairly steadily for the rest of the afternoon, but she didn't seem to get drunk. When dinnertime came, she ate her food again without pleasure or comment.

Sunset came and went—darkness settled over the town.

The ladies of the town had labored long over their cakes and fancy breads—now these foods were ready, but no one wanted to eat them.

Roger did not come to the Mayor's house, because he had no good news to bring.

Chapter 219

NEW LODGINGS

"You can sleep here," the Mayor said.

"You are very kind," Elaine replied, "but I must return to the inn."

"It is really no problem—"

"No."

Elaine stood up.

"Milady, wait!" The Mayor's voice was insistent.

Elaine looked at him with hard blue eyes and then it was as though she suddenly broke—she clutched the table for support—she looked down at the veins standing out on the backs of her hands. "What is it?" she whispered.

The Mayor came around and put an arm around Elaine. "It's nothing, dear lady, nothing's wrong. Look at me, it's alright—" Elaine looked up at his face with eyes filled with tears—and hope—the Mayor went on: "It's just a little surprise that Robin planned for you—come, I'll show you myself."

He helped Elaine into her sable coat, and put his own coat on—he took a torch from the wall and took Elaine's arm with his other hand. He led her out into the moonlit street.

"Let's go by the jetty," Elaine said.

"All right."

Roger and some other young men were still waiting there.

"Any news?" the Mayor asked.

"No Sir," Roger replied. "But we'll have someone on watch all night—we'll let you know as soon as Robin comes in."

"Do you know the stone cottage that I've been working on?

"Yes sir."

"Lady Marian will be sleeping there tonight. When Robin

comes in, bring the news to her first."

"Yes Sir!" Roger said, smiling—he imagined a scene where he brought the good news to Elaine in the middle of the night—in her excitement she would come to the door half dressed . . .

Elaine didn't know why she had to go to this cottage, but she didn't care enough to ask a question.

The Mayor took her over to the cottage, which wasn't far from the main dock. When the Mayor opened the door, she saw that there was a window on the seaward side—in the daytime she would be able to see the ships coming and going.

The Mayor used his torch to light the candles that his servant had set out earlier this day.

Elaine saw that her clothes were all here, neatly unpacked. She saw the fragile beauty of the thin nightgown on the bed.

"Your honeymoon cottage," the Mayor said, gesturing. "Robin asked me not to tell you until it was done."

The Mayor realized his mistake even as he spoke—he wished that he had not brought Elaine's clothes over here—he should have managed to get the clothes back to the inn somehow—anything was better than a bride alone in a honeymoon bed.

Elaine was crying without making any sound. She walked forward, blinded by tears, until she struck the side of the huge bed. Then she crawled up onto it—she lay facedown across its width, next to her nightgown—the bed was so large that her feet didn't even hang over the edge.

The Mayor came over and put a gentle hand on her back—he wanted somehow to comfort her, and make amends for the blunder of bringing her here—but Elaine was beyond comfort now.

"Please go," she said.

The Mayor flinched at the aching sorrow in her voice. He pulled his hand away from her.

"I'll send a maidservant over to assist you in the morning," he said.

Elaine's body was shaking under the sable coat. He realized that she was trying to hold back her sobs. He wanted to stay and help her—he knew that there was nothing he could do—he cursed himself for bringing her here.

"Good night, dear lady," he said—and then he quickly left the cottage, and closed the door behind him.

He thought that he could hear Elaine's sobs, unrestrained now, following him all the way back to his house.

Chapter 220

BLOOD IN THE SEA

Elaine didn't know exactly when she stopped crying. She just knew that the feelings of sadness and fear and loss were gradually pushed aside by the stronger emotion of anger—the black rage that she had felt on the first lonely night in St. Lyons came back, doubled and redoubled in force.

You're dead, Robin, she thought.

I hate you.

Elaine got up and began to pace around the room.

You've left me alone with my hate—I hate you—I hate your pride. I came back to you with no conditions, just my love and my body waiting to be taken—and you spurned me because of pride. You wanted money to build some palace for me—if I wanted money I would have stayed with Roland! I offered myself in a coach! You rejected me! You *wanted* me to wait, while you went off to be a hero—Louisa told you you couldn't do it—but you wouldn't listen to her—I saw you smile at Little John—you go off to fight fifty knights like it's just a game—you'll be back in a week—Ha! Ha!

Elaine felt the tears come again, suddenly, unexpectedly—she turned and savagely slammed both fists against the wall.

This was not the inn's smooth wooden wall protected by tapestry—this was hard unfinished stone.

The pain of impact was terrible—she cut both hands in several places.

Elaine stood quietly in the flickering light of the burned down candles. She held her hands up and watched the blood as it flowed in little curling rivulets down her hands, down her wrists, and finally down to her elbows, from where it dropped onto the floor.

"The blood," she said out loud, "the blood is with me. In three weeks there will be another full moon. The blood will flow again from my empty womb. I will never be filled.

"Even Sandra was given a child before Anton died.

"I have nothing."

Elaine opened the door of her cottage and stepped outside. She could just make out the figures of two young men with torches, standing near the jetty. She walked away from them, keeping parallel to the shore, until she was sure they couldn't see her—and then she turned toward the sea.

She walked across the rocky beach until the incoming waves lapped over her feet—and then she bent down and washed her bloody hands in the sea.

The salt burned her cuts but that didn't concern her—she gathered a double handful of the bitter water and raised it to her face—she washed away all traces of her own bitter tears.

She walked back into the stone cottage—she refused even to think of the name the Mayor had given it—she went inside and kicked off her wet slippers. She took off her sable coat and her dress and put them both on a chair—she lifted the beautiful nightgown off the bed and laid it carefully atop her dress.

She climbed naked into the big lonely bed—she pulled the heavy woolen blankets up over her body.

Elaine lay on her back, shivering—her wet feet seemed frozen and the rest of her wasn't much warmer—she felt the cold wind whip in off the sea through the open window.

She pulled the blankets all the way up over her face and hugged herself in the darkness. Gradually feeling came back to her feet—gradually warmth came back to her body—finally she was almost suffocating in a hot cave—but there was no reason to go out.

She screamed, she screamed again and again, but no one heard the sounds from inside the cottage, from under the blankets.

She stopped only when her throat was raw—and then the sense of suffocation became too much. She rolled over and squirmed until her head was just free of the blankets. Her tumbled golden hair protected her face.

She lay quietly for a long time and then she eased a hand down under her body. She cupped her womanhood and she spread her legs wide. She thought of Robin and she started to

rub herself—each stroke opened the fresh cuts on her hand—
she ground down into the pain, she needed the pain, she sought
love in pain—but finally nothing worked.

She could not come because she could not forget that she was
alone.

She abandoned her caresses—she lay still on her lonely bed,
too drained even to cry.

Sometime before dawn she fell asleep.

Chapter 221

FATHER

The Mayor, as he had promised, sent a maidservant to look after Elaine in the morning. The girl arrived shortly after sunrise. She put down her bucket of fresh water and knocked timidly at the cottage door. There was no answer, but the unlocked door swung inward a few inches. The girl pushed it open farther and looked inside. She saw Elaine, asleep on her bed—the lady's face showed the ravages of nearly unbearable sorrow. The maidservant did not have the heart to wake her. She picked up her bucket and quietly carried it inside—she had fresh towels too, and she laid them by Elaine's nightgown—she tiptoed back out and shut the door behind her.

Meanwhile the Mayor was down by the docks, talking to the fishermen.

No one had put out to sea yesterday—but the town could not afford (especially with winter coming on) another day of idleness.

The Mayor asked the men to spread their boats out as much as possible, in the hopes of sighting Duncan's craft—perhaps his boat was damaged in some way.

The men agreed to this request, of course, but privately they had their doubts. They knew that Duncan was a superb seaman—if he had got his boat close enough for them to see him, he would have found a way to sail it in.

Most likely he had never escaped London harbor . . .

The fishing boats put out to sea while Elaine slept—when she woke up about noon, and looked out her window, she saw not one boat at the docks.

Elaine looked around and noticed the fresh water and towels.

She washed herself, and then she considered her choice of clothes. There was the wrinkled red dress from yesterday, a selection of courtesan's outfits from Madame Genevieve, and Louisa's billowing white gown.

She did not feel like a bride or a courtesan—she pushed her nightgown aside, picked up the red dress, shook it, and put it on.

Her slippers were still wet but she put them on anyway. She didn't bother with her coat.

She walked quickly to the Mayor's house.

His servant let her in, and escorted her to his master—the Mayor was sitting very sadly on a single chair in his living room.

The servant discreetly withdrew to the kitchen.

Elaine went over and knelt down beside the Mayor. "I'm sorry," she said.

The Mayor reached out and stroked her hair, "Don't be, dear lady. It is I who should apologize—I should never have taken you to the cottage."

Elaine reached up and touched his hand. "I am sorry because I thought only of my own pain—I burdened you with my pain, and I never thought of your grandson. Please forgive me."

"There's nothing to forgive—and no reason for sorrow—my grandson will come back, and he'll bring Robin with him."

Elaine felt the tension of the old man's hand in her hair as he said that. He needs to believe in that hope, she thought. Perhaps I should believe as well.

She looked up at the Mayor's face and she tried to say something—but she choked on her words.

The Mayor made room for her on his chair. She snuggled up next to him and buried her face against him—she cried unashamedly like a very young child, and he held her as a father would—he used his handkerchief to dry her face—she hugged him desperately—she thought of her own father, but she had no picture of him in her mind—she thought of Father Ashendon, but he had never held her like this—she had been forced to make adult decisions since the age of four—she had never since truly been a child, until this moment—now she rested against an old, wise, loving man, he caressed her as he had caressed his daughters, fifty years ago—he held her just as though she were a child of four, he let her cry and he dried her tears, and he told her that everything would be all right.

"Everything will be all right," he said.

"Everything will be all right."

Finally she looked up with trust in her eyes, and she said, "Yes."

The Mayor kissed her forehead, and then he called to his servant.

That good fellow soon served a meal, which was lunch for the Mayor—and breakfast for Elaine.

Chapter 222

DOT

Late afternoon sunlight slanted through the Mayor's windows.

"Do you want to go down to the docks with me?" the Mayor asked Elaine.

"No, I couldn't bear it," Elaine replied. "Please take me back to the cottage."

"You could go to the inn if you like. I could—"

"No. I'm used to the cottage now."

"As you wish." The Mayor stood up and offered Elaine his hand.

Ten minutes later Elaine was in her cottage—the Mayor was waiting at the main dock—and the first fishing boat was coming in.

Elaine watched the boat—not the right boat—as it came in, and then she noticed something else—a sight of terrible sadness.

She saw a group of six come up behind the Mayor—they stopped before they reached him, as though they didn't want to disturb him—they huddled together: six women.

Elaine knew right away that she was looking at Duncan's wife, and the wives of his five crew members. She thought of the children, children sent off tonight to stay with their grandmothers, children asking questions—

Children whose lives will be destroyed.

NO!

Children who will never see their fathers again because of Robin's pride.

NO!

She forced the black thoughts away, and she forced herself to watch as the boats came in.

There was a ritual to each arrival. Each captain, seeing the Mayor waiting for him, would step ashore ahead of his crew. There would be a brief conversation—Elaine couldn't hear the words but she could read the expressions—she knew the meaning of heads shaking sadly back and forth: No, no, no sign of Duncan's boat—no sign of Robin Hood.

One boat after another, and each arrival was the same.

The six women clung to each other, and some of them cried.

Now all the boats were in—save one.

Elaine watched as the men began to divide up their catch.

None of the sailors paused in their work to look out to sea. They kept their eyes on the tools and fish before them.

Elaine understood: After a day of searching, scanning the horizon, hoping, they just couldn't bear to look out anymore.

Perhaps there was no reason to look out anymore.

The six women turned around and began to walk toward their homes.

The sun blazed red as it set.

Elaine was looking out a south window at the southern coast of England—a coast that angled, in this part of the world, a bit north of west.

So the red sun in the west appeared to plunge into the sea—the dying red light of day spread over the waves—and the dark water was turned to blood.

Elaine looked out at this ocean of blood—and she saw Robin pierced by fifty swords. She saw his red blood covering his green suit. She saw his head chopped from his body and mounted on a pike.

She closed her eyes and then she opened them and looked out again.

She stared deep into the bloody vision and saw a black dot—

She stared into the blood and saw a black dot with a white speck on top—

She slammed her body against the stone wall as she stuck her head out the window to look—

The black dot was a fly and the fly had white wings—

She pressed harder against the stone as though to touch the one coming toward her—

The fly was a rabbit with a white patch on his back—

The drowning sun cast its last light over the water, enough—

Enough to see that the rabbit was a horse being ridden by a splendid white knight—

A little boy who had come down to the docks to meet his father—a little boy whose most precious possession was a shirt with a hole in it—this boy tugged at his father's sleeve and said, "Look"—

The horse was a fishing boat with white sails and eight men aboard—

Everyone on the docks looked, as Elaine looked, all strained their eyes in the gathering darkness—

The eight men were Duncan, and his five sailors, and Little John, and Robin Hood.

Everyone on the docks yelled at once.

Six women stopped in their tracks, turned around and ran back. They added their highpitched cries of happiness to the men's roaring cheers, and so they created a tumult of noise that reverberated through the town even as it rolled out over the sea—the noise penetrated every house in St. Lyons, and within minutes, every house emptied.

From oldest to youngest, they all came out into the streets—they rushed to the docks to greet their green hero, Robin Hood.

Soon everyone was there by the water—everyone, that is, except for Elaine the Fair.

She stayed alone in her stone cottage, and she listened to the crowd, and she watched as the boat came in.

Chapter 223

WEDDING

Duncan stood proudly at the bow of his boat as he brought it in to the dock. He tossed some lines ashore, and about a hundred helpful citizens grabbed for them, causing great confusion.

Elaine watched the spectacle—and then she saw her man come up next to the Captain. Robin wore his bold suit of green, a bow was slung over his right shoulder, and he held a heavy bag with both hands. He stepped up on the rail and leaped—a quite credible jump, considering his burden—he flew over the first line of people (who were still fiddling with the lines) and landed right in front of the Mayor. Robin dropped his bag and the two men embraced—and then the crowd swarmed over both of them. Elaine was unable to catch a glimpse of green for the next few minutes.

Robin *had* succeeded in taking the King's gold—he had already counted and divided the booty at sea. He had given a handsome share to Duncan and his crew; the heavy bag he carried was loaded with gold for the town in general; Little John had been apportioned a generous percentage; and Robin had marked the rest—half the total take—for himself. His share and Little John's still rested inside the captured chest.

Now Little John and two of Duncan's sailors carried that extremely heavy chest off the ship—as soon as they touched the dock they had to drop it, for they were overwhelmed by wives and well wishers. The rest of the crew then jumped down—they too were quickly overwhelmed by those who loved them. Duncan waited until he saw that his boat was properly secured—and then he too leaped into the crowd. His grandfather hugged him first, and then his wife claimed him—she hugged him, hearing nothing while people yelled all around her.

For a while there was a mass disordered celebration—and then several men got the same idea at once, and they started to lift Robin. He sensed their intent—he picked up the heavy bag again. Now the men had to work twice as hard, but they managed to hoist Robin up onto their shoulders.

The sun was down now but the sky was still far lighter than the earth—Elaine could see Robin clearly now, silhouetted against that evening sky.

He said something that Elaine couldn't hear—something no one could hear—he waited, and gradually the turbulent crowd noticed their high held hero, and they deferred to him—they quieted down as they looked up expectantly.

Robin spoke now in a solid booming voice that even Elaine could hear easily. "Dear friends, I am so glad to be home!" The crowd roared but Robin waved them into quietude. "I always think of how you people saved me from death—well, today I want to give you some return for your kindness." Robin raised the heavy bag up over his head. His voice boomed even louder. "I have taken the King's gold, and now I am going to give it to those who deserve it the most! I give this bag of gold to your Mayor"—Robin handed the bag down to the old gentleman, who nearly collapsed when he felt the full weight of it—"and though he is the finest man I know, this gift is certainly not for him alone—this gift is for you!" The cheers started again but Robin shouted over them. "This gold is for every man, woman, and child in this town, the greatest town in England, St. Lyons!"

Elaine watched the beaming hero accept thanks and congratulations—and she cursed him. Not one word for me, she thought. He has made me suffer the agonies of the damned, and he does not come to me, and he is not even looking for me!

Elaine was wrong. There were private words that she had not been able to hear. When Robin had first alighted on the dock and embraced the Mayor, he had asked right away the only question that mattered to him: "Where's Elaine?"

The Mayor had answered quickly, "She's in the cottage—it's ready and she's ready—she's missed you terribly!"

Ever since then Robin had been aware—regardless of the way his head was turned—of the door to the stone cottage.

On the other side of that door, invisible to Robin, Elaine gathered all the rage that she had felt this last week.

When she was ready she opened the door—she hadn't bothered with her coat, and for a moment her scarlet dress was backlit by the candles in the cottage—Robin saw her right away, his whole body twisted toward her, and he fell off his perch.

He landed on his feet, and he looked—

The men who had held him up looked to see what had caught the attention of their hero—

Soon *everyone* was looking at Elaine the Fair.

She walked like a Queen down the avenue—she moved gracefully but slowly, and that gave a quick thinking blacksmith time to run to his forge and light a dozen torches—and then he ran back past Elaine, handing out the torches as he went. Men took the torches and held them aloft—they created a firelit pathway for Elaine—she walked between the blazing lights, and blazed with her own unearthly beauty—she walked toward the man all in green who had moved up to stand at the end of the torchlit path—a man with a smile on his face (he remembered the Mayor's words, 'she's ready', and so he thought of incredible delights)—Elaine had a slight smile on her face as she slowly approached her man—no one in the crowd breathed as she took her last steps up to him—Robin opened his arms wide to embrace his true love—and then Elaine took a last step forward with her left foot, she was so close that she almost stepped on Robin's toe, she was inside his guard just as he had taught her, she leaned forward into him and pivoted on that left foot and brought her right hand around inside his embracing arm, brought her hand around with all the force she possessed—she slapped Robin across the face, a staggering blow, the crack of impact like the sound of a mace on steel armor, one of Robin's knees buckled and he almost went down, but he was saved from that by her hand coming back the other way, the back of her hand smacked his right cheek this time, and this blow actually helped Robin, it straightened him up, as everyone watched in amazement and dead silence, and then Elaine spoke.

"Why did you make me wait?"

Robin shook his head to clear it, and then he gave Elaine a rather abashed smile, as though he were a small boy who had been found out. "I had to stop and buy you something."

"You what?" Elaine tried to slap Robin again but this time he caught her right hand easily with his left—with thumb and forefinger of his right hand he lifted a small box from a pocket in his suit of green.

"It took a long time to engrave it," Robin said as he handed the box to Elaine.

She took it—she stared down at the little box, almost frightened—Robin released her left hand, and she used it to slowly open the box—the people around craned their necks, trying to see—inside the box was a gold wedding ring.

"Let's see if it fits," Robin said.

"Not yet," Elaine said. She looked over at the Mayor, who stood watching with the bag of gold between his feet, and his arm around his grandson Duncan. "Lord Mayor," Elaine said, "you have been the father to me that I have never had. Will you give me away?"

"Of course, daughter," the old man replied, his whole face smiling. "Shall I call our priest?"

"No." Elaine's eyes were bright and clear. "We'll do it right now, as we are, before friends, before God."

"Yes," said the Mayor. He came over and embraced Elaine, and kissed both her cheeks—Robin used that moment to hand his bow to Little John—the Mayor turned around, holding Elaine's hand. Elaine had the little box in her other hand. She gave it back to Robin.

He took the ring out—it gleamed golden in the torchlight—he put the box back in his pocket.

"Robin, will you take my daughter as your wife?"

"I will," Robin said. He took Elaine's left hand in his, and slid the golden ring onto her third finger. It fit perfectly.

"Take care of her, my son," the Mayor said.

"I will," Robin said again, and he looked at Elaine, who was still staring down at the sparkling gold on her finger.

The Mayor continued the ceremony. "Dear daughter, will you take this man as your husband?"

Elaine looked up into Robin's eyes. "I will," she said.

Robin smiled—and then he suddenly threw his head back and roared: "I speak to you, O Lord, and I declare us married in Your eyes till death do us part!"

The people of St. Lyons roared with their own earthly approval—and then Robin drew Elaine into his embrace, and he kissed her mouth fiercely until she melted in his arms.

When he released her Little John was standing ready to shake Robin's hand and kiss the new bride's cheek.

The men of St. Lyons were eager to follow the big squire.

The Mayor could not make himself heard in the uproar, so he struggled over to the captured chest that Little John had left unguarded (the Mayor noticed on his way that Duncan was keeping a foot on the bag of the town's gold). The Mayor climbed up on the chest and so got his head above the throng. He cried, "Festival! Festival! Festival!" until all heard—the ladies remembered their day old bread and fancy cakes (no one tonight would complain that they were stale)—they went to fetch those treats while men brought out wine and spirits—the blacksmith kept himself busy by lighting more torches—now there was food and drink and light, and the wedding celebration truly began.

Robin paid no attention to the surrounding bustle. He danced with his bride as though they were alone.

Little John, assisted by the Mayor's servant, carried the heavy chest to the stone cottage. They stowed the chest inside, along with Robin's bow and John's sword. They lit a fire to keep the place warm for the honeymoon couple.

On the way back to the party, Little John was met by a pretty young girl, and he danced with her back to the docks.

He saw that Robin and Elaine were still dancing—swaying really—in the same spot where he had left them.

The bridal couple kissed long and often—they stared into each other's eyes—sometimes they simply looked down at their intertwined hands.

Then Robin would always turn Elaine's hand up, so they could both stare in wonder at the golden ring that symbolized their love.

Chapter 224

THE WEDDING NIGHT

An enchanted circle, perhaps five feet in diameter, seemed to have formed around the newlywed couple. The townspeople celebrated wildly outside of that circle—inside the circle Robin and Elaine swayed against each other, oblivious of the festivities. They danced within their private world—and then they both came to realize that they had danced enough.

Elaine stopped the motion of her body—Robin placed his hands firmly on either side of Elaine's face. He held her still, and he whispered, "I love you, Elaine," and then he kissed her, a kiss that was a foretaste of things to come. Elaine gave herself up to that kiss—she opened her mouth for her husband, she felt his tongue, she felt the strength of his body against her, she was ready for any suggestion, any order—Robin broke the kiss, intending to tell his bride that it was time to go home for the consummation of their love—but then he could not speak, for he felt the cold breath of evil on his back.

A shudder of fear ripped through Robin—he jerked his head around, but at first he saw only Little John's broad back close at hand—then he saw that a girl's pretty white arms were embracing his friend—the squire's bulk hid all the rest of the girl, but then perhaps she sensed Robin's interest—she went up on her toes—the top half of her face appeared over Little John's shoulder—she had soft brown hair, and a smooth white forehead, and eyes that had turned black in the night—eyes that were black with hatred—Robin looked into the eyes of another woman who loved him: Dorothy.

Elaine moved to one side to see the object of her man's sudden interest.

Dorothy saw her rival's movement—she softened her own face until she showed only the adoring expression that she had bestowed on Robin so many times before—she loved him, O she loved him so much and he had left her, but still that wasn't the worst—the worst was the whisper that she had heard when she had danced close with Little John—not Marian, no, Robin had called his bride by another name—he had taken *her* back! The faithless woman who left him—the one who was supposed to be dead—the one who broke his brave heart . . .

I heard you suffer, Dorothy thought. How can you take back the one who hurt you so? I would have been faithful till I died, I would always have loved you, even now I could make you happy—

Her thoughts went out to Robin as she remembered being on her knees before him, she remembered his hand touching her breasts—

Elaine saw that look of total adoration—then she looked up to see Robin's reaction, but saw only the back of his head, because he was still looking at the girl—on his wedding night! She dug her fingernails into Robin's arm and snapped, "Look at her too long and you'll lose me."

Robin turned around as Elaine ran off into the crowd. He cursed because he wanted to talk to Dorothy for a minute—he wanted to find out if that first shudder of fear had a real basis—but now Elaine was fast disappearing—he had to go after her.

Dorothy's eyes went black with hatred again as she watched Robin run off after Elaine the Fair.

Robin saw a glimmer of red—he raced toward it through the laughing crowd, feeling ridiculous—how can I lose my bride on my wedding night? he wondered—and then too he worried about Dorothy: what had that evil look meant?—but then Elaine moved again, he was obliged to keep following her, tripping over revelers—he realized that a new emotion was building in his heart, one he had never felt before—he was angry at Elaine, and growing angrier by the minute—and then he suddenly realized that he had lost her.

He looked in every direction but he could see no flash of red.

He felt a wave of fear crash in his heart, a shockwave of loss that drove anger and every other emotion away—he was left with a single purpose: Find her.

He ran full tilt through the crowd in front of him, he knocked people out of his way and he didn't care, he wasn't embarrassed, he just kept going, looking in every direction as he ran, people were scattering out of his way now, and then he saw a familiar figure, it was Duncan, grinning—the Captain pointed down an alley and Robin swerved and ran into its darkness—he saw a gleam of red at the lighted end near the waterfront—he realized that Elaine had led him in a circle as he turned on the speed—Elaine saw him coming and she ran too but there was no stopping Robin now, she could have had wings and she would not have been able to get away from Robin, he was closing on her, she was still running but she knew she couldn't get away, she did not want to get away, and so she stopped, panting, right in front of the door of their stone cottage.

Robin slowed when he saw her stop—he walked the last few yards—he came up in front of her and placed both his hands against the cottage's wooden door—he trapped Elaine between the two rigid bars of his arms.

Elaine looked up at her man, her breasts heaving from her run, her eyes frightened and yet deeply satisfied—she asked, "Dear husband, may I go in first? I wish to change."

Robin shoved the door inward with his two hands. Elaine trembled—Robin reached down and picked her up in the classical manner, one arm under her knees, his other arm supporting her back—he held her easily, he turned her so that her feet went first, and then he carried her across the threshold.

He didn't take her to the bed. He surprised her by setting her back down on her feet—he steadied her with his hands on her shoulders, and then he said, "Don't take too long."

Elaine trembled again as she watched her man turn and leave the room. He shut the door behind him.

The cottage had been warm from the fire Little John had started. Outside now, Robin could feel the cold air from the sea—but he didn't let it bother him.

He could not hear Elaine through the thick oaken door—but he could see ever brighter light seeping past the hinges, and he realized that Elaine was lighting all the candles inside.

He smiled: she wanted him to see her.

He waited until the quality of the light stopped changing—he waited a few minutes more—and then he could wait no longer.

Robin opened the door and entered the cottage. He turned as soon as he stepped in and locked the door. Only when the door was solidly barred did he turn back and look at his bride.

Elaine stood facing him in front of the huge bed.

She wore only the silk nightgown that had been made just for her—that had been made for this night.

The ladies had measured her well. When she stood straight, as she did now, the effect was perfect. Delicate thin straps crossed the bare skin of her shoulders and joined the low, lacy neckline. Her breasts were bare right to her nipples—and they were only covered by a fragile froth of lace. Every breath she took threatened to expose those hard excited peaks.

Robin let his eyes linger there—and then he looked down further at his bride's narrow waist. This was showed off by a purple ribbon pulled tight—but he noticed that it was carelessly tied—one tug would undo it.

He looked down further—Elaine's legs were parted and the ever so fragile silk was nearly transparent—he could see the faint shadow of Elaine's feminine triangle at the juncture of her thighs.

Robin looked up at her face.

He saw fear in Elaine's eyes—she was terribly afraid of getting what she had always wanted.

"You're beautiful," Robin said, but his voice had a hard tone—he was going to use that beauty.

Elaine's breathing got deeper and more erratic. Robin saw a flash of pink as one nipple fought with the lace that imprisoned it.

Elaine tried to speak, found she couldn't, swallowed and tried again.

"What are you going to do?"

Robin took a step nearer her and stopped. He looked over her body again.

"I'm going to fuck you," he said.

This was the man that Elaine had asked for in her secret heart—and she fought him, in a last desperate battle against happiness. She made her eyes turn cold, and she said, "No. You're going to make love with me."

Robin smiled at Elaine as though she were a foolish young girl—and then he shook his head. "No darling," he said, "that's what your other husbands did." He walked right up to her, undid the purple ribbon, and casually tossed it aside. "I'm not like them."

He looked down into Elaine's blue eyes and he saw the coldness melting, an anguished desire taking its place—he put both his hands over Elaine's breasts. He felt their heat, he felt her hard nipples pressing through the lace against his palms—and then he gathered the neckline of the nightgown together with his left hand, and he inserted the two rigid fingers of his right hand down in the cleavage between her breasts.

Elaine felt the two stiff fingers against her bare skin under the nightgown. She shuddered as she remembered her thought upon receiving this gift: Robin's going to tear it—

He did.

He ripped straight down with his right hand and he tore the beautiful garment in half from neckline to hem.

He opened the split garment, exposing her body—he freed her arms from the straps—he tossed the nightgown aside, and he looked at her.

Every inch of Elaine's nude body was quivering.

He picked her up easily then and laid her on her side on the bed—laid her like that so she could watch while he undressed.

He took his clothes off slowly, deliberately, the only sign of impatience being the way he threw each removed garment away from him.

Then the last bit of green hit the carpet, and Robin was naked, with his rigid manhood level with Elaine's face. He came over to her and plunged his right hand into her golden hair—he pulled her to him—her mouth opened for him and he forced himself in deep—he made her move her head to his pleasure, he made her suck for a long minute, and then he pulled away and rolled her over onto her back.

He looked leisurely down her body, and then he focused on her golden fleece and her just parted thighs. He seized her thighs with his big hands—he started to pull her legs apart, but he felt resistance in her body—he immediately raised his right hand and slapped her hard on the softness of her left inner thigh.

His hand left its red print there—Elaine gave one short cry and looked up at Robin's face—she looked at his gray eyes, and they were as hard as stone.

She spread her legs.

Robin saw right away how wet she was, how open, how ready—

Elaine saw him looking at her and she wanted to hide but she couldn't—she understood that she was being *known* by this man—

Robin climbed on to the bed over her and got between her

legs. He put one hand deliberately on the marked place on her left thigh, put his other hand on her right thigh, and he spread her wider.

Elaine didn't resist at all.

Robin came down and he put his manhood against the center of her femininity—he quivered too, for a moment—and then he drove inside of her.

Elaine felt him possess her, felt his weight come down on her, she felt that she would never be free again—she went wild, her nails tore at his back, she bit at his lips, her hips jerked against him—but there was nothing she could do anymore.

He just pinned her with his weight, and drove deeper into her soul—he smiled down at her through his bitten lips and she cried out, helplessly, and then she raised her head and kissed him where she had hurt him, and her hands tightened around his back now only for an embrace, and she pushed her hips up against him only to feel him better—he owned her, yes, O yes—

Robin slid his hands down under her buttocks and he dug his fingers into their softness—Elaine felt the sweet tender pain and she accepted it, she liked it, she belonged to him now, she belonged to him for ever and ever, she let all her love show in her eyes and she saw the fierce anguish in his—she felt his hard grip tighten even more on her buttocks—his manhood swelled within her as though searching for her womb—he was inside her, outside her, the boundaries between their bodies melted— he came in her, his sperm burst free inside of her—she felt his pleasure as though it were her own—it was her own—she came, shuddering, she hugged him savagely as he pleased her, he belonged to her, O yes he belonged to her as she belonged to him . . .

Robin was the first to recover and it took him quite a while. Finally he raised his head—his face was sweat-soaked, utterly relaxed, utterly happy—he looked down into Elaine's loving eyes, and he said, "A son!"

Elaine smiled up at him, her eyes twinkling with happiness— she laughed and shook her head.

"A daughter!" she said.

Chapter 225

DOROTHY

When Little John woke up the morning after Robin's wedding, he did not at first know where he was. He looked around the unfamiliar room—an inn somewhere—and then he saw the bloodstains on the sheet next to him and everything came back.

He remembered Dorothy.

He had known her, in childhood, as any boy from a small town knows a girl. She had been someone to chase, someone to tease—but certainly not a friend for such a manly little boy as he. Then he went away from her and their town of St. Lyons in the year 1187, when he was twelve (already the size of a man) and she was a child of eleven. Little John left to serve as the squire to Sir Warwick, a local knight who at that time had just inherited a vast estate in Aquitaine. The boy crossed the Channel with his new master, and he did not see England again for seven years.

When Sir Warwick heard of Richard Lionheart's triumphant return to England in the summer of 1194, he decided that it was time to pay homage to the King that he had never seen. He traveled with his squire to London—but when they got there, they discovered that Richard was off chasing Northmen, and a renegade knight, and Elaine the Fair.

Richard soon returned to London with some Norse heads, a new mantle of heroism, and an official version of the facts.

Sir Warwick believed every good word about the King.

Little John heard some different stories, and he formed his own opinion.

Specifically, Little John thought that Thomas, not Richard, was the hero of the tale. Little John argued with his master over this point—and so lost his position. He returned then to his home town, never imagining that the hero he had heard of awaited him there . . .

Serving Thomas—Robin Hood!—as he recovered, Little John met Dorothy again. How different she had become! She had grown and her body had filled out wonderfully—she was a beautiful young woman—and she was in love, not with the squire, but with her hero, Robin Hood.

Little John saw Robin kiss Dorothy once—but time went by and Robin never called her name in the mornings—he never came to love her.

Then last night Little John nearly bumped into Dorothy after he had stowed the gold in Robin's cottage. He was surprised then when Dorothy warmly greeted him—he was even more surprised when she asked him to dance. He took her in his arms and she eagerly returned his embrace—he kissed her and she did not protest.

She was certainly not the first girl who had wanted Robin and settled for him—he danced with her up the street, pausing often to kiss her, and he was happy.

When they came back to the main area of celebration people came from all sides to offer congratulations or food or wine—Little John graciously accepted all that was offered, especially the wine—he got happier by the minute, and he hardly noticed that Dorothy wasn't drinking herself, because he could think of little save her firm, close pressed body.

He didn't understand that her embrace was really an act of desperation—she wanted her breasts crushed hard against his chest so that she could forget the feeling of Robin's gentle fingers—she wanted Little John's leg pressed between hers so that she could threaten herself with the loss of the innocence that Robin had protected.

She worked her body against Little John, she deliberately inflamed him—she wanted him to take her, break her, destroy her—she wanted to be destroyed if she couldn't have Robin—but then she had a secret thought as well.

She thought that if Robin saw her like this he would strike Little John and save her—she thought that he would leave Lady Marian behind.

She maneuvered Little John up close to the wedded couple, and then she went up on her toes and looked over her partner's shoulder—she looked right at Robin, who was only a few feet away—but still oblivious of her—she saw him look lovingly at his bride, and she heard him whisper, "I love you, Elaine."

The revelation given in that name nearly drove Dorothy insane.

He had taken *her* back.

She hated Robin then—she hated Elaine—she ducked down and hid her face, because she wanted to die.

Then she felt Robin looking for her, and she raised her head again so that he could see what he had done to her.

She watched Robin run after Elaine and she knew that she would have to kill him.

She let Little John take her to the inn. He got a room and she covered her face and he took her inside.

Little John undressed her—she did not help or hinder him— she was cold and stiff now, but he did not notice, for he was fired and eager from wine and long contact with her body.

He took off his own clothes. He threw Dorothy on the bed and mounted her. He spread her legs—and then at the last moment she came back to herself, she awakened from Robin's betrayal to the knowledge of what was being done to her at this moment, she realized she *didn't* want it, she screamed "NO!" but Little John just slammed one hand over her mouth to stifle her screams, and he caught her flailing fists with his other big hand, he got a grip on her wrists and forced her arms back against the bed above her head—he drove into her, and he broke her, and he felt her scream again against his hand.

He looked down and saw the blood.

Remembering all this now, this morning, he was ashamed to recall how much the sight of her virgin's blood had excited him.

Then he had just plunged in deeper, knowing he was hurting her—he took his hand from her mouth and kissed her, he told her that he had made her a woman, he told her she was his woman now—she didn't answer and she didn't try to fight anymore and she didn't react at all when he came in her.

Then he was exhausted, and somehow fearful, and very drunk. He rolled off her—and she got up right away.

She dressed, unmindful of the blood on her thighs.

He said, "I'll see you home," but she just looked at him, looked through him, and then she left alone.

Little John let her go—he let the wine take him down—he fell asleep.

Now he was awake, and ashamed, and still frightened.

He went to Dorothy's parents' house. He explained that he had danced with Dorothy during the wedding celebration, but that he had lost her in the night. He asked if he might see their daughter again.

At this Dorothy's mother began to weep—her father told Little John that he hoped *someone* would see Dorothy soon.

She had not come home last night.

They were terribly worried because they didn't know where she was.

Chapter 226

ELAINE DEMANDS A STORY

After visiting Dorothy's parents Little John went to see Robin. He debated with himself all the way to the stone cottage as to whether or not he should tell Robin about Dorothy. He still had not made up his mind when he found himself before the strong oak door the Mayor had put in—he knocked, and so allowed circumstance to dictate his conduct.

There was no answer to his first knock, so he struck the door again. Finally he heard Robin's voice. "Who is it?"

"It's me," Little John answered, as was his custom—rarely in his travels with Robin could he identify himself by his true name.

Robin opened the door. Despite the length of time that he had taken to answer the knock, he was still only dressed in a pair of wide green trousers. Behind him the room was bright and well heated by a roaring fire.

Little John stepped inside at Robin's invitation and looked over at the big bed. He saw Elaine sitting up in the bed, her back against the headboard, holding the blanket that covered her up to her breasts—holding it so that it *just* covered her breasts—it was obvious that she was naked beneath that blanket.

Little John quickly looked back at Robin—his friend met his gaze with a grin—Robin was relaxed, the picture of happiness— Little John had *never* seen Robin look this happy before—the squire knew now that he could not speak of the shame and fear and blood of last night. What danger was there anyway? Little John asked himself. She's a naive girl who got more than she bargained for—she's probably just gone off to cry somewhere.

There's no reason to disturb Robin by talking about her—for myself, I should just try to forget her. I need another sort of woman—certainly no virgin—I'm sure I can find an experienced woman who could use a bit of gold, perhaps a young widow—Little John smiled at the thought, and he said, "Good morning, dear friends. I won't ask you how your night was—"

At this Elaine gave a low little laugh and sat up a bit straighter, so nearly uncovering herself—Little John looked at her and forgot what he was going to say and nearly forgot the purpose of his visit—he coughed to gain time and then he managed, "I'll just pick up my share and then I'll leave you two alone."

"Of course, Little John," Robin said. He opened the heavy chest that lay on the floor by the bed. Inside there was a great loose pile of sparkling gold coins—and Little John's well filled bag. Robin handed the bag to his squire.

"Thank you," Little John said. He turned to leave.

Robin thought of asking Little John about Dorothy, but after Elaine's reaction last night he didn't really want to say anything in front of her. Anyway, Little John looked cheerful enough—if there was any danger he certainly would have said something.

Little John headed for the door, glad that Robin hadn't asked any questions. He just wanted to get away and hide from his memories—but then Elaine stopped him.

"Little John," she said, "don't go yet."

He stopped just before the door—and then he reluctantly turned around. Elaine smiled at him and continued, "I want to know how you did it."

Little John's face turned ashen.

Robin didn't notice because he was gazing lovingly at his lady.

"What?" Little John asked weakly.

"The robbery of course," Elaine said. Robin caught something in her expression and he looked sharply at Little John—but now the squire had his face back under control. Elaine continued: "Now that I am married to Robin I want to know how these things are done—tell me exactly how you stole the King's gold."

Little John smiled broadly because this was a question he could answer. He was so relieved that he even sneaked a glance down at Elaine's breasts, just to check if she was still holding the blanket high enough.

"We just took it," Little John said to Elaine, as he admired her.

Elaine felt the heat of his gaze, and it excited her. She spoke to her husband. "Robin, I can't stay like this. Get me my nightgown, please."

Robin arched his eyebrows. "The one from last night, I assume," he said in a mocking voice.

"Of course," Elaine replied, just as if she had made the most natural request in the world.

Robin picked up the torn garment and handed it to Elaine.

She accepted it graciously and said, "Now if you gentlemen would just turn your backs for a moment . . ."

The men obeyed.

There was some delicate rustling, and then, "You can turn around now."

Elaine was still sitting up in bed as before, but now she had let the blanket fall to her waist. Above that she was covered—in a manner of speaking—by her nightgown. Indeed, the lower halves of her breasts and her nipples were concealed (barring any deep breaths)—but since Robin had torn the garment all the way down the front, there was a strip of bare white skin revealed from between her breasts to just above her navel, where the blanket's coverage began.

"I think there's more to the story than just 'taking it'," Elaine said to Little John, smiling merrily. "Perhaps Robin can help you fill in the gaps." She turned her smile on her husband. She patted either side of the bed with her hands—her nightgown fluttered with the movement. "Why don't you two men sit down here on the bed and just tell me everything from the beginning."

Robin wanted to tear the nightgown again. He dragged his eyes away from his wife and looked at Little John. The squire was staring at Elaine with a look of wonder on his face—all thoughts of Dorothy had been driven from his mind.

Robin said, "I don't think we have a choice, do we my good man?"

Little John looked over at his friend and shook his head. "No choice at all, Robin," he said. Then the squire looked back at Elaine, and the force of her femininity drew him as though he were a will-less puppet on a string. He walked over to the bed, and he sat down on one side of it at the feet of Elaine the Fair.

Robin shook his head too, watching his squire, and then he walked over to the other side of the bed and sat down opposite Little John.

Elaine looked from one to the other—and as she moved, the

gap between the torn halves of her nightgown opened a little wider.

"Which of you wants to go first?" she asked brightly.

Chapter 227

STORY OF A ROBBERY

"I'll start," Robin said. He looked hard at Elaine. "The robbery was really very simple. You yourself gave me the idea as to how it could be done, dearest Elaine."

"And what idea was that, good husband?" Elaine asked, still smiling.

Robin smiled back at her. "When I was a waiter, years ago, I served you but you didn't really see me, and you certainly didn't remember me. I was invisible to you then, dear wife."

Elaine reacted as though Robin had slapped her across the face. His words hurt her, exposed her—her smile seemed to break on her face—she lost all her confident teasing sensuality—she wanted to be covered.

"Please give me my dress, Robin."

"No. Stay as you are—and listen.

"Like you, the nobles of the court don't really see their servants. The lads who do the dirty work are simply invisible to them—a most useful fact, as far as I am concerned.

"You might think it hard to hide Little John—but even such a remarkable fellow as my friend becomes invisible (as a man) when he joins a crew of laborers. He is seen then as just a tool designed to obey orders and lift heavy things.

"I knew as soon as Louisa explained the Prince's plan that there was only one place to seize the chest of gold: when it was loaded onto the ship. Leaving the palace it would be loaded on the coach by the Prince's personal servants—and he might even know their names. But at the dock—would those fifty brave knights sully themselves, and bend their creaking armor, by lifting the chest themselves and carrying it onto the ship? Of course not! They'd tell a gang of dockworkers to do it.

"Little John, you tell the next part."

Little John looked over at Elaine. She was holding the torn halves of her nightgown together with one hand.

"Just as Robin told me to do," Little John said, "I went to London and I made my way to the docks. I did some drinking in the waterfront taverns, and I found out which crew loaded the royal ships. I picked a fight with the biggest and strongest member of that crew—I'm afraid I hurt him pretty badly. Anyway, to make a long story short, I got the job in his place, and then I worked on the docks through the days, and I waited through the nights, until Robin came and found me on Friday evening, the day before the gold was going out. We sat in a tavern then, to all appearances a dockworker and a fisherman, and we worked out how we would rob the King of England!"

Little John smiled brilliantly at Elaine. She didn't trust the bits of nightgown any more. She pulled the blanket up high to cover herself.

Robin took up the tale. "When Saturday morning came I was on Duncan's boat in the harbor. He had done some maneuvering in the night—we were quite close now to Richard's warship.

"On shore everything was in readiness—Little John knew his part, and I had also bribed an old beggar to scream just as soon as he saw the fire that I would soon light.

"The Prince's stately, well guarded procession came down to the dock. The knights swirled around in their armored might, and the pike men raised their weapons to the skies. The coach stopped at the edge of the dock. The waiting crew of workers—Little John among them—was ordered to lift out the chest. Those who gave the orders believed, as Louisa told us, that it would take four men to carry the chest.

"On the boat, meanwhile, I had finished my preparations. I had some hot burning coals in a bucket next to me. I had wrapped rags just below the points of several of my arrows. I dipped those arrows into the bucket and lit them—then I sent a half dozen flaming arrows into the sails of Richard's warship.

"No one saw my actions, for all were watching the ceremony on shore. The onlookers imagined the riches inside that so carefully protected chest—they gasped as they sensed its weight, for the four men carrying it had to set it down to catch their breath almost as soon as they got it out of the coach. Of course"—Robin winked at Little John—"I suspect that one of the men was not applying his full strength." Robin looked back at Elaine. "Anyway, it was at just that moment that my friendly beggar saw the flames—and he earned his pay.

"'FIRE!' he screamed. 'His Majesty's ship's on fire! The sails are burning! Fire!'

"Everyone looked up at the miraculous flames that seemed to have come from the heavens—and Little John, down on the ground, picked up the chest all by himself and ran."

"I nearly pulled my arms out running with that thing," Little John remembered, smiling.

"And when you tossed it in our boat we nearly sank. I never heard such a crash," Robin said to Little John.

Robin looked back at Elaine and said, "So that's how we did it, my dear. As we sailed away I pulled off my fisherman's clothes and revealed my suit of green. We heard many cries of 'Robin Hood!' from the shore—we heard curses from the knights, and cheers from the common people.

"We had a good wind, and the royal ship could not follow us with burned sails—we got away cleanly, and then, as you know Elaine, we stopped further down the coast so that I could have your ring made. I knew of a good jeweler in Folkestone—I think he did his best work for us."

"It was the engraving, you said, that took so long," said a rather subdued Elaine.

"Yes."

"I haven't even had a chance to look at it yet."

Elaine took the ring off and held it up to the light. She looked inside the band, and there she discovered the beautiful fine engraving—their names reached all the way around in one endless circle: Robin Hood—Elaine the Fair.

She looked at Robin and she wanted to throw the blanket off and let her nightgown fall open—then she remembered how he had hurt her with his words, and she wanted to strike him.

She put the ring back on.

"I thank both of you for telling me the story," Elaine said. "You are both true heroes."

"Thank you, Milady," Little John said. He got up. "I must go now."

Elaine nodded.

Robin saw his friend to the door—then he watched as Little John walked off down the street, tucking his bag of gold under his shirt.

Robin closed the door and locked the crossbar.

He looked around at Elaine, and he saw that she had thrown the blanket back down to her waist. Her nightgown was open even more than before—she was breathing heavily—he could see bright flashes of pink from each of her swollen nipples.

He looked up higher then, and he wasn't really surprised to see the look of cold rage on Elaine's face.

Chapter 228

PUNISHMENT

"You should not have spoken to me like that," Elaine said.

"I have no right to criticize you, dear wife?"

"Not in front of Little John."

Robin looked at the line of bare skin that showed between the torn halves of Elaine's nightgown. He walked over to her and inserted his left hand into that gap—he felt the heat of her body—he held his hand steady there between her breasts, and he looked down into Elaine's hard eyes and said, "But you can show yourself like this to him?"

Robin felt the motion of Elaine's breathing against his hand—he felt the side of each soft breast.

Elaine looked down at the hand that touched her. "You like to look at me."

"So does he—you should not have teased him like that."

"I was aware of your squire. Isn't that what you want, Robin? I *saw* him—and I let him see me."

"I did not mean in that way."

Robin was on the defensive now. Elaine pressed her advantage.

"Are you jealous because I let Little John look as you were never permitted before? Indeed, I did not even acknowledge you when you used to wait on me. Perhaps you should be jealous—Little John is a hero. You were just a waiter."

Elaine felt Robin's hand stiffen against her skin. She didn't look up at his face. She knew that she had gone too far. She was frightened—and terribly excited too. She waited in an ecstacy of fear—she could feel her own heart pounding against his hand—she felt lost when his hand left her but it was only to flick back the halves of her nightgown—he breasts were completely bare now for him, she could feel the tightness in her nipples, they were so hard they ached, she wanted his touch but still she wasn't exposed enough for him, he pulled the nightgown off her arms and threw it away, he threw the covering blanket off the bed—she was naked now and he would touch her yes—

Robin made her his prisoner. He seized her nipples with the thumb and forefinger of each of his hands—he tightened each terribly tender grip, and so captured Elaine's whole body—she trembled in his grasp, but she knew that she could not pull free without suffering great pain—she struggled to stay still, but she was trembling so much, and breathing so heavily, that she could not stop all motion—and every move she made increased the tension on her so sensitive flesh—she tried leaning forward, toward him—but then he pulled up sharply on her nipples, he lifted her breasts, she knew what he wanted—

She gave in.

She looked up at his face, and she was surprised to see that his gray eyes were not unkind. He was not angry with her—he would simply do what he thought necessary.

"I have to punish you, Elaine," he said.

Elaine shivered—she wasn't really trying to get away, but Robin tightened his grip nevertheless—Elaine felt a hot pain shoot up through her breasts—she gave a little cry and looked down at the powerful hands that held her—tears started down her face, and she spoke softly, still looking down at her husband's hands.

"Once Roland said he was going to spank me—but then he didn't do it."

Robin let go of Elaine's nipples. She covered their soreness with her hands as he spoke. "I told you already, darling," he said, "I'm not like him or any of the other men you've known."

Robin sat down next to his wife on the bed. He pulled her across him so that she lay face down over his lap. He gathered her wrists together and held them behind her back with his left hand. He raised his right knee slightly so that her soft white never marked bottom was the highest part of her body.

Elaine had held Sandra in the past in just this way. She had wondered what it would be like to be in Sandra's position. This morning she learned everything.

There was the fear first, and then the anticipation—he caressed her until she began to long for her punishment—and then it began. There was the shock of the first spank, the sudden humiliating pain—then more of the same, his hand coming down harder and harder, pain growing all the time, pain and heat, she was burning there and she couldn't even move, no escape and would he ever stop, she was hurt O she was burning dying—she couldn't feel anything but her helpless buttocks crimson now surely—

He stopped.

She wanted more than anything to reach back and rub the pain away—but he still held her wrists tightly with his left hand and he was not ready to let her go.

He forced her legs apart with his right hand—he touched her womanhood with his two rigid fingers and then he eased them inside her—yes, the way was easy, and somehow for Elaine this self-knowledge was the worst of all—she was wet, boiling with wet heat, she was ashamed and she couldn't help herself—she ground back against his fingers, she rose swiftly toward a sharp peak of pleasure, the pain behind driving her—

Robin took his fingers out and she cried in frustration—

He spanked her one more time, hard, right across the center of her buttocks—

She cried out again, but Robin heard the submission in her voice this time—he pushed her gently off his lap, and guided her into a kneeling position on the floor facing the bed—he pushed his trousers down and moved over until he was sitting right in front of her—Elaine looked through tear blurred eyes at the enormous column of his manhood—Robin put his right hand in her golden hair and said, "Serve me"—he pressed down on the back of her head and Elaine bent forward and took him in her mouth.

He used her for his pleasure—she submitted to his pleasure—when he came in her mouth he held her until she had swallowed all of his seed.

Chapter 229

HONEYMOON

Sandra had told Elaine, "He's a lot like you," and she was right.

Robin and Elaine were both proud, powerful people—they knew how extraordinary they were—they were both used to command.

They fought all through their honeymoon.

Robin was, as he said, unlike any other lover Elaine had known. His desire did not weaken his will—he simply refused to be less than a man. He made no obeisances before his wife's beauty—he admired her beauty, he appreciated and enjoyed it—but he did not think that her gifts gave her any superiority over himself.

In the past Elaine had been able to choose which man's favors she would accept—but now, loving Robin, she had no choice. She discovered that to bring Robin to her she had to give—she had to be a woman, as he was a man.

This was not always easy for the lady who had been the Duchess of Larraz.

Likewise, for Robin, her ceaseless challenge was not always easy to meet.

They would not have lasted one day together had they not loved each other so much.

They ended every battle in bed.

They had no interest in anyone besides themselves. Little John, for example, did not come to see them anymore, but they didn't miss him. They didn't notice when he began an affair with a pretty fortyish widow who lived down the street—they didn't know of the torments John suffered, even when he was held by his gentle lover's arms.

Little John kept thinking about Dorothy—he regretted a thousand times what he had done—he helped her parents search for her, without any success. All they could discover was that Dorothy had rented a horse on the morning following Robin's wedding—she had not brought the horse back. Little John paid the stable man for the loss of the animal—he made love to his kind older lady—he wished now that he had told Robin about Dorothy—he had never kept a secret from his friend before—but now, of course, it was too late to say anything.

Little John sometimes saw Robin and Elaine out walking together—during their honeymoon he never saw them apart— they strolled along, blind to the world . . .

Robin had never before lived every minute of the day with a woman. Even with Suleka he had gone out to battle every day. Now with Elaine he learned the minutiae of her existence, as she learned of his. They were so close that they were able to come together to become one glorious loving being—and they were close enough that they never missed when they chose to hurt each other. They fought—and then suffered pangs of separation when they were only two feet away—they came back together to kiss, and cursed between kisses—they nearly ripped the bed apart with the violence of their passion.

The Mayor had not bothered to put any cooking utensils in the house, which was wise, since Elaine never even thought of cooking. The lovers ate at any odd hour—sometimes they'd wander over to the inn in the middle of the night and persuade the innkeeper's wife to make them a meal—they bought hot fish to eat while they walked in the daytime—they would lick each other's greasy fingers and stroll back to their cottage, seeing no one, hearts pounding while they tried to make the anticipation last by walking slowly . . .

Robin learned every signal of Elaine's desire—Elaine learned every touch that made Robin's manhood rise. They wanted to know everything.

One day, two weeks after their marriage, Robin asked Elaine about her escape from Larraz.

Elaine told him about going to Madame Genevieve's brothel— she told him of the wig, and the beauty mark, and the love carriage.

Robin looked at her. "You're leaving something out," he said.

"Yes," Elaine replied, "but is it something you want to know?"

"Tell me," Robin said.

Elaine came close to him and kissed him, and looked into his eyes. "I will," she said. She kissed him again, and then she told the story. "After Madame's girls had transformed me, after the wig was fitted and my face painted and so on, they let me look in a mirror. I found myself looking at a courtesan—I had to smile, and my reflection smiled back with bold red lips—I became excited, staring at this self who was not me—I went over to see Madame Genevieve, and I asked her if I looked like I could work for her.

"She looked me over, not just my face, she looked at my body too—I might just as well have been naked—she looked at me for a long time, and then she took my hand—she gave me a little squeeze, as though to reassure me, and then she looked into my eyes and said, 'If you worked for me, my dear, then I could fire all the other girls and make more money on you alone!' "

Elaine smiled, remembering.

Robin said, "You liked that."

"Yes."

"If you were a whore you'd have to do everything."

"Not a whore, my love," Elaine said, raising her head in a regal manner, "a courtesan."

"The name does not change the occupation," Robin said. "Your body—all of your body—would belong to the man who paid for you."

"I belong to you."

"My"—Robin deliberately hesitated—"courtesan."

"Yes."

They had just come in from a walk. Elaine had thrown off her sable coat—all she was wearing (quite in keeping with their conversation) was a low cut courtesan's dress from Madame Genevieve's.

Robin opened the chest and took out a handful of gold pieces. He carried them over to the far side of the bed and laid them down on the blanket. "I want you to look at these while I have you," Robin said. "Get on the bed, face down, and pull your dress up to your waist."

Elaine stared at him from across the bed. Her eyes were a hard furious blue.

"Don't treat me like a whore," she snapped.

"No," Robin said calmly, meeting her eyes, "like a courtesan.

Now get on the bed—and do what I told you."

They fought a war with their eyes. The six feet of air between them seemed to crackle with lightning bolts—the gold on the bed blazed as if in answer to those explosions—Elaine cursed Robin silently for learning another of her secrets—she cursed him for knowing that this excited her—she kept cursing him even as she climbed on the bed—she crawled across it on hands and knees and then she let herself down—she put her chin on the bed just before the gold, but she didn't look down at the money—she kept her head tilted back so that she could look forward—she saw the tent that had formed in Robin's trousers—his manhood was level with her face and she wondered if Robin would use her mouth again, but then she remembered his second command and suddenly she *knew*—she pulled her dress up over her hips—Arthur had broken her maidenhead, and Roland had entered her mouth, even if he had never satisfied himself there—but there was one place where no man had ever touched her—Robin took his pants off in front of her and she looked at his manhood and she said, "It's too big," but he didn't answer—he walked around the bed, now he was behind her—she let him spread her legs—there was nothing she could do—she felt the bed move as he climbed up on it between her legs—one hand spread her wider, and then he guided himself into her soaking femininity—he seemed bigger than she could ever remember—he moved in her, just for a minute, and then he pulled out—she was expecting it but even so she shuddered with fear—she felt his big hands force her buttocks apart—she looked down, trembling, and there was the gold before her eyes—that wasn't right—his manhood touched her there—he was wet from her juices but still much too big—pressing—NO!—the gold swam before her eyes—not for that, no, only love—entering her GOD NO!

Elaine screamed and her arms thrashed wildly and she knocked all the gold off the bed—

As the gold rolled across the floor Robin drove into her to the hilt—

Elaine wanted to scream again but she couldn't, the breath had been driven from her body, he was on her, in her, stretching her, O God he filled her so much—

Elaine remembered Davila's pronouncement—he's done it, she thought, he's filled me and O God it hurts so much—why does he have to do this? She thought of the gold again and she felt a sudden rage in her heart—she tried to get free but he kept her pinned down, he was using her brutally, he was moving in her, pain whenever he moved, but the thought of being paid was even worse—she said, "Not as a whore, Robin—not as a whore!"—but he only laughed, he laughed easily as he plundered her, he drove deep and held himself still there, his laughter stopped then and he said, "You'll be a whore whenever I want you to be, my dear, *my* whore—I love you that way—and you'll be the grand lady again, soon enough, and I'll love you that way too—you're my woman and I love you in every form—I love you Elaine, I love you"—Robin had kept himself still all the time he was talking to her, but now he pulled out just a little, he eased the pressure, he lessened the fullness—he stayed like that while Elaine kept hearing his words in her mind: I love you Elaine, I love you—she wanted to give to him—she felt a strange desire for him—the pain was still there but she raised her hips—her spread buttocks bumped him, she pressed up against him to drive him deeper, she wanted to be filled again, always filled—her belly came up off the bed as she pressed back—Robin reached down underneath her and cupped her sweet soaking plum—he pressed down then and drove her down against his holding hand—she cried out, half pain, half pleasure—he raised up and she followed him again, she wanted him and now he knew of her desire—he thrust down into her even harder than before, he hurt her as he forced her down onto the pleasure of his hand, she was caught between two worlds and couldn't escape—

"I love you, Elaine," he said again, and then he curled his hand and put two fingers into her sweet place—

Elaine screamed into the blanket, she was filled like she had never been filled before, she felt Robin buck and come in her, she felt herself come, her body seemed to fly away, she could hear herself screaming as from a great distance—her screams gradually broke into discrete words—she listened to her own faraway voice—she was saying, "I love you Robin, I love you, I love you . . ."

It seemed to be a long time before she came back to herself. Robin softened and finally slipped out of her—there was new pain once he was gone—Elaine knew that she would be sore for days—Robin got off her back and lay on his side next to her—she turned to face him, wincing with the movement—he smiled at her and she found herself smiling back—he leaned forward and kissed her gently on the lips.

Chapter 230

ASSASSINS

Wednesday, October 18, 1196, three weeks after the wedding . . .

By this time Robin and Elaine were beginning to accept each other. In the midst of their violent passion there was also, occasionally, peace.

This morning began peacefully.

Robin woke up first—he looked over at Elaine's sleeping form. She was lying nude on her back—the fire in the hearth had burned down to coals but it still gave off enough heat to offset the breeze coming through the open window (Robin could never be bothered to fasten the blanket over it). Robin got up on his elbow so he could see his love better—he looked at her with an almost inexpressible tenderness.

He looked at her shut eyes and her parted lips—he looked at her breasts, and noticed that they seemed a little larger than usual—they stood up firmly even though she was on her back— he ran his eyes down the splendid incurving of her waist, he wanted to put his hands on either side of her there—but then he didn't want to disturb her, so he simply looked down further, he savored the sight of her curly golden fleece just above the juncture of her thighs—he looked too long and then he *had* to touch her—he reached out and very gently spread her thighs—her legs opened easily at his touch—he felt his breath go short as he looked at the traces of last night's lovemaking—he realized that he had become hard almost without noticing—he looked up and saw that Elaine's blue eyes were open now—she was staring at his risen manhood—she spread her legs wider, she looked up at his face then and whispered, "Good morning"—he smiled and got between her legs—he eased into her, she was wet, welcoming, he slid all the way into her as she wrapped her arms around him and hugged him tight, he put his mouth next to her ear and said, "I love you"—their spirits flowed together—

A thunderous crash nearly shattered their senses.

Robin looked at the source of the sound, the door cracked, the crossbar bent—

Someone just struck the door with a battering ram, Robin thought, and thank God for the Mayor and the good oak he used—but still it won't hold a second time—the villains have been staggered but they'll back up and try again—

Ten seconds.

Robin used them all.

One: He rolled off Elaine and reached for his bow that, with his quiver, hung from the bedpost—as he reached he started to speak—

Two: "Go out the window," he growled in a harsh whisper and Elaine, eyes wild, naked, started to get up—

Three: Robin had his bow in his left hand—he took an arrow from his quiver with his right as Elaine ran to the window—

Four: Robin nocked his arrow by feel as he watched Elaine start to climb up and put her head out—

Five: Elaine screamed as she looked down at a criminal archer—he was crouched under the window, looking and aiming up—Elaine was staring down at a nocked arrow aimed between her eyes—

Six: Robin dropped his bow at the sound of Elaine's scream and he seized the half filled chest of gold as Elaine yanked her head back inside—

Seven: "Duck!" Robin yelled at Elaine as he hurled the chest that in a calmer moment he could barely lift—

Eight: Elaine ducked as the heavy chest flew over her head like a missile flung by a catapult—Robin reached for his bow again—

Nine: The chest nicked the top part of the window, breaking its trajectory—it tipped over and down—the weight of flung gold in its front end guided its fierce plunge toward the archer's face as Robin raised his bow again—

Ten: The weighted chest drove the archer's head back—the sound of his neck snapping was just distinguishable before the second onslaught of the battering ram shattered the door.

Three men charged for Robin, guiding the steel capped ram

before them—

Robin yelled "Go!" to Elaine again as he drew back his still nocked arrow and pivoted to his left away from the ram—he released the arrow as the first man charged by him—the arrow tore through the villain's side and stopped his heart—the dead man kept charging, driven by his own impetus and the force of his two fellows behind—he hit the bed and splayed out across it, streaming blood—Robin took a step to his right and pulled out a second arrow as the other two villains dropped the clumsy ram and reached for their swords—Robin knew he had no time to nock this arrow so he just stepped forward and used it like a spear—he drove it right through the second one's neck just as that assassin raised his sword—the villain spun around like a pinwheel with the steel headed, green feathered arrow projecting from either side of his neck—Robin danced away from the dying assassin's blindly whirling sword—he stepped toward his quiver again as he threw his bow backward at the third assassin—Robin didn't see the man knock it away with his free hand but he could feel that the villain hadn't been slowed—a drawn breath indicated the killer's approach—too close! Robin had to jump away before he could get his hand on another arrow—the third assassin's sword slashed through the space that Robin had been in—the blade of the sword cut through the quiver and splintered the arrows within—Robin tried to break for the door but the second assassin's pinwheeling corpse chose that moment to topple in front of him—before Robin could get around the body the last villain moved to block his way—Robin tried to dance but the assassin used his sword well—he backed Robin up against the wall—the only comfort for Robin was that as he moved he saw that Elaine was no longer in the room—she must have gone out the window as he had told her—at least she'll be safe, he thought, and then his back hit the wall.

He was naked, unarmed, and trapped. He looked at the face of the man who wanted to kill him.

The assassin had dirty yellow hair and washed out blue eyes—his half open mouth quivered with the excitement of evil—he wielded his sword like an instrument of pleasure—he brought it around in a loving, curling swirl and then he faked low and thrust high and he skillfully stuck the point into Robin's chest no deeper than a quarter inch—he broke the skin and not much more, but Robin saw that the assassin's elbow was cocked behind the sword—he can straighten his arm faster than I can come around, Robin thought, so if I try to counter I'm dead—the assassin began to move then and Robin wondered if living was worse than dying—drool had formed in the assassin's open mouth and now it began to run down his chin as he prolonged his pleasure—he started to cut downward with the sword, opening a bloody track—his eyes began to brighten with anticipation as he looked down at Robin's wet limp manhood—his sword cut steadily downward through Robin's skin as it headed for that target—

The assassin grunted like a pig. His eyes rolled up and there was no light in them now—he choked, and then suddenly the drooling mouth was pouring blood—the point of a sword came out of his chest—he had been run through from behind—he dropped the sword that he had been cutting Robin with—Robin swung with his bare hand and knocked the falling blade away before it could cut his manhood—the assassin, dead on his feet, began to slowly crumple—and so, behind him, there was revealed Robin's savior: Elaine the Fair, in all her naked glory.

She had taken the broken-necked archer's sword and used it to save her husband's life. She let go of the hilt of that sword now—she left the weapon buried in that last assassin as his impaled corpse fell sideways onto the bloodstained rug.

"Is the one outside dead?" Robin asked quickly.

"Yes." Elaine looked at the bleeding line down Robin's chest. "Are you all right?"

"I'm fine," Robin said, but then he saw a movement past the door and he stepped by Elaine to look—he saw what could only be the assassin's coach heading away.

The coach got away but not the driver.

Little John had heard Elaine's scream—not love but terror—he had been swiving his widow, but then he had freed himself from her and put his pants on—he had buckled on his sword—he stepped out now and saw the coach coming toward him—

Robin could not see the driver because the body of the fleeing coach was in his way—but then he saw Little John and he knew that the driver would not escape—he only hoped that Little John would leave the driver alive so they could find out who was behind this attack—

Little John leaped onto the driver's seat as the coach went by—

Robin saw squire and driver come tumbling down off the other side of the coach—they fell in the road as the panicked horses ran off, dragging the empty vehicle.

The struggle in the road was brief and unequal—Little John had no intention of killing this foe—he simply made the driver his prisoner—he stood up, dragging his captive with him—

Robin had caught a glimpse when they tumbled off the coach but he hadn't wanted to believe his eyes then—

Now he had to face the truth. This driver of assassins was a woman. He had kissed the one who had betrayed him.

Elaine came up next to him and looked down the road at the disheveled woman in Little John's grasp.

Suddenly Elaine recognized her as the yearning young beauty who had disturbed their wedding celebration. "I remember her," she said. "What's her name?"

"Dorothy," Robin said.

Chapter 231

THE MAYOR'S SADNESS

Robin turned away from the sight of betrayal and looked back into his honeymoon cottage. It looked like a charnel house. There was one body on the bed, two on the floor, blood everywhere.

Robin knew that he and his love would never sleep in this house again. Perhaps it could be cleaned, but the illusion of safety that he had felt here was now forever shattered. Indeed, if he could be attacked in St. Lyons, then where in England would he be safe? Where could he and Elaine raise the children that would soon be coming?

"Are you all right, Robin?" Little John called.

Robin looked back at his friend. "We're fine. Hold your prisoner—we'll come out and see you in a moment."

Robin looked back at Elaine—he could see that she too was thinking about their future—and then he realized that they wouldn't even have a future to worry about had she not saved his life again. "You were right, Elaine," Robin said. "I did have need of your good sword arm. Thank you."

Elaine gave him a faint smile and looked back out at Dorothy.

Robin saw the direction of her look as he made up his mind about something else. "I'll tell you about Dorothy later," he said, "but what is more important, what is definite, is this: we will be leaving this country soon." Elaine looked up at Robin with new hope in her expression. He could see that this plan pleased her. Robin gestured toward the carnage. "This won't happen again. I promise you I'll find you a safe place."

Elaine touched his chest near his wound. "You were almost killed," she said.

"Don't worry about it," Robin said. He looked out into the street. The townsfolk (mostly women, since their husbands were out fishing) were coming out to see what had happened. Robin suddenly realized that he and Elaine were both quite naked. "Let's put some clothes on, darling," he said.

Elaine picked her way gingerly past the bodies. She put on her red dress, for she thought that if there were bloodstains on it they might not show too badly.

Robin put his pants and shoes on and picked up a shirt. Elaine looked over at him—he gestured to his wound, and said, "I know the Mayor keeps a few bottles of good whisky. I'll have him pour some on this before I put my shirt on."

Elaine nodded and offered Robin her hand.

He took it and led her out of the stone cottage.

The Mayor and his servant were out in the street now, talking to Little John. Then the servant took over custody of Dorothy and led her back toward the Mayor's house. Little John headed back to the widow's house to put on the rest of his clothes.

The Mayor continued down the street toward Robin and Elaine. As he approached, Robin noticed the enormous sadness in his eyes—a sadness, Robin first thought, because of the destruction of his town's hospitality—but then the far worse truth struck Robin like the blow of a fist—he knew exactly what weighed on the Mayor.

Dorothy certainly didn't know four professional assassins. She must have gone to the Prince, Robin thought. When he learns that his assassins have failed, will the vindictive Prince use his royal powers to crush this whole town?

Robin knew that he and Elaine could escape the Prince's wrath—but he also knew that he could not leave until he had devised a plan to save the living town that had befriended him.

Chapter 232

"WHAT DO YOU KNOW . . .?"

A half hour after the attack . . .

Robin, Little John, and Elaine all sat with the Mayor in the living room of his house. Dorothy, bound, was in the kitchen, watched over by the Mayor's manservant.

Dorothy's mother was right outside the house. She had begged the Mayor to be allowed in to see her daughter, but he had refused her request.

Dorothy's father, along with the rest of the town's fishermen, was out on the sea, still unaware of the violence that his daughter had brought to the town.

The four in the living room thought of that violence—thought of the consequences of that violence.

The Mayor spoke first. "Let me lay out the situation for you, my friends—please listen." The Mayor paused to look at each of his guests in turn, and then he continued. "I found a writ on one of the bodies. It called for the death of you, Robin, and Little John. It was signed by the Prince, and countersigned by Arthur the Assessor."

The Mayor was looking only at Robin now. "There is no need to ask Dorothy anything. We know that she has gone to the Prince. We can be sure that she told him all she knows about you—about us.

"Robin, we are eternally grateful for what you did to save our town two years ago—but then the situation was different in several ways. You were not yet the crown's sworn enemy; you had not yet transformed yourself into the 'Robin Hood' that we admire so much today; and finally, your successful recovery of our goods took place far outside of town. Neither you nor St.

Lyons was endangered by your heroic acts—then.

"But now our connection is known. Dorothy will have told the Prince—and the Assessor too, judging from the countersign—of your previous exploits. She will have told them how our town sheltered you. She has revealed your place of safety—she set you up for death."

The Mayor gave Robin a thin smile. "But you are a hard man to kill." The Mayor paused, and his smile vanished. There was sadness in his voice as he continued. "Our town does not have your skills, Robin. Nearly all our men leave town every day to fish. We will be helpless if an army is sent to seek vengeance against us—and that is a distinct possibility once word gets back to London that the assassins have failed. We must remember that both the Prince and the Assessor are vindictive men."

"The Assessor's power exists only as an adjunct to the crown," Robin said. "If we stop the Prince, we stop the Assessor."

"How do we stop the Prince?" the Mayor asked.

Robin looked at the floor—he didn't have the answer to that question.

Elaine did.

"We could take a walk," she said, "and perhaps while we're out we could let Dorothy's mother see her daughter for a while."

The Mayor was surprised by the look of confidence in Elaine's eyes. He felt a sudden surge of hope. She knows something, he thought, and she doesn't want Dorothy to hear it.

"A capital idea," the Mayor said. "I'll just speak to my man for a moment."

After a brief colloquy in the kitchen the Mayor reappeared to lead his friends outside. He stopped in front of Dorothy's mother, who looked up at him with pleading eyes.

"You may see your daughter now," the Mayor said coldly. "Tell her that unless we find a way to curb the Prince's vengeance, she will be responsible for the death of every person in St. Lyons—even you, good woman."

The mother sobbed and went inside.

The Mayor looked down the main street of his town. He saw women, children, old men—*everyone* who was not out fishing— he saw the fear on their faces—they were waiting for him, and he had no answer for them.

He remembered the confidence that he had seen in Elaine's blue eyes.

He trusted in that confidence—he waved calmly at his people, as if to say, 'Wait, everything will be all right.'

Then he led his little procession down the street, and the citizens stepped aside respectfully to let them pass.

The Mayor did not stop until he was out on the deserted docks. He turned then and faced Elaine, who was flanked by Robin and Little John.

The Mayor spoke only to the beautiful lady.

"What do you know about Prince John?" he asked.

Chapter 233

THE NATURE OF PRINCE JOHN

"I *know* the Prince," Elaine replied. "There is not one special secret that I know *about* the Prince—rather, I understand his character, I know what motivates him."

Everyone looked expectantly at Elaine.

"Unlike any of you, I lived close by the Prince for many years in the Palace of Bermondsey. I came to know that he is a man driven by fear.

"It is fear that makes him want to be King. He is afraid of his equals and superiors. He thinks that only as King can he be safe.

"When Richard returned from France, John fled to France rather than confront his elder brother. When Richard invaded France, and John was expected to fight with the French forces, he quickly switched back and begged mercy from Richard.

"He is always moved by the greater fear.

"When I first met him at the court I could see that he desired me."

"That was hardly unusual," Robin put in.

"What was unusual," Elaine said, continuing smoothly, "was that he never acted on his desire. Given his position, outranking my husband, any other man would have at least tried.

"But he was frightened—perhaps of me, or of the truly brave knights who admired me.

"Pursuing me would have put him at risk—so he contented himself with low class strumpets, and frightened boys, for those he could control.

"We need to show him that he is not in control. We need to frighten him."

Robin looked at Elaine, and his teeth flashed in a brief smile before he spoke. "You know the layout at Bermondsey, don't you?"

"Yes," Elaine replied.

"You know where the Prince sleeps, where he eats, where the guards are posted."

"Yes."

Robin turned to the Mayor. "We'll need some good paper, and pens, and a ruler for the drawings. I'll write the letter myself.

"We will make certain that no harm comes to St. Lyons—and then Elaine and I will leave you tonight. We will thank you forever, but we can not trouble you any more."

The Mayor looked from Robin to Elaine, back and forth. He saw how alike they were in their ferocity—he watched the hard slate of Robin's eyes shade into Elaine's icy blue orbs.

He shivered as he looked at these two young people that he loved.

They had killed in his town.

He was glad that they would go, and so leave St. Lyons in peace.

Little John was also looking at the great outlaw and the beautiful lady.

I don't think they want me to come with them, he thought.

He felt the cold wind striking his big frame, and he wanted to weep.

Chapter 234

DOROTHY REMEMBERS

Dorothy's mother embraced her daughter, who was bound with her hands behind her back. The mother pressed her tear stained face against her daughter's cool dry cheek.

"Tell me—please tell me why," the good mother sobbed.

Dorothy looked off into space—she did not see the walls that confined her, she did not notice the manservant who guarded her—she did not even feel her own bonds.

She traveled through time, and she remembered . . .

She had fallen in love with Robin before he could even raise his head—she knew that she still loved him even now. She could recall exactly the touch of his hand on her breasts—she could still feel his kiss on her lips.

She remembered two years of wasted dreams—and then Lady Marian arrived, and that was terrible, but still worse was the soon discovered truth that this woman was the unfaithful Elaine the Fair.

She felt that agony in her heart again now, as she saw herself going to the inn with Little John—she saw her own last struggle as he took her virginity—she remembered the pain as she rode to London with fresh blood on her thighs.

She remembered London—days or weeks with "helpful" courtiers who used her, abused her, and passed her around— she finally got to meet the Assessor, and what a loose skinned toad he was—she remembered being conducted to Prince John—O yes he wanted to hear what she had to say—he dismissed everyone so they could be alone—he listened carefully— and then, wildly excited by the thought of murder, he took her again and again on his fancy bed.

That was just two days past.

Dorothy remembered the trip down to St. Lyons: herself and four assassins in one carriage—they took turns with her all the way down, but she reacted not at all to their pleasures, and only slightly to their cruelties—her indifference had finally bored them.

They had let her sleep last night.

They made her drive this morning, so she could take them to Robin's house.

She remembered the attack.

One skulked over underneath the window. The other three charged with the battering ram—and then bounced back—in a quite comical manner—

I laughed then, Dorothy thought, I laughed when I saw them tumble, because I knew then they were all dead.

I watched as the assassin under the window looked up to meet his death—I watched the fools break the door on the second try, and through the opening I saw Robin—ah, he was beautiful in his nakedness—I watched as he slew two, and then the third trapped him—I knew that third man well—he had never been able to love unless he inflicted pain at the same time—I saw him try to hurt Robin like he hurt me, and I saw Elaine coming up behind him, and I even loved her at that moment—I rejoiced when she drove her sword through his back—

But then I dropped right down into despair, they would love each other forever now, I drove away and Little John caught me—

I am a prisoner now and my life is over.

What part of this story can I tell my mother?

What tiny part can I tell her?

Dorothy heard her mother begin to speak again, but she couldn't bear to listen. She shut out the pain of the present—she went back in time—she gave her spirit to a dream of love—she remembered Robin's gentle hand on her virgin breasts.

Chapter 235

A KISS GOOD-BYE

Several hours later, after Robin had completed his drawing and writing . . .

Robin came into the Mayor's kitchen, and dismissed the servant who was still standing guard there. Dorothy's mother had long since been sent out, so after the servant left, Robin and Dorothy were alone together.

Robin stepped over to the girl and undid her bonds. Dorothy brought her freed hands out in front of her and rubbed them together stiffly. She looked up at Robin with the eyes of a condemned prisoner who has finally begun to look forward to death.

Robin ignored her expression.

"Some men are going to take you to London," he said. "They'll leave you off at the palace. They'll give you this package"—Robin reached in his pocket and took out a thick envelope that was sealed with the official imprint of the town of St. Lyons—"and then you will take it in and give it to Prince John. Give it to no one else—just him.

"You do know the Prince now, don't you?"

Dorothy looked away, and her lips curved in a faint bitter smile. "Yes, I know him."

"Then you'll do it."

Dorothy turned back and looked defiantly at Robin.

"No," she said firmly.

Robin looked at her with his hard gray eyes—but he didn't say anything, so finally Dorothy spoke again.

"Robin, I have some idea of what's in your package—enough to know that after I give it to the Prince, he'll kill me." The bitter smile touched her lips again. "You see, Robin, I do know him."

Robin started to speak but Dorothy stopped him. "No, let me finish. You think that I am afraid of death, but you are wrong—I look forward to death, death is my only desire—but I want to choose my executioner."

Dorothy looked deep into Robin's eyes. "I don't want the Prince to kill me, my love—I want you to do it."

Robin shook his head back and forth. "I won't kill you, Dorothy—and the Prince won't either. The letter that I am sending with you contains explicit instructions that you are not to be harmed. If the Prince molests you in any way, I will learn of it—and he will die."

Dorothy looked up at this man that she had loved, and hated, and still loved.

"You want to save me—now?"

"I want to give you another chance," Robin said.

Dorothy looked down at the floor with terribly sad, loving eyes—Robin remembered her bending over his bed, two years ago in this very house.

Dorothy whispered, keeping her head down, "For me there is no other chance, only you."

"Then you'll do it for me," Robin said.

"Yes."

Robin put out his right hand and Dorothy took it in both of hers. She pulled his hand to her face—she rubbed her cheek against it, and then she turned it over and pressed her mouth to his palm. Robin felt her warm tongue tracing the line of his arrow scar—he felt a sudden ferocious desire for this girl—he pulled his hand away.

Dorothy looked up at him with eyes now so much older than her years.

Robin didn't want to look at those eyes—he looked down a little and he saw the mark of a fresh bruise on her cheek.

He looked down further at her mouth—

He forced himself to look up and meet her gaze.

They looked at each other for a long time.

"Is this good-bye?" Dorothy finally asked.

"Yes," Robin replied, "unless you fail to deliver the letter properly."

"What would happen then?" Dorothy asked.

"Then I would come and kill you," Robin said.

Dorothy shivered. "I don't think I really want that, O I don't know what I want—"

"You'll do what I want."

"Yes, Robin, yes, I'll deliver your letter—now just please hold me, please Robin please—"

Robin put the envelope back in his pocket and took her in his arms—she hugged him fiercely, desperately, she sought his lips—he kissed her, and she opened her mouth for him, she gave him everything that she could—the one kiss lasted for a long time, but finally the intensity eased, and Robin broke the sweet contact of lips on lips.

He pulled back a little—he put his hands on her shoulder so that he could hold her away from him—he looked into her eyes and he said, "Good-bye Dorothy."

Dorothy's eyes filled with tears—she could not say a word.

Robin turned and left her.

He walked back into the living room where the Mayor, Little John, and Elaine were waiting as before.

Robin addressed himself to the Mayor. "It's all right," he said. "She'll do as she's told."

Chapter 236

A WRIT, A LETTER, AND A CONVENT

Two days later, after Roger and Paul (the two intrepid lads who had rescued Elaine from the jetty) had delivered Dorothy to the Palace of Bermondsey, Prince John himself welcomed Dorothy into his bedchamber.

She handed him the envelope without a word.

The Prince saw the seal of St. Lyons and his hand began to shake. He looked up at Dorothy with fear and rage in his eyes— and then he suddenly screamed, "He lives!"

"Open it," Dorothy said calmly.

The Prince broke two of his long foppish fingernails before he managed to crack the seal—and by then he was holding the envelope upside down, so the papers inside fell out onto the floor.

Prince John got down on his knees on the royal carpet. He looked down at a series of exact drawings that showed the lay-out of the Palace of Bermondsey. There was an X on one draw-ing that indicated the room he crouched in now—under the X was this inscription: "Your bedchamber—an excellent place for silent assassination."

John grabbed frantically at the rest of the spilled drawings. He saw that all the guardposts in the palace were noted, as were the times for the changing of the guard. Only someone who had lived in Bermondsey for a long time could have drawn this map—John shook with fear as he tried to guess the identity of the enemy who lived in his home.

The terrified Prince did not consider the fact that the routines at the palace had not changed for years.

John found an official document under the last drawing. He

stared at it, uncomprehending, for a moment—until he suddenly realized that it was his own writ calling for the death of
Robin Hood.

He turned the paper over with trembling fingers.

There was a letter written on the back—John recoiled in horror from the clear bold signature at the bottom of that letter.

The Prince forced his eyes to move to the top of the page—but
then the writing seemed blurred, so he picked up the paper and
held it close to his face.

Dorothy watched the paper shake in John's hands as he read:

> My Dear John,
>   Your assassins are dead. They were hardly a
> challenge—I do hope you send more and better men
> next time. However, I must insist on one condition: you
> must not take any revenge against the town or any of
> the people of St. Lyons. You will have to curb the
> Assessor and your knights, because I will hold *you* per-
> sonally responsible if there is any attack on that town.
> My condition extends to my messenger—Dorothy is a
> citizen of St. Lyons—you must let her go free.
>   If you hurt Dorothy, or if you try *any* reprisal
> against St. Lyons, I will hear about it—and you will die.
>   Remember your chest of gold, guarded by hundreds of
> pike men and fifty knights? I took that.
>   Killing you would be far simpler. As you can see,
> I know every stone in your castle—every chink in your
> armor—my people watch every move you make.
>   Cross me—and you die.
>   Behave yourself, and you can continue trying to
> plunder the country—and I'll do my best to stop your
> agents—but you won't have to worry about the page
> lighting you to bed one night, the page who might
> suddenly strip off his livery to reveal a suit of green . . .
>   No, you don't want to think about that.
>   Tell Dorothy to go now.
>   Forget St. Lyons.
>   Try not to think about me.
>   Robin Hood

"Go," John said weakly from his kneeling position, "Go."
Dorothy left the room, and the palace, and walked into the

first convent that she found. She knelt before the Mother Superior.

"Please take me in, Good Mother," she begged.

"The Lord welcomes all of us, my child," that devout lady replied.

Dorothy took up residence in the convent. She lived there for five years. Then one day she got up very early, before morning prayers, and quietly walked out of the house of God that had sheltered her.

She began a new life.

Chapter 237

A SEA VOYAGE

St. Lyons . . .

The assassins had come in the morning.

Dorothy was sent off in late afternoon.

As night fell on the day of battle, after all the fishing boats had come in, Robin and Elaine prepared for their own departure.

Beryl had fixed Robin's quiver. He had procured arrows from a number of young men to fill it—his bow was undamaged.

Duncan's crew had unloaded their catch—and ever since they had been working hard, at Robin's request, to make the boat ready for a longer sea voyage. They had loaded foodstuffs and extra sails and Robin's heavy chest.

Robin and Little John had had a long private conversation with the Mayor. Little John, a native of St. Lyons, would stay on in the town for a while and be welcome. Robin and Elaine would leave the country altogether.

Now Robin and Little John embraced on the dock near Duncan's boat. "I'll be back," Robin whispered in the big man's ear. "It might be a year or so, but I'll return. I'll send a message to you through Baroness Louisa."

"I'll keep in touch with her," Little John replied.

The two men patted each other on the back with the awkwardness of men friends who have never really touched before—and then they disengaged, fighting their own emotions.

"Go in peace, my friend," Little John said.

Robin nodded, and stepped aside.

Elaine took his place. She put her hands on the squire's massive shoulders and went up on her toes and kissed him on the lips.

Little John lost the power of speech—but Elaine understood all that he wanted to say. She touched his cheek, and she gave him a smile—and then she walked over to stand by Robin.

Duncan called from the ship. "We're ready to go."

The Mayor left the crowd of townspeople at the end of the dock and walked up to Robin and Elaine. He embraced Robin, and kissed him on both cheeks—and then he smiled and let the outlaw go.

He turned to Elaine and took her in his arms. She was soft and small and fragile, she was just so terribly dear to him—he could hardly imagine that this sweet girl had recently wielded a sword with deadly effect—he was ashamed that just a few hours before he had *wanted* her to leave—

"My daughter, my daughter," he whispered in her ear.

Elaine kissed his old wrinkled cheek, and tasted the wetness there. She cried then herself, softly, but she spoke through her own tears: "You have become the father that I have always wanted—I love you, dear father, but you have given me away—I love you, but I must go now with my husband."

The Mayor gave Elaine one last loving hug, and then he released her.

"Go with God, dear daughter," he said.

Robin took Elaine's hand. He helped her climb onto Duncan's ship, and then he stepped aboard himself.

Duncan cast off—the whole town waved as the boat moved out into the harbor—one boy waved a shirt with a hole in it.

It was easy for Duncan to steer, for this was the first night of the full moon. Duncan used the lunar light to head the boat west—he set sail for Ireland, for the west coast of Ireland, which still resisted English rule.

The voyage took six days, for there was much bad weather. The pitching boat was most uncomfortable for Elaine. She was sick every day—though she remembered that she had had no trouble crossing the English Channel twice. She was upset that Robin had to see her in this condition—she was embarrassed when he had to hold her while she leaned over the side and threw up into the rolling sea.

The sky was overcast for most nights of the voyage, but occasionally the night clouds would part enough to give a glimpse of a magnificent full moon beaming down on them.

Elaine was too sick to appreciate the moon—but not so sick

that she failed to notice the tightness and new sensitivity of her breasts—sometimes even Robin's casual touch hurt them, and that wasn't right.

She went below one day when all the men were on deck—she took her dress down and held her breasts—they were hard and full and swollen—they were growing—she felt her breath catch in her throat as she remembered the moon—"No blood this month," she whispered softly to herself, "no blood—I carry new life inside me."

She smiled then—she felt very calm—she did up her dress properly, and made her way up to the deck to tell Robin.

She had to blink several times to adjust her eyes once she came topside, for the sun had suddenly come out and the light was almost blinding after her dark cabin. Finally she could see again—none of the men had yet noticed her. All of them, including Robin, were staring across the bright sea.

Elaine followed their gaze with her own eyes—she saw the coast of an isle as green as Robin's clothes—she saw her new home: Ireland.

Part VIII

Ireland

Chapter 238

ELAINE, MOLLY, AND PATRICK

June 28, 1197, inside the largest mansion in Connaught County, Ireland . . .

Elaine lay on her side, wearing only a nightgown, on the big bed that she shared with Robin. She watched as Molly, the midwife, left the room.

Molly, in her cheerful manner, had just told Elaine to relax—told her that the business of birth often took a long time. Molly had suggested that Elaine try to sleep, for she would need the strength later.

The door closed behind the midwife—Elaine heard Robin's deep questioning voice (though she could not distinguish the words) and then Molly's bright, higher pitched answer.

Elaine was relieved that she could hear no sign of worry in the midwife's voice. I suppose everything is all right, she thought. My daughter will just take her time.

Elaine had already been in labor for twelve hours, since just after sunup this morning. About every half hour she felt a great tightening—she could hardly call it pain—all through her already taut belly. She looked at Robin's hourglass—she was about due for another one. She wished that this one *would* really hurt, just as a sign that the baby was moving—but then that made her think of another worry—Molly had told her that the pathway down which the baby had to come had hardly opened at all.

Elaine told herself that everything was all right—she worried—she felt the pain, but O damn it really wasn't much of a pain—just the tightening as before—she put a hand on her hard swollen belly as the door opened and Robin came in.

"Another one?" he asked.

"Yes, but it's just the same."

Robin sat down on the side of the bed and took Elaine's hand.

"Molly says you ought to try to sleep, and I agree with her. It's almost dark outside now anyway and you've had a long day." Robin saw the resistance in Elaine's eyes. He continued, "Look, darling, Molly really doesn't think the baby will come until tomorrow. You've told me yourself the pains aren't too bad now. Just try to relax."

"I'll try," Elaine said, "but I don't think I can sleep."

"I'll lie down next to you."

"You're sweet, Robin," Elaine said, using his real name as she always did in private—though publicly he was now Patrick O'Dowd, a distant descendant of the great eleventh century Irish King, Brian Boru. "But I think I'd prefer to be alone for a while with our daughter—I want to talk to her, and prepare her for this great step into the world."

"You're still sure the baby will be a girl?"

Robin and Elaine had argued over the sex of their child all through Elaine's pregnancy.

"I'm sure," Elaine said, smiling.

Robin leaned down and kissed her. "I think you're wrong," he said.

Elaine shook her head.

"Are we going to fight even as our baby is being born?" Robin asked.

"Perhaps," Elaine replied—but she still had her smile.

Robin kissed her again.

"I'll leave you alone to talk to our son," he said, and exited quickly so as to have the last word.

Chapter 239

PRINCESS

Elaine put a hand on her big belly and spoke softly to the new soul inside, just as she had done all through her pregnancy.

"Hello, dearest daughter," she said. "I've been talking to you for months about your life to come—I've told you all the hopes and wishes I have for you, and I do believe you'll have a wonderful life.

"But perhaps now, while we have time, I should tell you of how you came to be here, to be born to these parents, in this house.

"You were conceived in love, little darling. Your father is the bravest and finest man I know—he showed me the joys of being a woman—he fulfilled me as he took his pleasure, and out of our happiness your soul was born.

"In another age we might have peacefully awaited your arrival—but these are dangerous times for a man like your father who stands for justice.

"Your father is brave and true—he is a hero of the English people—and at the same time he is considered an outlaw by the crown. When you are old enough to understand, I will explain all this to you. I will tell you of your father's secret name, the name that right now I can only whisper: Robin Hood. I will also tell you then of my own history, and of the name I no longer use: Marian, the name of my brave mother. I will tell you about her, and in addition I will tell you the story of a more distant ancestor—but all this must come to you in the future.

"For now I can only say that there was no safety for us in our native England—we had to find a place where you could grow up without fear.

"So we sailed to this green island country called Ireland—a country in the midst of a war against the occupying English army. You might think, as I did at first, that we had left the frying pan to leap into the fire, but such was not the case.

"You see, your father knew many facts of which I was unaware. He knew that Ireland is divided into counties, and each of the counties has its own King—indeed only once has there been one high King supreme above all, and that was the great Brian Boru, who drove out the Norsemen almost two hundred years ago. The point is, the country is as fragmented as it is embattled—this always gives opportunity to an experienced soldier.

"The best opportunity awaited us here at Connaught, for your father had heard that the brave people of this county still resisted English rule.

"We landed and soon after Robin bought a small house for me to rest in—not this one—and then he went out into the field.

"He fought—your father is a great warrior but never without cause—he fought this time for his family, and that is you, and that is me.

"Robin took the fine old Irish name of Patrick O'Dowd—that is the last name that will belong to you, dearest daughter—and he claimed a kinship with the great Brian Boru, which I believe is certainly true in spirit.

"Your father soon distinguished himself—he had gold and spirit and courage in abundance—he became a leader of the Irish rebels—he inspired the populace, he raised an army, and he drove the English troops our of Connaught.

"Now I do not think your father intended to become King— but he filled a space where there was no one, for the previous King of Connaught had been killed by the English years before, when he was still a youth without descendants.

"The people here saw Robin as their savior—they pressed their highest honor upon him, and he accepted his responsibility. We moved to this mansion, the traditional residence of the royalty of Connaught—your father was crowned as King Patrick O'Dowd, and I became Queen Elaine.

"So, my dearest one, that is a brief history of our last nine months—now we just wait for your birth. I tell you this: Do not fear to enter the world, for you have a mother and father who will love you forever—

"Come forth, little Princess . . ."

Chapter 240

A TUG AT THE HEART

Elaine talked to her still unborn babe all through the night. Whenever Robin or Molly or Bonnie (Elaine's lady in waiting) came to check on her, they found the expectant mother wide-awake, bright eyed and alert—which quite exhausted the rest of them. By morning's light, after Elaine had been in labor for a full twenty-four hours, both Molly and Bonnie were asleep. Robin came into his bedroom and lay down on the bed behind Elaine. He fitted his body to hers like a spoon to its mate.

"How are the pains?" he asked, as he put a strong arm around her taut belly.

"Just the same," Elaine replied. "They're no better, no worse—just about the same time interval too."

Robin yawned.

"You sound exhausted," Elaine said solicitously. "Why don't *you* try to rest for a while."

Robin snuggled sleepily against Elaine and kissed the back of her neck. "You're the one who's supposed to be tired," he said.

"I'm fine." Elaine put a hand over Robin's where he held her belly. "Just hold us—hold us just like you're doing, and I will wake you if anything happens."

"I love you," Robin said softly, and then he fell asleep.

Did the father's comforting presence give the baby courage?

All Elaine knew was that everything changed after Robin fell asleep.

The next contraction came early and it was far more than simple tightening—this was true, teeth grinding pain—there were three of these in the first hour after Robin went to sleep—labor had begun in earnest.

Elaine turned the hourglass over.

There were five in the second hour and each time Elaine wanted to cry out—but she thought of Robin fighting Brian with a broken hand, after days without sleep—she felt the comfort of his good hand on her clenching belly—she thought of the brave little girl inside who was seeking the light—the sand was out of the hourglass and she turned it over again, but now she couldn't count the pains anymore—they just seemed to come continuously—she would bear it just a little longer—pain—she began to get an urge to push, but she knew she shouldn't until she was open—she'd wait a little longer—pain—the last few grains of sand tumbled out—three hours of this—pain—I want to push but I'll wait—I'll just turn the hourglass over—she reached out but a pain hit her in mid-motion—her hand jerked and knocked the hourglass over—it struck the table with a sharp crack that woke Robin instantly—"What is it?" he asked, even as he was opening his eyes—Elaine watched the hourglass, amazingly unbroken, as it rolled off the table and fell soundlessly onto the rug—she felt something different, something strange—she was all wet—she remembered Sandra's story—

She said, "My water—" but that was all she got out before another pain hit her—

Robin didn't wait for her to finish the sentence.

"MOLLY!" he roared as he stood up. "Get in here!"

The midwife came rushing in, with Bonnie following. Molly took one look at Elaine and turned to Robin, intending to order him out—after all, a man should not see the secrets of birth. "Your Majesty," she began, "you must—"

"No," Robin interrupted. He gave Molly a look. "I'll stay here and see my baby born. Now do your job."

Molly ducked away from his gaze and turned up Elaine's nightgown. She sent Bonnie for some towels and then she began her examination.

Robin moved over to the head of the bed. He looked down at Elaine's face, and he took her hand.

Elaine gave her husband a grateful smile. She was glad he was staying—he was her love, her strength—she felt another pain and now she didn't have to grind her teeth—she just tried to crush Robin's hand but of course she couldn't do that—the pain was so much easier to bear with him holding her—now she felt Molly's fingers opening her, checking the baby—

"You've nearly done it all yourself, Your Majesty," the midwife said in an amazed voice. "His head is down, you're open—you're ready." Molly's voice became brisk and she dropped ceremony and titles. "Now I want you to push on the next one—now—Push!"

Elaine pushed and it felt so good—the pain had a purpose now—she pushed and thought that soon the midwife would be surprised—not 'his head' but *her* head—relax—wait—Push!—this will be easy . . .

Painful effortful time passed—

Why isn't anything happening? Elaine wondered—

Pain—Push!—relax—too tired—pain—Push!—

Nothing—

What's wrong?—

Pain—Push!—exhaustion—

Elaine had been in light labor—but she had been very tense—for twenty-four hours. She had had three hours of intense labor, intense pain—now she had been pushing for at least another hour and she couldn't get the baby's head through the tight canal, she was going into her twenty-ninth wakeful hour, this was harder than she had ever imagined—

Exhaustion—pain—Molly told her to push but she couldn't do it—nothing was happening anyway—

"Push, Your Majesty!" Molly said.

Robin heard the panic in the midwife's voice—and he saw something he didn't like in Elaine's eyes. She didn't seem to see him—she seemed to have drifted off—

He leaned over the bed and took his wife's other hand. Now he was balanced over her—he looked right down into Elaine's face—his gaze pierced her fog of pain and exhaustion—she looked up at his terrifying gray eyes and she tried to turn away, she tried to shake her head no, she couldn't stand it, no more, but he just kept looking at her, he held her with his eyes, his will was battering at her, she felt the pain rising in her again—No More!—if she could close her eyes she could sleep and get away from the pain—she heard Molly call, "Push!" from far away but she couldn't do it—she couldn't close her eyes either—Robin wouldn't let her—why did he want to hurt her like this?—he just looked at her—he had hurt her sometimes when they made love—he had entered her and helped make this child—his seed had joined with hers and now this child was struggling to be born—

The child will die if I don't get her out and Robin is not hurting me he's sending me his strength—

Elaine opened herself to Robin's gaze, she accepted his will into her spirit as she had accepted his manhood into her body—

His force poured into her and joined with her own—with Robin she could shove the exhaustion away, with Robin she could stand the pain, she could use the pain, and when Molly said, "Push!" again almost desperately she *could* push, she and Robin pushed together, she looked into his eyes, she felt the grip of his hands, their wills were locked in tandem now "Push!" and she pushed and she felt her child move, she was doing it, with Robin's strength pouring into her she could do it, "Push!" and she did, her own strength awakened now, surging, reserves pouring in from God knows where, "Push!" and yes another movement "Push!" and she felt her child touch the gateway— new pain there, lovely burning stretching pain and Molly's happy voice, "His head is coming through! Just wait a moment, Your Majesty!" the midwife almost singing as she checked the baby, everything fine, not caught in any way—"Bring him out now, Push!" and Elaine looked into Robin's eyes and gave a mighty push, she felt such a stretching but O not quite—"That's all right Your Majesty the next one now Push!" and she tried, she was stretched thin, burning up but then the contraction stopped and she hadn't quite done it—she felt Robin's hands tighten on hers, she felt a surge of his strength come from his heart to hers, she hardly heard Molly's call to push this time, she just listened to her own body listened to the contraction ris- ing on its wave of pain and she caught it just right and she pushed with all her heart and soul, she could do this, yes—

So easy—

The baby's head came free, then the shoulders, then the whole sweet slippery little infant fell out into Molly's hands.

Elaine felt Robin release her hands as he turned to look at their newly born child.

"It's a girl," Molly said quietly—she was worried because she knew Robin had wanted and expected a boy—Kings always wanted boys—

The little Princess filled her lungs with fresh air and let loose with a hearty cry.

The biggest smile of his life spread across Robin's face and all the women relaxed.

"We are blessed," Robin said.

Elaine lay her head back on her pillow and closed her eyes.

She felt loose and empty, totally relaxed—and totally happy. She listened to her daughter's cries as Molly cut and tied off the baby's umbilical cord—she felt Molly come around the side of the bed—she opened her eyes and there was her little beauty.

Elaine stared at this living miracle. She was perfect—every little finger perfect—every little toe perfect—perfectly beautiful little face with blue eyes and a sweet little nose and a little open rosebud mouth—

The baby cried.

Elaine reached out instinctively for her daughter—she gathered her babe into her hands, and at the first touch she felt a rush of love that was greater than she could ever have imagined. "I love you," she said to the child, "I love you, I love you sweet—"

She stopped because she realized that the baby did not yet have a name. She looked up at Robin. The huge smile still transformed his face. He was not a King or an outlaw or any sort of fighting man now—he was simply blissfully happy. He didn't notice that Elaine was looking at him because he was staring in awe at his tiny child—he reached down and touched her with gentle, wondering fingers.

"Sweet dear babe," he said.

Elaine looked down at her husband's caressing, protective hand on the baby girl—for just a second she thought of her father, who had never known this moment—she bent her head and kissed her child's forehead, and let her cheek rub Robin's wrist as she went down—then she looked up at her husband and asked, "What shall we call her?"

Robin looked at his wife as though he was surprised that she had asked such an absurdly obvious question. "We'll call her Sandra, of course," he said.

Elaine looked at Robin in amazement—and then her eyes just filled with tears. "How did you know?" she asked.

"I know you, darling," Robin said, "and I know that she is the one you miss the most."

Elaine was crying and her baby was crying. She needed to do something about both of those things. She handed the little girl to her husband. "Please hold her for a moment, my love," she said.

Robin took the squirming, crying baby and held her easily with his big hands.

Elaine wiped her eyes and undid the tied straps of her nightgown. She pulled the garment down so that her breasts were revealed—breasts that were as big and full as she had ever wanted, breasts that contained just what her baby wanted—she looked up with clear eyes and reached out for her daughter.

Robin gently laid the child into her hands.

"Princess Sandra," Elaine whispered, and then she drew the babe down to her breasts. Elaine offered the child a thick nipple—the baby fussed for a moment, and then the little rosebud mouth opened over the treat and clamped down. This was, indeed, just what she wanted.

The little Princess began to suck. Elaine felt the tug through her nipple, through her breast, and straight through to her heart.

EPILOGUE

Robin and Elaine had four children altogether. After Sandra, who was born on June 29, 1197, there came Myles on May 28, 1199, Elizabeth on February 10, 1202, and then Edward was born after a very difficult pregnancy on July 31, 1205. Elaine needed a few months to recover from that birth, though she did finally come back to full health and stunning beauty. She continued to make passionate love with Robin for the rest of their lives—but after Edward was born she never conceived again.

Each of the children, on the occasion of his or her twelfth birthday, was told the secrets of the family heritage. Robin would reveal his true name at that time, and explain his absences. Likewise Elaine would tell of her mother, and of her more distant ancestor, the Countess of St. Valery.

The first of Robin's aforementioned absences occurred when little Sandra was six months old. Robin sailed to England, packing his bow and a new suit of green. He linked up with Little John at Baroness Louisa's estate—then the two outlaws sallied forth. They struck hard at some of the Assessor's men, embarrassed a detachment of Prince John's soldiers, and straightened out a Baron who thought that greed had come back in fashion.

Then Robin left England, with a promise to Little John that he would return.

Robin kept his word.

He came back for similar forays about once a year, on an irregular schedule, until King John's death in 1216. Robin felt his duty as a beacon of resistance for the suffering English people—and on a personal level, the constant awareness of his presence kept John from ever moving against St. Lyons.

Each of Robin's raids was magnified in story—but none added so much to his legend as a certain exploit in the year 1207. King John (Richard Lionheart had been killed in 1199) had been busy looting the English churches that year so as to fill up the royal treasury and pay for fresh royal vices. Robin and Little John interrupted one such attack on a church—the two outlaws slew the six men who had been dispatched there by Arthur the Assessor. Only one monk actually witnessed the brief battle—he was a genial, corpulent friar named Tuck who had been sent out to gather wood, but who had found that task fatiguing—he had lain down to rest, in fact he slept until he was awakened by the clash of arms.

Then the good Friar Tuck saw a giant of a man, and a green outlaw, and he knew them at once as Little John and Robin Hood. He saw them defeat the forces of evil—the sight was like a revelation straight from God.

Friar Tuck did not return to his church. He felt that it was his duty to inform the world of this wonder, and so he became an itinerant preacher: he spread the gospel about the wonderful defender of right, Robin Hood. Friar Tuck was a popular guest in every village he visited—he was always given hospitality and wine by people who were hungry for news of their hero—Tuck solved the problem of having only one story to tell by adding artful embellishments—indeed, after several draughts of wine, the two minute battle he had witnessed often reached proportions analogous to the battle of Hastings! The good Friar conjured up thousands of King John's soldiers—he sent out hundreds of Merry Men to oppose them—he placed himself in the middle of the fray, where he called down God's blessings on the forces of right . . .

So the legends grew, and in these legends Robin was always linked with the beautiful Maid Marian. Women still offered themselves to Robin, and Robin still declined—and this was taken, quite correctly, as proof that Robin had a true love waiting for him in some enchanted place. The only woman who had actually traveled with Robin—Elaine, using the name of Marian—was remembered well for her beauty and her mystery. Robin was amused by the slight change given to her identity in legend: since Robin was a representative of the common folk oppressed by the nobility, Marian had had to lose her title. No longer a lady, she was now a maid—but she was always beautiful.

Robin's adventures in England seldom accounted for more than one month out of the year. The rest of his time he spent in Ireland, where, as King Patrick O'Dowd, he was more Irish than the Irish. He fought the English to a standstill whenever they tried to retake Connaught. He made such an impression on the English commanders that they eventually decided to leave well enough alone—they let the stubborn Irish keep that corner of their country.

Robin saw no contradiction in his action—both in England and Ireland he defended the local people against the same corrupt monarch—Robin's enemy was King John, not the good citizen (whether English or Irish) who just wanted to make a living.

As a monarch himself, Robin was both just and wise—and Elaine was a lovely and gracious Queen (a Queen, one might well add, who was quite capable of running the country whenever her husband mysteriously disappeared). Connaught, avoiding English oppression, prospered under Robin's rule. In particular, the little seacoast town of Westport, on Clew Bay, experienced a revival. This little town, the only free port on the island, began to attract international trade from merchants who did not wish to deal with the levies of the English crown.

Little John never joined Robin in Ireland. He stayed in England, drifting from woman to woman, waiting for Robin's messages, always keeping in touch with Baroness Louisa. Louisa and Little John had an interesting relationship—though Baroness and squire, when they were alone together they were simply friends untroubled by class. They were both lonely in their own way—they comforted each other, but there was no passion between them, at least not for many years.

Then finally things changed—perhaps because Louisa wanted a child before it was too late for her, perhaps because King John was pressing all the Barons and she needed a protector—perhaps Little John just finally grew up—perhaps there was no reason save a slow building love—in any case, when the two became aware of their mutual desire, they could barely restrain themselves long enough to marry—but they did just manage to follow the proper form.

Little John did add one original twist to the formal proceedings—he saw the civil war coming between Barons and King, with the outraged common folk fighting for their own survival—he didn't expect King John to live long and there was no successor on the horizon—he knew that in the darkness of anarchy to come, it would be every man for himself—he thought a title might help out in the impending turmoil, and so on his wedding day he simply declared himself a Baron—some looked askance at this claim, but then when they looked at the size of the gentleman himself, they lost all interest in challenging the new Baron.

So it came to pass that when the Barons did revolt against their King, when they presented their demands in that meadow at Runnymede, as King John stared at the document known as Magna Carta—at that fateful moment in history, a huge man, the Baron of Nottingham, came up to King John—and handed him a pen.

The King signed, and Little John, telling the story the next day to his pregnant Louisa, could not keep from laughing. "If only he knew," Little John chortled. "If only he knew!"

The child, Louisa's first and only, was born on July 15, 1215, one month exactly after the signing of the great Charter. Louisa weathered her labor well, though she was already forty-three years old. The child was healthy, a strong big boy—the proud parents named him Gawain, after the faithful knight of King Arthur's court.

Robin was very well informed about the collapse of English government toward the end of King John's reign. Like Little John, he saw the civil war coming—he knew that his native country would soon be torn apart—in the violence to come there would be no way to tell right from wrong, black from white.

Robin was pleased that Little John and Louisa had joined together—he visited them, and the little babe, once in the summer of the year 1216—Robin thought that with Louisa's estate, and Little John's fighting power, they had every chance of surviving the coming troubles.

But Robin saw no role for himself. He was forty-six years old when King John died on October 18, 1216, leaving behind a ravaged country without a leader.

Robin thought that perhaps he could raise an army, conquer England, and establish himself as King—but that was a young man's dream. Older, wiser now, he saw years of bloodshed—he saw the human cost of 'saving' England.

After that last visit to Little John and his family, Robin never set foot in England again. His conscience did not reproach him, for with King John dead and Arthur out of power, there was no longer any specific danger for St. Lyons.

The country as a whole would certainly go through a difficult period—but Robin believed that in time the resilient nation would rise again—and in time, he was proved right.

Robin narrowed his focus. His work was the governance of Connaught—his pleasure was to give all his love to his beautiful (if also spicy and sharp-tongued) wife and to his four marvelous children.

The first of these children, Sandra, had grown up like her mother to be an astonishing beauty. She had blue eyes and red hair (much brighter than Robin's auburn) and a temper still more fiery than her hair. Her mere existence seemed to cause riots among young men for miles around. Before she was twenty there had been dozens of duels fought over her—but she was capricious and cruel, and no suitor was able to retain her favor. Then came a sudden change, like a storm off the sea—she fell in love with a Venetian ship Captain who had docked at Westport—he was equally smitten with the beautiful Princess— the courtship that ensued was as ferociously passionate as it was brief—the Captain had soon to sail off, though Sandra refused to be parted from him—he likewise was ready to take her with him, regardless of legal or familial blessings—Robin and Elaine bowed to the force of love, a wedding was hastily arranged, Robin gave away his eldest daughter and Elaine cried.

The next day Sandra and her new husband set sail for Venice—and even Robin could be seen to shed a tear as the ship sailed away.

Elaine retired to her bedchamber on that day, the first of September, 1217—she cried, for she knew that she would always miss her daughter—but she also came to realize that day how much she missed the girl's namesake, the first Sandra, her lady in waiting, her lover, her dearest friend.

For years there had always been the sound of the name Sandra in the house—sweet memories floating on the sound— but now all that was gone.

Both Sandras seemed very far away now.

Elaine had had a succession of pretty young ladies in waiting since she had become Queen. She had been fond of them all— and they had all come to love their mistress (at least until they found the right man)—but none could replace the sweet girl who had known love and pain and birth and death with her.

Elaine sobbed anew.

Passing by was Myles—he was of an age, eighteen, when young men dream of saving beautiful damsels in distress—though they rarely find them. Now here was such a lady—he knocked and entered her bedchamber—he comforted his mother, and asked her the reason for her tears.

She told him a little about his sister's namesake—told him that she was so far away—but distance is nothing to a bold young Prince.

"Write her a letter," Myles said, "and I will take it to her."

Elaine looked in amazement at her little boy—and she saw a young man with his father's eyes who meant exactly what he said.

She sent the youth to see his father, to seek Robin's counsel—after he left she wrote the letter, the words just poured out from her heart—she let her tears fall as they might on the paper.

Robin helped outfit Myles for his journey—the whole family (save for Sandra honeymooning on the high seas) saw the young Prince off on his quest.

So then there were only two children left in that big house in Connaught, and they were growing rapidly.

Elizabeth was a sweet dark beauty, gentle in temperament: she reminded Elaine of her mother, dear beloved Marian. In time Elizabeth would marry the richest merchant in Westport—she lived a long and comfortable life.

Edward, on the other hand, chose never to be comfortable. From an early age he showed an aptitude for music and a propensity to wander. At the age of seventeen he left home abruptly to seek his fortune as a traveling troubadour—he wandered the world, playing, singing, and seducing—he led quite an eventful life.

Yet Edward was still a boy of twelve when Myles set off on his quest. The elder brother finally reached Larraz after some months and many difficulties. Myles knew about his mother's previous marriage to the Duke, and he had hoped to meet Roland—but the Duke's information was as accurate and wide ranging as ever. The young Prince was not granted an audience. Myles had the distinction of being the first visitor that Roland had ever turned away.

Myles discovered that while the Larrazian people loved their Duke—he was a wise and gentle ruler—they were saddened too, for there was no passion in their leader's life, no love, no

Duchess. Roland dressed all in black, Myles learned. The Duke governed, and he mourned—he did nothing else.

Myles could understand how the loss of his mother could so affect a man. He said a prayer for Roland, and then he set out to find Lady Sandra—but as it happened, she found him.

Lady Sandra, mother of five children now (young Anton plus four more from her present husband, Sir Gowan), was wandering alone through the grapevines near the palace. She took this walk often in the afternoons—she would eat a few grapes and remember Elaine, and tender loving kisses—this day her gentle reverie was interrupted by the sound of rough cruel voices.

She came out of the grapevines and saw three young Larrazian knights tormenting a young stranger. The three knights wore steel breastplates and they carried swords—the stranger had a sword, but no armor.

The stranger, who stood with his back to Sandra, had long flowing blond hair—and that was what his tormenters had seized on: they were loudly debating his masculinity.

Sandra began to walk toward the group—she saw the youth slowly, almost negligently, reach for his sword hilt—and then the heckling stopped abruptly. The three knights looked at each other uncertainly, and then real fear began to show on their faces.

What had the stranger done? He had touched his sword but he still hadn't drawn it.

The three knights turned and walked away.

Sandra felt herself drawn forward. She had to see this stranger's face. She walked by him, and then she turned around and looked right into his eyes—

She saw what the three knights had seen—

Terrifying gray eyes—only one man that she had known had eyes like that—

The blond hair must have come from his mother.

Sandra just stared at the beautiful young man—and then she began to cry.

Myle's gaze softened as he stepped closer to the attractive lady. "May I help you, Milady?" he asked.

Sandra spoke through her tears. "I believe I knew your mother and father. My name is Lady Sandra."

A great smile spread across Myle's face. "You are just the lady I have come to see! I am Prince Myles O'Dowd, son of King Patrick O'Dowd, better known to you as Robin Hood. My mother's name is Elaine, and yes, she is still fair." Myles grinned even more, as Sandra shook with emotion. "My mother has missed you all these years, she loves you, and she has entrusted me with a letter for you."

Myles started to reach into his shirt for the letter that he kept in a leather wallet next to his skin—but he stopped the gesture when he realized this was all too much for Lady Sandra—there would be time for the letter later—for right now he needed two arms to catch the lady whose knees were giving way.

The strong young Prince held the lady up—he hugged her, and comforted her, and kissed both her wet cheeks—and then finally she read the letter, and hours later she wrote her own reply.

Myles returned home with a letter as tear stained as the one he had brought.

A few adventurous years later, after many brief flings with 'eligible' ladies, Myles found his true love. She was a poor Irish girl named Kelly, the daughter of a chimneysweep. She helped out her father when he worked—Myles kissed her sooty face one day for luck, and he found beauty under the covering of ashes.

Soon after he made her his wife.

Some years after that Myles became King of Connaught. Whether this succession occurred because his father died, or whether Robin simply stepped down in favor of his eldest son, is a fact that has been lost both to history and legend.

Somewhere in the Irish mists, Robin and Elaine disappeared. Their bones are lost, their gravesites unmarked. One searches for their dust in vain.

Yet one has only to close one's eyes, and the legend lives on, as it lives on in the hearts of all men who have heard of it. There is Robin Hood, mankind's bright green hope, and by his side the beautiful Marian, the name a lovely remembrance for the mother who suffered for her daughter, as mothers have always sacrificed for their children.

With closed eyes, one can see the daughter who grew to be the most beautiful woman in the world—the lady who would seek love, and finally find it, and pass her beauty on to her children.

One can see, living and beautiful, the lady who was known as Elaine the Fair.